The Game... Jade

Rocío Blisswealth

The Game...Jade/Rocío Blisswealth
ISBN-13: 979-8-9914613-3-7
            979-8-9914613-5-1

Translation: Sandra E. Castellanos Guardiola
                sandra.ecg@guardiola.com.mx
Cover design by: Vanessa Blisswealth
Library of Congress Control Number: 2024918178
Printed in the United States of America
www.blisswealth.net

If, upon reaching the end of my story, you find yourself identifying with it—and believe me, I pray that it's not the case—you'll decide if it's a romance, a horror tale, or a 'next exit' signpost from your path, the most dreadful of your realities. I hope I haven't caught up with you too late.

Jade

Chapter I
Daniel Montalvo

Present day.

For the first time, I am on my way to face my tormentors. After all, it's nice to realize that I have the guts to do it, even though the odds of biting the dust are high. Maybe it's because how things play out could go in two different directions. I could die, it's true, but for the first time, I have the chance—a small one, but at least there's a chance—to recover everything I've lost. But honestly, a part of me wants to run away, but where to? Where could I hide so they wouldn't find me? There's no time left, no other way out. They always have beaten me. If they do it again, I'm not planning to get out of here alive. I'd rather die than keep dealing with this unbearable life. I am ready to fight for the things that still mean something though.

Monterrey, Mexico. Seventeen years old.

Ten traffic lights, four stop signs, here comes another one, as if this counting game is going to do anything to rein in the massive wave of anxiety running through my veins right now. I don't have the slightest idea how I have dominated my body so that it behaves with some normalcy during the last hours. This whole "lack of control" thing kicked in the moment I caught wind, thanks to the TV, that Daniel Montalvo was hitting up my town. Just saying his name sets off a riot of butterflies in my stomach, and that's one drawback. Anyway, let's get back to my story.

I've always been incredibly shy, and it's not some random thing. There are legit reasons for it, and I'll totally spill the tea on that later. But here's the thing: it was around eleven o'clock at night when I suddenly felt like a whole other person had taken over me. This new version of me had zero shyness and zero fear about whatever consequences might come my way. It was out there looking in every corner of the Earth for this businessman who was bringing Daniel Montalvo to the city. I was so caught up in this madness that I didn't even stop to think that, once I got the man   on the phone, I'd still need to work some serious charm to convince him to hook me up with a few seconds of Daniel Montalvo's time for an autograph. I know, I know, believe me, I know better than anyone that this whole thing sounds crazy. But seriously, around three in the morning, I managed to track down Mr. Carlos Garza himself.

That hour is seriously disrespectful when it comes to making a call to someone I've never met. But my grandma always told me that in life-or-death situations, you can ignore the clock. And trust me, my call felt like that, kinda sorta life or death, at least for me. Mr. Garza was really nice when he picked up the phone—the man is a saint. He coughed a couple of times and chuckled a bunch. Please don't even ask me to repeat what I blabbered because, first off, I only recall fragments; and secondly, it was such a jumble that I'd die of embarrassment by retelling it. Point is, he agreed to see me today at five in the evening, and yep, that's where I'm headed.

The first time I saw Daniel was while watching a Spanish TV show, around three years ago. Back then, at the ripe old age of fourteen, I'd never come across a guy—whether singer or actor—who could truly captivate me like he did. Though, I'll admit, my total obsession can be explained by his alluring good looks. It's like someone put in an absurd amount of effort to craft a guy with perfection as the ultimate goal, making sure every single detail was just right. Picture this: he's tall, like six feet and two inches tall, with jet-black hair that contrasts beautifully with his pale skin. His face has this chiseled, angular shape, and his eyes are this intense, striking blue. And that smile? It's the most extraordinary I have ever seen. Oh, and his body? Athletic and totally in sync with his face. It's like he's a moving piece of art—seriously, you can't look away. And here's the kicker: the guy can sing like a dream, and he's got the smarts to match. I mean, he can actually hold a conversation without sounding like he's reading from a "How to Not Sound Stupid on Camera" manual. He's the definition of perfection. Do you get me?

I'm still kind of baffled about what came over me. I mean, don't get me wrong, I'm into it, no doubt. But if you knew me better, you'd realize I'm not really the type to go all out like this. Usually, my emotional outbreaks are more like shy, scared, and anxious combos—and they love to team up. So, it's a little confusing why I suddenly decided to call up the businessman, convinced him to say yes, and now I'm on my way. It's totally out of character. Between the time Mr. Garza agreed and the actual meet-up—which, by the way, is a pretty big deal—my brain's been waging a full-on war against me. It's been trying to talk me out of it, but its efforts have been in vain. And as if that's not enough, my sister's been hammering the "You're nuts!" point for hours straight.

The Game…Jade

Groundbreaking news, right? Apparently, this kind of stuff isn't expected to happen to someone as "insignificant" as me.

Like, it was as if I needed her help to have reasons to feel tinier than I already did. My self-esteem? Oh, it's already set up camp way below ground level. Her words didn't exactly work magic to plunge me further down. At least, I must give myself credit. This time, her attempt didn't quite succeed in squashing my determination to do what I wanted. Sure, there'll be plenty of time for her to laugh it up later when I get back home empty-handed, without that prized autograph that's supposed to be the proof of my triumph. But, right now, I'm soaring on this cloud that's so far from reach. I heard her snarky remarks alright, but didn't quite hurt—well, at least not yet. It's like some weird kind of numbness has set in against that usual hurt.

Through the car windshield, I can see the hotel gardens where he's staying, completely swarmed by girls waiting for him. I mean, how many of them have already caught a glimpse of him? Why didn't I think of coming here at the crack of dawn just to watch him pass by and admire him from a distance? It's like whatever possessed me had no idea that was even an option.

Suddenly, I find myself in the hotel lobby. Okay, not quite like that, but honestly, I have no clue how I ended up here. I ask about Mr. Carlos Garza, and the guy at the reception desk gets this softer expression on his face—he's probably sick of being asked about Daniel. He makes a call to his room and mentions that he's expecting me. My legs seem to know exactly where they should be headed, which is great because I'm pretty lost.

I knock on the door, and this tall, fair-skinned guy with a mustache and a totally saintly expression opens it. He looks at me for what feels like forever without saying a word.

"Mr. Garza?" I venture.

"Jade, isn't that correct? Young lady, what on earth did you say to sway me? I'm not usually one for these kinds of situations. Come along with me."

I'm trying my best to keep up with him. He leads me over to the hotel lobby and tells me to wait for Daniel. He quickly instructs the security agents not to kick me out. I feel like everything is crashing down around me. What does that even mean? Shouldn't he be the one introducing me? He openly chuckles at my confusion.

"If he figures out I allowed you in, I'm going to be in major trouble. So, just stay here and act properly." 'Act properly' like, does he even know me?

Rocío Blisswealth

8

I mean, I'm not sure how to act in another way, and honestly, I don't really want to, either. He pauses for a second and looks back at me.

"I've got just a single piece of advice for you: be cautious around his manager. She's a bitch." Sorry, but those were his exact words. And, with that said, he takes off, not even giving me a chance to say thanks. And there I am, left totally freaked out.

I still can't figure out how this crazy shyness that's always hanging around has suddenly faded away. It's like it took a timeout from bugging me to let me get this far, but handling it all on my own? It feels impossible!

And now, I'm facing yet another issue. My brain is all like, "Run!" but my legs? They're acting like they've gone on strike. It's as if the blood that was rushing through them just moments ago has turned into lead. I'm watching them from a massive brown couch, and it's almost like they belong to someone else entirely. Like I'm telling someone else's legs to take off running. They don't listen to me, whether it's for good or bad.

I can't help but play out the absolute worst scenarios in my head. All the stuff that could go wrong the moment his manager strolls in and catches me right here, sitting. What's holding me back? Part of me screams to get up and leave, to shake off the nerves racing down my spine and this crazy nausea that's seriously the worst ever. But I can't bring myself to do it. I crave this; I admit it. I'm totally aware—I need those few seconds just to catch a glimpse of him, let my eyes soak it all in, even if it's a one-time thing. I'm not hoping for more than that.

Out of the blue, he walks in through the hotel lobby. He's way taller than I ever imagined, and his eyes are this deep, sweet shade of blue that just grabs you. Our eyes meet, and somehow, my legs actually decide to cooperate, carrying me towards him. My brain's racing, trying to come up with something to say—you know, something that won't make me sound like a total idiot. But let's be real. I've pretty much given up on the idea of saying anything remotely smart.

He's rocking blue jeans that totally sync up with his eyes, and his white shirt's sleeves are casually rolled up, like halfway to his elbows. And then, oh gods! He's making his way towards me. He strolls over, it's like he's got the feline grace thing going on. There's no way nature didn't take notes from this guy. His steps are just perfection. And then he hits me with this smile. I swear it's the kind that could light up an entire room, and before I know it, he's got

The Game...Jade

me wrapped up in his arms. I'm probably asleep and dreaming. But, you know, when I really think about it, my heart's pounding so crazily it's like it's trying to escape my chest... Yes, he's actually hugging me!

Just for a tiny moment, I find myself in the embrace of an actual angel, and I'm thanking the universe for making me exactly who I am. I've lost count of how many times I've wished I could be someone else. You know, stunning, super smart, anything other than me. But right now, I wouldn't trade a single thing, not even the tiniest bit of who I am or where I am, 'cause it's totally me— just as I am—that he's holding so close.

Out of nowhere, this awful doubt crashes into me and totally jolts me out of my dreamy state. What if he's got me all mixed up with someone else? Or, you know, what if he's actually waiting for a different person? Panic floods over me—I'm thinking he's going to be so disappointed when he realizes I'm not who he's expecting. A shiver goes right down my spine, and I kind of pull back just a little from his arms, enough so he can see my face or really see me. And right then and there, he smiles and asks for my name. This massive wave of relief washes over me. I'm scrambling to remember the answer to that seemingly simple yet totally complicated question.

"Jade," I reply. "My name is Jade."

Just at that moment, his manager walks over. Oh no, seriously? I'm still trying to piece my thoughts together to remember my own name, and now it's like my good luck is going to totally disappear. Daniel switches his focus to her.

"Look, Sara, she's Jade." It's like she's supposed to magically know who I am. She reaches out to say hello, and I follow suit. I guess my reflexes are starting to kick in again.

"Jade, it's my pleasure. I'm going to leave you here; I have some things to do. Rest assured, you're in capable hands."

Has everyone lost their minds or something? Was that the bitch I was supposed to watch out for? Those moments I've been longing for—the ones I've been begging the universe for the absolute best times ever—have probably slipped away into some ancient history by now. And yet, here I am, feeling like I've just walked into some alternate dimension or something. It's as if the universe is on my side, but I've always got this inner voice saying not to push my luck too far. And honestly, now isn't the perfect time to start testing those limits. So, even though it's a bit of a struggle, I'm, you know, trying to get myself back on track with my original idea. Well, okay, fine, I never really got around to totally forming a plan, but let's just pretend I had one, and this is me putting it into action. I dig into my bag and pull out a piece of paper, and then I somehow muster up the courage to ask for an autograph. And his response? It leaves me confused.

"Would it be alright if I handed it to you later? I've got a meeting lined up with my band. Would you be up for joining me?" I'm seriously out of breath, and I'm not even processing what's going on. And then, there's this voice—I swear, it's like coming from my own mouth, and it's saying that I really don't wanna be a bother.

"You're never a bother."

He says that, and seriously, all my doubts just poof away. It's like I'm standing there with two options: either I've officially lost my mind, or this whole thing is some kind of dream. Then he goes and reaches for my hand... and my hand is between his. Alright, this has to be a dream, and I'm going to relish every moment of it while it lasts. So, we walk into the room, and everyone's eyes are totally on me—the musicians are all staring at me. And then, one of them stands up and grabs a chair for me to sit in.

"Don't worry, I'll take this seat." I point over at this little stool. Honestly, what I'm thinking is that I just wanna take in every bit of him while this dream lasts. So, where I sit doesn't even matter much to me.

Daniel grins and leads me to the chair, the one meant for his musician. Then he sits down right next to me, and he even lets his hand rest on my arm, which is kind of unexpected. Okay, this is totally throwing off my theories. Maybe this isn't a dream after all? Maybe I'm officially going nuts. But you know what? I'm just going to enjoy every single second of this, theories or whatever can take a back seat. They were just me being curious, and honestly, I'm cool with either of them being true.

No matter how hard I try, I can't get into their conversation. I'm simply using this time to, you know, gaze at his athletic figure through my lucky eyes. And those words he said—you're never a bother—they're playing over and over in my mind, just like a cherished tune. They're the nicest compliment I've ever gotten. But there's this tiny voice in me that's questioning it. 'Cause, come on, he's only known me for a few minutes, right? How could he even tell if I'm annoying or not? But, whatever, none of that matters right now. At this moment, nothing else even counts.

The Game...Jade

"Don't worry, I have bodyguards. Plus, I just want to make sure you get to your car safe and sound."

He gently holds my waist and guides me towards the car, and honestly, I can't quite remember where it's parked exactly. But that's not surprising, considering I'm not even sure how I managed to make my way back to the hotel lobby. Yet, my legs seem to know the route, leading me somewhere—I'm just not entirely sure where.

The fresh scent of his cologne wraps around me, and I take two steps for every one of his. All I see are these blurry streaks of color forming like a sort of barrier we're walking within. I'm guessing those must be the fans hoping to catch a glimpse of him, though I have to admit, being in his arms sounds way more appealing right now. I'd rather hear the steady rhythm of his breath. Thankfully, he's holding me still because it kind of feels like my feet aren't touching the ground.

Finally, I spot the car, and the door is opened for me. Did he even ask for my car key? I can't remember. As I'm about to step inside, I realize he hasn't moved. Instead of moving aside for me to get in, he's just standing there, watching me with this smile on his lips. Oh, my goodness! He must have said something and is waiting for me to respond. What should I say?

He lifts his hand and gently rests it on the back of my neck, making me shift my focus from his eyes to his smile, which is getting closer. And there I am, not budging an inch. It's like my body's completely unsure what to do, and all I can think is: "Jade, no matter what, just keep your eyes open!"

His lips touch mine, and the kiss is so intense and lingers way longer than I thought was possible. Right then, in that second, and it's like everything changes—my whole world shifts; my imagination isn't big enough to calculate how much.

Now, after half a year has gone by, here I am, lying on my bed, just staring at the ceiling. Not that there's anything super interesting about it, but it's the perfect canvas for my thoughts to flow. And yes, as expected, I can't exactly piece together how I made it back from the concert. The whole show, even though it was amazing, feels like it's broken into bits in my mind. But there are these flashes that stand out so clearly: his totally captivating face, his perfectly toned body, and the fiery memory of our kiss—and that's more than I could've ever asked for.

Rocío Blisswealth

I was lost in my thoughts when suddenly my mom knocked on the door and came into my room—where I spent most of my time—and handed me a letter. The name on the sender line reads Daniel Montalvo.

Monterrey, Mexico. The day I was born.

I came into the world at 7 a.m. on a crisp March 5th morning. My mom, caught up in her worries inspired by countless movies, seemed to fear that I might be swapped for another newborn. She showered the clinic staff with all sorts of instructions and suggestions. The nurse, trying to reassure her, explained that her concerns were unfounded. I turned out to be the lone baby girl welcomed into the hospital that day; all the other arrivals were a bunch of newborn boys.

Two days later, I was brought to my grandparents' house—the same house we've called home for as far back as my memory stretches. They placed me in a crib right in Mom's room. Not too much time went by before she realized that something strange was happening with me.

Beneath the crib, a regular and repetitive sound begins to echo. According to Mom, it resembles the tick of an antique alarm clock, though this one resonates a touch louder than those old timepieces. Intrigued, she investigates, hoping to uncover its source, only to find nothing. Yet, that noise doesn't sit right with her; it's like a persistent reminder of a ticking time bomb. She tries to change the crib of place with me still in it, but she knows any movement might stir me from sleep. She carefully lifts me with one arm while using the other to relocate the crib, and abruptly, the noise ceases. Almost in perfect harmony, the noise stops, and my crying begins.

Noticing that I'm already awake, she moves the crib to the opposite end of the bedroom and places me there. It takes only three, maybe four seconds before the sound resumes its rhythm, and I drift back into a peaceful sleep. Fear grips her; she doesn't want to leave me alone there. Acting on instinct, she opens the door and calls for my grandma while she picks me up again, and I continue crying loudly. Two hours later, and without results, a sense of surrender sets in, and they return me to the crib, where the sound promptly begins its distinct, resonant notes once more.

Mom couldn't bear the thought of something endangering her baby's life. If such a threat existed, who or what could it be? And why? The questions linger without any clear answers. In the years that followed, during my early

The Game...Jade

childhood, that sound would become a constant companion in both my dreams and my mother's.

Monterrey, Mexico. Seventeen years old.

Life has changed for me since I met him. I feel stronger, more secure, and uniquely special. One day, my sister began harassing me. I don't even remember what she said, which is quite unusual for me, as I used to store her comments and replay them in my mind countless times until they became ingrained in me. Not anymore.

While Mara tries to talk to me, all I catch is a string of "blah, blah, blah." She's trying to get me to do something, but I can spot her intentions by the way her voice subtly rises when she's trying to pass off an order as a favor. I shift my attention towards her and reply.

"No." My words come out calmly.

"Why not?" Mara questions, her voice pitched even higher than usual.

"Because I simply don't want to."

The surprise leaves her speechless. My mother looks at me incredulously, and my grandma says:

"Oh, this day had to come." Almost as if she'd been secretly waiting for it.

Mom realized that day, that girl who used to be afraid of being punished by god for misbehaving no longer existed. And that's how it was. From those days on, I wouldn't have cared about divine punishment anymore—I had already been to heaven.

I left them behind and headed to my room, that place I had turned into... how can I put it? An altar, maybe? Yes, that sounds about right. I've covered my walls with every Daniel poster I could get my hands on—until there was no more space for either posters or walls. Whichever way I look, his face, his smile, his eyes—they're always there! This is my sanctuary, my haven. It's become my most cherished memory so far, and I'm determined to hold on to this feeling for as long as possible.

As my mom steps into the room, she's holding a letter, which she then passes to me. In an instant, my heart races up to my throat, its rhythmic and fast-paced beats eclipsing every other sound around me. An electric tingle courses through my entire body, and I'm left staring at the letter in my hands, captivated. I can only watch it as if I'm trying to reassure myself that it's truly real.

Rocío Blisswealth

Meanwhile, my mother's voice reaches me, as if speaking through a tin can, resonating deep within my ears.

"What's the matter?"

Just give me a few seconds, Mom. I'm not sure yet, but I'm guessing I'm a whirlwind of emotions—overwhelmed, surprised, and teetering on the brink of excitement to the point where I might even start hyperventilating.

What's going on with me? The most stunning guy in the world sent me a few lines—just as he said he would. Those same words I didn't take seriously at first. I mean, come on, who would? Believing that would have been way too naive of me. Good things like this never happen to me, yet here I am, holding a letter that's proving me wrong, at least in this instance, if it's even real. Incredibly, he thought of me, even if it was for a minute or maybe even longer.

My mom keeps looking at me, waiting for an answer. I need to respond with something, anything.

"Nothing, Mom, I'm not completely awake yet." I wave her off, eager to read the treasured letter without any interruptions.

Hello Jade,

The tour has been quite a journey, concerts, nights without sleep, endless interviews, and it's like a cycle starting anew in every city.

Back in Madrid now, fully engrossed in album promotion. Just wanted to let you know that Carmen, my aunt, will be your go-to when I'm tied up.

As we arranged, she's sent you my address. I'm looking forward to receiving your letter.

Sending you a warm and affectionate kiss,

Daniel Montalvo

These lines in his handwriting feel like a divine gift. It's a beautiful sort of anesthesia, making me sense his presence so strongly that I believe I can conquer anything—well, almost anything, except the courage to write back to him. Why, you might ask? I'm not entirely sure. I suppose my mind, caught up in relishing these emotions, leaves little space for the craziness that would let me respond. No, I'm not holding out for any expectations, and that's precisely why there's no room for disappointment. I'm okay with it—I'm happy, thoroughly happy. There's no other emotion swirling within me, and honestly, it's more than enough.

Monterrey, Mexico. Four years old.

This night stands out as the first time I truly experienced fear.

When I was four years old, my bedtime routine was less about adhering to a specific time and more about going to bed when sleepiness overtook me. With Mom always working, my grandma has been concerned about giving us the best education possible in terms of manners. However, she granted us certain exceptions, like not having a fixed bedtime. Mom succeeded in getting me to bed early, but unfortunately, I woke up shortly after, in the darkness, listening to the voices of my mom and sister talking to someone else, whom I can't see but who scares me. I started trembling but kept silent and paid attention.

"Is not responding to me." My mother whispers.

"But it does to me. I will ask him." That's my sister's voice, Mara, five years older than me. "Knock twice for 'yes' and once for 'no', okay?"

Two knocks resonate from beneath my bed, and her delighted laughter fills the air, causing my trembling to intensify. It's the first time I've noticed the sound emanating from beneath my bed, and I find myself thoroughly disliking it. They're both seated on Mom's bed, right beside mine. Meanwhile, I'm left all alone, buried under my blankets, which no longer feel like a shield against the creeping terror that leaves me frozen in place.

"I want to know who he's dating." My mother's voice can be heard.

"Not that way, it's only yes or no, remember?" my sister replies.

"Is he dating someone?"

Two knocks are heard. I am no longer capable of controlling this terror; I have a scream in my throat and finally let it out.

"No more! Don't ask him again! I don't want to hear it, I'm scared!". Amidst my sobs, the words burst out of me. Of course, I scared them, and my sister's irritated voice filled the room.

"Stop crying. It's not doing anything to you."

My mom tells me to go back to sleep and assures me that they won't ask anything anymore, but I find it hard to believe her. The tales of monsters

Rocío Blisswealth

under the bed suddenly feel like they were written just for me, becoming the reality in this room. No one can convince me that there's nothing there, not after hearing my mom and sister pose questions and receiving responses from... whatever it is.

With a quiet voice, I call for my grandma, but she doesn't hear me. Someone, please, get me out of here. My sister mocks me, and my mom remains motionless where she is. I can sense their anxiety. Somehow, they want to force me to fall asleep again so they can keep asking. I ask my mom to lie down with me for a minute while my fear subsides, but she doesn't. She asks me to close my eyes and try to sleep, and she doesn't move from where she is. I watch her; panic creeps up my blankets, enveloping me.

I begin to pray, feeling it's the only option left, even though I struggle to remember the Our Father that my grandma tried so hard to teach me. My desperate search continues for someone to hold me, to pull me out of this horror story.

And then, I see him in the dimness of my room. A young man, tall, dressed in jeans and a white T-shirt, as if he's passed through the wall. He walks towards me and slowly takes a seat at the foot of my bed. I can feel his body's movement as he does so; my eyes open wider and wider, and I hold my breath.

A smile—such a sweet smile! He reaches out his hand and rests it on my foot. Even though I'm tucked under the blankets, I can sense his warmth. It won't harm me, I'm certain. What a blessing it is to be at an age where I don't fully grasp the possibility that the sound beneath my bed and the young man seated at its edge could be two facets of the same being. Yet, the latter presence provides me with a reassuring comfort.

"How are you?" It's as if no one else hears it.

"I'm really scared." I manage to say in a soft voice, my words mixed with sobs.

"What scares you?" He asks in a gentle tone.

"The noise under my bed."

"Don't want to hear it anymore?" Keeps asking.

"Please, ask it to stop." I hope he can make it stop somehow.

"No more." He declares firmly, drawing closer to gently caress my head. He lies down beside me, wrapping me in his arms. Clinging tightly to his hand, which I can barely hold with mine, the fear vanishes. It's so calm now;

The Game...Jade

Now I'm in a bit of a pickle. My life is much more ordinary than most people's. What can I tell him that won't sound so boring?

"Daniel..." I start to answer. "I don't know what to tell you. When I'm not working, I usually find myself holed up in my room, reading. Oh, and listening to music." I look at him and wink; he knows that most of the music I listen to is his. He doesn't interrupt me; he wants me to keep going. But what the heck! What should I say? Of course, I must be careful because there's so much of my uneventful life that I can't share.

"I studied English in the United States."

"I know."

"How do you know that?"

"When I first saw you in Monterrey, do you remember?" How could I forget? Of course, I remember, but what surprises me is that he remembers, but that doesn't really clarify my point. "You were with me in the meeting with my band; it was in English, and you didn't have the slightest problem."

"Well, the truth is, that darn meeting could have been in Russian, and it wouldn't have made a difference to me." Shut up, Jade! Please. Too late; I've already said it, and my cheeks are screaming it. I gently shake my head from side to side.

"Oh, really? And why?" A mischievous smile begins to emerge; he's being rude!

"Let's just say my mind was wandering elsewhere while you guys were talking."

"Don't tell me. Where?" The smile is getting bigger and bigger, and now he raises an eyebrow; he is cornering me, but I'm not willing to let him win.

"I couldn't get over the surprise of being there, with you, with Daniel Montalvo."

"Daniel."

"That's what I said."

"To you, I'm just Daniel; the other one is a persona I put on when I go out to sing, but now, right here with you, I can just be Daniel."

And I let it be that way, just Daniel, and we talked for quite a while, sharing childhood anecdotes, school stories, and details about our families. He had a tough childhood, something I can relate to, even though the experiences we went through were quite different. He also doesn't get along with his father, but he adores his sisters, both younger than him.

I share with him my escapades from catholic school. My mom used to drop me off at kindergarten every day, and when she got home, she found me in the living room watching cartoons. Nobody ever knew how I did it, and I don't even remember, but eventually, Mom got tired of it and abandoned the idea of giving me a religious education. All of this makes him burst into laughter. Also, I share about the wonderful landscapes I saw when I studied in the United States and the passion I have for traveling, a passion he shares, too.

Without realizing it, I finish the fruit I had on my plate and get up to place it on the table. As I do, I catch him tracing my legs with his gaze, pausing at my feet. It's curious how our insecurities work; we instinctively gravitate toward the self-image we hold. This leads us to mentally revisit the entire list of flaws that life has given us, one after another, wondering why the person observing us hadn't noticed them before, like the length of our nose, the dryness of our hair, and so on. Ironically, it had to be my feet that caught his attention— thank you, Murphy's Law. And as if that weren't enough, he not only stares at them intently but also grins while doing so. What could he be thinking? I can't hold back any longer, so I decided to ask.

"What are you looking at?"

"Your feet." He answers with that blessed smile still on his lips.

"Alright, and what's up with them?" I return to the couch, hiding one of them as I sit on it.

"They're so small!" He keeps looking at the one that remained outside my makeshift hideout.

It's official; I could love this man with absolute passion and debauchery. The truth is, my feet aren't that small, but if that's what he thinks, I won't be the one to contradict him. We keep talking for a few more minutes, and finally, we get a call from the lobby to let us know they've arrived to pick us up. Our activities are about to start. Before leaving the room, he stops me by the arm.

"Gorgeous, who are you going to talk to about these days here?"

"Are you kidding? No one. Who would believe me?" I reply, laughing.

"I won't tell anyone either. I can't even believe you're here with me."

What? Are you serious? But he's the famous one, the unattainable one, the dream come true, it's him. I'm just, well, me, without any frills, without anything special worth mentioning. I look at him with absolute surprise. He smiles almost shyly and asks for a hug. Why does he think it's necessary to ask? I'm dying for one, too.

I move closer and wrap my arms around his back. I enjoy the sensation of his breath on my hair, and suddenly, it dawns on me that the Jade who left Monterrey has vanished here, in his arms. After this, I'll never be the same. What does it matter if no one knows? Who cares if no one believes me? I know, I believe it, and that's enough for me. He comes closer, placing his hand on the back of my neck, pulling me toward him, and kisses the tip of my nose, sending a shiver racing from my neck to my heels. He smiled slightly. Surely, he could feel it. Then he presses his lips against mine, and I respond. No, I'm most definitely not the same anymore.

We spent the entire afternoon at radio stations and once again, the same questions, over and over. However, I keep enjoying every minute as if it were the first day. When we left the last radio station, Paty bid us farewell.

"But how? Why are you leaving? What about your things?" I ask, surprised.

"They're already at home; I took them this morning." Probably, she did it while we were having breakfast. "Thank you very much for including me in all of this."

"I'm the one who can't thank you enough for all your attention. If it hadn't been for you, I wouldn't be here." I speak with complete honesty.

"I know that's not true, but still, thank you." She hugs me and asks me to stay in touch.

Daniel offers to take her home, but she declines and decides to take a cab. We get in the van and head back to the hotel. On our way, Daniel grew serious.

"We're leaving today too." He speaks.

"You and Raúl? I thought you were leaving tomorrow."

"Originally, but there was a change of plans. You're also leaving for Monterrey today on the last flight. I don't intend to leave you alone." He says without looking into my eyes, holding my hand in his.

"No, I'm leaving tomorrow by bus." I say firmly; he turns to look at me sweetly.

"I'm not going to leave you here alone, and I've already made arrangements. I didn't tell you because I knew you would refuse, but at least this time, indulge me, okay?"

It's useless; I couldn't refuse now, not when he looks at me that way. I feel like the world is crashing down on me. There's still sand left in my hourglass; it's not fair!

We arrive at the hotel, and Raúl is already waiting for us in the room. He looks much better, truly, absolutely healthy.

"How are you, kid?" He asks with a smile. "Have you already confirmed that this guy is unbearable?" I couldn't answer without exposing myself to one of Daniel's pranks, so I just smiled at him. "Sometimes there's no way to shake off his bad mood. Too much stress in the mix!"

"What's happening is that you don't know how to calm me down." Daniel says. "Only she can; ask her how." I had a feeling he wouldn't let me off the hook; he has to annoy me, even at a time like these. So, I strike back.

"With meditation, it's excellent, you know? But he has to do it headstand style so that the blood circulates to his brain. He still hasn't mastered it, so don't let him stop trying until he succeeds. Okay? It really works wonders on him." I smile.

I hear his laughter, and Raúl looks at us as if he doesn't understand anything. I want to etch his laughter into my memory because, from now on, it will be the only thing I have left. The darn balance, remember? The so-called yin and yang will make sure to collect from me every second.

We arrived at the airport and checked our luggage. Raúl hands me a box. I look at Daniel, and he winks at me; it's the music collection with which I'll have to pay the bribe that allowed me to be here up to this day. We head to a VIP waiting lounge where we can wait without the bustling crowd around us. We sit together, and Daniel starts stroking my hair.

"I'm going to miss you." He says quietly.

"And I even more." I answer.

"Are you going to write to me now?" He asks as he talks more and more softly.

"No, not now either." I replied.

"I knew it! You never change." He holds me in his arms.

"Believe me, I change. I've changed a lot."

The Game…Jade

We heard the boarding announcement for my flight. So, he clings to me with even more intensity, making it feel as though my skin might peel off my body. He kisses my head one last time and asks Raúl to accompany me to the waiting area. Raúl takes my hand, and we sprint down the hallway, as if I were in a hurry to board that wretched plane. I don't look back; it would just be too much for me.

I say goodbye to Raúl and thank him as I've never thanked anyone in this life for getting sick and granting me the opportunity to fulfill dreams I didn't even know I had. I hug him tightly, very tightly, desperately hoping to capture any trace of Daniel that might have rubbed off on him. I kiss his cheek and walk away to make my way toward the slaughterhouse.

Now I can feel it with absolute clarity, this pain. It's as if the light has gone out, plunging me into the most agonizing darkness, as if I had truly torn my skin to shreds in his arms. What does it matter now? What good could it possibly do me now? Who could touch it that would matter to me?

I can feel my arms growing numb, painfully aware that they can no longer wrap around his body, and my eyes search for the blue of his, but he's gone, too. He has been taken away from me just like everything else—his laughter, his scent, his breath, his very presence. And it hurts. An unbearable pain invades me, weighs me down, and I feel alone. For the first time, I know what it means to be truly alone.

It was in that last embrace, the one I painfully let go of, that my soul decided to split, to tear itself in two to remain with him and, at the same time, help me keep on living.

How could she not do it? Anything is better than going back to that room where she has lived, not knowing under what charges, condemned to coexist with demons, to serve them as a toy, without a break, without solace. I don't blame her; if there was one thing she dared to wish for, it was to stay with him, and she did, leaving only a piece inside me, large enough to feed the longing to see him again and reconnect with this part of me that accompanies him. The part that did manage to escape and go with him.

What is my brain doing, refusing to shut down? It's no longer necessary for it to remain active; that's needed when there's a life. But, in case my brain hasn't gotten the memo, I left mine down there, in those arms. So, as far as I'm concerned, it could very well consider its services finished. Yet, I keep breathing, just that—breathing repeatedly, aimlessly.

Rocío Blisswealth

The plane finally lands, and as I step outside with my suitcase in hand, the demon is waiting there for me, ready to mock me, I suppose. What other reason could he have for waiting? Except to intensify my suffering. I almost smile at him. Why doesn't he just end it with me once and for all? He only has to squeeze tightly until I stop breathing. Come on, why don't you make up your mind already?

End my own life? No, sorry, that's no longer an option. I left that behind willingly in Daniel's arms. You have to settle for what's left of me, this half-empty vessel; there's nothing else left, you can be sure of that.

Monterrey, Mexico. Sixteen years old.

Certainly, the night I tried to banish the demons from my room—with terrible results—I unwittingly opened the door to even greater terrors than the ones I was already experiencing. As soon as the demon left the room, and despite the fear of interrupting Mom and Mara's prayers without uttering a respectful "amen" in between, I rushed to the restroom to empty my stomach. Between the nausea provoked by the demon's proximity and his smell, and the uncontrollable trembling caused by this newfound sensation of not knowing, but rather intuiting, what I had just gotten myself into, I couldn't even hold my breath inside.

Of course, they went after me, so not only do I have to deal with trying to expel the contents of my stomach without losing valuable pieces of it in the process, but I also have to try to take a breath to answer them the dozen times they ask me if I'm okay. I'm not sure how many times I have answered yes; the air I manage to draw into my lungs is not enough for anything else, only for a "yes" from time to time and to help my stomach to continue vomiting.

I don't want to tell them what happened; in the end, they didn't see anything, and I've always preferred to keep them out of it all. I guess I see it as a sort of personal burden. I don't want to share anything that might put them at risk, but I will have to get out of the restroom at some point. At least, I hope so, and I can't think of any other alternative. I open the door, and they both look at me with eyes of terror.

"What happened?" Mara asks. I explain with the little voice I have left due to the damage to my throat.

The Game…Jade

The only response I receive is her diving more fervently into her Bible. Mom is not sure if what we did was right. I am sure it wasn't, and I'm just waiting for things to get worse. She looks at me and starts asking me questions that only show me how little she knows me.

"Jade." She asks with fear in her eyes. "Why don't you ever read the Bible?"

I try to come up with an answer that won't scare her more than she already is, but I want to be honest. I don't want to add to the fear she already feels for me, which isn't good. So, I responded.

"It's a book that scares me. I'm scared of god." I reply while looking at her in the eyes. She doesn't bother hiding her surprise and tries to correct me.

"Scared of god?! You mean fear of god." There's no turning back now. No matter what Mom might think of me, I have to keep going, and so I do.

"No, I'm terrified of him." I see her struggling to find something to say to me, but without letting her speak, I continue. "Mom, let's face it, there's something wrong with me as far back as I can remember, since I was born, or even before that. I swear I pray, or whatever you want to call it, but nobody answers me, nobody saves me, nothing." She wants to get closer to me and tries to hug me, but I don't allow it, just as I haven't allowed her for many years.

"What's happening is that you lack faith." She says, almost in a whisper, with an immense sense of disappointment in her voice.

"Faith?" I say, trying to control the volume of my voice to keep it low. "You've told me that faith is believing in what you can't see, right? Well, maybe you're right, because I believe in everything I can see. I'm surrounded by demons, don't you realize? No, Mom, it's not a lack of faith, it's more like... from where I am..." I can't control my voice anymore, and it starts to escape in shouts. "...from where I stand, from the day I was born, nobody can hear me, not even god! You know why? Because I live in hell!"

Chapter IV
A path strewn with corpses

Monterrey, Mexico. Eighteen years old.

This feeling is so strange. I can't even bounce back from it. Why am I feeling so wrecked? If I'm being real with myself, I never even dared to dream that this whole adventure could be an escape for me, you know? A way to break free from this prison in some way.

I always knew deep down that I'd go back to Monterrey. But now that I've shaken off those demons and had the chance to dive into that little bubble with just Daniel and me, everything else just feels ridiculously unbearable, painfully monotonous, and overwhelmingly boring. And, like some kind of self-defense thing my brain does in my everyday life that makes it hard to get close to anyone, I don't miss anyone either. I only switch up my life when someone beyond my family disappears from it, whether it's due to travel or, you know, passing away, which, to me, feels pretty much the same.

But, this time, nothing is the same. I'm in the taxi on my way home, with my demon right there next to me, which it's weird. He doesn't even look at me. Despite that, I can feel that Daniel is still on the plane. He's flying over that endless ocean, getting farther away from me. When am I going to get to see him again? My brain refuses to admit that it probably will never happen. Darn it! If only I could accept it, maybe I could stop sinking and put an end to this never-ending fall into this black hole that seems to go on forever. Maybe I could do something more than just breathe or, you know, just stop breathing altogether.

But no, not this time. This time, there's a tiny spark inside me, shouting its heart out, even though I can barely hear it, telling me to wait, to just wait for him. And it's exactly to that voice that I decide to hold on. How stupid, right? Just check the odds, Jade: they're a million to one! But I can't help it. I keep hearing that little voice in the distance, and it's the one I choose to pay attention to.

I finally arrive home, and they're waiting for me in the living room, eager to hear how it all went down. Mom and my sister are watching me closely

The Game…Jade

as if trying to read the outcome of these days in Mexico City from my face. They barrage me with questions.

One-word answers are my best bet right now; "Yes," "No," "Sometimes," "Pretty good." That's all they manage to get from me. I won't share this with them. Why would I? I don't need their harassment or their comments about how they would have handled various situations way better than I did. No, this is just for me. I won't let them invade my memories and twist them into accusations or reasons to pity me—they've got plenty of those already.

Mara tells me she saw Daniel on TV, and before she can mention why she's bringing it up, I stop her dead in her tracks.

"Don't talk about him." I say, my voice holding back a hint of anger. I don't want him tarnished by her words, his memory, his essence—none of it should be tainted.

"It's just that they said that Daniel..." She keeps ignoring me. She always has, but she's about to get a surprise.

"Mara. Don't you dare bring it up again, got it? I won't allow you to mention him in front of me." I let it all out now, not bothering to hide the anger, letting each of my words carry the weight, and I locked eyes with her. No, I'm giving her a stern look, and she gets the message loud and clear, shutting up on the spot.

"I'm really tired." I add, heading back to my room where his image hangs on every wall, waiting for me.

Mom says they have a lot to tell me, that Mara has discovered many things that can help me. Yes, right. Unless it's a bottle of cyanide, I doubt they can achieve anything. However, I don't bother responding to them; I just keep on trudging up the stairs.

I step into the room, and Daniel's eyes stare at me, multiplied across every poster, every photograph, every album. And it suddenly dawns on me; how did I not realize this before? They're just pieces of paper, dry and lifeless pieces of paper, yet right now, they offer me more comfort than my mother and sister, who are still chatting in the living room.

I lay down on the bed, seeking a touch of unconsciousness, anything to numb this pain, the sound of a voice echoing in my head: "How are you,

Rocío Blisswealth

90

gorgeous?" But it's not there. So finally, I fall asleep. The demons leave me alone. There will be time for everything.

Two nights later, I'm still in my room. I've hardly left this place except to go to work and deliver the albums that Daniel promised to my boss in exchange for letting me skip the office. I know I made him very happy; I had never seen him smile so much. Obviously, he bombarded me with questions, but the good thing is that I had rehearsed the answers to every single one of them. So, he got my supply of "Yes," "No," "Sometimes," "Pretty good," and seemed satisfied. I've never been very talkative, so I guess he didn't expect more.

Tonight, has been insanely tough. Instead of just feeling Daniel's absence a little less, it's like every second without him is even more unbearable. So, when Mom barges into my room, she's got my full attention.

"Jade, there's something you must do." She says. I've heard this line before, but then she continues. "Daniel needs your help."

The demon lurking in the corner of my room perks up and starts heading my way, and inside me, a little voice is screaming urgently:

"Jade, no!"

I sit up in bed, turn to look at the demon, and raise my hand to signal him to stop. I mutter under my breath, "Back off." Then, with a louder tone, I let out, "Everyone, just shut up!" Surprisingly, they both obeyed this time. Mom stays quiet, too.

"No, not you! Tell me what's going on." I'm freaking out, highly agitated, but she keeps going, trying to match the speed of her words with my impatience.

"You've never given us a chance to explain, but Mara has accomplished some incredible things in the last few months. We'll have time to explain how she found out, but that same darkness that's been weighing you down is affecting Daniel, too. If you don't help him, things won't turn out well for either of you."

She takes a deep breath, and honestly, at this point, my own life doesn't matter to me at all. But after how Daniel treated me, I can't let him suffer for something that I automatically assume is my own fault. Mom goes on.

"He needs to see you; there's something he wants to tell you." She sees that I'm about to interrupt her and goes on. "I don't mean you have to see him face-to-face; you know what I mean. Mara can guide you through it."

The Game...Jade

Yes, I'm well aware of what she's talking about; it's what's known as astral projection, which is very dangerous. You have to leave your body, and there's this real chance you won't make it back. But I don't even think about it; I stand up.

"Tell Mara to come; she can walk me through it as we go."

Mara steps into my room, a place that has been off-limits to her since I got back. I can see fear in her eyes; she no longer recognizes me. She used to have this power over me, but not anymore. I'm not the shy girl who was terrified just because she raised her voice, who took her criticism and harassment as if they were the word of god. No, now I scare her; she can tell I might get pretty damn fierce if she pushes the wrong buttons, and she's right. I know it, too.

"What do I have to do?" I ask impatiently, making it clear she needs to get straight to the point.

"Close your eyes and wait until you feel the energy in your body. You know how."

"What else?" That was my whole response.

"Someone will guide you, take you to him. After that, I don't know, only he will tell you what he wants. We will pray for you to come back."

"I don't care." That's all I say, shutting my eyes tight.

Moments later, a hand takes hold of mine; I catch a glimpse of the man from the corner of my eye. I grip his hand tightly, eager to reach Daniel wherever he may be. With each passing second, the voices of Mom and Mara fade into the distance, and I'm gone.

I start seeing things I've never seen before, and I can sense an icy sensation creeping up, slowly reaching up to my knees. Finally, we arrive at a place; I can't quite figure out if it's a house, a building, or something else entirely, but it's nothing I could have ever imagined. The entrance door is this massive thing made of thick planks. I turn toward my companion, ready to ask what's next, but before I can speak, he takes a step back, still holding my elbow. Got it; I'm on my own for this.

There's a being by the door, a tall figure in long, dark robes whose face I can't make out. It senses my presence, turns to the door, and swings it open for us. We walk through a long hallway, dimly lit by small lamps placed on the sides of the wall. The sensation of walking through icy water grows stronger inside, and my feet protest, though I pay them no attention. Along the hallway,

Rocío Blisswealth

there's an endless array of doors, and the bizarre part is that none of them look alike.

I pick up the pace, finally reaching a door with a small window. Through it, I can see him. My heart feels like it's trying to break free from my chest, and before I can say a word, he jumps up and rushes to the door.

"How are you, gorgeous?" He says with a voice barely above a whisper.

"Open the door, Daniel." I reply, pressing my palms against it.

"I can't. You've got to do it yourself." His eyes are filled with anguish. I push the door with effort, assuming it will be very difficult to open, but to my surprise, it glides open smoothly, like someone's just oiled it up. Daniel embraces me, or rather, clings to me. I hold his face in my hands to get a good look into his eyes.

"Daniel, what are you doing here?" The man who's with me barely lets me get a word out.

"Jade, there's no time for that."

Well, can someone at least fill me in on why I'm here then? Because, honestly, I have no idea. Guessing my thoughts, Daniel takes my hands in his.

"I want to ask you for a favor. I've got something I need you to hold on to for me. There are folks out there looking to cause me harm, but if you've got it, they won't be able to get to me. Would you do me a favor and keep it safe?" I can clearly see there's a plea in his eyes. I don't question anything, absolutely nothing. I give him the only answer I have.

"Yes."

The man accompanying me acts fast and approaches Daniel. With a gentle motion, he reaches inside his chest, and I barely suppress a horrified scream. Strangely, Daniel doesn't seem to be in pain. He extracts an oval-shaped sphere about the size of a small glass. It looks like it's made of some kind of lead crystal material, smooth but not see-through. It's glowing brightly, and Daniel just stares at it.

Next, he turns his attention to me. Of course, I expected this. I mean, he wouldn't just stuff it in my backpack, right? With the tip of his finger, he cracks open my chest, slicing a vertical line from my heart down to my stomach. My surprise couldn't be greater; I feel a slight pain as I watch him carefully nestle that thing inside my chest, and then he seals up the wound as if he's welding it shut. The sphere moves inside me, just a little, and then I no longer feel it, as if

The Game...Jade

it's always been there. The cold has risen higher, almost reaching my waist. He turns his attention back to Daniel.

"Hurry! You must get out of here."

Daniel comes over, gives me a kiss and rushes out the door. That catches me off guard. For some reason, I thought he couldn't leave this place. The cold keeps rising, freezing me down to the bone, even though I am aware that my bones are not with me. The man takes my hand and looks around.

"Don't pay attention to anything and run."

Run? My legs are asleep, but I spot that guardian-like being from the door heading our way, and it can't be for anything good. So, we quickly left that place. When we got back home, Mom and Mara were still there, and he settled me back into my body.

What a heavy load! How does anyone even breathe under all this weight? I hear a deafening noise that slowly fades, and then I can recognize it, or at least I think I can; it seems to be the blood flowing through my veins.

"I need to sit down." That's all I can manage to say; I'm struggling to speak as if my tongue were stuck to the roof of my mouth. As I crash onto the bed, they both watch me closely.

"What happened?" Mom asks. I try to give them a quick rundown of what happened, but they seem pleased. Whatever they were aiming for, they've achieved it. I tell them I'm going to sleep, and they leave me alone.

My gaze fixes on the room's ceiling, and a soothing calm washes over me. I feel that the void inside me, the one that has tormented me for the past few days, is gone, replaced by a strange warmth within me. It's a weird sensation, like there's a force hugging me from the inside out, from deep within my body to the surface of my skin.

I can breathe freely now; the air doesn't feel suffocating anymore, and I can be patient. I'm eager to see him again, but it's not that agonizing desperation anymore; I am calm. I bring my hands to my face and take a deep breath; they smell like him, his cologne. I smile peacefully, close my eyes, and finally drift off to sleep.

Monterrey, Mexico. Seventeen years old.

Rocío Blisswealth

When I think about my schoolmates' lives, I've realized that things just don't roll the same way for them as they do for me. I'm convinced that yin and yang are real, and some things are just better off left alone.

I tried to get the demons out of my room—or rather out of my house—because they've gone and spread themselves all over the place. Mara has seen them. Not that I'm throwing a party about it, but that's how it happened. This whole deal made her jump, in a single leap, the seven steps she needed to reach the ground floor, as she was unable to control her terror.

It had to happen, and in the end, it was she who did the research that led us to our ridiculous attempts to put out a volcano with a glass of lemonade—that's pretty much how I saw it. And, of course, they took everything into consideration, and it will be used against her; we'll have to be careful in the future.

I had this wild idea of asking Daniel Montalvo for an autograph, somehow using up all the good luck that had been saved up for me during these seventeen years of life. For some reason, I had never used my luck until that day. Obviously, everything turned out amazingly, but there was a price to pay; I knew it, and the time had come.

The first event that marked a turning point was when our father passed away. He hadn't been living with us for years and only stayed in touch with Mara through phone calls. Until one morning, we got a call: the one that said he was in the hospital, seriously ill, and probably had just a few hours left to live. It's funny; I don't even know how many relationships he had in his life or how many kids, but on that day, he was all alone.

Mom decided to see him, and honestly, I'll never get why. She asked Mara to go with her, but she said no. I couldn't quite grasp her attitude, but the real shocker was still to come. I surprised myself when I asked Mom if I could go. I felt like I had to see him. Of course, the first shocked face was mine, then theirs, but Mom didn't want to go alone, so she agreed. We got to the hospital; she went in to see him, and as I was about to follow, that voice that's always been in my ear spoke up:

"Don't go inside, just watch." So that's what I do. And there he is in that hospital bed, without the strength that always accompanied him, morally and physically diminished, but most of all, alone. He pushed me away until it was no longer necessary, distancing the only person who might have shown him compassion in his final moments; the only one who could have eased his

The Game…Jade

loneliness, the only one, as incredible as it sounds, capable of stalling his death and healing him. But that requires loving the person, and in my case, there's not even a trace of pity left for him. I see him, and nothing hurts anymore. That's the saddest part.

With this death, Mara is the one who suffers the most. One of us had to witness it, and there I was, at the door of that hospital's room, watching as the only thing that hadn't left him yet, his soul, abandoned him. Mara and I share the same blood, and later in my life, I realized that blood had to serve as a witness.

Next on the list was me. I had a debt to be paid, and I could sense it, although I never imagined how high the cost of my happiness would be. Two months after Dad's passing, death arrived to take away what meant the most to me: the only thing that could cover the steep cost of my good luck.

I get home from work and see the ambulance parked at the door. I ran in only to see my grandpa lying on a stretcher, ready to be taken to the hospital. I approach him, and he tells me that it's just a pain, maybe the appendix, but he doesn't want me to worry. He thinks he'll be back home tomorrow.

But deep down, I know it is not like that; this time, the terror takes hold of me. A man is walking alongside him, right by the stretcher, whom everyone else seems to pass through without even noticing. He sees me and simply shakes his head as a sign of denial. My grandpa won't come back, and now I know.

Mom is going to ride with him in the ambulance, but why her? She can't do anything for him. I have to go; I need to prevent his death. The man approaches me.

I always fulfilled his wishes, whatever he wanted. I always put it before my own will, and this won't be the first time I disobey him; everything will go the way he wants it. I spot the man and quietly request.

"Make sure he's in the best place possible."

He nods, and I know he will. They left through that door, never to return.

This loss is mine, and here I am, witnessing it. For my own good, I didn't see his soul depart from him; it would have been too much for me. I stay in the living room of the house, where anguish and pain take hold of me.

However, it doesn't end here; they don't plan on stopping. And tonight, three months after my grandpa's passing, death chooses to come to my house once again.

Rocío Blisswealth

A scream from my mom wakes me up, thrusting me fully into the terror that loss means to me. I rush to the bathroom to find Mom bent over my grandma's unconscious body. I move closer to touch her, but she won't allow it; she wants me to call an ambulance. What the heck! She doesn't need an ambulance; she needs me! It wouldn't be the first time I stopped this; the first time she would be completely healthy again.

But she insists on the ambulance, alright, I'll call it, but it won't do any good; I'll be the one to stop this, not them. But they won't let me get close. Mara is also there with her. Gods! Why won't they let me get close? I just need to touch her for a minute, just that, one damn minute, but they won't allow it. I don't understand why.

The ambulance arrives; they put her on the stretcher and head to the hospital. I watch them go with the last hope of helping her, healing her, keeping her by my side... They didn't let me do it. She stays in the hospital for one more day; however, Mom makes up excuses to keep me away from my grandma, and she succeeds.

I'll never see her again, and I'll have to go on without them. Who will listen to me now? No one. This loss is definitely mine because no one else in the house seems to notice it. But one thing is certain: this awakens in me, for the first time in my life, a beast that only desires revenge. I never thought I'd be capable of wanting vengeance with much more intensity than I'm capable of love. And now I know I have a balance in my favor; they've tilted the scales in my direction. They will have to pay, and they will, as soon as I find out who I need to collect from and learn how to do it. I won't stop; there's no doubt about that. I've just discovered that revenge is a much more powerful engine than love; you can give up on love but not on revenge.

Tonight, I'm going to bed trying to figure out what my life will be like from now on. I'm trying to learn everything I can about karma, horoscopes, and esoteric matters I can find. Meanwhile, Mom and my sister are trying to dive more effectively into biblical matters. I don't even bother trying; it doesn't seem to have worked for me before, and according to that book, everything I'm capable of isn't very religious, to say the least.

From my point of view, they should set aside their attempts to help me because my attitude is far from noble or peaceful. According to them, that's how religious people should be, and I'm the furthest thing from that image. First of all, I want nothing more than revenge, and I'm not about to turn the other cheek because I don't have any cheeks left that haven't been slapped repeatedly. And secondly, simply because I feel like it, just because.

In these past few months, I've learned a lot. I've already managed to get rid of a lot of demons in my room. Honestly, they weren't very big. I'd consider them more like minor imps. But anyway, demons are demons, and it drove me crazy that they had turned my house into their playground. That's why I sent them, literally, straight to hell. All of this is on Mara's advice. Who believes that's where they should go? So, if there are any complaints about their vacation destination, kindly direct them to her, okay?

However, they expect me to do everything with love, ha! As if I had plenty of reasons to feel it. No, honestly, every word I say is fueled by an unstoppable fury, and strangely, it seems to work just fine. As for the bigger demon, well, it's still there, harassing me, but I'll find a way to get rid of it.

I'm so lost in my thoughts that I don't even notice when Mom enters the room, startling me as she starts talking. I don't even get a chance to calm down before she makes me feel like there's a heavy weight in my stomach.

"Jade, you must do something! The doctor just called me; he already has the test results, and it's serious. Look at me. My arms don't respond. If you don't stop this, I'm going to die."

When will the day come when I don't feel this damn knot in my stomach? I don't understand what it's about; my grandparents are gone. Whatever needed to be settled, they paid with their lives, and I still feel like I'm owed something. The scales are still tilted in my favor. Those damned demons are playing rough, and it turns out I don't know how to play. Mom looks at me with a worried expression, and I wish I had some time to think, to try to figure out what's happening. However, it seems that time is always working against me. Everything needs to be done urgently and without thought, especially without thinking. That's how mistakes happen.

Maybe it's just a matter of healing her; it can't be that serious, but what if it is? Lately, they've been right about what they say, and now is not the time for doubts. I get out of bed and put a hand over Mom; it's been so long since I touched her that even her skin feels strange to me. Driven by the anger I feel, the energy quickly overflows from my hands and flows into her. She can feel it, and she looks at me with surprise. It's done; it will be several years; the voice tells me.

Rocío Blisswealth

The next morning, they call the doctor to confirm, despite his astonishment, that Mom is in perfect health. She and Mara are very happy, and honestly, so am I. Finally, I feel like I've managed to beat them. Now, at least, I'm also in the game. I'm no longer sitting on the bench watching my family fall apart.

For the past few months, my life has become a path strewn with corpses. A path that Mom won't be a part of, at least not for a few more years. By then, I will have learned and will know what to do, or at least I hope so.

Monterrey, Mexico. Eighteen years old.

It's weird, you know? Most of the people who are locked up in psychiatric institutions are the ones who believe they can see things or people that no one else can see. It's been such a strong awareness within me that no one outside my family knows what I can see, let alone what I can pull off. And yes, I've had my moments of thinking I'm losing it, especially these days when I came back from Mexico City. My mind keeps making me doubt if I just imagined it all, that it never really happened, and maybe Daniel doesn't even exist. I mean, obviously, he is real; thousands of people can vouch for it. I mean, well, you get what I'm saying.

Maybe somewhere deep inside, I'm scared that if everything I remember from those days is true, what's it going to cost me? Incredible things come at a price, usually human lives; at least, that's been the case for me, and I'm not down to lose anyone else.

The only option I can think of is to keep battling it out, to keep fighting without taking a break. But how long can I keep that up? How much longer can I shield my family from these kinds of attacks? What will happen the day I can't make it in time? The day they're too strong or too many for me to handle. I'm holed up in my room for hours on end, probably even more than before, just thinking, reading, trying to find some information about what to do, but I don't find anything.

There's no instruction manual for people like me, and even if there was, no one bothered to hand it over. I can feel this energy surging through me, and it's beyond frustrating not knowing what to do with it. For years, pretty much my whole life, I hardly ever used it, mostly to help my grandma heal; that's the truth. My grandpa didn't let me do the same for him, and that's why I've grown

The Game…Jade

up believing that this gift, or whatever you want to call it, shouldn't be thrown around recklessly.

However, all the time I've been dealing with this pain and anger, I haven't really stopped to think about the darn responsibility; I just go all out on anything that moves. But even with all that, the biggest demon is still hanging out in my room, and I haven't even scratched the surface. What am I missing here? I managed to save my mom from death, so why the heck hadn't that demon disappeared? It should be way simpler.

So, last night, I dozed off without even realizing it. Lately, falling asleep hasn't been as tough, and in the middle of all this madness, I've started to find some sort of balance, I guess. I can't really say I've found peace or anything. I wouldn't even know how to describe it. But here's the deal: nothing's been different, same old demons, same old nightmares, and the same anxiety every morning when I wake up. Other than that, everything had been the same until last night.

I can't help but think it was all some crazy dream, even though it didn't quite feel like one. I open my eyes, and I'm just lounging in this massive white rocking chair with cushions so comfy you'd think they're made of clouds. There's this cool fern right in front of me, and behind it, a giant window with small square panes. Through it, I can see a pool with clear water, tons of grass, and flowers everywhere.

I turn my head and spot a door leading to a big living room; I'm guessing I'm in some kind of indoor garden setup. I get up from the chair and start wandering through the house, the living room, and the huge kitchen until I reach the door that opens up to the garden. It's kind of strange, though. There's no one around, even though I can hear music and people chatting from where I am. And there's this subtle scent of incense in the air.

A beautiful, red-furred dog comes up to me, all excited to see me, wagging its tail rapidly from side to side. It runs off to fetch its ball, inviting me to play, but I'm just not in the mood, so I give it a pat on the head instead. It joins me as I wander around barefoot through the garden, and I can feel the dew-covered grass leaves brushing against the soles of my feet.

I turn around, following a small hedge made up of blue plumbago blooms, and finally, I can trace where the music is coming from, which has gradually grown louder. In a spacious room, a group of young people plays an

Rocío Blisswealth

array of musical instruments. Their eyes focused on what appears to be sheet music as they rehearse a song.

My eyes lock on the sight I've been yearning to see for the past few days—Daniel is seated right in the middle of them, holding more of those sheets in his hands. He's wearing shorts and a shirt in the same shade of blue as the flowers, which happen to be the exact color of his eyes.

My heart's pounding like crazy; it's incredible how vivid my emotions are. The dog with me starts barking at the window, and Daniel turns to look at it. Our eyes meet for just a second, and right at that moment, I wake up.

I felt so frustrated, desperately wanting to go back to sleep and pick up the dream right where I had left it. But no matter how hard I tried; it was impossible. Sadly, I'm starting to believe that from now on, this will be the only way I'll get to see him, in my dreams.

I had to take a shower to fully snap out of it; this was one of those dreams where, even after a few minutes, you still think they were real. But there I was, in my bed in Monterrey.

Later in the day, when I got home from work, Mom told me that a guy named Miguel Ángel had called me. He works at Daniel's record company and apparently has something for me. Without wasting a minute, I called him, hoping he was still available. Once I introduced myself, he told me that the Mexico City record company crew, on Daniel's orders, wanted to hand me the new songs on a CD.

"On Daniel's orders." That phrase kept echoing in my head. He's still thinking about me, even if just a little. I ask him when I can swing by, and he offers to drop it off at my place. Apparently, he lives nearby. Fantastic! I won't have to wait any longer; I'm dying to listen to it.

Twenty minutes later, he shows up with the CD in hand. I invite him to sit down and offer up something to drink. I didn't really want to do it, my manners were holding me back from diving into the music right away. But, in the end, he brought it all the way here, so I can't help it. Our conversation revolves around Daniel. Miguel has been working at the record company for over two years, so he knows the ins and outs—Daniel's career, the gossip in the magazines, you name it. He shared anecdotes and trivia about Daniel that I'd never heard before, which made it easier to cope with missing him so much.

I actually enjoyed his visit a lot. It's been ages since I've had a chat with someone about things that aren't related to work or demons. Besides, he's been doing most of the talking, and I've just been tuning in.

It's getting late, so we agree to catch up in a few days, and he finally takes off. I couldn't hold back my excitement any longer, so I rushed to my room to listen to the songs. By the way, these won't be released to the public for another three months.

I pop the CD into the player and listen to his voice, that voice that's like a healing salve to me. It takes me back to a place and time when I was completely happy in his arms, with his breath gently rustling my hair. Without a doubt, these songs are the best I've ever heard from him. They're going to be a massive hit; I just know it.

Out of nowhere, I crank up the volume, pay close attention, and replay the song. Those notes, I know them; they were playing when the dog... No, I don't want to think about it. This can't be real, and I don't want any more signs confirming that I'm losing my mind. Daniel, you never told me about your dog's breed, and honestly, I'd rather not know.

As the days pass, Miguel Ángel keeps swinging by, bringing me photos, posters, and magazines with articles about Daniel—things he uses as an excuse to hang out. I guess we've kind of become friends because our talks aren't just about Daniel anymore. They've gradually expanded into other aspects of our lives, especially his. I'm trying to act like any other girl my age would, but honestly, I don't have a clue what that's supposed to be like. So, I've just been winging it, and I think I'm doing pretty okay.

It'd be way simpler if this guy read more than just the sports section in the Sunday paper. There are so many things we could talk about. Yes, I know, I'm comparing him to Daniel, but don't worry, there's no real comparison. Take Daniel, for example; he's got these top-notch legs, while this poor guy, well, he's got, what should we call them? Just limbs that get him from one place to another. They don't exactly give him that agile, feline-like grace. Anyway, I should probably stop there before I completely tear him apart.

However, you can tell he's a decent person, well, friend material at least, so I'll make an effort to look amazed while he explains what a corner kick is. May god save me from that; it's all for the sake of bringing a bit of normalcy into my life. I haven't given up hope just yet.

Rocío Blisswealth

It seems there are still some hopes that Mara hasn't given up on either. Lately, she's been trying to get a little closer to me. She's dying to know what went down between Daniel and me. Now and then, she throws out questions like, "Were you hanging out with him all day?" Stuff like that. I think she believes she's got a clear picture of what happened, but I know she doesn't because I couldn't have even imagined it myself. Still, I never respond; I don't even resort to one-word answers anymore. I just let her bump into my silence, nothing more. I don't feel up to telling her anything; I don't want her hounding me with questions she wouldn't believe the answers to, anyway.

I can tell she's really keen on getting me to shift my focus from demons to other things, like people, for instance, and Mom shares the same thought. Whenever Miguel Ángel calls, they pull me away from whatever I'm doing to make sure I pick up. I've wanted to believe that they're afraid that if I don't see Daniel again, the depression might get so overwhelming that it'll drag me down. Honestly, I've thought about that too and I'm trying hard not to think about him so much. I wish my mind would help me think logically, knowing that I won't see him again—at least, I don't plan on seeking him out. But then I get swept back to the memory of that voice shouting at me to wait for him, and that's exactly what I want to do. It's really hard to decide to let go of that hope; the alternatives are simply unacceptable.

While I'm reading in the garden, Mara approaches me.

"Are you busy?" She asks.

"No. What's up?" I pause my reading, thinking that, most likely, she has some information about a demon she wants me to deal with. I'll gladly do it.

"I met two guys at Tec de Monterrey; they're from Wisconsin and need directions to some spots they want to visit in the city. You know my English is quite limited, and I thought maybe you... could do me that favor?" It's, if I recall correctly, the first time she's asked me for a favor. After her recent divorce, she's been dating some men, and I guess one of these young guys caught her eye, and she wants a chance to see him again.

"Sure." I replied, it's a good thing I did because those guys are already on their way and will be here in ten minutes.

So, there are these two guys, both around 22 years old, William, who I'm pretty sure my sister is into, and David. Seriously, their Spanish skills are almost non-existent. The conversation starts off with what they're interested in, poor guys! They had this idea of exploring Monterrey as tourists, but even though I'm totally in love with this city, there isn't all that much to see from a touristy standpoint. Two or three days should be enough.

Once I've done my part, I'm thinking about how to say goodbye. But since Mara is trying to chat with William, David has shifted his attention to me.

"That book totally blew my mind when I read it." He points at the book I've been reading, which I didn't even get a chance to put away.

"Really? I just started it, but I love how this author writes." Finally, someone who's on the same page with books, I thought, and the idea of leaving vanished from my mind.

We got into a chill conversation about what we've both read and our thoughts on them. I have no idea how or when it happened, but I found myself sharing my time in a U.S. school and how I eventually decided to bounce back to Mexico, even though I loved his country. He told me about his family, his life in Wisconsin, and his studies here. I'm not sure how much time has passed, but William tells him they should leave. They've got classes tomorrow, and it's gotten pretty late.

"Can I see you tomorrow?" He asks with a smile.

"I'll be holding it down right here at 8:00 if that works for you." He nodded. William didn't set up a date with my sister, so that didn't work out, but I think I've got a new friend, someone who doesn't mind if I don't know what a corner kick is.

At least life is throwing a little of normalcy my way. I've always craved what most people seem to have: peace, and above all, I've envied those lucky enough to have friends to lean on for distraction. So, I'm planning to cherish every moment of this.

Still, stepping into my room remains a real struggle. I chose it, I know, and I could easily strip away all of Daniel's photos and posters, but the thing is, I can't. Here are my reasons: One, my walls would suddenly be stark naked, and I'd need to buy paint, which I can't afford. Two, I'd have to find something else to fill all those empty spaces, and I don't have time for that. And three, I can't bring myself to accept not seeing him anymore. That's the most powerful reason. One of these days, I tried, I mean, I really tried to do it, but the tears wouldn't let me find the nails holding them up. It felt like ripping him away from my side all over again, and I just couldn't. I've already lost him once; I don't think I can handle losing him twice.

Rocío Blisswealth

Somehow, I yearn to live a different life, any life really, except for mine. But the thing is, mine includes him. What am I going to do? For the sake of my mental well-being, I need to move on. I know he won't come back, not here, not with me. It'd be too good to be true. I cry myself to sleep. It's become a habit every time he crosses my mind.

Hours later, I sensed a movement on my bed. I'm awake, but my eyes remain closed as I wait to see if it vanishes. But no, it's still there, and I can't resist any longer. I finally gather the courage to open my eyes... Daniel?

"How are you, gorgeous?"

"Hello..." The soft light sneaking in through the curtain makes his eyes appear black instead of blue. But apart from that, what I can make out of his silhouette is as incredible as always. I shut my eyes and hold my breath.

"What are you doing?" He asks softly.

"I'm trying to capture this dream. I've never dreamt of you so vividly before." Finally, I sit up in bed, and he edges closer to me. He caresses my hair and lets out a laugh.

"What's going on?" I ask.

"Don't you ever mess up your hair?"

"Never, it's bad manners." He laughs heartily; it's such a delight to hear his laughter.

"I've missed you so much. Everything feels different without you." He keeps running his fingers through my hair.

"On the contrary, everything's the same for me when you're not around. You were the one who made the difference."

"Not anymore?"

"No, not anymore."

"Why would you say that? Jade, I'm here with you."

"Daniel, don't you get it? This is all I have left of you, just dreams. Nothing more, and I'm trying to be realistic." I pause when I see his eyes, those sweet eyes that cloud with sadness as they hear me.

"Jade, please don't say that. Don't push me aside; I need you."

It's amazing how, not even in my wildest dreams, I can gather the guts to make the first move to touch him. All I really want is to hug him tight. Somehow, I stretch out my hand and gently stroke his cheek. He leans his face into my hand, cradling it against his neck, and shuts his eyes.

The Game...Jade

"Daniel, don't mind me. Even though I'm trying, I'm not getting anywhere. I miss you so much every single day. When I say I'm trying to be realistic, that's all I'm doing—just trying and failing."

"Indeed?" He says, half-opening his eyes.

"Never for more than two seconds."

"Could you cease your efforts? For my sake?" He smiles slightly, and I can't help but return the smile. What wouldn't I do for him? Almost anything but this I want to keep attempting. As I didn't reply, he inched a little closer.

"May I request a hug from you, Jade?" He asks, his hand softly caressing my arm. I make an effort to get up and move closer to him.

"No, just shift that way." He presses my shoulder to turn me around. Slowly, he leans against my back. Oh my gosh! What an amazing feeling! He wraps his arm around my waist and pulls me in close. Resting his head in his hand, he watches me, and I can't control it. I tremble. I can feel his breath on my neck as I search for the hand that's embracing me and intertwine our fingers. I don't dare to turn; he's so close, it's too much for my nerves. What a silly thing! It's just a dream! It's frustrating that this shyness still affects me even when I'm asleep, and I can't even bring myself to turn my head to see him. Regardless, I won't look; I'm sure he's trying to hide his laughter.

"I'll stay with you until you fall asleep, alright?" Seriously, do I even get the choice to disagree? Ha! Don't make me laugh.

"I don't think I'll be able to fall asleep."

"Of course. Why do you say no?" He plants a soft kiss on my cheek.

"Because I'm already asleep! How else could I dream of you? I don't want you to go, and if I fall asleep, you'll be gone. So, assuming I was awake, I still wouldn't be able to sleep."

"You'll manage. I'll tell you a story."

I can only hope it's incredibly boring; otherwise, I doubt I'll be able to sleep. I hear his gentle voice right next to my ear, and I drift off to sleep for the second time, this time within my dream. I didn't get to hear the story; it must be a déjà vu like I've lived through this before.

Months pass, and David drops by almost every day. We've really gotten to know each other, and there are some things I've never talked to him about, and I probably never will, but it doesn't really matter. He's filled me in on his family stuff and his plans. I've always been intrigued by how people make future plans; it can all change in seconds and wreck those plans. Nevertheless, deep down, I think having it gives them a sense of control over their lives.

I've noticed that David's plans include me, which leaves me with some seriously mixed-up feelings that are tough to deal with. Back when I was dating Joseph in high school, and he talked about wanting to marry me, all I felt was fear, not excitement, like other girls in my shoes. I couldn't even picture planning a wedding, marriage, kids. Kids who might inherit my gift. I couldn't do that to a child. So, that's why I decided to break up with him.

Also, all of this is just a guess. David could mean the only chance I've ever had to enjoy a normal life. If only I could gain some control over the demons, maybe I could lead a life like everyone else—it would be incredible.

David is a smart and incredibly attractive man, tall with auburn hair and striking green eyes. He's been a lifelong enthusiast of water sports, which has given his body an enviable muscular tone and incredibly smooth skin. His father, blessed be him, has instilled a deep respect for women, turning him into a true gentleman. Combine that with his excellent sense of humor, he easily qualifies as a great catch. I could potentially fall for him. Well, maybe not that easily. If it were that simple, I'd already be head over heels, wouldn't I?

It's tough to let your heart wander toward someone new without Daniel occupying your thoughts, and I still haven't managed to do so despite my best efforts. Every time I go a day or two without thinking about him, he reappears on television in one of his videos, graces the cover of a magazine, or, even better, invades one of those vivid dreams where he visits my room. It's a cycle, and I need to start over with the challenging task of descending from the clouds and planting my feet firmly on the ground. I make efforts to remind myself that Daniel is a dream, a wonderful and sweet dream, while David could be my reality. A reality that would make me happy, not overjoyed, I know, but at least happy, and I think I could live with that. Although, I'm aware that he deserves someone who genuinely loves him, not someone who merely settles for him. Maybe I can learn to love him. I truly believe that.

On a different note, poor Miguel Ángel keeps insisting on finding me, even though I've attempted to reduce our relationship to phone calls. Lately, his focus on me has intensified, and I sense he might be on the verge of proposing we try dating. I don't want him to waste his time; I could never be his girlfriend. I can't find any common ground between us, except for the fact that his work is connected to Daniel's career. Beyond that, my only interest in him is as a friend, and I don't want him to waste his time on me.

It's already Saturday, and David came to visit me. He invited me to dinner at one of my favorite places and stayed a bit longer to chat. He finds it hard to leave me, and I can see it in his eyes, which I like.

Inside the house, my mom calls me. Miguel has been calling all afternoon. She knows he'll call again soon, but she's going to bed, so I'll have to answer the phone; there's no other choice. I can't let it ring when everyone else is asleep.

I step out to join David, who now holds my hand for the first time. I kind of liked the feeling. Suddenly, the phone rang again, unbelievable! This guy really has a knack for bad timing. I turn to answer it.

"Hello?"

"Jade?"

"Yes."

"Hi, it's Miguel. Can we talk?"

"I'm sorry, Miguel, it's late, and I'm tired. Can we do this tomorrow?"

"You're too tired to talk to me, but not for your little boyfriend, huh?" He's spying on me! I'm filled with anger.

"Miguel, you have no right. We'll talk later."

"Don't hang up on me, Jade!"

But I ended the call and returned to David, trying to hide my frustration. He approaches me and kisses me on the cheek.

"Jade, there's something I want to ask you." He looks at me, and I remain silent. "In less than a month, I must go back to Wisconsin, and I just can't imagine leaving without you. I know it may sound sudden, but I've thought about it a lot, and it's what I want most. Will you marry me?"

I couldn't believe it; I didn't think his feelings towards me were this serious. I wanted this, but I assumed he would propose a relationship, although time, of course, always seems to be against me.

Without letting me say anything, the phone starts ringing again, which infuriates me. But I appreciate the opportunity to think, even if only for a few seconds, about what David has just asked me. I go into the house and pick up the receiver, ready to put an end to what's left of my friendship with Miguel.

"Hello?"

"How are you, gorgeous?"

"Daniel!"

Rocío Blisswealth

Chapter V
Thirty days, seven hours, and some very, very long minutes

In the blink of an eye, I can feel how my heart dilates and compresses, beating at an unbelievable speed. My lungs, at last, fill with air completely, as they do when they come out of the water after having been there for a minute. But I stopped breathing more than six months ago. David peeks out the door, smiles, and points his finger at me to come closer.

"Give me a second, Daniel." I say.

"If you're tied up, I'll give you a bell later." He replies.

"No, please, it's just a second." I plead.

"I'll be right here, waiting." He says.

Oh my gosh, what am I going to tell him? I approach the door with those dreadful seconds ticking away. What should I do?

"I know you have issues with someone on the phone. How about I look for you tomorrow? Think about what I told you, okay?"

"I will. See you tomorrow." I say, kissing him on the cheek.

I don't even wait for him to leave; I close the door behind me and rush to the phone. Who am I kidding? Suddenly, I can see all my efforts to build a normal life crumble before my eyes. Nothing can last if its foundations are made of sand. Just hearing his voice, his wonderful voice, makes me thankful that blood still courses through my veins despite being apart from him for so long. This time, it's not a dream; it's real. I can hear his breathing on this blessed device I hold in my hand, though it's quite a struggle. This return to life has me trembling like a leaf in the wind from head to toe. I try to find my voice among the whirlwind of emotions, and finally, I find it.

"Daniel?" I ask.

"Here I am, gorgeous. How are you?" He responds.

I can distinctly feel how his voice affects me; it's as if it gradually courses through my body, igniting every single one of my cells. There's no doubt that the part of me that's in him has rejoined me, and my body, which had stayed behind, welcomes them both. I'm already smiling, unable to contain it.

"Alright, how about you?"

The Game...Jade

"I do what I can... This is where you're supposed to say, 'And you do quite a lot, Daniel.'"

"Sorry, I forgot! What tone do you want it in?"

"One day, Jade, one day."

"I hope you plan on living for a long time because to be honest, I think that day is still very, very far away."

He bursts into laughter like he always does when I try my best not to acknowledge how attractive the physique that he was blessed with is. I lean back on the couch and just enjoy this call. For a moment, I paused to ponder the reason behind it, but who cares? Not me, that's for sure.

"I miss you." He speaks more seriously.

"I don't."

"That's a bit twisted! Couldn't you at least fib a little and tell me you miss me too?"

"Remember, I don't lie." I laugh, trying to decide if I should tell him what I'm really thinking. Well, what the heck. "The truth is, I haven't had a chance to miss you. I dream of you so often that, to be honest, you were starting to get annoying."

"Well, this conversation is beginning to get intriguing. And what do you dream about?"

Aha! Here comes that mischievous smile. Yes, I know you can't hear it, but it's there, I know it.

"Forget it; my lips are sealed. You've shared so many secrets with me only to make me promise not to tell anyone. So, to prove my trustworthiness, I won't spill the beans."

"If there's one thing I'm sure of, it's that you're trustworthy; that's the reason for this call, apart from hearing your sweet voice. Jade, I want to ask for a favor."

I don't know what it's about, but the answer is yes, no matter what. I can't bear to dive back into this way of life, which feels more like death. I need strength and oxygen; I need him.

"In a few months, I'll be embarking on a tour of your country. The business executives need to organize it, and I'd like you to take charge of the logistics, then meet us in Mexico City and carry it out. I need you. I know you already have a job, but would you leave it? For me?"

It's strange how he asks things as if he's certain I'm going to say no.

Rocío Blisswealth

"Do you think I can pull this off successfully?"

"If anyone can do it, it's you."

"In that case, the answer is yes."

It seems like he's finally catching his breath, and now he's just bugging me for the rest of the call. One thing I've always enjoyed about our conversations is that they're mostly filled with funny situations. I love hearing him crack up and join in on the laughter. Life's too short. I don't see why we can't make it lighter.

He's telling me that someone will call me sometime next week to fill me in on the details, and these days leading up to it, I can use them to organize my stuff. And let me tell you, I've got plenty to sort. I have to set aside this phony life I've got going here and jump into his world. Everything seems pretty straightforward, except for that chat I must have with David to turn down his marriage proposal. As always, the clock's ticking fast. Is time relative, or is it just relative when it comes to me?

I make my way up the stairs to my bedroom at the end of the hall. Right before reaching the door, there's a huge full-length mirror that reflects your image as you head towards the rooms. Mara's got this thing where she turns on the light every time she walks by; she says she wants to see clearly to avoid tripping. Truth is, she doesn't want to catch another glimpse of the demon that once greeted her from this hallway. She's convinced she saw it because it was dark. I know it's not true. Light or dark, it's all the same to them. They're just there, end of story. Although, yes, for some reason, that mirror in the dark does look creepier. Today, though, it looks different. Even though I don't pay much attention to my surroundings anymore, I can tell something's off. Something has changed, and I don't know what it is. I enter my room, and that's when it hits me. My demon is not there. I freeze, still gripping the doorknob.

"Hello?" I hear myself saying, how crazy! The last thing I want is for someone to respond. I take two more steps without turning on the light, nothing. I shut the door, and as I do, I catch sight of the mirror. It sends shivers down my spine; I can't see anything in it, but I'm scared out of my mind.

Finally, I turn on the light and continue searching, but still nothing. I open the closet; he's not there either. Something's not right. Jade, don't be ridiculous. You've always wished for him to vanish, and now you're worried about not finding him. Just go to sleep already!

The Game…Jade

Without knowing how I somehow managed to drift off to sleep. It is the weird ability my brain has picked up lately, this knack for disconnecting. A couple of hours later, I woke up startled and trembling. Why? It doesn't take even a minute before I figure out why. Through the door, I can hear the sound of wings flapping, just as if a bird were trapped in the hallway. But it doesn't sound like regular bird feathers; it's more like the flutter of a bat's wings, like membranes.

I, who usually keep a tight rein on my emotions, am shaking uncontrollably. The only thing my brain allows me to think is that the noise I'm hearing is too substantial to come from any ordinary animal. The intensity with which it resonates suggests it is something massive and definitely not an animal. Tears stream down my face without me being able to stop them. I don't make a sound; not a whimper escapes me. I just feel them coursing down my cheeks.

I climb out of bed, sensing that something is coming for me, and I'd rather be the one to decide whether to open the door. In the end, nothing will stop it, and I don't want to wait around for it to make an appearance. Reaching the door, my sweaty palms cause the doorknob to slip. The flapping sounds are growing faint, but I manage to get the door open.

Someone, help me! The first thing I see are his eyes in the huge mirror, not reflecting, but emanating from within it. He's using it as an entry point, from goodness knows where, right into my house. He stares at me with those huge bloodshot yellow eyes and emerges from the mirror slowly, step by step, the same steps I take backwards. His head nearly grazes the room's ceiling, and he's tucked his wings behind his back. I dare to imagine that if he were to spread them, we wouldn't even fit in here.

He tilts his colossal head, scrutinizing me, and bursts into laughter—a laughter that sends a shiver down my spine, showcasing long rows of yellow, foul-smelling teeth. He sniffs the air around me, prompting even more laughter. I can't take my eyes off him. He begins to speak with a voice so gravelly that it's almost inaudible, given its depth.

"I HAVE KNOWN YOU FOR COUNTLESS CENTURIES. YOUR FEEBLENESS ENDURES, YET YOUR ARROGANCE PERSISTS UNDIMINISHED." Unable to stay silent, I respond.

"Hundreds of years, really? You can't count." His shouts almost burst my eardrums.

Rocío Blisswealth

"YOUR BLOOD, I'VE KNOWN YOUR BLOOD FOR HUNDREDS OF YEARS, STUPID LITTLE GIRL!"

I suppose it must be true because I feel a surge of strength coursing through me, though I don't know where it's coming from. It's not true, I know. I can vividly recall my grandparents' faces in my mind as if it were today. I want to shout at him, insult him, if possible, match his arrogance before I die at his hands. I guess that's what he's here for, but I won't go down without a fight. Suddenly, I sense a presence behind me. Damn, they're playing dirty.

I sneak a glance out of the corner of my eye, and relief washes over me. It's the guy who comforted me as a child, whom I'll call Ángel from now on. He doesn't look at me; he keeps his eyes fixed on the visitor. I can hear the demon exhale in annoyance through his nostrils.

"HELLO. JOINING THE GAME, ARE WE?" He speaks, looking directly at Ángel. Without responding to him, he whispers in my ear.

"Command him to leave; it's not time for him to be here yet!" I suppose he can read my thoughts because he instructs me. "Don't engage with him, Jade. Don't provoke him."

I haven't even managed to get the other one out of here, who is much smaller. And now you want me to order this one to leave without provoking him? I don't know how I'll do that. Gradually, I gain control over my trembling, at least in my voice.

"Leave this place and return to where you belong. It's not time yet." He lets out a loud laugh and moves closer to me. This isn't working. Suddenly, an idea strikes me, and I look him straight in the eyes. "You've known my blood for hundreds of years; you're aware it's not time yet. I command you."

I close my eyes, bracing myself for the blow that would shatter my feigned courage. But it never comes.

He flaps his membranous wings and exhales heavily through his massive nostrils. He no longer laughs, turns around, and goes back into the mirror. Before disappearing, he says.

"I'LL SEE YOU SOON WHEN THE TIME COMES." He didn't need to say it; I know it will happen. Ángel watches me and smiles gently. Now that I can see him clearly, I realize nothing about him has changed. I have one thing to say to him.

"Tell my grandparents this one's for them." At least today, I won't have to see them; I know it's a victory for my grandma.

The Game…Jade

Now I understand why the demon in my bedroom wasn't present. He did what animals do when they sense a hurricane approaching—he fled! Coward. I now grasp that even among them, hierarchies exist. Only one question haunts me now: What will I do when the time finally arrives? When will that be, and who decides it? I don't know.

This visit has put my brain to the test, and no, I couldn't sleep for even five minutes. My mind has been racing, replaying the events of a single night all again.

I was worried about what I should say to David. I don't want to hurt him; he's been kind to me. The fact that I can't reciprocate his feelings forces me, at the very least, to take our conversation seriously to not cause him any harm. He doesn't deserve it; his only fault is not being Daniel Montalvo.

As for Daniel, I just gave him a positive response about a task I have no clue how to handle. I know I lack the necessary skills entirely. I simply tagged along; that's the truth. If I claimed I worked with him, it would be an exaggeration. Five days during which I could observe how certain things are done, but nothing related to a concert tour. I don't know why he trusts me with this, and I'm already starting to feel scared. Nothing would hurt me more than letting down his trust. And, as always, I wonder, why me? There are surely plenty of people who would give their souls for this opportunity, so he doesn't pick me due to a lack of options. So, what's the reason?

What leads him to choose the least qualified person? I can't think of anything. This is a situation I'll have to face in a few days, and I'll need to discover what I'm truly capable of. I think this scares me more than dealing with demons.

Speaking of them, the one tonight filled me with an incredible terror. Just remembering his image makes my stomach churn. I'm dying to smash that mirror until there's not a trace left, but well, it's just an idea, like others. I won't dare to go through with it. I wish I knew how he's known my blood for hundreds of years; I suppose it has something to do with Clemen. This must be the damn creature that scared him to death. I felt a deep sense of satisfaction; I chased him away. I finally managed to get one out of my house, and this was the biggest I've seen. That's right. They're getting bigger every time.

Ángel keeps reminding me that it's not the right time yet. Time for what? Who determines it? What forced the demon to obey me? And once again, what am I going to do when the time comes? More importantly, who's supposed to inform me when that blessed moment occurs? I mean, I guess someone will have to tell me something, or do they just want me to find myself suddenly in the twilight zone? I don't think so.

The demon asked Ángel if he had already joined the Game. Please! Don't tell me this is a game because I just felt like the ball: voiceless, without a vote. I'm there, and I'm the essential part of the match. Without me, there's no fun. I just have something to say about it... I'm sorry, I don't dare to say it, but you can imagine it, right? Anyway, if this fight between angels and demons doesn't kill me, gastritis surely will, and believe me, if I don't have it already, I'm heading there flying.

A few days ago, I came to realize that there's no nice or gentle way to tell someone who loves you that you don't feel the same way. David, however, acted like the true gentleman he was and assured me that he'd be there for me no matter what.

I appreciate his words for what they're worth. Ever since my grandparents passed away, I hadn't felt what it's like to have someone there for me; it's been quite the opposite. I'm so sorry I can't love him, but I believe the god he trusts saved him from me. He doesn't deserve someone as damaged as I am, and I can see that myself. Just for that reason, I was glad to see him go.

As for the job, my boss mentioned that he saw it coming; after working with me, no one would let me go, and that included him. However, he knew he didn't have a choice. It feels so strange to hear that people hold me in such high regard. I've always had such a low opinion of myself that I automatically think they must be mistaken. Anyway, I appreciated it.

I find myself sitting in a waiting room, surrounded by walls covered in dark wood and decorated with paintings that must be great works of art. I'm not an art expert, but I don't like the idea that frames cost more than the artwork itself, and they look pretty expensive, so works of art. The room is furnished with large leather couches, and right in front of me is a low table stacked with entertainment magazines from all over the world. In the center, there's a stunning white orchid in a small vase.

A couple of days ago, Carmen got in touch with me, on behalf of Daniel, to give me all the nitty-gritty details of my trip. Dates, times, airlines and hotels, the address of the company, and nothing else. She even asked if I had any doubts about anything. When I told her that basically everything was a giant question mark for me, she seemed to be amused.

"I'm sure you'll do great." That was her entire response.

Well, it's a good thing you think that way. You have no idea how relieved I am to hear that. Like I said, I am crazy. How else would I throw myself into this battle without a gun? That's pretty much the story of my life.

I watch as a group of people enter a conference room, all of them men so far, and any one of them old enough to be my father. Right from the start, I don't like this at all. They don't even bother to look at me. Of course, why would they? They don't expect to deal with me; I mean nothing to them. I'm nobody, period. Everyone is dressed in these fancy suits, especially when compared to my outfit, which is, how should I put it? Let's just say it's very youthful and leave it at that.

A young lady wearing shoes that probably cost more than my entire round trip, I'm sure of it, gestures for me to enter the conference room. Once I'm seated in my oversized chair, she asks if I'd like something to drink. Ha ha, I can barely get my saliva down. Imagine what would happen if I tried to drink water or something else.

"No, thanks." I reply as she leaves me there to face my fate.

Ten pairs of eyes remain fixed on me in silence. Suddenly, one of the businessmen speaks up and introduces me to the others, but there are no warm greetings, just something that sounds like subdued grunts or coughs. I'm clearly in their territory, and I'm sorry, really sorry.

The meeting kicks off, and they start handing over the schedule with all the details about the tour they've already planned. I try to read as fast as I can, and I come across a line that mentions we'll have to take a ten-hour bus ride after one concert to reach the next city. I pause; common sense tells me that's the stupidest idea. None of them will be traveling with us. Well, it's time; there's no way to come out of this looking good, so what the heck?
Daniel didn't choose them; he chose me for a reason, and I'm ready to prove that his decision was the right one.

"Excuse me? About this ten-hour trip..." I try to ask.

"What's the issue with that?" One of them impatiently responds.

"We should find a way to change it to a flight; this will be way too exhausting for..."

That's enough; they don't even let me finish, and they all erupt in unison against me. Alright, I think this is as far as I've gotten, not one step further.

Rocío Blisswealth

"We'd better call Montalvo; we can't work like this!"

And without warning, they already have him on the line. You can't imagine how polite they were; they let me greet him first. Of course, they want to witness my humiliation, well, so be it.

"Hey, gorgeous! Glad you called. Are you already in the meeting?" Gods! What's in store for me now?

"Yes, Daniel, they wanted me to call you because..."

"I assumed they would. Actually, I was expecting the call. I'm on speaker, right? Fabulous! I want everyone to hear clearly what I'm about to say. Dear gentlemen, the girl you have in front of you has more intelligence, insight, and business acumen in her pinky finger than all of you combined, who, let's face it, are a bunch of..." Here he started spouting a bunch of swear words that I won't repeat. "...Unfortunately, you're the ones in charge of this tour. She's my voice at that table where you're sitting, displaying your utter incompetence. She dictates, determines, and decides what's best for me. So do yourselves a favor, shut your mouths, and pay attention. If she doesn't sign those papers, there's no tour! Is everything clear? I hope so, but if not, Jade can surely repeat it for you; she also has a remarkable memory."

It didn't take him longer than thirty seconds, and he left them all speechless. As for me, I felt like I grew at least seventy centimeters during that speech. Daniel, we both know it's just a bluff, but still, thank you.

"Jade?"

"Yes, Daniel."

"Enjoy your day, gorgeous. Call me as soon as you've finished sorting out the mess they've brewed. I'm sorry you're a victim of so much stupidity but get used to it. It happens all the time: different places, same idiocy."

"Thanks, I'll call you later."

I could only hear, no, let me correct that, we could hear his laughter as he hung up. Daniel enjoyed all of this; I enjoyed it even more. My grandma taught me that you shouldn't kick someone when they're down. Why? Why? Right now, I have a group of ten huge trees in front of me, and I'd love to do just that: chop them into firewood. No, tiny pieces. What am I saying: sawdust to be trampled in a rodeo, while it gets dirty with all sorts of disgusting things.

But you already know me. I'll do what my grandma taught me. There's no doubt that good manners are a burden I'll have to learn to get rid of someday. For now, I'll focus on doing what I think is best for Daniel, and I hope that's enough. There are so many details to coordinate, and I suppose these men are crossing their fingers, praying to the saint of their choice, that I make a mistake. I won't give them the satisfaction; I'll do my best.

Three hours later, I leave the meeting, and one of the businessmen approaches me.

"What a boss you have!"

"I know. He has rather a temper."

"He stood up for you because he knows what you're made of." He continued.

"Thanks." That's all I said, but I really appreciated him noticing how hard it was for me to be polite; my grandma would've been proud.

As soon as the man left me alone, the girl with the expensive shoes came up to me and told me I could go into a small room where she would connect me with Daniel. Those were magic words, and of course, I followed her.

"Jade? How did it go?"

"You mean before or after the massacre?"

"Tell me everything, please." He says with a voice choked with laughter.

"Poor guys, Daniel. I think you left them with a serious desire to change their lucrative profession and go into a monastery." I can only hear more laughter. "Daniel. What will we do if I screwed up something, or worse, everything?" I asked with concern in my voice, and he just kept on laughing and responding.

"Screw up? Never. Everything will go splendidly; stop worrying. And now, tell me something. Did you get revenge?"

"Revenge on who?"

"On that bunch of idiots."

"How did you know they treated me badly?"

"It was to be expected; it's their style. They love to think they are more important than they actually are."

"No, I didn't seek revenge. You did it for me. I've always known that revenge is in someone else's hands, and today, you proved me right. Thank you so much; I can't express how grateful I am."

"It was a pleasure, anytime you need it."

Rocío Blisswealth

118

He encourages me to enjoy my trip back to Monterrey and mentions that Carmen will be calling in a few days to fill me in on all the tour details. I know that, based on the dates and times we just organized, the tour will start in four weeks. Daniel wants me to be in Mexico City three days before it begins to finalize details. He'll be arriving here one day after that date so we can go through the specifics together. I'll be seeing him in thirty days, seven hours, and some very, very long minutes.

I hang up the phone and sit there for a moment, thinking about what just happened. I spent the last three hours organizing Daniel Montalvo's tour. It's going to be the most important and expansive tour he's embarked on in my country since I met him. What's even better, judging by those men's expressions, I achieved good results. If not, their mocking faces would have been immediate, I'm sure. This achievement makes me experience a sensation that feels quite unfamiliar to me; I feel confident. But what really made me incredibly satisfied was the phone call. If I'm not wrong, we all have dreams, especially when we're little, of some kind of superhero who will protect us from those who torment us. Well, today, Daniel was my superhero, and I could witness how, by fiercely confronting these people, in my mind, he was defending me from my schoolmates, from the teachers who frightened me, from demons, and above all, from Mara.

My grandpa always used to tell me not to pay attention to what she said, as it wasn't true. However, and I think you'll agree with me, it's always easier to believe the bad things said about us, and the good always seems unbelievable. But not today. Today, everything was wonderfully different, and I could see how these men bowed their heads before me as a sign of respect; it was simply delightful.

In that conference room, I shed the armor that hid who I truly am, or at least I could see the person I want to be from now on. That person who Daniel, with his faith in me, has convinced me that I am.

I learned that no matter who you are or who you think you are, there is always someone above or below you. Someone not only willing, but eager to teach you a lesson and put you in your place. Someone yearning to morally crush you and turn you into a human wreck, just because they can, by exercising their power.

I saw those men lower their gaze to hide it from me, and I know that my satisfaction came at a high price: their complete and utter humiliation. I find

The Game...Jade

myself entangled in two diametrically opposed feelings; I experience the joy of triumph and deep pity for those people who, at their age, were humiliated by a twenty-five-year-old. A young man who relished tearing down their pride and the pedestal they had climbed on to look down on others. After what I saw today, I don't think that arrogance will ever rear its head again.

Let's go back to the concept of yin and yang; everything has a price. I believe that arrogance has a higher cost. I will continue to enjoy the gift of this newfound self-assurance, knowing that I must tread carefully.

I've spent the last month counting the days, one by one, without figuring out how to make them pass by a little faster. I even made several trips to the pool, not to swim but to achieve the wonderful tan on my skin that I'd always wanted, and I finally did it. But, in the end, all deadlines will be fulfilled, and now I'm in Mexico City. I've gone over, reviewed, and corrected everything I could think of regarding the tour. Mr. Rogelio, appointed by the record company to be our support during it, has been incredibly kind to me. According to him, news of everything that happened in that conference room has spread like wildfire. I still wonder how it became known; I didn't say anything, and I highly doubt that any of those present wanted to relive the situation by sharing it with a third party. So, it must have been Daniel, right? It must be helpful for him that people refrain from provoking his temper.

As for me, this has set a precedent. They see me as someone who wouldn't deliberately harm anyone but is very attentive to Daniel's well-being. For that, I have his unconditional support, and since no one wants to upset him, everything is going incredibly well for me.

Rogelio tells me we'll head to the airport early and grab dinner there. Daniel's flight, as often happens with international flights, will arrive late at night. I prefer it that way; there won't be as many people, I hope. I doubt I'll be able to eat anything; it's been months since I've seen him, and my nerves are wreaking havoc on my stomach. I feel somewhat worse than the first time I saw him in Monterrey. Back then, I had no idea what to expect, or rather, I didn't expect anything at all. Now, it's the same, though I've been waiting for this moment for so long, and I'm dying to see him, to touch him. Well, to be more precise, for him to touch me because I won't do it. I couldn't. My newly gained self-assurance doesn't seem to apply to him, okay? He'll obviously be tired and maybe in a bad mood from the trip, and... It's better if I stop thinking; I'm not achieving anything.

Rocío Blisswealth

As Rogelio is finishing his meal, he deliberates between requesting the bill or having one last coffee. Suddenly, my heart starts racing, and it feels like my ears are popping. For a moment, I see myself seated on an airplane, one that has just touched down and is opening its doors. I can't wait any longer, so I stand up.

"Are you going to the restroom?" Rogelio asks.

"No, I'm going to welcome Daniel."

"Don't worry; the plane won't land for another twenty minutes."

"No, it's already landed. Are you coming with me, or will you catch up later?" I don't know if it was the assumption that I had my very own radar or Rogelio's desire not to leave me alone at the airport at two in the morning, but he leaves a generous tip on the table that will surely make the waitress very happy and then follows me as I hurry through the corridors.

I don't even dare to doubt what I'm feeling; I'm absolutely sure he's already landed, and I need to see him. The sensation I'm going through is akin to the anticipation on Christmas Eve when you know that, upon waking up, the gifts will be under the tree. Or like that sinking feeling in your stomach when you take an endless drop on a roller coaster, or maybe a tad of both. I can't take it anymore! Someone, do something. I'm sprinting through the airport corridors as if I'm about to miss a flight, and poor Rogelio is trying to keep up as best as he can.

Once again, I can see a place I'm not in, people everywhere approaching him for autographs, but for heaven's sake, just leave him alone. Can't they show some courtesy? Scratch that; not even courtesy, but at least some mercy? It's hopeless; he stops to give them autographs, accompanied by an attempt at a smile. Oh no, no photos, please.

I reach the international departures gate, try to slow down, and almost collide with one of the guards. He looks at me as if I've committed a crime and points out that I can't go any further. Gods! Doesn't he understand my desperation? I have to see him.

Passengers start emerging through the massive door, one, two, ten. Where are you, Daniel? A lady who has just exited stands next to me.

"Do you know who's on the plane? Daniel Montalvo, can you believe it?" She observes me, and since she doesn't get a response from me, she continues. "If you stay here a little longer, you might see him. He's not coming out because he has a lot of luggage, and they need to inspect it all."

"In that case, I'll wait here and see if I'm lucky."

"Why don't you tell her you know him?" Rogelio asks in a hushed voice.

"Are you crazy? She wouldn't believe me, and besides, I need her to keep quiet." My anxiety is increasing. How much anxiety can the heart endure before it bursts? No idea, but I'm pretty sure I'm close to the breaking point. My eyes are focused on the doors ahead, although I can see the baggage carousels. Someone, please, collect his bags already!

I bend and unbend my knees while I stand in the same spot. Let me run, okay? Just until I find him. The guard gives me a menacing look, but I don't care. I rub my hands; I should try to control myself, but it's impossible. Suddenly, voices start rising louder than usual, and then I spot him through the glass, among the other passengers, almost one hundred feet away from me.

There's a burst of shouts from the surrounding people, but I can barely hear them over the other sounds in my mind. Daniel is heading toward the massive automatic doors. A man accompanying him asks him to wait, but he doesn't respond. Two uniformed guards approach him and order him to stop, but he keeps walking with his gaze fixed on me. Those sweet eyes that I adore.

I can see his lips moving. "Hello, gorgeous," he says, accompanying his words with that glorious smile of his. I don't know how much longer I can hold back; I want... no, I need to run to him. His movements are slow, and I can see that although the guards haven't dared to touch him yet, they are following closely.

Little by little, he approaches the doors, still smiling. Rogelio won't stop asking me what Daniel is up to, but I don't even bother turning to look at him; my eyes remain fixed on Daniel. A person, loaded with suitcases, reaches the doors, and they open. Without anyone being able to stop him, Daniel slips through, edging ahead of the passenger. The guards inside attempt to restrain him, but it's too late. The doors close once more, affording him the split-second he needed to reach me. Complete silence falls over that huge reception area. The lady next to me drops her jaw when she sees him approaching. He comes running and stops right in front of me.

"Jade, hug me, just hug me."

Finally, I throw myself into his arms, holding him with all the strength I've gathered during these months of missing him so much. I bury my face under his chin as he strokes my hair. Everyone else ceases to exist. Gradually, I feel

Rocío Blisswealth

that overwhelming thirst for him subsiding, much like the intense thirst that fades after that first sip of ice-cold water. There's no more anxiety or desperation, only an overwhelming sense of joy at being wrapped in his scent once again. How did I survive all this time? I don't know; all I know is that I'm finally home.

I lift my face; he seeks my eyes, smiles, and sighs. The security guards arrive with grim faces and ask him, as politely as possible, to follow them since they haven't inspected his luggage, and he can't leave either.

"I'll accompany you wherever you like, officer, but she's coming with me. Believe me. If I let go of her, even for a minute, she vanishes. You wouldn't want that to happen, would you?" He takes my hand and leads me into the baggage area, and no one argues with his decision. What did the people who were there do? I didn't even notice them. By the way, poor Rogelio wasn't allowed to enter; he had to wait for us outside. The wait is long, but I don't mind; I'm already with him. He watches me closely and says, stroking my arm.

"What an edible color you have!" Taking my hand to his mouth, he bites me slowly, not letting go, increasing the pressure with each passing moment.

With my free hand, I trace his side; he looks at me and smiles with his eyes, his mouth still busy. Once I find the spot I'm looking for, right above his waist, I pinch it with all my strength. His eyes open wide, and laughter forces him to release my hand.

"Daniel, didn't anyone teach you to respect people's personal space when you were little?" I rub my hand. He helps me and sees his teeth marks on it.

"All the time, so now I'm getting even; you better watch out."

"Does that mean you're threatening me?"

"No, it's not a threat. It's a promise!" Fortunately, it's going to be a long tour. Once they finish checking his luggage, they call him to sign some papers. A very tall young man with beautiful black eyes approaches me.

"Hey Jade, I've been missing you. How's it going, kid?" He extends his arms to hug me.

"Hi, Raúl!"

"I've been finding comfort all this time by looking at your photos. I showed them to everyone so they could get to know you."

The Game…Jade

I turn my head and see many pairs of eyes watching me and smiling. They are part of their crew, and I know I don't know any of them, but they all greet me warmly. I continue with my questions.

"Photos? What photos? I don't have any pictures with Daniel. You must be confused."

"Of course, I'm not. How could I confuse you with someone else, kid?"

Daniel approaches and takes me by the nape of my neck. I'm dying to ask him which pictures Raúl is referring to, but there will be time.

"Ready, gorgeous? Let's go to the hotel; I'm starving." Without thinking twice, I hid both hands behind my back.

"I'm going in the other van!" I hear his laughter and feel the impact of his hug; it's still just as rough, or even more.

"Coward! No way, I missed you so so much that now I won't leave your side for a minute, you hear me?"

"This is going to be a long tour."

"That's right, gorgeous. Get ready."

By the time we arrive at the hotel, it's nearly four in the morning. While Daniel settles into the suite, I order some food. Raúl and Rogelio stay with us, and we take advantage of the time to go over the first seven days of the tour, which will last for two months. There will be fifty concerts during that time. As everyone's eyes scan the pages, line by line, I wait anxiously, fearing they might find something devastating, a massive mistake; thankfully, that's not the case.

"Fantastic job, you handled it like a pro." Daniel comments, with Raúl agreeing.

"No, Daniel, it's better than that. Recall we've encountered supposed 'professionals' who ended up being complete morons with initiative. This is top-notch work; everything will work out just fine."

"Thank you." I breathe a sigh of relief.

I recline on a couch, way too comfortable for me at this hour, and I watch them talk about the album's promotion in Europe and how well everything has gone. My gaze settles on Daniel. That darn habit of dreaming about him in my bedroom leads me to close my eyes without thinking, their voices lulling me. I'm not sure how much time passes, but I feel Daniel's fingers brushing the hair off my forehead, and I open my eyes. Rogelio and Raúl have left; how embarrassing, I couldn't help it. He speaks to me softly.

"I'm sorry; I forgot it's the middle of the night for you. There are still hours to go before we start our activities. Go to bed, get some sleep."

"I must have fallen asleep without realizing it. I'm sorry, I'll go to my room."

"Are you sure? You seem really tired. You could lie down here."

"No, I can't." I reply, smiling.

"Why not, Jade?"

"Because my bed's over there."

"Oh, I see. Yours is personalized."

"Of course. Did you expect anything less?"

"Absolutely nothing less. You deserve that and more. Come on; I'll walk you over."

He takes my hand and leads me down the hallway; only Raúl's suite is between his and mine. I open the door, and he stops me, cupping my nape and turning me around. I meet his eyes, and he stares at me intently.

"You're the purest thing I've ever known, as I told you once before, like a breath of fresh air."

He kisses me slowly. For me, fresh air is him, air without which I can't breathe. I'm off to sleep.

I've pretty much lived my whole life in Monterrey, except for that one season I spent in the United States. However, I always felt like an outsider, even in my own city, as if I were just passing through. Here, though, with Daniel by my side, I've found my place. I feel totally at home, like everything and every place knows me. It's all so familiar, even this hotel room I've never been in before, and most importantly, Daniel's closeness. I have no idea how long this will last, but I'm going to enjoy every moment of it, especially since my demons stayed back at home again. Poor Mara.

It's two in the afternoon, and I'm ready to start the day. Our first stop is at the record company's office. I walk into Daniel's room, and to my surprise, I see a gigantic teddy bear right smack in the middle of the suite's living room. Let me break down what "massive" means to me. This darn thing is about five feet tall, and its body's also about five feet in diameter since it's sitting down. So, I think you'll agree with me that it's ginormous. As soon as I step into the room, I hear Daniel's voice coming from behind the bear, and I can't even see him.

"Hello, gorgeous!"

"This is ridiculous! Whose genius idea was this?"

"It was my fan club's. Jade, what should we do?"

"Oh no, so now I have to figure out how to get rid of this gift, too?"

"No, of course not, but please, help me out. Don't be like that." I guess Daniel's fans, eager to show their immense love for him, never thought that this gift, no matter how much he liked it, would never leave the hotel. At least it's not going to be part of his luggage. But because this gift is so special, it wasn't just a matter of getting rid of it either. Besides, how would we even do that? Daniel had this idea that not only seemed brilliant to me but also gave me a deeper look into who he is, well, at least one side of him.

Our gazes got lost in the bear, trying to figure out what to do with it, when the room's service lady walked in, and Daniel's eyes instantly lit up.

"Hello! What's your name, ma'am?"

"My name is Gloria, sir, at your service." She replied with absolute shyness.

"Gloria, can I ask you something? Do you have kids?" He asked with enthusiasm.

"Yes, sir, a six-year-old girl, well, turns seven tomorrow." She answered almost without looking at him.

"Gloria, could you do me a favor?"

"Whatever you'd like, sir, just ask."

"What if I send this bear to your daughter as a gift? Would you be okay with her accepting it?" She looks at the bear, examining every inch of it without responding. Daniel gives her a few more seconds.

"Is something the matter?"

"Sir, it's just that I wouldn't know how to get it home."

"Don't worry about that; I'll arrange for it to be delivered. Moreover, what time do you finish work today?"

"In a couple of hours, sir."

"Well, that settles it. You'll be taken home with the bear in a van. Thank you very much, Gloria."

She looked at him with great curiosity; I guess she was surprised that he was thanking her. If the dear lady only knew the favor she was doing, perhaps she would have understood everything more clearly.

"No, sir, thank you." Finally, she smiled.

Daniel's satisfied expression was quite evident. We arranged a van to take Gloria and the hefty cargo to her house, and, to top it off, he ordered a cake from the hotel restaurant for the birthday girl. I'm sure it's going to be a joyful birthday celebration.

Once that matter was sorted out, we set off more calmly towards the record company. Rogelio was already waiting for us in the hotel lobby to accompany us. It's amusing to be constantly escorted by bodyguards; I can see that for Daniel, it's the most normal thing in the world, but I'm still struggling to get used to it, especially pretending they're not even there. Daniel barely even exchanges a glance with them, but Raúl, on the other hand, positions himself next to me and warmly greets me. I'm glad to think that, at least, I'll have someone to chat with during the long waits.

We travel in the van, and Rogelio talks about the tremendous success of the new album. Sales figures and radio requests have been very high, and the tour is already showing sold-out dates in various cities. That reminds me of something, and I turn to Rogelio.

"By the way, I forgot to thank you for sending the album to my house; it was very kind of you."

Daniel, seated next to me, suddenly tenses up; it's as if, for a moment, he stopped breathing. I'm not sure what it was, but I can clearly tell that something didn't sit right with him.

"Jade, you have nothing to be thankful for. Daniel requested that we send it to Monterrey's office for you to pick up, and I'm glad you received it." Rogelio smiles, but something seems off.

"That's what I meant; I didn't have to go. Miguel Ángel lives near my house, and he brought it to me. In fact, he occasionally calls me to pass me the latest news about you." I mention the last part, addressing Daniel. Maybe they could show their appreciation to the young man with a bonus, I think.

But Daniel's tone turns serious, matching his already furrowed brow, as he speaks with heavy sarcasm in each sentence.

"No doubt, Rogelio, we'll have to thank that young man for his kindness. Imagine taking the trouble to deliver it to her doorstep, and not only that, calling her from time to time. I'd love to do it in person."

"You'll be able to do it very soon; Miguel Ángel is at the office to receive instructions regarding the tour. He's waiting for us." Rogelio says, now very serious.

The Game...Jade

"Fantastic!" Was Daniel's only response, leaving me still in the dark about what was going on.

Minutes later, we arrive at the offices and are promptly led into the conference room. The atmosphere remains tense, and I take advantage of Raúl's proximity to ask him very quietly.

"What's going on?"

"Nothing for you to fret about. Daniel is quite apprehensive, especially when it comes to what's important to him, and, well, you'll catch on soon enough." Raúl replies.

"Soon enough? Find out what?"

Right at that moment, Miguel Ángel enters the room, quickly makes his way to me, and hugs me. We exchange greetings, but Rogelio steps in, separating us. He firmly grips Miguel's arm, guiding him to a different side of the room. Daniel moves closer to them, turning his back to me to talk to Miguel face to face. Although I can't make out their words, I observe Miguel's expression gradually hardening, his gaze fixed on Daniel, occasionally flicking towards me. I attempt to join them, but Raúl steps in and asks if I want something to drink. I don't respond and continue walking towards them. He then tries to take my arm, but I shoot him a furious look.

"Don't touch me." That was all I said, and he withdrew his arm, but he didn't let me advance.

I can't help but compare this scene to the countless times I witnessed back in junior high when a teacher would notice a student overstepping boundaries with one of us and promptly take them aside for a stern talk. However, it just can't be the same; it would be completely and entirely ridiculous.

Their conversation, or should I say, Daniel's monologue, ends, and Miguel doesn't look my way again. Instead, he takes a seat at the far end of the table, burying himself in the papers they're distributing. Daniel approaches me. Noticing that I'm serious, asks, "What's the matter, gorgeous?" He places a paternal kiss on my forehead; that is a gesture that, right now, seems unbearable to me.

"I don't know, you tell me." I reply without being able to soften my tone.

"Absolutely nothing that could remotely be important. Everything's spot on."

Rocío Blisswealth

He smiles, although this time it's not sweet; it's rather mocking. I guess for him, all this is entirely unimportant. However, I can see the guy who had been my friend until now, despite the disagreements we've had, sitting across from me without even looking my way. And all because of him, Daniel. I don't know what he said, but he distanced himself from me, and that annoys me. I don't think he has the right to make such decisions regarding my life, or does he?

He sits next to me, resting his arm on the back of my chair. I can picture it in my mind—for everyone around us, I'm his extension, a part of him, something like... his property? The mere thought angers me; I've never experienced the feeling of belonging to another person. I've always believed that one should never consider someone as property. Now, he's revealing another side of himself—he's possessive, and I'm not sure I like the idea.

He reaches my hand under the table, and I instinctively withdraw it. I can sense his surprise. He searches for my gaze, but I pretend to be deeply engrossed in reading the papers in front of me, even though I have no clue what they're about.

"Jade?"

"The meeting has already started. The least you can do is show some respect and pay attention; don't you think?" I reply, unable to contain my increasing anger as the minutes tick by.

Chapter VI
Oh, my bad, excuse me, Mother Teresa

The meeting keeps going, and I'm trying my best to calm down, unsuccessfully. My grandpa always used to say that anger clouds your mind, especially when you need to think clearly, and I know he's right. However, I find it impossible to put it into practice.

Why am I feeling like this? Maybe because I've always had a hard time making friends. So many things get in my way whenever I try, and I hate the idea of people just bailing on me. And then there's Daniel, treating me like I'm five years old, like I need someone to babysit me. I've been fighting for years not to live up to the image my sister has of me—that I'm completely and utterly stupid. And now Daniel is pushing me to that point, making me feel like this helpless little dumb girl who can't decipher who to hang out with and needs help to figure it out.

If they know something about Miguel that I don't, wouldn't it be right to inform me without making me look like an idiot? To let me step back or something. I don't belong to anyone; I never have, and I'm not planning on it, either. If they had the faintest idea of the things I've had to deal with, they wouldn't even think about trying to defend me.

As the meeting is ending, I know Miguel will slip out the door without giving me a chance to clear things up and, of course, without even trying to say bye to me. That's what's going to bother me the most. He'll have to respect what Daniel decided, regardless of what I think about it.

That's it! The voice of the man. They wouldn't even listen to mine because it's not coming from a man. That's what makes me furious: that a man is the one deciding for me. Well, I won't allow it. And Rogelio, who jumped on Daniel's side, giving a damn about his employee, will pay for it.

"What do you think of that idea, Jade?" I hear one of the advertising campaign directors interrupting my thoughts. I guess they think I have no clue what they're talking about, but that's not true. I've been paying attention to this stuff.

"The idea of giving fans t-shirts that look like Daniel has worn them? Terrible. I mean, do you guys really think a bunch of girls, who know every outfit Daniel's ever worn, wouldn't see through the lie? And even if you pull it off, those clothes can't be brand new, right?" To everyone's surprise, because of my brutal honesty, Daniel responds.

"We could give it a wash to make it look used, you know."

"Oh, of course. And who's supposed to do the laundry?" Daniel, you better be careful with your answer.

"Rogelio!" He responds with a smile, trying to make me laugh.

"Of course, I forgot he's the one handling your dirty laundry now. In that case, you've already got it all figured out without asking. How considerate!" I look Daniel directly in the eyes; I want to make my point clearly, and I know he understands exactly what I mean. He holds my gaze, but the smile disappears.

I get up to leave the room, and I give Miguel a look, but he doesn't even dare look at me. Coward! Maybe I don't want your friendship after all. Raúl walks me out; he better not think of escorting me to the restroom, right? Well, who knows, maybe he would. Probably another order from the boss, so I don't slip down the drain, and then who's going to decide which t-shirt brand to buy? That'd be a disaster!

Instead of heading back to the conference room, I head to the reception area and just take a seat. Raúl's watching me, grinning, but nothing's funny to me right now. So, still annoyed, I ask.

"What's so funny?"

"Now I see why Daniel's got such an eye on you."

"Oh, really? According to you, what makes me worthy of such high honor?" I've always wondered.

"Well, among other things, which aren't my place to spill, nobody can really match up to him. He pretty much calls the shots, and you, well, let's just say you're not keen on willingly stepping into the corral if you catch my drift. When it comes to you, there are just two choices: convince you to come in willingly or leave you out, hoping you'll still be around by morning. But taming you? I think that's a lost cause, and marking you as his property? Even less likely! He'd be thrilled if he could pull it off. But you're like a wild horse that can't stand the saddle, and you keep fighting to get rid of it, along with the rider. I mean, look at what you just did in there—you left him hanging, and in the process, you knocked the pride out of quite a few others. They're going to learn to respect you from here on out. That really gets under his skin. Jade, mind if I ask you a question?"

"Go ahead."

"Do you really care about being friends with that guy?"

"I kind of thought so, but after seeing his reaction, I know it's a no-go. But that's not the point here. It's on me to decide, not Daniel." Raúl keeps looking at me like I'm some weird and wild creature he can suddenly get close to without getting hurt.

The meeting wraps up, and people start leaving in small groups. Daniel and Rogelio are the last to leave, still discussing tour details, which officially kicked off today. Raúl and I stand up and head over to the van. Daniel's chilling, taking photos with some employees from the record company. I slide into the seat, making space for Raúl to sit beside me. He watches me closely.

"Remember when I told you he calls the shots?"

"Ye."

"I'm not like you, Jade; for me, he still does." And with that, he takes a seat in the back. He set his stance, and I'm okay with it. Daniel comes over and asks me.

"Can I sit beside you?" He's just serious, not furious.

"Sure thing." I reply with the same seriousness.

During the ride to the hotel, Daniel stays, how shall I put it? On his side of the seat, acting like there's this imaginary line he doesn't dare cross, avoiding touching me. He's staring straight ahead, biting his lip now and then. Obviously, he doesn't know what to expect, and neither do I. If he knew me, he'd know I'm not into staying pissed longer than it takes to get my point across, and I've already done that. As for him, I've got no clue how he's reacting, but I know it won't be long before I find out.

Once we hit the hotel, which we roll up to without saying a word, we walk down the hallway to our rooms. We swing by his suite first; he stops, and I keep on walking towards mine. As I reach my door, I search for my key in my pocket, and when I look up, I see him posted up next to me, leaning against the wall, looking like he's carrying the weight of the world on his shoulders.

"What's up?" I ask grudgingly.

"Can I hang out in your suite for a moment? I'd like to..." He doesn't turn to look at me and doesn't finish the sentence.

Here comes the lecture; I'm not exactly great at taking those. I just pop the door open and motion for him to come in. He slumps into the couch and still doesn't look at me. I pick the nearby couch and get ready to listen. He takes almost a minute before saying anything. It's getting on my nerves, but finally, he speaks.

"Jade, I'm pretty impulsive, you know. I don't do things to hurt, but sometimes, when I try to do the right thing, it doesn't turn out as I expected. Especially when it comes to you, it's like I'm always walking on quicksand. I felt that young guy had crossed a line with you, and I wanted to put a stop to it. I never thought it would hurt you. I..." I cut him off during a pause.

"Hurt me? You didn't. You know so little about me."

"Oh, really?" He replies, sounding kind of relieved when he hears me calm. Finally, he turns to look at me.

"No, it takes way more than some impulsive move to get to me. All you did was exasperate me."

He goes quiet, so I keep it going.

"Daniel, I don't handle it well when people step on me at all. Just like you, I don't like it, and I make it clear. I'm not afraid to speak my mind anymore. You probably noticed. There's something I'd like you to understand; I don't know what kind of women you're used to dealing with, but the ones I've seen around you so far would be willing to let themselves be skinned alive for one of your smiles and say thanks afterward. I should warn you, though, if that's what you're expecting from me, it's not going to happen. You once told me that with me, you could just be Daniel. Well, be careful what you wish for; it might come true."

He faintly smiles; it's evident he didn't expect any of this, but I don't know how to react any other way, and whether he likes it or not, he's the one who made me this way. Maybe a few months ago, I would have acted very differently, all submissive and afraid he'd bounce on me. Not anymore. Time can't turn back. He says nothing, so I keep talking.

"You and I both know that your reaction had nothing to do with me."

"No? Then, with whom?" He asks, annoyed.

"I made it very clear that Miguel was nothing but nice to me. Oh, but since you seem to think I'm your property, your reaction was all about getting mad that he acted without your authorization. Admit it, the last thing on your mind was to find out if he was kind or had crossed the line, as you put it. At least, it didn't matter to you that he crossed the line with me. He crossed your line, not mine."

Once again, he remains silent. I can see him crossing his arms over his chest, trying to put a barrier between us. I'm definitely hitting the bullseye. And, you know what they say, silence speaks volumes, so I keep it going.

"Daniel, you have no rights over me, no ownership badge, at least not that I know of. I'm here because I choose to be; there's no one twisting my arm. Doesn't that count for something? And you know what? Not all my anger was because of you, honestly. Of course, it was also because I realized that, no matter your motivations, you made it clear that this guy wasn't worth my time. If he couldn't even face you to at least say goodbye when leaving, his so-called friendship, if it even existed, doesn't interest me—he's just a coward. Maybe I would've figured that out over time, or maybe not. Who knows. But you didn't need to step in. I appreciate the good intentions, but it wasn't necessary; none of this was needed." He thinks for a few seconds, loosening his grip on his arms, and looks at me directly in the eyes this time.

"It won't happen again, or at least I'll give it my best shot."

"Thanks, I guess." I hope he has something to say because I've rambled on enough.

"Jade, are you here because you want to be?" I can't believe it! I just poured my heart out in one of my best speeches, and this is what he picks up on? Out of everything I said, he focused on the one sentence that was going to boost his ego. I swear, dealing with him is impossible.

"That's right, no one's twisting my arm. And man, it's tough dealing with you. Seriously, now that I think about it, why am I here?" I smile, trying to lighten the mood that got pretty heavy while I was talking. It surprises me to see a hint of sadness in his eyes; I've never seen that before. I think he's struggling to say something.

"Please don't be upset with me. I can't bear it."

"I stopped being mad a while ago." I say very softly.

He looks at me and sighs as if a weight has been lifted from his shoulders. He leaves his spot and settles next to me on the couch, resuming his habit of playing with my hands.

As silence brings calm back to the room, I can't help but think that what I did today, facing him openly, deserves some kind of trophy. And that must be having him sit next to me. All I can focus on is how his black outfit delicately contours his body, moving subtly with each breath, now deep. That human-like movement might be the only thing that gives his image a touch of reality because the dark contrast against his pale skin makes him look like a perfectly smooth and warm statue. Especially now, as he gently caresses my fingers with his, his eyes remaining closed as if granting me permission to admire him freely.

This silence between us and the depth of my thoughts startles me a bit when, with one of his graceful moves, he slides his leg over mine, letting it rest there, allowing me to become part of the picture my eyes are beholding. It's as if the statue has come to life. Having him so close lets his scent envelop me. Gods! It's almost unfair for one person to exude so much perfection. I still can't believe how I managed to set aside all my feelings to confront him and speak to him as I did. A trophy, no doubt. At this moment, he breaks the silence to ask me a question.

"Do you really think they'd let themselves be skinned?" I can't help it, and I burst into laughter, which he joins. He is crazy!

A little while later, we entered the hotel's dining room, an area reserved exclusively for us and off-limits to regular guests. This is the first time we'll dine with all the musicians and tour staff, and it's a big crowd—people Daniel considers as family. They greet me warmly, even though my interaction with them doesn't go beyond greetings and polite phrases.

Daniel sits to my right and Raúl to my left, but, come on, how am I supposed to get to know the others if I can't get closer to them, and vice versa? Well, the tour is just getting started, so I suppose there will be time to make friends. In front of us are sited two of the musicians who, as I understand, have been with Daniel since the beginning of his career, Sebastián and Julio—I think that's the other guy's name, but their accents make it tough for me to catch everything, especially when they're all talking at once in their group.

I can see that they, like me, practice the prison-style table manners that seem to be universal—guard your food, or Daniel will devour it! They laughed heartily when Daniel sweetly asked me if I was going to eat my mashed potatoes, and I responded with a growl. I'm determined to set things straight from the start.

"She learns fast." Sebastián remarks.

During dessert, Sebastián asks me for some tour details, something I just can't remember, so I reach for my agenda, which is actually the broadest extension of my memory. Meanwhile, Daniel talks about some renovations he's doing in his house, a place I've never been to, as everyone knows. He's enthusiastic about how everything's turning out.

"But what area are you changing?" Sebastián asks.

"The reception area of the recording studio and one wall in my bedroom." Daniel replies.

"I see. And what are you doing to the bedroom?"

"I'm refurbishing the columns; have you ever seen them?"

"Yes. And why don't you remove those columns? They're just for show, right?"

Daniel has just taken a bite of his dessert, so he can't speak, and I don't give him a chance to answer. That's when I find myself speaking again, as if it's someone else's voice, although at first, I don't realize what I'm saying.

"He can't remove them because they support the beams. The room has very high ceilings and needs the extra support." I continued searching for the information Sebastián asked for.

It seems that from that moment on, everyone included me in the conversation, even though I kept flipping through the pages of my agenda, still looking for the elusive information.

"But don't you reckon the wood above the fireplace would look better if it were a pinch darker?" Sebastián asks.

"I don't know; it's a matter of taste, I suppose. I like it the way it is." Oops! I still can't find the date, and it's driving me crazy.

"And what do you think about Daniel's bloody habit of sleeping with his dog?" Sebastián continues with the interrogation, but why isn't Daniel answering?

"Tiber is adorable, with that sweet face and that beautiful reddish hair. Besides, he's very well-behaved. I wouldn't have the heart to leave him outside."

And then it hits me, I'm completely in the dark about all that stuff, or at least, I really shouldn't know any of it. I've never been there, only in dreams. I was overwhelmed by the same feeling as when Daniel questioned me about his sister's accident, but this time, I accessed information without even thinking. I go quiet, frozen in place, scared to tear my eyes away from that darn agenda.

Slowly, I widen my eyes and pay full attention. That's when I noticed that the people around me were all quiet, staring at me with intrigue. Sebastián smiles in a way I can't quite figure out. I turn my head to Raúl, and he's still eating, trying to ignore everything that just happened, like he was totally expecting it.

There's no way out of this. I turn to look at Daniel. He's leaned in close to me, surprised by my answers, and now I know he's the one who encouraged Sebastián to keep bombarding me with questions. He raises his right eyebrow, curious, and without saying a word, he smiles widely, almost about to burst into laughter, clearly at my expense. I think the only thing holding him back is the situation this afternoon; he doesn't want to make me angry. In a hushed voice, trying (and failing miserably) to stifle his laughter, he says.

"Jade?" And now, what do I do? I literally turn to look at the ceiling of the room, hoping someone will say something, anything.

"I thought you'd never been there." Sebastián also says, laughing.

"I've never been." That's all I can manage to answer.

"But the bedroom, the beams, and Tiber, it all adds up. How's that...?"

Darn it, I don't know! I wish I knew how I know, and I could use that to my advantage, but I have no freaking clue! Quit staring at me, I hear Raúl responding to Sebastián.

"Well, do you really think there's no TV, magazines, or paparazzi here? Give Jade a break already. Don't be so stubborn, boy!"

Thanks, Raúl. I love you from today, that's for sure. Daniel keeps smiling and shifts his stare to someone else. They pick up the conversation where they left off, and I don't even remember what the heck I was searching for in that agenda anymore.

Moments later, Daniel leans in and plants a big kiss on my cheek while he puts his arm around my shoulders. He whispers to me in secret.

"You're absolutely spot on. No one would have the heart to let Tiber sleep outside. I never leave him out there, but you already knew that, didn't you?" He grins and keeps his lips pressed against my cheek. I'm pretty sure he can feel my face heating up with each passing second.

The next morning, we set off for the airport, bound for our first destination in the far south of the country. Now I understand the role these bodyguards play in all this. Just trying to leave the hotel, mind you, I said "trying" felt like an impossible mission. I never imagined the sheer number of people outside, hoping for a chance to see him up close. For the first time, I'm feeling scared being here. The crowd is absolutely ecstatic, and I think I'd prefer to stay at the hotel, at least until they disperse. Though I know that's not possible if I want to go with them.

Daniel meets up with the people from the record company and the bodyguards, giving them last-minute instructions. He calls Raúl aside and gives him directions, pointing at me. Surely, he'll be responsible for my safety. We better get out of here soon; I'm getting more nervous by the minute.

"Tuck your hair into your shirt." Raúl instructs, helping me with it.

"Are you serious? You don't really think that..." I start to say, but he interrupts.

"Jade, I'm begging you, just go along today, don't make it any harder." He pleads.

Two bodyguards are leading the way for the group, with all the musicians trailing behind them, forming a protective circle around Daniel. Meanwhile, there are a bunch more bodyguards surrounding them all. I'm at the back of the group with Raúl right behind me, his arms outstretched like a human shield on both sides. When one of the men up front gives the signal, we start walking quickly, staying close together. For me, it's like wading into a turbulent wave when the sea is rough. The tour bus is just a few feet away. I know it's there, but I've already lost sight of it. We're swallowed by a sea of screams and reaching hands, all trying to get a piece of Daniel, the musicians, or anyone else. I can see Raúl doing his best to push people away, at least far enough for us to barely squeeze through.

After stumbling, getting bumped, and having our clothes tugged, we finally managed to get on the bus. Once inside, we scramble to our seats as fast as we can. I can still hear screams that, by a small margin, are louder than those from outside, but these are asking if everyone is okay. So far, there are no casualties. But the second part of the storm is yet to come; people are pounding on the tour bus, and at times, it feels like they might shatter the windows. They flood the interior of the bus with an endless barrage of camera flashes resembling lightning strikes. As if someone yelled, "Take cover," suddenly everyone crouches between the seats, or should I say, they're fortifying themselves, preparing for whatever might happen.

Without training in dealing with such chaos, I'm lost in the scene before me. Raúl grabs me by the back of my neck and pulls me down on the seat, placing my head on his lap and shielding me with his body. Gods! Is this for real? Don't these people realize what they're doing? First of all, they're scaring

138

us half to death! Well, I don't know about the others, but they sure are scaring me! What's wrong with them?

Finally, the tour bus starts moving, and the screams grow fainter. Raúl moves away from me, and as I look up, I see that he's bleeding from a deep scratch on his chin. Yet, the first thing he does is ask if I'm okay. I take a tissue from my bag and wipe away the blood trickling from his wound. That injury was meant for me; I'm so sorry. Raúl smiles and tries to reassure me.

"Don't worry, sweetheart, it's just part of the job. No big deal." I spot Daniel walking the length of the bus, checking on everyone, and quickly reaching us.

"How are you?" He asks, sounding concerned.

"I'm fine, but Raúl..." I don't get to finish as Raúl cuts in.

"It's all good, Daniel, nothing to stress about, but that was wild. They've never been like this. Why do you think...?"

"I don't know. We'll be more careful in the future." He says, gesturing towards me with his eyes, not wanting me to get more nervous than I already am. Raúl immediately falls silent, and Daniel continues.

"Jade, I forgot to tell you something. When we're in these situations, stay as far away from me as possible; next to me is the most dangerous place. Don't take any chances, okay?"

"I don't agree, but do I have a choice?"

"I'm sorry, gorgeous, but no. Behave well, obey Raúl, please."

"Alright."

We arrive at the airport terminal, and fear washes over me again. Raúl takes my hand, and he can feel that I'm trembling. He stops for a moment and hugs me. I think he finds it a bit endearing to see me like this and tries to calm me down.

"Jade, nothing's going to happen. Airport security is tighter, and they're keeping an eye on our arrival. Plus, we'll be entering through another gate. However, don't stray too far from us; now we'll have to deal with the passengers, but they're more chill, so relax."

"Oh yes, I'm as calm as can be. You have no idea."

He chuckles and leads me off the tour bus. Thankfully, there aren't many people around, and even the few who are here watch us with curiosity, they don't approach us. We enter a VIP waiting lounge, and as the doors close, I finally start to feel at ease. Daniel is sitting, ordering something to drink, and

The Game...Jade

he signals me to join him with a wave of his hand. Without moving an inch from my spot, I use my index finger to decline. He smiles, raising an eyebrow, and heads my way.

"Why don't you want to come sit with me, gorgeous?"

"You just told me that being next to you is the riskiest place, and sorry, but the last battle is still too fresh. I don't want to imagine that one of those crazed fans of yours might pop out from behind the couch armed to the teeth. No, thanks, I'm good here. You can go back to the other side if you want. It's not that I'm kicking you out, but..."

Without needing Daniel to ask, the person who was sitting next to me offers up their seat, which he takes immediately. He takes my hand and speaks softly.

"They're scary, aren't they?"

"Absolutely terrifying; it felt like we were escaping from somewhere, and they weren't willing to let us go."

"I know but let me tell you something. Everything will go very well; the tour you organized will be fantastic. Even so, everything that could go wrong, things beyond our control, is likely to go wrong. It can't be perfect. We'll have to deal with that."

"I hope so. It's just that these people are insane. I never imagined..."

"It's funny. I know those people have a fondness for me, but when we're together, the hysteria spreads, and they try to touch me with such fervor that they'd gladly hold a piece of me if it were possible."

"Do you think it's the same everywhere?"

"Let's hope not; in any case, we have to keep our fingers crossed."

I don't say anything, and he continues.

"Let's say this is the tour's own little slice of hell. The interesting thing is that the same people who put us through this chaos will be the ones to elevate us to glory when we hit the stage. You'll see; it's an incredible experience. In the showbiz world, we refer to them as 'The Monster with a Thousand Heads.' When they see you on stage, the energy they unleash is monumental and mind-blowing. But don't dare to get closer; they'll act just as you witnessed today."

"Well, for me, it was the 'hairy beast with a hundred fingers.' What a nightmare! I've never been touched so much." He smiles, knowing I'm trying to be brave. I had a tough time, but others had it worse, and I don't want to complain anymore.

Rocío Blisswealth

"You're adorable. Have I already told you?"

"Yes, I'm sorry. It's just something I can't control." I respond with a feigned and exaggerated tone of annoyance. He bursts into laughter.

"Poor you; it must be hell living with all that charm."

"You have no idea; it's a constant risk. By the way, Daniel, could you please go back to your seat?"

"No."

"Alright." Raúl, who had been sticking close to me, chimes in with a smile.

"Since when so resigned?"

"Shh! I'm trying to be compassionate here. This poor guy is scared to death; he doesn't want to be alone, so I'm letting him stay here." I reply in a whisper.

"Oh, my bad, excuse me, Mother Teresa."

We boarded the plane without a hitch, and the journey was peaceful. In fact, I actually dig flying; it has a strangely calming effect on me, which isn't the case for most people. I genuinely enjoy the whole experience. Daniel leans in close to my ear, maybe so the other passengers can't hear him.

"Hey, gorgeous, I forgot to tell you something."

"Oh no, please. What now?"

"I hope you've fully recovered from this morning's incident."

"Um, well... Why?"

"We've got the toughest part ahead. How do I explain it to you?"

"Just spill it out, even if it hurts. I've already accepted it."

"Alright, if that's what you fancy. The press is waiting for us."

"Oh, the mighty fourth estate."

"Exactly."

"I'm not great at praying, but if you want, I can give it a shot."

"No, just keep it in mind."

"I know. They can either make you or break you."

"Not quite that. The farthest place from me is the safest."

"Got it."

"Raúl, make sure she's alright, and don't let those photographers get anywhere near her, no matter what, got it?" He spoke in a serious tone directed at him.

"Don't worry, Daniel, consider it done."

The Game…Jade

He turns around and exits the plane, striding towards them—the reporters who are already waiting with wide smiles and metaphorical swords drawn. They're taking bets on who will win the story that'll make headlines in the entertainment section, and they'll sign their names under it, trying to claim a piece of his success.

Flashes, hundreds of flashes that blind him. A barrage of shouted questions, some louder than others. I have to admit; he handles them like a pro, turning on the charm, flashing that amazing smile of his, cracking a joke here and there, and they're eating out of his hand. Today, everything has gone well. Everything was in his favor.

Raúl keeps his promise and gets me out of there safe and sound without being captured on camera. Why would that be, though? I mean, why would Daniel be so specific about that? Who would even care about having pictures of me? Oh, wait, now I remember what Raúl told me, that Daniel has some. Since we're alone, without Daniel, I figure it's a good time to ask.

"Raúl, what are those pictures Daniel has of me like?"

"Jade, maybe it's just easier if you ask him, alright? You already know him, it's his deal, and I wouldn't want to..."

"Don't worry, I was just curious."

"I get it, my bad, don't give me that look, alright? You're making it pretty tricky for me to turn you down."

I didn't even realize I was giving him some kind of special look. Oh well, never mind, he won't say anything. I'll find the right moment to ask Daniel; I wish he'll tell me something, or at least I hope so.

Finally, I'm starting to see the magic that goes into a performance. Despite the countless things to consider making everything run smoothly, once everything starts falling into place, there's this incredible vibe to it.

The auditorium we're in is massive and absolutely gorgeous, and from what I've seen so far, it's got amazing acoustics. Daniel has been rehearsing for almost an hour, checking one microphone after another while the tech crew is tweaking the massive number of lights that add to this whole magic. I have no idea where to stand; during the promotional tour, I figured that leaning against a wall didn't get in anyone's way, but here, I don't know what to do. If I just sit somewhere, it will seem like I'm not doing anything. Yes, I know, I'm not really doing much, but I don't want everyone to know, right?

My entire job is just keeping an eye on Daniel during the show, which won't start for a few more hours. I feel lost. Rehearsal wraps up, and Daniel sends the musicians off to rest a moment before they come back. He stays on stage, firing up the computer that's got all the tracks pre-recorded in case of any issues.

"Jade, come on, join me." He says.

The stage floor is all wood, and it creaks with each step I take. The view from here is just mind-blowing; I can't even find words for it. Even now, with all those empty seats, it sends a tingling sensation down my spine.

"Take a seat here." He says, pointing to one of the giant speakers. I jump into place.

He presses a button on the computer, and I hear some chords. It's a melody I'd recognize anywhere—it's my song. Daniel takes his place next to me and starts singing softly, just for me. I can feel the stage vibrating beneath us; it's almost like it's breathing as if it's alive. If it is, it's welcoming us, and I can feel it.

He wraps his leg around mine at the ankle and looks right into my eyes. His voice is gentle, his gaze so sweet. This is one of those moments I wish I could lock in a box and revisit it whenever I want. It's like a dream, no, even more than that.

I get shivers down my spine, and I want to touch his face, but I don't dare; I just stare at him.

The song comes to an end, and Daniel takes my hand and kisses it. Goosebumps pop up, and I quickly pull my hand away, and he gives me that mischievous smile of his.

"Thanks." I can't think of anything else to say.

He tilts his head, getting closer, his nose brushing my temple, and he places a quick kiss on my cheekbone. I tremble a little.

"It was a pleasure. Care to explain the goosebumps?"

Now I notice his gaze is fixed on my arm. Unfortunately, like the intense redness that's now flooding my face, these are reactions I can't control, no matter how hard I try. Embarrassed, I answer.

"I knew you wouldn't let me get away with that." I lower my gaze, but I can't help but laugh.

"Just tell me what caused it, please." He says, his lips brushing against my cheek. Gods! This is only making it harder for me to keep my composure.

The Game…Jade

"Why does it matter? Just leave me alone." I replied, annoyed.

"Please." He gets closer, holding me tightly to his side.

"Excitement." I jump down from the speaker and move away from him, trying futilely to hide my eyes, but I can't; he follows me. His ego's clearly hungry, no doubt about that.

"Because of... being on stage?" He corners me.

"Not exactly." I refuse to let him get away with it.

"Then so?"

He's chasing me and trapping me in his arms so I can't escape. He wants the answer he's been waiting for, to hear me say that I really like him. He knows, but it's not enough; his ego wants to hear it from me, letter by letter. I don't want to; I don't even know why.

My skin reacts more intensely as if it's eager to please him. He notices and runs his fingers down my arm. I get it, okay! Believe me, I get it! Stop pointing out the obvious, will you? My brain finally finds something to tell him, not the truth he's expecting, but still a truth, and it lets me say it while looking into his eyes.

"No one's ever given me such an incredible gift. I can't listen to it without getting all emotional, and today, the way you sang it, with me so close, made it even more special." I look away from him, though my body remains close. He tightens his grip even more. Still smiling, he sighs, not giving up just yet.

"I'm glad it's special to you. It was special for me too, but goosebumps, gorgeous?" He takes my chin and forces me to look into his eyes.

"I get them quite often."

"Liar! You're a liar, but it's all good. That's how I love you."

"I don't."

His hearty laugh makes it clear he didn't believe me at all. That's okay; I didn't believe in myself either. Wait a moment... did he say, "I love you?" Oh, my goodness! How could I say I don't? I must really need my head examined.

Hours later, the lights blaze to life, and it's like the same switch ignites the cheers of the packed crowd. The musicians kickstart the magic with a single chord, and the stage resonates with the audience. It's intense, a palpable roar from where I'm standing. I can't gauge how powerful the music must be to drown out the crowd's excitement, but it makes the floor vibrate like a beating heart. Daniel's right beside me, bouncing in place as if he's about to run a race. He says it's just that—a race against himself, one he must win every day.

A note, which I still can't recognize, is the starting pistol, and Daniel rushes to the stage, ready to conquer it all, determined to win. All eyes are fixed only on him, the cheers are deafening, and everything else fades away. One song follows the next, and the enthusiasm never wanes.

During a break, as the musicians show off their immense talent, Daniel exits the stage to grab a drink and change in a matter of seconds. His clothes practically adhere to his body, soaked as they are, that they cling to him like tape. It's a marathon he's running out there, but he's happy. I've never seen him this way before. This feeds his spirit and sustains him. Now I understand why artists refuse to retire; after experiencing this, it must be a kind of death to be without it.

It's odd how this auditorium makes me feel. I imagine it as a living being, constantly waiting for someone to make it resonate like this. And when it does happen, when someone with "the gift" steps on the stage, the place embraces them, melds with them, and stands ready to triumph alongside them, to live through them the very purpose for which it was created: greatness. "At last!" it must say in a world filled with mediocrity, where people boast of talents they entirely lack. Finally, someone emerges, truly blessed by the gods, someone who possesses it. The one who has what it takes to shine like this, to captivate the masses, that beast that roars with a mere gesture, with a smile so human yet not.

Poor auditorium. How many times can it experience a moment like this? I don't think very often, which is why it enjoys it. This amplifies its essence and feeds upon it, much like Daniel. It gathers strength for another long wait, for the arrival of someone else blessed with that gift. In my country, in the entertainment industry, they call it "dwarf." I regret to inform you that, from my point of view, most artists I've seen barely ascend to gnome status without offending gnomes, of course. Genuine "dwarf" artists must be quite rare; they are the ones who win Oscars, Emmys, Grammys, Nobles, and so on. When you look at the numbers, there are very few. The rest is just that, the rest. Cannon fodder, destined to be torn apart by these stages, lays bare their lack of talent before the world, which ultimately assigns them their place in nothingness. That must be painful, though I know none of them would ever admit it. To them, we, the public, are a bunch of ignorant people who fail to grasp their talent. Perhaps if they had it, maybe we could try to understand it, but, well, it's a never-ending story.

Human nature is complicated. How do you tell someone who feels deserving of an Oscar, convinced they were a superstar in their past life, that in this one, they ended up as nothing more than a cashier or a driver? Oh, of course, they attribute all their greatness to past lives. Who could verify that information? Watching Daniel on stage, everything becomes so clear to me. He's right to enjoy it; for however long it lasts, it will have been worth every moment.

The show comes to an end, drowning in an endless sea of applause. The audience is ecstatic, not wanting it to finish. However, Daniel has already come out three times to say goodbye with more songs, and I doubt he can keep on his feet much longer. Finally, he waves his arms and bids farewell to the city, expressing gratitude for the extraordinary experience it has given him. The crowd's roars erupt once more as the final curtain falls. I didn't think he'd still have any energy left, but I was wrong. Adrenaline has taken over him, and he continues to jump, sharing hugs with the crew and showering them with praise for a phenomenal night.

We make our way back to the hotel, and the atmosphere on the tour bus is absolutely festive. It's impossible not to get caught up in all the joy. We all gather for a late-night feast at the hotel's restaurant, even though it's nearly 2:00 in the morning, and the place is completely empty. It's incredible how much food we've managed to consume. It's strange; I hadn't even realized how hungry I was. I'm almost embarrassed by how much I could keep eating—oh, the horror!

Once my hunger is satisfied, I notice something I have completely overlooked until now. In any other situation, I'd never have dared to sit at the table without washing my hands. Funny how things change; if my grandma saw me now, I wouldn't just be talking about hands. We've just emerged from the sauna that the concert turned into. We sweated, and we sweated endlessly. Each spotlight is a thousand watts or so, and I've lost count of how many there are, but they were a lot. That means one thing: it was hot! And if we add in the fact that everyone's been leaping and dancing without a break in a city where daytime temperatures easily hit 100 degrees Fahrenheit, well, the situation is that we all stink! That's for sure, and it must be pretty obvious to anyone not in the group—poor waitstaff! How embarrassing!

Rocío Blisswealth

I guess it might have been wiser to hit the showers directly and dine after, but waiting wasn't really an option. I start feeling uncomfortable and get up from my seat as if it were the signal everyone had been waiting for. The table clears within seconds, and we all make our way to our respective rooms. Daniel walks alongside me and Raúl toward the suites. I'm relieved that this time, he doesn't take my hand. Not because of him, I honestly wouldn't mind, but my skin feels tacky. I know it's pretty gross, but that's how it is.

Now, the adrenaline has all but faded away, and we're dragging our feet down the hallway along with the rest of our worn-out selves. We exchanged goodnight wishes, and finally, I made it to the bathroom. I pass the mirror without even glancing. It would be embarrassing by any chance, so I step directly into the shower. As the warm water washes over me, I struggle more and more to lift the shampoo bottle, which it is so minuscule. If this was only the first concert, I can't help but wonder what we'd be like at the end of this tour. They might need to scoop us up from the last stage with a spoon. It's amazing to compare how I feel now with the boundless energy that surged through me just a few hours ago. I've never experimented with drugs, but it must be something akin to this, a supernatural high.

With some effort, I change into my pajamas and call the operator to set my wake-up call. We have to be at the airport by noon. As soon as I hang up the phone, it rings again. No, please, what now?

"Yes?"

"Hello."

"Hi, Daniel. Is everything okay?"

"Absolutely, gorgeous."

"Oh, okay." I don't understand why he's calling, but I love it.

"I didn't want to sleep without thanking you."

"Thanks? For what?"

"For everything, for being here because you want to."

"It's a pleasure." It truly is. I can't think of anywhere else I'd rather be.

"I want you to know that I notice everything you do, every detail; I see it. I heard you tell Raúl that you only contribute with tiny details that seem like drops, but to me, they're an ocean. You take an interest in my things. That, to me, means a lot more than that. I don't know how to thank you."

"You just did."

"Sleep well, gorgeous. See you in a few hours."

The Game...Jade

"You too, rest."

As I said, I've never used drugs, but what he makes me feel must be similar to getting high. It's like diving into happiness, as refreshing as cool water. This time, it's the most delicious sleeping pill.

I can't believe he took the time to call me and thank me, when it is him who is making my dreams come true, allowing me to be by his side, every passing hour proofs the fact that he doesn't need me. Anyone could do what I do.

We've already completed ten concerts. I'm sorry, but I've completely lost track of the days; our schedules have turned into total chaos, so this is the new way I've learned to measure time. Today's afternoon has been spent on what seems like an endless bus ride. There was simply no alternative. The city we were headed to lacked an airport, and the closest one just wasn't suitable for our needs.

Our travel hours have multiplied due to the torrential rain, and the road we're traveling on is covered with rocks and mud along extensive stretches. We've come to a complete stop. There's no way to go on. The driver approached Daniel and delivered the news that a landslide had obstructed the road, and the tour bus couldn't pass through. It seemed like this was as far as we could go. I could see the desperation in his eyes; there has to be a way, and if there is, he'll find it. He turned to the driver.

"How far are we from the venue?"

"Daniel, even if that landslide wasn't blocking us, we wouldn't have made it in time; we've lost too much of it."

He then went over to Sebastián and talked to him for a few minutes; I guess they're weighing our options. Then he comes over to me.

"Get a plastic bag and put some clean clothes in it."

"Daniel, the clothing was sent in the other truck. I'm not even sure if they made it to the auditorium."

"Anything will be fine, don't worry about the outfits." I wasn't sure what he had in mind, but I obeyed as quickly as I could. All we had at hand were jeans and t-shirts. I suppose for him and Sebastián, as I didn't see anyone else making a move. He kept arguing with the driver; I think Daniel's idea didn't convince him, however, there was no way to stop him.

Rocío Blisswealth

Outside the tour bus, the rain keeps pouring relentlessly, and Daniel approaches the door. Is he planning to go outside? This is serious. I could hear his voice from there.

"Raúl, Jade, let's go."

Sebastián was already standing behind him with his guitar, and I got up from my seat. Raúl grabbed the bag with the clothes, and we followed him. I'm starting to worry; what was he planning to do? When we reached him, I overheard the driver expressing concern about me joining them. It's dangerous; the whole situation is a risk.

"You guys are men, Daniel, but this girl. Are you sure?"

"Are you afraid, Jade?" I don't even know what he means.

"No." That's my only response.

"That's what I thought; let's go."

We step out to face the downpour. As we separated from the tour bus, I could see there was a small space where cars could pass through. I think I know what he's trying to do. A few minutes later, a heavy-duty double-cabin pickup truck passed by. Despite the road conditions, it managed to move smoothly. Daniel signaled for them to stop. The young guys inside couldn't believe their eyes, and I could hear their excitement through the open window as they greeted Daniel with a mix of enthusiasm and playful obscenities. Typical guys! He did it! They would take us to the auditorium, and we crammed into the vehicle like sardines, speeding off toward the event venue.

Upon arrival, the organizers greeted us. The concert was supposed to have started twenty minutes ago, and they were considering canceling it. The audience inside was loudly demanding Daniel's presence. They couldn't help but notice our bedraggled state. But what can be done? However, there was no stopping Daniel; he rushed inside. Canceling is out of the question! He'll sing no matter what. By the way, he asked me to arrange special seating for our honored guests—the young people who had rescued us, of course. They were overjoyed. When I made it to the dressing room, Daniel was already changing.

"How do I look?" He asks with a broad smile.

"Seriously?" I turned to see my soaked reflection in the mirror and replied. "Just like me, with a little less mud."

"Then I look fantastic." He laughs.

"Jade, you know why I do it, don't you?" Over time, I had come to understand him, and yes, I knew why he was doing it.

The Game...Jade

"For the people, you wouldn't leave them waiting, would you? You won't let them down."

He comes over to give me a hug, and I quickly block him by placing my hand on his chest. I can't let him get all dirty again, especially since we don't have any spare clothes left. He heads onto the stage, and it goes all quiet. Carefully, he grabs the microphone and starts explaining to the audience what went down. They know their roads better than anyone else, and the applause erupts in no time. If they give the green light, the concert will go acoustic, just Daniel and his guitarist. The crowd goes crazy; I think they're totally into the idea, and so am I. The organizers breathe a sigh of relief.

Two hours later, the show wraps up, and the audience burst into applause. Honestly, I can say that this is probably the longest applause he's received on this entire tour—it's a pretty big deal. People are beyond thankful, and the press is showering him with praise from their box. That's how stars are born.

Today, I admire him more than ever, if that's even possible. He's not the kind to rest on his laurels or dish out excuses. No, he goes beyond the possible and does what's necessary to make things work. From my point of view, that's how a guy should roll, someone you can always count on.

We finally arrive at the hotel, this time straight to our rooms. I can't stress enough how much we need a shower right now. Raúl asked for our keys at the front desk and the poor staff looked at us like they were ready to deny us entry. I don't even want to picture what I look like at this point. Daniel suggests we all meet up for dinner after we've freshened up, so a few minutes later, we find ourselves in the hallway, making our way to the dining area.

As we head down, we can overhear conversations that suddenly turn into enthusiastic applause when people see us. The whole crew, the ones who are pretty much family when we're on the road, totally get what we accomplished today, and they're showering us with congrats. I struggle to let go of Daniel's hand and join in the applause. Raúl joins me as we take our seats. They're drowning in a sea of hugs, and it's clear they're bursting with genuine pride. Today, they gave us a lesson about love of art and passion for what we do.

We don't eat much this time around. The exhaustion we're feeling is different—it's more emotional than physical, I think. Daniel is happy but quieter than usual. We say goodnight and start heading to get to sleep when he stops me by grabbing my arm.

"Jade, are you quite tired?" He asks in a very low voice.

"What do you need, Daniel?" I'm surprised to see his eyes welling up.

"I don't know, just fancy a chat." He says.

I guess there were just way too many emotions today. We enter his suite, and he follows me in. He closes the door and stands there, in the middle of the room, staring at the floor. And for the first time, I'm the one who takes a step closer to him. I cup his face in my hands, and he closes his eyes, keeping them hidden from me. I tiptoe and plant a kiss on his cheek. Suddenly, he wraps me up in a tight hug, and I lock my arms around his neck. He buries his face in the hair falling over my shoulder, and I can literally feel his chest heaving as he finally let go of all the tears he'd been holding back so hard. He's trembling. I hug him really tight, running my fingers through his hair. I don't say anything, honestly, because nothing comes to my mind; instead, I try to comfort him with my hug as the minutes slip away.

He eases up on the hug, and I gently pull back to see his face. He's still hiding his eyes from me. I wipe away his tears using the tips of my fingers, and without letting go, he leans in, resting his forehead against mine.

"Th… thank you." He finally says, his voice still wavering.

"You're welcome." He opens his eyes, and I'm left speechless. I need to create some distance. Crying is like a yawn; it's contagious, and I always run away from anything that might set me off. Unfortunately, I'm falling victim to a pretty severe case of it right now.

"Thank you." He says again, this time looking into my eyes.

"No worries." I say, dropping my arms and heading over to a couch. He follows me. I can feel the tears trying to take hold of my throat, choking me up. Please, don't let it go any further. Having him this close and in such an emotional state caught me off guard, and right now, I just can't find a way to escape those memories that are buried deep in my mind. They're too painful to face, but they've somehow decided to come back. I really need to think about something else.

"Jade, I'm used to experiencing the weight of my emotions, the highs and lows, all on my own, and sometimes, it can be quite a heavy burden. Today, it has become too much to bear, and I felt the need to share it, but it's only with you that I feel I can truly open up. Do you understand me?"

The Game…Jade

"Better than you think." I don't lift my gaze from the floor. I rubbed my hands against my thighs, and he watched the restless movement as he continued to talk.

"I'm sorry your family is far away. I mean, for being here and having to put up with me." He smiles, apologizing.

Daniel, if you only knew that my most loyal companion is a demon I haven't been able to get rid of, and right now, he's probably the one who misses me the most. I'm not on a good path, not at all. This journey takes me through the darkest corners of my life, where I've avoided shedding tears. Finding the right words with this tight throat is challenging.

"Don't worry about that."

"Who do you miss the most?" His voice still carried the effects of his crying.

"My grandparents." Images of my grandparents flooded my thoughts, and controlling my emotions became increasingly difficult. Darn it! I need to get out of here.

"Why don't you give them a call?" His voice has turned into a sea of sweetness I don't want to plunge into.

"Since months ago, they have been in a place with no phone." My voice has definitely changed.

"I'm sorry." He reaches out to take my hand. I know he can clearly see me falling apart while I'm still trying to hold myself together.

"Me too." I withdraw my hand and furrow my brow, puzzled by my own reaction.

"How did they pass away, gorgeous?" At what point did the conversation take this turn, focusing on me? I don't like it. My feelings were locked behind walls I had strengthened over the years. Believe me, Daniel, I had no intention of letting them escape now. Doing so would only make it impossible to contain them, and this was neither the time nor the place. I don't want to talk anymore, especially not about my grandparents; it hurts too much.

"Could we talk about something else, please?" I ask, almost pleadingly, without looking at him or responding directly. He watches me carefully and slowly reaches out to touch my arm, a gesture I mirror to keep him out of reach.

"Gorgeous, let me give you a hug." He whispers.

"No, Daniel, please don't touch me." I have lost hope of meeting his gaze, making it clear just how overwhelmed I feel. If I allow him to hug me

Rocío Blisswealth

right now, I'd lose the battle against the emotional breakdown that's looming, and I'd rather face it alone.

"What if I ask you kindly?" He inches closer to me.

"Please, don't ask me... I just want to go to sleep."

"Did I say something wrong?" He asks, concerned, though I had a feeling he sensed there was something else going on.

"No."

"Jade, did I offend you in any way?"

"No, Daniel, it's just that I need to go. I don't want to talk anymore."

"Why do I feel like you're trying to escape from me? Seriously, gorgeous. Wouldn't you prefer us to talk?"

I get up to leave the room, to escape, as he put it; that word seemed fitting. However, he reaches the door before I could open it. He strokes my hair, prompting me to turn away. I try to take a step back but bump with the door behind me, grabbing the handle tightly. What's wrong with me? Surprised, he becomes serious. He's never seen me like this before. He raises his hands and waves them in front of me, showing that he has no intention of touching me.

"Just let me tell you something, alright?" Summoning all my strength, I looked him in the eyes, wanting so badly to hug him, but I couldn't. No, not without letting this overwhelming feeling inside me take over. Resting his palms against the door to ensure he doesn't touch me; he kisses me on the lips.

"I'm here." He says with his lips still brushing against mine.

"I know." My voice is barely audible.

"Really?"

"Yes."

I don't have the strength to say anything else. He gets it and respects my choice, stepping aside to give me space. I open the door and step outside just in time for him not to see the first tears slipping down my cheeks.

As soon as I get to the room, I totally give up on those useless attempts to hold back the tears. I grieved my grandparents when they passed, but with a mourning fueled by anger and frustration, knowing I could have done something to help them. However, I never allowed that pain to overwhelm me; I know my limits perfectly.

Daniel, without even realizing it, dragged me into this really tough emotional spot; with the mood he sunk into, he exposed me to my own feelings. It may sound odd, I know, but holding him in my arms made it even harder to keep it together. Today, the emotions I had been avoiding overwhelmed me, and it was impossible to evade them. And these tears, I have no clue where they're coming from.

I know Daniel is just a few feet away. I wish I could let him hug me while I let it all out. Until now, the only witness to my tears has been my demon, who seems to enjoy it whenever I fall apart. Having someone by my side, offering even at least pity, just a little, would have been a welcome change, but oh, how embarrassing!

I've truly bewildered him, poor guy; I'll have to explain everything to him tomorrow. What a nightmare! If only I could have controlled myself a bit better, maybe I could've handled the situation more gracefully, less hysterically. But I ended up making a complete fool of myself by running away, and knowing him, he won't let me forget it. Just what I needed, to give him more material for teasing me. Although, on second thought, crying in front of him would have been even more embarrassing, and I managed to avoid that, so it's not all bad.

One of the perks of crying excessively is that it usually leads to a deep slumber. Another one would be... well, there really isn't another. The main downside, I think, is the inevitable swelling of your eyes, unless of course, one of your hobbies is boxing. I know, now you are probably thinking about all those remedies you've heard of to reduce eye puffiness, from cucumber and potato slices to, embarrassingly enough, hemorrhoid cream. Yes, you heard that right, a model's secret. Well, no, I've spent the last forty-five minutes trying them all, and they're useless.

There's a knock at the door. Please, anyone but Daniel! I'm not ready to talk to him; I'll need about a month or so. I reach the door and open it, and Raúl strides in without waiting for an invitation.

"Good morning, Jade." He avoids making eye contact, which I appreciate.

"Hello..."

"I've got a little something for you today, and trust me, it's going to come in real handy."

"A gift? But..."

He extends his hand, revealing a pair of completely dark sunglasses. I never wear them; they annoy me, but today... I might just end up falling in love with this man.

"Thank you."

Rocío Blisswealth

154

"You see, there's quite a crowd out there, and these shades will help you carve out your own space just a bit."

"So that's why people wear them. I get it now."

I put them on, and finally, I can relax. Raúl watches me. I wonder what he is thinking? He steps closer and looks at me. I know he said the glasses would help me isolate myself; could he be testing how much I can see through them?

"Jade, we'll be making our way to Monterrey soon."

"I know. Why do you say that?"

"Now, I understand, being away from family for so long can be tough, but you've gotta know. We all care about you a lot here. Things just wouldn't be the same without you, that's for sure."

Now I get it, Daniel probably explained my irritated eyes, ones he's never seen but can imagine, with a bout of melancholy. It's a bit cheesy, honestly, a little too much for my taste, but strangely convincing. After all, in my hometown, we'd say, "I'm the gal," the only one in this whole group. I guess people expect us to be all sentimental and corny, you know, everything in shades of pink. Ugh! I hate that image. I mean, come on! I deal with demons. Anyway, as ridiculous as it makes me feel, that excuse works like a charm; I didn't even have one myself, so I won't argue with it.

"Raúl, I can't even thank you enough for everything you do for me."

"Kid, it's part of my job; no need to thank me."

"I know, but you always go above and beyond, like today with the sunglasses. I really appreciate you." He smiles.

"Are you ready?"

"Nope."

"Seriously? What's missing?"

"A paper bag."

"A paper bag. For what?"

"To put it over my head." I let out a hearty laugh.

"Come on! But you're rocking it; go ahead, I've got your back."

I'm sorry, Raúl, but there are no bodyguards for this kind of mission. We head out into the hallway and run into all of Daniel's musicians, who are walking ahead, followed by hotel staff carrying a bunch of suitcases. Sebastián is the first to come up to me.

"Blimey, those glasses suit you brilliantly. What's the story behind them?"

The Game…Jade

"I'm trying to hide behind them."

"Hide from who?"

"From myself."

"Well, I wouldn't have guessed. Good luck with that! Let me know if you manage it. Come to think of it, there are times when I'd love to give it a try."

"Promise."

We reach the hotel lobby, and that's when I see Daniel, standing there in shorts and a bright orange t-shirt that makes his eyes pop. Raúl approaches him and whispers something in his ear; he nods. Then, he turns toward me, and he stares right straight at the sunglasses. I keep my eyes on him; there aren'tmany places to hide my embarrassment, so, as my grandma used to say, "I have to hold a tiger by the tail."

He walks over to me, stops a few steps away, and then shows me his hands. With a slow movement, he places them behind his back and smiles. Annoying. I totally saw this coming; he had no intention of leaving me alone. Slowly, with almost mime-like movements, he kisses me on the cheek.

"Good morning, gorgeous."

"Is it?"

"Of course! Look at that beautiful sun, oh! But you've seen it. Isn't that right? Is that why the glasses?" He's getting on my nerves, thanks; I work much better this way.

"No, actually, with that t-shirt, you didn't leave me any other choice; my pupils protested."

"I see." He smiles broadly. "Sorry, you can't have it all in life, and today, I'm putting all my effort into not touching you, so my outfit took a backseat."

"Well, god is great! He finally decided to rid me of you, huh?"

"No, miracles are saved for another day. Today, you've only escaped my hands; I'll keep them away from you."

"Well, it's a start."

"You're in quite a hurry to get rid of me. Mind if I ask why this decision? You're missing out on all of this." He smiles, gesturing towards his body.

"I'm glad to see you have such a high opinion of yourself. But, like I told you before, I'm not missing out; I'm just avoiding it! Oh, and as for my decision, you might find it hard to believe I'd let go of something so marvelous." I emphasize the last part by pointing at his body, just like he did earlier. "It's not that I'm a martyr or anything; it's just that despite how awful it could be for me, I've found out that you give me allergies."

"Strange. In this life, I've caused all sorts of reactions in people, but an allergy? No, that's new. And can you tell me what symptoms I'm causing?"

"How? Haven't you noticed? My eyes are watering!"

Laughter bursts out around us; Sebastián, Raúl, and a couple of other musicians couldn't help but overhear our conversation and start chuckling. Sebastián approaches Raúl.

"I told you; she picks up things fast." Daniel, still with his hands hidden behind his back, whispers in my ear.

"Evil." He smiles.

Finally, we get on the tour bus; it's going to be a short trip, about four hours or so, though it'll probably feel much longer for me. Once on board, I head to my usual seat at the back of the vehicle, which I usually share with Raúl or Sebastián in shifts. I only sit next to Daniel during flights because he prefers to stretch out and sleep, and he just doesn't feel comfortable with anyone else. However, this time, no one came over to sit with me. I see Raúl a few seats ahead.

"Aren't you coming with me?"

"Not today, kid."

"Raúl, please don't leave me alone."

"But you're doing great. Keep on this track, and everything will be fine."

He replies with a smile and settles in to enjoy the show. Oh boy, I can already imagine what's in store for me.

I take a seat by the window and wait. A few seconds later, Daniel arrives and sits down next to me. This time, there's no escaping.

Chapter VII
And that, ladies and gentlemen, that's how gossip is made

He keeps staring straight ahead while everyone else gets ready to watch a movie that, I'm pretty sure, we've all seen before a bunch of times. The seats in front of us are conveniently empty, and he takes a deep breath, exhaling slowly, pursing his lips as if preparing to whistle.

"Forgive me. Would you?" I was expecting anything, like teasing or maybe even a scolding, but not this. I give him a surprised expression.

"Forgive you? Why?"

"For whatever I did to you last night. I'm rather sorry about it." He looks down at his hands to avoid looking at me.

"Daniel, come on! That... it had nothing to do with you."

"It had nothing to do with me?! Gorgeous, if my memory serves me right, I was the sole company you had." He says with a half-smile.

I can't help but laugh, part out of nervousness and part because of the silliness of what I just said. I turn in my seat to face him, and for that, I take off my glasses and put them on my head like a headband; I don't care how my eyes look anymore.

"I have nothing to forgive you for. What I mean is, you didn't do anything to me, so there's no need to apologize."

"However, something happened, didn't it? Something that upset you." He's already noticed my teary eyes and avoids looking at me.

"Yes, but it was nothing. Can we just drop it?"

"No, I'm sorry. I got rather furious last night, you know? I got furious with myself." His eyes wander to the front of the tour bus or perhaps even further.

"But I already told you that..." I get interrupted.

"I got angry because I realized that I've spent so much time with you, and I never really took the time to get to know you. Jade, I didn't even know about your grandparents, and it must be recent. I mean, we already knew each other when it happened, right?"

I slowly nod my head, and he sighs, continuing.

Rocío Blisswealth

"This is embarrassing. Now that I think about it, I realize you've spent hours and hours with me, and I didn't notice a thing about you. Yet, I can remember the conversations we've had, and all you've done is listen to me. And you still say there's no reason for me to ask for your forgiveness, so I don't know what would be."

"I like to listen." I reply quietly.

"Do you always do that?" He asks, raising an eyebrow.

"Most of the time."

"I won't forgive myself for this. How did I not realize?" He starts cracking his fingers, a thing he does when something bothers him.

"Daniel, what can I say? The way things have happened has been perfect for me. I'm kind of... my mom says I'm self-absorbed. I rarely talk about myself, hardly at all. Everything was fine for me like this, and even though I appreciate how you feel, I still think you have nothing to apologize for." He looks at me for a couple of seconds, furrowing his brow, then shakes his head in disagreement.

"Self-absorbed? There's none of that in you. Let me ask you something, not to bother you, I promise. What happened last night?" I've got no other choice but to speak up. That's how I'll prevent any misunderstandings, or at least, I hope so.

"Have you ever had that thing where you yawn just because you see someone else yawning?"

"Yes."

"Okay, that happens to me with crying. Since I see that you feel guilty, let me tell you, I didn't notice until last night. I didn't know, and I didn't force myself to keep you company or anything like that; I was genuinely happy to be with you until my throat tightened up. I felt like crying if that makes sense."

"Perfectly clear, thanks." He looks at me. Maybe a little hurt would be the word for it.

"Well, I was trying to keep that in check, and I think I would have, but then you asked me who I missed more, and everything got out of hand."

"Your grandparents." His voice is barely audible.

"That's right."

"Does it still hurt a lot?"

"I doubt it will ever stop hurting."

"Was it an illness?" He's afraid to ask.

The Game...Jade

"Not exactly. Well, in a way. To me, it was a lost battle; I don't know how to explain it. It's frustrating."

"Why didn't you let me touch you? You kept pulling away from me." Slowly, he focuses his eyes on mine.

"I'm not sure." He raises an eyebrow and observes me. "Honestly, it felt like if you touched me, you'd bring down the walls that were already crumbling on their own." My response seems to intrigue him; the furrow in his brow doesn't ease up.

"Why not let that happen?"

"No, not that. I mean, no." I shake my head from side to side.

"Jade..."

"I've never cried in front of someone, and I don't like the idea."

"Not even with your grandparents?"

"How do you think that I would have worried them? Of course not!"

"And with someone else? I don't know."

"Daniel." I'm getting impatient; I don't want him to insist on this point.

"There might be someone." His voice starts to sound concerned.

"Who says that?"

"I don't know. Life has its moments, both uplifting and challenging, but going through them alone doesn't quite cut it. Take last night. It helped because..."

"I'm glad for that, but still, that's not for me."

He keeps his gaze locked on my eyes as if he's asking something, and at the same time, not. He lifts the corners of his lips slightly in a very poor attempt at a smile.

"I realize how little I know about you. I'm truly sorry, and this time, it's not an excuse; it genuinely pains me. I've missed out on so much!" He says while stroking my hair.

"It's not like that." Once again, he doesn't seem to hear me.

"At this moment, I see you as a gift that, through the sheer act of not unwrapping it, has ended up sealed, with no one having the pleasure of discovering what lies within. And yet, I've received so much from you; I've never known anyone quite like you. You just give; it's natural to you. And I haven't managed to give back even a little, if not nothing."

"It's not like that, really, Daniel. You've done more than you could imagine."

Rocío Blisswealth

"I wonder if you'll ever allow me to explore this maze." He says, placing his hand on my chest over my heart.

"You wouldn't like it; the parts that aren't boring are filled with monsters." I smile softly. It's obvious he doesn't believe me. After a moment's hesitation, as if testing the waters, he asks another question.

"What were your grandparents like?"

"They were sensational, loving, polite, funny, and great conversationalists; always there for me. I can tell you with certainty that if you've seen anything good in me as a person, it's all because of them."

"They must have invested a great deal in you; they accumulated a lot of things." He caresses my cheek and leaves his hand on my neck.

"Thank you." The conversation is growing uncomfortable for me, and I can't see an end in sight. So, I decided to take a shortcut.

"You had assured me that you would keep your hands away from me." He knows what I'm trying to do. Finally, he smiles, and it's a very sweet smile.

"I lied." He waits a few seconds. "Jade, one last thing. If at any point... well, I mean... I'm here for you, you know that, don't you?" He places his hand on my neck, snuggling my nape.

"I know."

Finally, after nearly a month of non-stop touring, we've got a day off. Can you believe it? A whole day! But, as luck would have it, there's always a catch. We somehow found an interview with a national newspaper on our agenda, and there's no way to cancel it since we don't have the phone. So, our well-deserved rest is going to be interrupted, although hopefully briefly.

As I enter Daniel's suite, I discover him dressed—well, if you can call it that. No, that sounds too fancy. Let's say he's wearing a pair of pants that have been at the bottom of a suitcase for many days, clean but... Also, he's got on a shirt that seems to have rested in the same corner, and its color has absolutely nothing to do with the pants. His shoes are electric blue sneakers. Can't help but wonder, where did he get those? As soon as he sees me, he smiles.

"I know what you're thinking. Hold your fire! Let me explain."

"Alright."

"It's our day off, isn't it?"

"Yes, and?"

"So, I had this idea that for the reporter who shows up, we'd give him some archive photos from the suitcase and inform him that, since I'm not all dolled up, they can't snap pictures of me. What do you think?"

"Daniel, I suppose there's no way in the world I can convince you otherwise, even to just take a shower."

"But I already did. I've had a bath!"

"Oh, my bad. It's just that you're pretty good at covering it up, well..."

"I swear, I've already showered! And no, there's no way to convince me otherwise; I'm tired." He says with a pitiful look.

"Aw, poor thing."

Apparently, I've got no choice but to give in. It would embarrass me, but if he's not bothered by it, and he's the one with the interview, then so be it.

I take a seat, and just like any other Sunday, even if it isn't one, we plop ourselves on a couch to watch TV. We doze off during a movie until we decide to order some food.

"You know, I've got this feeling he isn't going to make it. It's way past five, and that meet-up was supposed to go down at four." Raúl tells us.

"Excellent, we'll just indulge in our laziness. Raúl, please order a bottle of red wine."

We feast heartily, and everyone, except for me, has several glasses of wine. Obviously, Daniel teases me about how little I drink, but I've never been much of a drinker, and I don't think now's the right time to start, especially when I have no idea how it might affect me.

The daylight slowly retreats from the window, leaving us alone with the TV. We don't even talk anymore; we're falling asleep, even though it's only 7:00 in the evening. Or is it nighttime? I've never been sure. At that moment, there's a knock on the door. Raúl gets up and goes to answer it, probably out of habit. He does so, and Daniel and I hear the reporter's voice, whom we now spot in person, apologizing for being late while the photographer starts snapping away.

In a split second, Daniel jumps off the couch and turns on the lamp on his right, and I do the same with the one on the left. Raúl raises his voice, instructing them not to take any pictures. The reporters stare at us in astonishment; they don't know what's going on, and neither do we. However, after seeing Daniel's struggle to get rid of his glass of wine, they exchange

Rocío Blisswealth

glances, and of course, I'm caught in the crossfire. The temptation to click their cameras must be irresistible.

"I'm sorry. I don't want photos, not even one!" Daniel says seriously, then turns to Raúl. "Escort her to her room; we'll catch up later."

Gods! My imagination is totally clueless about what they must have thought. Thankfully, Raúl took it upon himself to explain to me the whole scenario these gentlemen saw. We were on the couch, the room all dimmed, wine glasses in hand, and then a request to accompany me to my room for a later visit. Looking at it that way, even I don't believe it was just an innocent afternoon of lazing around. So, there we were, stuck in my room, waiting, with nothing else to do. Daniel is going to deal with them all on his own.

Almost half an hour later, the door opens, and Daniel walks in, drowning in laughter.

"Can someone fill me in on what the hell I just said?" He asks.

"Well, you told them we'd see both later. Oh, and not to take pictures, of course. That's basically it." I respond, and at this point, we're all laughing.

"Well, it wasn't just what you said, but how you said it. What went down?" Raúl asks.

"I honestly don't even know anymore; they bombarded me with questions. Why was I so camera-shy? Was it because I wanted to maintain your anonymity?" Daniel explains.

"What anonymity?!" I practically shout.

"What do you think? Yours, of course!" He replies.

"But, seriously, no one needs to keep anything for me!"

"Haha, that was the case until today; now you're officially one of us. But even though that was the truth, they weren't buying my story about looking terrible. I tried diverting their attention with their lateness, but that didn't cut it. They asked me for your name."

"Daniel…" He gives me a mischievous look, and he continues.

"I didn't give it to them, of course; that would've led them straight to the song and a media scandal that I'd rather keep you out of."

"You're such a sweetheart."

"I know. Somehow, I managed to show them the door. Let's see what the newspapers have to say tomorrow because they certainly didn't leave with any conviction."

"We acted like total maniacs." Raúl laughs.

The Game…Jade

"I know, it just caught me off guard." Daniel turns to me, suddenly serious, almost as serious as I am. "If you want, call your home, gorgeous. Give them a heads up."

"Of course not! Are you crazy? Mara would be over the moon and look for the first reporter to tell her side of the story and get famous. I'm worried about you."

"No need to worry, then." He continues to laugh. What's so funny? I have no idea.

"Who's Mara?" Raúl whispers.

"Her sister, I think." Daniel replies in the same tone.

The next morning, I caught a flight to Monterrey, our next stop on the tour. My flight leaves very early, while Daniel and the rest of the crew leave at noon. The reason is that he wanted to give me some time to visit my family. He won't admit it, but he's still concerned about the reporters. That's why, as soon as I set foot in the airport, I checked the newspaper, and there was nothing there. Raúl says sometimes they don't release a story until they gather more information or make one up.

However, my biggest concern is something else. I know Mara, maybe even better than she knows herself. And I know perfectly well that her desire for the spotlight would not allow her to stay quiet if the opportunity to make a name for herself arose. I need to make sure she stays silent. This time, the demon didn't wait for me at the airport, which is odd. I can't quite figure out how they've left me in peace for so long, but I'm grateful for it.

When I get home, the ones to come out to greet me are my two nephews and my niece. They know I always come bearing gifts, so even before saying hello, they snatch the small suitcase I slung over my shoulder and open it on the living room floor. Mom is happy to see me; dealing with Mara must be tough when I'm not around. I mean, I'm the one who takes care of every spiritual plan she comes up with, and in my absence, she gets hysterical. I'm sorry, but today I don't have time for that, though not without
some guilt, to be honest. Regardless of anything, I've always seen them not as my family but as my responsibility.

My grandma always talked to me about god and what he expected from us. Needless to say, I don't feel worthy of expecting anything from him. Still, the mere hope that one day he might grant me a peaceful life always led me to the point where they wanted me to be. I resisted, but always, in some way, they got what they wanted. But not today, no matter how serious it might be. This is my time with Daniel, and it's something even the demons respect, so they'll have to as well.

"Would you like to take a break? Your room is all set."

"No, Mom, I'm sorry. I have to go back to the airport in a few minutes to pick up Daniel. I can't stay."

"Aren't you going to stay here?" Mara asks, annoyed.

"No, work schedules are completely unpredictable, so I have to be available all the time."

"We've been closely following the tour; it's the biggest thing happening in the entertainment scene in the country right now, so they're giving it extensive coverage."

"Speaking of that, Mara, there's something I want to talk to you both about. A couple of reporters are very interested in finding out my role in the tour. Since they didn't get information directly from Daniel, I don't know what they're capable of, so..."

"Don't you worry," Mara replies, determined and cheerful. "If anyone from the press gets in touch with us, I'll make sure to explain that it's just work, so they'll leave you alone."

I can't help but smile; I know her so well. What's worse is that I don't think she even realizes what she's doing. Mom looks pleased; she will finally stand up for me like a true sister. I doubt it.

"No, Mara, that's exactly what I don't want you to do, none of you. Honestly, I don't think it will come to this point, I mean, reaching the family, but if it does, all you have to do is say that you don't know anything, okay? Please."

"Are you sure? Don't you think it would be better...?"

"No, it's already decided; let's leave it at that."

"Alright. But tell us, how's it been going?" I spend the next hour sharing tour anecdotes with them, which they seem to enjoy a lot. In return, they overwhelm me with all kinds of recommendations about food, vitamins, and even moisturizers. A few minutes later, I say goodbye and head back to the airport. I still have a month left, and I will enjoy every second of it.

On the road, I mentally replayed the conversation I had with Daniel last night before going to sleep. He asked me how many tickets I wanted for the show.

The Game...Jade

"Tickets? Why would I want tickets, Daniel?"

"I know you're not a fan of me giving you anything, but it's the Monterrey concert. Wouldn't you like to invite your friends? Just tell me how many you want, gorgeous."

"Well, I guess I'd love to invite my friends if I had any. But no, I had some coworkers I chatted with sometimes, not enough to invite them. I also have some former schoolmates, but I lost touch with them a long time ago. Do you really want me to continue?"

The way he looked at me was hard to describe, not in disbelief, but rather with a touch of pain. Yes, that's what I think it was.

"You weren't kidding! You were serious when you told me you didn't have any friends. It can't be; it shouldn't be like this." He said while gently stroking my head.

"Well, Daniel, it's not that big of a deal."

"How can it not be? It's important, Jade. It's not good to be alone."

"Sometimes it's preferable, believe me." I said, distancing myself slightly from him.

"What do you mean? Gorgeous, consider that..."

"You're not thinking of giving me a lecture about it, are you? I've already told you that not everyone works the same way."

"Just give me one reason, one good reason, and I'll leave you alone."

"Daniel, people leave. They always leave, so I avoid goodbyes."

"I'm here, and..." He stopped halfway through the sentence, he's leaving too.

"See?" It sounded like a reproach, and it was.

"Life, especially yours, is so misguided. Considering all that you can offer, it's insane." He replied, seemingly upset, but I don't think it was directed at me.

"You overestimate me, Daniel, not a single ticket, okay?"

"I get it, not a single ticket."

It annoys me when he treats me like that. I know one thing for sure: no one, except the person living it, truly knows what their life is like and the reasons behind certain things. I suppose if I explained my darker side to him, it might make things easier or incredibly more complicated. I wouldn't know until I mentioned it, and since I don't plan on doing that, I'll remain in doubt.

Rocío Blisswealth

Lost in these thoughts, I finally reach the airport, where a representative from the record company is waiting for me. Just in case doubt gnaws at you, no, it's not Miguel to make sure I don't have any access problems. We make our way to the waiting area, and I can see a group of reporters with cameras and microphones, the usual. One of them recognizes me; we were classmates in school, and he approaches to greet me.

"Hey, Jade. Remember me?"

"Hi, how are you?"

"Just here working, you know. I spotted you from afar a few months back. You're still living in Málaga, right?" That's the name of the street where I live.

"Yes, but how do you remember that?"

"You know, elephant memory. Hey, how long have you been with Montalvo?"

"It's been a while, but how do you know that...?"

"Someone from the record company told me, and of course, there can't be too many Jades. I connected the dots. Don't worry; your secret is safe with me."

"How kind. Either way, it's no secret, but thanks."

"Maybe you can lend me a hand for an exclusive."

I knew it. Luckily, at that very moment, Daniel's plane lands, and I don't get a chance to respond. Once again, I get lost in the whirlwind of reporters, bodyguards, fans, and a lot of people. We make it to the van, and Raúl asks us.

"Did you see him?"

"Who?" Daniel asks.

"Yesterday's reporter, he was here, among the others."

"Of course not. It can't be."

"Of course he was! He can, and he was, so let's get ready; he's still on the hunt."

The reporter had overheard my conversation with my former schoolmate and had also pieced things together. I know this because the next morning, the national newspaper's entertainment section included a column whose text said, among other things, something in between these lines:

The Game...Jade

* Daniel Montalvo is performing today in the city of Monterrey, and he will be in excellent company. A fortunate Spanish young lady originally from Málaga, with whom he has been in a relationship for several months, will be at the concert as a special guest.

We'll see how his fans take this news. Her name? Jade, of course! Just like his most famous song. They have been seen together in other cities, and we can confirm that they enjoy their limited free time with good food and exquisite red wine. We witnessed one of their outings, and as expected, we were not allowed to take photographs. *

Seriously, the way it all unfolded was brilliant. And that, ladies and gentlemen, that's how gossip is made. A few minutes after the newspaper came out, Mara called me.

"Images of Daniel with you at the airport are all over the local TV stations, not to mention the newspaper article, and the phone hasn't stopped ringing despite the late hour. What should I do?"

"Nothing, I already told you. You don't know anything, just don't pick up, Mara."

"Alright, but it's going to be tough, not to mention frustrating."

"Don't worry, the reporters will be after Daniel for his statements, and they'll stop calling the house soon."

"Which reporters?"

"The ones who've been calling. Or... who has been calling?"

"Only one reporter called, claiming to be your friend, saying you promised him an exclusive when he spotted you at the airport. But I mean your actual friends."

I'm sure of one thing: I don't have friends, so who the heck has been calling my house?

"Mara, focus. Give me details, please."

"Alright. We've received about fifty calls, men and women saying they're your friends or that they know you from school or previous jobs. They want to chat with you, see if they can get tickets through you, make sure you'll be at the concert tonight, and some even want to know if you're staying here to drop by and say hello."

"I see, Mara, you know me, you know that many people aren't my friends."

"Well, you see, César, Ricardo, Claudia, Verónica called. Those are the names I remember. So, should I not say anything to them?"

Rocío Blisswealth

168

"I'll make it easy for you. Let the kids handle it. Let them say I don't live there anymore."

"Alright, but please give me a heads-up before you leave so I can find out what went down, okay?"

"Sure, I'll call you later."

Daniel enters my room, and I'm still sitting on the bed with the headset in my hand. He doesn't say anything; he watches me from the corner where he chooses to sit. I know he's there, but I still can't muster enough concentration to snap out of my thoughts and greet him. He rises slowly and comes closer to me; I know he's searching for my gaze, but it's lost far from here. He takes the phone from my hand, and it takes some effort as I grip it tightly. Finally, he manages to free it and puts it back in its place. That's when I see him, and I fake a smile to greet him.

"Hi."

"Are you alright?" He asks very seriously.

"Yes. No, that's not true, but don't worry; I'll be fine soon."

"Soon enough to bury all those feelings somewhere deep down, huh?"

"That's right."

"Jade, please tell me what's wrong. Allow me to be here for you." He looks at me with a sad gaze, and I don't want him to feel pushed aside, so, trying to stay calm, I attempt to explain. I start pacing around the room like a caged lion, and he follows me with his gaze.

"You're not going to like it; I'm furious." I mutter.

"With me?"

"No."

"Did I do something?"

"Definitely not." I shake my head from side to side.

"So, I guess I'm ready to take on all the rage you're toting. Go on."

"Mara called; the newspaper article came out, and on top of that, there are pictures of us at the airport on local channels."

"I already figured as much."

"The phone at home hasn't stopped ringing; it's going crazy."

"I'm sorry."

"No, that doesn't matter. I think, despite everything, it's something she's enjoying, but…"

"Has the press been calling?"

The Game…Jade

"No."

"Then who has?"

"Daniel, if you stop interrupting me, maybe I'll get to that point."

"Sorry, please continue."

"According to Mara, by now, we've received around fifty calls at home. All of them are from people who claim to be my friends from junior high, from previous jobs, who knows! She can only recall a few names, and yes, I recognize them, but that's it—I know who they are, but I can't picture their faces. I could run into them in a hallway, and they wouldn't even look familiar. You get me?"

"Yes."

"They want to know if I'll be at the concert, which, obviously, thanks to them, I have no intention of attending." He furrows his brow but says nothing. "They say they want to come by and say hello, for what reason?! I haven't seen them in years! Heck, I never paid them any attention; to me, they were mere shadows, and I didn't exist to them either. Yet, they had the nerve to ask Mara if I could get them tickets to come see you. Idiots! Why would I do that?"

"They must be assuming that..."

"What thing? They're my friends? Then my concept of friendship is way, way off. Over the years, I've seen them, over and over, hurting each other, hurling insults that I'd consider fit for the bitterest of enemies, and then ignoring them, all in order not to be alone. It's pathetic."

"Some people out there find loneliness more terrifying than death itself."

"I can get that, Daniel, but tell me this: can they really consider themselves accompanied when their relationships leave them feeling empty inside? Isn't the whole point of friendship about nurturing your inner self? And besides, is that what friendship means to them? Something to rely on when they need stuff? Something material, I mean. Like concert tickets?"

"Now I understand how you're feeling; I've been there."

"I can imagine."

He follows me around the room and tries to hug me. I stay still; I don't want to take it out on him, but his touch irritates me. I'm boiling inside.

"Jade, let me attempt something."

"Okay." I reply quietly.

"Locate your anger within you." He speaks very softly in my ear. "As if it's a tangible thing."

Rocío Blisswealth

"Okay." I don't know what he's planning, but I want to give it a try.

"Now, release it."

The names of the people who had called home were swirling in my head, and then, they just vanished, along with the anger, and I let out a sigh of relief, a long one.

"That was easy, wasn't it?"

"But how?"

"Let me see you."

He takes my face in his hands and looks into my eyes carefully, smiles with that amazing smile of his, and kisses me firmly.

"It's back."

"What thing?"

"The magic in your gaze."

"Really?"

"Absolutely, it's right there, looking at me from your eyes. Can you see it?"

"Daniel..."

"Give it a try; you might catch a glimpse in my eyes if you come close enough."

I think I saw something winking at me in the reflection of his beautiful blue eyes just before he kissed me again, but I'm not entirely sure; it doesn't matter now.

The day dragged on, and I only left my room to join them for the soundcheck. I don't want to go to the concert; the mere thought of dealing with people whose faces I want to spit on annoys me. Yet, as far as I understand, I must go because I made a promise to Daniel. I have no idea when I did such a thing, but I always stick to my word, so here I am, left with no choice. Funny how things turned out; I never imagined I'd end up at a Daniel Montalvo concert, only because I had no other option.

This will be the first time I get to experience a concert from the audience's perspective. The previous ones I watched from the stage's sidelines, and it's an entirely different experience. You see more of the crowd than the singer, and that changes everything. For the first time in months, I'm feeling the nerves, those same nerves I felt the first time I saw him.

I make it to the concert after a long battle to persuade Raúl to stay backstage and let me venture out alone. Neither he nor Daniel wanted it that way, but when I pointed out that attending with Daniel Montalvo's bodyguard would attract even more attention, they saw reason and agreed to let me go.

I find my seat just minutes before the lights go out. As I walk down the hallway, people wave at me, but I ignore them and keep walking, hoping the lights go out soon to escape the curious stares. The two girls to my right already asked if they knew me from somewhere. Of course, I said no, but I figured it was best not to attract too much attention to myself.

The stage looks so different from here, much larger and imposing. The musicians take their places, illuminated only by a soft blue light. Obviously, I'm in the front row. And I say obviously because Daniel picked my seat for tonight, so all of them could see me clearly. Sebastián winks at me, and the girls next to me see it, so they turn to look at me. I'm going to kill him later, of course, but for now, I'm not planning on moving from where I am.

The lights explode, and the music's intensity grows along with my excitement. It's unbelievable; I've seen this concert nearly thirty times, but I can't seem to control it. Daniel takes the stage, and the hysteria begins. He's right in front of me, yet the distance between the stage and my seat makes everything look different. The saying goes, "Familiarity breeds contempt." Today, more than ever, I understand the truth behind that expression. By spending time with Daniel, I've learned to see him as just that, Daniel. Without the celebrity facade that the spotlights project during the concert, without the myth, the unreality.

Now, I see him as I did on television years ago; once again, I can appreciate the harmony of his figure. Everything has the perfect proportions for his height. As he dances to the rhythm of the music, his jet-black hair shines brilliantly under the spotlight, and his skin takes on a paler tone than usual, so smooth and so perfect that I can't find another way to describe it, but as the statue I talked to you about a while ago. If it weren't for his remarkable agility on stage, he could easily pass for a sculpture, a true work of art.

As it often happens to me, I find myself lost in the images and sounds. Just for once, I wish I could face the person responsible for my being here, the one who caused this incredible happiness I've ever been able to experience in my life, and thank him for all this, though honestly, I don't know if I deserve it. Suddenly, Daniel runs his fingers from the top of his face down, barely touching it with his fingertips—a gentle caress he gives me when I'm lost in thought—and smiles at me. Butterflies flutter inside my stomach; I wink back at him.

Rocío Blisswealth

Daniel, don't distract me; let me be a mere spectator, even if just this once. I'm paying all the attention I can.

It's in these moments when I can pull back and see the bigger picture that everything takes on a sense of unreality for me. It's here that I wonder if all of this might be a dream, if my imagination took flight during one of his songs, creating every detail, every experience, every kiss in my mind. The fifth song ends, and Daniel leaves the stage for his first costume change. I can imagine the rush at which everything is moving backstage. He returns with another song, and a hand lands on my shoulder, startling me. I turn to find Raúl crouching beside me.

"Jade, I'm sorry." He says in a low voice.

"What's happening, Raúl?"

"The thing is, we can't find Daniel's towels."

"Raúl, they're in the suitcase I packed, and I double-checked that they were loaded on the tour bus. Go get them, will you?"

"Sure thing, sorry again."

He leaves, disappearing through a small door at the side of the auditorium, which I hadn't noticed until now. This won't be the same anymore; I won't be able to help but keep an eye on that damn little door from now on.

The concert continues, and I return to my contemplative attitude. My task has become more challenging now that the people around me can't stop looking at me with a questioning look. I try not to pay attention to them, but, well, at least I'm trying.

Daniel keeps singing one song, then another, and I'm already singing along with the rest of the audience. I wish I had a lighter in hand; I know precisely which series of songs is up next, and a lighter would create the perfect ambiance. Suddenly, Raúl's hand again.

"Jade."

"And now what?"

"Sorry, but..."

"Stop apologizing already! I'm not going to forgive you, anyway."

"Daniel asked me for his water bottles, and I just can't find them."

"Did you find the towels?"

"Yes."

"Really?"

"I swear."

The Game...Jade

"And you didn't see the bottles?"

"I wouldn't be asking you if I did."

"Well, then you need to get your sight, touch, and even your sense of smell checked because the bottles were wrapped in the towels, liar. Just leave me alone; you promised."

"Alright, I'm leaving now."

This isn't just hard anymore; it's mission impossible. The girls next to me inch closer and ask if I'm Jade. I pretended not to hear them over the blaring music, but they weren't buying it. They've got Raúl pinned down, and I guess they will be thinking about his next move. Please! Let me enjoy the concert. In three songs, just three, Daniel will be singing my song, and I want to hear it from here.

I sing along to the next song; I know it well. And as the next one starts, that's right, you guessed it! Here comes Raúl again. It's relentless; he's not planning to give me a break. Everyone around me is watching closely. I'm so angry.

"Jade." He says secretly.

"Just shut up! It doesn't matter anymore! What is it now? Can't find his right shoe, or is it his left? Step aside!"

Raúl doesn't say a word anymore. I stand up furiously from my seat, and before taking a step, I turn on myself and face the girls next to me.

"That's right, I'm Jade! Happy now?"

I kept going, sprinting past Raúl to disappear through that damn door. Anyone who crosses my path won't enjoy it, that's for sure. I reach my usual spot next to the stage; no one speaks to me. They've had time to get to know me, and they know it wouldn't be a smart move. Daniel is finishing the second song; you know, the next one is mine, and I won't be able to hear it from down there. I hate them all.

My song begins; Daniel winks at me, but he gets no response from me. What was so hard about letting me see the entire concert from my seat? He doesn't need me here for anything; Raúl can handle everything perfectly. This is the result of how spoiled he is. He's going to pay for this! I step aside, staying out of his line of sight. If he's up for annoying people, I can do it, too.

"Jade, you mad?" Raúl asks.

"Well, today seems to be the day for dumb questions. Do you have them written down, or are they a product of your brilliant intellect?"

"That's what I thought." He steps away.

That part of the show ends, and Daniel comes out to change. He asks Raúl about me, and Raúl points out where I am. He looks at me and blows a kiss. I turn my head the other way; anything is more attractive right now. I'm furious.

He runs over to me, hugs me tight, and kisses my cheek, which only angers me more. I guess anger doesn't come across so eloquently when nobody seems to notice. Being ignored just makes you angrier. At least, that's how it feels to me.

"Yikes! You're all sweaty. Back off, Daniel!"

I only hear his loud laughter next to my ear, and he heads back to the stage. The last part of the concert is already underway, the applause rings out, and the closing songs begin; the ones Daniel uses to bid farewell until I finally hear, "Goodbye, Monterrey!"

"Are we leaving?" Raúl asks without looking me in the eye. I'm aware he just followed Daniel's orders, but I couldn't care less.

I get up from the step I was sitting on and walk outside to board the bus. Everyone is settling in, and I take a seat next to Sebastián. Daniel boards shortly after.

"Not sitting with me?"

"Wow, your deductive skills are impressive."

"It's alright. Sebastián, mind if I switch places?" He says, smiling. I give Sebastián a threatening look; if he dares to move, I'll hit him, that's for sure.

"Sorry, mate, but this girl and I have a conversation pending, so..."

He just earned my respect. Daniel continues to his seat and leaves me alone. I know it will only be until we reach the hotel, but for now, it's enough. Once there, I entered my room as quickly as possible. Two minutes later, the phone rings.

"Jade, are you coming to dinner with us?" I hear Raúl's voice.

"I'm not hungry, thanks." I'm sure that if I ate something now, I'd get sick.

"I'm really sorry about the concert." I simply don't respond. If I did, it would be worse; all I can think of are rude remarks. I've decided to stay quiet until my anger subsides, so I hang up.

The Game...Jade

After a bath and changing into my pajamas, I decided to give Mara a call. We've got an early start tomorrow, and I know there won't be time then. According to her, letting the kids answer the phone paid off; people got tired as the day went on and eventually stopped calling. Other than that, everything seems to be going okay. As I say goodbye to her, Daniel steps into my room and sits next to me. I end my call, promising to call frequently, and hang up.

"It feels like stepping into quicksand. Will I ever learn how to act around you?"

He's next to me, without the playful attitude from the show, yet I don't look at him, and I don't respond at all. He'll have to be the one to speak.

"I've grown accustomed to having you with me during the show; I can't shake the feeling when you're not there. I don't like it. Raúl... Oh, I should mention he didn't want to do what I asked. He did it all grudgingly. Please don't be angry with him because of me."

"So, the big guy already went to you with the gossip that I'm mad at him? That's all I needed, a crybaby!" I sigh in annoyance.

Despite my frustration, he can't help but smile, probably thinking about the image of Raúl that my words painted in his head.

"I was trying to help you understand that you're not like the audience; there's no distance imposed by a stage between you and me. You don't need to buy a ticket to see me; you have me here whenever you want. You're part of this, just like the rest of us." I put my anger aside for a moment; I want him to understand this, so I look him in the eyes and interrupt.

"I know, I've always known."

"Seriously?"

"The day I met you, it felt like the character from my favorite movie had reached out of the screen, grabbed my hand, and pulled me into the film. Since then, I've known. Believe me, I'm aware of where I am; I repeat, I know all of that."

"Then why did you tell me at the beginning of the tour that you wanted to be a spectator at the Monterrey concert? I never understood the reason; I still don't. There was no need. I thought it was just a whim." He says, with a certain annoyance in his voice, as if trying to explain to a five-year-old that Santa didn't get the Barbie doll she wanted, and she'll have to settle for another.

"You never got it, did you?"

"No, never."

Rocío Blisswealth

"Maybe you should've started by asking the real question."

"What do you mean?"

"Did you ever think to ask me why? I don't remember you ever doing that."

He stared at me with wide eyes, then lowered his gaze, a bit embarrassed, and asked.

"Why did you want to be in the audience?"

"Well, you see, I wanted, even if just for a couple of hours, to go back to where I came from and appreciate what I have and what I am now. I wanted to see you again, with all the glitz and glam that surrounds you when the lights come on, and reconnect with that image of yours that, from the back of the stage, has faded a bit, or maybe a lot, perhaps. I wanted to witness the artist Daniel Montalvo, and be able to admire, once more, all that you can achieve when you step onto a stage. After seeing all that, even without understanding why I was here, I would've sat on this same bed, taking a moment just to feel special. As special as you made me feel that first day, which, as the months passed, I started to forget."

I continued. "I hate the idea that I'm getting used to being here because it would be like living on top of Mount Fujiyama; not being able to see it, I would stop appreciating how wonderful it is. I wanted to renew my perspective on everything I'm experiencing, which is normal for you, but for me... Well, that's all I wanted." He looks at me with disbelief. I'm not sure if that's what he expected. I don't think it is.

"No way. And I messed it up for you."

"Yes."

"But you don't need that. You're very special, you just are. It annoys me that you can't feel it."

"Daniel, can you feel the color of your eyes?"

"No."

"But they are of an incredible and crystal-clear blue that..."

"Well, no, I can't feel it."

"To me, it seems so intense that I don't understand how you don't feel it."

"I get it now."

"You did it that day. I'm not saying I believe it, but true or not, you made me feel special. Can you blame me for wanting to feel it again?"

The Game...Jade

"I didn't know. I'm sorry, I shouldn't have, but I promise in the next concert, no one will bother you."

"It doesn't matter anymore. I won't do it again. There won't be another one for me."

"Of course, there will be! The day after tomorrow, there's another one, and I'll make sure of it."

"Daniel, it won't be Monterrey anymore. It won't. Besides, let's face it, you can't do without me. I'm sorry. I knew this would happen sooner or later. You couldn't help but act like a spoiled child; it's part of my charm." He laughed heartily; I was glad because things were getting really tense. He took my hand.

"It had to be Monterrey, no other place, right? It's incredible; every time I think I know you, I realize how far I am from doing so. While I see only the surface, you reach the depths."

"You called me whimsical."

"And you, a spoiled child." He extended his hand towards me and then said, "Are we even now?" I shook it and nodded my head as I replied.

"No, I win."

If I had been allowed to see the concert the way I wanted, would it have changed my perspective on him at all? I guess I'll never know.

Chapter VIII
Well, no, Jade, much more than just two little bits

The next morning, we rolled into one of the biggest states in my country, where the excitement of seeing Daniel was massive. As the tour bus pulled into the hotel, we saw cars parked along the way, filled with fans holding up signs declaring their undying love. It's mind-blowing how many people admire him; I guess today's concert will be unforgettable.

The trip was fun; Raúl has been bugging me for calling him a crybaby. When I mentioned I had only said it to Daniel, he rolled his eyes and asked, "Did you really have to tell him, considering how he is?" He had a point; I knew Daniel would have a blast teasing him with that nickname, and I would enjoy that too, so I can't help but laugh.

Meanwhile, Sebastián finds it hilarious when Daniel and Raúl talk about me. According to him, they're convinced they've cracked the code into my thoughts. But every time they make one of those statements, they hit a dead end, and I prove them wrong.

"And do you know me?" I asked. Laughing, he replied.

"Know you? No, mate! I'm already doubting you're even from this planet, but I never go around boasting the opposite. That's a big difference; I'm more down-to-earth."

Wow, I never thought I'd be so weird. Well, okay, that's a lie; I've always known I am, but I never realized it was this much. Finally, we reached the hotel, and as usual, Raúl escorted me, both of us ready to rush inside. The entrance is packed with people, making it a hard task. It reminded me of the first time I did this running with them, but I'm not as scared anymore. I tucked my hair inside my shirt, and Raúl stood right next to me. On the count of three, we ran inside. People blocked our way, and we were caught in the crowd.

I said I wasn't scared, right? Call me fickle because I've changed my mind. I felt Raúl's arm on one side and Sebastián's on the other; the rest I couldn't even recognize. We finally broke free from the crowd, not without some punches from Raúl, I have to admit, and we entered the hotel where security barred the way for them from following.

Once inside, while the hotel staff take care of sorting our luggage into the right rooms, Sebastián, Raúl, and I enter Daniel's room. He smiles, scanning us from head to toe. Suddenly, his eyes fixate on me, and he looks alarmed.

"Jade, turn around."

"Turn around? Why? What's going on?"

In a split second, he was by my side, gripping my shoulders and turning me around to inspect my back, his voice rising.

"I said, turn around, I tell you! No arguing."

Normally, I might have protested his tone, but not today; he's out of control, and I won't contradict him. His hands quickly tracked my back, pausing when one of his fingers touched my skin. But how? Was my shirt torn? Or was there something else going on? He continues his inspection, repeating the process three, no, four more times. He turns me around again, throwing me off balance, and I stumble. He grabs my arm, still checking me. He pauses once more, and with a determined look, he looks for Raúl. The moment he spots him, he charges at him like a raging bull, slamming him against the wall almost three feet behind them. Grabbing his shirt, he shakes him against the wall, his voice never ceasing to shout.

"I told you to look after her. Her, you idiot! Is that so hard to understand?"

Raúl could easily defend himself; he practices several martial arts. But he sees me, and his gaze drops to the ground. He won't do it; he won't lift a finger against Daniel. He feels guilty. I throw myself to stop Daniel, but Sebastián stops me, holding me by the waist.

"Not now, Jade, not now."

Daniel keeps yelling at Raúl, although I know he's holding back so he doesn't hit him, well, doesn't hit him anymore.

"I don't matter, you idiot, it's her! It's her they shouldn't harm! I told you once, and a thousand times, I told you." Finally, Sebastián steps in.

"Daniel, mate, they didn't do anything to her; she's alright."

"What do you mean they didn't harm her? Her clothes are slashed with scissors! Scissors! Do you get it? They didn't harm her because they weren't allowed to, but not thanks to you."

Not allowed? By whom? I let go of Sebastián and approach Daniel. Slowly, I take one of his fists; he releases Raúl's shirt and takes a step back, heavily breathing as he tries to calm down. Raúl and Sebastián leave the room,

Rocío Blisswealth

and I approach him very slowly. I hug him around the waist, and then he hugs me tightly.

"Jade, tell me you're okay. Just tell me you're okay, please." He pleads in a whisper.

"Daniel, nothing happened to me. Seriously, I'm fine."

He kisses me on the forehead repeatedly, and I feel his hands run down my back again, this time more carefully.

"Daniel, stop examining me, okay? Nothing happened to me. I'm fine. Agree?"

"I'm sorry, I'm so sorry, Jade."

"Daniel, please! It was nothing, just drop it, will you? You're tickling me. Besides, it wasn't your fault or anyone else's."

"I should've protected you… I must protect you."

"As much as I appreciate your efforts to do that, I have to tell you, nobody has ever taken care of me, and yet, here I am, in one piece, and trust me, I've been through some stuff." I reply, trying to make him smile.

"But whatever happened to you before, it wasn't my fault. This is."

"This isn't either; stop with the fatalistic attitude. Please, Daniel, I'm whole. There was no bloodshed."

"Don't talk like that." He gets upset.

"Alright, I can see nothing I say makes you laugh."

"I'm sorry. I just can't think of anything else right now."

"Fine, you leave me no choice…" He looks at me, intrigued, and I continue, taking on a more serious tone.

"I never thought this would be necessary, but desperate times call for desperate measures. You have something of mine, and I want it back right now."

"I have…? What do I have of yours?"

"Oh, now you don't remember; how convenient." He starts to smile, although he still doesn't know what I mean yet.

"No, I don't remember. I'm sorry."

"A while back, you stole a kiss from me, and I just don't want you keeping it anymore. I demand its full return, with interest, at this moment."

"So, that's it. And you want it right now, with interest, you say?" He moves closer very slowly, and it makes me nervous, but there's no turning back now.

The Game…Jade

"Yes, you've kept it for quite a while, so the accrued interest must be sky-high. If you keep it, you'd owe me, and you wouldn't want that, would you?" My voice trembles slightly.

"No, of course not. Are you sure you want it?" He finally smiles, that mischievous smile I adore.

"Yes, I'm sure, right n..."

Without a second thought, he pulls me close and kisses me deeply. Gods! I'm really enjoying this interest thing; I think I finally managed to distract him. No, he didn't forget. His hand gently traces down my back, and it's not a caress. Unbelievable! I can't help but laugh, and he does, too.

"Fool."

"I just wanted to make sure."

"I'm leaving."

"Where to? Are you off just as I'm settling my debts?"

"To change my shirt; this one seems too tempting for you. Goodbye." I open the door and spot Raúl waiting for me in the hallway. He looks very serious, but I'm not in the mood for another scene. Plus, curiosity gnaws at me, maybe even more than it does at Daniel. Raúl starts talking, but without listening, I grab his hand.

"Come with me." I say, leading him down the hallway. He follows me to my room, which I never reached with all the hustle and bustle. We enter, and I search for the nearest full-length mirror. I stand with my back to it, pulling the shirt from the front to inspect the cuts. There are five gashes spread all over my back, large enough for two of my fingers to fit in each. I'm about to do something that terrifies me, so I ask Raúl for help.

"Help me lift my shirt; I want to check my back." He lifts it almost up to my neck, and I turn to look. Nothing. Absolutely nothing. I just don't get it; those scissors should have cut me at least once. I don't understand how they didn't reach my skin; they were clearly meant to hurt me. And it happened fast—we weren't in the chaos for more than thirty or forty seconds. I rule out, of course, that someone might have cut it at another moment. It was brand new; I unpacked it this morning, and it was perfectly fine. I don't know what happened.

"I'm right when I tell Daniel that if anyone among us doesn't need bodyguards, it's you. Nobody could have protected you from this. In fact, we didn't. It's like someone just got in the way, right between you and those scissors."

"I don't understand."

"Jade, I'm deeply embarrassed."

"Raúl, let's not go there, I beg you. I'm just curious, that's all. If anyone is to blame, it's the person who had the scissors in their hand, no one else. I even had to ask Daniel for a kiss just to distract him. Honestly, I don't plan to do that with you. Are we clear?"

"What? You asked him for a ki...? Yes, right! That's a good one!" Raúl bursts into laughter.

"It's true. Why won't you believe me?" Well, at least I made him laugh, even though I'm not sure why.

A short while later, we gathered for lunch. I'm intrigued to see how Daniel and Raúl will act around each other after that intense clash. I've thought about a bunch of different scenarios, but they never fail to surprise me. We bump into Daniel, and Raúl casually says hi, effortlessly blending into the conversation like nothing had happened.

I approach Daniel, pleased to satisfy my curiosity. This time, I have a lot of questions I want to ask him, and I'm hoping to get at least some answers. He keeps talking to the others, acting like nothing went down. It's definitely a really mature attitude, which contrasts so much with how everything blew up just a little while ago.

"Daniel."

"What's up, gorgeous?" He smiles.

"Can I ask you something?"

"Anything."

"Why did you say they hadn't done anything to me because they weren't allowed to?" I ask, my voice barely above a whisper.

He remains silent for a few seconds, looking ahead, and then he responds, speaking very softly.

"I've always had this feeling that people like you have some sort of protection. Today could've turned nasty if there wasn't someone watching your back. I'm quite certain of that. It's hard to put into words; it's just a gut feeling I've got."

"And who were you referring to?" He closes his eyes as if something hurts.

"To those bloody fools who attempted to harm you."

"Hmm. And what do you mean when you refer to people like me?" I want to take advantage of the fact that he's answering me, which doesn't happen very often.

"Jade, we're circling back to what we talked about before; it's difficult to make you see it if you can't appreciate yourself. What can I say? These are just convictions I hold. Like when I tell you, I don't like having my picture taken. My grandma always said they snatch a piece of your soul, and I genuinely buy into that. It's somewhat akin to what I feel."

"Are you saying that, according to what you believe, nothing bad can happen to me?"

"That's right, and in a way, it extends to the people you're fond of... Don't mind me, gorgeous; I'm still not over my anger."

"So, if you believe that, why did you get so angry with Raúl? In the end, it doesn't matter if he takes care of me or not, right?"

"I never plan to put you at risk."

"Oh, well, in that case, if what protects me, according to your words, extends to the people I'm fond of, then..." He turns to look at me and raises an eyebrow.

"Then what, gorgeous?"

Gods! As far as I know, that's enough. Why do I need to tell him? Yet, I want to, but it's difficult for me.

"Well, then, you don't have to worry." I say, staring at my teacup. He doesn't take it as a joke. He just asks a question.

"Can I assume that you're fond of me a bit?"

"A little." I repeat, still not looking at him. He comes closer, rests his forehead against mine, and takes my hand.

"You, on the other hand, have no idea how fond I am of you."

"I guess, two little bits, right?"

"And why should it be just two?"

"Oh, well, because you're all about doing things in a big way." I answer with my eyes fixed on the damn cup. He starts laughing and grabs my chin to force me to look into his eyes.

"Well, no, Jade, much more than just two little bits."

"Thank you."

"You don't owe me any thanks, Jade ..."

Rocío Blisswealth

"What?"

"Now, will you admit that I'm handsome?"

"No, not now either."

"Why not? We're amid confessions, aren't we?"

"Turns out that wouldn't be a confession; it would be a lie." He starts laughing and hugs me.

The rest of the afternoon and the concert passed without incidents, which was a relief; it's been too many emotions for one day, all kinds of feelings. After the concert, Daniel's manager will be paying him a visit. As I understand it, he's in town and wants to say hello. He'll be accompanied by one of the top national singers, whom he also manages. I think Daniel and this young man have had the chance to work together on some projects before, and I suppose they'll have a lot to talk about, which makes me extremely happy; it means I can go to sleep at least a couple of hours earlier than usual.

Once back at the hotel, Raúl asks if I'll go with them; my answer is a definite and resounding no. However, when Daniel asked, my answer varied, just a little, to "If you think it's necessary." He laughed it off and released me from the commitment. Raúl follows me a few steps, attempting to leave the room, but he didn't get far before Daniel told him he was referring only to me, not both of us. I stifle my laughter, but I think he heard me as I peacefully retreated into the arms of Morpheus.

In the morning, I get ready in a hurry because last night we didn't have a chance to go over the schedule, and there are always last-minute decisions to be made. I find it odd that neither Raúl nor Daniel have called me like they do every day. Surely, the evening stretched into the early hours of the morning, and I'd have the pleasure of waking them up.

I reach Daniel's room and knock on the door; I hear his voice, wide awake, inviting me in. I open the door, take a step inside, and freeze from head to toe. My smile disappears. Daniel notices and furrows his eyebrows.

"Good morning, gorgeous. Come in. Let me introduce you." I manage to compose myself enough to take two short steps and get a little closer: just a little. Raúl closes the door behind me. A man is sitting in front of Daniel, but my attention is stunned by this man's bodyguard. It is a demon much like the one in my room, who straightened up the moment I entered and approached his... 'boss'?

The Game...Jade

"You must be Jade." He says, getting up and extending his hand to greet me. Do I really have to shake his hand? I don't want to. But still, I do, and he smiles, holding my hand. "I'm Salvador, Daniel's manager. A pleasure to meet you! I've been dying to get to know you; I've heard so much about you."

The demon seizes the opportunity to sniff the air around me, then grins. As he does this, the foul smell that surrounds him envelops me. Gods, I'm going to vomit.

I try to speak, but I can't. I just release my hand from his and manage a weak smile. Daniel is staring at me; I don't know what to do. Slowly, the demon walks around the room, dragging his feet while never losing sight of me. It's curious; I know them well. He won't physically harm me, but I don't know what effect his presence might have on Raúl or Daniel, and it's for them, I fear.

"Take a seat, gorgeous." Daniel says, trying to figure out what's going on.

The demon approaches where Daniel is sitting. Trying to act more naturally, I head straight for that couch, positioning myself between Daniel and him. His reaction intrigues me a lot. As I get closer, he takes two big steps back and retreats against the wall behind Salvador. Very strange.

"Would you like something to drink?" Daniel asks. I finally manage to respond.

"No, thanks. I had breakfast a few minutes ago. I just wanted to go over a few things with you, but we can do it later. Nothing's urgent."

"Marvelous." Salvador responds. "We were here yesterday. Víctor Arredondo and I came to dine with you. Why didn't you join us, darling?"

What do you mean by 'join us'? They came to have dinner with Daniel; I have no business there. There's something about this man's way of calling me 'darling' that I find annoying.

"I'm sorry. I assumed you had important matters to discuss, considering the high-profile artists at the table. I didn't want to be a bother."

"But you never cause any trouble, dear! It would have been fantastic to introduce you to Víctor; he would have liked to meet you."

"You're very kind." How does this man know I never bother if he has never seen me before? And meeting Víctor Arredondo, to be honest, I couldn't care less.

"Do you enjoy his music?"

"Whose music?" I ask somewhat absentmindedly.

Rocío Blisswealth

"Victor's, of course. Or do you only indulge in Daniel's songs?" He asks, ending with a laugh.

"I only listen to Daniel's." I reply seriously.

"Well, out of loyalty?"

"Perhaps it's just xenocentrism. I guess that's what we can call it." I think I preempted his arguments because he finally fell silent, watching me.

Daniel doesn't take his eyes off me. What is he thinking? That I'm rude, most likely, at the very least. He turns his gaze to Raúl.

"Raúl, fancy joining Jade to sort through the schedule and see if you can make some progress? Salvador and I will wrap up in a few minutes, but time's catching up with us, regardless."

We stand up, but the demon just stays put, completely ignoring us. I suppose he's just here as a mere companion. What interesting friends Daniel has.

"It was a pleasure meeting you, darling. I do hope we can meet again very soon."

"Let her go now, Salvador. Can't you hear we're in a rush?"

"Excuse us, oh, and it's Jade. That's my name, Jade." I step out, followed by Raúl.

"Wow, Jade, you really couldn't stand Salvador, huh? For a moment there, I thought you were going to puke." He bursts into laughter.

"It was pretty obvious, huh? I couldn't help it; I mean, my attempts to be polite were completely in vain." Now I'm feeling distressed.

"No, you were polite, but with a totally disgusted face. I could barely keep from laughing, darling." He repeats the last part in the same tone Salvador used.

"Just shut up, please! I'm already feeling embarrassed enough."

Daniel arrives at my room. I don't even want to imagine the huge problem awaiting me; I'd rather not even look at him. I waited a couple of seconds and nothing. When I finally lift my eyes, I spot him, hearing his laughter, followed by Raúl's.

"Gorgeous, I thought you were going to throw up! I get that you don't fancy him; he's kind of a bore, but you had a look of pure disgust on your face."

"Daniel, I'm really sorry; it's just that..."

"No, don't bother apologizing; it was bloody brilliant watching him crumble because you didn't take a liking to him, achieving absolutely nothing.

The Game...Jade

I mean, trying to introduce you to Víctor, of all people. But, on a serious note, why did he rub you up the wrong way so much?"

"He has a... a very unpleasant aura."

"So, you can read auras, and you never mentioned it?"

"I can only see it when it's as unpleasant as his. Oh, I'm sorry." I cover my mouth with my hand.

"I already told you, no need to apologize; it was a riot. Let it go."

"But he's your manager."

"Just forget about it, alright?"

No, I can't just forget it. That was the first demon I've seen since I left Monterrey, and I can't just ignore it. I had never seen them in connection with anyone other than me, and what worries me most is that it's someone so close to Daniel.

While they go over the schedule, I try to replay the events. Why did the demon back off? And how come he's accompanying Salvador? That's a fact I can't ignore. I never took the time to think about them because they were strictly related to me. However, today, I saw one just visiting. Could it be a coincidence? If it was, he recognized me as soon as he smelled the air around me. Will he be informing others of my whereabouts? I think they do know because it must be the main topic of conversations between Mom and Mara.

I've been so absorbed in enjoying all this time that I haven't even paid attention. I haven't checked around for them—what if they show up? I'll have to be more careful, but if I find them, how will I know if they're here for me or someone else?

When we reach our next destination and get settled, I receive a call from the president of a fan club. They are Paty's friends and got in touch with me through the record company, so everything should be safe. Daniel had t-shirts and mugs made to give them, and I'll meet them in the hotel lobby to hand them over. I owe so much to Paty that, at least through them, I want to give back a little of everything she did for me.

With the hotel staff's help, I take the elevator down, carrying the stuff I'm about to hand over. The door opens, and they are there—almost twenty girls who look at me like I'm some surreal creature as if something from Daniel has somehow rubbed off on me, and they can sense it.

I sit in one of the small lounges in the lobby, and they form a circle around me, sitting on the remaining couches, some on the coffee table, and the rest on the floor. They couldn't care less; they had a ton of questions and just wanted to hear my story no matter what.

The president steps up and greets me, but I ask her to let me hand over my packages before we chat. I crack open the box and start giving out stuff—first, the t-shirts, which were more than enough for everyone, and then the mugs; luckily, they were just the right amount. Daniel included signed photos and a few albums for them to raffle. It amuses me to see them caressing the items as if they were treasures. As if they were an extension of Daniel.

That reminds me of the time I got his letter and kept it in my dresser drawer. I took it out countless times just to touch it. I didn't need to read it; I knew every word by heart. Still, having it gave me a sense of happiness; I guess I can understand them. Once the box is empty, I get ready to hear what they have to say. The president speaks up.

"You're Jade, right?"

"That's right."

"Paty has told us a lot about you, shared the story, you know?"

"What story?"

"The one about how you met Daniel in Monterrey, and now you're here." She says the last part with a hint of admiration in her voice.

"Oh, that, well, I..." Before I can think of something to say, another girl jumps in.

"It must be incredible, isn't it?"

"What do you mean?"

"Having him around all the time."

She's got a point; it is. It's exactly what I wanted to remember in Monterrey; this is what I don't want to take for granted.

"Yes, it really is."

"I knew it! It had to be."

The rest of the girls hit me with questions, from "What's Daniel's favorite food?" to "What's his favorite soccer team?" and a thousand more. I try to answer as fully as I can. My time with them is almost over, and I don't know how to say goodbye; I've had a lot of fun.

Suddenly, I see them smiling and getting really quiet. I feel a hand patting my head. I look up, and there's Daniel, grinning. He gestured to the girls to keep quiet, and, of course, they obeyed.

"How long have you been there?"

The Game...Jade

"A little while." One of the girls, in a show of loyalty to me, adds.

"More than a little, I'd say." Daniel looks at her with an accusing look.

"Hey! Don't grass me up. I leave you with her for a few minutes, and she's already got you wrapped around her finger, huh?"

Laughter fills the air around us.

"Make a little space for me, would ya?" He sits next to me. "Raúl asked if I wanted to come down with bodyguards, but I said it wasn't necessary. You girls look out for me, don't you?"

"Of course!" They all answer at the same time.

I lean towards the girl who sided with me, and I ask her in secret.

"How long was he there? I mean, what did he hear?"

"Don't worry, just from the soccer team onwards, nothing important."

"Thanks."

"You're welcome." She replies with a knowing smile. I guess that makes us friends or something like that.

Daniel talks with them for a while, snapping as many photos as he can, and then says goodbye, hugging each one as if they were old friends. That's what I love about him; he's grateful. He knows that the most important thing to them is the time they get with him, and he gives them as much as he can. My new friend comes up to me and whispers in my ear.

"You give hope to all of us." She said.

I just smiled back at her; what could I say? I say my goodbyes as well and walk away with Daniel towards the elevator; he places his hand on my back.

"Not now, Daniel. This time is just for them, and I don't want them to remember you with me, but the time they spent in your company. You're

all theirs now." I insist.

"Alright." We continue walking side by side, not touching. Yet, as soon as we step into the elevator and the doors close, he stretches his arms as far as the space allows and shouts with a wide smile.

"Alright, gorgeous, I'm all yours now!"

Gods! Seriously? What have I done to deserve all this? Such a terrible temptation. I look at him, raise an eyebrow, and with a smile, I reply.

"Well, there's no doubt I'm a lucky girl, very lucky." I move closer slowly, place my hand on his chest, and as soon as he lowers his head to kiss me, I continue. "However, I won't be taking advantage of my luck today. I'll save it for another time." Just then, with perfect timing, as if we were in a play, the elevator door opened. I turn my back away from him and start walking down the hallway. Laughing, he hugs me tightly.

"You're wicked, you know that?"

"So I've been told."

It looks like we've got some free time, around three hours, enough for a long shower. I can't remember the last time I spent more than ten minutes under the shower. And honestly, it seems I need a waxing session. Wearing jeans all the time helps hide... well, you know, my legs, but I like to be prepared in case I decide to wear a skirt; you never know.

Besides that, I mean, once I'm done with the whole vanity routine, I'll have some time to think. I'm hoping that if I can just take a few moments to ponder everything that's happening to me, maybe, just maybe, I'll figure out the reasons behind some things.

Once out of the bathroom, I lie down on the bed and let my mind wander through ideas—that's all. Everything's so mixed up that I can't seem to find a clear train of thought to follow. Ever since I met Daniel, my life, and even my sense of who I am, has changed a lot; I hardly recognize myself anymore. Thinking back on it, I've always been quite isolated; I never managed to find common ground with other people. To be honest, most people annoy me; they worry about whether their boyfriend called them, or if they'll pass an exam they didn't study for, or if taxes will be higher starting January, and things like that, which don't really matter. Life keeps going, no matter how these things turn out, yet they're missing out, just letting it pass, waiting for a call from someone who is actually living life to a greater extent than they are.

Despite being aware of this, I didn't do much to change my life; I didn't believe it was possible until I met Daniel and discovered my place—this place, which seems almost unattainable to most people. Yet, I fit right in perfectly; no one treats me differently, which means I don't come off as weird, and I enjoy it immensely. Still, I can't ignore the possible reason for my presence here. Daniel knows about the things I can do; he brought some of them to the surface when I didn't even know they existed, and others seem to be known only to him. How can he know so much about me in that aspect? We never talked about it, but it's there. Could it be that for him, these kinds of things are normal? I would love to know; maybe I could talk to someone about it and learn a couple of things.

Another thing I'd like to know is, how did the demons end up here? Well, I never thought that the joy of their company was exclusively mine, but seeing them elsewhere does bring some relief. Still, I wonder, what privileges does Salvador have that make them protect him? Because I clearly saw his demon doing just that.

The one in my room has been terrorizing me my whole life. So, what's the difference then? Even though my grandma insisted that everything was either black or white, never gray or any other shade in between, I still don't quite believe that's entirely true. The demon I saw coming out of the mirror made it clear that he recognized the scent of my blood from hundreds of years ago. That makes me lean more toward the concept of karma, especially since the one I saw with Salvador didn't react until he sniffed the air around me. I'd love to understand how they handle these demons, at least to keep them away from me; that would be more than enough for me.

Another strand in this intricate web. Being here, I feel like I don't have to watch my back around anyone. I'm not just sharing my time with a group of people I can genuinely call friends; I've shared so much with them in just a month and a half, way more than I ever did with my neighbors or schoolmates over the years. While it's true that they don't know much about me, not directly from me at least, I sense it's only a matter of time, not trust, before they find out how I am because, until now, none of them makes me feel the slightest bit of distrust.

I guess that's pretty clear since, as I said, I've been on the road with them for almost a month and a half, working with them, well, living with them, and I've never felt this secure ever before; it's an incredible feeling. But what I can't wrap my head around is how, after being suspicious of my own shadow for as long as I can remember, now I'm totally letting my guard down.

Time's slipping away, and, like always, I'm stuck in the same place. I keep wondering if I'll ever find answers to all my questions. Maybe if I could draw a line between the tangible world and the spiritual one, I might discover something, but the trouble is, I can't tell which is which anymore. When I'm face-to-face with a demon, nothing else feels real; on tour, this is my reality, and in Monterrey, that is the reality. Where does one end and the other begin? Or are they the same? I wish I had answers to that, too. There's a knock at the door; it's Daniel, I can tell.

"Come in."

"Hey there, gorgeous! Did you get some rest?"

"A lot, actually."

Rocío Blisswealth

"Did you sleep?"

"I meditated." A smile appears on his face. "Daniel, don't start."

"Alright, just a heads up: we're having dinner in a moment. Nothing fancy, just us lot, but the grub's cooked up by this brilliant chef whose food I absolutely adore. Sure, you could stick to your rest, but trust me, you don't wanna miss out on this." I watch him and let out a mischievous smirk, his eyes shine in a special way.

"What are you laughing at?"

"I wonder..."

"What?" He asks, raising an eyebrow.

"Are you implying that this chef here has been responsible for feeding the temple right in front of me?"

I caress his cheek with the tip of my finger. I did it! He didn't see it coming, and his face turned completely red. I never imagined it would work; he knows it. He closes his eyes and smiles very gently.

"You're calling me handsome."

"No."

"Of course you are!"

No, Daniel, I'm not calling you handsome. I referred to you as a temple, you know, like those majestic ones in some cities here, adorned with intricate gold details. I'm basically calling you a National Monument, that's all.

"No, it's not like that. Haven't you heard that the human body is like a sacred temple for each person? It deserves to be cherished and looked after. I've told you before: you might have an overly generous opinion of yourself, but trust me, I'm not that indulgent."

Laughter overwhelms him, and he throws himself at me. I haven't gotten up from the bed yet, but even as I try to join in his laughter, there's no way for me to catch my breath.

"Daniel," I say in a whisper. "You're suffocating me."

"You deserve it for being so... so mean!" He continues laughing. "See you in a while." He leaves the room, letting me enjoy my mischief.

Before the big dinner, I head down to the hotel lobby to grab some magazines. We're leaving this city early tomorrow, and once again, it's back on the tour bus. I swear, if I have to sit through that darn movie again, I might as well just die.

As I enter the store, I start browsing through the magazines. I notice the lady at the counter struggling with a young man; he doesn't speak Spanish, and she doesn't understand a word of English. I step in and ask if I can help. The girl looks at me like I've just saved her life. After the purchase, I leave the store, and he follows me, asking where to buy a few other things. We ended up chatting for a while.

Before I get the chance to ask him what brought him to the city, I hear a commotion near the elevators. I turn to see what's going on, and I spot a rock singer who, as far as I know, is in the midst of a concert tour in the country. The last time I spoke to Mara, she asked if I'd seen him. She told me we've crossed paths with him during the tour in several cities. When I said I had no idea, she couldn't believe it, considering he's supposedly the sexiest man on Earth. Luckily, she didn't mention the most handsome, or we'd have been in for an epic debate. The sexiest, well, I can accept that. In fact, I stand by it. If there's someone sexier than him, I haven't laid eyes on them.

He's really tall, with long, tousled blond hair, a sharp angular face, and his way of talking is loud, I mean really loud, and he moves—oh my god, his moves! His fashion sense is a riot of colors, colors, and more colors, making it impossible for him to blend in. I find it incredibly hard to tear my eyes away from him. What time will he leave and head wherever he's going? I'd like to continue my conversation; John, that's the name of the guy I'm talking to, stands up. Of course, with all this noise, talking is impossible. The noise keeps going, and this singer is getting closer and closer to us. That's all I needed; to be right on the path to that "wherever" I mentioned earlier.

He stops right in front of me, and before I can react, he hugs me. Suddenly, his arms are around my neck, and one of his legs—yes, one of his legs—is wrapped around mine! What's wrong with this man? Mara is going to hate me for this, that's for sure. Oh, because you bet I'm going to tell her! I struggle to free myself from his grasp, and that's when he greets me. About time, seriously, what a guy.

"Hey! How are you?" He says.

"Good afternoon. Would you be so kind as to let me go?"

"Why?" Can you believe such rudeness? Why? Like, seriously?

"Because I say so, that's why."

"Are you John's friend?" He asks, still not releasing me.

Rocío Blisswealth

John does his best to catch him up, considering how uncomfortable the situation is—uncomfortable only for me, apparently. Turns out, he's his assistant, making it increasingly difficult for me to escape this man in the near future. I manage to place one of my hands on his chest and push him away. His laughter echoes throughout the lobby. The only thing that could make this situation worse is if Raúl, Sebastián, or, even worse, Daniel, came down looking for me. The teasing would never end.

"I just met him. Tell me one thing: are you always this familiar?"

"Don't you like being hugged? That's weird; you'd be the first woman I've met who feels that way with me."

"I really don't. But I've always been weird; I prefer guys who are quieter. For you, it must be simply incomprehensible, sorry. Also, I can't handle so much attractiveness in one person; it seems unfair. So, I'd rather you keep a bit more distance." I smile widely; I guess my explanation satisfies him as long as I acknowledge the abundance of his qualities.

"Well, I don't prefer it; sorry, too." He puts his arm around my waist. This guy is impossible. He knows he's handsome; he really is.

"What do you do?" John asks.

"I work with Daniel Montalvo. Do you know him?"

"Never heard of him." The rock star replies, winking at me. He knows who he is; he just doesn't care. "However, he must be one lucky idiot."

I manage to free myself from his arm and say goodbye. He smiles and bids farewell, too, in the same loud voice in which he greeted me. I only turn to say goodbye to John and get into the elevator. Crazy! I can't believe it. I better go to the safety of Daniel's room; I run the risk of bumping into him again. By the way, I never asked which floor he's staying on.

Everyone is in the suite, ready for dinner. One of two things: either this chef is truly amazing, or everyone, including me, is starving. That's an advantage; in case I don't like the food, which, knowing me, is quite common, I'll eat it, anyway. During these weeks, I've learned to ignore my taste buds and satisfy my hunger without caring about the taste of food. As soon as I enter the room, Daniel turns to me.

"There you are! Where have you gotten into?" His voice shows anxiety.

"I went to buy some magazines."

"Buy magazines? Where?"

I'm not used to anyone questioning where I've been or what I've been doing; maybe that's why it bothers me so much, even coming from Daniel. Especially if he talks with that authoritative tone I hate; I've heard it from Mara enough times to allow anyone else to use it on me. I'd be crazy.

"Out there." That is all I say.

"What do you mean, out there? Where did you go? You didn't leave the hotel, did you?"

I don't reply. I head to the table to find someone to talk to, although, from what I can see, Daniel plans to follow me and continue the interrogation.

"I didn't hear you." He says, raising his voice a little.

"Maybe because I didn't answer." I'm starting to be rude.

"Oh, and may I know why?" He's already upset; oops, if only he knew how much I care.

"I'm not used to being interrogated."

"Don't tell me your family never asks where you've been."

"Never."

"Not even your grandfather?" Don't try to use that weapon, Daniel.

"He wouldn't dare."

"What do you mean...? Why?"

"Because he was a gentleman."

There was silence in that room; when Daniel asks a question, you answer. No one dares to confront him, even if there's a good reason. Well, I'm not like everyone else, and if he gets mad, he has two options: get mad and get over it because I'm not impressed by his screams in the least. All eyes are on me; that's right, no one dares to look at him.

"You're accusing me of being disrespectful?" He continues with a raised voice.

"I think the more appropriate word would be rude."

"I care about you." He lowers his voice a little.

"Aha, now it turns out that's what they call being nosy."

"It's true, Jade."

"Wow, couldn't you try to be more consistent with what you say and what you do? Because, according to you, nothing bad can happen to me. Wasn't that what you said?"

"Yes."

"Great, end of discussion. I'm very hungry." I sit down in front of him, breathing heavily; Raúl sits next to me.

"He's still hanging on, waiting for you to spill the beans."

"I know."

"Will you?"

"No."

"Jade, so where were you?"

"That's none of your business!"

"That's a good spot."

The food, as it turns out, was fantastic. I have to thank Daniel for warning the chef about my seafood allergy, which led to him preparing the most delicious meat I have ever tasted. The rest of the people joyously devoured large amounts of fish. Finally, the chef joined us for a cup of coffee. He is a truly nice Spaniard. Even so, he did not want to share any of his recipes. It doesn't matter; I don't cook, not even if my life depended on it.

I slept better than I had in a long time after that dinner. It was to be expected, considering our hearty meal. However, our bus had to leave at dawn to arrive on time at our next destination, so I had to leave the bed while it was still dark. We gathered in the lobby, and Daniel approached me. I greeted him with a kiss on the cheek, and he just smiled. I hope that means he'll let the matter drop. Oh no! The elevator door opened, and the rock star stepped out, followed by John. Well, let it be whatever fate decides. He saw me, and I quickly moved away from Daniel. I didn't want to find myself in the dilemma of having to introduce them. The rocker smiled at me. Gods, he is so sexy! Why do some people seem to have it all while others have nothing? It still seems unfair to me.

Daniel keeps an eye on me; I see Raúl and hope my gaze is clear when I express that he better not dare to approach. He hesitates but stays in his place. Well done, Raúl, well done. Then, as if an explosion had occurred, the rocker's screams filled the air as though I were a hundred feet away.

"Hello, beautiful. How are you?" he greets me, hugging me... let's say, with more intensity than yesterday. I suppose that by now, we are old acquaintances. I don't resist; it's what they're expecting, any sign of my discomfort for them to come to my rescue. No, I won't. He hugs me around the waist and keeps me in front of him so I can't see anyone else. Without letting go, I greet John, who smiles with a certain amount of embarrassment. He knows that all of this makes me uncomfortable.

The Game...Jade

"Fine, thanks."

"What?" He asks.

"You asked me how I am."

"Oh, that wasn't a question. I don't need to ask something so obvious."

"You are crazy."

"Are you leaving already?" I don't answer him; I just watch him.

"Why don't you answer me?"

"Oh, my bad, was that a question? Okay, yes, I'm leaving."

"See you soon."

"Definitely."

Finally, he let go after kissing me on both cheeks repeatedly and stroking my hair. I bid goodbye to John, but not before telling him not to worry; he's crazy, and I've accepted him that way—he's harmless. I turn around and find several pairs of eyes watching me, all except Daniel, who pretends to check the agenda. I rejoin the group, and we head towards the tour bus. Sebastián approaches me and asks if I want to share a seat with him. That indicates he'll be in charge of getting the information Daniel wants. Ha! That'll only happen if I allow it.

"Jade, that man is..."

"Yes."

"I didn't know that..."

"That's right."

"Blimey!"

That's the kind of conversation I like; direct, concise, and to the point. Once on the bus, I pull out one of my magazines and offer it to him. He looks at it strangely; it's an ordinary magazine. He won't think I'd buy a car magazine, or worse, a craft one, right? I respect people who have the patience to do either, but it's definitely not my thing.

"What's up?" I ask.

"Oh, it's just... was the thing about the magazines true?"

"Yes. Why?"

"I figured it was just a cover, and you were really with that rocker dude." He wants to find out where I was, but I'm not going to please him.

"Do you want the magazine or not?"

The screen in front of us lights up, announcing as a "World Premiere" the darn movie they've played ad nauseam, just slightly newer than the Cerro de la Silla. Sebastián snatches the magazine from my hands and starts leafing through it. Anything is better than this.

Everything seems calm as we reach the next city. Daniel has returned to his usual self, and his good mood is back. Everything appears normal until we reach the hotel room, and I answer a phone call.

"Dani..."

"Who's that, gorgeous?"

"It's your dad; he's in the lobby."

I know he's not thrilled by the news; it's as pleasant as if my own dad were paying me a visit. Nothing good will come out of this. His face pales, he becomes serious, and he picks up the phone, but it's too late; the man has already hung up. He's knocking on the door. Raúl and I head towards the door on the opposite side of the room, which connects to Raúl's suite. Daniel grabs my arm, "Don't go, trust me, he'll like to meet you." It sounds like he needs moral support. Fine. Suddenly, I feel like the seasonal outfit of a mannequin on display. Daniel opens the door.

"Oh! Finally, you deigned to open. Were you on the other side of the palace? You took your sweet time."

I underestimated it when I said it would be like my dad coming; it is him, wrapped in another skin, arrogant, and with an astronomical ability to belittle those around him. Daniel, I'm sorry to inform you that if you don't let me out of here —and fast—this is going to end worse than I thought!

"How are you? What brings you here?" Daniel asks.

"I came to see my son, or what, can't I?"

"I suppose you can. Let me introduce you; you already know Raúl. This is Jade."

"Girl, nice to meet you. Tell me, aren't you bored working with him?" He points at Daniel with his index finger as if he were an object.

"No, sir, not at all." I restrain myself; I restrain myself.

"But don't call me sir; my name is Daniel."

"I'm glad you mentioned it; my name is not 'girl' either. My name is Jade, sir." Daniel smiles, his father does too, although it looks more like a grimace. He keeps talking, and I find it increasingly hard to hold back until I don't.

The Game...Jade

"I still don't understand what the hell people see in him; I don't find him that amusing." He says, referring to Daniel. Enough! I can't take it anymore.

"It's not surprising; it's the same with jewels. To a jeweler's eye, they're works of art. To us, ordinary people, they're just stones." I'm sorry, I'm sorry, I'm sorry. No, it's not true. I don't regret it at all; he finally fell silent.

We'll eat together, but what's my fault in this? It's sure to end in indigestion or something worse, but I won't escape a stomachache. I watch him as we eat; thankfully, there's hardly a trace of him in Daniel. Still, there's something in the bone structure that reveals the same genes passed through there. He's been very successful in every business he's undertaken, and it's obvious he can't forgive Daniel for pursuing things he considers not just frivolous but also temporary. Daniel shows discomfort through every pore, and I see him struggling not to lose the image of an upright man he has in front of us. At the same time, his father strives to portray him as a fool with every sentence. Don't these kinds of men realize that they've lit the fire in which their children are slowly cooking a simmering hatred and that someday they'll have the pleasure of making them eat it?

I still remember, with absolute clarity, what I felt when I saw my dad on his deathbed—nothing, absolutely nothing. And now, seeing Daniel, I'm glad I shut the door on all his nonsense before he could do to me the damage this man has done to him, a damage so palpable.

The man has a way with people. He can be pleasant and polite to anyone except Daniel. If only I had met him under different circumstances, maybe I could have enjoyed his company. My dad was like that too, adored by those who knew him, with exceptions like the one you're aware of. He keeps talking for a while until silence settles in, and I seize the moment to express my gratitude for the delightful meal and bid my farewell. I couldn't find more patience; I wanted to escape to the nearest restroom and throw up. Raúl is also taking his leave, giving them a few minutes alone to talk, assuming they have something to say to each other. I'm not sure. Only a few minutes after I reach my room, Daniel opens the door, saying nothing for a few seconds.

"He's gone."

"That's great." For anyone else, this would be outrageously rude, but not for him; in this, we are alike.

"Jade, can I have a hug?"

Rocío Blisswealth

"Look at that. Just today, I have a special offer on hugs, so I could give you up to two."

"How generous! And could you trade that substantial amount for one long, long, long one?"

"Let me see. Well! You're in luck; I still have one of those left."

He comes over, and I hug him very, very tight, tighter than ever before; I know he needs it. But how long does 'long' mean? I don't know, but I hope it lasts a very long time, truly.

I had never seen Daniel so down. It's hard for me to believe how similar our fathers are. Yet, I managed to push mine away. Daniel chose to leave, even if it meant he'd see him less often and have to deal with him only a few times a year.

That's suffering it for me all the same, though I can get it. We'd rather run from problems than face them. We know what we should do; surely, we've played out countless scenarios in our minds, analyzing every kind of situation, and in our thoughts, we succeed. But when the time comes to face those problems, fear grips us, and we'd rather put it off for later. I know this all too well because that was my situation with Mara, at least until something became more important to me than myself. The sad truth, and I know this perfectly well, is that the love we feel for ourselves isn't enough to free us from what bothers us. We get used to it, convinced it's a cross we must bear—what a stupidity!

Society, religion, and even our families fill us with guilt. We're supposed to love family, love each other, turn the other cheek, and, of course, to be afraid of being left alone. Who knows how many other expectations. I'm not sure if those kinds of things are what drive Daniel to tolerate that man who, by a twist of fate, turned out to be his father. If that's the case, I'm glad I cut ties with mine a long time ago.

Deep down, because of my grandma's teachings about being good to go to heaven, I wondered if I had made the right choice. Thanks to Daniel's father's visit, I know I did, and from today, I feel much lighter. In the end, I never hurt him; I simply didn't allow him to harm me. It's not about being a punching bag for those people. I know I didn't do all I could have. Perhaps my sin lies in my omission, but I can live with that.

Tonight, will be the last concert of the tour around the country, and tomorrow, we'll be heading back to Mexico City. Our schedule for the next fifteen days of concerts is crazy. We have to meet with every single member of the press who registered in advance to interview Daniel, and that's not even considering the television appearances. As a result, the concerts will probably be the easiest part of our days. We better start taking vitamins, or we might not even make it to day three.

We reached the airport terminal around noon, a terrible time if you're Daniel Montalvo. When the flight is at night, the crowd welcoming him diminishes significantly; at this hour, it feels like a nightmare. Rogelio, the record company director, is waiting for us, trying to lighten the situation. He has brought security to assist us at the airport, anticipating it would be difficult; I could sense it. Stepping out the door, we were immediately engulfed by the screams; we couldn't hear anything anymore. Raúl wasn't with me; now, I was under the care of three bodyguards I don't know. It seemed like their sole mission was to get me out of there and into the car as quickly as possible, in one piece; nothing else mattered.

I lost sight of Daniel, Raúl, or any familiar face. My arms are held by large hands, and my feet barely touch the ground. Amidst the chaos, a hand stretches out and gently touches my face. I could only watch as one of the men holding me, yanked their hand away with a grip that must have been very painful. I tried to keep moving, but I couldn't; someone halted me by grabbing my waistband. An elbow to the face of that guy frees me from his grip, but was it necessary? I asked the man, but he didn't respond. I supposed it was.

A few minutes later, they tossed me into the limousine. Why a limousine? Daniel won't like this; he hates all these ostentatious displays. He doesn't even wear branded clothes because he feels ridiculous doing so. In front of me, there are Raúl and Andrés, another musician, both looking pretty beaten up from what I can see; it seems like we've all had a rough time. A few seconds later, Daniel steps into the vehicle, in even worse condition than the three of us. Enraged, he starts ranting against everyone; even the color of the limousine disgusted him.

"The press was insistent on getting an interview right here amidst all of this. Don't they have an appointment with me early tomorrow?"

"How on earth did you pull off slipping away from them?" Raúl asked.

"I didn't do it; it was the fans. They noticed I was about to go head-to-head with one of the reporters, and one of the girls closest to me asked if they should take care of it. Without a second thought, I said yes."

"And what happened?" I asked, watching as he started to smile.

"I have no idea. They're dreadful, truly wild. They must have riot training; I just saw the reporters vanish from my sight, and I had no clue what happened next. They seized the chance to get me out of there. Jade, sort them out for dinner, alright?"

"For the reporters? Do you plan on taking responsibility?"

"Of course not! I owe it to the fans."

"Oh, splendid, don't worry; I'll handle it." I watch him rubbing his neck, his face contorted in pain.

"Daniel, is something wrong?"

"I don't know yet; I think I got hurt. I feel one of the muscles in my neck is really swollen, and the pain is getting worse."

"Do you want me to call the doctor when we get to the hotel?"

"I'll take a bath first, and we'll see if it eases a bit, alright?"

I sat on the bed, waiting for him to come out of the shower. When he finally did, I could see that the back of his neck was starting to turn purple. I got angry, picked up the phone, and contacted the hotel doctor. I knew Daniel didn't want to see him yet, but I needed to know what I could give him.

"Daniel, the doctor prefers to see you, but you'll probably have to take anti-inflammatory meds and wear a neck brace, at least for a few days."

"Gorgeous, anti-inflammatories knock you out. I can't do interviews like that and risk being accused of performing drugged or something even worse. And as for the neck brace, how do you expect me to put on a show with that? Not a chance."

"What if we cancel the interviews?" I suggested, and without waiting, I answered along with him in unison.

"Of course not!" He asserted.

"That's right, gorgeous. I'll lie down for a while, and we'll see if it gets better."

I leave the room, knowing he won't feel better; it's only going to get worse if he doesn't take care of himself, but he won't. I pace around my room endlessly, trying to figure out what to do. Nervously, I rub my hands together, feeling a gentle tingling sensation.

No, no, I can't do it; I haven't done it in years, and my grandfather didn't like it. The tingling intensifies, but I resist, continuing my restless pacing. I'm sorry, Grandpa, truly, I am. I rush out the door and knock on Daniel's room; he answers in a muffled voice.

"Daniel, will you let me try something?" I ask anxiously.

"What, gorgeous?" He winces, trying to turn to look at me.

"It's like a massa... Oh, let me try, okay? Lie face down." I'm surprised when I see his back; the purple hue has already spread across the entire upper area. I sit on the bed and place my hands on his neck, which by now are burning; he winces at my touch, but seconds later, he sighs. In reality, I'm just caressing him; I've never given a massage in my life, but I can clearly feel how the energy leaves my hands and seeps into his skin. Minutes later, the purple tone starts giving way to a pale pinkish tone.

Thank you! Thank you! His breathing deepens. He had let his arm drop down from the bed, and his hand rested with his fingers touching the floor. I startle when, as he lifts them, he grabs my ankle.

"Jade, you've got the hands of an angel. I don't feel any pain anymore."

"Don't get too confident, Daniel; this is temporary. You have to take care of yourself." I get up from the bed; he turns to rest his head on the pillow and watches me. He points to the side of the bed he just vacated and asks me to sit next to him. Now, how do I explain?

"I never knew you were good at massages."

"I don't know, it's just, well, I... Daniel..."

"Yes?"

"Why don't you take a nap for a while?"

"I just wanted..."

"What do you need?" He smiles. "Oh, no, forget it. You don't need anything. Go to sleep; I'll see you later."

"Jade, I need a kiss. If you don't give it to me, the treatment won't be complete, and the pain might return, and we'd have to start all over again. Ever seen kids being kissed on their wounds to heal them?"

"How incredibly cheesy! Besides, you said kids, didn't you? I have to inform you that your childhood is on a very, very distant horizon. So, no, the pain won't return; don't worry." I try to stand up, and he traps my wrist; the patient has certainly recovered!

"You won't do it, even if I beg you from my sickbed?"

"But didn't you just tell me that you're not in pain anymore? Whatever. Which of the two versions is the lie, then?" I see him, and I start laughing. He sits up next to me, takes me by the neck, and kisses me softly.

Rocío Blisswealth

"Thank you." He caresses my face the way only he knows how, trailing his fingers down from top to bottom, sending shivers down my spine. "Will you ever tell me what you did?"

"As my grandma would say, I just showed you some affection."

He kisses me once more before letting go. I turn off the light as I leave so he can sleep and quickly head back to my room. Every time I did something like I did today, guilt would claw at me in different intensities, and doubt always crept in, not knowing if I should use what I had or not, but not today. Today, my mind is filled with different thoughts, and among them, there's one I don't want to think about. The only one I refuse to hear, even though something deep inside me screams it. I futilely cover my ears; the voice comes from within, impossible to silence. My gift functions with love; I must love the person for it to work, and I don't want to love him.

Chapter IX
Sweetheart, you sure know how to appreciate a gift

Today, I really wish my grandparents were alive. Who else could I talk to about this? If I even dared mention this to Mom or Mara, it would be a huge scandal. They would think I'm stupid, obviously, I know that. It is completely insane; that's why I refuse to accept it.

My grandma would see things differently; she'd help me not be so terrified. Why didn't this happen with David? I would have said yes to his marriage proposal, and by now, I'd probably be a housewife somewhere in the States, living a simple, happy life, I guess. But what kind of future can I have now? None.

If only Daniel didn't treat me the way he does, it would be easier for me to put some distance between us. But I can't. I need to be closer to him every time. No one has ever treated me... No, that's not true. Some guys treated me like he does, but they weren't him. That's the difference. I never loved them because they weren't him, with all the baggage his DNA carries, with the perfect combination of things and attributes that I find extremely attractive: sweet to the point of being captivating. It's like he was specifically designed for me, with his soul perfectly tailored to mine.

What's even worse is that I'm not in love with him; that would be easy to handle, just a crush, an excitement, a madness. No, what I'm feeling is far more complicated, more profound. It's about overlooking the flaws of the other person or even growing to love those imperfections alongside them. It's being willing to do almost anything for that other person. It's a genuine bond.

Well, if there's one thing I'm good at, it's hiding what I think and feel. So, I'll keep doing it. I just hope this overwhelming mix of emotions I've recently discovered doesn't end up slipping out in an attempt to reach him, because I'll do whatever it takes to stop it.

This morning, we went back to the TV station. My entrance this time wasn't as spectacular as the first time I came, but I enjoyed it just the same. This place holds wonderful memories for me. We'll be on a music show where Daniel will be a guest, sharing the stage with another singer, Pablo, who's also Spanish.

Rocío Blisswealth

The recordings begin, and everything is going on as usual. I watch Daniel sing, and the other artist, Pablo, comes over and greets me. He's really friendly, and I love his songs, so we chatted for a few minutes. Raúl watches me from the other side of the set, but he knows that he'd better stay away.

"Pablo, how many songs do you still have to record?"

"I've already finished recording them."

"So, does that mean you have to go? I'm sorry; it wasn't my intention to hold you back."

"Hold me back? No way! I stayed because I wanted to."

"Thanks, by the way, I'm Jade. I work with Daniel Montalvo."

"I know."

"Seriously?"

"Yes."

I turn to check the monitor, and I notice some errors in the projection; Daniel is not going to be happy about this. Raúl approaches when he realizes the same mistake; he will tell Daniel and let the bomb explode because that is for sure: there will be bloodshed. I continue talking with Pablo, and Raúl comes back.

"Jade, come with me, please."

I scan the set, and I can see Daniel very upset, staring at Pablo with eyes full of hatred. Well, what's up with this guy? The worst part is that when he acts like this, it's when I most refuse to let him get what he wants.

"I'll be there in a minute, Raúl."

"The thing is..."

"Believe me, I know exactly what's going on. I'll be there in a minute or two."

Pablo smiles. I guess he finds it amusing that I openly refuse to please my boss, a boss who apparently hates him; I didn't know it.

"Do you know Daniel yet?"

"Yes, we've known each other for quite some time."

"And you two don't get along, right?"

"I thought we did, at least until today." That doesn't sound good. It's probably best if I say goodbye to avoid any further trouble.

"Pablo, I have to go. It's been nice meeting you."

"Believe me, Jade, the pleasure has been mine."

"Thanks. See you." I reply, although I'm pretty sure I'll never see him again. I don't know how, but I just know.

I step into the dressing room and find Daniel truly furious. He's taking the production mistake to the extreme, yelling at the top of his lungs. I stop at the door and watch him. Okay, he's angry, but in my opinion, it's not that big of a deal, nothing that can't be fixed in a few minutes. I take a seat and observe the entire scene, like someone watching the rain without getting wet; he fails to impress me. He kicks one of the dressing room tables into pieces, and I remain here, undaunted.

While he keeps yelling, a man who had once dined with us here walks in. It hits me now: if my calculations are right, this man must be the president or the owner of the TV station; no wonder everyone worships him. He sees me very calmly while pieces of objects fly around the room. Daniel has turned into a real Tasmanian devil. I just smile at him, and he does the same. Poor man, he probably assumes I'm used to witnessing these kinds of outbursts, but no, this is the first one. However, I've seen kids in the supermarket when their parents refuse to buy them something, and yes, the reaction is quite similar. It evokes the same response in me as children's shows do: it makes me laugh, but I keep it in; I'm not stupid.

"What's going on, Daniel? How can I assist you?" He asks, using a condescending tone.

"It's outrageous the way they're treating me! Initially, they invited me onto the show, and then, once I was here, they dropped the bombshell that I have to share the stage with another singer. Am I not good enough for this? And then, they freely do whatever they want while I'm performing. They socialize with others, neglect their responsibilities, and these are the results."

Clearly, the last sentences were aimed specifically at me. It's going to be hard for me to hold back my laughter if he keeps going down this path. I can spot emotional blackmail a mile away and take a twisted pleasure in amplifying its sting. I hope he tones it down soon or redirects his aggression toward someone less dangerous than me.

"Daniel, don't worry, I'll sort it out right away. If you have the time and you're not too tired, we can record another show, making the necessary adjustments. How does that sound?"

Gods! How do they indulge his whims like this? That's why he's the way he is. The place is crawling with celebrities, and I highly doubt that this man takes his time to come and calm them down during a tantrum. Besides, I find it hard to believe they treat everyone the same way. What makes Daniel so special? Because I doubt the man is interested in the same qualities as I am.

"Fine." He responds.

"Fantastic! I'll give instructions to start again. Get organized and let us know when you want to begin; everything will be ready by then."

The man exits the dressing room, and I stand up to prepare the clothes Daniel will wear for the rerun of the show. The outfit he's wearing is covered in dust, and he can't use it. I don't look at him; he's sitting on a large couch with his arms stretched wide. Judging by what I know about body language, his posture means he's not afraid of me. Well, great, I'm not afraid of him either. I can feel his gaze on me as I move around the room. He tries to control his breathing before speaking to me.

"Jade..."

"Yes?"

Raúl steps into the dressing room to ask for instructions, but Daniel ignores him and keeps talking. Raúl looks at me with a pleading expression. I'm sorry, my friend; I won't back down on the treatment I expect from people, no matter who they are. If he behaves, so will I. If not...

"Where were you?"

"Here and there." He looks at me and makes a face of disgust.

"I get irritated when I look for you and you're not by my side."

I turn to face him directly; I know it bothers him when I do that. He's used to intimidating people with his simple tone of voice.

"You don't want me to believe all this pitiful attitude is because of me, do you? How embarrassing, Daniel!"

"Whether it was or not, it doesn't matter now. I just expect you to be by my side when I..."

"When you want? Is that how you planned to finish that sentence? Choose your words carefully, Daniel."

"When I'm looking for you." His voice is deep.

"You've seen too much TV. I used to watch Star Trek, too, you know? But I was pretty clear that teleportation was just sci-fi. Anyway, in any case, you'll be the first to know if I ever learn how to do it, though I doubt I'll use it to show up wherever you look for me."

The Game...Jade

He watches me, and the muscles in his jaw move frantically. He keeps his mouth shut so as not to tell me everything he's thinking; the knuckles of his hands begin to turn white from the pressure he exerts on the couch. Seeing he doesn't say anything, I continue under Raúl's accusing gaze.

"I've already left your outfit in the bathroom; I'm guessing you'll take a shower."

"At times, you're exasperating."

"I guess those times coincide with the moments when I tell you what you don't want to hear. Am I wrong?"

"It's possible."

"Well, look at that; I wasn't like this before. You made me this way! So those times must be when we're most alike."

Raúl can't help it and laughs. I was right! It is in these moments that we are most alike; he sees himself as if in a mirror and is annoyed by the stubborn attitude I adopt. Daniel laughs and turns to look at him.

"Do you think we look alike a lot, Raúl? What's your take?"

"In moments like this, you're like two peas in a pod."

"I suppose I've passed on to you the worst of me."

"You gave me what I needed, the half I didn't have, that was all."

Finally, he puts a smile on his face. No matter how, he's got me here, and I guess that's what matters to him: I don't think he cares about the way he did it, even if it meant making a monumental fool of himself.

"Come here, gorgeous. Can I have a kiss?" He says softly and smiles.

"Oh, no, please. A kiss, no less! Now it turns out that, since you're over the tantrum, you want everything to be as it was before. I don't think so."

"It wasn't a tantrum! It was genuine rage. And truth be told, I wanted a kiss. No, I still want one. You understand what that implies, Jade; I'll pursue you until you grant it to me."

"No, it means I won't give it to you. Remember what I told you earlier about your childhood, which was a long way off? Well, I'll take it back. Grow up!"

I step out into the set and see a swarm of people bustling around like ants, making sure everything is set up on time. That is, on Daniel's cue. The camera director comes up to me, asking if he is ready to start because they still need a few minutes. Once I tell him that Daniel still needs to finish his bath and go through makeup, he sighs in relief. Raúl comes over, smiling.

Rocío Blisswealth

210

"Jade, what would we do without you?" He says.

My mind fixates on a single thought. It's not like that; it's exactly the opposite. What would I do without them? The same old thing, going back to my room, to that horror story where I'm attacked by demons, where I've lost everything except a shred of sanity. A horror story where I don't know how to defend myself, and all I do is wait, wait until I find out who the new demon will be that comes to play with this toy.

If that's the price I've had to pay for the fairy tale I live, even if it's only for short periods, it's all worth it. Somehow, in a way I can't fathom, I found a crack in the walls and managed to escape and change. I'm not the same anymore; yes, it's been worth the effort. Unnoticed, tears fill my eyes. Surprised, Raúl hugs me and buries my face in his neck; he doesn't say or ask anything, just strokes my hair.

Suddenly, I feel another pair of arms wrapping around me, joining Raúl's, until they form a sandwich with me in the middle. It's Daniel, precisely the person I didn't want. With his voice so low that only I can hear him, he says playfully:

"Gorgeous, it's alright. If you don't want to kiss me, you don't have to. I won't push anymore, I promise."

Now, instead of tears, laughter chokes me. I turn around, grasp Daniel's chin with both hands and pull him towards me, giving him a loud kiss on the lips. His eyes widen, and his jaw drops open.

"You kissed me! You kissed me right in front of everyone. Raúl, you did see it, didn't you? Of course, you did!"

"Well, you see, Daniel, it's so dark in here that, honestly, I didn't see a thing." Raúl responds, trying to contain his laughter.

"That means my kisses don't bother you. I was beginning to worry."

"No, it just means I'm becoming a masochist."

He takes my hands and leans in to hug me tightly, bringing his lips close to my ear.

"Gorgeous; are you alright?"

"Yes."

"Sure?"

"Sure."

"Sometimes I feel like I'm asking too much of you."

"You give just as much."

The Game...Jade

"I don't think so."

They call him to go back and shoot everything again; we'll be here for a couple more hours. I head to one end of the set and sit on the floor, just like I used to when I first met him. One of the production technicians, who are always incredibly kind to me, comes over with a chair and offers it to me. He smiles when I tell him I prefer the floor; it brings back good memories.

"What if I bring you a cushion? Would that interrupt the flow of good memories?"

"No, I don't think so."

"Alright."

He runs off and brings me a plush blue cushion. I take it and sit on it; it's genuinely comfortable. Now, I just hope I don't fall asleep.

I overhear another of the technicians asking if I'm Daniel's assistant, and him replying that no, apparently, I'm his little sister. I find it hilarious; the guy must have heard us arguing, there's no doubt about it. Not to take any credit away from the crew, but now I understand all the attention. They don't want to face the lion.

I settled in, ready to admire that amazing man I just kissed, and yes, for the first time, I was the one who made the move; to be honest, I stole it from him. Well, every now and then, one carrot for all the sticks. The darkness of the set allows me to focus my eyes on him without any distractions. His music has always had a calming effect on me, so my heart rate gradually slows down, and I relish every moment of his performance.

Sitting here, I can't believe my luck. One of the things my grandma used to say was that every human being is given a bottle of luck at birth. Some sip it slowly, some accidentally break the bottle and never get to use it. But she was worried that I hadn't even uncorked mine yet. She was probably right; I was waiting for this moment. My soul must have known that it would come someday, and I would need all my good luck, not just a small part, but all of it.

I can see this man, who seems to possess an endless well of talent, singing, dancing, smiling in a way only he can, receiving standing ovations, and then, when the cameras fade, winking at me. Tell me if that isn't luck. Me, who never dared to dream of anything more than an autograph. Me, who was always the weird one out, even to my family. Me, who used to spend almost all my time alone, now spends nearly all of it with him, just me. The song ends, and as if he could hear my thoughts, he rushes over, bends down, and kisses me on the nose.

Rocío Blisswealth

"Don't fall asleep, gorgeous." He says. I smile, and he responds in kind.

The entire situation becomes more confusing by the minute. Still, even as I continue to mull over thousands of questions about the "whys" and "hows" of my presence here, moments like the one I have now are enough to make everything crystal clear. It doesn't matter because I'm not willing to give up anything—not his company, not his closeness, not his laughter, not even his outbursts—the ability to love him without expecting anything in return. That's the truth. Remember I told you I managed to cling to some sanity? Well, that's what allows me to enjoy everything without expecting anything more. What will happen next? Like I said, it doesn't matter.

One thing I've discovered is that I'm getting closer to the image my grandpa had of me. Every time he faced my shyness, which was quite often, he used to tell me that I could do anything I set my mind to because I had everything inside me to achieve it. Once, when I replied that he was wrong, he said very seriously that, unfortunately, it was I who was wrong. He couldn't fathom how, being a tiger, someone had convinced me that I was a Chihuahua, one of those little dogs that quivers at everything. Not being able to please him always hurt me; I just hope he has a small window from where he can see how much I've changed. I owe him that.

Daniel finishes for the second time, though he's happier with the outcome, according to him. Raúl walks over to where I am and extends his hand to help me up. I shake the cushion, return it to the guy who had lent it to me, and head towards the dressing room. Raúl takes my hand.

"Trust me, sweetheart, you don't want to go there. We're better off waiting for Daniel outside."

I look at him with a puzzled expression, and that's when he discreetly points towards a small group of people blocking the dressing room hallway. I get what he means; among them is the rockstar. Well, lucky me! I want to assume this is part of good fortune, but I'll let it slide.

"You're absolutely right; I don't want to walk past there."

He smiles, and we run in the opposite direction, down the hallway, as far away from the noisy rocker as possible. I'm not in the mood to deal with him today; if only his fans could hear me, but well, it's the truth.

"We managed to sneak out without him spotting you. You know what Daniel calls people like them?"

"Who?"

"The folks who come up to you, like the rockstar or Pablo."

"How?"

"Vultures."

"Vultures? Why?"

"He says they all want a piece of you."

"Raúl, I think your boss is going crazy."

"I don't think so; when it comes to figuring people out, he's pretty sharp, I can vouch for that. The only one he's never been able to figure out is you."

"Well, that's good. At least I have that advantage over him."

The days we have left on tour are flying by. Lots of artists have visited Daniel, not to mention the press appointments—it's been the same routine with both groups. In other words, some of these artists are friends with Daniel, and he welcomes them warmly until he gets tired or fed up, whichever comes first. Then he asks us to politely end the meeting in the best way possible.

Others want to collaborate with him on projects, and he always says it's a fantastic idea. He promises to talk to the record company staff about it. And yes, he does talk, but what he actually says is that they will have to deal with him if they dare to arrange a collaboration with any of them.

For me, it's a lot of fun, even though someone flipped the script on me. I mean, these are usually famous people, Mexicans, or foreigners, and you know, I've always wanted the chance to meet them in person, to see how different they are from the image on camera. I thought this was my chance, but no, I hardly get to do it. Apparently, I'm the one who piques their curiosity because they rarely see someone new in the group. This annoys Daniel, and he refuses to let them meet me, even though I'm around almost all the time. He doesn't even allow me to leave him with Raúl to go watch TV or something. One of them openly asked him if he would introduce us, and Daniel simply said no and changed the subject.

By the way, Raúl and I found a great way to have fun. As soon as we receive the list of artists who will be meeting him during the day, we start betting between us and the band on how long Daniel will tolerate their presence before getting rid of them. The range is from ten minutes to over an hour. Most don't last more than fifteen minutes. One poor woman only stayed with him for four minutes—can you imagine? Four! Before he asked her, without getting help from anyone, to leave. Anyway, this is a lot of fun, and I'm winning.

Rocío Blisswealth

Today, for instance, I got a huge scolding from Daniel when he found out about our game. I still can't figure out where the information leaked. He asked how we could organize such a game without inviting him to participate. I explained that since the decision entirely depended on him, he would always win, and it wouldn't be fair. Almost crying with laughter, he emphasized that these were underground bets, and here I was worrying about the legality of the event. Maybe he's right.

As for dealing with the press, what can I say? Most of the reporters who've interviewed him repeatedly ask the same set of questions over and over again. It seems like they've been handed out as templates, and they've memorized them down because even the phrasing is exactly the same. Very boring, but in the world of fame, it's a necessary evil or an indispensable one.

This morning, I talked to Mom; they're eagerly awaiting my return. I don't know why, but I suppose they'll fill me at the moment I step foot back in Monterrey. It's kind of funny—I thought the more time I spent with Daniel, the harder it would be for me to say goodbye. So, it surprised me that I'm feeling strangely okay about letting him go.

These are emotions I don't know how to explain. Returning to Monterrey this time doesn't scare me like it did before. I don't know. Seeing Salvador's demon retreat as I approached has given me renewed hope that things are changing. Somehow, I feel like I have a purpose in my life. Until now, the only one I had was getting Daniel's autograph, and that went pretty well. The new one has the main goal of completely freeing my life from demons. I know it's a huge task, and I won't have support from those involved, but I've made up my mind.

One thing's for certain: I'm not stuck in the victim mindset anymore; I'm ready to fight. I don't know exactly how yet, but the willingness to fight is the first step, and that's huge. So, now we'll see how it plays out. It's strange to possess such strength and not know where it comes from or how it works. Still, I'm more than willing to experiment until I achieve something—anything—to keep the things I have now. Let's see if my grandpa was right; he used to say I could achieve anything I set my mind to.

I tag along with Daniel while he says goodbye on TV shows; he still has a few gigs left, but the record company insists on getting everything done in advance. They refuse to admit that Daniel's personal promotion always leads to more concerts, thanks to high ticket sales, resulting in increased record sales and financial gains for everyone involved. He's a walking gold mine.

Today, he received several gold and platinum records for his best-selling albums. I have no idea how he plans to carry them all; thankfully, that's not my concern anymore. This, along with the stack of gifts in his room, accumulated over the past two months. Truth be told, he has also given me gifts, one in particular.

Last night, he gave me a pendant with his initials in gold. When I saw it, I couldn't help but think back to what Raúl once said, how Daniel would love to mark me as his property. I laughed, and he clearly thought I loved it.

"You're planning to wear it, right?"

"No. Actually, I plan to leave it as a decoration at the bottom of my jewelry box."

"Jade, I'm being serious." He said, his smile fading.

"So am I, Daniel. You just need to ask me to get your name tattooed."

"I wouldn't do that." He said, a little embarrassed.

"Then you got the initials wrong. Mine are JA, not DM."

"Just wear it, so you'll remember me when I'm not around."

"It's a shame, Daniel…" I said sadly.

"What's a shame?" He asked, more serious now.

"That, after all this time, you know so little about me that you think I need something like this to keep you in my thoughts. It's a real shame but thank you for thinking of me." He just looked down and walked away from me for a few minutes. Raúl, however, came over to bug me.

"Sweetheart, you sure know how to appreciate a gift."

"I had nothing to be thankful for; the gift was for himself, not for me, and you know it well." His eyes showed some embarrassment, too, and he finally decided to leave me alone.

Once the interviews were over, we made our way back to the hotel, just Daniel, Raúl, and me, without any bodyguards. They don't usually tag along when we visit the TV station because it's unnecessary; the access there is so restricted that bringing them would be absurd.

Once we stepped into the hotel, we walked through the enormous lobby. When we reached halfway to the elevator, a shout pierced the air: "DANIEEEL!" It quickly echoed and spread, reaching us from all directions.

We had no idea, but it turned out there was a women's convention in the hotel, and suddenly, we found ourselves surrounded by them.

Within seconds, I saw the hotel security staff trying to reach us, but it was simply impossible. Daniel grabbed my hand, and Raúl took the other. We retreated slowly, like someone escaping from a wild animal, except there were many, hundreds.

All I could think was, "Please, somebody, help us." And before I could finish the thought, I saw them—a sight that turned my fear into sheer terror in an instant. Hordes of demons pushed through the crowd, filling the air with their putrid stench.

Now, I understood that we wouldn't escape. I wanted to shut my eyes, but I couldn't; I needed to know what they would do. They were getting closer, and I could see the fear in Raúl and Daniel's eyes, no less than mine. I held their hands as tightly as I could. I dared not lose sight of the demons; I followed their path toward us. I couldn't see the people anymore; they had blocked my view as they approached closer and closer. Why now? Why, when they had us at their disposal all this time? They could have done it at any other moment. Why now, with so many witnesses? My throat tightened. Daniel tried to shield me with his body.

Just when I thought I couldn't hold my breath any longer, I witnessed something that left me breathless. The demons, acting unlike anything I had ever seen before, turned around. I couldn't believe it! They were holding the people back. But why? Without finding an answer, I heard a voice in my head screaming at me, "Run!" I couldn't wrap my head around what was going on, so I yelled to Raúl and Daniel what the voice was telling me.

"Run! Run!"

I resist turning my back on the demons; even now, I don't trust them. If this is a trap, we'll figure it out real quick. For now, this escape is our only option. We sprint towards the elevator; a hotel employee holds it open for us. We rush in so fast we slam into the back wall, and the doors close too slowly, giving me time to see them once again, blocking people's way, who continue to scream hysterically. Inside, all you can hear is us panting hard. Daniel reaches out, putting his hand on my shoulder.

"Are you alright, Jade?"

"I'm not sure. What just happened?"

"I don't know either, but I swear I'll figure it out."

The Game...Jade

"Me too." We step out of the elevator, quickly checking both ends of the hallway before rushing toward the room.

I can't seem to catch my breath. How did my worst enemies end up being my guardians? And if the situation was truly so dangerous, why didn't the other one, the angel who has helped me in these kinds of situations, show up? If I don't regain control soon, I'm pretty sure I'll start hyperventilating.

Daniel hugs me, trying his best to calm me down. All I do is search over his shoulder for those yellow eyes I know so well. I know they're around here somewhere, yet for some reason I can't understand, I can't spot them. Without even realizing it, I press my hands against his sides and gently push him away, trying to clear my line of sight. I have to find them. His hands gently cup my face.

"Jade, close your eyes."

"No, Daniel."

"Please, just do it for me."

"I swear I can't." I say, with anxiety in my voice.

"Yes, you can."

"Daniel, please don't push it; it's not a good time."

"It's not a good time for what?! For me to touch you?" He sounds really annoyed.

"Not a good time for anyone to touch me; let me calm down, okay?"

"Once again, your bloody habit of facing everything alone." He backs away, frustrated, and sits down, doing nothing but watch me as I try to wrap my head around why the demons did what they did. Now, am I supposed to feel grateful to them? It's downright ridiculous! The idea makes me burst into laughter uncontrollably. I can't even imagine myself thanking them. Should I bake them a cake? Or maybe send them flowers? Raúl and Daniel stare at me, surprised.

"What's going on, Jade? Why the laughter?" Raúl asks.

"I don't know." I manage to reply, laughter bubbling up and choking my words. There's no way for me to explain to them what's causing it.

"She's just venting, you know." Daniel says, laughing too.

We laughed until tears streamed down our faces, and even for a few minutes after that. We could have continued if it weren't for a knock on the door. It's the hotel manager checking to see if we're okay. I don't want to imagine what the poor man thought, seeing us still laughing like that. He almost

Rocío Blisswealth

218

joined in; I think the only thing stopping him was realizing how inappropriate it would be, given what had just happened.

The man showers us with apologies, which Daniel accepts. His mood has shifted since a few minutes ago. Also, the apologies come with plates of delicious food and two huge bottles of the best champagne. So, we forgive him! According to Daniel, everything's been forgotten. I don't think it's exactly that, but my mouth is full, so I'm not about to argue.

The rest of the evening is rather calming; let's say nothing out of the ordinary happens anymore. Raúl says goodnight and goes off to rest. I try to do the same, but Daniel asks me to stay for a while. He starts talking, recapping the tour and everything that's happened between us, until he gets to the point he really wants to address.

"Jade, why are you like this?" His face becomes serious as he asks.

"Like what? How?" I inquire.

"I couldn't even begin to explain it."

"You mean when I tell you things you don't want to hear?"

"Yes. That, and when you don't let me get close to you."

"Well, how would you like me to be, Daniel?" I speak, annoyed.

"It's not about whether I'm okay with it or not. I just can't wrap my head around it, and sometimes it really gets to me, like it did today."

"In that case, I'll try to explain, if you'll let me." I say, attempting to soften my tone. He's not lying; his eyes show the pain I've caused him.

"Please."

"Daniel, I'm not someone who goes around touching people to express my feelings, and I don't like it when others do it to me, either. It makes me uncomfortable, and sometimes, it can even bother me. I don't understand why physical contact is necessary."

"Your mother must find it quite a challenge dealing with you in that aspect."

"Don't worry about her; she hasn't touched me in years, many years."

"That can't be right, Jade." He says, growing indignant and furrowing his brow.

"It is, but we're not talking about her now." He doesn't say more, and I continue my explanation. "I get that, like most people, all of this seems really weird and beyond your understanding. But for me, it's more important to feel like I can count on someone without having to measure our love through hugs or kisses. It just doesn't work that way for me."

"If that sort of contact isn't crucial for you, then how do you feel when I touch you?" He struggles to ask this question.

"I like it, I like it a lot. The sensation is strange to me but comfortable. The feeling you bring is nice and warm. Daniel, don't get me wrong; that contact isn't something I can't live without. However, when it comes to you, I enjoy it. That's just how it is, at least most of the time." I need to be crystal clear, as clear as he was when he asked me, gods! Talking about feelings I've never learned to handle is incredibly hard; my hands sweat, and I wipe them on my pants.

"Most of the time. So, can you let me know when you don't appreciate it?" He asks very seriously.

"Let me think. When I'm trying to concentrate on something or when I'm trying to control a strong emotion like anger or fear. In those moments, your closeness feels suffocating and genuinely annoying, especially when you insist on doing things your way, and I end up making you feel bad. There are just too many things to handle all at once. The only way I can regain my stability after something unpleasant is by retreating to my space and, as you say, my 'bloody habit of facing everything alone.' It's the only way I know how to do it."

"And when I touch you, I interrupt your flow."

"Yes, actually, can I tell you something? When moments like that happen, and you hug me, what I do is count." He looks at me with a questioning face. "Yes, from one to ten or more if I need to, to distract myself and not ask you to back off. I couldn't hold back today. I'm sorry."

"Today, it wasn't just a request to let go; you pushed me away." He says without looking me in the eye, in a rather clear, angry tone.

"I trust you more now. I couldn't help it; I'm really sorry."

"Well, let me tell you, I find trust quite hateful." He smiles a little when he says this. "Is it the trust that makes you speak so candidly to me?"

"Daniel, I talk to you like this because, in front of you, I show exactly who I am. When you ask me something, I tell you the truth, nice or not, uncensored. I never felt the need to use those damn filters that people use in diplomatic situations, the ones I've always had to use with everyone. I answer what I'm thinking, as it is, as I'm doing now."

"Always?"

"Always. I know I'm weird, Daniel. I'd rather just live by myself and not worry about being all polite at specific times or if I hurt someone by not saying hi, stuff like that. Personal relationships aren't really my thing. But with you, I got wrapped up without even realizing it."

"But I've noticed you've been quite sociable these past two months." He comments with a certain tone of reproach in his voice; I expected it.

"That's easy when I can pretend to be a regular person. All I have to think about is being polite or nice, and after that, I just forget about the conversation and the person." He gives me this little half-smile and raises an eyebrow. As always, the ego. I watch him for a second and then carry on. "However, if what you want from me, and I mean it, is for me to act in a more conventional, more normal way, you just have to ask for it. I can do it perfectly; I've done it my whole life until now."

"No, not that; it wouldn't be you. But there's still something I'm not quite getting. Can I come closer, or...?" Okay, Daniel, let me break it down for you, even if I have to use pears and apples.

"I thought I already explained, but if you need me to be clearer, even a few weeks ago, I wouldn't have been able to. I don't know where the embarrassment that held me back went. So, Daniel, I can be straight with you: I love it when you hug and kiss me, almost always. It's not just something I enjoy; I look forward to it. Got it?"

"Almost always." He repeats the phrase as if he wants to erase it.

"Exactly."

"Jade, I've got something to confess, and it's mostly because of how brutally honest you are with me. I tend to bury what I feel as deeply as I can out of shame or, well, maybe out of fear of being rejected. But I want you to understand that I enjoy it when you initiate physical contact, having you close. Yet, there are moments when I try to get closer, and you push me away, like today. To avoid getting hurt, I would like you to do it without me having to ask, at least occasionally, so I don't feel like I'm forcing you, but rather that it's something you also crave. Would you be open to that?" His eyes finally meet mine.

"Yes, I promise. Why didn't you tell me?"

"Was that all I needed to do?!" I don't answer him; I just smile. He smiles back, too.

The Game...Jade

"Is everything better now? Please, Daniel, don't doubt about it, waiting for me to say or do something. Trust me, I'm being totally honest; I won't even notice, no matter how hard I try." He looks at me and smiles warmly.

"To be honest, I'd rather not ask anything else." He paused for a moment, noticing the furrow in my brow. "And now it's my turn to explain why, isn't it?"

"If you don't mind."

"When you react in ways I don't expect, which happens quite frequently, I always take some time to try to figure out what the cause was. I form a hypothesis or several. I find myself hesitating to ask often, waiting until I've thought about it a lot for a couple of reasons. One, I know you'll respond with the uncensored honesty you always use with me, and sometimes I don't feel up to handling it. And two, your answer always reminds me how far off the mark I was, nowhere near what you were thinking. It frustrates me to have to admit to myself that I haven't made any headway in my mission to know you. I even asked once if I could ever unravel the mysteries of that maze." He points at my heart with his index finger. "Now I think I never will. It's sad; I really wish I could."

"I'm sorry, Daniel. I don't know what else to say so you can understand me. For me, everything is normal as it is. I learned I'm weird just by hearing it all my life, not because I can notice the difference. But I no longer search for answers to most of my questions about my nature, simply because I grew tired of finding none. Perhaps if you accept me the way I've embraced myself, everything will be easier."

"Can I move in closer now?"

"Yes." He stands up and sits down next to me.

"You're not weird, Jade. You're genuinely intriguing. I consider myself incredibly lucky to know you, to be able to get closer than the rest."

He falls silent, holding my hand, his fingers tracing its lines as if he's reading it. I look at him, and I can see that he's sad. I can't imagine why. I ask, trying to inject seriousness into my voice.

"Daniel, would this be a good time to tell you that you're handsome?"

"Seriously?" I start laughing...

"Of course not."

He joins in my laughter and pulls me into a hug. There's a brief silence, and then he asks.

"What number are you on?"

"Don't interrupt me. Ten, eleven, twelve."

"I knew it! I'm making progress. Finally got something right."

Two days later, I found myself in my room, closing my suitcase. This time, they're leaving a couple of hours ahead of me. It's only been two months, but believe me, these past weeks have felt like a lifetime. I'm calm; I know I'll see him again sooner than I think. I just know it. A young man comes in to collect my bags, and I quickly scan the room to make sure I haven't forgotten anything.

I make my way to Daniel's suite to fulfill a promise. He's still getting ready, his hair damp, dressed in those light blue jeans and the white shirt I adore. I approach him, and he starts giving me hundreds of last-minute instructions as if phones didn't exist. I pretend to pay attention. Moving closer, I place my hands on his sides; his lips keep moving. I hope it's not something important because I'm not hearing a word. I stare directly into his eyes, those enchanting blue springs, and see my reflection. My hands travel a little further to his back, drawing me closer to him. His smile starts to form, but he doesn't stop talking. What a man!

"Daniel…"

"Yes?"

"Would you mind shutting up for a moment?" He looks surprised.

"Why, gorgeous?"

"So, I can kiss you. I've been trying for a while now, and you won't stop."

He narrows his eyes, and at last, he goes quiet. His face lights up with the mischievous smile he wears so well. He stays still, letting me take the lead. I rise slightly on my tiptoes, press my lips against his, and he receives my kiss; a sweet, lingering kiss, enough for two goodbyes and maybe a couple of hellos. I cup his chin in my hands and release his lips. He tilts his forehead to meet mine and sighs.

"Thank you." What else could I say to him?

"It was my pleasure."

A couple of hours later, his flight takes off to the other side of the world, the opposite side from where I am, but this time, it doesn't hurt. Of course, I miss him from the moment his embrace broke as he hurried towards the plane, leaving me here. But this time, he doesn't entirely leave. Honestly, I don't stay

The Game…Jade

entirely here either. I arrive in Monterrey and step into the house; the phone is ringing. Mara answers while I greet my mother, my nephews, and my niece.

"Jade, it's for you."

Gods! I haven't even taken the second step in my house, and they're already calling me. The question is, who?

"Hello."

"Jade?"

"It's me. Who's speaking?"

"Salvador, Daniel's manager. May we speak?"

Chapter X
Please, don't leave me alone, too

I can't imagine what reason this guy could have for calling me, but seriously, he's a master of surprises. If someone had told me I'd be talking to him on the phone, I would never have believed it.

Suddenly, there's this voice in my head saying, "Just say no, no matter what." Alright, let's see what this is all about.

"Good evening, Salvador. How can I help you?"

"I do apologize for intruding; I assume you've recently arrived in Monterrey."

"Yes, I'm literally walking in the door. By the way, how'd you get my number?"

"Oh, well, I do have my connections, but of course, I've sworn to secrecy. I hope you don't mind." Of course, I mind, but I know he won't tell me, so I don't press further.

"So, tell me, what do I owe the honor of your call?"

"Well, let me enlighten you. In a couple of days, Víctor Arredondo will be putting on an exclusive concert at a Monterrey hotel, and he has reserved a table just for you to join us. You might consider gracing us with your presence, perhaps alongside your friends or a chosen family member; the table is yours. Feel free to arrange the seats as you like. What do you say? Will you honor us with your attendance? Víctor is really looking forward to meeting you."

"Wow, that's sweet of him. But sadly, I can't make it to the concert. Either way, please thank him for thinking of me and extending such a nice invite." Daniel, you should be proud; in just this call, I'm throwing around more diplomatic phrases than during the entire tour.

"What a pity; I suppose with your recent arrival in Monterrey, you must have an abundance of tasks to attend to. Is there even the slightest chance you could set aside one of those matters, creating an opening in your busy schedule for us?"

"Sir, I don't mean to be rude, but the tour just ended, and you know how it is. We were pushed to the limit, and now all I've got energy for is collapsing into my bed. Honestly, I'm not planning on leaving it for at least a week if I can help it. Obviously, I'm trusting you not to spill to Mr. Arredondo about why I'm saying no. You get me, right?"

"Certainly, but, I'll reiterate, it's truly a pity. Perhaps another time."

"Yes, perhaps later I'll get the chance to personally thank Mr. Arredondo for his kindness. And thanks to you, too, for taking the trouble to call."

"Have a delightful evening, Jade."

"Good night."

Voice, you really didn't need to worry; I would have said no anyway. I can't stand this guy. Just the thought of having to greet him, or worse, having him and his crew sit at my table, drains me even more than I already am. Who was the moron who gave him my number?

Once again, my niece and nephews, like vultures, have descended on my suitcases, hunting for their gifts. Mom and Mara usher me into the living room, treating me like a visitor, trying to see what they can squeeze out of me. This time, things are different. My determination to rid myself of these demons is rock-solid, and for that, I need their help. They are the only people who, out of resignation or routine, will hear me out without trying to toss me into a psych ward. And both of them have all the time in the world to tackle the daunting research task I need.

I spent the first hour sharing all the tour anecdotes with them, which they complemented with every detail published in the media. Gradually, I started telling them about Salvador's visit and his bodyguard. I study their reactions carefully; I want to know what ground I'm treading on.

For the first time, Mara watches me, not with reproach or curiosity—I couldn't quite read her expression, but it's no longer hostile. Slowly, she begins to speak, mentioning that during this time, they've had the opportunity to find out a lot of things. They know that what I see are indeed demons, that I've been seeing them since I was a kid, and they're already exploring the possibilities I might have to get rid of them.

They also understand that it all ties back to the unique abilities I possess, which we haven't sought reasons for, but they are not common. According to Mom, there are people, experts in these supernatural things, who have offered their help to put an end to this, and she wants to know if I would be willing to meet them.

Absolutely not. I couldn't tell you why, but just the thought of being a subject of study for those people, whoever they are, sends a chill down my spine. However, if they want to be in touch with them and pass the information to me, I have no problem with that. Mara eagerly agrees; for them, who have always been so emotionally distant from me, this is an opportunity to get closer. Perhaps they think the space left by my grandparents is up for grabs, and maybe they could fill it. But no, neither available nor empty. That place will never be for anyone else.

I've never let my guard down, except with Daniel, and despite this need for my family's support, there's still a part of me that remains strictly under my control: Daniel Montalvo and everything related to him. That's just mine; everything else, I'll have to lay out on the table sooner or later.

Mara asks if the call I received was from that man, Salvador. As soon as I confirmed and explained the reason for the call, she quickly asked me what my response was. Once she sees a smile forming on my face, she understands it is a negative response. The recommendations to stay away from that kind of person don't take long to come, as if I didn't already know.

Finally, the conversation drifts into much smoother territory, the rockstar. It occurred to me to tell Mara that I had already forgotten about it. Wrong! How could that be possible? I use this discussion as an excuse to stand up and make my way to my bedroom. Even with my sister's voice echoing two steps behind me, I manage to enter and close the door; everything is exactly the same.

The demon spots me as I enter; he heads to his corner and stays there, not looking at me, eyes downcast. It's a strange feeling seeing him like this. The images of what his colleagues did for me, for us, at the hotel, make me see him differently, with less fear, maybe. They shielded us from serious harm; it must be true, or else they wouldn't have intervened.

Anyway, even though I have many questions to ask him, I don't dare. My grandma used to say you don't negotiate with the devil. Lucky me! From what I've heard, not with the devil, ghosts, or fortune-tellers either, anyone who could help me, at least that's what I think. Angels, I don't know, I think they're getting farther away, further each time.

I close my eyes, hoping to make the most of the night and sleep for a full eight hours—the first time in months. I glance at him; I'm not as scared of him anymore.

The Game…Jade

Well, I don't think I achieved my goal of those blessed eight hours of sleep. I can feel my niece climb onto the bed, starting to move around to wake me up. The moment she sees me smiling, she signals that there's a phone call for me. Another one? And who now? With an air of self-importance, she informs me that a lady is calling me from Spain. I quickly pick up the receiver, and she steps out to hang up the extension, successfully completing her receptionist duties.

"Hello..."

"Hello, sweetheart! Did you manage to get some rest?"

"Carmen! What a pleasure to hear from you! You've left me hanging for so long."

"I didn't mean to interrupt; I know you had tons of work on your plate."

"Oh, come on! I had nothing of that sort; all the weight was on Daniel's shoulders. I was just an observer."

"Well, you see, the version I heard doesn't quite match yours. Daniel couldn't stop talking about you and everything you both did these past couple of months. Of course, he emphasized how you never wanted to humor him by saying he's handsome, ha-ha-ha."

"I've told him that no matter how much I appreciate him, I won't lie."

"You're absolutely right; honesty is key! Besides, with the whole family playing along, it's more than enough." Our laughter echoed across continents.

"I see you get me."

"I heard you've already met Salvador, and you almost vomited."

"Gods! Yes, that's true, and I almost did it yesterday, too." Carmen falls silent for a moment before asking in a more serious tone. "What do you mean, Jade?"

"He called me yesterday. I had just walked in the door, and they transferred his call to me."

"And what...? I mean, some task from Daniel, I suppose."

"No, not at all. He wanted to invite me to the concert that Víctor Arredondo is presenting in my city the day after tomorrow."

"I see. And who will you be going with?"

"Do you think I would accept to attend? First of all, I don't even know this Víctor. But if he's anything like Salvador, I have zero interest in accepting

228

an invitation from him anywhere. Besides, I don't know; there's something about all this that I don't like."

"Well, Jade, unfortunately, I have to hang up, but I'm glad to hear you're doing well and starting your recovery process. We'll be in touch more often, I promise. Take care of yourself."

"I will, you too. Thanks for calling, Carmen."

"Ciao."

At least now I know that Daniel arrived safely in Spain. Knowing him, he'll probably sleep for a couple of days. I decided to follow his lead. I roll over, squeeze my eyes shut, and try to fall asleep again. I'm so tired; it shouldn't be hard... zzz.

I sense someone watching me, and I open my eyes. My niece is standing next to me again.

"Let me sleep a little longer." I plead.

"Okay, even if it's been a long time. But what do I say to Daniel? Should I tell him to call back later?"

"No, no, I'm awake now. Hang up the phone, please, little one."

"Sure, but I already knew that." She says and runs off.

"Daniel?"

"That's right, gorgeous. Were you hoping for someone else?"

"Anyone but you. I thought you'd be in the arms of Morpheus by now."

"Well, obviously not. First things first, I wanted to find out how you did when you arrived in Monterrey. One can never predict your adventures; maybe you decided to go on a little escapade, and if so, I was planning to give you a good scolding for not inviting me."

"No, never that. I hate going on adventures."

"But would you have invited me if you had gone?"

"Yes, Daniel, of course, I would invite you. In fact, I wouldn't dare to go without you."

"Thanks."

"Crazy."

"I heard you're being invited to a concert."

"Another place I wouldn't dare to go without you."

"No, Jade, I'm serious."

"I am serious too, Daniel. That guy, Salvador, creeps me out."

"I thought he disgusted you."

"That too. What I'd like to know is, how did he get my phone number?"

"I'd like to know that, too. Gorgeous, would it be too much to ask you to give me all the details about his call? I'm dead curious."

"Not at all; let me try to remember."

I start telling him about the call, going into all the details I can remember, but all I hear in response is his heavy breathing. I finish my story, and he still doesn't say anything.

"Daniel? Don't you plan on congratulating me?"

"Gorgeous, I got confused. Congratulate you?"

"Seriously, Daniel, count yourself lucky that I don't have you in front of me because if I did, I bet you wouldn't escape a kick!"

"Gorgeous, I don't know..."

"The entire conversation was absolutely and totally diplomatic. I poured politeness into every sentence I said to that unfriendly guy, and don't I deserve congratulations? Can you believe it?! Let's see when I do it again. Probably never!" His laughter sounds like sweet music in my ears. He shakes off his distraction and keeps talking.

"My bad, gorgeous. How rude of me. That call doesn't deserve congratulations; it deserves a standing ovation, and right now, I'm on my feet."

"Thank you, thank you, but it's not that big of a deal."

"Crazy."

"I know, it's contagious; spending so much time with you, those are the results."

"We should find out who passed the craziness on to whom, because I'm not sure you're faring well in that department."

"You're wrong; I thought I made it clear that I'm weird, but crazy, not at all!"

"I miss you, gorgeous." Butterflies fluttered in my stomach uncontrollably; I thought I had gotten used to this, but I was wrong.

"I miss you too, Daniel, a lot."

"Sending you a massive kiss. Be good, please."

"I'll send you two, and well, I'll try. I'll let you know if I succeed, but behaving well, I've never quite mastered that."

"As long as you give it a shot, I'm cool for now. Take care, I'll call you soon."

Rocío Blisswealth

He hung up. He didn't like Salvador's call at all. All hell is going to break loose. Good, I can't stand that guy. I go downstairs to the kitchen; I don't know how long I've slept, and now another pressing need demands my attention—I'm starving! I grab the first edible thing I find in the fridge; Mara approaches and asks what I plan to do. I'm sorry, but our conversation will have to wait until at least tomorrow. All I want is to get back to bed. It's as if my body insists on repaying the countless hours of sleep I owe it.

She gets upset. She's in a hurry for me to start my activities, but I'm aware it all demands a lot of energy from me, something I lack entirely right now. I need to rest. She insists, but my answer is the same. I've managed to anger her; I'm sorry, there's no way I can do it; my eyelids are heavy.

Before leaving the kitchen, she asks what Daniel wants. She assumes that I'll open up about it now; she couldn't be more wrong. Not a single word comes out. Her warnings come quickly; if I'm not willing to share information, how can I expect her to help me? Her words fall on deaf ears; I've already decided that this matter is mine alone. Besides, I still have to test the help she can provide. After that, I'll know what to share and what to keep to myself. I walk upstairs as if my room is pulling me with the force of a giant magnet, and I surrender back into bed, slipping almost immediately into a deep, restless sleep.

I wake up, surprised to find myself shrouded in darkness. It's strange; it couldn't have been more than two in the afternoon when I fell asleep, or at least, it didn't feel like much time had passed. I try to focus my sight to see my surroundings more clearly. I blink hard, becoming aware of where I am, far from my room and Monterrey. I recognize this garden, even though I've never seen it in such darkness.

The near-total absence of sound is odd; even in the dead of night, I should hear at least a cricket, but there's nothing. I start walking on the grass, feeling the dew's cool dampness underfoot, the texture of the ground, the path lined with overgrown bushes—wilder than the last time I saw them. I'm sure of where I am now. It's Daniel's house. I stop, and the humidity becomes colder with each passing second. I can feel it up to my ankles like ice-cold water. Fear creeps from my feet to the nape of my neck, settling like thorns at the base of my skull. A sob catches in my throat, and I force it back. Not here, please. Let him not be here.

The Game…Jade

I can hear footsteps behind me, barely audible on the grass. I don't make a single move, hoping they haven't spotted me yet. With a whimper, Tíber sidles up to me, crying like a puppy. I crouch down next to him, cradling his head in my hands, trying to calm him, but it's useless—he senses it too; it's here.

In a very low voice, I ask him to lead me to Daniel. In response, he wags his tail once and heads towards the house. He almost drags himself to the ground; I can clearly see he doesn't want to do it, but he'd give his life for his master. The determination that makes me enter the house instead of running away makes me wonder if maybe I'm capable of the same.

We approach the house; I can't see a single light on. Tíber's sense of smell will have to guide me. Or rather, mine will. The awful stench of that demon has already reached my nose. Shivers run down my spine, tensing my shoulders to the point of unbearable pain. I can't feel my feet, but I keep moving. The smell grows stronger; if I can't control my breathing, I'll vomit.

My hands find a wooden door. The smell seeps out like smoke; even Tíber starts to retch; he wants to vomit. In almost inaudible words, even to myself, I ask him to step back. He doesn't, but he seems to understand me because he stays still. I press my ear to the door and listen—that horrible, guttural voice is screaming furiously. I can't understand what it's saying, the door is too thick. I turn the handle gently and push; it slides open a few inches before halting, revealing the most terrifying scene before me.

The semi-darkness is softened by the moonlight streaming in through the window; the tree leaves outside dance, casting shadows that seem to conspire, adding an even more macabre touch to my vision. The demon that came out of the mirror a few months ago, huge, skeletal, with wrinkled grayish skin resembling cardboard and intense yellow eyes, is holding Daniel by the neck, lifting him until his feet dangle in the air. Daniel fights back; his breathing is ragged amidst the struggle; he's covered in sweat, and his hair sticks to his forehead. The veins on his temples pulse so hard I can see them clearly from where I stand.

Its demonic voice fills the room, spewing insults while he shakes Daniel like a puppet. Now I understand what he's shouting, with all the strength his lungs allow, if he even has lungs. He asks the same question again and again: "Where is it? Tell me where." Daniel gives no response, clenching his jaw in determination. The demon raises his free hand, effortlessly sinking it into

Rocío Blisswealth

Daniel's chest like butter, rummaging inside him as if searching desperately in a drawer.

Daniel tries to stifle a cry of pain that slips through his teeth; he won't hold out much longer. Unable to control myself, or rather, without reason to do so, I slam the door wide open. I have no idea what I'm going to do; I just want him to let him go. The demon is visibly shocked to see me, enough to release Daniel with both hands. He crumples to the ground, offering no resistance at all; the impact sounds sharp against the tiles.

I have his full attention now; his gaze is fixed on me, and he remains still. It's as if he has completely forgotten about Daniel, good. Tíber rushes into the room, emitting a strange mix of growls and whimpers, sniffing at Daniel insistently until he manages to make him open his eyes. As soon as he regains enough consciousness, his eyes widen in shock at seeing me. The demon takes a step forward and grins, displaying the long rows of yellowed teeth that have haunted my nightmares for several months now.

"WE MEET AGAIN, FOOLISH GIRL. HOW DARE YOU...?" I want to run, but I see Daniel still struggling on the ground, fighting unconsciousness. I can't leave him. I stare the demon straight in the eyes, tossing him a bait, something I know will be irresistible: my arrogance.

"How dare I? Not for pleasure, that's for sure. In this life, there's nothing more satisfying than your absence."

He scowls, his expression sharpens, and he slowly turns his head to look at Daniel. Tíber responds with a series of grunts, positioning himself over Daniel's chest and standing between the demon and him. There's no doubt that he'd sacrifice himself for his master. The question remains: am I capable of the same?

"SO, IT'S HIM." He reaches out to touch Daniel, and I react instinctively.

"Leave him, you idiot!" I shout.

Daniel opens his eyes, this time for longer. I don't recognize his voice; it's just a series of gasps his throat can produce. Yet, he manages to warn me.

"Jade, no, run, go back. He can't touch you while you're there." That's all he says before falling unconscious again.

I need to make sure this damn demon took the bait; I'm not going anywhere, leaving him here with Daniel. Infuriated, he takes a step toward me. That's it; he'll follow me. I turn away regretfully. I need to know how Daniel is doing. For now, it's enough to know he's alive, and Tíber is with him— It's more than I could say at other times. I run through the corridors as fast as my numb legs allow. I've lost my sense of direction; I don't know where I'm going. I have to get to the garden.

I can't waste time looking back, but I hear the demon's ropes dragging on the floor, pursuing me frantically. For moments, I feel him tugging at my clothes when he manages to get close enough, only to trigger an adrenaline rush so intense that it propels me faster ahead, momentarily freeing me from his grasp.

I tear myself away from that place and crash heavily back into my body. I can't control my breathing; my heart feels like it's about to leap out of my mouth. I open my eyes and search for the demon that always accompanies me; he's incredibly restless. I know this is just the beginning; he's coming for me. At that moment, the other one appeared by my bed, filling the room with his shouts.

"WHERE IS IT? YOU KNOW! STOP AIDING HIM."

I don't answer him, mainly because fear has left me breathless. He paces around the room; I have no idea what this is about. He turns and lunges at me, only to be repelled by an invisible wall. His cry floods the house; I don't understand how no one hears it. They should have come to help me by now, I think.

"EVEN IF I CAN'T LAY A FINGER ON YOU, I CAN STILL KILL YOU, GIRL. I DON'T NEED TO TOUCH YOU FOR THAT." With just a raised hand, he makes me feel an inexplicable pain all along my spine. I squirm on the bed. I don't know how much longer I can take this; all I know is that I must resist if I want to help Daniel, and at this moment, there's nothing I want more than that.

The demon keeps attacking me, taking turns inflicting pain, not letting any part of my body escape him—my head, legs, hands, stomach, and back to the beginning. I try to stifle my screams, but the tears running down my cheeks have already soaked my pillow.

"RELEASE HIM! RELEASE HIM, YOU FOOLISH GIRL! I SHALL END YOU! I SHALL END BOTH OF YOU!" He storms out of the room, snarling. I don't know where he's gone, but I take the chance to catch my breath in this brief pause from so much pain. I look at my demon and ask him, addressing him for the first time, hoping for some answers.

"What would happen if I let go of Daniel? If I didn't help him?" He can't believe I'm talking to him. He looks into my eyes and lets me hear his voice for the first time, his incredibly deep voice.

"HE WOULD DIE."

"And if I hold on to him?"

"YOU COULD DIE, DEPENDING ON YOUR ENDURANCE."

"Alright, thanks." A snort is all he gives in response; we're definitely not friends, that much is clear. He just despises the other demon more than he does me. I guess that's my silver lining. He watches me carefully.

"WILL YOU RELEASE HIM?"

"No." He laughs mockingly; he can't believe I prefer this pain over letting go of Daniel. He simply doesn't understand.

"FOOLISH GIRL, HE WILL KILL YOU. WHY DON'T YOU RELEASE HIM ALREADY? YOU WILL, SOONER OR LATER."

"If he dies, if he ceases to exist, I'd rather be dead, too. Can't you see? I won't let him go. It's worth the fight." The demon returns for another round of torment. I now have a reason to endure it.

The next morning, Mom walks into the room. I must look terrible; I can see it in her expression.

"Jade, do you want me to call the doctor?"

"No, Mom, he can't help me. This will be over soon." Or at least I hope so.

"But what's happening?" I resist telling her, but I can't hold back anymore. I don't have the strength to come up with a lie. Besides, if she and my sister try to help me, she'd better have some information.

"I'm helping Daniel resist an attack."

"A demonic attack! Is that true? You're crazy! Jade, stop that. Let go of him; don't help him anymore!"

"No!"

"Oh, my god! Have you gone crazy?"

"If I let go, he'll die."

"Maybe that would be for the best."

"I won't let him die like I let my grandparents go. I won't do it." She slams the door as she storms out of the room, never to return. But the demon does return. It seems he only lets me rest so that I don't die without revealing what he wants to know. I'm glad I don't know what it is. If I did, maybe I wouldn't be able to keep it quiet. He attacks me more intensely, or maybe it just feels that way due to the length of his assaults. What an incredible ability to cause pain, and how much pleasure is reflected in his eyes as he does it. How many hours have passed already? It's the second day, maybe the third. He lets go of me again, as if tossing something useless to the ground and leaves. I wonder where he goes every time. My demon seems to sense what I'm thinking.

"HE'S INTERROGATING DANIEL. HE'S IN WORSE CONDITION THAN YOU, BUT HE'S NOT SAYING ANYTHING." His words fill me with unbearable fear, a true terror that he might not resist and die at the hands of the demon. I can barely speak through my sobs.

"Not saying anything about what?" He doesn't answer.

"THIS TORTURE WILL BE THE LAST." The demon hears his voice as he enters the room, and he only looks at him with indignation, shouting for him to get out. I look at him with pleading in my eyes.

"Please, don't leave me alone, too." He stays in his corner, ignoring the orders of the senior demon. I don't know if it's to please me or to defy the demon he hates so much. I don't know, but in this sharp pain that penetrates my skin through every pore and my moans, the only comfort I can feel is his presence, his icy demonic presence. There is no one else, only him and the hope that Daniel will endure this, and that there is still some life left in his body, some life to hold me once more.

The demon stops and asks, for the umpteenth time, where is what he's looking for. Where did we put it? My gaze is fixed on the wall, and my breath is no longer enough to fill my lungs, not even halfway. I am in that physical state where you feel like you might fade away from one moment to the next; I have longed for it for many hours, but the pain couldn't pierce the veil of unconsciousness. No, he wouldn't allow it; his only pleasure during these long and fruitless hours would disappear, and then what would his amusement be?

"STUPID, BOTH OF YOU ARE FOOLS. DON'T YOU REALIZE THIS WILL CONTINUE? I'M LEAVING FOR NOW. JUST LISTEN: I WON'T REST

UNTIL I KILL YOU BOTH!"

I inhale deeply, filling my lungs to the bottom; I've breathed in his putrid smell for so many hours that I don't notice it anymore. Slowly, I turn my head to look at him. I want to see his horrible eyes; I would like to smile, but the corners of my lips refuse to release the grimace of pain they've adopted for so many hours. However, inside me, a huge smile spreads, reflecting my

Rocío Blisswealth

immense satisfaction. I look for my voice, and when I find it, I take the opportunity to make a comment, one that obviously isn't what he expects.

"Kill us, you say? Then he's still alive, and your time is up, idiot."

His screams make the room tremble, and me along with it. My demon is restless; he looks furious at me for provoking such an aggressive reaction, one that could cause him serious harm. I don't care. Only one thing has kept me alive during the endless hours of this brutal attack: being able to prevent Daniel from dying in the process. If that were to happen, the demon wouldn't speak of his death as a possibility in the future, but as my ultimate failure. No, he's not part of my path strewn with corpses. I did manage to save him. Nothing else matters anymore; the pain finally fades, and I black out.

Hours later, I started feeling sensations returning to my body. It must be very late because the usual sounds of cars outside my bedroom window are absent. I'm dying of thirst. My senses slowly come back, and I start to process what I'm feeling. There's a gentle hand running through my hair from behind; I recognize the touch, even though it's been ages since I felt it. I attempt to speak, but my throat hurts terribly. I don't think I've swallowed in hours; it's completely dry.

"Rest." He says very softly.

"Ángel?"

"Is that how you've decided to call me?"

"I don't know; let me see you."

He leans over my shoulder, letting me see his face, his sweet face. Nothing has changed since the first time I remember seeing him, back when I was about four years old, right here in this room.

"Yes, you are Ángel." I say, my voice is still barely audible.

"Alright."

"Where were you when that damn creature almost succeeded in killing me?" I reproach.

"Where I've always been, preventing him from succeeding."

"I would have been comforted to see you."

"He would have seen me too, and that wouldn't have helped you."

"I didn't consider that."

"It hurts me so much to see you like this; you're completely covered in wounds." He feels sorry for me; I can see it in his eyes. He continues to caress me delicately, careful not to inflict more pain.

The Game…Jade

"It doesn't matter; they're not visible to the naked eye."

"I can see all of them."

"I know, I mean, you get it. Besides, these wounds mean a victory. I'll wear the scars proudly, even if no one else can see them."

Suddenly, the terror that let me rest during the time I was unconscious returned to my stomach. Anxiously, I ask him.

"Because... it was a victory, right? Daniel is alive."

"He is."

"Then, yes."

"Jade, you shouldn't have."

"Ángel, I won't allow them to take away what I want once more. I prefer..."

"I know, believe me, I know. Sleep now, I'll help you heal. Do you need anything else?"

"Yes." He looks at me very seriously, assuming I'll ask for something for Daniel, but that's not it. He's alive, and he'll take time to recover from this; I can imagine that. My soul will return to my body when I can hear his voice again, and that will be resolved with a phone call. What I want is something else.

"Tell my grandma and Clemen that the damn demon didn't kill me. They'll be glad to know. And tell my grandpa that this time, I finally confronted him, that's all. No, one more thing, Ángel, how long did we hold out?"

"Seventy hours; try to get some sleep."

This time, I sleep for real, without the haze of unconsciousness and the stench of the demon around me. I forgot to tell Ángel that I want a dog, too. Such incredible courage!

Wow! I had no idea how many muscles my body has until now that each and every one of them hurts. It's hard to understand how a spiritual attack, so to speak, can mess up my physical body this way. Like I told Ángel, there is not a single visible wound, not to human eyes, but today, I can feel them all.

Even though I'm still in pain, my mind is in a hurry to fully kick into gear. There is a swirl of feelings and thoughts inside of me that I want to analyze. I'm still scared, more than I've ever been, and the emptiness I feel in my stomach keeps coming in as a constant reminder that whatever the demon was looking for, he's still pending, and he won't just let it slip away.

Despite that, I've learned something from this experience: everything has its time. He had his moment to attack us, and when it was over, much to his regret, he had to leave. That's something. I don't know how this might help me, but I treasure any kind of information I can use in the future. If there's another attack, I know that I will only have to resist for a while; they are not permanent.

I'm slowly getting up from bed; it feels like the mattress has glued itself to my skin, even through the clothes I'm wearing. Another overwhelming feeling inside me, so powerful that it can push fear aside for long stretches, is the immense satisfaction of having helped Daniel. I faced the demon, resisted his attack, and I'm here alive to talk about it. Okay, I don't have anyone to tell. But I could do it.

I don't know what would have happened if he had died. I've never considered suicide; my grandma managed to convince me it was one of god's most hated sins. But maybe because of the comfort Ángel provides, I've always felt I owe something to that god my grandma believed in, even if it's just not taking my own life.

But what would life mean if Daniel weren't in it? Worse still, if I hadn't been able to do something for him. It would be reliving the death of my grandparents, and I couldn't bear it, especially considering the only thing that gives me strength to keep going is the time I spend with Daniel. So, maybe not suicide, but would letting me die be just as serious? I don't think so, not if the reason for living is gone; it's something worth thinking about, just in case.

The third and most powerful feeling that has settled within me is the determination to fight. Just once, I want to be the one who attacks. I want to be the one who has the power to inflict pain and relish in it, holding that damned demon in my hands for seventy hours. I still don't know how we managed to resist for so long. I wish I could be the one witnessing the terror in the eyes of the other.

The demon didn't achieve what it set out to do, but it enjoyed using all his endowed weapons on us, inadvertently accomplishing something in the process, something it didn't intend at all. It stirred greed within me, a profound greed for that kind of power. If there's anything within me that I can tap into to save Daniel, to save myself, and to put an end to every demon I can, I will, without a doubt.

I'm already sitting on the bed, and I place my feet on the floor. What a delightful sensation to feel the coolness of the tiles under my feet. How many unnoticed things are there in our daily lives? I compare this to what happens when we catch a cold; suddenly, we realize we can breathe freely, but due to the illness, we can't anymore. It's the same: peace, calmness, the air free from unpleasantness, sleeping peacefully, the ability to feel hunger in a stomach not quivering under the weight of fear. We value these things only when we no longer have them.

My bedroom door creaks open just a bit, and I can see a little eye no more than 3 feet from the ground, followed by a smile lacking the two front teeth.

"Are you going to go for a bath?" The little one asks. Gods! It must be imperative when a seven-year-old girl considers it so important.

"Yes, I will."

"Are you feeling okay now?"

"Yeap."

"Well, Mara and Luz are waiting for you." She refers to her mom and grandma, but she has always just called them by their first names. I think that speaks of the blurry bond between them.

"Alright, little one, tell them I'll join them here after my bath, okay?"

"Okay, bye." She closes the door, which was never fully open, and runs off to deliver the message.

I take a slow shower. No matter how much I try, speed remains out of my reach. My tired muscles find some relief under the comforting warmth of the shower droplets. I wish I had a balm to soothe my aches, but my grandma was the one who knew about those things, and I doubt there's anything like it left in the house. As I step out of the bathroom, the little one peeks in again from the door opposite my bedroom.

"Jade, come here; you have a call." She says, smiling.

I entered my mother's room, the one that used to belong to my grandparents, to answer the phone. I pick up with total reluctance.

"Hello," I say.

"Hey, gorgeous!"

His voice, though tired, still manages to stir butterflies in my stomach. A tear slides down my cheek; he's okay.

"Daniel..."

"Are you alright, Jade?"

"Recovering. And you?"

"When I got home, well, I think it hit us..." I know exactly what he's referring to, but we never openly talk about those things. We both understand, just like in the past, but we don't bring it up; it's too frightening.

"All the exhaustion."

"Yes, Jade, how are you?" I can hear his voice breaking while my tears keep rolling down my face.

"I'm okay, sweetheart, and after some sleep, I'll be much better. Don't worry. But how about you? How do you feel?"

"Better now that I hear your voice. I couldn't sleep without talking to you first." He can't speak further; the tears won't allow it.

"We're fine, Daniel."

"I miss you terribly, and I want you to remember how much I love you."

"I know, two little bits. I remember it well."

"Far more than just two little bits. I'll call you soon, rest."

"You too. Daniel..."

"Yes, gorgeous?"

"Give Tíber a kiss for me, would you?"

"I will, without a doubt."

"Thank you."

I hung up the phone. I couldn't have received a better balm for my soul than hearing his voice, worrying about me, and expressing his love. He might not know how much I love him, or perhaps he does. My eyes are getting closed after the shower, but this time, I won't yield to my body's exhaustion. There are many important things to do, matters of life and death.

I headed towards what, until a few days ago, was the scene of my worst nightmares. Now, I can view my bedroom differently; it will still be the battleground, but this time, I'll be the one taking the first step. I already have a victory under my belt and his affection. I need nothing more.

As soon as I open the door, I can see Mom and Mara sitting on the bed, waiting for me.

"Are you ready?" Mom asks.

"I am. What do I need to do?"

The Game...Jade

Chapter XI
I guess this can save us the introductions

The conversation between us is crucial to figure out how we're going to roll from now on. They've never really known me. They knew who I was, or at least, knew what to expect from me until a couple of years ago. Now, I'm pretty sure they have no clue.

For me, life is split into 'before Daniel' and 'after Daniel.' They barely know anything about this new Jade, but I guess we got to find some common ground.

First things first, I got to lay my cards on the table to avoid drama later on. So, when I see Mara about to speak, I wave my hand to let me go first. She looks surprised but stays quiet, and I take the lead.

"I want to set some ground rules for these talks, so you know how far I'm willing to go and where it's not advisable for you to get involved. I am not going to let anyone ask me about or get involved in my work with Daniel under any circumstances. I won't accept any complaints, warnings, opinions, or anything related to situations like the one I went down the past three days."

Mom is not thrilled that I'm keeping them out of the most important stuff in my life—I can see it on her face—but that's non-negotiable. Mara just found out she's got to figure out how to deal with me. Fair warning, no tricks. So, I keep going with my announcements.

"I know you helped me out with something related to him a few months ago, but from now on, that territory's mine alone."

No objections, so I keep going.

"I won't ask for permission or anything. I'm going to do what I have to do, and I'll only go along with what I'm okay with. It's going to be useless trying to talk me into doing something I don't want to do. And just so we're clear, I won't be dealing with anyone else so they can figure out why these demons are harassing me. I've always known that's what they are, and whatever you're asking me to do, it better start from that point; I don't want to waste my time. I'm willing to patiently listen to everything you have to say, if it makes sense to me, for as long as it takes. This time, I'm up for anything."

They know it; they've seen the havoc a demon has wreaked on me and my strong determination to keep fighting. They're aware I haven't eaten in three days, and I don't even remember having a sip of water, but here I am, just like I told them, ready for anything. I guess that emphasizes how serious I am.

"The information I have so far is this: The demon that attacked me had already reached out to me a few months ago. He said he'd been familiar with my bloodline for a hundred years, or maybe even more, I don't know, and that he'd return when the time was right, which was three days ago. Another thing I found out then is that it can't touch me, not physically, I mean. On the other hand, demons seem to have a timing for things. What is it? I have no idea, and somehow, I'm immune to it."

"But then, it can follow us, too. We share your same blood." Mara says with terror in her eyes.

"It would have done that already, from what Grandma told me. This has happened in the family before; however, it only chooses one member. I don't know the reason, but the rest of the family seems to ignore it. If that weren't the case, you'd see what I've been able to see since I can remember. Don't worry, Mara."

"Grandma told you?" Mom asks, surprised.

"Yes, she told me about... Well, there'll be time for that later. Another thing I've figured out is that there are various types of demons; I don't know how many of different sizes, I mean. The one who attacked me is almost seven feet tall, and the ones that come in and out of my room are barely five feet tall."

"The ones in your bedroom?" Mara's voice trembles.

"Yes."

"When do they come?"

"Well..." I can't help but smile a little, noticing the fear she's experiencing, something I've been dealing with since I was a kid. "Right now, one of them, the usual one, is sitting there." I point to the corner of my room. "I guess I'm his assignment. I don't remember him being absent much."

They look to the corner, fear overtaking them; the terror in their eyes is unmistakable. The demon stares at them and snorts, as is his custom when something annoys him. What nonsense! Here I am, talking about that demon as if he were a pet.

"Why don't you get him out of here?" Mom asks. "We once told you how to do it." Her fear becomes evident in the tremor of her voice.

"Well, there are things that are easier said than done. If I remember correctly, attempting to get him to leave cost me dearly. It's not that simple, Mom, at least not for me, not yet. Hopefully, someday."

My words bring them some relief, but my mind can only replay the desperate way I begged that same demon not to leave me alone just a few hours ago.

"But how can we talk about all this with him here? Just think about what he could do." Mara speaks up.

"That's what I wish—being able to imagine what he could do. I don't know why he never leaves here, even when I travel, he..."

"You mean he stays here when you travel? But why? Good lord!"

I can't help but let out a chuckle; my grandpa was right; he always said I laughed even in the worst moments. Well, maybe not that much, but this situation does amuse me.

"Well, yes, he stays, and no, 'good lord' isn't exactly the right expression." I smile.

"Don't mock me, seeing that he's there, how can you laugh?" She responds indignantly.

"Mara, I'm twenty-one, which means he's been here for at least twenty years, and now you're scared? If I hadn't told you anything, you still wouldn't have noticed. Besides, if I recall correctly, you two are more than familiar with him."

Rocío Blisswealth

Both of them look at me with incredulous expressions. How could I dare to suggest something so monstrous, like the idea that they have something to do with demons? But I'm about to remind them.

"Do you remember the sounds under my bed when I was little? Could it have been him making them? It's possible, which means you already know each other. Because I doubt god spent his time down there with his many occupations. Though back then, it was me who was scared, not you. You seemed quite comfortable asking him questions."

I can't stop the sarcasm from slipping out, a skill I've recently learned to master. They say, 'If you run with wolves, you learn to howl,' and I've just spent two months with the alpha wolf and the rest of the pack. Masters in the art of sarcasm, among other things. Both of their eyes widen even further, and they can't stop looking at the corner. I know perfectly well it's an issue they'd rather not remember, but I've never forgotten it.

I want them to know they've dealt with demons, too. Or who did they think was answering them? An angel? I'm sorry, but I don't think so. I've always sensed that both of them blame me for what I can see, not in the healing sense, of course. But while I can see them, I would never think of asking them anything to satisfy my morbid curiosity. Someday, I had to tell them, and what better time than now?

"I guess this can save us the introductions. So far, they haven't managed to kill me, but that doesn't mean they'll stop trying. The only thing I fear is that now that a bigger one has appeared, a larger one, I mean, it might signify the start of another phase. I barely withstood the one from these past few days, not without a considerable amount of help, from what I've managed to find out."

"Help? What are you talking about?" Mom asks with her voice barely there. It must be terrible to face things with such graphic detail. I guess in her demonology classes, or whatever they're called, they haven't told her about real-life experiences, only the sweet theory. I hate to break it to her, but now, her nightmares about me are going to be more vivid than ever. She's probably picturing the help I'm talking about coming from a witch or something. I'm not sure if what she's about to hear will make it better or worse.

"There's another being, I don't know what to call it, whom I've also seen in situations where I've been incredibly frightened. In those moments, I can see him; he helps me calm down and protects me. I don't know to what extent, but I believe if I didn't die yesterday, it was thanks to him."

Their eyes are on me to the point where I think they've almost forgotten about the demon watching them. Mom clings to her Bible as if clutching at straws. To me, it's like a kid holding their teddy bear for safety—it's just a book with no more power than the information it holds. By the way she holds it, I sincerely hope the information inside is worth that trust.

"That must be an angel; it can't be anything else." Mara sounds truly hopeful.

"I don't know, I can't be sure of anything anymore. According to Grandma, angels and demons don't coexist, yet I see these two here, in this very space. Neither of them runs away in the presence of the other. I don't know, but I'm grateful. He knows it; I told him yesterday."

"But do you talk to him?" Mom sounds calmer.

"With both."

"But, Jade, you don't talk to the devil." We say this simultaneously, showing her that I know this information by heart.

"Mom, I need you to understand that I'm not telling you a horror story; this," I point to my room, covered with posters of Daniel and, of course, the demon, "It's my reality, the only one I know, and in it, everything comes together. Things aren't just black and white; they mix in some parts, creating gray areas, you know? I will talk to both of them."

"How long have you been seeing this angel?" Mom's question is directed at a topic I don't want to touch, not today, not ever.

"Since I was very young." Is all I'm going to say. I don't want to open that door; I wouldn't be able to close it again. We would have to go back to the times when they used to ask things to the noise under my bed—a very painful memory, even now.

"Does anyone else know about this?" Mara asks.

"No one, absolutely no one, and it will stay that way." Obviously, they want to know if I've told Daniel anything. Who else among my many friends could they mean? But no, I've never shared this with him; that's the truth. Even though we both know it, we'll probably never talk about it. Some things are better left alone, and this is one of them.

They look at each other, then at me, and finally at the demon in the corner. For Mom, it must be terrible to find out that her youngest daughter talks to demons. But It's Mara who speaks up.

"Jade, we've been looking into the abilities you have, like healing people and such. All of this has attracted the attention of demons, which is why you find it almost impossible to get rid of them. Each time you stand up to them, when you face them, it's as if..."

"Like if I were earning points."

"Yes, it's like you're building up this scorecard, and that's when the angels step in to defend you. But if you succumb into the demons and join their side, they won't protect you anymore. Your gifts must be used for the right side, or you might end up losing them."

"The right side."

"Jade, those gifts are meant for good, and there are demons out there fighting to keep you from using them the way you're supposed to. You've become an adult, and it's time for you to decide whom you're going to serve."

"Now that I have to make a choice... what if I just do nothing? Would I lose them? It's worth thinking about, right? Not having them would cancel out the demonic persecution, wouldn't it? And I could finally know what normal feels like, just for once."

Mom's face twists with anguish; she never imagined that I didn't consider myself normal, let alone the idea of wanting to be. Mara keeps going; there are things they want, just like me, to be said once and for all.

The Game...Jade

"Jade, unfortunately, you don't have that choice. Demons don't know how to act around you; some attack you and others defend you, right? I guess it's the same deal with the angels."

I try my best to keep my face neutral. It took me years to maintain a calm appearance in the presence of demons, and I've usually been successful. But this situation is different. When someone wants to keep a secret and you know how it goes among regular people, they spill the tea to their closest friends, swearing them to secrecy. It's impossible to figure out how the info leaked and became public knowledge.

In my case, I'm the only one who knows about what happened with the demons defending us at the hotel, and I'm absolutely sure I didn't tell either of them.

My head starts to spin. I used to think they'd recently turned into religious fanatics, their actions lacking any real credibility. Now, I'm not so sure. I keep my mouth shut; anything I say would just confirm what they're saying, and that would automatically put me in a position where I have to accept everything else, and I'm just not ready for that yet.

"Jade, we know it's true, just like we know that when you're with Daniel, at least most of the time, you don't see them. They've been given orders to stay away from you."

Gods! This is all too much; my mind is racing, dismissing one theory after another. The top one on the list is that they implanted a chip in me when I was very young, tracking my every move and knowing everything I did. The second, which freaks me out the most, is the idea that they are actually upping their connection with god, and he assigned angels to keep an eye on me.

I mean, if the demon in my room is in charge of me—and I don't doubt that anymore—why wouldn't god do the same? Not for me, of course, but maybe for them. Perhaps they've turned all goody-goody or something. "When you're with Daniel," that's a bait I can't ignore. I can almost taste it in my mouth; I'm choosing my words as carefully as I can.

"Orders to leave me alone."

Mara gains new confidence and keeps talking. Until now, she wasn't even sure if her words were making any sense in my head, but now she knows they are and can't miss this chance. She speaks slowly, trying to keep my attention.

"They have orders to leave you alone because the moments you spend with Daniel are a gift, a reward for your resistance against demons, and they're not allowed to interfere and ruin it. Once you're in the house, well, somehow, this space belongs to them, and that's when they come after you. That's precisely what we aim to prevent."

No one ever hinted that they had a clue about what's going on in my life, let alone what's going through my head. My grandma knew what I might be going through from past references, but she was never sure about anything. I can't fathom how they know all of this. Mara could be making educated guesses, but it's the accuracy that blows my mind. She's not just throwing ideas out there; she is convinced of what she's saying. And, even against my will, I'm sure of what she's saying, too.

Everything makes sense now—the bizarre way demons react to me and, above all, the amazing moments I've spent with Daniel. I've even labeled it a godsend, and I'm fully aware that this situation is anything but normal.

This friendship that sprouted between Daniel and me out of thin air has many shades of something beyond the ordinary. In fact, he knows things about me, and he doesn't seem to mind how weird I am.

I can't hear anything else but the pounding of my own blood, matching the speed at which my heart pumps it. The sound is loud enough to drown out everything else, allowing me to focus only on my own words. What if everything Mara says is true?

"Jade, a lot has gone down in our family, and we've been unraveling some of it, including this situation with you. We need to stick together to find a way to break you free from this. It's definitely getting worse, and just looking at you, we can tell. I've never seen you like this, scared perhaps, but... this has brought you very near to death; we know it."

I'm aware, too. I see Mom looking into my eyes, trying to uncover what I'm thinking. My brain drills into me, hitting me with the words Daniel once said, "Life has its moments, both uplifting and challenging, but going through them alone doesn't quite cut it."

Back then, it felt impossible to imagine someone being there for me in these situations. Honestly, I've never had someone close to me in my life since my grandparents passed away. I know Daniel is around; he's reminded me numerous times, but it's different. I wouldn't talk to him about this even though we both knew. I don't know why; it's like sharing a dark secret, being part of a murder plot, or something even worse—that's the vibe it gives me.

Still, just the thought of having someone who has an idea of what I'm going through is appealing. Maybe it's the hope that someone else might watch me die in case everything goes as badly as I fear, and those won't be demon eyes that I see last. The chance to see some compassion, even in a pair of human eyes, and not having to beg a demon once again to endure the disgust I cause them; to stay and keep me company while their superior torments me, sounds intriguing, to say the least.

Unable to help it, I seek out my demon. I want to hear his opinion on all of this. Hope starts to tempt me, and I would love to surrender completely into its arms. But the distrust within me runs so deep that, yes, I want a demon's perspective, something to balance the scales. I search for his eyes, but his stare is fixed on the floor; he won't look at me anymore. The decision will have to be mine alone. Darn it! It must be the infamous coming-of-age thing, but the one getting the short end of the stick is me, no matter how you look at it.

I'm so tired, not just physically, from these past few days but also, morally, I feel incredibly satisfied. I'm tired of a life where I have no one to talk to, although, to be honest, I can't imagine telling them anything. Maybe if I started by listening, it would be easier. Talking; that's something they're pretty good at.

Maybe if I focus on listening, I might achieve something. And if that's the case, if I could make my demon-free life—the one I've only enjoyed briefly—become something permanent, or, speaking more cautiously, prevail for longer periods where they stay away, it would be heavenly; at least for me.

"Should I respond now?"

Mom smiles slightly. I haven't said no; that's something. I'm aware of that, too. Mara replies:

"No, right now, the most important thing is for you to rest and recover from these days. Once you decide what you want to do, we can focus on that. I mean, if you want our help or if you prefer to handle things on your own."

"It's possible I might not, but I want to think about it."

Mom reaches out to touch my hair as a caress, and I pull away immediately. I'm definitely not ready for that much closeness. Mara understands; she, especially, has never touched me except accidentally, and I hope that doesn't change.

"Mom, let her rest. She needs sleep." She says, urging her to leave the room. I keep my eyes closed, unable to fall asleep. I have a lot to ponder. Grandma, what would you do in my place?

If I can't consider the demons' opinions, then I have no choice but to consider the perspectives of two people who are the most important in my life: my grandma and, of course, Daniel. I don't know what Grandma would say in this particular case, but from what I could see, she was always willing to help, especially when it came to family. Without a doubt, it was for that very reason that she, along with my grandpa, took care of me. And perhaps the most important thing to consider is her unwavering faith in god.

However, there are many things about that faith that I doubt when I think about it a little. The demon killed Clemen, and no one could stop it. On the other hand, I know for sure that my grandma, unable to do anything else, prayed for me constantly. And maybe, just maybe, even when the demon attacks me, it hasn't been able to finish me off because her prayers made me more resilient. It's a possibility.

As for what Daniel might think about family unity, well, he doesn't like me being alone. He says it's not good, and I'm not sure how to take that; it has always seemed easier to me, although life seemed different when my grandparents were around. Daniel might be right about that, even though Mom and Mara aren't even remotely like my grandparents were.

Now, if I didn't consider so many factors and just focused on what happened in these last three days, of course, seeing it all just the way I see it: a demon attacked me with all its might, and an angel intervened to prevent its attack from being deadly. That's it. I didn't ask for either of them; they're just here. I can't just remove them from my life either; they're a part of it. I don't know the "whys" and the "hows," and I need help to understand what's happening to me, even if it's just a little; whether I'm ready or not to face it, it's going to happen. I used to think it would be a relief if this managed to kill me; it would have meant being reunited with my grandparents. Now, it would only mean leaving Daniel behind, and I can't do that.

So, I have no other choice. I'll accept their help, and if this really has something to do with god—a matter downright terrifying from my point of view—I just hope I can live up to his expectations, which have always felt like too much for a mere human like me. But if, as Mara said, my reward for resisting the demons is time with Daniel, that might lead me to think that god not only exists but is truly magnificent. Just this situation might make me take a leap of faith as monumental as the world itself.

Well, I've made up my mind. I'll let them help me, and even though it's completely against my analytical nature, I'll have to pay attention, try to learn, and, most importantly, do what they ask without complaining, trusting them blindly. If I give in to my doubts, I'll end up dead sooner than I can say it. But if I can delay that moment for however long, it means more time with Daniel. How amazing.

Just before closing my eyes to finally sleep, a thought hits me, making the pit in my stomach come to life again. I always used to think the times when my dreams magically transported me to Daniel's house, or brought him to my room, were just that—incredible dreams.

Of course, I doubted everything when Sebastián, right after the tour started, asked me questions about Daniel's house, and I answered all of them with a hundred percent accuracy. I was so embarrassed then, having to admit I'd actually been there because I wanted to be. That was the only way I could project myself.

But this time, the demon followed me here, which means the projection works both ways. Daniel's words were, "He can't touch you while you're there." It wasn't a dream, I'm sure of it. So, the times Daniel has been here, he truly has been here; I didn't just dream it.

Gods! How many times have I paced around the room in the last few hours? I feel like the most ridiculous person on the planet. Anyone else in my shoes would be exploring the possibilities this could mean. Daniel can come here, not as something unconscious, but perfectly controlled. He can find out what I'm really thinking or ask me about things I don't want him to know, and I would talk about it, thinking it's just a dream. Or he could find out about my dealings with the demons. I don't know if, being a projection, he could see them. Well, a regular person would think about that, but not me, and that's the most embarrassing part.

All that's on my mind are the outfits I've worn to sleep when he's been here. How dreadful! They're the most comfortable ones I have, so they're the most horrifying ones you can imagine! You can picture them, right? We all have one or more, I know, but can you imagine wearing it in front of someone who, for you, is the most incredible being to ever walk the planet? I bet you can't! How awful! Please say you understand, even just a little.

It's weird. I can't remember what he was wearing, and honestly, why does it even matter? Nothing could overshadow his impressive shape. I've seen him in mismatched, totally crumpled clothes, and even though I've teased him, deep down, I know it doesn't matter at all. One look into those fabulous eyes and everything else just fades away; if you manage to shift your stare a little towards his face, or even more, his spectacular body, ha!

How could I remember what he was wearing? One thing's for sure: they definitely weren't shorts. Trust me, I'd remember that no matter what. Unlike me, well, I barely mess up my hair when I sleep. That's something, isn't it? Who am I kidding? Now, my brain is racing over what I could wear, just in case. Oh, but of course! I plan to fix this disaster; I don't have much, if anything, to wear. Why have I never bought a glamorous gown? Easy, why would I need one? I'm more of a shorts and t-shirts kind of sleepwear girl, that is, if I can find any shorts. Usually, it's just the shi... Ugh, I don't want to think about it anymore.

I know! A while ago, I bought this oversized t-shirt that says Monterrey, stretched all the way across. It's really wide, imagine, so the word Monterrey, in big letters, fits and still has plenty of space. It's like it belongs to a ten-feet-tall giant, so it covers me almost down to my knees. I don't know why they've become trendy; I guess because they're comfy, and they serve my purpose perfectly. I can practically run inside it, and no one would notice, perfect! I know, I know, my original plan was a glamorous gown, but remember I don't have one? This one, at least, is new.

I jump out of bed, find it at the bottom of the drawer, and put it on. I'm not taking any more chances. Now, I'll try to shut down my brain so it won't give me any more surprises, and I'll sleep as much as I can. Mara's schedule will make the tour look like child's play, I'm sure of that, and I need all the rest I can get. Honestly, it feels like I haven't slept in ages. At least now, I'm, if not satisfied, then at least calm about my outfit. I roll over in bed and see the demon. If he could laugh, I can just imagine his laughter.

What an incredible feeling it is to sleep peacefully. Maybe for you it's something common, so much that you hardly even notice it. How lucky you are! I check the edge of my curtain, where the dawn light usually seeps through, trying to figure out how much longer I can sleep. It's still dark; I can be quite lucky sometimes.

Rocío Blisswealth

I shift on my mattress, searching for a position that will quickly whisk me away into dreamland. But as I turn, in the spot where my second pillow should be, I see his eyes—those blessed eyes that just a few hours ago I thought I'd never see again. I fought hard to resist the attack, just for this moment, to see them and find my reflection in them. Due to the darkness, I can't see it, but I know it's there.

As I watch him, my mind replays all the anguish I experienced during those damn seventy hours. I didn't care about the physical pain it could cause me; the only thing I couldn't bear was the thought of him not making it and his presence fading away forever, leaving me in the deepest void imaginable.

He makes an effort, which is evident, and draws a soft smile on his lips. However, I can't reciprocate. The lump in my throat is using the strength that could move the muscles of my lips just to stay where it is. He remains still; I reach out my hand to his chest and place it there, afraid that the image might vanish at my touch. My fingertips gently stroke the area beneath which his heart beats, strong and clear. I press my hand against it; I need to confirm it's still there; he keeps allowing me to examine him.

My hand travels to his face; I need to feel the warmth of his skin. As my index finger brushes it, treating it like an invaluable treasure, a tear escapes from my eyes, and he catches it with his hand. I have completely lost the embarrassment of crying in his presence. Now, all I care about is not losing sight of him. He holds my face with the tips of his fingers, guiding my gaze to his. Despite his gentle smile, his incredible eyes have also welled up. He moves his forehead to touch mine, and I can no longer contain the fear of losing him that I've bottled up during these days.

"Come near me, Jade. Hug me, please."

In one swift motion, I move closer to him and press my body against his side, resting my head on his shoulder. He hugs me tightly, releasing the pressure I've been carrying from this pressure cooker I've become without realizing it until I could touch him. I cry, burying my face in his neck, and at the same time, he, amidst sobs, keeps kissing my head and holding me close with all his strength.

This, precisely this, is what terrifies me—the thought of losing the chance to be so close to him that not even a tattoo could fit between us. Close enough to experience absolute peace, replacing my anguish. If there were any doubts about my plans from now on, this moment in his arms would dissolve them completely. If after every confrontation, every fight that awaits me, if after all that, I can come here to this space under his neck and recover myself, I have no objections.

I'll do whatever it takes, just as I said before, without a word of complaint, to keep this man walking the face of the earth. I couldn't live any other way; once I've been in his arms, there's no turning back, not even a chance.

My breathing has steadied, leaving behind the jagged sobs, and has become deep. It took me longer than him to reach this point; his breath on my hair had settled into a calm rhythm for a while now.

"I had to see you just to ensure you're alright." He says, not letting go of me.

"I told you I was, but I'm glad you wanted to check." I pull back, grabbing the pillow to prop up my head and admire him. Now, he smiles with a stronger commitment, using all the muscles in his face, not just his lips. He turns on his side to face me.

His eyes are focused on my t-shirt—luckily, I changed! He tugs it sideways to read it.

"Monterrey? Worried you might lose your way? I recall you used to leave a little note on the nightstand during the tour just to remember the city you were in."

"Yes, well... Daniel, how do you know I used to leave a note on the nightstand if I'd remove it when I got up?" A playful smile forms on his lips from side to side. "Forget it; I don't want to know, don't tell me!"

"It looks exceptionally comfortable, delightful."

"It is."

"Will you give it to me?"

"No."

"Selfish, if I may ask, why not?"

"Well, it happens to be the best pajama I have."

"Really? Quite avant-garde, aren't you?" He smiles a little more.

"No, just fashion-unaware, I suppose."

"Well, I must wholeheartedly commend your lack of fashion sense; I love that shirt."

"Me too. And now that you've caught me being selfish, I don't have to pretend. I won't give it to you, and that's my final word."

"You needn't actually give it to me. We both fit inside it. Want to see?" He lightly brushes his fingers against the edge of the shirt, around my thighs, as if he's about to lift it. My heart starts racing like it's in a high-speed race. In a split second, I grab the shirt's edge with both hands, sit on the bed, pull my knees up to my chin, and with almost no effort, I stretch it out, covering myself all the way down to my ankles. I wrap my legs with both arms, intertwining my hands around my forearms. In short, I become a human knot, with the shirt in the middle.

"I won't verify that; I trust you completely. Thank you very much." His laughter bursts out instantly; the bed shakes, almost throwing me off balance, but I hold my ground, not moving an inch. I'm starting to get the hang of these projections; only the people involved can pick up on them; otherwise, someone would have already come to find out why there's so much fuss. Although, if my mom overheard, she'd probably assume it was some lively chat between the demon and me, in which case, she wouldn't dare to enter. And that works just fine for me.

His loud laughter continues overwhelming me; I'm quite foolish, I know, but that's just me. What can I do? As soon as he catches his breath, he kneels next to me, pulling me into his arms, all without me budging an inch.

"You're adorable! I simply adore you; did you know that?"

"Of course I do! Do you think it's easy to survive being like this? I face this every minute; it's downright unbearable, I've told you before."

"Please, don't ever change."

The Game…Jade

He kisses me, the very kiss I'd been longing for since he arrived, and one I didn't dare to request due to the tears. It's a kiss that feels like heaven. I quickly free my hands and wrap my arms around his waist. When he lets go of my lips, he lies back again and asks me to do the same; I nestle my head on his shoulder.

"Rest well, my gorgeous; you need it."

"When I wake up, you'll be gone, won't you?"

"That's right."

"Alright, you too rest."

I tilt my face up to him, and he leans in to kiss me; seconds later, I've fallen asleep. Really, I can be quite lucky sometimes.

Rocío Blisswealth

Chapter XII
Open in case of emergency

I wake up feeling brand new, with an absolute determination to do exactly what I'm told. After a bath, I search for Mara around the house. To my surprise, I found Mom in the kitchen, cooking breakfast. Mom, despite liking it, never cooks. In fact, she's hardly ever at home. I guess things have changed around here, and I just hadn't noticed.

She tells me that Mara left early but will be back around noon. Perfect, I've got plenty of time. I sit down, and Mom hands me a plate of food. I can't help but feel like I'm on tour; I really don't care what she serves. I'm so hungry that it doesn't matter; I just eat it.

I let her know I'll be out for a couple of hours but will be back right at 12:00. I grab some money and dash out; there's something I urgently need to get. Once at the store, I bought another shirt exactly like mine and some packaging to mail it. The only thing the store clerk has that might work for me is a tin can with the label "Open in case of emergency" on the front. It works for me. The lady packs it up, waits for me to prepare a note to put inside, and seals it. The note says:

Hey Daniel!

I've got insider info that you love these shirts· Hope you enjoy this one!

Jade

I've got the address memorized ever since he wrote me that letter, even though I'd never used it before. The post office is really close to home, so I head there, and once I arrive, I find out it'll take seven days for the package to reach his hands. Imagine being that t-shirt inside the can! I could touch all over his skin without him ever suspecting a thing, of course.

When I got home, I found Mara at the door; she'd just arrived and asked if I was ready. Absolutely, there's no time like the present. We pass by the kitchen, and we ask Mom to come with us. She grabs her Bible and follows us upstairs. Once we reach the hallway, Mara asks:

"Don't you think it's better if we gather in Mom's room?"

"I'm sorry, it has to be mine. I don't feel comfortable anywhere else."

"But, Jade, the demon is there." Mom says anxiously.

"Mom, they're everywhere; you just can't see them. Besides, since you can't see this one either, just pretend he's not there, okay? Please."

"Mom, it'll be wherever she prefers." Mara says in an authoritative tone, and Mom reluctantly agrees.

I have to admit, even though I've had terrifying moments in my room, Daniel's photos are plastered on my walls, too. They remind me of all the good things I could enjoy if I manage to defeat the demons; I need to have them close by. As for the demon, it doesn't scare me anymore; it makes me feel accompanied. I guess this situation is weird, but in the bizarre world I live in, it's just another one of my quirks. The truly strange part is that I'm about to wage war against his kind, yet, at least to my eye, it doesn't belong to that group. Honestly, I'd like to keep this one with me, but I doubt they'll let me.

Once in the room, I try to ignore the demon's corner to avoid feeling guilty, and focus my gaze on a poster of Daniel, my favorite one. He's sitting directly facing me, dressed all in white. That makes his eyes incredibly striking, and it feels like he's watching me. Maybe that's why I love it; he makes me feel accompanied too.

Mara takes a seat in front of me and tries to explain about a bunch of demons that have been in the family, but I don't pay her any attention.

"Mara, just tell me what I have to do. Keep it short, please."

"I wanted to clarify why they're here with us, and look, what..." I can see my demon getting restless; he moves from his corner and dashes to another, growling a few times and staring at me. I'm sorry, darling, but I won't stop now.

"Mara, they'll be here soon. Trust me, there's no time."

Mom reaches out her hand for me to take, and Mara does the same. It seems they hold hands when they pray. I hope it's not necessary to make this work because, honestly, it's just asking too much of me; I can't do it.

"What do I have to do? Tell me now! Without hands, Mara, it has to work without hands."

Whatever they have planned, it will work; I can sense it because the tingling in my hands has never been this intense. And this time, I can feel it all the way up to my elbows; I'm pretty sure I could count from one to ten, and it would still work.

"It's a scripture you need to recite."

"Mara, we tried that once, and it didn't work. Are you sure?"

"I am, I am. Please, just read it!"

I see them coming through the walls, almost as if the walls were made of smoke; they effortlessly pass through. I never heard them speak anything other than my language, but not this time. They keep repeating a set of words that sound like Latin to me over and over again. One by one, they make their way through the walls of my room, which, despite being spacious, now feels tiny. They're all totally different from one another; there are four of them so far. My demon has curled up in his corner, covering his ears with his hands, whimpering in a way he never has before.

Another one shows up, yelling at the top of his lungs, reciting the same incantations. I guess they're supposed to have some effect on me, but until now, all they've managed to do is scare me, and that's not news; I'm used to feeling that way.

Suddenly, I heard Mara's voice. "I'm scared." She's on the verge of tears. And how could she not be? These damn demons seem capable of anything, and they're willing to prove it. Even if she can't see them, she can feel them. For the first time, I feel sorry for them; they are about to face something they are completely unaware of, no matter how much they have heard about it. I remember at this moment that Ángel said he tried to prevent them from killing me, so I must be the one they're protecting. I reach out and grab Mara tightly by the arm; she doesn't move, frozen in her spot. I pull her harder and push her behind me; I do the same with Mom, and they both stand there, tears rolling down their cheeks, unable to pray. Concentrating isn't easy when you're being screamed at, and fear takes over. But somehow, Mara manages to hold the paper with the writing so I can see it.

A sixth demon enters, joining the prayers of the others, staring at me with fury in his eyes. I can only see them—they're enormous; their bald heads are grazing the ceiling. Because of the darkness they've created, I can't really make out their color, but their skin seems wrinkled and damp, with a slimy, foul-smelling liquid dripping down their bodies.

A couple of them have twisted and hunched backs, making their faces much closer to mine than the others. Another, in particular, catches my eye—

its chest, visible through its clothing, is somewhat transparent, revealing a fluorescent liquid in reddish tones that swirls inside, forming small whirlpools, moving rapidly when it gives me a look. Their eyes are all yellowish, but right now, they appear bloodshot. Some have sharp teeth, while others lack them entirely. Three of them have bony hands, covered only by rough skin, and the rest have plump hands. Yet, all of them have four limbs, a body, and a head with two eyes, a nose, and a mouth; in other words, their appearance is humanoid.

Mara shakes the paper in front of me; she probably thinks I'm frozen, but no, I'm just waiting, listening to my instincts, to that voice screaming at me that there are seven now. One is missing, and I have to wait until they're all together. I have no doubts anymore; it will work.

"Wait, Mara, it's not time yet, just a few more seconds."

She nods and keeps holding the paper for me to see. And just as I said, only a few seconds later, the seventh, the most terrifying and repulsive of all, enters, chanting the same incantations. It moves closer, placing its hideous face just inches away from mine, letting drool drip from its chin and chest, all the while never stopping its prayers, the same ones as the others. It is making me feel nauseous; it stinks so bad! Its skin is reddish, like the shade of raw meat, and that's exactly how it looks as if its body had been entirely stripped of its skin. Something inside my chest jumps as if trying to escape. They are getting closer, and I can see Mom and Mara, who stand behind me with their eyes closed. The demons are flailing and trembling, never stopping for a second, reciting the same unintelligible words.

Suddenly, I realized this is my moment, the opportunity I longed for to have them, just like the other damned one had Daniel and me, torturing us. It's not the same demon, but what does it matter? If this works, I'll be waiting for it. I can't help but smile, and one of them lets out a howl that echoes through the room. Their prayers intensify, and I notice something I've never seen before—there's a tremor, even if it's slight, in their hands. The tingling has spread throughout my entire body, and I tremble too, partly from the force of this energy, partly from the fear it instills in me. I raise my chin to look them in the eyes. A thousand things can go wrong, and it leaves a hollow feeling in my stomach. I assume Ángel is somewhere helping me, but what if he isn't? My feet start to grow cold, and the sensation of wading into icy water returns. I'm scared, please; I can't afford to falter now.

Rocío Blisswealth

262

I turn my gaze towards Mara's paper; she notices and brings it closer to me. The voice inside me screams over the demonic chants, "Seven times! Repeat it seven times!"

I begin, not paying much attention to the words. I read it once; the howls become so intense that I can barely hear my own voice, and the air starts swirling within the room. Two times, they react as if they're being jolted with pain in their hideous bodies; now they know what we felt for seventy hours. One of them, the reddish-skinned one, lunges at me, trying to make me stop; it startles me, and he almost succeeds, but he runs into the same invisible barrier that stopped the previous one. Thank you, Ángel!

With all the fear in the world, I continue, three times, four, five. Three of them collapse to the ground due to the intense pain my words inflict upon them. They turn to look at me; hatred is all I can perceive from them; they are incapable of begging for mercy, only to hate me even more. Six times, their bodies tremble, and my demon screams along with them. Their disgusting skins finally reveal the destruction caused by what I'm doing, opening up with huge wounds that pierce them all over, oozing a nauseating fluid that, as it drips onto the floor, intensifies the coldness in my feet, creeping up towards my calves. Seven times.

I can't understand what's happening; their bodies twist amid screams, like when clothes are flipped inside out when pulled over the head. Their mouths, which, although enormous, are not big enough for this, tear apart completely, revealing the interior of their bodies while the outside remains hidden. At the end of the horrifying process, the bloody masses of skin left on my bedroom floor keep moving, struggling to return to their original forms, producing noises resembling a hungry stomach. Terror makes me tremble uncontrollably; the sight of this is simply horrifying. Finally, they stop moving, blending slowly into the darkness they had created, and with it, they fade away. There are no more cries, no more prayers; the air has calmed, and the awful stench has dissipated.

My body stays still, and my breathing steadies. I turn around to see Mara and Mom. Surprisingly, the breeze was real; I never would have guessed. I always thought those things only happened in my head, but there's proof in the way the wind tousled their hair. They are terrified; I don't know what they felt, but they definitely didn't see it coming.

"Okay, those aren't there anymore."

The Game…Jade

"Are they gone?" Mom asks, still teary.

"Yes, they are. What else do I need to do?"

"But isn't that enough?" Mara is surprised, still catching her breath.

"It's not that; it's just that if they have to leave, well…"

"We need to investigate; you'll have to give me a few hours."

"Weren't you scared?" Mom asks.

"More than you can imagine."

"I don't know how you pulled it off."

"I didn't do anything, Mom. I mean, it didn't come from me."

"I know. I'm certain that god bestowed it upon you, and he's the one safeguarding you. I can't imagine what you saw, but if it's anything like what we felt, it must have been horrendous."

"Well, god made sure I didn't fall victim to the terror they cause, although it's a whole different story when you see them with the advantage on your side, not in the position of their toy. This time, they couldn't lay a finger on me."

I can see the pain in her eyes, but now is not the time for pity. According to my watch, more than forty-five minutes had passed; it didn't feel that way to me. In my perception, everything happened in just a couple of minutes.

"Jade…"

"What's up, Mom?"

"The one here…" She points to the demon's corner. "Is he gone?" No, he's not gone because the problem wasn't with him. I needed to address him specifically, and I didn't. It didn't take much effort to include him in the demon-disappearing act, but I simply chose not to. I look at him, and he looks back at me. He knows he's still here because I wanted it that way; however, there's not the slightest hint of gratitude in his eyes. I couldn't care less.

"No."

"Why haven't you dealt with him yet?"

"Not yet."

"But, Jade, for the love of god."

"I'm sorry, Mom, but I haven't grown that love yet. So, if that's the reason I should get him out of here, it won't happen today."

"But, considering what happened?"

"Mom, today was against his enemies, right? I mean, god's enemies. I just acted as a hitman, and he gave me the weapons I needed. The rest will take time, and if he clearly approves of it, I don't see why you shouldn't."

"Mom, Jade is right; god doesn't seem to mind. Let everything happen in its own time. Come. Let's go to the kitchen so you can help me find out more information." Mara takes her out of my room.

I can't bring myself to be without him; he has been my only company for a long time. What does it matter if he doesn't thank me? What does it matter if I'm not essential to him? I don't keep him because he needs me but because I, even though it hurts to admit it, do need him so that I don't feel so alone.

"Mara, tell me something. Do you still think my time with Daniel is a compensation for what I do?" I ask as she leaves my room.

"Without a doubt."

"Then ask god what else he wants me to do; I want to keep racking up points."

It's been days since the whole seven demons showdown, and let me tell you, Mara put together her list like it was Santa's wish list or something. I've spent hours getting rid of demons I've never seen before, but always hoping that among them, the damn mirror one shows up so I can finally take it down. No luck yet, though. Sometimes, I'm the one on the prowl. As soon as a demon realizes it's next on the list, it barges into my room, trying to stop me. And honestly, I still can't shake off the fear they provoke me, so I'd rather be the one attacking first. Alongside these demons I've never seen, I've come across names of ancestors I've never heard of either. Seriously, what has my family been up to for so many generations? I can't imagine how they've dug up all this information.

The little one says the phone in my room is just a decoration, and honestly, she's right—I never bother picking it up. Calls are hardly ever for me, so I muted it. That way, when the door opens and I see her eyes, I can already guess what's up. I just smile and throw myself on the bed, grabbing the receiver.

"Hello?"

"Sweetheart, how are you?"

"Carmen! All good, what about you?"

"Oh, I'm doing well, but there's a question on our minds, and I thought I'd give you a call to get it cleared up, alright?"

"Sure thing. What's up?"

"Could you explain, with all the dots and commas, what an 'emergency case' means to you?" I can't hold back the laugh, making it impossible to answer.

"My bad, Carmen. Did Daniel not pop the can?"

"No, dear, the can arrived a couple of hours ago. When he showed it to me, I asked him to open it. He looked deadly serious and said, 'No, it's for an emergency case.' Okay, I said, and when would that be? To which he replied, 'That's what I'd like to know.'"

"But, Carmen, it's just packaging."

"Oh, let me tell you, an hour later, his sister came for a visit, found him sitting with the can on his lap, asked what it was, and he said, 'A gift, I suppose.' Naturally, she asked him to open it to see what was inside, receiving the same response as I did."

"Carmen..."

"I should warn you; he doesn't know I'm calling you. When I suggested talking to you, he refused, thinking you'd probably laugh at him, and he preferred to figure it out himself. But it's been two hours with it on his lap, and he's gotten nowhere. So, his sister and I decided to give you a call."

"Well, thanks for that. Let me tell you, when I went to the store, I asked for packaging I could mail, and that was the only one they had. The front slogan was the least of my worries."

"I thought so."

"Do me a favor, tell Daniel the CIA just called urgently, saying if he doesn't pop the can within three hours upon arrival, the inside will self-destruct, and he'll never know what's in it. Sounds good?"

"Fantastic. Jade, thanks a million."

"Don't mention it. Feel free to call whenever."

"I will. Sending you a big kiss."

"For you too."

No way! This guy never stops surprising me. How can he take the phrase "in case of emergency" so literally? It's mad subjective, totally different depending on who's reading it. Although, with me, he probably thought it was some special defense against demons or something. I can't stop laughing.

It's been almost a month since I got back home, and I've never felt so comfortable within these walls. Mom and Mara are thrilled about the big task we've accomplished. I guess, according to the religion they fervently profess

Rocío Blisswealth

(which, by the way, I have no clue about the denomination because I stopped paying attention to that a long time ago), they're on the brink of heading to heaven, shoes and all, when the time comes, no doubt.

Their perspective and mine differ completely. For them, they're carrying out a task assigned by god. But for me, it's all about breaking free from my tormentors, ditching real enemies, and if, in the process, I can do a service that earns me some points, even better!

However, what excites me the most is thinking that none of them can attack Daniel like the previous one did—by the way, how sneaky is the darn one. When I get frustrated because their hunt doesn't bring him here, I spend long hours sitting on my bed in the dark, with the door open so I can peep at the mirror, just waiting. Usually, I sit on my hands to keep them from shaking, and I check out my demon every now and then. I know he won't sit still if he senses him coming, and sure, nothing's happening yet, but the day will come when I face him, I just know.

I'm dying to see Daniel. There are no upcoming gigs in Mexico, and I have no idea how long I'll have to wait. If it weren't for his nighttime visits, the wait would be totally unbearable. By the way, in case you're wondering, he opened the can! He had his t-shirt on during one of the occasions he came to see me—the only time I've noticed what he was wearing. I suppose you can imagine; I burst into laughter the moment I saw him. He tried every trick to shut me up until he finally caved and joined in my laughter, all while still teasing me for sending him packages with messages that were impossible to decipher.

Now that his visits are more frequent, I can tell that the projections can't fill the gap that's growing in my chest as time goes on without seeing him. It must be like talking on the phone with someone you really miss; the voice just isn't the same as having the person there. I can hug him, even crash in his arms, but it still feels like a phone call. I can feel his love, but it doesn't quite fill me up. I don't know if that makes sense.

The bottom line is, I miss him more every day. I listen to his music as much as I can; it makes me feel at ease. Still, I'm hanging in there, that's all. I would've preferred not getting so used to him. In fact, I tried not to, but that ship has sailed; I can't even breathe if he's not by my side. The more time I spend with him, the stronger the need to have him close becomes. After two months with him on tour and soaking up his vibes, I'm seriously missing him now.

The Game...Jade

There are moments when the knot in my throat struggles to escape as sobs. I still hold it back, but it's becoming increasingly challenging to keep it under control. In the meantime, until I get to see him again, I mean, I don't cut the demons any slack. I can't help but wonder, will I ever get rid of them? I don't mean all the demons out there, just the ones connected to my family. I'd like to know. I go to sleep, hoping that Daniel will arrive, but he doesn't show up. Where are you?

The sound of the phone from Mom's bedroom wakes me up; it must be six in the morning. No one answers. Darn it! I have to do it myself.

"Hello." I say with a hoarse voice from sleep.

"Darling, did I wake you up?"

"Carmen! Don't worry. How are you?" Oh, please, I hope she called to get me in touch with Daniel.

"Well, sweetheart, and I have excellent news for you."

"What are you talking about, Carmen?"

"Daniel just arrived in Mexico City."

"Are you serious?!"

"Yes, he didn't want to let you know to give you a surprise; he said he owes it to you. You have a plane ticket waiting for you at the airport; your flight leaves in three hours. Is that enough time, or should I change it?"

"No, Carmen! No need. I'll make it in time."

"Great, then I'll let Raúl know to wait for you at Mexico City airport. Do you need anything?"

"Nothing, thank you so much; we'll talk soon."

"Of course, have fun."

The room is spinning again; it better stop soon because I need to pack my suitcase. I jump up and run to the shower. Luckily, during the tour, I got enough training to be ready in a matter of minutes. I tidy up my room and pack my suitcase, which I'm proud to say I can do within a time limit, and I boast of never leaving anything behind. Money, IDs, agenda, a pair of jeans, two t-shirts, and three sweaters, underwear, toiletries, a slightly more formal outfit just in case, of course, my favorite gown and boots, they work for every occasion, or almost.

I slip into my jeans, a white turtleneck sweater, and sneakers. From my room, I call a taxi; it will take ten minutes to arrive, more than enough time to let Mom and Mara know I'm leaving. I don't think they'll like the idea.

Rocío Blisswealth

268

I walk into Mom's room; she has just woken up and is surprised to see me bathed and ready at this hour.

"Where are you going so early?"

"To Mexico City; I'll call you from there."

Without giving her time to react, I go downstairs to Mara's room, suitcase in hand. Mom keeps talking behind me, but I've decided not to pay attention.

"Mara." I woke her up. "I'm going to Mexico City; I'll call you later."

"But why are you leaving? You're going with Daniel, aren't you?" She asks, annoyed. I control my anger, but she can see it in my eyes.

"We agreed that this topic was beyond your reach. Well, that hasn't changed at all; it's none of your business."

"No, it's just that..."

"If what worries you is that a demon shows up, tell it where I am and to come find me. After all, I can get rid of them on my own now." The taxi I ordered honks, and I run out; they don't try to catch up with me anymore.

Everything was going great, at least for this past month. Things at home were calm until today when the most important thing for me returned to the scene. On the journey, I contemplate the idea of accumulating points. Will god truly consider what I do? As I'm less than two hours away from finally being able to hug Daniel, I'm starting to believe it.

Mom keeps pushing the idea that I should love god, but my grandma's phrase about fearing him fits me better. For me, the concept of love is hard to understand, especially when it comes to god. I don't know him; people say many things about him, and depending on their religious beliefs, the image they paint of him can be very different. But when I reflect on my feelings, it's more about respect that I have for him. Even though my belief in the existence of demons is stronger than anything else, and I understand that everything has its opposite side, I can't doubt his existence. Mom insists that he loves me, but I find it hard to believe because why have I been so attacked by demons my whole life?

Ángel, however, is always there looking out for me; I'm sure of that, and he's definitely not a demon. So, he must belong to the other side, the good ones, which means that god must have sent him; I suppose they do not rule themselves. So, that makes me think that god is concerned about what might

The Game...Jade

happen to me. I don't get it all, but yes, I think I respect him simply because he's trying to keep me alive.

Airplanes are supposed to fly very fast, or else they'd crash, right? So why does it feel like this one is completely static in the same place? To make things worse, two seats ahead of me, there's a couple with a two-year-old who's turned our flight into a screaming concert. This does not make the minutes longer; it makes them stretch into eternity. Can someone please do us a favor and cover his mouth?

My chest burns, and something inside it doesn't stop moving; probably the anxiety of finally seeing Daniel that just won't give me a break. The passenger next to me looks at me, first in the eyes, then at the knee. I get it. I can't stop tapping my right foot up and down, and he must be getting annoyed. I say sorry and make an effort to stay still. I look out the window and see some movement; we are getting closer to the city, finally!

The anxiety turns into anguish, and I don't understand why. I think about Daniel; I want to see him, make sure he's okay, that the demon didn't harm him in any way. That's it; I haven't seen him since the attack, not in person, I mean. And I know the wounds won't be visible. But still, I'm convinced I can somehow measure the damage done. I'm sure of that; I just need to see him.

They announce that we're landing. My suitcase rests in the overhead compartment; I chose not to check in with the luggage because I knew it would gobble up precious time. The plane door opens, and I stand up, slinging the bag over my shoulder. I wish people would move faster.

Oh no! The couple with the screaming kid rushes ahead, blocking the aisle with their bags and suitcases. Not this time; they've annoyed me throughout the entire flight, and I won't allow them to do it any longer. Taking a step forward, I hop over one of their bags and the toddler from hell. The idea of turning around to apologize briefly crossed my mind, but that wouldn't be real. I just keep going. From the corner of my eye, I see the rest of the passengers doing the same until the couple decides to move their child from the aisle. I don't get why parents believe everyone is obliged to put up with their children; we're not.

For anyone familiar with it, the hallways at the Mexico City airport are extremely long, and people usually take their time walking unless they fear missing a flight connection. So, imagine I'm on the verge of missing a flight because, like the last time he showed up, I'm about to run. But this time, I'm not eager to see him; it's a mix of anxiety creeping in. Clutching my suitcase tightly, I sprint through the halls; my sneakers practically make no sound as I go.

I quickly reach the passenger exit, where the crowd is not letting me through. It doesn't matter; I won't ask for permission. I keep walking, and they eventually move aside until I reach the doors, which open to let me out. I dash out of the area, as if pursued by something, but it's the opposite; someone is waiting for me. Without slowing down, arms surround me, bringing me to a complete stop.

"Whoa, Jade, hold up! I'm right here."

Like waking up from a trance, I shift my gaze, locking eyes with Raúl. I ditch my attempt to keep running; anxiety and anguish are still running high. Putting in some effort but keeping it real, I smile at him and throw myself into his arms. I've missed him so much, too.

"Hey there, beautiful, the car is waiting for us." Without letting go of his arms, we make our way to the car, and once we're there, I can finally say hi properly.

"I couldn't wait to see you, Raúl!"

"Me too, kid. It's wild how you have this way of making people miss you, like, almost to the point where it's just too much to handle." He replies with a huge smile on his lips.

"I don't think you all missed me as much as I missed you."

"That's open for debate. Picture this: the moment Daniel called me, asking if I'd roll with him to see you, I straight-up ditched another plan just to be here with you." He keeps smiling. "And guess what? We racked up several thousand miles in the air while you barely scratched five hundred and ninety, or something like that, not even six hundred."

Feeling a knot in my throat, I reach out and gently touch his face, stopping at his chin and tracing his beard—a clear sign he didn't bother with a shave before showing up; it tickles the palm of my hand. My eyes get misty, but I fight to hold back the tears; I should be happy, not dealing with this hollow feeling inside. I pull his face closer to mine and plant kisses on both cheeks.

"I care about you a lot, Raúl."

The Game...Jade

"Okay, fine, you win. On your planet, five hundred and ninety miles are somehow more than several thousand." He smiles softly. "I knew you'd be very sensitive."

"And how did you know?"

"Daniel's in the same boat. Had to twist his arm to keep him at the hotel while I hustled over to pick you up. Suddenly, he's all smiles, and sometimes, like you're doing now, he just can't stop saying he's gotta see you."

"Thank you."

"Thanks, but why, lovely?"

"For everything, for coming to see me, for rolling with him, for saying what you just did, for missing me."

"Well, you're welcome. All those things are a pleasure." He throws his arm around my shoulders, kind of easing up the race of my heart, which has more horsepower than the car we're riding in.

I can already see the hotel; my lungs release air as if something's hitting me. Raúl smiles, probably checking if I can breathe again. I'd forgotten how good it feels to breathe when I'm close to Daniel. My lungs must remember because they're already trying to fill up with his scent, like a fish taken out of the water for a few seconds—intense and desperate. The car halts completely, and Raúl hands me the room key.

"Go ahead, kid, he's waiting for you."

I grab the key, ready to sprint, but he stops me by the wrist, warning me not to run or the hotel security will give me a hard time. Okay, okay, I'll behave. At least I'll give it a shot.

I step into the lobby, walking quickly, but keeping it within the bounds of decency. When I reach the elevator, the guard addresses me.

"Miss..."

Without waiting for any indication, I flash the room key, letting him know I'm a hotel guest and I won't be slowing down.

"I just wanted to wish you a good morning."

"Oh, I'm sorry. Good morning to you, too." I better keep myself in check; I'm making a fool of myself.

The elevator door opens, revealing the long hallway ahead. Why does my life seem to be filled with never-ending corridors? I guess it adds to the suspense. I check the room number on the key; I know this hotel well. It's one of the last rooms, and why not? Of course, it would be one of the last; someone

Rocío Blisswealth

wants me to die of anxiety before reaching the door. My chest tightens, and I struggle to catch my breath. The hallway yards zoom by under my feet, and at last, I reach the door. I raise my hand to knock, even though I have the key; I wouldn't dare enter without doing so. The door swings open before my knuckles touch it, and for a fraction of a second, I see his eyes, and then I meld into his arms, finally able to breathe.

He wraps his arm around my waist and, with the other, cradles my head in his hand, pressing me against him. In his arms, without needing to see his face, I can feel the damage that damn demon caused him as if I could see it in an X-ray. The area of his chest is full of scars, his arms, and his face too, though it suffered the least damage; it's all there. Tears stream down my face as he gently strokes my hair.

"I wanted to see you; I wanted to see you." He speaks softly.

I know that as soon as I separate from him and can see his body facing me in this dimension we move through, it will be impossible for me to estimate this again. My tears flow until they land on his shoulder. However, this time, my crying isn't born of pain; it's pure rage, and I find it easier to control. Now, it's him who takes the longest to calm down. I don't mind; I have all the time in the world to hug him. Once he's calm, he cups my face in his hands and looks straight into my eyes, smiling as he says, "There you are," as if my body, tied to his waist, wasn't enough proof. He always searches for what he sees moving inside my pupils. I do the same, looking for my reflection; yes, that's there too.

"Daniel, how many days will you be here?" I ask, afraid that it's only for a few hours.

"Three."

"And what are the plans for these days?"

"I have no idea, gorgeous. I'm just here to see you. Honestly, I can't come up with any plans; probably something Raúl prepared to explain why I'm here in case some reporter caught sight of me. But, you know, we always manage to slip away." I can hear him starting to smile.

"Well, that means I can stay here longer, then."

"Here?" He asks, frowning and looking around the room.

"No, here." I reply, lifting my hand and placing it on his chest. I really need this time with him; there will be an opportunity for anything once I recover from this absence.

"Please, feel free to stay as long as you want."

The Game...Jade

We curl up on the couch, and he slides his leg over mine, pulling me closer. I enjoy feeling him breathe and his gasp running through my hair, knowing that he is alive and healthy, at least to the extent of our human bodies. However, the total count of the wounds of his non-physical body has been burned into my memory. I'll go through them one by one; I'll find a way to locate that damn creature. Everything I've learned should help me get rid of him, to finish him before he decides to keep looking for what he didn't find on the first try. It has to be like that because I'm not going to stop looking for him. Probably, the damned one doesn't know it yet, but sooner or later, I'll find him. Today, I've become his worst enemy.

Rocío Blisswealth

Chapter XIII
But I guess, confession for confession

After spending a good chunk of minutes figuring out how to kick that demon to the afterlife, I've decided I'm not letting his vibe ruin this amazing time I've longed for so much. I'm focusing on the much more pleasant image of the guy I've got sitting next to me, so close that I finally get what sets his real presence apart from the version projected in my room.

My right arm is resting behind his back, at waist level, and my left arm wraps around until my hands meet in a circle. My head rests on his shoulder, and his arms hold me tightly at shoulder level. From here, I can hear his heart beating, maybe a hint louder than his projection, as if it's more on the surface, almost at the chest's forefront. The scent of his cologne, a dry and deep woodsy smell, wafts around, saturating my clothes and hair, something that doesn't happen with his other version. I guess you only carry the bare essentials during projection, and maybe the scent isn't that crucial, but this one is so delicious that it would totally be worth carrying.

I lift my face to kiss his chin, and against my lips, I feel the soft pins of his beard starting to show up. The veins in his neck match his moves with his breath, and I can hear the air flooding in, then emptying his lungs in long, deep pauses. The details, that is, the details of the functioning of a human body, are the ones that are not evident in projections. They are all those small things that are a normal part of our lives, everything that allows us to see that a human being is going through their day. It is what is not shown when you have projected yourself. I suppose it would be hugging a wax statue, but with warmth.

I love that he wears cowboy boots; they give him that bad-boy look that fascinates me, especially with the way he's been letting his hair grow since the tour started, now almost covering his neck like a chill chinchilla fur. His sky-blue cotton shirt wrinkles easily, a victim of my hugs, mirroring my tendency to cling to him, gently outlining his torso as if caressing it. Today, I don't feel the slightest bit of envy; I can do it too.

Luckily, the anxiety that hit me on the plane has almost completely disappeared. His chest shakes easily, and I hear laughter rising to his throat.

The Game…Jade

"Thanks for my gift."

"Did you like it?" I ask, joining in the laughter.

"I absolutely love it."

"I'm so glad, especially after the struggles to send it to you."

"What struggles?" He asks, intrigued.

"Oh, but can you imagine it's super easy for the CIA to grant you permits to send something straight from Monterrey to your lap?"

"I'll murder Carmen!" His laughter intensifies.

"Don't you dare, Daniel!" Catching his breath, he asks.

"You haven't spilled whether you enjoyed yours yet."

"My gift?"

"Of course."

"Daniel..."

I start to worry; I don't remember receiving anything. He lifts my chin to look at me, laughs, and points to his body from head to toe.

"Well, isn't this plenty for you? I mean, it wasn't a walk in the park to snag the permits for all of this to cruise the ocean and drop straight onto your legs." With the leg resting on mine, he applies pressure to prove his point. "And there's a bonus; knowing you, you wouldn't let me purchase you a thing, and truth be told, I've had all of this, in fact, for quite a few years already."

"Wow, you're splendid!" I caress his cheek and let a huge smile break out before he can question what I think. "As soon as I get to Monterrey, I'll swing by the store for a box of t-shirts. If this is your way of returning the favor, I say one box, make it two!"

He squints his eyes, smiles, and sighs, holding my chin with his fingertips, talking to me by brushing my lips.

"I've told you that I'm rather fond of you, haven't I?"

"Sometimes."

He seals my words with his lips, and a few seconds later, he interrupts the kiss.

"And are you fond of me?"

I find it pretty amusing the somewhat childish way he asks certain things as if he's qualifying his question with a not-so-subtle tone of reproach. I try not to laugh as I answer him.

"I've told you. A little bit."

Rocío Blisswealth

"But seriously, haven't I at least upgraded to the category of two little bits yet?"

"With today's gift, and not that I'm materialistic, but, honestly, it was super generous, you're almost at two little bits."

"Almost."

"Uh-huh."

"Alright, I'll give it my best shot to bridge the gap between 'almost' and 'two.'" He brings his lips close to mine and continues with the kiss he interrupted a minute ago. Gods! If he keeps this up, he'll quickly reach three or four little bits. Maybe even five.

I move a little away from him and practically request permission, like in a classroom style, to go to the restroom. He smiles and sets me free. Resting in his arms is genuinely delightful, but the body craves movement, and he rises from the couch as I do.

Suddenly, memories flood back of those magazines that used to rest on Mara's bedside table when I was a kid, filled with pictures of stunning models in the arms of the latest heartthrobs. I always believed it was their looks that brought them such luck. I finish brushing my hair, and I know it's not like that at all. I never considered myself glamorous; I barely wear makeup, and let's not even get into the whole fashion scene. However, the most handsome guy in the world is waiting for me in the other room, confirming that luck doesn't give a damn about your appearance.

I open the door and find him sitting on the armrest of the couch, eyes shut. It seems like he's thinking about something pleasant, judging by the soft smile on his lips. I walk in front of him, trying not to make a sound to let his thoughts flow. I'm startled when, without opening his eyes, he grabs me around the waist, pulling me into his arms and closing them around me. Without any resistance, I nestle against him, and he places his ear on my chest, squeezing me tight.

"Let me listen." He says in a hushed voice, almost fearing that whatever he wants to hear might escape with the volume of his voice.

Naturally, I comply. I don't make a single sound except for my breathing, and I quickly find something to occupy my hands. As he listens to a sound that seemingly takes longer to fade away than I thought, I start running my fingertips over his forehead, then down his nose, his cheeks, his lips, and along the contour of his hair—basically, everything within my reach. I stroke the incredibly smooth texture of his skin, and suddenly, a memory rushes back. The image of the demon lifting him into the air, grabbing him by the neck, showing its sharp claws just seconds before cutting off his chest. It was so close to destroying all of this that I now gently touch with my fingertips. I shudder, but his soft voice dissolves the haunting memory.

"Do you know what I'm listening to?"

"No, will you tell me?"

"Yes, I'm listening to myself."

"Really? And how did you get there?"

There's a knock on the door, and Raúl's voice makes itself heard, asking if he can come in. My right foot instinctively takes a step backward; I've always reserved my displays of affection for moments when we're alone. His arms hold me tighter and, seeing the futility of my efforts to pull away, I return my foot to its original position. He looks up a little with his eyes only half-open.

"Hold steady, it's fine. Come in, Raúl."

I can feel my face flush immediately, and I hide my gaze in his hair. Raúl, however, showing off his discretion, pretends not to pay attention to us, although it must seem strange to him to see us so close. Daniel laughs to himself; I can feel the movement of his ribs, and he hugs me tighter.

"Do you know what I'm up to, Raúl?"

"I suppose anything I come up with will be wrong, so why don't you both enlighten me?"

"I'm listening to myself."

"Of course, I should have figured, and Jade is like your own personal player, isn't she?"

"Not exactly, but she mentioned I'm in there." He points to my chest with a finger, not moving an inch away from me.

"Did I tell you that? I don't remember." I replied, surprised.

"Do you remember the day I gave you a ring on the phone right after the tour wrapped up?"

How can I forget it? That's when we both wanted to find out if the other had survived.

"Yes." I don't know where he's going with this.

"How did you affectionately call me? Tell it to Raúl and let him say if I'm right or wrong."

It's incredible how this man has the ability to extract from my conversations, regardless of the context, be it a joke or from the depths of my anxieties, the exact phrase that feeds his ego. My face must be purple right now. However, instead of attacking him, as is my custom, I please him. In a low voice, I stroke his face and repeat, more for him than for Raúl.

"Sweetheart, I called you sweetheart." I reply, resting my chin on his head.

"Thanks, gorgeous." Closing his eyes, he places a kiss right at the level of my heart, then, turning to Raúl asks: "I should be there, right?"

"Sure thing, brother. Now tell me, what are you talking yourself about?"

"That this girl needs a bit more social action. Can you believe it? Since she got back home, she hasn't even hit the cinema."

I look at him surprised: that's true; I haven't been to the movies; my recreational activities have been slightly more violent. But how does he know? Well, maybe it's not that hard. He gets up from where he is, without letting go of me, gives me a loud kiss on my lips and then smiles mischievously. He picks up on my chameleon-like shift in facial colors that he's giving me a hard time. Drawing near in a low voice, he warns me.

"We'll talk about this later." He places the tip of his accusatory finger on the part of my cheek that shows a deeper red. "You've got me feeling like you're a bit embarrassed to be seen with me. Got a lot to explain, gorgeous!" I only have a guilty smile for an answer. The truth is that, yes, I am ashamed, but for now, our discussion will have to wait.

Daniel asks Raúl to order something to eat and ends his request by saying:

"Jade is starving."

"So, I'm starving, huh? And did you tell yourself that, too?"

"No, gorgeous, your stomach told me that."

"Don't tell me; I didn't hear anything."

"I was closer to it than you, and I've got to confess, it seems to trust me more than you."

"Well then, take care of it, feed it."

"You talk about your stomach like it's some kind of pet." Raúl points out.

"There's a portion of truth in that, especially if you could hear the growls." Daniel comes forward to answer him with a laugh. I can't contain myself, and I punch him in the arm; I only get him to laugh more intensely and for Raúl to join him in his laughter. I'll figure out how to annoy him in revenge.

The afternoon has been delightful. For the first time, the three of us are getting some hangout time without time pressures or fixed plans—that's all saved for tomorrow. And while that tomorrow arrives, time is mine.

Raúl looks at us, still chomping down the massive piece of meat he stuffed in his mouth. I totally forgot that on the road, they eat as if there's no tomorrow because you never know if there's going to be a chance to grab a bite the next day. However, his eyes are smiling, even if his mouth isn't free enough to join the party.

"Hey Raúl, what's so funny?" I ask.

"I om noph loghing." That's kind of how he replies, still with his mouth full.

"Totally; your eyes do the talking."

Daniel looks up to check him out, and they lock eyes in total complicity, nodding almost secretly.

"Great, would you be so kind as to include me in your silent conversation?"

Raúl finishes his bite and clears his throat before responding to me.

"Jade, I was just thinking about how damn right Daniel was when he rang me up to tag along. I went to check on him, and let me tell you, he wasn't himself. We've known each other for many years, and I can easily pick up on when something's throwing him off."

I stare at Daniel, trying to figure out if he thinks Raúl is oversharing, but he just reaches over, grabs a strand of my hair, and tucks it behind my ear, showing no sign of annoyance by the change in topic. So, I go back to Raúl.

"So, once we got everything lined up to come over, he started to ease up. Said he'd be back to his old self after kicking it with you for a few hours."

It catches me off guard how genuine he is about it. I was anxious to see him, but those feelings were all mine, not shared with anyone, mostly because there was no one to share them with. Still, I appreciate that Daniel doesn't mind Raúl talking to me about this.

"That's why it cracks me up to see he was totally right; you both bounced back."

"Both?" Daniel asks, turning to look at me.

Rocío Blisswealth

Gods! My face is flushing red again. I wouldn't want Raúl to spill about my previous near-crazy state, but I guess, confession for confession. I don't bother trying to stop him.

"While waiting for her at the airport, she almost zoomed past without noticing me. I had to grab her by the arms, put the brakes on her, and man, those eyes of hers? Same look as yours, straight-up desperation. It just wasn't the Jade I know."

Daniel caresses my cheek. I'm not sure how much Raúl knows about what we went through at the end of the tour, but I doubt he knows exactly what led us to that state. We do know. Not caring that Raúl is here, I bring my hand closer and take his, pressing it on my face, and close my eyes. I want to feel the glorious warmth of his twenty-eight years, still coursing through his lifeline that the demon couldn't interrupt. It's all I needed.

"That's why I'm telling you both snapped back to your true selves." Raúl concludes with a big smile.

"She's my oxygen, brother, and I was drowning. Now you know. Let's make the next trip a non-stop flight, alright?"

"I promise." Raúl places a hand over his heart.

"Gorgeous, got some shopping plans for tomorrow. Fancy coming along?"

"I'm in. What do you need?"

"The new album's hitting shelves soon, and I'm eyeing some breezy outfits for the beach photoshoot. What better place to get some incredible outfit than here?" He grins, using a mischievous smile I haven't seen before. "And later on, we could catch Víctor Arredondo's concert. Up for it?"

"Don't tell me that's your way of expanding my social horizons. What an idea! Who comes up with this stuff? No way, I'm staying, thank you."

"But, how? I thought you liked Salvador." He laughs.

"Of course, but you know? Tomorrow night, I'll be indisposed, for sure. What a shame."

"It's a bit of a bummer, but I've got to show up. Got a few things to sort with Salvador and this guy Víctor. Mind if I leave you alone for a little while?"

"Not at all, don't worry." Using my sarcastic tone, I add. "Enjoy yourself."

"Evil."

The Game...Jade

Raúl says his goodbyes late into the night; he'll call at 9:00 to get us ready for breakfast. Is he going to be the one to wake us up? That's a twist in my routine; usually, I'm the one waking everyone up. I guess, for now, I'm not officially on duty.

The hours felt like minutes, and inevitably, the moment to head to bed was drawing near. I'm about to lose sight of him for those hours, even though I'm aware he's just a few feet away. Anxiety starts bubbling up inside me. It's ridiculous; during the tour, bedtime was a welcome break, even if only for a short while. Now, I'd give anything not to need sleep. I refuse to stop seeing him, having him so close.

He starts pacing the room, and I recognize that measured walk that always comes with a furrowed brow. To make things worse, he rolls up his shirt sleeves, almost reaching his elbows; this isn't good. He wants to say something and doesn't know how. The heaviness settles in my stomach, and a shiver travels down my spine. I watch and wait, but he doesn't muster the courage to open his mouth. The suspense is killing me, so I'm the one who takes the lead.

"Daniel, is something wrong?"

He looks surprised; he wasn't aware I'd been following him with my eyes. I think he forgot I was here while he was turning his thoughts over. He genuinely smiles, and now, the tables have turned—I'm the one taken by surprise. What's the worry then if his smile can surface so easily? Why does he have all the symptoms that something is troubling him? Still smiling, he turns to me. Just his presence makes my skin tingle. He takes me by the arm, turns me until my back is against his chest, and hugs me. His heart is racing; I can feel it. What's wrong with him? Finally, he speaks quietly.

"Gorgeous, I've got a favor to ask." Great, but he'll have to do it face-to-face; I want to see his eyes because if it's bothering him this much, it has to be serious. I turn away from him, put my hands on his ribs, and look him straight in the eye.

"How can I help you?"

His smile holds steady, but he narrows his eyes almost to the point that I can't see them. Yet he knows that if my gaze is fixed on him, I won't let him hide them. I am surprised to see a slight pink hue appear on his cheeks. Due to the whiteness of his skin, this is not easily seen. The only thing that surpasses this blush is when anger triggers those tones, and in that case, the color is much more intense. Daniel, speak now!

Rocío Blisswealth

"Do you trust me?" I roll my eyes to show him how stupid his question is.

"Yes." His smile falters. He tries to get serious but fails.

"I know you'll think I'm a bit pampered, and you're likely to tell me to grow up and all those things you usually throw at me when I'm about to pull something like this, but…"

"Daniel, you're rambling." I'm still waiting; he's speechless. "Apparently, you're the one who doesn't trust me, or it wouldn't be so hard for you to ask me for something, anything." He finally gets serious and opens his eyes, allowing me to see them.

"I've missed you a lot. The days after the tour were utter rubbish for me, and all I craved was being right here with you. I don't want to lose sight of you, you know? I worry that if I do…" His voice deepens. "I'm not going to ask you to come to the concert, as I get what it means to you. However, I'd like to… Jade, don't read anything more into my words; I wouldn't dream of putting you in a spot that makes you uncomfortable. You're like pure air, as I've said before, and that's why I'm at a loss on how to ask you without you thinking that…"

"What, Daniel? You're scaring me." I speak softly, trying to get him to say it outright and break free from those haunting memories. His voice barely reaches me.

"Stay with me tonight. Don't get me wrong; maybe I'm just feeling a little nostalgic, and I'd like to chat."

"Daniel, haven't you stopped to think that, perhaps, the favor could be mutual?" I reply with relief in my voice; I don't want to be apart from him, either.

"Seriously?" He says with a sigh.

"Yes, I thought the image Raúl painted of my expression spoke for itself. Just a few minutes ago, I regretted that it was bedtime, and I'd miss that time with you. It hasn't been an easy stage for me either, so what were you thinking?"

"I don't know. I've always considered you're quite strong, not really needing…"

"Not needing you? I hope I don't disappoint you, but there are times when I'm not, and this is one of them. And, as you can see, I trust you; of course, I can stay."

"Come here, gorgeous." He presses my body against his and kisses me. I furrow my brow as a question occurs to me that I should ask him.

"Daniel, do you snore?"

"You'll figure it out." He replies with laughter. "Let's get your luggage." He takes a key from the table.

"Give me that key; I want it handy in case I decide to desert."

"Gorgeous, you wouldn't!"

I just laugh and wink at him, letting him know that no, but I'm not very sure. I sleep with a demon in my bedroom, but he doesn't snore! He sees me smiling, walking down the hallway towards what would have been my suite.

"There's something I need you to clarify once we're back in the room."

"Damn it!" It slips out without thinking; I had already forgotten. He looks at me sternly.

"Swear all you like, miss, you won't escape this one." He sometimes sounds like my grandpa.

Obviously, I put on my Monterrey gown, and he wears a black sleeveless shirt and pants of the same color. I think I've seen both garments under the dim light that comes through the curtains in my bedroom, but the memory is vague. I'm so glad to see him that I hurry to hug him, losing sight of his clothes.

I always thought the beds in this hotel were excessively large. Still today, it seems like this one measures the size of a fifty-cent coin. It's a good thing I'll be sitting because his image is so striking; I don't think I could stand upright. He sits cross-legged on the bed and offers me the space in front of him, allowing me to rest my back. Great, we're face to face for the interrogation, just as he said; I won't be able to escape this.

"Jade, do you feel embarrassed being seen with me?" He shoots straight, serious, but calm, at least.

"No, Daniel, it's not like that, and you know it." I let my words out without losing sight of his eyes; I want him to know that what I say is true. I already know him, and he asks this question very seriously.

"No, Jade, it's just that I'm not sure. When Raúl knocked on the door, you tried to pull away from me."

"I know, but it's not that I'm embarrassed to be seen with you; it was the situation."

"Did it seem like we were up to something shameful? Gorgeous, I'd be incapable of..."

"Oh, gods! Daniel. No, let me break it down for you."

"I'm listening. If memory serves me right, we've got the entire night ahead."

"Alright, I'll try to give you the quick and dirty version, anyway. Just a heads up, my grandparents raised me. According to my grandma's teachings, it's totally tacky to show affection as a couple in public. She used to say those moments should stay private."

"Times have changed, gorgeous."

"I think I'm the one who stayed stuck in the past. Don't get me wrong, I'm cool with everyone else doing their thing, but when it's about me, that's when the drama starts."

"So, does that imply you'll never kiss me in public?" I almost laughed. Why would I even want to do that? But he's still serious; it's one of the things that bothers him, so I'll hold back the laughter.

"No, probably not going to happen."

"And if by chance I did, would you back away?"

"I thought you wouldn't do something that would make me uncomfortable." I'm throwing the same lines he used a few minutes ago, I know, but he said it.

"No, gorgeous, I'm not attempting to force you into anything. I'm still trying to..."

"Find the way out of this maze."

"Yes, perhaps it's a bit daft, but I'm still trying to get a sense of who you are. I just want to feel like I'm on solid ground and not sinking in..."

"Quicksand." Can't help the pain in my voice as I jump in and finish his sentence; wish there was an easier way for him to get to know me. He can hear it in my voice because he rushes to tell me with a sweet tone.

"Not as much anymore, but it's as if you're from another planet or another century."

"Wow, thanks, how encouraging! Daniel, as long as my way of being doesn't hurt you, I'd like to keep it. It feels right to me." I try to smile at him.

"Please, don't change. Just grant me the time to fathom you, alright?" He keeps firing questions. "Tell me one thing, your other boyfriend..." I look at him, raising an eyebrow, other what? "I say, your previous boyfriend, didn't he take issue with you on this matter?

"No, well, he was never really my boyfriend." Now, he's the one raising an eyebrow. "What I mean is, even when he was just my

friend, he skipped the whole dating thing and went straight to asking for my hand. So..."

"He proposed to you?! But you're only twenty-one!"

"Legal age here and in China."

"That's madness. You say no, right?"

I don't respond, just roll my eyes; sometimes he can be so absurd. He smiles sheepishly and keeps going.

"Alright, there's another thing I'd like to know if you're up for it."

"What's it about?"

"You don't like to be touched."

"Nope, don't like it, and if I recall correctly, we've already covered that topic."

"We haven't covered it; may I carry on?" I don't answer; he'll do it anyway. "You mentioned once that your mother hasn't touched you in years. Any chance you'd share how many?" I pause for a second, counting on my fingers.

"Seventeen, more or less. And I can sense the next question coming: why? Isn't that right?" His stare shifts to his hands.

"Well, indeed, that was it, but I won't ask if it doesn't sit well with you. It's just bloody frustrating that circumstances are this way for someone like you. I can't quite fathom it, Jade. How long since someone last touched you?"

"Not counting Raúl, you, and the accidental contacts you might have with someone, it's been about three years, maybe."

He squints, shakes his head from side to side, sighs, and continues asking.

"What goes through your mind when someone does it?" His eyes are completely closed.

"It makes me anxious; it freaks me out having people so close, I feel vulnerable." It's funny; I had never stopped to analyze exactly what I felt. I just know it bothers me, almost always.

"Is it a challenge for you to let me touch you?"

Rocío Blisswealth

"Daniel, we've already talked about this." I don't know why he insists on this topic. It's starting to bug me, and he can hear it in my voice.

"Come on, Jade. Spill it for me, please."

"Alright, but this will be the last time we discuss this, okay?" He nods in agreement, so I continue. "When my grandparents touched me, I was oblivious to their touch; it was as familiar as if it were my own hands doing it. You've got that kind of touch."

The truth is, his touch, for me, is like a sedative applied through my skin, but I won't tell him that. Pretending to sort out his feet, he lowers his gaze and hides it from me. He mulls it over for a moment, then changes the subject.

"I'm glad you agreed to spend the night with me; your trust in me speaks volumes. Things I don't deserve, you trust me thoroughly not to try... I mean, the image you've got of me makes me change, makes me want to be up to scratch."

"There was no reason for me to say no; I didn't want to. Besides, you're not trying to... nothing. You would've told me by now."

"I'm a guy, gorgeous." He looks down at his hands and continues in a very hushed voice. "And you... you." He lifts his eyes very slowly, locking on mine, which I can feel are wide open with surprise. Me? But I've always been that simple.

"Me?!" I ask in a whisper. He raises an eyebrow and smiles gently; I guess he expected some annoyance from me, but no, there's just surprise.

"Jade." He speaks surprised by my reaction, not expecting it. I don't understand why not; he's the most wonderful man on the face of the earth, and I'm just me. He smiles as if apologizing.

"You've had a boyfriend before. I suppose, with them, with someone." I shake my head slowly from side to side and close my eyes. Now I get it; he thinks my dating included a physical relationship. Well, Daniel, it wasn't like that. I open my eyes to look at him; his eyes are fixed on me, his brow is furrowed, and his hands are clenched into fists.

"Don't assume anything." I say in a low voice.

I never thought my face could turn a more intense shade of red, but here we are. I also didn't think my situation would be something to be embarrassed about. It was just a decision I made because no one ever made me feel what I feel when I am next to him. Maybe that's what embarrasses me a little—the intensity of what I'm capable of feeling for him. His eyes remained fixed on mine as if he couldn't look away. I try to escape his gaze, which is impossible, so I end up facing it. He still doesn't speak; he just watches me closely. That's the problem—every time he looks at me, he doesn't just see me. That's when I knew I looked like a being from another planet.

"Daniel, can we change the subject?"

He startles when he hears my voice; even though he was staring at me, he wasn't really here. What was he thinking? He pulls himself together and answers me.

"Jade, you are... I'm not going to start explaining because you'll probably regret agreeing to stay with me. I would understand if you... but I swear I'm not trying anything."

"I already told you I have no doubt about that. No, don't explain anything to me; leave it at that." What I don't dare to tell him is that I won't believe him anyway; I still can't wrap my head around what he just told me. Come on! If I can't even believe he is here. We look straight into each other's eyes for a long time, and he breaks the silence to tell me:

"And you also sense why."

"You're waiting for something. To figure me out?" He squints.

"Not exactly, Jade." He observes my eyes, still fixed on his. "You know there's a bond between us. You know that, don't you?"

"Yes, I am fond of you, and you are fond of me."

"There are bonds much stronger than love; I need to fortify ours so that, despite anything, it becomes one of those."

He notices my eyes calm down when listening to him; that speaks of time, which he plans to dedicate to establishing bonds with me. Sounds perfect to me; he keeps talking.

"Once I achieve it, you'll be the first to know." He winks at me.

Gods! Daniel, don't do that, please, not now that the currency that this bed has become is tiny to me. My skin tingles and I use my gaze to check out the palm of my hand with such care that it seems as if I had never seen it before. Obviously, the skin on my face changes its hue rapidly until it stops in burgundy red.

"You know, gorgeous? Your cheeks betray you; they clearly reveal the changes in your mood." He smiles, raising an eyebrow.

288

Daniel, but where is your chivalry? Oh, but of course, making use of it would mean not being able to annoy me, and that's something you're not going to miss out on, hateful!

"Yes, it also happens to me, even when I get angry."

"Oh, 'also.' So, what's it for now?" Jade, shut up already! And stop digging your own grave; you can't think straight. Daniel, lower that eyebrow now! And stop tormenting me. Well, it just so happens that the most attractive man in the world is sitting at the foot of my bed, in his pajamas, no less, and smelling delicious. If we add to that the fact that the air has disappeared from this room, I don't know where it went, but something, or someone, stole it because I can't find a little to fill my lungs. Or is he just the one who takes my breath away? Yes, that sounds more logical; if I think about it a little more, it will be impossible for me to breathe again.

"Stop bothering me, Daniel." I beg. He smiles and bites his lip—well, at least he's lowered his eyebrow.

"I want to try something, gorgeous. Would you allow me?"

"What do you mean?"

"I want to try communicating in your language."

"Sorry?" I shake my head; now I'm lost.

"I express my feelings through touch. For me, a hug is the most commonly used resource, and I would like to try to do it as you do. It's a challenge I've set for myself."

"Without touching me."

"Exactly."

"Okay. What do you want me to do?"

"Nothing at all, just listen to me. Maybe one thing, can you close your eyes?"

"Close my eyes?"

"Gorgeous, don't make it any harder for me; I'm not used to doing this."

I close them and get ready to listen to him; I can hear his breathing rushing. He's nervous, and I'm still waiting.

"Jade…" His voice is slow. "I want you to know that I'm here. Whenever you need me, I'm here." His voice lacks firmness; it's clear that he has a hard time expressing certain things.

Something right in the center of my chest starts to spin very hard, recognizes his voice, and lets me know that what he says is true. That part of

The Game…Jade

me is his, or rather, that part of him lives inside me, and it recognizes him. Although it doesn't make the slightest attempt to make the three-foot leap necessary to lodge itself again inside his chest, that part of him binds us.

I bring my hand to it, right over that space, and I can feel the tapping much faster than my own heartbeat, which I sense in the background. He knows, and I know, he's with me, just as he just said. He found a way not to leave me alone; I'm never alone. I don't know how, but he accompanies me wherever I go.

"You're not alone. I need you to understand that. I found you, and I'm here with you. You're unlike anything I've ever known, pure air, basically that. Pure air. I love you so much." A tear runs down my cheek; the bed moves when Daniel tries to get closer to me.

"Not yet." I say very softly, reaching out and placing my palm in front of me to make him stop. "Don't touch me yet."

I don't want to open my eyes, and I know that if he touches me, I won't be able to feel it anymore; the sensation will be lost, and I want to know what it is. I hear his voice inside me repeating, "Whenever you need me, I'm here," as tears continue to well up. No one ever bothered to express something like that to me. It doesn't matter; who could have said it with sincerity? As genuinely as I feel it now. As serious as it is at this moment. He's here with every breath, every fleeting second of the day, with me. Despite the tears, I smile.

"There are bonds stronger than love," were his words. I never felt anything stronger than this. A sob catches in my throat, making it difficult to breathe, but I don't mind. I enjoy so much that my crying doesn't stop. My hand feels through my chest, and at times, it slows down its movement until it stops. However, my inner self still feels it.

I slowly open my eyes; I can barely see him through the tears. He's worried; I get up and go to the foot of the bed where he is. I stop at his back, and he gives me the freedom to act without moving. I stroke his hair.

"Daniel, can I now speak to you in your language?"
"Are you alright, gorgeous?" He asks, somewhat distressed.

"Better than ever. May I?"

"Whatever you want."

I pull his hand, leading him to stand in front of me, and he complies without opening his eyes. Reaching the level of his waist, I run my hands to his back, letting the energy I can't quite contain flow through his skin and my hands with an unexpected intensity as if it's in search of something. Just as if it has been waiting for him, it pours into him, and I hug him tightly; soon, it has spread through his entire body.

I move closer and kiss his chin; I feel him tense; he's clenching his teeth, trembling from head to toe. I'm used to it, but he's not. When I open my eyes, I notice a gentle smile on his lips even though his eyes remain closed; he can withstand it. His hands clench my clothing tightly at my waist. If I tried to move, I'm sure it wouldn't be possible. In a low voice, I say:

"I'm here too, whenever you need me."

I rise on my tiptoes, pressing my lips against his, and he playfully bites them in response. The smile he evokes frees them from the pressure he is holding them with. With effort, I slowly close the palms of my hands in a process that takes a couple of minutes. He relaxes again and kisses me once more. Finally free from his lips, I speak to him in the thread of voice that I have left after all.

"Thank you."

He sits down on the bed as if his legs were no longer supporting him, watching me as I wipe the tears from my face with my fingertips.

"Jade, I've... never. Your hands possess an incredible knack for self-expression!"

"I just tried to make you feel the same way you make me feel."

His face lights up with a wonderful smile, and he asks, holding my face with both hands.

"Did I achieve it? Did I finally get there, gorgeous?"

"I heard everything, even what you didn't say."

"Wonderful."

"Daniel, I'm really sleepy. Do you mind if I lie down?" This energy usually leaves me exhausted in seconds.

"I'm quite tired as well; I'll join you. Gorgeous, you should use your hands more frequently."

"I don't think so."

As I turn off the light, I can only hear his voice in the darkness from the other end of the bed.

"Jade, how much fondness was that?"

"Well, you received level 'two and a half little bits.'"

The Game...Jade

"Incredible. I aspire to reach level ten."

Level ten is for demons, Daniel. I couldn't apply it to you. Unless my intention is for your body to be turned inside out, and with the outside being so fantastically attractive, why would I want to leave the inside exposed?

"Someday, maybe."

"I'll consider that a promise."

The sudden darkness gives an air of unreality to his voice. I don't want to think I'm imagining it; I want him close, like in my room. I reach out in the gloom and touch his chest; his arms come around me, and he draws me closer, sliding his hand around the back of my neck until I settle on his shoulder, cradling my face on his neck.

"Goodnight."

"Goodnight, Daniel." I intertwine my fingers with his. Now, I can finally sleep. Seconds later, I heard his voice very softly.

"Fifteen, sixteen, seventeen..."

"I thought you were sleepy."

"I am."

"Then, aren't they sheep you're counting?"

"No, I do the same as you, I count."

"But, the same as me? When?"

Now I understand; when he hugs me, and it's not a good time, I start counting.

"Gorgeous, why do you have to make things so complicated?" He laughs.

"Daniel, I'm sorry." I try to get up to move away from him, but he won't let me; he holds me where I am.

"I'm playing, Jade! Stay here; I enjoy teasing you, that's all. Besides, counting really works. Don't budge; please, go to sleep." He kisses my nose.

"Go to sleep, of course. It turns out that I'm the one doing the hard things. Where is the blessed key, Daniel? I give up! I'm going to my room; I'm no longer interested in finding out if you snore."

His laughter echoes in the room; he laughs so much that it's hard for him to catch his breath, but he continues to hold me.

"You're adorable!" He keeps laughing, and now, how does he expect me to sleep? Crazy!

Six, seven, eight rings. So much noise! The phone! It's probably Raúl calling to wake us up. I half-open my eyes, and Daniel is already reaching out to grab the receiver. He looks so good! The perfection with which he was created sends butterflies swirling in my stomach; it's an awesome, giddy feeling. Normally, he's not hanging around when I wake up, so this is a pretty sweet change.

"Hello." Gods! His voice isn't hoarse; it comes from the grave. He listens for a few seconds and continues, "Need a couple more hours, brother." He keeps listening. "No, it's fine, I'll wake her up." Daniel, stop, stop, please! I silently shout at him with my eyes. He smiles and places his finger on my lips so that I don't speak, and that soothes me. Then he finishes his sentence, "She's right here with me."

"Arrgh!" I growl, cover my head with the sheets, and turn my back to him.

With one of his feline movements, he slides until he's attached to my back, burying his face between my neck and wrapping one of his arms around me. His body shakes with laughter that's threatening to choke him, but he manages to control it a little and says in my ear:

"I suppose under these sheets, your face is totally red. Am I off the mark?" I don't answer; he's getting on my nerves so early. "You still bothered about what Raúl might think?"

"If you think about the possibilities of what he might think, I suppose so." I mumble from my hiding place under the sheets.

"And the most plausible possibility would be that we loved each other last night, right?" I'm surprised that my heart stays in place; with the speed at which it runs, it should be rolling on the mattress by now. I was thinking of revealing my face, but honestly, I'm already regretting it.

"I suppose."

"And tell me, gorgeous, wouldn't that be the truth? No one had ever given me so much in a hug, ever. So, if Raúl were to ask me directly, I wouldn't dare to answer in the negative. Would you?" I uncover my head and turn to look at him; he's right.

"No."

"Give your capillary vessels a break and sleep a little longer, will you?" It's unbelievable. I didn't think I'd make it; however, just a few minutes later, my eyelids weighed a ton, and I was asleep again.

The Game…Jade

I totally lost track of time and crashed out like a log. It's been ages since I slept this well. I crack open my eyes, and there's Daniel, knocked out cold right next to me. I sneak out of bed, trying not to make a sound, and head into the shower. He's got a permanent Prince Charming vibe, and at least I'd like to be cleaned up when he wakes up. I mean, no birds are dressing me like Cinderella, but hey, I'll take what I can get.

I threw on some jeans and boots, this time with a black sweater. Mom's not a fan of me wearing funeral colors, but I'm loving it. Finish up with some makeup, and I almost drop my mirror when Daniel startles me with a talk. I didn't even notice he woke up.

"Morning."

"Good morning. You scared me, Daniel. I didn't want to wake you. How long have you been watching me?"

"Since you chose to give your skin a run with makeup. You don't need it; you're stunning."

"Thanks."

"And then?"

"And then, what?"

"Do I snore?"

"Oh, come on. Do you really think I could've noticed? I didn't sleep last night; I died."

"You'll get another shot at figuring that out tonight, no worries."

"Fair enough."

A huge smile lights up his face as he watches me.

"What are you laughing at?"

"Well, that you…"

My expression turns into total surprise. I don't want to ask, scared of what he might say, but I have to know.

"Do I snore?"

"Nah! That wouldn't have been half as fun."

This time, I didn't blush. I don't need a mirror to know my cheeks are a pale wax color. What the heck did I do? No, I don't dare ask this time. I just stare at him, wide-eyed; his laughter's now a barely contained chuckle. I might cry if he doesn't spill it soon. Maybe I'll cry even after he does; tears seem kind of inevitable.

Rocío Blisswealth

"You chatter away in your sleep, gorgeous." Laughter cuts through his words. Okay, now my face definitely must reveal my stress.

I'm completely speechless; my voice simply disappeared, and I can't find it. I think about the endless possibilities of what I might have said. Seriously, anything and everything. Why won't the ground just open up and swallow me whole? I'm feeling dizzy; I instinctively shield my face with both hands.

In a split second, he's sitting on the same stool where I am, wrapping his arms around me, still laughing, thoroughly enjoying seeing me so embarrassed. Gathering courage, I lower my hands and look at him.

"What did I say, Daniel?" His laughter eases off, and his tone turns sweet. He plants a kiss on my cheek.

"Tíber is doing just fine, gorgeous."

Now I get it; clearly, when my subconscious took over my thoughts, it brought to the surface the ones that were causing me the most stress. The image of Tíber, stepping in between the demon and Daniel to prevent him from being killed, is etched in my mind. I try to shake off the sadness that memory brings; I say nothing.

"Don't worry, Jade; besides that, I didn't catch much. No matter how many times I asked you what you said, you refused to repeat it, so I missed out on a chunk of the monologue; it was like a dodgy tuning. Just to set your mind at ease, Tíber has dived into a new relationship. His girlfriend goes by the name Laila, and she's lovely."

"Next time, if I ever manage to sleep around you again, just ignore my monologue and go to sleep, okay? Oh, and cheers for the good news;
give him congrats from me."

"I swear, I made that promise to you last night, don't you remember?" Well, no, absolutely nothing. It's probably all stashed away in some hidden drawer in my subconscious. He gets up, arranges his clothes ready for a shower, then turns back toward me at the bathroom door.

"I've got a confession to make. This morning, when Raúl called..."

"Yes?"

"The call had ended by the time I mentioned you were with me."

"Darn it, Daniel!" I grab my brush and throw it at him. He dodges, and it barely brushes his hair before crashing against the bathroom wall. He quickly

The Game...Jade

shuts the door, and all I can hear is his laughter. I bang on the door to yell at him.

"Daniel, you better hope Raúl gets here before you come out. You're going to need bodyguards!"

It's pointless to wear out my throat; I'm just giving him more reason to laugh. Several minutes have passed, and the shower's water sounds are gone, but his laughter persists. How rude. He comes out of the bathroom, casually combing his hair with my brush—the audacity. He's got on light blue jeans, a dark blue silky sweater, and cowboy boots. He decided not to shave, amping up that bad boy image I brought up earlier, and the woodsy scent just makes me feel that everything about him, even his fragrance, is in-san-ely per-fect. It's not fair; I already forgot why I was mad in the first place.

He kneels in front of me, placing his hands on my knees. My heart is racing, and I keep reminding my lungs to keep breathing because the room has just gone crazy, and it won't stop spinning; I don't want to get dizzy. He remains there at my feet, not saying a word, simply smiling, gently squeezing my knees.

"And then?"

I can't even manage a questioning look. I should ask, "And then, what?" But here I am, once again breathless and, therefore, voiceless, watching him there, inches away from me. He bites his lip and smiles.

"Should I shout for Raúl to come and rescue me? I've been terribly rude to you, fully aware of it. One thing in my defense is that I adore witnessing you all flustered; it's rather charming, I must say. On my planet, that's not a sight you come across often; actually, you don't come across it at all. Therefore, enduring whatever punishment you've chosen is worthwhile. Here I am. What is it? I won't put up a fight."

My eyes got lost in the electric blue of his gaze. Punishment? What punishment? I can't think of anything; it's the result of depriving my brain of oxygen for so long that my neurons are dying. I lift my hand and slowly stroke his eyebrow until I reach his cheekbone, almost as if hypnotized. I run the tip of my index finger over his lips, much like I do in his photographs, and enjoy the sweet smile they still evoke. During my journey, he bites my finger, disrupting my state of hypnosis a little. He releases it immediately, and I continue, lifting it to the bridge of his nose. Of all the features of his face, all so perfect to me, his nose just drives me crazy.

Rocío Blisswealth

I place my fingers at the base of his neck and slide them gently through his hair, pulling him toward me as I lean forward to reduce the space between us. As he said, he doesn't put up any resistance; instead, he's very cooperative. He offers me his lips, a tempting offer indeed, but that's not my goal. I rise a little and plant a long kiss on the bridge of his nose while he presses his fingers against my knees.

He sighs and brings his lips close to me again. I narrow my eyes and smile as I see him come closer. I'm sorry, Daniel, I was after your nose, that's all. I get up from the bench I am on.

"Shall we go?"

He drops to the ground with his arms clutched against his ribs as if they were going to disarm because of the extremity of his laughter; I watch it from where I am. There's a knock at the door, and I slowly make my way to the door, being careful not to step on him. He's still rolling around there on the carpet, and once I see Raúl through the peephole, I open it to let him in.

He looks at Daniel with curiosity, lying on the floor, laughing uncontrollably. He asks me with his eyes what's going on. I just shrug, letting him know that I have no idea.

"Good morning."

"Hello." I replied.

"Are we leaving?"

"Sure, let's go." Daniel answers, jumping up from the floor, and continues laughing. He throws himself at me, hugging me tightly.

"Jade, did you get training to inflict torture, or does it come naturally to you? You're wicked."

"What did I do?" I ask with an innocent look.

"Brother, just as you see her, all innocent-looking, she's a bit wicked. I swear!"

"What's up with him, Jade?"

"He's crazy, you know, that's how he woke up."

Maybe he's right; I'm evil because I didn't think about it. With what neurons could I have thought about it? I acted on instinct, smile satisfied and started walking beside him.

Walking through the streets of Mexico City with him has a completely different vibe. I had this whole picture in my head of us scouring the entire Zona

Rosa for dozens of outfits for the photoshoot, but that wasn't the case. He selected precisely what he needed, and that was the only thing he bought.

I'll admit, when we met up in the car to head to the stores, I was a little nervous. The experiences from the tour, especially the confrontations with the public, weren't very pleasant. However, we've been here for a few hours now, and things have been surprisingly calm. The shop assistants treat us like celebs, they go all out to assist him and us as a bonus.

He's asked me a couple of times if I want anything, but I just shake my head and continue handing him clothes that I think will look great on him. Come to think of it, he could probably make a sack look stylish. He corners me by the shelves and throws a question at me under his breath, almost like a grunt.

"Why won't you let me treat you to anything?"

"Because I don't need anything. You brought me everything I needed as a gift."

I think my response pleases him as he smiles and leaves me alone. The shop ladies go above and beyond to attend him, so he throws a question that causes a stir among them.

"Ladies, am I handsome?"

Raúl and I burst into laughter at the sudden uproar of the girls who respond in unison:

"Very handsome!"

He approaches one of them, takes her by the elbow, and pulls her over to me.

"Give us a hand and repeat it in front of her because, you see, she keeps insisting I'm not, and as a result, she never tells me. So please..." He points at me with a graceful gesture of his hand. The girl looks at me stunned—probably wondering how I could dare to deny the obvious attractiveness. She stands in front of me and, looking at him, repeats.

"Very handsome!" Daniel eyes me, looking all self-satisfied, waiting for my opinion.

"Did you notice, Daniel? How fake that sounded!" And then I turn to the young lady, who is already starting to laugh. "Don't worry; he does this all the time, and the result is always the same. We need to find him someone who can lie really well."

Laughter explodes, and Daniel steps up to me, joining in.

"I said, you're wicked! You are going to pay for this!"

Rocío Blisswealth

A couple of hours later, we pull up at a restaurant they're familiar with. After settling into a table at the back, Daniel orders a bunch of dishes from the menu, insisting that I try them all. Cheese, meats, sausages—everything is top-notch. The red wine he chose, from a famous Spanish brand, is like a gentle kiss on the taste buds. When I share my thoughts on the wine, he pops the question.

"What's your favorite drink, gorgeous?"

"Without a doubt, this wine." I replied. They both look at me, expecting me to elaborate on my answer. "Champagne, I guess. Back when my grandpa was around, we'd raise a toast on New Year's Eve."

Their expressions turn totally uncertain, and not having a clue about what to say next, I just stay quiet, watching them. After their focus shifts away from me, they shoot each other these puzzled looks. Finally, Daniel asks.

"You're not into drinking?"

"No."

"And from what I've seen, you're not a smoker either." Raúl points out.

"No, I have never smoked." I continue, totally calm, sipping the rest of my wine, not understanding why it seems so strange to them.

"I hate to be nosy, but I've got to ask. Have you experimented with any substances, gorgeous?" It amuses me how surprised they are. I can't imagine what they've been thinking all this time.

"Let me think..." I keep them hanging, and then I smile. "No, Daniel, nothing stronger than aspirin."

"Mind if I ask why?"

"What?"

"I mean, I've got this sense that your family's given you the freedom to make your own decisions, especially since your grandparents are no longer around. You're of legal age, and having studied abroad, I don't know, you could basically do whatever without anyone knowing. Why haven't you, then?"

"Well, that's exactly it, Daniel. It was my decision, and I just didn't feel like doing it."

"You're at the age to make all the wrong moves in your life, and yet, you've opted for the right ones. I don't know how you manage it."

"I'm thinking that maybe they weren't so right after all. Look at missing out on this wine; it genuinely stirs up huge regrets."

They keep watching me now as if I'm genuinely from another planet; this makes me question my own choices. I've never felt pressured to make decisions about these things, I guess, simply because I could've done whatever I wanted, and no one would have cared. Maybe that took away the excitement of being rebellious. I've always been responsible for myself, and if I got into any kind of trouble, I had to get out of it on my own. The fewer complications, the less trouble to get out of—it's that simple.

Raúl smiles and suggests a few wine brands that, according to him, outshine this one. I can't imagine such a delight. Daniel is sitting in front of me, lost in thought. I give a gentle tap on his shoe with the tip of my foot to make him turn and look at me. He does, and I wink at him. He responds in the same way, but his gaze is somewhat sad. He looks back down at his plate but doesn't touch anything on it.

Shortly after, we left the restaurant for the hotel. It's already getting dark, and he needs to prepare for the damn concert. As he gets into the car, Raúl takes the seat by the driver; perfect, I can ask him what's going on.

I take his hand, intertwining my fingers with his. He switches hands and puts his arm around my shoulders, pulling me closer, resting his forehead on my temple with a long sigh. With my free hand, I gently caress his face.

"Daniel, what's going on? I said something I shouldn't have, right?"

"No, gorgeous, not at all."

"Then?"

He doesn't move, and I can still feel his breath on my cheek as he, I suppose, thinks about what he has to say.

"I'm contemplating all the decisions I've made, and if I had been even a tad like you, I would never have gone through with them." I remain silent, unsure of what to say, waiting to see how far he'll go. "I've always seen you as a breath of fresh air. However, today, that takes on a different meaning. Your way of thinking is so clear, and even your body is so healthy that, in comparison, I don't want to know how I would appear in your eyes if I told you everything."

"Is that what you're worried about? You can stop; I never concern myself with such petty stuff. Daniel, I don't go around looking at a person's CV to see if they suit me as a friend."

"Maybe you should, Jade."

"Oh, really? So, is that why you're always interrogating me? Do you want to know if I suit you as a friend? Well, now I know!"

"I never went down that path, and even if I had, everything about you, both physically and mentally, is pure—completely pure." He says it in a tone of voice that irritates me.

"Cut it out with the nonsense, Daniel." I grab his arm and pull it away from my shoulders. "Everyone, absolutely everyone, has skeletons in the closet, and I regret to inform you that your interrogations haven't even scratched the surface of mine. Maybe it should be you questioning your friendship with me." He squeezes my hand without giving me a chance to let go, and I continue.

"Besides, if the point is that I'm too clean for your taste, let me warn you that I'm not giving up on our friendship, so... How much older are you than me? Seven years, right? Perfect! I've got plenty of time to catch up, and I might as well start now, so you don't feel sooo uncomfortable around me." My breathing has become irregular; he really makes me angry. The car pulls up at the hotel; I swing the door open and step out hastily, and he trails behind me.

I enter the lobby and walk in the opposite direction of the elevators; he easily catches up with me and stops me by the arm. I don't resist; I don't want to make a scene in front of people.

"Where are you off to, Jade?" He asks in a low voice.

"To the hotel store."

"Where?"

"That's where they sell cigarettes, isn't it? Well, if I'm going to catch up with you, I can't think of a better way to start. Will you join me to inaugurate the pack? Let's just say it will be the starting flag."

"No, please don't do this; come with me."

I follow him to the room; no wonder Raúl has disappeared from the map; it was to be expected. We go in, and I haven't been able to control my anger.

"You seem really upset."

"I prefer it; I work better this way when someone hurts me." He stares at me with great surprise in his eyes. He reaches out to me, and I take a step back; I don't feel like having him close. He tries again, with the same result; he stays still.

"I didn't think, I didn't mean... Jade, I wasn't referring to you."

"'Pure, completely pure.' Those were your words, Daniel." I repeat, practically spitting out the words.

"And is that offensive, gorgeous?"

The Game...Jade

"Anything can sound terribly offensive when mentioned in the tone you used, with contempt."

He closes his eyes and sighs, rubbing his face with his hands, and with a more measured tone, he continues.

"It was, but to me. I can't help but feel, more strongly than before, that when I come to you, I contaminate you, and it makes me feel dirty like I don't deserve..."

"Stop talking about deserving, will you? Who decides if someone deserves something or not, and how much is it worth anyway? You're a masochist, no doubt about it; you love to torment yourself." I say a bit calmer.

"Please, I know from experience that your perspective often differs from mine, but this one, in particular, can't be drastically distinct. I must seem to you..."

"There's only one thing I'm sure of, and it's the only thing I care about when it comes to you."

"What is it?"

"Every decision I've made in my life, good, bad, or terrible, led me to this moment, here, with you. I wouldn't change a single one of them. I am pleased with the result, and I'm not going to ruin it thinking nonsense." He remains silent, and I continue talking. "There's something I must confess, Daniel. When you leave, you cease to exist for me. I don't think about what you do or who you're with; you just disappear and come back to life when you call me or when I see you again. I don't agonize over how many pieces make up your life or whether they're of good quality. The only piece that matters is the one where I can be with you, and believe me, that piece of your life that you've shared with me doesn't contaminate me; it nourishes me and makes me happy. The rest doesn't exist."

He takes a small step in my direction. I don't move. Seconds later, he extends his arm. When he sees that I don't reject him, he comes to me and hugs me.

"On the contrary, for me, it's entirely the opposite; I'm always thinking where you are or what you're up to. I can't help but worry." I let out a sigh of annoyance.

"Same point, different day. Aren't you the one who claims that nothing can happen to me because I'm taken care of? I don't understand you, Daniel?"

Rocío Blisswealth

302

"I know, but I'm still not entirely convinced." He takes my face in his hands and, looking straight into my eyes, he adds. "Gorgeous, I didn't mean to hurt you, never, believe me. Can you forgive me?"

"Yes."

"Do you know what I think? That what you consider skeletons in your closet are actually teddy bears."

"Well, they can be scary! Daniel, promise me something. When you leave and lose sight of me, think that I am succumbing in the arms of vices and perdition to catch up with you, okay?"

"And you say I shouldn't worry."

"Daniel!"

"I mean, it's quite splendid."

"Deal then."

"I am fond of you, Jade."

"Of course."

He finally laughs and kisses me. With a kiss like that, do you still think something else might matter to me? If I can't even think clearly.

He showers to head to the concert. I'll be alone because, obviously, Raúl is going with him. He puts the finishing touches on his hair. I go through the TV channels, trying to find something I like, then I opt for something that might interest me, and I end up staying on the channel that I find less boring. Why is it that on Saturdays, there's nothing good to watch? I've come to think that movie theaters pay a fee to television stations so that they don't show anything worthwhile, forcing us to leave our homes and go to them.

I settle into the couch. He watches me through the mirror, I pretend I don't see him. I don't want to give him a chance to convince me to go to the concert; I don't have the slightest desire to do so. A few hours ago, I was a little scared to think that Daniel would be so close to Salvador's demon, but for years, he has been, and there has been nothing to regret. Therefore, I stay calm. He keeps his look fixed on me.

"Jade..."

"Hmm."

"If you get hungry, go ahead and order whatever you want."

"With what I ate, it would be ridiculous, but thanks."

"Very well, and..."

The Game...Jade

"I know, Grandpa, I can't play with matches or stick pebbles up my nose." I answer with a face of absolute seriousness.

"I realize you're not a child. Did you just call me 'Grandpa'?"

"Ok, then, I won't use your absence to invite a boy into the suite."

"You better not!"

"Daniel, isn't it quite late for you already?"

"I've got no intention of listening to Victor's songs. The more I skip out on the concert, the better for me, Jade..."

"Now what?" I say in a very obvious tone of annoyance.

"Will you be waiting awake for me?"

"Yes."

Raúl knocks on the door and finally takes him away. If given more time, he might leave me in charge of the hotel manager; he's definitely out of his mind.

Why did I agree to wait awake for him? Considering my TV options, I'll probably fall asleep in the next hour. To pass the time, I take a long shower and put on my pajamas. However, even in my PJs, I feel cold, and my most logical option is to get under the covers. Well, I tried, for the record.

I'm awakened by the sound of the electronic keys at the door beeping to give me a heads-up; I sit up slightly on the pillows. Daniel walks in, stops at the foot of the bed, and crosses his arms, wearing a huge smile.

"You said you would wait awake for me."

"I never said I wouldn't sleep while you arrived, did I? And now I'm wide awake."

"I'll freshen up and join you."

He goes into the bathroom and comes out dressed in shorts and a t-shirt. Why did they have to be shorts?!

"Make room for me, gorgeous." He slips under the covers and sits next to me.

"How did it go?"

"Well, depending on how you look at it. I fired my manager."

"Really? And is that good or bad?"

"It's great; I was tired of that guy."

"Then, congratulations."

"Thank you. Gorgeous, I want you to listen to the songs from my new album if you're not too tired."

Rocío Blisswealth

"Not at all; and how am I going to listen to them?"

He smiles with that wonderful smile of his and, partially closing his eyes, he clears his throat.

"Is this for real? I'm going to have my own private concert!"

"Very private. There's nothing more private than this."

I sit with my legs crossed, turning more towards him. He takes my hand and talks about everything, from the song's name to the reason why it was selected for the CD and sings just for me.

He took quite a marked turn in his music; they are no longer just romantic ballads. The lyrics of his songs now also include heartbreak and separation—they are much deeper, with a very intense emotional charge. I get goosebumps listening to him, and, still singing, he caresses my arm to lessen the effect.

After the last song, he leans on the pillow, resting his head on his hand, and adjusts the other pillow for me to lie down. I do it immediately and allow myself to be lulled.

"End of the CD. Did you enjoy your concert?"

"Very much."

"I'm glad because it's the birthday gift I owed you."

"You didn't owe me anything; you weren't here on my birthday." I express my surprise.

"But I wanted to give you something, and you make it difficult for me. So, after much thought, I came up with this idea: a concert just for you. Happy birthday, gorgeous!"

"It is, Daniel. A very happy one, thank you."

"No need to thank me." He says, brushing my lips, and kisses me, a long, sweet goodnight kiss.

Certainly, the best things in life can't be bought with money. Perhaps, for someone offering the right price, it would be relatively easy to get a private concert from Daniel, but it wouldn't be the same. Surely, he would present it from a stage, no matter how small, and not between the covers like with me. Every day, I love him more. What a gift!

Almost at sunset, we arrived at the airport minutes before the deadline to check our tickets; they were on their airline, heading to Spain, and I was on mine with a much closer destination. We manage to spend the last few minutes together, and Raúl smiles, promising that we will see each other soon. Please, god, listen to him! The seconds got lost in hugs, and we rushed off to our respective flights.

Now, it's time to face the monster waiting at my house. Mara! She must not be happy at all. I'll make sure to put on some earplugs before I get there, just until her anger passes.

I mentally go over this wonderful weekend; it changed my mood completely. The gifts I received, which I won't be able to tell anyone about, have given me all the strength I needed to continue my hunt. If you thought I had forgotten, well, you are completely wrong; I will find that damn demon wherever he is.

Rocío Blisswealth

Chapter XIV
You don't know what you have until it's gone

On my way home, the taxi driver keeps chatting away, but it doesn't matter. My thoughts are racing so fast that I hardly hear him. I've reduced myself to nodding my head from time to time, instinctively responding when necessary. So far, I haven't missed a beat.

My three-day vacation is about to come to an end, and I need to refocus on the work that is most urgent for me right now: dealing with the demons. If my calculations are correct, Mara must have a list of tasks ready for me, tasks that I must carry out even tonight if need be. She always operates like that; everything must be done right away, and I don't ever argue. I know that as soon as the demons catch wind of it (and trust me, they always do), the one being called in shows up to stop me. So far, none of them have succeeded, but I wouldn't want to lose that advantage.

I'm squeezing in the minutes when I can still break down and openly enjoy the events of these days. The moment I step foot in the house, my vacation is officially done. Once I'm there, I don't want to let god down on what he's expecting from me. Yup, I'm starting to buy into the idea that he's behind all this—at least for the good stuff. My grandma believed in that, and I always trusted her good judgment.

Plus, after a few days like the ones I've just spent with Daniel, without demonic interruptions until my soul was completely restored, I'm pretty sure that, as Mara says, god plans that for me as a kind of reward. He must know me very well; there's nothing better for me than that.

All this gives me a deep feeling of gratitude, and it's messing with my head. Gratitude, at least for me, is a seriously heavy load because, sooner or later, it's payback time. I'm thinking about all the gifts I got, especially one that I might have received without noticing until now. I feel absolutely happy in my own skin; I wouldn't change myself for anyone. After years of wanting to be someone else, this is very valuable to me. I love every atom of this body that Daniel holds so tightly, mainly because this body, and none other, shares a seriously special bond with him.

Even the fact that most of the things that go down in my life, both for good or worse, are light years away from normal. I don't care anymore. Normal or not, it happens, and even that I assume now with some calm—well, maybe "resignation" is the right word.

We all have a role to play in this world, or at least, that's what I believe, and I guess I'm already on the road to figuring out mine. And when it comes to gratitude, mine is focused on performing that role as best as possible, doing what, according to my mom and Mara, god expects of me. I think Daniel is right; I tend to make things difficult, not just for him but for myself, too. What a task awaits me.

As the cab pulls up, my firing squad, aka Mom and Mara, are sitting in the rocking chairs at the front of the house. They are surprised to see me, of course. Sure, I said I would call them from Mexico City, and I didn't, partly because I forgot and then because I didn't want to ruin a single minute of those three days listening to their gripes.

There is something I don't understand about their attitude. They assure me that time with Daniel is like a reward that god gives me. So, what is the problem then? Seems a bit arrogant for them to think he should adjust his schedule with whatever suits them, don't you think?

I almost wish I could tell the driver to flip a U-turn and take me back to the airport! But where would I go? I have nowhere to go, so I get out of the car, and the man takes my luggage out of the trunk and hands it to me. They get up from where they are and come to greet me. They won't think of hugging me, will they? No, Mara grabs my suitcase and carries it inside the house. She greets me like nothing has happened. I've got my repertoire of one-word answers ready, but they change the questions.

"What's that fragrance? It smells delicious." Mara says.

"It's, uh, must be Daniel's lotion." I reply, a little taken aback by her attitude.

"Come closer; let me smell it." She comes close to my neck, at a safe enough distance not to touch me. "Mmm... Absolutely delightful, woody notes, isn't it?"

"I guess so."

"He must have given you quite the hug for you to carry this scent; even your hair holds it."

Rocío Blisswealth

308

Mara, don't start; I'm not talking about that, and you know it. Seizing the moment while my niece is hovering over my suitcase, I tell her:

"Little one, they're in my bag; candies, grab them." Without a second thought, she grabs my bag and runs off.

"And how is Daniel doing?" Mom asks.

What kind of question is that? What's going on here? They know those are exactly the kind of questions they agreed not to ask. What's this all about?

"Fine." I say, taking off my boots and putting on the slippers the kid brought me.

"Thanks, little one, hand over my bag." She smirks with her nearly toothless grin; I'm starting to think my bag has become a victim of kiddo-napping.

"I put it in your room." She answers, her exaggerated sneer making it seem like she's the one who spent these days with Daniel, not me. She's missing some teeth.

"Thanks."

"Jade, how did it go? What did you do?" Mom interrogates me.

"Fine, Mom, there were some loose ends to tie up. The new album is dropping soon."

That should be enough; I'm not saying anything more. I choose to steer the conversation elsewhere; they're trying to stick to areas they think I'm interested in, and I'll do the same.

"What's new? What do I have to do?"

"We've got some details, but we can talk about that tomorrow. You must be starving. Want something to eat?" Mom heads to the kitchen.

"No, Mom, we ate really late. I'm not hungry, thanks."

"Alright."

"We saw Daniel at Víctor Arredondo's concert." Mara chimes in. "You didn't attend, did you?"

"No, I didn't want to go."

"Good call. We were worried Daniel would force you to go, and with the manager's demons, it's better that you didn't go."

"Daniel doesn't make me do anything; he wouldn't. I didn't want to go, didn't go, and it's just one demon."

"What's that supposed to mean?"

The Game...Jade

"It's just one demon, Salvador's demon. You said, 'the demons,' but it's just one."

"It's the same."

"No, it's not. And he doesn't represent him anymore; Daniel fired him."

"Well, that's a relief; he was getting too close to you." I can't help but laugh. He was the farthest from me, but whatever.

"I'm heading to my room."

"So soon? You just got here." Mom says.

"I want to unpack, and if there's nothing I have to do right away, I'm going to take a shower."

"Alright then. If you need anything, we're here for you."

I grab my suitcase and head up the stairs. Once in the hallway, I don't turn on the light. I walk slowly to the mirror, which reflects me in the dim light. However, it's not my image that I'm looking for. I press my hand against the glass, searching for some sensation that might give me a clue, something that tells me I have him within reach, but there's nothing.

"Are you there?" I mutter. "Answer me, damn it." Nothing, no change at all. I'll be waiting. Among the numerous tasks Mara surely has for me, this one is especially important: tracking down this demon until I find it.

The door to my room is open. I place my suitcase on the bed and turn on the light. Out of the corner of my eye, I see my demon, loyal as always, still there. It's a silly thought, I know, but it makes me happy to see it. I search for more comfortable clothes and, grabbing the sweater by the waist, I pull it over my head. Gods! Its scent overwhelms me; no wonder Mara mentioned it— smells delicious, it's true. I pause for a few seconds before tossing it into the laundry basket. Upon second thought, I fold it and stash it in a plastic bag. I hope this preserves the scent as much as possible. With the days I'm about to face, I'll surely need to feel Daniel closer. I open the drawer to put it away when there's a knock on the door.

"May I come in?" Mom asks.

I guess they changed their minds about waiting until tomorrow to start working.

"Go ahead."

She looks at me, takes a pair of pants from my suitcase, and goes to hang them on a hook. I don't think she came to help me unpack.

"What's up, Mom? Do you want us to do something now?"

Rocío Blisswealth

310

"Well, actually, I wanted to talk to you about something that worries me."

She takes a seat on my bed and glances toward the demon's corner, a futile effort since she'll never see it. With the palm of her hand, she gently taps the space next to her, indicating that I should sit. I do, just not too close.

"What's bothering you?"

"I've noticed that Daniel has become very close to you, maybe even closer than anyone else." For a moment, I recall the bond between us. However, Mom's thoughts navigate more physical than emotional seas, and she concludes her idea. "Close enough to give you a hug." I don't even blink; I keep silent and wait. "I'm wondering, how far he has gone."

Does she really expect me to answer? I can't shake off the surprise of what she's asking me, I guess, based on the claim she has as my mom. But since when does she care?

"Have you slept with him?" She looks at me.

I have no intention of answering, and besides, the answer would be, "Yes, Mom, I've slept with him," emphasizing the word "slept." Judging by the look in her eyes, she wouldn't believe me. My grandma would, and I could tell her how incredibly happy I was those nights, but when it comes to Mom, her position is crystal clear.

"Mom, you're not thinking of giving me 'the talk' at this point, are you? That's what my teachers took care of at school a long time ago because, if you haven't noticed, I turned twenty-one." Obviously, I didn't answer, and I'm not going to. Annoyed, she continues to pressure me.

"I just want you to be aware of all the problems you could get involved in; you see what happened with Mara." How could I forget? Mara got pregnant really young, flipping our lives upside down.

"You have nothing to worry about with me, Mom. Let's drop this."

"No, Jade, I need to know."

"I already told you not to worry, okay?"

"Despite all my efforts to guide Mara, she never took heed, and now you might come up with a...."

What am I going to come up with? A stupidity? Is that what she means? Since when are my problems hers? If I had chosen to be physically involved with Daniel, I would have taken all the necessary precautions, just like I handle every situation in my life. I'm aware that if a problem arises, I would be the one to deal with it alone, no one else, especially not her.

"I'm not coming up with anything. I repeat, don't worry, Mom."

I try to hold my anger; I don't want to argue with her. I'm making a superhuman effort to understand her belated concern, but it's hard for me. I'm infuriated by the way she's handling this because it comes off more as morbid curiosity than genuine concern for whatever consequences might happen. I can't help it.

"But you see, Mara didn't follow my advice."

"Well, you haven't given me any yet, so I couldn't ignore them."

"Of course I did."

"No, Mom, my grandma gave me the advice, and I followed it."

Damn! I knew it. It's hard for me to control myself, and I've already said something that must be painful for her, or at least I thought it would, even though her reaction doesn't show pain, just anger.

"Fine, Jade, you know what you're doing. If you don't want to tell me, then don't."

"I won't bring up topics related to Daniel again, Mom; it will be healthier for all of us. Also, I find it funny that it's now that you worry about this. I remind you that I had a boyfriend in the United States, and the surveillance in the dorms was quite relaxed."

And no, even back then, she wouldn't have had anything to worry about. The image of Mara pregnant was so fresh for me at that age that I agreed with my boyfriend not to get physically involved until our relationship was firmer. And since that never happened, consequently, the rest didn't either. However, it's true, why is it that she cares until now?

"Rest. Mara will look for you in the morning."

"Of course."

My demon watches her walk away; I get up to close the door. I think about how my grandma used to handle any matter with me. She always made me feel worthy of all her trust, and I, at the same time, always tried to live up to what she thought of me. And I don't mean that she thought sex was bad; she never made me see it that way. She just didn't think much of it; it was just another topic in our conversations.

I imagine, if she were alive, what this conversation would have been like. I would have run to her bedroom and said, "Grandma, let me tell you that

I slept with Daniel." And her first question would surely have been, "Oh, dear, and do tell me, does he snore?" I would have told her every situation, in detail: the long hours hugging his athletic body, my private concert, and, above all, what I enjoy the most, his laughter. But she is no longer here, and no one will ever be like her.

After a bath, there's nothing better to do than go to sleep, and that's exactly what I do. This bed, though smaller than the hotel ones, feels enormous today. When is Daniel coming? I miss him even more now. The curtains sway with the wind, but I don't bother getting up to close the windows. I'm not cold, and, honestly, I'm too lazy to move. I turn to the other side and forget about it.

Images rush through my mind too quickly. Seconds later, they slow down, and even though the lighting is low, I can focus more sharply on the ones in front of me.

I'm home, and it looks like there's no light, or maybe no one has turned it on yet. However, the glow from the streetlamps lets me see my surroundings pretty clearly. I take it step by step, checking the different rooms for someone, but they're all empty.

In the living room, my grandpa is sitting, reading the newspaper. I hadn't noticed him; I mean, I hadn't even dreamed of him since he passed away. I rush over, kneeling beside him. He smiles, showing me the newspaper page. Gently, I move it away from me and set it aside. There are so many things I want to ask him, but he brings the page back, pointing to a headline with his fingertip. I pay attention; it's the entertainment section with photos of Daniel. "This section carries special significance for you," he says. I smile; obviously, he is aware of my life, maybe more than I think.

Screams echo from upstairs. I look back at my grandpa; he's still smiling, unaware of anything wrong. I run upstairs, and as I reach the hallway, the screams become clearer, and I can identify them—it's Mom and Mara in my bedroom. I try to reach them, but something grabs my attention, the mirror doesn't reflect my image; there's only darkness in it. The screams intensify, and I don't know what to do. I don't want to let this damn thing escape; he's outside, he entered the house, but where?

I throw myself against my room's door and swing it wide open. They're huddled in a corner, curled up on the floor, screaming non-stop. Mom looks at me; her eyes are bulging like Clemen's, still seeing something behind me. An icy wind runs down my spine; I turn around, and then I see him. Yes, he has

The Game...Jade

come out of the mirror, and his mere presence terrifies them to the point that it could kill them. He smiles when he sees me.

My demon also dashes through the bedroom, at times getting between them and the demon, just like Tíber did with Daniel. The demon in the mirror says, "THAT LIZARD KNOWS YOU BETTER THAN ANY OTHER. IT'S ALREADY STARTED SCURRYING, AFRAID OF THE TORMENT YOU CAN UNLEASH. FOOLISH, DON'T YOU REALIZE? YOU'RE DEFENDING A DEMON FROM ME."

He takes a step to get closer to them, and I stand in his way. I want to provoke him to follow me. I managed to gather some energy in my hand and place it on his chest. His scream of pain almost deafens me; he runs after me, leaving Mom, Mara, and my demon alone.

The house contracts and expands like a heart; it's almost like it's alive. It makes it very difficult for me to move forward; I'm stumbling and almost fall a couple of times. The demon is hot on my heels, and I know I'll have to face him soon. But what's happening to me? The energy seems to be gone; I simply can't find the strength to use it. Please, don't fail me now.

In my run, I stumble upon a door I've never seen before. I'm surprised that, from the room it leads to, I hear Daniel's voice singing softly the same concert he gave me in the hotel bed. The demon corners me, leaving me no choice but to go through it, finding myself in that room where I find Daniel. No! I don't want to lead the demon back to him. Without slowing down, I try to turn and get out, hoping the demon hasn't spotted him yet. But there's nothing; I stop abruptly, looking around—he's gone. Where did he go? I can't wrap my head around it.

Daniel comes closer, hugging me from behind as usual. I feel his breath on my hair, and slowly, I calm down enough to turn and face him. I want to see his eyes; I need to make sure he's okay.

I chill out when I see his calm face. He smiles, and I gently caress his face with the back of my hand, locking eyes with him to find my reflection. It's the dim light or some weird trick, but I can't see myself; there's only a deep blue where his eyes used to hold light. Panic grips me; he keeps smiling with the sweetest smile I've ever seen. I hear a voice saying, "Focus, Jade, focus on the details."

I control my terror as much as possible to study him closely. It's not a projection; every minor detail is there, but what's happening? I reach around his back to hug him tightly, and that's when I notice it—my hands can't find the contours of his body. Instead, they sink into his clothes, responding to the pressure as I attempt to hug him. I step back; everything seems normal at first sight. I reach for the buttons on his shirt, and with my fingers, I find them. Daniel still smiles. Quickly, I unbutton a couple, and I can't see his skin. In desperation, I yank at his shirt's buttons to expose his chest, only to find nothing there—his head and clothes are placed over a skeleton! And all the while, that gentle smile lingers on his face.

My own scream wakes me up. I'm on my bed, drenched in sweat and panting. I struggle to breathe; my throat is burning from the desperate attempt to do so. Leaning on my elbows, I let my head fall back, puffing as I keep trying. Slowly, a thread of air manages to sneak into my lungs, helping me breathe, first with difficulty, then rapidly until, minutes later, I'm still struggling to normalize my breathing.

My tears won't let up, and they've already soaked the top of my pajamas. Ángel, please talk to me. What's going on? Nothing, absolutely nothing, or anyone responds. I lay back on the pillow; usually, nightmares stick around in my mind for a few minutes and then fade away, but I want this one gone completely. I'd like to hold onto the part about my grandpa, but if I have to erase it along with everything else just to shake off this terror, so be it. Two hours later, every second, every detail, every terror is still playing in my head. Please let it be morning already.

Time feels like it's dragging on painfully slow, but after what seems like an eternity, the dawn light finally starts to filter through my bedroom's thick curtains. Aware that my worst fears emerge regardless of the time, I've never really cared whether it's day or night for any of my fears to start fading away. However, this light does bring a bit of relief, maybe because of the contrast with the cold gloom of my nightmare.

It's not like I've never had nightmares before; unfortunately, I could count them by the hundreds. But this one was completely different, more real. The fact that I can't shake off even the smallest detail really gets to me. My throat aches from the struggle to breathe; I can't remember another nightmare that triggered a terror like this. Now that I analyze everything carefully; to be honest, I've replayed the images in my head a hundred times. It's not the demon that terrifies me; I've faced him, and he couldn't have messed with me like this. It's the looming possibility of him taking Mom's or Mara's life.

Today, I realized I won't let them fall into his clutches. I can't stand to see them suffer what Daniel and I went through. They're walking on minefields. Every time they stand next to me during a demonic battle, I'm putting them at risk; they could get killed. Just the other night, when the seven demons attacked, something serious could have happened if I hadn't spotted the demons getting too close to them. I need to be more careful; I won't let them be around anymore. I'll have to handle things on my own.

Digging into the details, I avoid reaching the part of this nightmare that leaves me breathless—Daniel. My hands tremble at the mere memory of his shapeless body, except for the skeleton inside. I wish I could make sense of it, but I've got no clue whether it holds any meaning or not. That image is etched so vividly in my mind that shivers still race down my spine every time my brain dares to replay it, whether in full or in fragments—the outcome remains the same: fear and anguish.

I rub my hands together, trying to convince them not to do what they desperately want. Their only intention is to dial a phone number, etched in my memory like stone, and ask for Daniel. How many seconds would it take to check on him? But I'm not going to invade that timeframe where he doesn't exist for me; after all, Carmen would call me if something bad happened. Would she? Of course, she would! Jade, don't start tormenting yourself with nonsense.

It was just a nightmare. I've repeated it to myself like... How many minutes are there in four hours? Well, at least that many times. The phrase has lost its meaning, and my brain keeps using it as a defense mechanism. It's useless; my common sense has already convinced me that, while it was a nightmare, it has nothing in common with the others I've had. And yes, there's an underlying theme that would be worth analyzing if only an expert would teach me how.

An idea strikes me; I need to know how much reality is in that dream. Mom still hasn't woken up, so I have some time to figure it out. I jump out of bed and reach the door, opening it slowly to check the mirror. I approach step by step, unsure if demons can pick up sounds like footsteps or if they have their own way of detecting my presence. Either way, it's better not to take any chances.

I examine it carefully; it looks so different from the one in my nightmare that I could swear it's a completely different mirror. I place my palms against it and sense the energy flowing through it. Perfect, at least that part of the dream wasn't real; if it appeared, I would have needed something to defend myself.

"Are you there?" I ask, and when I don't get an answer, I continue. "Are you there? Why won't you come out?" I sense someone is listening. "Get out of there, damn it, get out so that…"

"Focus on the details, Jade!"

I take a giant step backward, away from the mirror. A scream rises to my throat, and I stifle it, covering my mouth with both hands. I'm too close to Mom's bedroom, and the last thing I need is for her to think that madness has now been added to my extensive repertoire of virtues.

I step into the room and shut the door behind me, looking around, and there's nothing more than the usual. However, it was Ángel's voice; it's unmistakable, at least for me.

"Ángel? Where are you?" I whisper.

"Focus on the details, Jade."

"I haven't been able to do anything else all night. Why won't you let me see you?"

Nothing, not another word, and, of course, he doesn't show up. Okay, I try to recover from the scare he gave me. I don't know why, given that I was prepared to face the demon, but anyway, one more thing that I will have to control. Now, on top of all this, I have to zero in on the details—damn it! What details is he talking about? I've already gone over the dream at least a hundred times. Besides, my suspicions are now confirmed; it wasn't just a nightmare. If I have details to analyze, it's because there's something important within that dream, but what is it?

Seeing my room completely illuminated by the sunlight, I decided to plunge back into the realm of dreams. Fear makes my stomach tremble, and I wish I knew what Ángel wants me to discover about the details of my nightmare, but my eyelids refuse to stay open.

There's a knock on the door, and it's Mom urging me to wake up. Why so early? I feel like I just slept a few minutes, but according to the clock on my nightstand, it's been three hours. It can't be; it's as if I sat in front of a blank screen when I went to sleep. I didn't dream anything at all, and that's even stranger than the nightmare I had. We always dream of something, even meaningless things, but even so, there are usually images, not a void like the one I'm facing now.

The Game…Jade

Mom stands in the doorway, watching me, asking what's wrong. I make up a smile, unsure of what to say. I'd also like to know what's happening to me. I assure her I'll be ready soon, and she leaves me alone. I scan every space in my bedroom. There's something weird about it, but I can't pinpoint it. My demon is not calm; he joins his hands and intertwines his fingers. Perhaps that gesture could go unnoticed by anyone who didn't know it, but it's not a typical move for him.

I ask him what's going on, and he doesn't look up; he keeps looking at his hands. I no longer have any doubts; something serious is happening. That dream was not a coincidence; I must pay attention to it, special attention to details, just as Ángel said. I know he is trying to help me; the least I can do is follow his orders. I put on my jeans and a t-shirt and stand in front of the mirror; nothing, no changes. Okay, in that case, the details.

The obvious thing would be to think about Grandpa; the detail would be to focus on the newspaper he held with pictures of Daniel. They were photos from concerts I went to, and I don't know what to infer from that. Should I be more aware of what he does? I can't be anymore, but, well, I can try. Or maybe, since my grandparents are no longer alive, could he be a replacement for them in my life? No, I don't think so.

Regarding Mom and Mara getting attacked by the demon in the mirror, Mom's eyes pop out like Clemen's. Could it mean she's in danger like him? Very likely. But I've just decided to stop putting them in the line of fire. The demon in the mirror is signaling I'm protecting another demon from him. I know, I know, and I've refused to do a thing about it. Is this god's way of telling me I should get rid of it? Just the thought of doing something final with it troubles me; I don't want to be left alone. Then I remember the night at the hotel with Daniel and how I could realize that I'd never be alone again. Fine, I'll obey; I'll kick it out of here today. The mere idea hurts.

Daniel, his empty image, just his skeleton, makes my stomach turn. The most disturbing thing about this is that, despite my terror, he kept on smiling, oblivious to everything. I think this dream part is about his connection with me. I'm the only one standing between the demons and him, and luckily, he's clueless about it all. One step at a time, I'll figure out how to protect him. There's got to be a way, but for now, let's see what Mara's up to. I head to the kitchen, not for food—my stomach is shut tight—but to find them. Mara's having breakfast, Mom offers me something to eat, and I just go for juice.

Rocío Blisswealth

318

Through the kitchen window, I see the backyard, filled with plants Grandma planted when she was alive. I like picturing her strolling among them, watering and chatting with them. My grandpa took care of the fruit trees; he had a real knack for it. Case in point, the avocados in the bowl in the middle of the table are straight from his tree. Sitting here, having breakfast with them, was always nice, even enjoyable, and it's only now that I realize it. Grandma always said, "You don't know what you have until it's gone." Today, more than ever, that saying is true. I was happy. I could enjoy my food in peace; today, I can't even take a bite.

I watch Mom searching for something in the fridge and Mara munching on her cereal while reading the entertainment section of the newspaper. Last night's nightmare has made me feel incredibly responsible for whatever might happen to them. As humans, we have this innate knack for etching every harm against us in our minds. That's why, ever since that night when I was four, gripped by panic and finding zero support in them, I've hated having them close. But hey, it's not like they chose to have a daughter or sister like me—someone burdened by demons—who's now brought persecution into their lives. If they didn't know me, they wouldn't have to suffer. Their lives would be demon-free if only I could free myself.

I'm wondering how much of their bad luck is tied to their relationship with me, and I feel like I'm some kind of bird of ill omen. At least I get the days granted with Daniel—days that, for me, are worth a lifetime. But for them? I wonder if they've ever achieved what they want, I mean, to that extent. Something that leaves them totally satisfied. I don't know much about their lives, but I doubt it.

It wouldn't be fair if I defended Daniel against everything and not them. They share my blood; they're my family. And I have to admit they've invested a lot of time figuring out how to help me. They're wading into territories without a shred of training—well, just like me, but at least I know how to handle a defense that frees me from demons, a defense they don't have. Yet, they keep pushing forward as if there's some advantage for them in all this. I know for sure that if my grandparents were alive, they wouldn't expect anything less from me than taking care of the family, and I can't afford to let them down. I don't know if one day, by some twisted fate, I end up in the clutches of those cursed demons. What would I say to them when I see them? No, I wouldn't be able to face them.

The Game...Jade

"Mara, what do we need to do?"

She lifts her eyes from the newspaper and looks at me. Even my tone of voice has changed. That's right, I've changed, and I'm about to prove it.

"Well, I've got a few demon names we might want to rid ourselves of, but do you have anything in mind?"

"You see, I've been thinking it's about time to get rid of the demon in my bedroom. I'm adding it to the mix." Mom's reaction doesn't take long; her joy is so palpable that her face lights up with a huge smile. That hurts me even more, but I couldn't expect her to mourn it, right? I probably will.

"I have to see that!"

"Mom, I remind you that you've never seen it; I don't think that will change now."

"You know what I mean."

"Yes, I know." I hesitate a bit and ask. "Mom, is there a commandment that says I can't be profit-seeking?"

"A commandm... what do you mean?"

"Just answer me." If there is, she probably knows it.

"No, Jade, there's no such thing."

"Great, because there's something I need you to tell god."

"You can tell him yourself; just do it."

"No. I doubt he'll hear me. Would you do me that favor?"

"I promise. What do you want me to tell him?"

"Since my job has turned out to be a good bargaining chip between us, I want to make it clear that I'm very interested in continuing to rack up points. He knows what I want."

"Very well, I'll tell him. Don't worry."

"Another thing, Mara, I need you to write down the names. You know, of the demons. From now on, I'll do it alone."

Both of their voices reflect deep anguish as they scramble to be heard, but Mara's voice is the one I hear most clearly.

"Why do you want to do that, Jade? You need our support."

"No, Mara, you're taking too many risks. I have to go through this, but you don't."

"Just this once." Mom replies. "It's important to me. Please, Jade, let us be present."

Rocío Blisswealth

I guess she's been eagerly looking forward to this day ever since she found out about my demon. I think about it; I shouldn't, but I agree one last time.

"Okay, Mom, just this once. I hope I don't mess up."

We stand up from the table and head upstairs to my room. Upon entering, I refuse to look at my demon; facing him would only make it harder to banish him from this place. I start shaking from head to toe. Mara starts mentioning the names, which I repeat, and at the end of her list, I turn to face my demon. He looks up and stares at me, rising as if preparing for his departure. His stare was cold, devoid of any expression. Inside me, I scream at him with all my strength, 'Please! Ask me not to do it. In fact, you don't need to if you don't want to; just let me see in your eyes, for once, that you want to stay with me. Despite everything, I'll stop. I beg you.' But nothing, he does absolutely nothing.

I finish what I have to say, and unlike the other demons I've dealt with under these circumstances, he doesn't scream or destroy himself; he simply disappears, and that's it. I didn't want to cause him unnecessary pain. I'm a fool, I know, still defending the demon, but no, it was like seeking the most merciful way for a death row inmate to meet their end. After his companionship, it's the least I could do for him, spare him agony.

I walk and take a seat in the chair resting in the corner opposite his. I say nothing. Mom couldn't be happier; she probably achieved something she had prayed for during endless nights. If she doesn't applaud, it's probably out of respect for the grief that has just fallen upon me. She doesn't understand it, I'm sure, but at least she doesn't question it anymore. For her, it must be just another of my quirks. They turn to look at themselves and almost congratulate each other. I just watch them, and out of the corner of my eye, I check his place—he's gone.

Spain.

"I'm going to see her; I can't stay like this."

"DANIEL, IF WE'RE PROVIDING YOU WITH THIS INFORMATION, IT'S NOT FOR YOU TO ACT RECKLESSLY BUT TO BEHAVE APPROPRIATELY; THERE'S TOO MUCH AT STAKE."

The Game…Jade

"And what do they expect me to do? Shall I stay here, abandoning her to fate, letting anyone who finds her tear her apart? All for the sake of stealing a fragment of what she possesses."

"DANIEL, SHE MUST NEED YOU. IF YOU MAKE FREQUENT APPEARANCES, SHE MIGHT GROW WEARY AND…"

"And what about me? I can't remain here without her, thinking about everything that might happen. I need her."

"YOU'VE ALREADY MADE A TERRIBLE MISTAKE BY DISMISSING YOUR MANAGER, DANIEL. PLEASE, STOP; WE'VE BEEN VERY CLEAR WITH YOU."

"He wanted to draw her closer to Víctor. I won't permit them to use her."

"DANIEL, THE MOST CRUCIAL ASPECT IN ALL OF THIS IS THAT THE DECISION IS HERS; IT WILL ALWAYS BE THAT WAY. NOTHING WORKS WITHOUT HER WILL."

"I want to ask her to come with me."

"DANIEL, UNDERSTAND! THINK RATIONALLY; SHE MUST ASK YOU. IF YOU DO IT, YOU VIOLATE ONE OF THE MOST IMPORTANT LAWS THAT GOVERN US—FREE WILL. YOU WOULD LOSE EVERYTHING. CALM DOWN, PLEASE."

"She's so prudent; she'll never do it."

"THAT'S A DISADVANTAGE FOR US. NEVERTHELESS, YOU'VE DONE MUCH MORE THAN YOU SHOULD HAVE. TO BEGIN WITH, YOU SHOULDN'T GET SO INVOLVED WITH HER; KEEP YOUR DISTANCE."

"You don't understand that I can't. I need her like the very air I breathe."

"DANIEL, GRASP THIS: HER PRESENCE IS ADDICTIVE. ONCE YOU'VE HAD HER CLOSE, THE MORE TIME YOU SPEND WITH HER, THE MORE INDISPENSABLE SHE SEEMS. IT'S ONE OF THEIR CHARACTERISTICS. BEING AS CLOSE AS YOU ARE IS VERY RISKY."

"I'm sorry. I'm heading to see her."

"HE CAN RESIST HER; OUTSIDE OF HIS ADDICTION, IT DOESN'T SEEM TO AFFECT HIM PHYSICALLY." Another demon talks to Daniel's guardian.

"I CAN SEE THAT, BUT IF IT'S NOT CONTROLLED, WE ARE THE ONES IN DANGER."

Monterrey.

Rocío Blisswealth

I went to bed very early; I can still hear a lot of activity in the street, people passing by, chatting happily, completely oblivious to how I feel. I've had to cry over many losses, and of all of them, losing my demon makes the least sense. To begin with, obviously, he was a demon and nothing good could be expected from him. Still, he stuck with me through my whole life, the only one who never ditched me, not due to detachment or death. That's another point; he couldn't die, so he would have never left me alone. For a long time, I was scared, but lately, I started to need him. I repeat he wouldn't have died unless I had been the one to destroy him, and I did. I can't forgive myself.

I'm lying on my bed with my eyes closed, I don't want to open them because the empty space he left pains me even more. I notice how the street sounds rebound off the walls, just like they do in empty houses, where the echo takes the lead, followed closely by loneliness. I feel guilty; that's the truth. Besides, there's another feeling I can't shake off; I feel that something very terrible is coming, and I have no idea what it could be. The nightmare continues to haunt me; yes, maybe that's what it is.

There's movement in my room, as if a soft breeze made its way in, causing a ripple through the surrounding air. I open my eyes and see Daniel approaching my bed. I jump up and throw myself into his arms, seeking the comfort that only he is capable of giving me. He greets me with a kiss so intense that if anyone saw us, they would think we haven't seen each other for a long time.

The first thing I do, as soon as I can put my hands on him, is trace the outline of his back with the palms of my hands; apparently, everything is still there in its usual place. He takes my chin in both hands and smiles; I know what he's doing, looking for the usual, what he sees in my eyes, and apparently, it's still in the same place.

"Hello, gorgeous!" He says in a whisper.

"Hello. I'm so glad to see you."

"Did you miss me?"

"Always." I look into his eyes, unable to help but look down at his chest from time to time. I can't forget how his body looked in my nightmare.

"What's bothering you, Jade?"

"I need to ask you a favor, and I'm afraid it might sound like a huge audacity on my part."

The Game…Jade

"None of that. Whatever you want." I smile, embarrassed. How do I ask him without leading his thoughts in the wrong direction?

"It turns out that I had a nightmare, and in it, your body was... No, I mean that..."

"And that's what's troubling you."

"A lot."

He watches me closely; I guess the anguish etched on my face is enough to show him that there's sincerity in the request I'm about to make. Without waiting for me to ask, he seizes the buttons of his shirt with his fingers and begins to undo them. In any other situation, I might take this opportunity to admire the perfection of his body. However, the distress from my dream has become so real for me that I can feel my throat tightly closing up due to the tears wanting to escape. It's stupid, I know, but I'm still expecting to see the skeleton.

Furrowing his brow, he not only unbuttons his shirt, but sheds it entirely. My eyes stay fixed on his ribs, watching them as they ascend and descend to make room for his lungs.

"Jade..." I don't respond. I keep watching his body, trying to erase from my mind the most horrifying part of my nightmare—that emptiness. He reaches out, taking my hand and backing it with his own, gently tracing his ribs. This gives me time to accept this reality and dispel the nightmare. He stops it over his chest, and a tear escapes my eyes.

He leans back, pulling my body towards him, placing me at his side, arranging my arm across his chest so I can still feel his heart, his breath, his warmth—everything that assures me he is there, complete. Once the anguish fades, I can finally speak.

"Thank you."

"You've got nothing to be thankful for. If anything, it's me who has no way to thank you for worrying about me like this."

"I'm glad to do it."

"Excuse me?" He laughs.

"Oh, that wasn't what I meant. I mean, I can't help it."

"Jade, come on, admit it. It was my belly button you were really looking for, wasn't it?" He continues laughing.

"Why on earth would I be looking for your belly button, Daniel?"

Rocío Blisswealth

"Well, to find out, once and for all, whether I'm human or some kind of alien. Wasn't that right?"

"Daniel."

"Yes?"

"There are more options than science fiction movies; you should try them."

"Never! They're my favorites. By the way, gorgeous, have you seen the one about the Martians that just came out?"

"Not for anything in the world, but I bet you're going to tell me about it, aren't you?"

"Since you insist, get comfortable."

"I'm very comfortable, thank you."

"Great. So, it all starts on a dark night, and..." I close my eyes to avoid looking into the corner where my demon used to be; lulled by his voice, sleep overtakes me. I think I stayed at "a dark night." I love you, Daniel.

The Game...Jade

Chapter XV
Like when I leave, and I cease to exist

"Jade."

"Mmm…"

"Jade." Daniel keeps whispering in my ear.

"What's up?"

I half-open my eyes and see him lying on his side, facing me, propped up on his elbow. I can see him very clearly. It's daytime; he stayed with me!

"There's a knock at the door." He says with that mischievous smile of his.

"What?! Daniel, you can't be here. Get out." I reply discreetly.

"I don't think so, gorgeous."

My stomach knots as I watch the door slowly open, just enough for Mara to peek in, staring straight at me since the bed is right in front of the door.

"Jade."

"Yes."

"I'm sorry, but it's getting late, and Mom's wondering if you'll join us for breakfast."

"Sure, I'm starving."

"Great, I'll get the water heating for the coffee while you head downstairs."

"You hate coffee, gorgeous. Doesn't she know?" He asks, as if nothing happened. I don't look at him; he leans in and kisses my cheek.

"I don't drink coffee, Mara." He gently brushes my hair back from my forehead, making me nervous, and I hesitate to answer.

"It's true. Jade, are you okay?" Daniel starts laughing and watches me very, very closely.

"The thing is, I've been having nightmares lately, and I still can't shake off last night's."

"Ouch." Daniel complains, making a pained face, as if I had hit him—well, I did, just his ego.

"We'll be downstairs waiting for you." Finally, she closes the door.

"I hate you, Daniel Montalvo."

"And I adore you, Jade Arias. See you tonight."

Rocío Blisswealth

"Really? Are you coming?"

"Do you want me to?" He asks with a spark in his eyes.

"Of course, always."

"See you tonight, then." He blows me a kiss as he disappears through the door.

My eyes fixate, without even thinking, on the corner where my demon used to be. Now that Daniel is gone, taking the comfort he offered last night, it feels like a burning dagger. I can't bear to see that empty space. Maybe if they had given me a heads-up about the risks I was exposing myself to by having him here, it would all make some sense. The way I see it now is like I've senselessly killed someone—someone I actually liked, someone I needed, and I still need.

I head downstairs for breakfast. Despite the pain I feel, my stomach feels hungry. I haven't eaten well for several days, coupled with some days of not eating at all. I need to catch up on my meals; there's no time for getting sick right now.

Mom and Mara are chatting in the kitchen. I'm concerned about the smell of coffee that has spread throughout the house. I hate coffee in all its forms, and I just hope I won't offend Mom by turning it down. I reminded Mara that I don't drink it, but I'm not sure if she remembered to tell Mom. I sit at the table, and I notice a biscuit with butter in front of me. I love them so much that I might even brush aside how nauseating coffee is to me if it turns out to be the only thing to drink. However, Mom places a large glass of lemonade with two ice cubes in front of me. Not one, not three, but two ice cubes. As strange as it may sound, this is my favorite breakfast, and I haven't had it like that since my grandma was alive. She was the only one who gave it to me without a fuss and the usual lecture about how bread, mixed with water, would cause me to have worms in my stomach. I don't get why people come up with so much nonsense to force us to eat what we don't like.

Now I understand why certain foods are called comfort food. It's like when you've been away from home for a long time, and your family sends you something they've prepared—there's a sense of calm that few things can provide. Strangely enough, biscuits with lemonade have that effect on me; they comfort me, and my pain eases. By the end of breakfast, my mood has shifted.

Mom recalls this story from the day of a party when a demon threw me—well, the official version was that I fell from the tree. When they asked me what I wanted to eat, I kept repeating, "Biscuits with lemonade." This concerned the doctor so much that he banned me from eating such a thing, but I kept asking for it. Grandpa, feeling sorry for me, would sneak my favorite breakfast into my bed every morning, and I happily ate it. Everything went smoothly until the next doctor's visit. He asked if I had been given biscuits with lemonade for lunch, and I firmly said no. The doctor smiled, pleased, until I added, "Not for lunch, only for breakfast."

I start laughing as I remember my grandpa's expression when he heard me say that. He didn't know where to look; all I could see was my grandma, who, under the accusing gaze of the doctor, glared at him. Despite everyone knowing that the blessed breakfast was a tag-team effort—she prepared it, and Grandpa delivered it to me. Mom and Mara, who strangely remember the story, join in the laughter. I can't recall another time when we all three shared a laugh like this.

It's been a week now, and the task Mara set up for me to carry out goes smoothly, without delays or issues. It keeps me busy and gives me more reasons to spend time outside my room. I miss my demon; I can't help it. However, the nights are a different story. I sit cross-legged with Daniel in front of me, in the same position, aligning his knees with mine, capturing my entire field of vision. I wish it could be like this forever.

"Gorgeous, may I ask you something?"

"Of course."

"Is there something in that corner of the room that particularly grabs your attention?" He points towards the demon's corner.

"Why do you ask?"

"For the past few days, while we're talking, you keep glancing over there. And last night, while I was still awake, you suddenly got up, looking toward that corner. When I asked about it, you said, 'He hasn't returned, Daniel,' and that's all. I asked you, but you didn't mention anything more; you simply shed a tear."

"Well… what happens is that, right in that corner, I had a gift someone gave me since I was a child. A few days ago, I got rid of it, and I miss it a lot." That explanation was the only one I could think of.

"And why did you get rid of it if obviously you didn't want to?"

"To please Mom."

"But, gorgeous, there are times when you must say no."

Rocío Blisswealth

"Daniel, coincidentally, that has always been my answer to her, but this time I wanted to please her. Besides, she was right. There are things we need to let go of, even if it hurts, for the right reasons."

"I can accept that when the reasons align with your own, not someone else's. Jade, would it help if I stood in that corner? I could remain motionless and pretend I'm your... What was it? A teddy bear?" He takes the typical position of those toys, with his arms wide open as if trying to give a hug that they can't complete.

I can't believe how sweet this man can be with me. No, Daniel, it wasn't a teddy bear; it was a demon, yet I needed it because it was always with me. That's all. If only I could tell you. What would you think about it? What would be your opinion in this world where you and I live, where unreality is the most real thing for us, where you leave your body every night to sleep next to me? What would you think?

"No, Daniel, I'm actually in the process of..."

"Of forgetting it."

"I couldn't, never, but I am in the process of making it hurt less. And for that, even though it weighs heavily on me, I've got to keep looking at that empty spot frequently until my body gets used to this pain and shifts it to another place; not so much on the surface, but within my subconscious."

"Like when I leave, and I cease to exist."

"You got it."

"Do I hurt you the same way?"

"No."

He takes my hands and brings his face closer, searching for my eyes; he is interested in knowing what I think. For the first time, he has managed to deduce one of my deepest thoughts, and he does not intend to change the subject. He is still waiting for me to clarify my answer.

"When I finally decided to let him go, definitively, I mean, I knew it would hurt, but not to the point of wishing for death. No, you don't hurt me the same way."

He takes my hands to his lips and kisses them repeatedly, sighs long but doesn't say a word. I guess I took him to a cliff.

"I'm sorry, Daniel, I didn't mean to..."

"What are you sorry about, Jade? Reciprocate my feelings? Is that what you wouldn't want to do? I can't be without you. I know I'm stating the bleeding

The Game...Jade

obvious; I don't even venture out of here anymore, but that's what I wanted to hear. More than anything. So, no need to apologize for putting it out there, please."

"I didn't know that…"

"Of course, gorgeous! I do this with everyone."

"Honestly, Daniel, I hope not. You'd spend the day unconscious."

"Come here." He grabs me by the back of the neck, and without finding the slightest resistance from me, he brings me closer to him to kiss me. With the same movement, he gently throws me on the bed and places himself on top of me without separating his lips from mine. I pull away from him and ask him, laughing.

"Daniel, I had the idea that what you wanted most was for me to tell you that you are handsome."

"That's the second thing, and right now, I'm working on it."

"Apparently, you're a supporter of lost causes."

"I never give up. Jade, be silent; I want to kiss you."

It's been a few weeks since the whole demon episode, and it doesn't hurt as much anymore. I've even found myself spending entire afternoons in my room without feeling the weight of his absence. So, it's no longer his emptiness that is the main reason for expanding my territory to other areas of the house. My relationship with Mom and Mara, especially with Mom, has become closer.

It seems like her motherly instinct has led her to recall, or perhaps invent, a way to treat me that I find quite comfortable. However, confidences are still excluded from our conversations, so she is still unaware that I share my bedroom with Daniel almost every night. I doubt she'd be thrilled to know he's my nocturnal visitor, but, as Grandma used to say, 'Out of sight, out of mind,' and everything has improved between us. Do I allow her to touch me? No. Fortunately, she doesn't attempt it anymore. That's another reason why I don't keep as much distance from her—my personal space feels secure.

Today is Saturday, and the kids are at home. The little one rushes up to me, mentioning that I've got a call. First off, she makes it clear it's a local call, not long-distance. However, she insists that I do want to answer it.

"Hello."

"Hi. Jade?" A man's voice I don't recognize answers.

"Yes, who's speaking?"

"It's Jorge from high school. Do you remember me?"

"Of course, Jorge." Not really, I mean. "How can I help you?"

"Jade, I hate to be a bother, but if I recall correctly, you're into dogs, aren't you?"

"That's correct."

"You know, this is an act of sheer desperation, or I wouldn't dare to call you. I actually had to dig up your phone number from old directories."

"What's it about, Jorge?"

"My dog had a few puppies, and sadly, she passed away. One by one, the puppies have been dying, leaving just one behind, but I don't believe he has much time left, either. I'm at a loss for what to do. Would you be open to considering adopting him?"

"Jorge, do you remember where I live?"

"Yes."

"Bring him as soon as you can."

"I'm on my way."

Obviously, Jorge had already told the little one about everything because she smiles and asks:

"Should I bring my doll's cradle?"

"Excellent idea."

And yes, it was. The puppy is so tiny it barely covers the palm of my hand, black and white, with spots like a cow. That's right, he looks like a tiny calf. The little one decided to take the daytime shift, and I, of course, the nighttime one, to feed him every hour with a dropper.

At night, Daniel comes into my room and finds me sitting with the cradle to my side. He smiles, intrigued, and goes to see inside, only to find the puppy sleeping peacefully between scarves.

"Gorgeous, what is this?"

"What does it look like?"

"A toy." He says, smiling.

"Well, you're looking at none other than Tíber II."

"Brilliant! But is he alive then?"

"Of course! And it's been quite a challenge; the mom died, and we have to feed him every hour."

"I'll handle the next shift! What do you say?"

"That will be in forty-five minutes, more or less."

The Game...Jade

"Very well."

As soon as the puppy moved a little, he hurried to pick him up and patiently fed him. He's so fond of dogs that he didn't let me take care of him; he insisted on looking after him today, and I'll handle it tomorrow. Of course, I can't wait to see if he truly allows me to do it.

Tíber is a month old now, and I'm still holding onto the hope that one day, he'll decide to grow. Daniel says that once we start giving him solid food, his growth will take off, but I'm finding it hard to believe him. One afternoon, we lost him, and we all went to great lengths to find him. Fortunately, we succeeded; he was asleep inside a shoe. On another occasion, we searched the place until we finally spotted him seated beneath the bed. Despite his head not reaching the bottom and everything seeming gigantic to him, he seems very comfortable down there. I wish it weren't the case, as it allows him to go on adventures around the bedroom very easily, and I'm afraid of accidentally stepping on him. Seriously!

Of course, whenever there's a need to go up or down any stairs, we end up carrying him. And he has gotten so used to it that he doesn't make the slightest effort to reach them. Just as Daniel puts it, he's treated like royalty, and we, of course, are his loyal subjects.

Tíber may be tiny; however, despite his size in contrast to my demon, he has succeeded in distracting me greatly from the void left behind. Being so small, everything he does is funny, and that really helps. It's hard to feel down when you have to focus all your attention on this little creature that resembles more of a wind-up toy.

At least he no longer needs to be fed every hour; he sleeps through the night in the cradle gifted by the little one's doll, who seems old enough to sleep in her own bed. That makes me happy, especially considering how troubled I was thinking about how little sleep Daniel was getting as he chose to care for the dog instead of getting some rest. He says it's because he loves doing it, but I'm more inclined to think it's because he doesn't have faith in my nursing or veterinary skills or something like that—he just doesn't trust me.

Spain.

Daniel's house, empty despite the time of the day, resonates with the voices of two demons waiting for his return.

Rocío Blisswealth

"HE HASN'T STOPPED GOING TO SEE HER A SINGLE NIGHT. WITH THE WAY THINGS ARE GOING, THAT IS TRULY SERIOUS."

"HE KNOWS. HOWEVER, HE HASN'T TAKEN INTO ACCOUNT OUR INSTRUCTIONS; THERE'S NO WAY TO CONVINCE HIM THAT IT'S NOT IN HIS BEST INTEREST."

"IT MIGHT BE WISER NOT TO PRESS FURTHER; THAT COULD LEAD HIM TO DECIDE TO VISIT HER, PERSONALLY, I MEAN, AND THAT WOULDN'T JUST BE SERIOUS BUT TRULY DANGEROUS FOR THE LORDS AND FOR US."

"FAME IS LIKE THAT, COMPELLING, IRRESISTIBLE."

"BUT HE ALREADY HAS ENOUGH EMBEDDED IN HIS BODY TO FORM A QUITE SOLID CAREER WITHOUT THE NEED TO BE THERE, WITH HER, ALL THE TIME."

"HOWEVER, ONE CAN NEVER HAVE ENOUGH FAME."

"AND DIDN'T THEY INFORM DANIEL THAT ALL OF THIS SERVES A HIGHER PURPOSE? HE CAN'T ALLOW HIMSELF TO BE SWAYED BY WHAT SHE PROVOKES IN HIM."

"THE FEELING IS ADDICTIVE. HE KNOWS PERFECTLY WELL WHAT HE HAS TO DO; HE SIMPLY DOESN'T WANT TO OBEY."

"I ASSUMED HE WAS MORE STABLE."

"WE ALL BELIEVED IT WHEN SHE PRESENTED HER EVALUATION; SHE MADE US BELIEVE HE WAS THE IDEAL CANDIDATE FOR THIS."

"AND NOW HE'S ABOUT TO RUIN EVERYTHING."

"WE WILL TRY TO PREVENT IT; WE WILL TAKE HIM TO VISIT THEM."

"WHAT DO YOU MEAN? ALMOST NO ONE ACHIEVES THAT."

"IT WAS THEY WHO REQUESTED IT, NOT HIM."

"IS HE AWARE OF THIS?"

"NO, IT'S BETTER TO ACT UNEXPECTEDLY."

"HE WON'T LIKE IT."

"THAT'S THE LEAST IMPORTANT THING."

The Game…Jade

England.

The journey to England turned out to be longer than Daniel expected, especially considering that no one took his wishes into account. After landing at the airport, he was ushered into a large black van capable of off-road travel, and that's exactly what it did. His companions, two men in gray suits with the appearance of bodyguards, didn't utter a single word during the journey. I'm not sure if it was because they weren't allowed to or simply didn't want to. Either way, all of this adds to the tension, which already has him on edge.

Their final destination is a small island right in the heart of England, deep in its forests. You heard right, an island resting on a huge lake, just large enough to house a mansion, which can only be reached by crossing the water surrounding it. Few humans know of its existence, and even fewer have managed to enter and leave it with their hearts still beating, and Daniel knows this. He hoped he would never have to set foot on it, but he's willing to do so even if his life is at risk. He knew this from the moment he accepted all this, and now it's time to prove it.

He rubs his hands against his clothes, trying to wipe away the sweat profusely oozing from them. It's easier for him, with the training the press has given him, to control everything from his breathing to his facial expression. But sweat, that's another thing.

They step out of the van to board a small boat, just big enough for the three of them. This final stretch is short, and the boat approaches the shore quickly; however, it stops just three feet away from reaching it. Daniel looks at his companions; even if he made an effort, he wouldn't be able to jump the gap between them and solid ground without getting his feet wet. According to their instructions, that's precisely what the maneuver is about.

It's an absolute requirement to take off your shoes and dip your feet in the water. And, without giving it a second thought, he does it. Contrary to what he expected, the water isn't freezing like the entire environment around him; it's at the exact temperature of his skin, and he can hardly feel it. With this done, he walks barefoot down the wide corridor flanked by bushes leading to the house. Once inside, he explores the enormous halls with sturdy Roman-style columns and marble walls in various shades from beige to white, forming the backdrop for captivating works of art. Under different circumstances, Daniel might have taken a moment to admire it all, but in his jittery state, it's just random paint patches scattered here and there.

His attention is captured, however, by one of his favorite paintings, Francesco Hayez's 'The Kiss.' The sheer beauty of it captures him, and almost involuntarily, he exclaims:

"What an extraordinary copy!" One of the bodyguards stifles a laugh.

"The copy is in the museum; only the lords could afford the original."

He moves on, pretending not to hear. This mansion screams excess within these walls. Of course, thinking about those reaches just to adorn a wall is overwhelming.

They reach a massive mahogany door with gold fittings, and one of the accompanying men opens it, indicating for him to enter. Before doing so, Daniel rubs his hands against his pants once again and takes a step forward.

Any area of the house he had explored earlier doesn't compare to the sumptuousness of this room. It's practically bare, featuring three wide steps leading down to the space where they await him. His gaze stops, contemplating the sensational work on the floor in front of him. The mosaics create figures of different colors, resembling a stained-glass window, their meaning unknown to him but surely serving some important purpose—everything here has a purpose. The unique gleam of these mosaics gives the illusion of reflecting light like a mirror. Descending the third step, Daniel realizes why—they're covered in water.

Five men are waiting for him; Daniel has never seen them before. Even though he knew about their existence, his imagination couldn't quite stretch enough to prepare him for what was right in front of his eyes. They all share similar physical traits as if a blood bond ties them together, but their unique features make them easily distinguishable. They are tall, probably over six feet. They have very short and well-groomed gray hair. Their attire, composed of pants and sweaters made from natural fibers, boasts light tones—beige, sand, white. None of them wears a watch or any other type of jewelry.

Daniel finds it impossible to guess their ages, and that sends shivers down his spine. Their thinness and the tone of their skin make it seem like they've never seen sunlight, so pale that their clothing colors seem dark in contrast. Even Daniel's fair skin appears rosy next to them. Moreover, it is so thin that veins can be seen through it on their foreheads, necks, and even eyelids, giving them a truly eerie appearance.

The Game…Jade

As soon as he dips both feet in the water, a collective soft sigh and plenty of expressions of contentment fill the air, though not directed at him but exchanged among themselves. Daniel looks around and notices that each of the five lords, as the bodyguard called them, has their left foot in the water, with the right one resting on a rung of their throne-style chair. The chairs are exactly the same, except for a plant carved into the wood on the back of each one, featuring their names in Latin. Only he has both feet in the water, and there's no other way to approach. One of the men stands up and greets him with a skeletal hand; it appears he will lead the conversation while the others merely observe.

"*Good afternoon, Daniel.*"

"Why have you brought me to this place?" He asks with fear in his voice.

"*Let's not lose our manners, young man.*"

"Good afternoon." He mumbles in response.

"*Thank you. I will proceed to answer your question then. We were somewhat eager to see you. The situation between you and Jade is far from what was initially planned before you met her, I mean. And we want to know the reason for such a serious deviation from the previously outlined plan.*" After a great effort, he manages to control his voice and then responds.

"I wouldn't say the deviation was overly grave; I merely implemented a few changes that, ultimately, only impacted me. After all, I'm the one spending more time with her and no one else."

"*You're wrong, Daniel; you're not alone in this. As I understand, you were instructed before it all began about the vital importance of accuracy in carrying out the plans. Therefore, the fact that you deviate from the original plan is serious, very dangerous, whether you consider it so or not.*"

"Why is it dangerous?" He asks, more to gain time than out of doubt.

"*Alright, Daniel, I'll explain it to you again, in case the person who carried that responsibility on their shoulders did not do so with the dedication that task required.*

Jade carries in her DNA an exceptional combination that does not repeat frequently. She is what we know as a Spiritual Nexus, a union of things that surely escape your understanding, but it means she is a point of incredible and inexhaustible energy. There are geographical areas with such forces, but when it comes to a human, her gifts can achieve incredible feats.

The combination of the blood flowing through her veins results in access to Fame; the energy she produces attracts it as an unavoidable consequence. Regardless of time or space, it envelops you. This, without taking into account the other benefits her energy produces, such as having the most inspired muse on the continent imprisoned and having access to her inspiration permanently, as in your case. Someone as gifted as her can make several careers flourish at once without deteriorating at all. That's why she's so special.

All of that is for you if you decide to adhere to the rules and distance yourself from her. This is because one of the drawbacks of her gift is that her presence is so addictive that it draws you towards her. However, being in constant contact with her can cause such a terrible spiritual and physical deterioration that it can end you much more quickly than normal. The only way her energy won't affect you is if you don't covet it, if you stay close to her without using it, and we both know that's not your case. That's why we seek your help; none of us would survive a direct approach. But you already know all this, don't you, Daniel? Your clock started ticking several months ago, and you're enjoying its sweetness. Howe..."

"I know that, but..."

The gentleman, upon being interrupted, locks eyes with Daniel and takes a few seconds to control his anger, then continues.

"*The youth have forgotten the gift of patience, my friends, and our dear Daniel is a clear example of a total lack of it.*"

"What she has given me doesn't only benefit me." He reproaches them.

"*That is absolutely true; however, the tone in which you mention it suggests that you had no idea this would happen. Weren't they clear enough with you, Daniel?*"

"Yes, I was aware, but..."

"*Splendid, it is essential that you are perfectly aware of all the points concerning Jade to simplify our conversation. Our priority in bringing you closer to her is and always has been to obtain what she produces so that such an extraordinary gift does not come to waste; that would be a real pity, almost a sin. That is why these plans were carefully drawn since her conception, taking care of her, accompanying her every step of the way, twenty-four hours a day, and now you seem not to give them the proper importance.*"

The Game...Jade

"She hasn't been given the opportunity to choose who she wants to give it to. No one has bothered to find out what her wish is." He speaks, annoyed.

"It is true, and that is why we will be eternally grateful to you. If it were not for you, who turned out to be the perfect bait for her, that opportunity would have presented itself to her under another skin. It has been you, Daniel, you, and no one else who has not allowed her eyes to be looking for another opportunity. Her love, which you have cultivated with such dedication, will not allow her to divert that energy to other points that could cause a disadvantage for us. You are our access to her gift, and we will know how to use it in the best way without causing her any harm. Daniel, if that is what concerns you, she won't even notice.

I just want it to be clear that everything in excess ends up being harmful; we are not prepared to withstand the amount of energy that you are sending our way, and everything could start to turn against us. We must be sensible, Daniel."

"I don't feel any negative effects on me."

"I'm glad to know that; it speaks of the success of carrying out our purposes. That's what you were designed for, you and others who were waiting for the same opportunity you received. The situation was that she chose you, as simple as that."

"What do you expect from me?"

"As a matter of principle, conclude the exchange as soon as possible. Could you explain why you haven't done it? Given your background, we assumed that taking Jade to bed, offering her your body, and thus paying for what she gives you would be quite simple for you. I just can't explain it. Besides, she attracts you, doesn't she? In the hotel in Mexico, you slept next to her. I mean, why resist? She wouldn't have refused if you had asked; you wouldn't even have had to force her."

"You have no idea what she's like; I had never met someone quite like her. And forcing her? She places absolute trust in me; I couldn't bring myself to do it knowing what she would be getting in return, the fact that she wouldn't have the option to change her mind if she wished."

"That would indeed be the case. I thought you would be glad to have the assurance that the supply of energy, and with it, fame, would never stop. I must admit that the last thing I expected to find in you would be scruples, Daniel, what nonsense. Consider that, upon completing the exchange, you could

finally distance yourself from her permanently and indulge in the life of debauchery that you always led. Doesn't that sound fantastic?"

"No, it doesn't sit right with me. So, I won't be doing it. Tell me, what exactly do you want from me?"

"Under the present circumstances, to distance yourself from her. Not definitively, of course, but you should limit your visits to no more than one night every two months; that would be enough."

"Not for me." He lifts his gaze and stares at them; his look is challenging. It's the first time he's confronted with the possibility of losing or, worse, letting go of what matters most to him. Despite the stakes, he finds the courage to continue.

"What if I choose not to obey?"

"What?! That's not possible! That's inconceivable!" The other four characters shout.

"Gentlemen, calm down, please!" Once calm is restored, he continues. *"We would proceed with our plan without you, without sparing any resources as we have done so far. We can't afford to have you mess it all up. We know well the raw material we work with, Daniel; everything we use is considered disposable from the beginning until it proves to be worth something. You are not indispensable."*

"Actually, I believe it is me who no longer requires you all. As you know, I have enough energy imbued in me to…"

"I praise your confidence, Daniel; as always, free will govern us, and we will respect yours. If that is your decision, at this moment, we consider our relationship terminated, and you are free to go wherever you please. However, I deem it necessary to give you a warning. We have invested too much time in Jade, enough to strive our utmost to achieve a favorable culmination of the plans we meticulously laid out. You can be assured that we will fight to see them fulfilled by any means necessary."

"You mentioned she had chosen me."

"And so she did, but everything can change, Daniel. You know, her will is what matters; girls, at her age, are fickle. And if you don't keep a proper distance from her, everything will eventually fade away. Remember, it is her will that keeps the effect of her gift alive on others. As for you, I deeply regret making such a grave mistake in judging you. Perhaps you are not as resilient

after all. Fame has driven some people crazy, and others have gone mad after losing it, having tasted its sweetness. I hope that's not your case."

"Which of the two cases are you referring to?"

"Both, my dear Daniel, both of them. Either way, you know where to find us if, at some point, we are necessary to you. I suppose I don't have to remind you that the confidentiality oaths you agreed to in your first meeting with one of our envoys are still in force. The decision is yours regarding what you want to do from now on, but the oaths remain until death. Obviously, the discretion we wish to emphasize refers to your conversations with Jade. If you were not to respect that agreement, your life would have absolutely no value to us anymore."

"Is that a threat?"

"Of course it is, Daniel! Well, I am pleased that my words are entirely clear to you."

"I'll bear that in mind. May I go now?"

"Yes, Daniel, I suppose you want to run back to her side. Honestly, I understand you, really understand you. I am savoring the energy she produces, a real delicacy, undoubtedly." He says this, pointing to the water covering the floor, and concludes. *"It must be delightful, enjoying it day after day, and at the same time, distressing to constantly remember the fragility of her nature, to depend strictly on the will of a young girl. A difficult, very difficult task, although surely this will be easy for you. Enjoy it, Daniel."*

Out of nowhere, one of the bodyguards swings the door open, holding it there for him. The journey back to the boat goes down just like when he first arrived—peacefully. And despite the fear gripping him, there's no violence or anything. Once on board, they hand him a towel to dry his feet and give him back his shoes.

Daniel can't shake the thought that if they intended to harm him or make him disappear, it'd be days before anyone noticed. Just think about it: the people who're supposed to be tied to him think he's in Spain; obviously, they didn't give him the chance to let anyone know where he was headed.

As the van rolls away from the island, the fear of death eases up. They've had plenty of time to end him if that was the plan. Now, it all boils down to an image stuck in his mind that sends shivers down his spine, and no matter what he does, it's going to stick with him for a while. An image that reminds him of the day he realized how pure Jade is compared to him, that is always calling the shots without considering where he's heading.

When the offer of incredible fame came knocking, he didn't give it a second thought—or any thought at all—before accepting every single clause they threw at him. If he had taken a few minutes to think it over, he might have figured out that a regular human can't pull off that kind of achievement. And if he couldn't come through with what he was supposed to give her in return, or if that wasn't really what she was after (just like what went down), it wouldn't be a trade, but more like a heist, totally different from what they first made him believe. A heist on a girl who has no clue about what she's losing or who she's losing it to. Even though, deep down, he knows that even considering all that, he would've still said yes. But maybe, just maybe, if he had seen the image that is haunting him today, he might've hesitated, put a brake on it, and let someone else take the fall for the sin.

During the conversation he had on the island, he was horrified seeing how the bodies of these men changed up as they absorbed the energy coming from him—Jade's gift, something she gave only to him, not them, that's for sure. The visible veins disappeared under a pale, no longer transparent, hue on their skin and their bodies; well, he could swear they even gained some weight in the process. They appeared to breathe more deeply, inhaling her energy. For them, just like for him, Jade is pure air, something they can't live without. They're not willing to give it up.

Fears he never imagined now overwhelm him. They've tasted what she produces, and they're going after her like predators after a gazelle, all because he stirred them up to do so. Why didn't he stick to the rules while figuring out how to protect her and keep her out of their reach? As always, he had to act without thinking. Damn it! What danger has he now put her in?

He saw her challenge a demon to follow her, all just to keep it away from him, to save his life. And now, he's exposing her to even greater dangers, ones he's not sure she can face without losing her own life in the process. They'll keep fighting for their prey, snatching her away; he can't bear to lose her anymore.

He needs to get home. The hours are ticking away; soon, it will be time for Jade to wait for him to sleep, and it will be impossible for him to be there. He's terrified to think of what they plan to do when he arrives with her. No doubt, they won't waste a single moment—the plans, even now, must already be set. He'll likely be late, and even if he manages to get there to face whatever they send for her, what could he do? Nothing, absolutely nothing. As soon as he steps into the house, he rushes to his room and locks the door. It's challenging for him to concentrate enough to project himself and get to Jade, yet despite everything, he keeps trying.

Monterrey.

It's three in the morning, and Daniel is nowhere to be found. I pace around my room, mentally going through all the possible reasons why he's not showing up tonight. The album is about to drop, and surely, the promotion is swallowing up most of his time—photo shoots, autograph sessions, parties.

But no, deep down, I can feel a sharp sense of panic coming from him—the same fear he felt the day the demon attacked him. However, this time, I can't shake off the nerves and sleep to reach his house, and my patience is wearing thin. If he doesn't show up soon, I'll grab the phone and give him a call; after all, it's ten in the morning in Spain.

Finally, I feel a breeze at my back and turn around just in time for him to hold me in his arms. He hugs me tightly, and I can feel his heart racing faster than usual. Tíber lets out a soft whimper from the bed; surely, he feels it, too. Pulling away, Daniel lifts my chin to meet my eyes and gently caresses my face from forehead to chin with his fingertips, smiling. This caress is his usual greeting, and looking into his eyes, I can sense his mood, which is usually calm. However, this time, it's not calmness but anguish, a bitter anguish that I see in his eyes.

"Hey." He says, almost in a sigh.

"Daniel, are you okay?"

"Now I am."

He guides me to the bed, pulling me closer until my face is partially hidden in his neck. I hug him, feeling the intensity of his breath. Tíber comes close from the other side, struggling to climb onto his chest. Daniel takes him in his hand, places him on himself, and the dog curls up right above his heart. I think both of us interpret the animal's movement as an effort to hug him despite his tiny size. Daniel pets him and says, "Thanks, Tíber," to which the little creature responds by licking his finger.

Rocío Blisswealth

I can't be at ease, contrary to what usually happens. Tonight, the closer I am to him, the more unsettled I feel. I sit up and rest my arm on my elbow, holding my head at a height that allows me to look him in the eyes. He doesn't let me see them, keeping them partially closed. I move closer to his cheek and kiss him; he turns and kisses my lips for a long while until I can feel his breathing calming down, and he looks at me. His gaze is sad; his fingers intertwined with mine don't allow me any freedom to move them at all.

"Aren't you going to ask me about anything?" He says in a hushed voice.

"I'm waiting."

"What thing?"

"It's pretty clear that you're feeling uneasy, and I don't want to bother you. For now, I just want you to know that I'm here, and I believe you already know that, don't you? Later, when you're feeling calmer, you can share with me or not. I know perfectly well that not everything in your life is within my reach." He extends his free hand and strokes my hair.

"I'm a bit scared, gorgeous, and at this moment, I couldn't find the words to explain to you what scares me. The only comfort I find is in you. I don't know what I would do if..." He presses my hand even more.

"Daniel, unfortunately, life is full of unpleasant things; that's just the way it is, but we can't live in fear. We've got enough on our plate dealing with those... circumstances when they come. No need to jump the gun, you know?"

"Jade, the album will be released soon, and the promotional tours are about to kick off. We'll be together day and night, regardless if they like it or not."

"As long as it doesn't bother you, everything is fine."

"Of course not, gorgeous. How could you say that?" He finally laughs even though the laughter only reaches his lips, his gaze is still sad. Tíber lets out a loud snore, too loud for something so tiny. We start laughing, this time more eagerly, and the dog wakes up. We have a good time playing with him until both he and Daniel yawn and snuggle up next to me. Daniel is one thing, but Tíber—I'm afraid to crush him, so I take him carefully and return him to his cradle.

Daniel sighs and starts falling asleep, although his sleep is quite restless. He keeps holding my hand, and I have had no success in my attempts to release it from his. As he sleeps next to me, I try to think, what is he afraid of? What's the worst that could happen to him? My thoughts inevitably turn to the image of the demon holding him. Losing him would be the worst thing for me, but when it comes to him, I don't know.

If I have to go by what I can sense, it would mean not being able to return here with me. That idea seems extremely egocentric, and I have always been against allowing myself such naïve thoughts. I've made plenty of mistakes, and I know I still make them, but it brings me some comfort to believe that I don't do it on purpose. But the feeling within him is strong enough for me to recognize it clearly, and I don't intend to ignore it either. So, considering that, what precisely is he afraid of losing by not returning here? I need to figure out how to protect him if I can. I really hope I can.

Rocío Blisswealth

Chapter XVI
All's fair in love and war

England.

After Daniel left, the mansion was filled with buzzing discussions. Clearly, these men are used to, on one hand, getting their way and, on the other, being obeyed without question. Therefore, Daniel's attitude has caused a stir among them. They expected that their mere presence would have such an impact on him that he would reconsider his mistakes and comply with their wishes. However, he doesn't care anymore about all that stuff he agreed to when the talks were just theoretical. In practice, after meeting Jade, everything has drastically changed, and these beings have just come to realize it.

Since their real names are unknown, and to simplify detailing their conversations, I'll refer to them by the name of the plant carved into each of their chairs, with Boxwood being the one who spoke directly to Daniel. They have stood up and are still wading through the water in the hall, absorbing the remnants of the energy.

Boxwood: What went wrong?

Grapevine: To begin, when she assessed him, she was confident that, driven by his desire for fame, he would be able to withstand what Jade projects and strictly adhere to the parameters he must follow. However, his attitude is far from compliant.

Boxwood: Many mistakes have been made with them. I foresaw something, or perhaps everything, going wrong.

Ebony: What do you mean?

Boxwood: Demons were tasked to watch over them.

Ebony: The angel is watching over her, too! It was our right!

Boxwood: I'm not referring to that; I mean the fact that the demon in charge made a terrible mistake by attacking them.

Ebony: He did what he deemed fit. He noticed that Daniel had seriously disobeyed and attempted to rectify the issue in time, but at that moment, Jade appeared. I still can't fathom how she can connect with Daniel in that manner; in theory, that's not possible.

The Game…Jade

Olive: Forget about theories. In principle, the demon should have ignored her, but he didn't. Not only that, but he also dared to attack her, putting the considerable investment we've made in her at serious risk. Moreover, he exposed himself, revealing as a threat to both of them.

Ebony: To a certain extent, he acted logically, carefully measuring his attacks to avoid causing severe damage. Furthermore, it would have been fatal to let her go and make Daniel see that she wouldn't suffer consequences for her actions. The demon felt he would respond better if he saw her vulnerable. He also couldn't allow Jade to feel free from his attacks, seeing Daniel as the sole victim, because she would rush to defend him, and we all know what that could bring us. We can't afford uncontrolled bursts of her energy, either willingly or unwillingly; in both cases, that would be fatal for us. Fortunately, she's unaware of that fact, like many others.

Olive: It all sounds great; however, that demon failed to discern the reason behind Daniel's disobedience. Despite the seventy hours he took to do so, he couldn't get a single word out of him. Instead, he incited Jade to seek him constantly, making it impossible for him to perform the task for which we trained him so carefully. Furthermore, knowing as well as we do that this girl is anything but vulnerable. He won't be able to carry out his assignment anymore, and training another demon at this point would be impossible. He has followed her blood for centuries and knows all her strengths and, more importantly, her weaknesses. We need him there, and he can't be close without her noticing and attempting to end him, which, with a slight effort on her part, would be feasible.

Grapevine: Perhaps, despite all that, it may not be necessary to look for another option; perhaps we can still use him.

Ebony: How?

Grapevine: Placing him in a location where it's not easy for her to detect him.

Boxwood: That's practically impossible; she has a special sense to find them.

Grapevine: Not always; there are times when, out of habit, she responds more to her senses than her instincts. I still think that maybe we could make her not notice.

Mistletoe: Alright, let's not waste time then. What are the next steps from now on? I suppose it's evident to all of us what we're losing, and without

Daniel's will, we can bid farewell to Jade's gift. At least, I'm not willing to lose it now.

Grapevine: *That's out of the question! There's no turning back, only a change of plans.*

Mistletoe: *Fantastic! I'm listening.*

Grapevine: *According to the demon, when she has time alone, her instinct leads her in the right path. We will prevent her from having time to do so. Lately, she has focused on intense demonic tracking, and that consumes a lot of her time. That area will be useful for us from now on. Besides, in that realm, many mistakes can be made, and we will ensure that happens.*

Ebony: *Who could we rely on?*

Grapevine: *We have no other choice. She doesn't trust anyone, has no friends; it will have to be the demons; we don't have other resource for now. We tried once to bring her closer to Victor, and Daniel made sure to keep her completely away from him. He knows our moves and has put herself on the defensive.*

Mistletoe: *But demons, sooner or later, make mistakes. Like the day they allowed her to see them protect her from the crowd. They could ruin everything.*

Grapevine: *We'll be clear enough, especially with one of them who is already in the place that suits us best. On that occasion, his mistake was due to the imperative need to protect her life, but you're right; she shouldn't have seen them.*

Olive: *Very well, and as for Daniel, what will happen to him? I suppose you haven't just let him go as if nothing happened.*

Boxwood: *Of course not! It's easy to assume that by now he has suffered a violent death, or am I wrong?*

Grapevine: *Friends, I regret to inform you that you're both wrong. Yes, as unbelievable as it may seem, we let him go as if nothing happened, and no, he has not suffered a violent death. The situation with him has changed drastically; Jade is protecting him so intensely that the moment I approached to greet him, I knew, by touching him, that I could not be angry with him without her making me pay.*

Ebony: *How?! She made him immune to us! How the hell did she know how to do that?*

The Game...Jade

Grapevine: That's the problem; she doesn't know how to do it deliberately; she just does it.

Ebony: So, what are we going to do?

Grapevine: We will use him without Daniel realizing it, without giving him time to feel afraid. That would be the trigger for Jade.

Boxwood: That's impossible; we no longer have control over his will anymore, remember?

Grapevine: If we have her, this is like a marriage: Daniel signed with us and gave us his free will; we will use it, even against himself. All's fair in love and war. In the end, he is already enjoying what we provide.

Boxwood: Jade provides it for him.

Grapevine: That's right, but if it weren't for us, he would never have met her, and he wouldn't know how to use that gift.

Mistletoe: Undoubtedly, this will be a war. Among all my concerns, we must be aware that her angel is also there twenty-four hours a day. And there is one thing that stands out above the rest—Daniel possesses the most powerful weapon, Jade.

Grapevine: We will not allow him to use her; she will soon be on our side and away from him.

Ebony: She won't distance herself from him so easily.

Grapevine: I never said it would be easy; it never is. Now, bring Sara; it is imperative that we talk to her. There are too many loose ends in this, and she has to take matters into her own hands.

Monterrey.

I couldn't shut my eyes the whole night; I was worried about Daniel's condition. I've seen him tossing and turning for hours, spinning around in bed, left and right, gripping my hand the whole time, making it even harder for me to catch some sleep. I think when he sleeps, he totally forgets that my hand is attached to the rest of my arm. He pulled it up and down without any mercy. If I wasn't so worried seeing him like this, I would've definitely woken him up to let go.

Right now, he's lying on his side, facing me, and his right hand is holding mine under his chin. Now and then, he squeezes it tighter, as if I tried to pull away, and then let go a bit again. Not enough for me to free it completely, just a little, so I guess my blood can keep flowing. Other times, he turns around,

Rocío Blisswealth

348

facing away from me, wrapping my arm around his chest, putting my hand over his heart, and I'm stuck to his back, but he doesn't seem to notice.

Sometimes, his face shows pain, and then anger. I don't know which feeling I prefer; the second one works pretty well for me. It gives me a sense of security, feels just right, and almost instantly makes me feel better. But when it comes to him, I don't know what's best.

With the free hand, I gently stroke his face and listen to him whispering words I don't get. What I do catch is my name; he keeps saying it, although I'm not sure if he's talking to me or about me. I hate this feeling, like I'm the cause of all his problems, when all I really want is the opposite.

Suddenly, he shudders, and opens his eyes wide, locking onto mine. He squeezes my hand hard enough to hurt, and I let out an "ouch" that he doesn't pay much attention to. Without letting go, he tries to get closer to me, then realizes the force he's using and releases me. You can clearly see his fingers marked in red against my usual pale skin. It's only at this moment that he wakes up completely, his expression changing from anger to concern.

"I'm sorry, Jade. Truly, I am. How long have I held you? Why didn't you ask me to release you? You should have woken me up."

I smile and watch him massaging my hand, trying to erase the imprints of his fingers on it, which seem to be tattooed because they don't give way at all.

"Daniel, don't worry. My skin marks at the slightest touch and these marks will be there for a few more minutes, whether you keep massaging or not, so..." He stops the massage, and I continue. "So, if I can choose, continue with the massage; it feels really good."

He smiles embarrassedly and continues the therapy while I keep answering his questions.

"How long did you hold on to me? Well, pretty much since you fell asleep. Why didn't I ask you to let me go? Probably because I didn't want you to. I'm a bit of a masochist, you know, and I didn't wake you up because I wanted you to rest. How are you feeling?"

"More or less, but I know there's a way I could feel even better. Will you lend a hand?"

"Yes, what do I have to do?"

"Can I have a hug from you, Jade?" He asks, just like the first time. His gaze saddens, and I don't want him to fall into that gloom again.

The Game...Jade

"That depends, sweetheart."

"And what does it depend on, gorgeous?" He smiles slightly.

"Well, you see, lately, I've been out there dishing out hugs every which way, and it's caused a hug shortage. I've run out of the short ones and even the medium-sized ones."

"Then?"

"I only have a long, long one left. Do you want it?"

"Absolutely." He reaches his arm out to me, but I interrupt his movement by raising my hand as a sign that I'm not done yet. He stops and furrows his brow.

"I'm sorry, Daniel, but this time, it'll cost you."

"Go on! And do you think my funds are sufficient to cover the cost?"

"You're lucky; I'm up for a trade."

"Brilliant! What's the deal? What have I got that might catch your interest?"

He finally smiled mischievously. It's not the same smile that has always fascinated me, but it's pretty close.

"Well, it's not exactly about something I'm interested in; it's more like something I need with irresistible desperation. Can I have one of your kisses, Daniel?"

"They're all yours, Jade; you can have them all."

"Agre…" I don't have time to say anything; he lunges at me and kisses me while I play my part in the trade by hugging him as tight as I can. Almost without separating his lips from mine, he asks, pretending to be angry.

"Can I know who the bloody hell you've been hugging?"

"No."

"What do you mean n… Why not?" He straightens up to look me in the eyes.

"It's a state secret. If I tell you, I'd have to kill you." He smiles and bites my lip.

"Jade…"

"Yes?"

"You mentioned needing my kiss…"

"Desperately."

"Really?"

"I have no reason to lie to you."

Rocío Blisswealth

"Well, let's not chatter any longer."

I get the feeling that what he was about to tell me wasn't this. However, I know that if I press him, he won't say anything. So, I just go along with it, responding to his kisses. This time is very different; they had always been filled with sweetness, but today they are desperate. It's hard to explain, like each one carries a message of fear, anguish, and rage. As minutes pass, sweetness begins to break through until he kisses me again, as he always does.

There's a detail that catches my attention. Whenever Daniel enters my room, he's in sleepwear. Today, however, he's wearing blue jeans, a light cream sweater, and sneakers—daytime clothing. Why wouldn't he change? I figured he thought it was too late, but I didn't dare to ask.

Later, it's time for him to go. It's getting late, and I know he has many things to do. Honestly, so do I. The little one needed a costume for a school party, and I promised her I'd get it. Knowing her, she won't take long to come and wake me up so I can take her. So, it'll be either her or Tíber, who is already making noise from his crib, not forgetting, of course, Mara and her checklist. Daniel gets up to leave, not without repeatedly confirming he'll be back tonight, this time at the usual hour.

"Daniel, I know the new album is dropping soon, and I have a hunch about the upcoming promotion. Don't worry if you can't make it one of these days. I don't like the idea, but I understand."

He takes a seat next to me and holds my hand, which has finally returned to its usual color.

"Jade, there are moments when I hate how much you respect my career and my life. I almost wish you'd ask me to return without fail, and then I..."

Suddenly, I recognize the words, and they bring me back to a painful image that is fresh in my memory. That's more or less what I begged my demon to do, and he did nothing to stay with me. I suppose his motivations weren't that noble, but I know what I'd get by asking.

"You would, I know, but no, Daniel, I'm not capable of doing that."

"Not even for me?"

"Especially for you."

He kisses me and leaves. I keep thinking about the truth of the words I just told him. For me, even before myself, he comes first.

The Game...Jade

It's been several nights since Daniel was late. Despite his busy schedule, he's been showing up without a hitch. Even his mood has almost returned to normal, maybe a little more apprehensive. He bombards me with constant questions, and unlike my usual practice of never explaining my actions to anyone at all, I find myself answering him. It's just that I don't want to cause him more distress, and there's something about me that seems to worry him a lot. After all, there's not much I can tell him, considering that the demon realm, the most extensive part of my life, is completely off-limits in our conversations. That leaves very, very little to share. Fortunately, I've always enjoyed reading, giving me plenty of things to talk about.

A few days ago, I said it's not worth worrying about the future and suffering ahead of time, but I find it impossible to follow my own advice. Used to stuff always taking a turn for the worse, the voice of my subconscious keeps warning me that the way things are playing out is not normal. I'm still on the lookout for the demon in the mirror; I know perfectly well it's a potential threat to Daniel and me, maybe the biggest one I'm aware of, but it's still on the loose, and I can't find him.

I'm also worried about the state he arrived in a few nights ago and the fear I sensed from him before. It bothers me not knowing what I'm dealing with, even though I'm sure it's something terrible. I can't even prepare myself to face it since I have no idea what it is. On second thought, even if I knew, how would I prepare? I've never figured out how to, and no matter how hard I try, I simply stick to Mara's instructions. I haven't taken the initiative in the attacks, and, to add to that, I don't know who to attack. I'm still on guard, keeping an eye out for any shifts, but there's nothing. At least this allows me to feel like I have control over something, probably not, but I like to feel that way.

With all this burden occupying my entire subconscious, and a good part of my conscious mind, the rest of my attention is dedicated entirely to Daniel. I don't know if it's happened to you, but even when I try to maintain a balanced life—between my work against demons (you remember the point accumulation, right?), my newly begun family life, and my relationship, if I can call it that, with Daniel—the latter always ends up leading over the rest. If things with Daniel are calm or even happy, the rest of my life adjusts accordingly, and everything feels simple and even exciting for me.

On the contrary, when things with him get distressing, this feeling spreads to everything else, and I end up getting caught up in paranoia. So, now

Rocío Blisswealth

352

that he's found his calm again, mostly at least, everything feels peaceful for me, too. I can enjoy his presence more without worrying about analyzing changes in his gaze or the tones in his voice.

Being in this mood lets me pick up one of the activities I enjoy the most: my absolute dedication to fully appreciating his incredible attractiveness. I simply love watching him, and lately, I haven't had time for it. When I'm not hanging with Mom and Mara, it's Daniel keeping me company. But with him right in front of me, I don't dare to look at him as freely as I do when he's not around.

Take right now, for example. I'm lounging on a couch in my bedroom, from which I can see all my posters, especially the one where Daniel is dressed in white; my favorite. His eyes, this shade of blue that I'm pretty sure I've never seen before—like a light, bright blue, with the edge of his iris rocking a much darker shade that totally emphasizes their brightness—are looking at me, but not really.

I get up to get a closer look at the poster, as if I don't know every detail by heart, and I stand right in front of it. I hadn't noticed before; it's life-sized, exactly like Daniel, and maybe that's another reason why it's my favorite. It doesn't take many seconds before I'm stoked about the image before me.

I take a moment to figure out what I feel when I see him like this. When he's with me in any of his versions, it's more familiar; maybe it sounds weird, but even more down-to-earth. I remember the day he told me that with me, he could just be Daniel, without the whole act he puts on for shows. And now I see the difference it makes, at least for me. We all look and feel different in our everyday clothes compared to evening wear; it's something like that. However, when it comes to him, the difference is not determined by the outfit because he could easily go on stage in his regular clothes and completely transform as soon as that spotlight hits him.

I walk up to the poster, and my stomach butterflies take flight. How is this even possible? I think I'm starting to get the difference—the part of him that allures me on a whole other level, the one that got me hooked the first time I laid eyes on him, it's like his second skin: Daniel Montalvo. Daniel fills me up emotionally, and if I can throw in a comparison, he's that go-to cloth in our closet that we've grown to love because it's so comfy, and we just can't live without it.

The Game…Jade

Daniel Montalvo, on the other hand, is like that amazing outfit for a night out that makes us look fabulous. Daniel is the one who wraps me up and caresses me until I fall asleep, the one I'm totally at ease with. Daniel Montalvo exudes sensuality and talent; he's the one with the velvety voice singing to me from the stage, making me feel incredibly special. He is unreachable, out of the ordinary. I deeply love the first one, but the second one excites me beyond words.

I keep staring at his eyes on the poster, letting myself get lost in this fascination. The butterflies have spread throughout my body, just itching to reach out and touch him with my fingertips, sliding my fingers over that silky smooth skin. Obviously, this only happens in my imagination, though. When he's right in front of me, I focus on reciprocating his advances; that's it.

Even in my daydreams, I can only pull this off with the singer. With Daniel, the decorum rules—as my grandma would call "modesty"—won't let me blatantly admire him as if he's mine, just placed in front of me to feed my eyes. Everything feels better with his picture; his eyes don't catch mine; he can't judge me. I'm completely free to enjoy...

The image on the poster changes slightly, like when a leaf falls from a branch and disturbs the mirror-like surface of a completely still lake. Daniel slides through that wall precisely, takes a step forward, and stops just less than one feet from me.

Unable to snap out of the trance, I let myself drown in the sensation that the photo has come to life. I let out a short gasp of amazement, almost like a sigh, admiring the third dimension his features have taken on.

He takes a short step forward, and I, surprised, instinctively step back, my gaze lost in him. He turns his head to see what I was looking at on the wall encountering his own image on the poster. Finally, he seems to understand my blissful expression. He looks at me with a soft smile as if he doesn't want to distort the image of himself, raising his right eyebrow and locking eyes with me.

Damn! At this point, my gaze is way too obvious, and unfortunately, in the name of decency, I direct it to the floor. With quite some difficulty, I become aware that Daniel has already arrived and is standing in front of me, flesh and bone, or almost.

As he places his hands on my neck, a shiver runs down my spine. With his thumbs under my chin, he tries to lift my face to meet my eyes. I'm sorry,

Rocío Blisswealth

354

Daniel, I'm not ready; I resist, and he stops insisting. He brings his lips close to my ear.

"Missed me, gorgeous?"

I don't respond; I rest my forehead on his shoulder, hiding my face from him, and let out a sigh. Honestly, I lost track, and I wasn't expecting him anymore. I forgot that I only had a few minutes for my admiration. I feel my freedom being trapped under the chains of good manners, and I try to regain my composure.

Now, I have no choice but to thank the almost darkness of my room because when I set aside my boldness, embarrassment takes over me, causing my capillaries to blush on my cheeks. I don't want to talk, Daniel. Couldn't you have taken a little longer? My eyes hadn't had enough of you.

His hands are still on my neck; he has entwined his fingers at the nape, and I'm sure he can feel the rapid beating of my heart. His lips are still closed, almost brushing against my ear, and his breath sends shivers down my skin.

"Jade..."

Two more minutes, Daniel; I just wish I could speak with more than a whisper.

"Gorgeous."

My hands, which are at his sides, slide to his back, and I lift my chin, aiming to slide it over his shoulder to hide my face from his gaze.

"Do you prefer me to keep quiet?"

I just nod, and he gently strokes my hair, my ear, and my shoulder, but he doesn't say a word. It's hard for me to recover because the moment he hugged me, his image on the wall took over my entire field of vision, along with a bunch of sensations. I close my eyes and try to count, but it doesn't work; my heart still hasn't returned to its normal rhythm, and my cheeks haven't regained their color. I know this because the warmth accompanying the intensity of the hue remains. I can't stay silent any longer; it's ridiculous. I turn my head slightly and kiss his cheek.

"Hi." I venture to say, not entirely sure if my voice has fully returned to my throat, but it seems normal.

"Hey, gorgeous. Everything alright?"

"Yes."

"But something's wrong, isn't it?"

"Nothing."

The Game...Jade

"So, nothing at all, huh? Jade, let me see you." He takes a step back, but I don't move away from his shoulder, and he ends up staying where he is. He takes a moment to think and then continues.

"Jade, there's something about you that I find utterly essential. Your gaze, gorgeous, your gaze in all its shades. I like deciphering everything you're capable of expressing with it. There are times when just locking eyes with you is sufficient, and I can sense your thoughts. It doesn't occur very often, but it captivates me when it does. Besides, I enjoy it when I discover a new glance, like a moment ago when I arrived, and you regarded me in a way you've never done before, or perhaps you have, but no..."

These are the moments when it's incredibly hard for me to please him; doing so puts me in a seriously vulnerable position, and given how vulnerable I've always felt, it bothers me to know that I'm the one who's put myself there. Still, considering how weird most of my reactions seem to him and the lectures I've faced because of it, it's better to face it now, even though I hate the idea.

I would have preferred that this gaze, full of contemplation towards him, remained anonymous, as my best-kept secret; well, one of them, but there's no other way out now. I place my hands on either side of his face, and with the intensity of that gaze in my pupils, I lock eyes with him, screaming with them, "You captivate me, Daniel!" He goes quiet, scrutinizing me, and his eyebrows rise in astonishment. He squints his eyes and softens his gaze; now, he looks at me with the same scrutiny with which I was looking at the poster a few minutes ago. He sighs and then tells me, in a very soft voice:

"Yes, that one's new, and it absolutely drives me wild. Why keep it hidden from me?" I smile without saying anything. I don't want to dive back into the topic of the upbringing I received because I'd have to be very clear in my explanation to tell him that he captivates me, even more explicitly than my gaze. He knows, I just don't feel like saying it out loud. I won't venture into that area; now it's for modesty.
It's not like telling him I love him; this is purely physical. I can't resist his appeal, and that's not a feeling; it's a sensation. Seeing that I don't respond, he keeps talking, answering his own question.

"Alright, just because, I suppose. Well, thanks for this gift. It's a delight for me to witness how you perceive me, how I reflect in your eyes, and attempt to align myself with that image. Although, I think there are moments when you're exceptionally kind to me, like now. Have I ever truly lived up to it?"

Rocío Blisswealth

Oh no, Daniel! I'm not falling for your game. We're not starting a conversation that will only serve to feed your ego. With what I've just done, I've already fed it like it's Christmas; I'm not going to give him dessert now, it would be never-ending. I take a step back, release him, and turn towards the bed. He stops me by the arm.

"Alright, got it. I've had enough, haven't I?" He smiles. Well! He really understood; we're making some serious progress.

"Now, allow me."

"What thing, Daniel?" I ask, still trying to hide my eyes.

"Express my gratitude for such a beautiful gift."

He leads me to his photograph and leans against it, giving me the sensation that the picture came to life. I lose myself in my trance as he gently brushes my lips and kisses me.

I wish I could freeze this moment and stay here, just like we are now, where nothing around me matters. But within me, so close to the surface that I can't ignore it, there's a voice telling me that everything is 'too good,' if such an expression exists, that my life isn't like this and I'm about to find out. But that will come later, and I'll have to face whatever is waiting for me, but not right now.

I've gotten into the routine of heading downstairs for breakfast as soon as I catch a whiff of activity in the kitchen. I spent time with Mom and Mara while they filled me in on the day's plans. I guess we could call it the Prep Talk. Usually, these go smoothly; however, just as the inner voice warned, life is gearing up to prove that when things seem too good, it's time to brace for a reality check. Ready or not, I hear the starting bell.

Through the door leading to the garden, a huge demon makes its appearance. Its dark clothes reveal only its hands resembling dry branches, and the hood, partially covering its head, can't let me see its eyes, so I have no idea what it's looking at or who. Its scent isn't the usual vomit-like odor I'm used to; that's strange. However, it smells more like acid; I can't pinpoint it precisely, but it stings my nostrils.

It positions itself behind Mara, who is in front of me, fixing its gaze on her, not turning away for a second. I wait for a moment to see if it tries something, but nothing; it just stays there. I hold back the urge to kick it out; I don't want to provoke something I have no idea how to handle. I turn to look at

The Game...Jade

Mara and Mom, but neither of them senses or sees a thing. This part bothers me the most—being able to see them and having no one to discuss it with.

"I need to go to the room, Mara. Can you hand me the list?"

"Sure, I'll bring it to you." She gets up to fetch it, and the demon follows her less than a step away. I stay in the kitchen, wondering whether I should tell Mom or not; I don't want to worry her. She already has enough dealing with a daughter haunted by demons, and besides, I want to see if, with what I'm about to do, the demon will leave, allowing me to ease my worries. Mara returns with the list, and her companion follows closely.

I run upstairs to find out if the demon is following me, at least to try to stop what I'm about to do, but no, it remains downstairs. I close the door to my room and start repeating the words I've committed to memory—the phrases don't change, only the names of the demons. Before concluding, I address the demon accompanying Mara. I finish and swing open the door, dashing downstairs to check if it's gone. But before I can take a step, I bump into Ángel; I stop abruptly, and before I can ask, he says:

"It hasn't left, Jade, and it won't." His face is serious, way too much.

"No, Ángel, please no. What did I do wrong?"

"You didn't do anything wrong. No matter what you do, Jade, it always works. It's just that this time, he's not looking for you."

"You have to do something, Ángel, please help me! You know perfectly well they're all I have. Don't let me lose anyone else."

"Jade, I can't interfere. It has its reasons for being here, just like I do." Furious, I ran downstairs; it's true, it's still here.

It's been several days, and I'm just fed up with the demon tagging along wherever Mara goes. I've tried everything and repeated the operation dozens of times, and nothing has changed. I need time to ponder something, and I don't have it. I'm constantly keeping an eye on Mara, trying to decipher what the heck he's planning, but I end up with no answers. I know she's in real danger; I feel it in the air. I just hope I can be there the moment it tries something because I won't stay idle; I have to do something.

Daniel hasn't missed a single night in my room; that's a real relief because, even when I don't tell him what's happening, just seeing him well soothes me and distracts me for a while. Even under these circumstances, if it's in his arms, I manage to get several hours of sleep. Today, however, it has been harder for me to stay calm. I keep hearing Ángel's words in my head, "It has its reasons for being here, just like I do." I gather that the demon's reasons undoubtedly involve an attack, and if he wanted to attack me, he would've done so by now. But Ángel also said, "He's not looking for you." Probably not, but the purpose is the same: to hurt me through the people I love.

An idea crosses my mind; maybe it doesn't make sense, but I must try. I can't just sit here doing nothing. I look for Mom in her room:

"Mom, I have to tell you something."

"What's going on, Jade?"

"I don't want you to be scared, but there's been a demon following Mara for a few days now. Very closely."

"Get him off her, Jade! What are you waiting for?" She says on the verge of tears.

"I already tried, Mom. It doesn't work."

"So, what are we going to do?"

"I have an idea. Do you think someone from your church would take her in? I need to get her out of here. Obviously, you'd have to explain to them what it's about; anyway, you know what to tell them. But I think if we send her to a place where, due to their faith in god, the demon doesn't feel so comfortable, maybe he'll leave her alone."

Mom makes arrangements with one of her church friends. Contrary to what I thought, the lady is more than willing to take her in and face Satan like her biblical heroes, if necessary, to help her. According to Mom, the lady even felt flattered that she had considered her for this. Gods! I never thought there would be people who could enjoy the possibility of facing a demon. Maybe I should have visited that church a long time ago.

I really hope the blessed lady knows what she's getting into and that her faith is not just for show because, if there's one thing I'm sure of, it's that the demon won't listen to what she says; it'll focus on what she truly feels. And if there's no such faith within her, the problem she's adopting is colossal.

Mom takes charge of talking to Mara; obviously, she is terrified, but this helps convince her to accept what Mom is proposing. She heads to her room and packs a suitcase for several days; that should be enough to find out if this maneuver serves any purpose.

I watch her leave in a taxi, with the demon following closely behind. Shortly after, the church lady calls Mom to inform her that they organized a prayer group at her house to pray for Mara, and everything seems to be calm. It sounds good; I still hope this will work, but deep down, the feeling inside me is that everything is about to get worse.

Hours later, I find myself in bed, discussing the album release with Daniel. Around two in the morning, the phone rings. I freeze for a few seconds, and then I jump out of bed; it's bad news, I know.

"I'll be right back." I ran to Mom's room.

I open the door and see her sitting on her bed, staring blankly, with a total absence of color on her face.

"It's Mara; Mrs. Rosy has passed away in her sleep while in bed. Mara heard her expressing discomfort because they shared the same room, and when she approached, there was no response. She checked her pulse, and that's when she realized. Members from the prayer group are on their way there."

"Mom, tell her to take a taxi and come back. If she stays there, the demon will kill them all, and that will be very hard to explain."

I return to the room and explain to Daniel that there is a problem with Mom's friend; the lady just died, and they are waiting for Mom at her house. I'm going to accompany her, and he has to leave. That demon will be very angry, and I don't want him near Daniel. I'll have to face it, but I want him out of all of this. He gets up from the bed and rushes to hug me, resting his forehead against mine.

"Are you sure, Jade? Wouldn't you fancy having me stick around a bit more?"

"I would prefer that, Daniel, but I have to go. I'll see you tomorrow, okay?"

"Jade, I am fond of you, and I'm here for you; always keep that in mind." I put my hands on his cheeks and kiss him forcefully.

"I know, Daniel, I know well. Thank you." He turns to leave, and I stop him by the hand. "I... am fond of you, too." He comes back and kisses me once more, smiling.

"Thanks, gorgeous. I needed to hear you say that." And I needed to tell you, Daniel, just because, when that demon walks through the door, following Mara, I don't know what might happen. I don't know if I'll be here tomorrow when you return, and I need you to know that I have feelings for you. Although, what I really wanted to tell you was "I love you," but I didn't dare. I hope I won't regret it.

Rocío Blisswealth

Mara returns almost an hour later, entering with the demon following closely. He doesn't notice me, keeping his gaze fixed on her as if it were an animal tracking its prey. If that's the case, what is it waiting for? Why hasn't it attacked yet? She is as pale as paper, undoubtedly having faced death, experiencing, for the first time, what I've endured multiple times—watching someone pay the price for trying to help her. She looks at me occasionally; I know she wants to ask me a lot of questions, but she refrains from doing so.

"Throughout the afternoon, everything went well."

"Did she complain about anything before going to sleep?" Mom asks.

"Not at all. She was quite well, and we chatted for a long time. She even moved my bed into her bedroom so we could talk."

"I still can't believe it; I've known her for years, and she was always the healthiest woman I've seen. Besides, she was no more than fifty."

"It wasn't a natural death, Mom." Mara replies, clearly annoyed.

"Alright, I'm sorry. Jade, is there anything we can do?" The demon turns to look at me for the first time.

"No, Mom, nothing for now." I hear the voice in my head screaming, Stay out of it, Jade! Don't intervene!

"But maybe you should try. You have to do it." The demon doesn't lose sight of me, and I fear that my own cowardice echoes these words in my mind because I feel terribly threatened by it, waiting for me to attempt to attack it.

"Mom, I can't do anything right now; please don't put me in this position."

I climb the stairs to go to my room, passing by the mirror. More out of habit than desire, I look into it searching for the other, the one I could act against, but there is nothing.

Tears stream down my face; I cannot accept the idea of not being able to do anything for her. She has invested so much time trying to help me, and now I feel completely useless. What good is it for me to know what I can do? What's the point if I will lose someone again, and I won't be able to defend her? What's the use of it?

"Ángel! Where are you? Talk to me, please."

"Jade, calm down." He replies as he appears next to me.

"How can you ask me to calm down? We both know what is going to happen. Unfortunately, I know, and I'm not okay with it."

"Jade, even though you're aware of what's happening, it's best not to intervene. This situation doesn't concern you directly, and getting involved could have serious consequences. Don't interfere. Trust your instincts, Jade. Don't think— feel."

"No, I don't like what you're saying, Ángel. I'm going to talk to him. We'll see if there's anything I can offer in exchange for leaving her alone." I head to the door to my room, but Ángel blocks my way.

"Yes, it is. There's something he would consider, Jade, and I'm sorry, but I must prioritize your well-being, and I can't allow you to go to such lengths for her." He raises his hand and covers my face.

England.

Sara, Daniel's first manager, arrives on the island, and the ritual is the same for everyone. She crosses the water on the boat, and once her shoes are removed, she dips her feet. She turns to one of the bodyguards and asks:

"When was Daniel here?"

"A few days ago."

"Now I understand why they made me come. They must not be in a good mood."

"No, ma'am, they're not."

"Thank you."

She is escorted through the mansion to the Elements Vault, where the five lords are already waiting, seated in their large chairs, this time with both feet in the water. Showing confidence, she enters the hall and descends the steps until her feet are immersed, flashing a smile.

Sara: Good afternoon.

Boxwood: *They are not even remotely good, Sara; things with Daniel are quite dire.*

Sara: I knew upon arriving that he was here. How dare he...?

Boxwood: *You know perfectly well that no one would dare without our permission, Sara. We were the ones who had him brought here, not without a significant amount of resistance on his part.*

Sara: I see.

Boxwood: *Your reports about him led us to believe he was ready for such a special assignment as Jade.*

Rocío Blisswealth

Sara: It was never my intention to confuse you. When I interviewed him and throughout the time we shared after that, he acted with extreme obedience. I can even say he displayed a certain submission.

Ebony: So, when did the change that he's showing now occur?

Sara: I informed you the same day we met Jade that he was no longer the same. He invited her to the meeting with the musicians, got her address, and couldn't distance himself from her. Later on, you referred him to Salvador, and we know how that ended.

Boxwood: It was imperative that you focused on urgent matters; we thought Jade's issue had already been settled.

Sara: I must admit that I also believed that would be the case and that Daniel would come to his senses when he felt the first impacts of her energy on him. However, it doesn't affect him. I didn't think that would be possible.

Ebony: Too many things are happening that we didn't believe possible, but we don't have time to waste. We know he spends a significant part of the night with her; however, we are receiving less and less energy each time. That needs to be fixed. Therefore, you might have to get involved again.

Sara: There's no problem with that; I can look for him, although I don't think he'll tell me anything. The last time I saw him, a couple of months ago, I asked about Jade, and he avoided answering me. I regret to tell you that his thirst for fame has taken him too far. He always knew and agreed that Jade's energy would be used for our purposes, including his own, but I believe greed now consumes him, and he's not willing to share.

Boxwood: That's foolish! The energy she emanates will take him wherever he needs to go, whether complete or fragmented, the result is the same. Therefore, it can be divided into parts that seem convenient to us. Wasn't all of this explained to him?

Sara: He knows well; I was very precise in providing all the information he would need to comply with all the rules. What I think is that it's not the energy that worries him, but her.

Ebony: Impossible! That would be deadly for everyone; we must prevent it at all costs. I know how to do it, but he could suffer damage.

Sara: Him?

Boxwood: Let's set sentimentality aside, Sara. You've always had an extreme preference for Daniel, and I fear that may have influenced your selection over other candidates. However, you must remember that, like

The Game…Jade

everyone else, he is disposable. There's something else you are unaware of. Now, she protects him. That's why it's more risky, yet, as long as she is not in danger, we will proceed.

Sara: It's true; that can complicate things if she's protecting him. Are you sure she won't notice what you're planning to do?

Boxwood: *We do not underestimate her; her instinct is too strong for our convenience. However, by acting cunningly, everything can be achieved. The demon knows her weaknesses well, and we will try to attack them one by one, so as not to give her time to think about defending herself.*

Sara: Well, considering that both Daniel and Jade have broken all the molds, you are thinking of extreme measures. Aren't we risking Jade with all this?

Boxwood: *No, she is not in any physical danger.*

Sara: She isn't, he is.

Ebony: *You care too much, Sara, that can be detrimental. We must remember that she has information in Daniel's songs; she could anticipate us. We won't stop for him, giving her a chance to destroy us.*

Sara: She hasn't discovered the information. We could achieve it without harming him, I mean. He could be useful to us later, perhaps as leverage against her at some point.

Ebony: *She hasn't found out yet, but I fear that Daniel, in an effort to put her out of our reach, might be able to show her things that she might have overlooked until now. He seriously worries us.*

Sara: He wouldn't dare.

Ebony: *That's what we thought before, and you see. He is not trustworthy, Sara, but you're right; he might serve us later. We could, perhaps, use him as leverage in our favor. I'll try to set him aside, but I think I already have exactly what I need. We will take action.*

Sara: Shall we do it immediately?

Ebony: *No, he needs to be convinced that we won't do anything against him, for fear of what Jade could do to us. At some point, he will lower his guard, and then we will act.*

Boxwood: *We cannot let time pass; she might learn to attack.*

Sara: We can't rush either.

Boxwood: *I agree, let's outline a plan.*

Monterrey.

Rocío Blisswealth

I find myself sitting in one of the rocking chairs in front of the house, watching the cars cruise down the avenue. The little one is right in front of me. I must have gotten lost in one of my thoughts because I don't remember how I got here.

"Jade, can you hear me?"

"Yes, little one, yes. What's up?"

I see her looking worried. Did it really take her some effort to snap me out of my trance? Well, what was I even thinking?

"Jade, Mara is dead." This must be a nightmare. I was keeping an eye on that; besides, Mara was at the house of... No, no, no, she came back because the demon killed that lady. The demon returned with her, and... darn it! I can't remember anything else.

"No, little one, of course not. Mara is fine."

"I'm telling you, Jade. Luz is crying, and she says she's gone." I feel a hole in my stomach and snap to the reality of what's happening. I have to stop this; it might not be too late. Not again, please!

I ask the girl to stay there. I run down the hallway to Mara's room, and even before I get there, I can hear Mom crying.

Two demons are talking in the hallway, but Jade can't hear them.

"IS EVERYTHING READY?"

"EVERYTHING. SHE JUST FOUND OUT, BUT IT'S ALREADY TOO LATE FOR HER TO ACT."

"HOW DID HE STOP HER? I THOUGHT HE WOULD LET HER ACT."

"HE DIDN'T WANT TO RISK LOSING HER; SHE'S NOT READY TO FACE SOMETHING SO STRONG YET."

"BUT, OF COURSE, SHE'S READY! SHE COULD DO IT WITH EASE."

"I MEAN, SHE DOESN'T KNOW SHE CAN."

"AND NOW THEY'LL MAKE SURE SHE NEVER KNOWS."

"AT LEAST THEY'RE GOING TO TRY."

"WE MUST GIVE NOTICE OF WHAT IS HAPPENING HERE; THIS WASN'T CONSIDERED IN THE PLANS, THAT THERE WOULD BE INVOLVEMENT BY EXTERNAL MEANS. THEY'RE NOT GOING TO LIKE IT."

The Game...Jade

Chapter XVII
Wake up, Daniel. You can't change your stripes

My eyes are locked onto one of Daniel's images, and this time, not because I'm deep into one of my thoughtful moments. Weirdly enough, it's just a spot where my eyes stopped, giving my mind some time to clear up.

I try to go over the events since Mara arrived from Mrs. Rosy's house, probably around four in the morning, and the moment the little one jolted me awake—let's call it that—at four in the afternoon. What went down in those twelve hours? Where did I lose track? Or what have I done since then?

I remember her showing up with the demon by her side. I also recall Mom asking me to do something and the demon's threatening look, waiting for me to make a move, and that's it. Twelve hours later, the terrible feeling in my gut and my sprint down the hallway, Mom's crying, and the scene when I opened the door to find Mara sitting on the bed, smiling at me.

Mom was crying, thanking god for bringing her back. She claims Mara died, had no pulse, and didn't breathe for about three minutes. But Mara is now perfectly healthy, no trace of the demon, and, of course, she doesn't remember dying.

I figured god, seeing me lost in my own dumbness, decided to take matters into his own hands, either to resurrect Mara, if she was dead, or to heal her if she was unconscious. So, I'm totally thankful. Now I know I don't have to take care of them; he's got them covered. That leads me to a bunch of questions. Why didn't he take care of my grandparents like that? I needed them, too. And what happened to me during all those hours? Where did I go?

I've spent almost two hours trying to get Ángel to show up and get answers to at least one of these questions. But, as usual, he doesn't appear unless I'm in serious trouble, and I guess that's not the case here. Still, I'm scared—a lot—but I can't put my finger on why. And I really want to cry, like I haven't in a long time. It makes me sick feeling some bad stuff heading my way, and not having the slightest idea of what I'm going to face. All my senses are screaming that it's going to be the worst thing that's happened to me so far, and I can think of a bunch of terrible things—any of them could be true.

However, I strive to feel grateful. As I've told you before, gratitude weighs heavily on me, and when it comes to being thankful to god, that burden significantly increases. I think god did me a huge favor today by preventing me from having to face that demon after my vain attempts to get rid of him. He somehow saved Mara's life. Because of the gift he granted me, I suppose he expected me to do it, but I couldn't succeed; all my attempts failed. So, I keep trying to fill my thoughts with gratitude, but I can't. A single image invades my mind: I saw my grandparents die, and it would have cost him nothing to bring them back to me.

I step out of my room and can hear Mom and Mara's voices chatting from the living room; everything is in order. Why do I feel so miserable then? I stop in front of the mirror and place my hand on it. Where are you, damn demon? Maybe confronting you would make me feel... I mean, I wouldn't feel so useless. As usual, there's no reply. I turn around and retreat into my room; I startle when Daniel greets me. Since my demon is no longer here, I've lost the habit of encountering someone in my bedroom.

This time, I'm not in the mood to pretend. I think it would be better for him to leave and come back in a few days when I'm better company. But I need him so much that I don't dare to suggest it. My appearance must be quite revealing because he approaches very slowly. I raise my hand, showing him my palm as a signal to stop. Even so, I muster an attempt at a smile. I turn around and close the door; he takes a seat on the couch, and I sit on the bed.

"What's wrong, gorgeous?"

"Daniel, I wish I could tell you, I swear, but I don't know."

"What happened?"

"Nothing, everything is fine; it's just that, I don't know how to explain it. It's something I feel. It's silly, don't mind me."

"No, it's not. What are you feeling?"

"You'll get mad."

"Is it that awful?"

"Yes."

"Trust me, Jade, tell me, please."

"Okay, it turns out that today is one of those days when I miss my grandparents a lot, but this time, the feeling is so intense that I wish I could be with them. I can't find a purpose in being here." I can see him struggling not to interrupt me, and I continue with this half-truth, which is all I dare to tell him. "I feel completely useless, stuck in this thick fog that surrounds me, filling me with anguish and pain that I don't know where it comes from. I'm drowning in it, Daniel."

He remains completely silent, knowing that if he interrupts me, I won't pick up the topic again. But I can see the sadness in his eyes caused by my words, and I understand. However, I'm not done yet. I lock eyes with him and continue.

"I'm falling apart, and I don't know why, nor can I get out of this pit I've fallen into. It's like a whirlpool dragging me from below, and each time it's getting harder for me to resurface and catch my breath—so hard that I'd rather give up. There's a single thought that tips the balance, urging me to strive to stay here, to fight to push this anguish aside. To see you, Daniel. Just that, seeing you."

I whisper the last sentence, using the last breath within me. I cover my lips with the tips of my fingers to hide the tremor that has taken hold of them, no longer allowing me to speak. At the same time, a knot forms in my throat. I've been holding back tears for several hours, and with Daniel before me, looking at me with those wonderful eyes that show a mix of distress and sweetness, I can't hold it in any longer.

With excessively slow movements, he slides from the couch to fall on his knees, and with short steps, he approaches me very slowly. I shake my head from side to side as a sign of refusal; even now, I prefer him not to get closer. I've cried with him on other occasions, but never under the weight of such inexplicable pain. I don't want to touch him, and at the same time, I'm dying for him to hug me.

I can feel how his body, as it moves towards me, disperses the thick fog that covers me, as if it were water, creating a passage through which he can sneak in and get closer to touch me. He touches my knee with his hand, and I stop resisting, drawn to him like a magnet. Trembling intensely, I slip off the bed and sit on the floor next to him, wrapping my arms around his waist with the same force as an addict must cling to the syringe that will give him peace again.

I lean my head against his chest, and as he hugs me with one arm, with the other, gently strokes my hair. He leans in and repeatedly kisses my head, not speaking, just allowing me to vent, to let out a large part of this anguish that I swallowed while drowning in it during the long hours of the afternoon.

Rocío Blisswealth

Once my crying becomes more subdued, at least enough for me to hear something other than my own sobs, he continues to caress me while starting to speak.

"Jade, stop dwelling on all this pain, and please, put aside the longing to be with your grandparents. Hold onto me; I'm here for you, and I won't abandon you. I beg you, cling to me. Do you think you can do that?"

"You must think I'm crazy; well, I believe it too." I say with a voice still interrupted by sobs.

"Actually, I'm quite amazed that, with all this on your shoulders, you're still keeping it together."

"What's happening to me, Daniel?"

"I'm not sure, gorgeous, but let's try not to think about it any longer. Let's go to bed; you need some rest."

I grab some tissues from the box on my dresser and wipe away the havoc that the mixture of makeup and tears left on my face. Daniel comes over and takes one too. It was not until that moment that I realized that tears were running down his face along with mine. I hug him gently and, taking his face in my hands, I pull him close to meet his eyes, and I kiss him. His lips curve into a faint smile, and he remains with his eyes closed for a few more moments.

I breathe slowly a few times; I can feel that the anguish, the pain, even the terrible sense of threat upon me have lessened, not disappeared, but dropped to a level I can bear, maybe even ignore them if I try. It is now that, as I experience this relief, I am ashamed of involving Daniel in my problems.

"I'm sorry, Daniel, I didn't mean to..." He takes my face in his hands to make sure I give him my full attention.

"Jade, listen up. Never regret allowing me to be present when you need me. Today, you made me feel like I'm a part of your life, and that's important to me."

"It's just that I'd prefer to keep you away from the bad in it."

"Recall that in the explanation you shared about your feelings, you made me part of it and, at last, I've managed to fill a space for you. To be, in some way, significant in your life, and I'm glad I was here to witness it."

"Daniel, you are more than that." No more, I can't say anything more for today, not under these circumstances.

"And you are to me, Jade. You have no idea how much." He lies down beside me and continues to stroke my hair, kissing me and holding close to me.

The Game...Jade

My eyes feel heavy, perhaps from crying, and I fall asleep. As soon as he realizes I'm asleep, he turns around, gets out of bed, and disappears.

Spain.

Daniel gets up from bed and rushes to the phone. He immediately contacts the director of the record company in Spain and tells him to move up the promotional tour in Mexico. The director assures him that everything is ready, and they are just waiting for him to set the date. The earliest it can take place is next Tuesday, just a four-day wait. He requests plane tickets, making it clear that Jade's flight is from Monterrey, Mexico. The tour coordinator will get in touch in a few minutes to share the ticket and reservation details; there shouldn't be any problem. He thanks him and hangs up the phone.

He looks for Raúl's phone numbers; he needs to locate him immediately to accompany him. As he reaches for the receiver, the ringing interrupts his movement.

"Oh, bother! Who could it be now? Where did I leave my mobile?"

"Daniel, are you awake?" Carmen asks from the other side of the door.

"Yes, do come in, Carmen."

"Hello, son. You have a call."

"Thanks. The record company said they would call me in a few minutes. Figured it would take longer." He picks up the receiver, and before he answers, Carmen rushes to tell him in a very low voice, so that only he can hear her.

"No, Daniel, it's not from the record company; it's Sara." One of the people he doesn't want to talk to; however, it's already too late, she has already heard his voice.

"Hello." Carmen leaves the room and closes the door behind her.

"How's the most dashing man to ever set foot on this planet?"

"Sara..." Seriousness is all that his voice conveys.

"Hello there. Expecting a call from the record company, are we? Let me guess, you're off to Mexico."

"That's right."

"I gather you must be missing Jade, am I right?"

"The promotional tour is a crucial part of the success of the new album; it's been planned for quite some time."

"We both know that the crucial part of your success is Jade, not the promotional tour." Well, Sara, so this conversation is going to happen with the cards laid out on the table.

"But the tour helps everything appear normal."

"Daniel, you can imagine I've been thoroughly briefed on the situation. I thought I could rely on your good judgment concerning Jade. We invested countless hours planning this, Daniel. You knew exactly how it would be, and you agreed to stick to the plan."

"You laid out your vision for how it would unfold; however, in reality, things turned out to be quite different. True, I agreed to follow the plan, but when the actual scenario presented itself so differently from your description, I had no choice but to act accordingly."

"You mean Jade."

"Sara, you presented her to me as raw material, someone possessing an extraordinary gift. And all it took was for me to persuade her, through my physical appeal, to give it to me."

"And that's precisely what she is, Daniel, raw material."

"No, Sara, she's a girl who, despite her intelligence, has no idea of what she is, and I have to snatch her gift away to distribute it as loot among all of us, a pack of hyenas."

"From my understanding, you didn't have to steal anything. Let's not exaggerate, Daniel. Just as I told you, your physical attractiveness led her to willingly surrender her gift to you."

"You're mistaken, Sara. Jade sees the humanity in me, making my physical appeal, as you put it, secondary. However, that's beside the point; it doesn't mitigate the offense. She remains oblivious to her true nature, and I... It pains me to know that she's feeding an entire tribe, unaware of what she's losing."

"Don't be foolish, Daniel. She's not losing anything; she's an endless source. Can't you see? Instead of someone else taking her energy, it might as well be us, don't you think?"

"And if what she produces holds such value, can you explain to me then why the necessity to assault her? She's being torn apart, Sara."

"It's not us, Daniel. There are many others coveting what she possesses, and they're taking matters into their own hands. Remember, all of this started long before you even met her."

The Game…Jade

"I don't believe you, Sara. I'm heading to Mexico, I will try to figure out what's really happening, and the moment I get the lowdown, if it turns out you're pulling the strings behind this…"

"Daniel, don't you dare utter one of your stupid threats. Consider this carefully and gain the proper perspective. Don't jeopardize everything you've managed to achieve so far, including the rest of your thriving career. There are still remarkable accomplishments awaiting you."

"The perspective you're referring to is seeing Jade as some sort of object."

"Yes, that would certainly simplify things."

"I'm sorry, Sara. I hate to let you down. Maybe when you interviewed me, I gave the impression of being much more selfish, and back then, I undoubtedly was. But now that I've had a chance to see the image she has of me, I've got no option but to try to live up to her expectations. I like the image she's formed of me, and I'm trying to be the man she wants me to be."

"Perhaps if she truly knew who you really are."

"I was, Sara, I was."

"Wake up, Daniel. You can't change your stripes."

"Things have changed, Sara. Why is it such a struggle for you to wrap your head around it? Jade isn't what you said, and I'm not the same anymore. I caught a glimpse of myself in her eyes, and I liked it. Now, I'll do whatever it takes to be the man she sees in me."

"Raw material, Daniel. We're discussing raw material here, and the substance that forms you is waste; remember that. The only thing you possess is your exterior, and they went to great lengths to make it appealing! However, all for the purpose of pleasing her. You're not meant to get close enough for her to see inside you; she won't like it, I assure you!"

"You're lying, Sara! You're trying to push me away from her."

"I don't need to, Daniel. You're handling that aspect quite well, and you're on the right path, but just to lose everything."

"Why are you doing this, Sara?" Daniel's pain is evident in his tone of voice. Sara softens hers before responding.

"Daniel, perhaps you don't realize it, but I'm trying to rescue you. They were ready to go to any lengths, and I managed to persuade them that you have the capacity to regain your senses. You weren't supposed to get so close to her;

Rocío Blisswealth

what I'm telling you is the truth, Daniel. Only maintaining a certain distance will keep you attractive in her eyes. Isn't that what you want?"

"You're trying to persuade me because you're talking driven by..." He stops before completing the sentence he shouldn't have said; it's not in his best interest to anger Sara.

"Out of jealousy? Is that what you're implying? Well, yes, you're right. I've always declared myself your most fervent admirer, captivated by your extraordinary appeal. But do you know something? There's a vast difference between her and me; I know perfectly well what lies beneath your exterior, all the challenges you've faced in pursuit of something as frivolous as fame, and yet, it doesn't bother me. I fancy you a great deal, and I've never made an effort to hide it. What would be the point? However, she, as you've mentioned, believes in a version of you that isn't real. If she has shown any affection towards you, it's not for the real Daniel that only I know. She's drawn to the image she's created in her mind. I wonder if she'd dare to approach you if she knew it was you who handed her over to us."

"Sara, please."

"I'm merely highlighting the obvious, Daniel, what you mustn't forget. I believe it would be wiser for you to return to your wicked ways, the wicked I adore, and make the most of this girl who..."

"Sara, got a load of things to get on with, if you don't mind."

"Alright, Daniel, go to Mexico and bid her farewell. Not forever, just take a step back, and you'll see how much better you feel. You lack the strength to achieve the transformation you're after. Being close to her might make you believe otherwise, but we both know where you come from, and that's practically impossible for someone like you."

"Goodbye, Sara."

"Until next time, Daniel."

He hangs up the phone, shrouded in the same anguish that surrounded Jade a few hours ago. He will travel to Mexico and do everything possible to turn that lost cause into an achievement. He will lose himself again in Jade's eyes and let her influence act on him, helping him to accomplish it. He can almost hear what Sara would say to him if she knew his thoughts. "Brilliant, Daniel, absolutely brilliant. You keep the girl and everything she produces; all for yourself, don't you? And do you think you've ceased to be petty? Just take a glance in the mirror and confess, if you dare, what your true motivations are."

In an attempt to dispel the fog around him, he gets up to leave the room. He has decided to personally go find Raúl; a tad of fresh air will do him good. On his way out of the house, he passes by a large mirror. No, he doesn't dare; he walks past without looking at himself.

Monterrey.

I wake up after a few hours of a very deep sleep. Daniel is no longer around; as expected, the promotional tour got him tied up. I take a couple of deep breaths, and the distressing feeling from yesterday has almost completely disappeared. Surprisingly, the voice inside me speaks to me. "Jade, keep situations involving Daniel to yourself until it's imminent to talk about them." Gods! What's this all about now? "Okay," I responded. Finally, that's one thing that comes easily to me. The phone rings, and I pick it up before the first ring ends.

"Hello, can I speak to Jade, please?"

"It's me, Carmen. How are you?"

"Hello, darling. Great, what about you?"

"Very good, thank you."

"I have good news for you."

"Just what I need."

"Daniel arrives in Mexico City on Monday morning to start the promotional tour. Your flight departs from Monterrey the same day at 7:00 a.m., and they will be waiting for you at the airport."

"No need, Carmen. Please tell Daniel that there's no need to wait for me. If I'm not mistaken, his flight will arrive around five in the morning, and that means they'll have to wait for me a little over three hours. I can take a taxi and meet them at the hotel." I hear Carmen's laughter from the other end of the line. She waits a few seconds and then continues.

"It's surprising. Daniel mentioned, almost in the same words, that you would say that, so I already have the answer. He said, and I quote, 'Don't be stubborn, gorgeous. We'll see you at the airport, and that's my final word.'"

"Wow, that means I don't have a chance to argue the point anymore."

"Oh, no, but of course you can! Daniel is not willing to listen to you, but I am. Go on, Jade, argue with me all you want. I'll listen to you carefully, then I'll pity you, and I'll tell you that you're absolutely right, but Daniel is very authoritarian and doesn't want to give in, and we'll meet again at the starting point. Still, if it helps, let it out, child, I hear you."

"Thank you, Carmen, but it's not fun this way. I like arguing with him; it's funny when he gets angry."

"He says you're the one who gets really funny fighting."

"What? No way! I'm violent and reckless when I'm angry."

"He also mentioned that, in those moments, it was better to agree with you, so, for the sake of your anger. I know, Jade, you're absolutely right." Laughter overwhelms both of us, and we spend some time controlling ourselves to be able to conclude the call.

"It's not fair, Carmen; this takes all the fun out of it."

"Well, you'll see, maybe for you, because I'm having a lot of fun."

"At my expense."

"It's true. I'm sorry, dear."

"Just kidding, Carmen. Thanks for calling me; it's always nice to hear your voice."

"It brings me great joy to give you a call, Jade. Daniel speaks so fondly of you that I almost feel like we've already met."

"Really? He talks about me?"

"Frequently, this young man cares a lot about you."

"And I care about him."

"I know. I'm well aware of it. Jade, I must end the call now. It was delightful to hear from you."

"I send you a big hug, Carmen."

"You too." I can barely hang up the receiver, and someone knocks on my door.

"Come in." Mara opens it, as healthy and calm as always.

"Jade, are you awake? Was it the call for you?"

"Yes."

"Who was it?" Once again, the voice inside me, this time more urgent than a few minutes ago, makes itself heard. "Jade, keep situations involving Daniel to yourself."

"The guy who gave me Tíber wanted to know if he pulled through." I managed to answer.

"Oh, I'm glad you had good news for him. Can I come in?"

"Of course."

The Game...Jade

"I have a list of things to do."

"But are you feeling better now? I thought..."

"This can't wait." She hands me a sheet with several names.

"Mara, these are people's names, not demons. Why do we have to act against them? I don't think..."

"Jade, these people are against us. They're our enemies, and we have to finish them."

"And what have they done? I don't recognize some of these names. How could they have done something to me then?"

"Mom will explain it to you. I'm going to call her." Mom doesn't take long to appear; it turns out they discovered that these people caused serious harm to our family—unhappiness, loneliness, anguish, pain, death, who knows! And where was I while all this was happening? It's true that my life has never been normal, but I don't remember suffering what they say. And while I lost even my grandparents, I don't believe these people had any interest in taking them away from me, and I doubt even more that these people had anything to do with the demons that have paraded through my life. No, this doesn't sound right to me; some of these people are already elderly, and this would not only affect them but also their descendants.

"Mom."

"Jade, please. I keep praying to god, just as you asked me, to consider everything you do. Help us. You're finding your place and what god has for you. Wouldn't you like us to be calm and happy, just like you? You can do it."

With her words, she brings back the commitment I made between them and me, a commitment in which, if I can protect Daniel, why not them? In addition, I still haven't recovered from the bad taste in my mouth that the news of her sudden death and recovery left me, without me having done anything to help her in something so serious. I promised myself that I would do what I could to help them without hesitation, and that's exactly what I'll do.

"Okay, hand me the sheet."

"Jade, I trust that god will take into account everything you do."

They leave me alone. I stand up to tackle this task, and I do it effortlessly. However, when it comes to dealing with demons, I can see them coming, getting angry, and hurling all kinds of insults at me before vanishing. With these people, there's nothing visible, just a lingering sense of darkness.

I'm not sure if I'm making myself clear, but there are situations where you feel lighter, and this is not one of those.

This is the kind of situation that makes me question how much I really know about what I'm doing, and the truth is, I know nothing. It often feels like I'm a switch, something I can toggle on or off at will, and it isn't that simple. But just like with electrical energy, I turn it on without the slightest idea, and honestly, I'm not concerned about where that energy comes from.

Things get complicated when the object to be destroyed presents challenges. I have no idea what options I have or how I can use this energy more effectively. Many times, I've wished for a manual that explains how to use it, but I doubt it exists. So, I'm here, still at the same point where I've remained for years, with no sight of this circumstance changing.

Four days, well, three days and some hours, is all I have to wait to see Daniel. I'm certain he won't appear in my room until that day arrives. That's how it has always been; once Carmen calls, I don't see him until we meet at the agreed-upon place. There's no doubt these upcoming days will feel eternal and incredibly long.

How insanely huge the room feels now that he's not around; even Tíber seems to miss him. He spends long minutes staring at the walls, hoping Daniel will appear until he gets tired, and sleep finally seizes him. I'm not so lucky; for the past few months, having him in my room has been a true blessing. However, the fact that he's not here keeps me from drifting into sleep. I hear more intently to all those noises that, when he's present, I don't pay attention to. Like the noise of cars outside, people passing by the sidewalk, and even parts of their conversations when their steps bring them near my windows, and, above all, the sounds within these four walls.

Over the past few days, this space has become a gathering spot for many... many things I could not describe exactly. I mean, they could be ghosts or demons, but as I can't see them, I still have my doubts. It's strange—I hear whispers, footsteps, and a lot of commotion around me as if I were in a room surrounded by people. Fear? No, I'm not scared of them; I'm actually quite curious. Since they spend long hours here, I suppose they feel the same curiosity about me.

Several times, I've tried to ask them something, you know, the typical question from horror movies, "Who's there?" A stupid question, of course. Whoever is there, always with bad intentions, isn't going to answer. But I had to give it a shot. Anyway, no one answers, still, the whispers and movements cease, sometimes for up to an hour.

My mind wanders through all the theories that can come to mind. As you can imagine, I'm not the kind of person who questions the ideas I hear, no matter how bizarre they may seem. My life is like that, and if I were to doubt such things, I'd have to doubt everything else, and then my life would be turned upside down. So, since it took me a long time to accept it as it is—a life where dreams and nightmares are possible—I analyze all the theories.

I kind of like the one that says our world consists of multiple dimensions, all occupying the same space. That means that the surrounding noises are from people who, in another dimension, share this place. And I say I only like it partially because if those people are aware of my presence, as I suspect they are, where does my privacy go? Honestly, I don't even dare to change my clothes here anymore. I've taken the ridiculous habit of changing in the bathroom, ridiculous, considering I supposedly have the room to myself.

Another theory I've tossed around is that a bunch of ghosts have figured out this is a good place to live or hang out or whatever they do. However, this theory also has flaws. I've never had trouble seeing them, and in this case, I don't see a thing, so I've had to discard it.

Perhaps the one I find most distasteful is the one that leads me to think that I am a specimen under study. Someone tossed me into various scenarios to see what I came up with in each case. It's not about doing right or wrong things; it's simply about observing my reactions for some purpose I still can't figure out. In this case, the voices I hear would belong to those who are watching me. I hate feeling that way, like a toy of someone that I can't confront. I think I'd rather prefer the demons; at least I can see them, whether to kill or be killed, like in a bullfight.

I know that many people consider it a barbaric practice. But having found myself in that position multiple times, locked in a ring with a demon to see what I could do with it while it stabbed me with banderillas, I find the idea fascinating that both the bull and the bullfighter dance with death, each having an equal chance of killing the other. They develop their strength, endurance, cunning, and courage. Most importantly, courage, which, for me, doesn't mean the absence of fear within them but the guts not to pay it any attention and move forward.

Rocío Blisswealth

I know these lines of thought don't really lead me anywhere, but I have to do something during all the time I can't fall asleep. Another thing that catches my attention a lot is the fact that the very moment Daniel arrives, there's silence, and I hear nothing else, just him. I think it's because my focus on him is so intense that there's no room left in my head for anything else. Since the blessed day I met him, he has always been a remedy for all my troubles. When he's present, except on very rare occasions, I don't see demons, ghosts, or hear voices of people I can't see, nothing. In the incredible normalcy of being in his company, everything is fantastic. That does scare me; because, for me, all the good things have turned out to be very brief, and I don't want this to end.

I look at my watch. It can't be; I hadn't considered this theory. I think I've been part of the Twilight Zone for a few minutes now. Every time I check the clock, it reads exactly the same time. If anything, and I have my doubts about this, the minute hand manages, with a lot of effort, to drag itself to mark another minute, then reverts to its previous position. There's no doubt that watch could be a very effective torture weapon, especially now when I am eagerly anticipating boarding that plane, arriving at Mexico City airport, and seeing him.

Gods! I always thought my stomach was the size of my fist, as my grandpa used to say, but that can't be possible because the emptiness I feel inside it is enormous. So, if I go by this feeling, my stomach encompasses almost the entirety of my body. I can't wait to see him; I always experience this vertigo when the hour approaches, to see him in flesh and blood, at last! I suppose I'm unforgivable; I enjoy his presence every night, and I've already told you it's a blessing. But I've also explained the difference between projection and reality, and now I eagerly long to see the real him. I have a lot to tell him.

Finally, the 72 hours of these three days stopped wandering around my watch and, exhausted, disappeared one by one. Each of them took a toll on my stomach and patience, leaving them both in a bad state. I've lost track of what it means to have a calm stomach, and my patience, we'd better not talk about it.

Luckily, an odd thing happened this morning, giving me some peace. After deciding it was the longest I could wait to let Mom and Mara know that I was leaving, twenty-four hours in advance, I threw the bomb on the breakfast table, making sure beforehand that there were no sharp objects that could take me down before I got to see him. They looked at me and, with smiles on their

The Game...Jade

faces, wished me a good trip and that we did very well. Unusual, isn't it? Especially if I consider the reactions that Mara has had in the past. I don't care; I won't question this very favorable change. I accept it, period.

I'm going to bed, continuing the countdown. In nine hours, my plane will be taking off, and an hour later, I'll be with him. I would give anything to be able to sleep a little, at least. I want to be able to see him with my eyes wide open.

"Would you like something to drink?"

"Nothing, thank you very much."

"Can I bring you anything else?"

"No, thank you." The flight attendant couldn't bring me what I need, someone who has been in a VIP lounge at the airport for a couple of hours. If that were possible, I would have asked him from the moment I boarded the plane.

This time, I've tried to be very conscious not to disturb my neighbors with the involuntary movements that my legs start making in a desperate and futile attempt to arrive more quickly. I focus on breathing slowly and keep my fingernails away from my mouth. I have never had the habit of biting them, and I don't want to start now.

We landed! I still don't know how we did it without having a panic attack in the air. A few times, I caught myself with my hand on the seatbelt clasp as if it were a duel between the rest of the passengers and me to see who could unfasten it more quickly. I would pull it away, grip the armrest tightly, and then return to the seatbelt. And, of course, I was the fastest; also, I was careful to ask for the first seat at the front of the plane. If Daniel finds out, I won't escape a good scolding.

He has always said that the safest seats are those located over the wings of the plane. I don't know how much sense that makes. If the plane crashes to the ground, for example, I think it doesn't matter exactly where you are; the result will be the same, to a greater or lesser extent. Rather, I think he makes up ideas that reassure him, and in that case, they are the safest, without a doubt.

I cross the small aisle between the plane and the airport reception area. The wind from Mexico City caresses my face for a moment. It's cold, and my blouse is kind of light; I didn't remember that. My thickest sweaters are inside my suitcase, and I'm not going to waste precious thirty or forty seconds pulling

Rocío Blisswealth

380

one out and putting it on. Of course not! I ask one of the flight attendants for directions to the VIP lounges.

"I'm heading in that direction; I can escort you."

"You don't have to. Just tell me how to get there, please."

"Just keep going straight until the end of the hallway and then turn right twice. Are you sure you don't want me to come with you?"

"Thanks, but you couldn't catch up with me." I shout once I start running, and I'm not lying. I know he won't make it; he's not in the same hurry as I am.

To the end of the hallway, right, right. About sixty-five feet in front of me, I can see the doors to the different VIP lounges. Gods! I forgot to ask Carmen in which one I would see him. One of the doors opens, and Raúl peeks his head out, sees me, and gives a big smile.

I stop my run and start walking quickly, but not running. I'd like to slow down my heart rate, although I don't know if the elevated pulse is due to the distance I ran or my anxiety to see him. If it's the latter, it will be totally useless to slow down; only he can soothe my heartbeats. I reach the door, and Raúl steps forward to hug me.

"Hey, Jade! Good to see you!"

"You too, Raúl; I've missed you a lot." I say, pressing myself against his chest.

As soon as he lets go, I open the door and step inside the waiting room; to my surprise, it's empty. I turn around to face Raúl.

"Where's Daniel?" I ask.

My breath has stopped. I don't like surprises, especially when they concern me; they're usually not good, and in this case, I'm terrified not to see Daniel where he's supposed to be. It was useless to stop my run; my heart wants to burst out of my chest, and my hands are trembling so much that Raúl can't take his eyes off them.

I know the possibilities are endless, from him being in the restroom to heading to the hotel for some reason, or, no, please! Not having come to Mexico at all. I don't know what expression I have, but Raúl keeps a close eye on me, and his smile vanishes. Why isn't he answering me?

A peculiar weight settles on my shoulders; I turn my gaze to the side and see someone has draped a coat over them. I recognize it perfectly: it's Daniel's.

The Game…Jade

"Here I am, gorgeous. Raúl said you were without a sweater, and I can't have you catching a cold." He wraps his arms around my waist, and I quickly clasp my cold hands around them. "How was the flight?" He asks with his chin resting on my right shoulder, and I raise my hand to caress his cheek.

"Long, too long."

"Seemed endless for me as well."

My heart, with a single leap, restores its regular rhythm, and my lungs have already found the oxygen they were missing.

"Let me fix this for you. Slip your hands through the sleeves."

He takes the coat off my shoulders and helps me slide my arms. I don't think it's a good idea; the height difference between him and me is also reflected in the difference in length between his limbs and mine. No matter how hard I try to get my fingers out of the sleeve's end, I can't do it, at least not very successfully.

Only my fingertips reach the end, poking out of the sleeves. Clearly, the coat, instead of looking as elegant on me as it does on him, appears as if it's hanging on a hook, prompting Daniel to burst into laughter. He stands in front of me, taking one of my hands, and folds the sleeve until it's completely uncovered, then repeats the process with the other. Holding it at shoulder height, he attempts to arrange it without success. Bringing his hands to the lapels, he crosses it over my chest. I furrow my brow, wondering if he really expects to make me look somewhat good.

Twisting my mouth to the side, I assess the poor outcome of his efforts. He tries to control his laughter, but he can't anymore. He hugs me tightly, and his laughter resonates in my chest.

"You look absolutely adorable."

"Daniel, your definition of adorable is starting to worry me." I can hear Raúl's laughter joining his.

"I'm sorry, Jade. Let me fetch you something else." I stop him by the lapels.

"No, Daniel, I love this one."

"Why?"

"It smells like you. Makes me feel closer, so I'm keeping it on."

"Closer than this?" He says, squeezing me tightly.

"Ouch! Maybe not, but I'll still leave it on."

We leave the airport and arrive at the hotel, where the record company staff is already waiting for us to take charge of the promotional tour. One of the girls comes out to greet us and welcome him. Raúl and I check-in, and someone from the hotel staff is already taking care of our luggage, handing us the keys.

"Daniel, feel like heading up to the room for a few minutes?" Raúl asks.

"Yes, let's go."

"I'll accompany you, Daniel, so I can pass on the details for this evening." Says the girl from the record company. Daniel turns around to face her, visibly upset.

"Maybe they didn't brief you on how I operate. Firstly, you've got no business in my room, and secondly, instructions for this afternoon and any other workday don't come through me. You'll be dealing directly with Jade, not me, and everything's laid out in writing, not verbally. On top of that, the three of us just got here after a marathon flight with a time change, so a little understanding would be appreciated for the few minutes we plan to take to freshen up before diving into activities. I don't see an issue; I've known for days that everything's been meticulously planned, considering we might need these moments. Am I wrong?"

"No, sir, you're not wrong. Take your time; we'll be waiting here." The girl responds with a completely red face. A serious mistake, a bad start.

"Thank you." He turns around, and we enter the elevator. Neither Raúl nor I say a word; Daniel is very strict about people trying to take liberties that don't belong to them.

"Are you going to give me a telling off, gorgeous?"

"No, it's better that the girl knows what to expect at the beginning of the tour, not at the end when the discomfort overwhelms you."

The elevator door opens, and we walk down the hallway towards the rooms. This time, mine is between theirs. Daniel continues talking as we reach his door; I stop to listen, and Raúl keeps walking.

"I'm relieved it doesn't bother you. After all, it was your fault I didn't let her in." He enters his suite, and I follow, surprised.

"Was it my fault? And can you tell me why?" He reaches out his hand, lightly taps on the door, closes it, and gently pushes me against it until we're just a few inches apart.

"I didn't fancy taking the chance that what you once spilled to me might be true." He brushes his nose against mine.

The Game...Jade

"What did I say? About what?" I say, almost breathless, after the fluttering butterflies have completely covered my lungs.

"That if there was a crowd, you wouldn't allow me to do this."

He presses against me and kisses me slowly. After a minute, he lifts his head and looks into my eyes, waiting for my answer. Gods! He insists that I think after one of his kisses.

"That's right, and she would be the crowd."

"Do you own up to your guilt?"

"I admit it."

"Brilliant. Can we carry on?"

"No, she's waiting for us downstairs."

"In the end, that woman is meant for me to hate her." I take another couple of minutes to change my coat and put on one of my sweaters. Even though I look adorable with it, I discovered that I attract a lot of attention. People from the record company didn't stop looking at me, and I don't like being in the spotlight.

We went down to the hotel reception, and the girl, whom I later found out was called Susana, approached me. This time, with a very different attitude, she wanted to make me aware of the details of the tour. The first stop will be at the record company, where a meeting will be held to inform Daniel about the achievements of the last album and the forecasts for the new one. Susana is very worried because she doesn't have anything in writing, as Daniel asked her to. I would like to tell her that it doesn't matter, but I can't contradict his orders, so I tell her to give it to me as soon as possible. For now, it will be enough for us to write everything down on my agenda; after all, that's what I always do. We spend the journey to our destination making notes in it—well, I've made them because Susana is in a state of nerves that doesn't allow her to control her hand very well.

When we get to the record company, she's in a hurry to get out of the van and get ahead of us. Well, I guess it's to warn people about Daniel's mood, although the others have nothing to fear, I think. Before the vehicle comes to a complete stop, Susana opens the door, jumps down, and while Daniel, Raúl, and I slide out of the seats to do the same, she slams the door, leaving us inside and just inches away from catching my foot in the process. If it weren't for my reflexes being pretty good, this wouldn't amuse me at all.

384

I can't stop laughing as I watch her rush into the offices; she didn't even realize what she did. I turn to Daniel, seething and spouting all sorts of profanities. After a few seconds, Susana comes running out again, covering her mouth with her hand, unable to believe what she just did. Daniel asks me to stop laughing, but I can't. Just seeing her a nervous wreck makes it all too funny. Poor girl, now she managed to anger Daniel for real.

Raúl opens the door before she does, and we descend. Susana is in front of Daniel, and I can clearly see the color draining from her cheeks. It's incredible how the same person can provoke such disparate sensations in her and me. She doesn't manage to say anything; she just steps aside and lets us go inside. Daniel is still fuming.

"Calm down, Daniel; she didn't do it on purpose."

"It nearly ended up hurting you." He's still furious.

"But she didn't; she's nervous."

"Well, she should control herself."

"How about we all control ourselves?"

"In case you haven't noticed, I've got myself under control." We enter the boardroom, and Rogelio welcomes us along with a group of people, each in charge of a different aspect of the release of the new album. The atmosphere there is festive; obviously, the news they have for us are very good. Rogelio sits next to me, letting each of these people inform Daniel about the excellent news regarding his career. We take the opportunity to catch up on the circumstances that are more important to us—namely, gossip. He leans close to my ear and asks:

"How's everything been going with Susana?"

"Why do you ask?"

"It's her first promotional tour. She's only been working with us for three or four months, and..."

"What's the matter?"

"When we informed her that she would be taking over Daniel's tour, she started jumping around the table. I had to ask her to compose herself and maintain a more professional demeanor. Still, I could see her legs trembling, even though she was sitting. I wasn't entirely certain if she could keep it together, especially considering Daniel's lack of tolerance. So, what's your take? Should we stick with the plan or consider a change?"

The Game...Jade

Right now, I remember the meeting to organize Daniel's tour, the one where the executives belittled and humiliated me until, over the phone, he put them in their place or even lower. Maybe much lower. If it hadn't been for that, my insecurity wouldn't have allowed me to move forward, either personally or professionally, sure that they were right in treating me that way. I can't do any less for Susana; I just hope that she really makes an effort to control herself.

"Daniel hasn't said anything about it; let's give her time to see how it evolves."

"Uh-oh. What did she do?"

"Let's give it time, Rogelio; we've just arrived."

"Jade, whatever it is, you'll give me a call, won't you?"

"I promise."

Rogelio straightens up in his chair and seems to pay attention; however, his lips move constantly, though he makes no sound. I don't know if he's praying or what he's saying, but he looks worried, poor guy.

I look away from Rogelio as I feel Daniel squeezing my hand under the table. I see him smiling broadly; the news about his career are really great. This means that the promotional tour will be extensive, and we better get ready. I congratulate him and approach Susana; I want to check the lists. Something tells me I'll have to do her job and mine if I want to preserve her mental health.

Indeed, the list includes practically all the radio stations and TV shows that cover entertainment. This is where my worries start: she scheduled meetings with Daniel for lunch and dinner almost every day of the tour, with people whose identities I don't know, so I asked her.

"Susana, who are these people?" She looks terrified and starts sweating profusely.

"What do you mean, who are they? They are upper hierarchy people related to the record company."

"Okay, first lesson: people in the upper hierarchy don't give us a damn, and you can't book meals with Daniel unless he asks for it; otherwise, the answer is no." Her lips are shaking; she just looks at me and doesn't say anything, so I continue. "Susana, you must call these people and tell them that you made a mistake, that Daniel's schedule does not allow him to have lunch or dinner with them, and for no reason, make him look bad; blame me. Anything is better than this reaching Rogelio's ears. And don't worry; nothing bad will happen. If any of them complain to the record company, tell them that I was the one who denied Daniel, and I asked you to apologize to them, okay?"

"But it is my fault."

"It's nobody's fault; you didn't know. Now get out of here and make those calls, without leaving anything pending, please." Daniel looks at me, still smiling. Let's hope he stays that way.

Chapter XVIII
Well, blame yourself

The evening was long; we visited many radio stations, and as usual, we didn't eat anything at all. However, all of that is common, and it doesn't catch us by surprise. Poor Susana spent the afternoon apologizing for every little thing, and when she realized we wouldn't have time to eat, she almost died. Daniel can endure everything the tour throws at him with good humor, but she turns out to be quite annoying. I've attempted to talk to her, but all it does is bring tears to her eyes, so I gave up.

We arrived at the hotel quite late, especially considering that, for Daniel, due to the time difference, it was almost dawn. He gets out of the van somewhat uncomfortably; he realizes that Susana was watching him through the rear mirror for most of the journey. I know she likes him a lot, and it must be terrible that things are going so awful for her. If I put myself in her shoes, that's genuinely a tragedy, especially after how happy she was when she got the news that he would be her assignment. I feel sorry for her, the same way I would for myself in her place.

Finally, she leaves, and I hope tomorrow is better for her sake and ours. We're dead tired and say goodnight in the hallway to head to our rooms. Daniel walks me to my door, kisses me on the cheek, and winks. Raúl comes up to me and wishes me goodnight. I open the door and step in.

How horrible it is to have to do things despite the tiredness; even the simple act of unpacking seems exhausting. I take out my pajamas and step into the shower. After an afternoon with Susana, I definitely need to relax. While I take a bath, I try to calm myself so I can appreciate being here; it's something I never want to cease enjoying, no matter what. I use Susana's situation to remind myself that things could have turned out like hers for me and that the first time I saw him could have been a disaster instead of the marvel my life became. Daniel is here, just one door away; I can see him and hug him as much as I want.

I finish combing my hair while singing one of his songs, my

favorite; it soothes me, and I open the door to head to bed. Now I can finally sleep.

"Jade."

Rocío Blisswealth

I turn towards the bed and behold the sight of Daniel's incredible body, already under the sheets of my bed, covering him up to the waist. How much I've wanted to see him! Just like that, calmly enough to glide my eyes over his face and his well-toned arms. I know I've had him with me all day, but when there are people around, I avoid fixing my eyes on him, keeping everything at a professional level. However, now, in the privacy of my room, I can fill my eyes with his image.

"Did I scare you?"

"Daniel! Of course, you scared me." Somehow, I have to justify the seconds it took me to react that his presence wasn't just an ornament on the bed.

"Sorry, gorgeous, weren't you expecting me?"

"It's just that... the rooms, and the luggage, and no, I wasn't expecting you."

"Well, blame yourself."

"It's my fault. Again?"

"Oh, undoubtedly."

"And now, what am I to blame for?" I ask, smiling.

"Well, for having to sneak into your room. Since you don't want Raúl to find out, well..." He says with a solemn tone. "I have to do it clandestinely."

"Poor you, you're undoubtedly a martyr. I can imagine the effort it took to hide to go through the door that connects our rooms without anyone seeing you."

"It took more effort for me to keep anyone from knowing I'd be spending the night here."

"And didn't you think that at least I had to know?"

"But I did give you a wink, gorgeous!"

"Of course! The wink, I forgot that clue. My apologies."

"I forgive you on one condition." He says, smiling.

"Oh, really?"

"Yep."

"And what is that condition?"

"Well, come over here and give me a kiss so I can catch some sleep." He points to the space next to him and pats it with his hand.

"You mean I have to pay for my sins with a sacrifice. Hmm... sounds logical."

The Game...Jade

"That's right, but it has to be a sacrifice worthy of forgiveness." I lift the sheet and lie down next to him, tapping my chest with my fist.

"Through my fault, through my fault, through my most grievous fault." I give him a huge kiss before asking. "How am I doing?"

"What do you think?"

"Well, in my opinion, I must be forgiven by now because I've reached heaven." He starts laughing.

"You smell so good!"

"I've heard that's how I smell."

"Gorgeous."

"Yes?"

"I missed you."

"I missed you more." I spend a few minutes enjoying having him so close before telling him. "Daniel."

"Yes?"

"Can I ask you a favor?"

"Anything you want."

"Could you be a little more patient with Susana?"

"Gorgeous, that girl is infuriating."

"If she weren't, I wouldn't have to ask you for patience, would I?"

"Don't you think it would be better to do without her cooperation? I perfectly realize that you're the one instructing her in practically everything."

"I know, but I would like to give her another chance. She gets very nervous because she can't pull things off the way she wants."

"Exactly, not a single thing goes right for her, and another chance would mean..."

"And have you ever wondered why she can't get a single thing right?"

"Oh, but is there a reason for her incompetence? I thought it was by birth."

"No, you're the reason. She likes you a lot, and she can't control herself. I try to put myself in her place, and I feel sorry for her."

"Gorgeous, pity is the worst feeling you can express for someone. Alright, I won't make any promises because, you know me, patience isn't my strong suit, but I'll give it a shot."

"Thank you."

"And tell me one thing, then. You must like me a lot, too. I guess that's why you put yourself in her shoes." He laughs.

"I said I was trying to put myself in her place. As inconceivable as it may seem, there are people on this planet who can find you attractive, and I try to understand them. As my grandma used to say, 'There's no accounting for taste'..." His laughter interrupts me.

"So, you don't fancy me, then. And how come you're putting up with being here, cuddled up with me, all night?"

"Well, you see, my intention is to go to heaven someday; with how badly I've always behaved, I better make... How did you say it? 'Sacrifices worthy of forgiveness.'"

"Well, if I am your penance, I won't stand in the way of helping you achieve your goal. To heaven, you say? Well, that sounds a fair bit away, so come over here, sinner." With his index finger, he lifts my chin and kisses me, and I, what can I do! All for the sake of getting to heaven, although, as I said before, I'm already in it, but I don't plan on reminding him of that.

The wake-up call rings punctually at 8:00 a.m., and without thinking twice, I get out of bed, preferring not to take those blessed five minutes and risk them turning into two hours. Daniel is still sound asleep. I walk around the bed to get closer to him, and I remember the time when returning from Cuernavaca. He laid down on my lap to rest, and I was able to caress him for the first time. His features are so perfect, and he looks so peaceful that I bring my hand closer, and with the tips of my fingers, I caress him gently as I did that time. This is a better way to spend those five minutes I decided not to take to keep sleeping. I kiss his cheek; he opens those blessed eyes that seem to take my breath away and smiles. He pulls me towards him and kisses me on the lips.

"Come, stay for a bit."

"Of course not; we have just enough time. I'll get in the shower and come wake you up again; make the most of these minutes of grace."

"No! I refuse outright; I'm not going. I... my stomach hurts a lot. Will you stay until I feel better?"

"It's not school, Daniel, and I'm not going to call to lie to them that you feel bad. Do you take advantage of these minutes, or do you get in the shower first?"

"Why can't I stay?" He says with a pitiful voice while covering his face with the sheet.

The Game...Jade

"Because you're a famous singer, very responsible and disciplined. You're Daniel Montalvo, remember?"

"I've got no clue what you're on about."

"So now you have amnesia. Well, I'm going to take a bath, and we'll see if your memories come back in the meantime."

He rolls over, hugs the pillow, and sighs before going back to sleep. Gods! I want to go back there and nestle beside him, but no, someone has to be sane!

I don't think it took me more than ten minutes to get ready, but as soon as I got back into the room, I heard his deep, slow breathing. I can't believe it! He's fallen asleep again.

"Daniel…"

"What is it?"

"Get out of bed and in the shower!"

"I'm very sleepy."

"Fine, you asked for it." I head towards the door.

"Where are you off to?"

"For ice." There are his laughs again; with his voice interrupted by them, he says:

"You wouldn't dare, gorgeous!"

"Put me to the test, Daniel Montalvo."

"Oh no, you're already getting mad. I'm coming, I'm coming."

After a lightning-fast breakfast, we headed down to the lobby to meet Raúl and Susana. She looks terrible, with a face like a fresh corpse; surely, she didn't sleep at all last night.

I search for an answer to my furrowed brow, but Raúl just shrugs, indicating that he knows nothing. What could have happened to this girl? What worries me the most is that, if her performance yesterday was achieved in her right mind, I can only imagine what awaits us now that she looks like a zombie.

However, despite her deplorable state, her face somehow lights up when she sees Daniel. I know exactly what she's feeling.

"Good morning."

"Good morning." We both respond.

"Susana, have you had breakfast yet?" I ask, even though my question should probably be, are you okay?

Rocío Blisswealth

"To be honest, I didn't have time, and I've decided to imitate you; seeing how you both manage to go without eating for a long time." Daniel comes up to me and whispers in my ear:

"Why didn't she find the time? With all the hours she was clearly awake, wasn't it enough for her?" I give him a nudge in the ribs.

"You promised, Daniel." I reproach.

"Alright." He slightly raises his voice and addresses her: "Susana, something you should know is that we manage to hold our ground because we never let a good breakfast slip through our fingers. If you're thinking of keeping up, maybe that's a good place to start." He speaks to her in the tone my grandpa used when he wanted to point out, in a certain situation, that he was right, and I was not.

"Oh, I didn't know, tomorrow..." She opens the van door for us to get in; I suppose she wants to remedy the slammed door incident we fell victim to yesterday. However, it makes Raúl and Daniel very uncomfortable. Raúl stares at her in the eyes, and more seriously than I've seen him today, he tells her:

"Susanna, neither Daniel nor I are used to having a lady open the door for us. Could you humor us and let us stick to our old-school ways, no matter how outdated they might seem to you, so we can handle that?"

"Yes, but... Sure, I..."

"Thank you."

As soon as we get into the vehicle, Susana hands me a large envelope with an impressive number of pages. I have no idea what it's about, and I look up to meet her gaze. Underneath the terrible shadows formed by her huge dark circles, I can see that she looks at me with an air of self-satisfaction.

"Oh, thanks."

"But open it!" She says it as if it were a gift.

I tear open the envelope, and as I sift through the pages, I can see that it's our itinerary for the rest of the tour, meticulously detailed hour by hour, including all the data she could think of. And that's the reason she stayed up all night. I feel so guilty; I didn't explain myself well. Much of this is unnecessary, and the poor thing didn't get any sleep. Definitely, I'm not planning to tell her.

"Susana, this is incredible. I don't even know how to thank you."

Daniel, seated in front of us, turns to look at me and rolls his eyes. Without Susana seeing, I shoot him an annoyed frown and he turns away so I can't see his face. Raúl disguises his laughter with a poorly feigned cough and stares out the window at the passing avenue.

"You're welcome." She's happy; well, at least I don't feel that bad about it.

The first item on the well-organized list is at the TV station. Daniel will be featured on a widely-watched morning show in the country, perhaps the most popular, and the host is an exceptionally intelligent man. That's a relief; it's not always the case, and Daniel has been through quite a lot. However, the show lasts four hours, during which Daniel will be there for at least three. As soon as we arrive, Susana rushes out of the van and opens the door for us to exit. As she does so, she's met with Raúl's accusatory stare, prompting her to immediately close it again.

"Sorry, I forgot."

"And why shut it again if she has already popped it open?" Daniel asks irritably, but at least in a hushed voice.

"This girl appears to have left her brain back on the pillow." Raúl complains.

"Remember, she hasn't slept." Daniel starts chuckling.

"Blimey, then where on earth could she have left it?" He joins Daniel's laughter.

"The question isn't where, but when." They laugh.

I don't dare to defend her. What can I say? At least they're making fun of it, but they're not being aggressive for now. Finally, we get out and enter the studio. The host comes out to greet us, warmly welcoming us and starting a friendly conversation with Daniel. He's mentally sharp, so his jokes are very amusing, and they encourage Daniel to reciprocate. The result is that we all have a lot of fun. They offer us some breakfast; there's a small buffet with fruits and pastries. I approach to serve a plate with a small variety of things on it. Daniel looks at me with a puzzled expression; after all, we had breakfast at the hotel, and he finds it strange that I'm so willing to keep eating. However, he nods in understanding when I approach Susana and hand it over. She looks at me very embarrassed.

"But Jade, you really didn't have to."

"Susana, it's Daniel's orders." Magic words. "Do you plan on disobeying him?"

"No, not at all." She grabs the plate and starts eating eagerly.

Minutes before the show begins, the studio plunges into almost total darkness. Susana came up to me, saying she had some phone calls to make, and the host said she could use his office. Perfect, she'll be out of Daniel's reach, at least for a while. Raúl comes over and gives me a shoulder hug.

"Raúl."

"Spill it, beautiful."

"Was I like that?"

"Like Susana?"

"Yes."

"Would've been the logical move, but it looks like you had this uncanny knack for getting into Daniel's head. Always one step ahead, knowing what he wanted. And when you didn't roll with his plan, it was clear it was something you didn't want to do. We always found that amusing. So no, you were never like her."

"I feel..."

"Sorry for her, I get it."

"I know it's unpleasant, but I can't help it."

He hugs me tight and plants a kiss on my head. I know perfectly well that it's not in my hands to help her; she gets very nervous, and that annoys Daniel. There's not much I can pull off in dealing with that. She has to control herself, and I honestly don't know if she can do it.

The show starts, and I take my usual place in a corner on the floor—my favorite spot where I can watch the show unfold and admire Daniel, all while recalling my favorite memories. During a commercial break, the host instructs a technician to get me a chair. Daniel interrupts, asking if he can bring me one of the cushions decorating the room.

"But, buddy, are you sure? The wait's going to be long."

"It's a sort of ritual. Can I?"

"Sure thing."

He grabs the cushion and brings it over, squatting in front of me, balancing himself by holding my knees. The touch of his hands, even through my jeans, sends shivers down my spine, and I lock eyes with his.

"Gorgeous, don't mean to break into your meditation, but I reckon you'll be more at ease that way."

"Thanks." I wink at him.

The Game...Jade

The show ended after four hours; I can't believe how quickly it passed. I deeply appreciate this man's cleverness; he managed to make the show not just brief but also entertaining. The lights come on, and as the host says his goodbyes, I look around for Susana. During the time I was watching Daniel, I didn't notice her absence. Now, where could she have gone?

"Raúl, have you seen Susana?"

"I figured you dispatched her for something."

"No, the last thing she mentioned was that she had to make some calls. After that, I didn't see her again."

Daniel approaches with the host, intrigued by my worried expression.

"What's going on, Jade?"

"I can't find Susana."

"Is she the gal from the record company? She dropped by my office to make a call; come with me." Says the host.

We walked with him down a long hallway until we reached this spacious office dominated by subtle lighting and oversized leather couches. Before going in, through the window, we spot Susana, knocked out in the desk chair. Her head is tilted to the side, resting on the backrest, holding the phone receiver, and snoring! Yes, you can hear her snores from where we are. The host grins, but Daniel isn't as thrilled. I stand in front of him, and placing my hands on his sides, I beg him.

"Daniel, please, I'll wake her up." He leans in and whispers in my ear:

"Only if you give me a kiss on the lips, right here, right now."

Seriously, he sure knows how to apply pressure. Still, I don't want him to scold her in front of us. I look him in the eyes and give him a gentle smile.

"Fine."

"Are you serious?" He asks, surprised.

"If that's what I have to do, then yes."

"Don't worry; I can tell it means a lot to you. Let's go." He puts his index finger to his lips, signaling us to keep quiet, and we enter the office. Standing around the desk, he asks me in a hushed tone:

"What's the birthday tune they play around here?"

"'Las Mañanitas'"? I ask, intrigued.

"That's the one! You start, and we'll follow." The host is clearly enjoying the moment, and I begin to sing.

"Estas son las mañanitas, que cantaba el rey David.

A las muchachas bonitas, se las cantamos aquí.

Despierta, mi bien despierta, mira que ya amaneció.

[2]Ya los pajarillos cantan, la luna ya se metió."

Everyone started joining my voice, to which I added intensity when I saw Susana wasn't opening her eyes. Eventually, she did, only to find herself holding the receiver and facing a chorus consisting of Daniel, Raúl, the host, his secretary, and me. At first, her expression was one of confusion, not fully realizing where she was. Then her face turned beet red, and we all burst into laughter, a laughter in which she eventually joined, after all.

She got up from the couch and gathered her things to leave when she realized she still had the receiver in her hand. She observed it closely, as if pleading for it to reveal who she was talking to when she fell asleep. Nothing. She hung it up. We walked with the host's secretary towards the exit, and I lost count of how many times Susana had apologized. The first few times, I responded, but then I let her words fall into the void.

We reached the parking lot, and I could see Daniel talking to the van driver. Raúl hurried to open the door and help us get in. Once inside, Susana stared at her planner and didn't move it from there, not an inch.

"Don José, now we're heading towards..." She tells the driver.

"Don't worry, miss, I know where we're going."

"Thanks."

After a few minutes, we entered a neighborhood near the TV station, and the van came to a stop in front of a house. I asked Raúl where we were, and he simply gestured for me to stay quiet. Gods! What are they up to now? Susana, realizing that we stopped, turns towards the window, and her eyes widen.

"What are we doing in... my house?" She asks, with anguish in her voice. Honestly, I'm starting to feel anxious too. Daniel turned to her, and in a sweet, almost affectionate tone, addressed her.

"Susana, I'm extremely embarrassed with you. Clearly, you're exhausted, and that's on us, no doubt. I'm about to throw a request your way. Fair warning, if you're not up for it, it'll turn into a direct order. Head back home, get some rest, have a good meal, and meet us early at the hotel tomorrow. I get it; it's going to be tougher for Jade as she has to do without your help and company for the rest of the day. But, I reckon she'll manage the sacrifice if she

---

[2] The song says: "Wake up, my love, wake up. Look, it's already dawn."

The Game...Jade

knows she'll have you in the morning, alright?" Susana turns to look at me, and I nod to let her know it's not a problem.

"Thank you very much." She seems to apologize with her gaze for being so tired. "I don't know how you guys can withstand this pace."

"We sleep." Daniel replies with a smile.

She smiles back, not fully believing that's true. I can see that it's hard for her to stop looking at Daniel for the rest of the day, but it doesn't matter whether she stays or not—literally, she can't stay awake. As soon as we move away from her house, Raúl stretches his arms, relaxing, and sighs.

"Thanks, brother."

Daniel, who has taken Susana's seat next to me, smiles widely, and I can't resist expressing my gratitude for what he just did in a way that leaves no doubt about how much I appreciate it. Without giving him time for anything, I cup his face in my hands and plant my lips on his for a resounding kiss. He raises his hands in surprise and responds with that wonderful smile I adore.

"Yes, Daniel, thank you. Thank you so much." I say, almost breathless.

Now, he quickly leans towards me, probably not wanting to miss the moment and let embarrassment take over. He takes my face in his hands and responds to my kiss with an even better one.

"Thanks to you, gorgeous. Thank you very much."

As soon as he separates from me, embarrassment wraps around me. Starting from my face, it makes my blood rush through my skin until it takes on the already well-known red hue. I turn slowly to see Raúl, who looks at me in surprise and smiles.

"I'm sorry." I say, dying of embarrassment.

Daniel can't stop laughing and grabs me, intertwining his hands at the back of my neck, hiding my face under his neck.

"Raúl, tell me she's not irresistible!"

"Brother, I'm still in the dark about what you did, but what a kiss, kid! You throw in an 'I'm sorry' in there?"

"Yes, that's what she's saying. Apologizing to you for including you in her gratitude expression. Can you believe it?"

"I swear I've seen a reaction like that in some old movie. What's the apology about?"

Still with my face hidden in Daniel's neck, I reach out to the back seat, putting my fingers over Raúl's mouth to make him stop. It's harder for me to control myself if he keeps discussing the point.

"Alright, I'll zip it." He says, still with my fingers on his lips.

I lift my head and start counting. I just hope to reach a decent number before we get to where we're going. Twelve, thirteen, fourteen. Daniel reaches out his hand and takes mine, a subtle move unnoticed by anyone else but us. I look into his eyes, and he smiles. I guess I can hold hands "in public" if Don José can't see us without losing sight of the road, and Raúl, in his relaxed position in the back seat, can't see our hands. Yes, I suppose I can. I give his fingers a slight squeeze, and as he sighs, he smiles sweetly and deliberately looks away from me, helping me hide my mischief.

It's amazing how much time life has gifted me with this man I love so much. Usually, I'm an observant person, paying attention to what's happening around me. For example, I've always been struck by the type of relationship my grandparents achieved, sharing more than fifty years of their lives and having spent much more time together than apart. For some wonderful and strange reason, they found each other, and knew how to choose or wait for the right person. I don't know.

However, I've started to see this as a miracle, something I've never witnessed happen again. My mom never quite pulled it off, and her life always seemed to carry that unhappiness, or so it seems to me. And, just like her, everyone around me settles in their relationships, choosing someone merely because they don't want to wait for the right person. It must be terribly frustrating for both sides of a couple to realize they're not each other's dream, just settling for second best. How do you even live with that?

That's why I've tried to keep my expectations about Daniel very clear. I don't know how long he'll be in my life, but I'm not planning on letting go of a single second of this experience, which is a miracle to me. Hoping for it to last long would be asking for too much. That'd be pushing for one more miracle, and I don't believe I deserve it.

By holding his fingers with mine, I try to absorb his warmth, his essence, and the minutes I keep accumulating in that special space in my mind where I store everything related to him. I know very well that I'll never get enough of his essence. People call it chemistry between two individuals, and I recognize that my whole being needs his in a gut-wrenching way just to make it to the next breath.

Yet, deep down, I brace myself for what happens to everyone. I would never dare to dream, even to come close to what my grandparents were able to achieve, so my brain carefully dedicates itself to cherishing the minutes with him. They are my lifeline when facing demons, when I'm alone under the terrible weight of the awareness that I've always been like this, except when I'm with him. And they are when I allow myself to hear the inner voice screaming at me to be careful. It never clarifies what to be careful about, but I can easily imagine it. Daniel is a dream come true, at least mine, and I let my heart overflow, pouring out love for him without reason and measure.

Well, that's not entirely true; there is a reason. He gave me something no one else did, a part of him that stays with me and fades the feeling of loneliness I learned to recognize when I was in his arms. He gave me a reason to live when, after my grandparents passed away, all I would have wanted was to follow them. Perhaps I would have found the way and the courage to do so. He gave me the only thing I can now identify as love—strong, intense, present, always present. All of that has been given to me by this incredible man who travels by my side. And yet, I guess I'll be like everyone else; one day, I won't be with him anymore. It would be the most logical thing, considering my life and his, nothing more, and I try to prepare myself. I just hope that whatever separates me from him ends me, because I couldn't live without him. Not anymore. I love him very much.

Daniel slides into the seat and gets closer to me, but I'm so lost in my thoughts that I don't even notice. He runs his fingers through my hair, and even then, I don't snap out of my contemplation.

"Jade." He says in a low voice.

Finally, I became aware and locked eyes with him, surprised to find him so close to me.

"Hey there. Where were you?"

"Not too far, but I'm here now. Did you want to tell me something?"

"I'd quite like to fathom what's running through your mind."

"Seriously, Daniel?"

"There are moments, like just a bit ago, when you delve into some thought that engulfs you and whisks you away from here. I've always been curious to know what it's all about."

Rocío Blisswealth

"Well, I don't know if the other times I've been thinking the same as now."

"Fair point. So, would you mind sharing what you were pondering just now?"

"Yes, only..."

"Later."

"Yes."

"What if you end up forgetting?"

"I couldn't."

"You swear you'll tell me."

"I do."

"Alright, I'll wait."

"Patiently."

"Oh, heavens no! Not ever."

It's true, patience isn't his strongest suit, and I guess I get that. He's been gifted with so many virtues that patience just doesn't seem to fit in. Yes, that must be it.

The promotional visits are finally over, at least for today. I shouldn't have let my thoughts take me to such dark corners of my mind, those murky lakes where I sink, surrounded by the feeling that I'll lose Daniel sooner or later.

I spent the afternoon dealing with them, trying, with little success, to stay afloat. Today is one of those days when I wish I could make a pact with someone who could promise that if I lose him, they'd summon a massive demon to let me get out of this world with a single blow. That is if the pain doesn't get to me first. But I don't know anyone with those kinds of connections in the spiritual realm.

I step into the shower and rush to get ready. I know Daniel will enter my room in a few minutes, and I don't want to waste time. I brush my wet hair, hearing his voice as he crosses the door that connects our suites, singing my song. I toss the brush on a shelf and rush to get out.

I smile at the sight of him. What better cure is there for all my troubles than having him right here with me? He keeps singing as he folds the sheet for us to lie down. I can't move; all I can do is watch him as I feel my inner self-healing and renewing until I'm filled with hope. I focus on enjoying his presence; he's here now, and that's all that should matter.

"Why does it take you ages in the bath, gorgeous?"

"Is that what it seems like to you?"

"I'm always ready before you."

The Game...Jade

"That's because I do it intentionally, unlike you. I have the feeling that... Let me check behind your ears; I doubt you'll ever reach that spot."

"Of course, I do!" He claims, laughing, and comes closer, holding his ear so I can see the back.

"Hmm, just what I thought."

"What's there?" He continues laughing.

"Endless things."

"No way! Seriously? Like what?" He asks, his voice cracking with laughter.

"Come closer; let me get a good look." Once he's close enough, I kiss him right there, and his laughter continues. "Daniel, I need a hug from you. Can I have one?"

He stares into my eyes, and his laughter disappears, giving way to a smile.

"You know they're all yours. Take them whenever you want, though I love that you bother to ask for them."

He wraps his arms around me, and I entangle my hands around his waist. Finally, my brain unplugs, making way for that awesome feeling of his closeness. I bury my face in his neck and let all my love flow his way. I have nothing, absolutely nothing better to do.

The days have passed almost unnoticed and too quickly; everything has become a blur in my mind. We traveled through several cities promoting the album, even though I still think all that promo was unnecessary. The album's already topping the charts everywhere, awards for high sales stacking up, and time's running out.

A good piece of news was finding out that Susana would only be with us in Mexico City; she couldn't follow us to the rest of the cities, thanks to Rogelio's intervention, I guess. That made everything easier. Thanks to this fact, Daniel regained his good mood and has been sweeter than ever, if that's even possible.

However, I still feel like I need to spend as much time with him as I can, as if my hourglass is dropping the last grains without me being able to stop it, and that's exactly what I've been doing. Last night, for example, I couldn't close my eyes, and I spent the night just listening to Daniel's deep breaths while watching him sleep. He keeps that habit of grabbing one of my hands until he falls asleep, and he doesn't let go all night. Is a situation more than pleasurable for me, always eager for his touch. One time, I tried to let go, just out of curiosity. I wanted to find out, one, if I could do it, as he sometimes holds me very tightly; and two, I wanted to know what he would do if he noticed. I took the tips of his fingers with my free hand and tried to lift them for freedom of movement, and right then, Daniel held me tight again and said in a hush:

"Please, don't." His breathing became uneven, and I regretted terribly what I tried. It took a few minutes for his breathing to get back to normal, and he finally freed up some space between my fingers, letting the blood flow again. I was starting to think that if he didn't do it soon, I'd have to wake him up just to get some feeling back in my hand.

I filled my eyes with him, with the incredible perfection of his features. It gives me the feeling that a god is sleeping beside me. I am deeply grateful to be the one there, without going over, once again, the never-ending questions that pop up every time I marvel at how unreal it is that someone so stunning actually exists. I no longer allow myself to waste time on that; I don't have time to spare, I never have.

Tonight, we're heading back home; actually, the suitcases are already loaded up in the van while he finishes his performance on the show that's live right now. The studio is already dim, getting ready to kick off, and in a few seconds, the signs will light up, inviting us to keep silent with a soft, red glow. Daniel comes up to me, trapping me in one of the corners of the studio, the one with the least light. He leans against the wall, placing his hands on either side of my shoulders, giving me no way out, and whispers in a very low voice:

"Gorgeous, I can't take it any longer. Are you going to spill or what?"

"What I was thinking?"

"Please."

"I'll tell you, but first, guess what it was."

"Since we dropped Susana off at her place, I reckon it's got something to do with her. Are you comparing yourself to her, thinking I fancy you just like her?" He smirks playfully.

"Not exactly. I was thinking more about something that sets me apart from her."

"To me, you're completely different, but what do you mean?"

For a split second, my eyes lock on his, and for the first time, even with him so close, my heart beats at a normal rhythm, and my breathing is steady, measured. My cheeks stay cool, with a perfectly normal hue for me. I can be

The Game...Jade

honest and lay it all bare, without fear, in a natural way. It's the only thing that's not forced, and that doesn't make me feel the slightest bit awkward. What my eyes have been screaming at him for a few months now and, I don't know why, I didn't dare to tell him earlier. There's no longer a voice yelling at me to be careful, just silence and the peace in his eyes. Nothing matters more to me than letting him know what I was thinking that day, which is the same thing I think and feel every twenty-four hours of the day.

"She just likes you. On the other hand, I love you, Daniel. That's what I was thinking."

His eyes, a deep blue lit up by the blessed red light that just turned on, narrow fixedly on mine, and it seemed like time stood still in his sigh. He didn't expect it; he was left speechless, and just as I thought, I don't regret or feel sorry for telling him. It's been a relief to finally say those words.

He already knew it, but he didn't believe it was possible to hear it from my lips, that I could clearly see. Obviously, I'll never add the rest of my thoughts, the dark part that makes me think I might lose him, especially because I know he doesn't belong to me. But whatever, I don't care if he belongs to the whole world; I belong to him, no doubt. Daniel starts to smile, his eyes shining brightly.

"Jade!"

"It's showtime, Daniel. They're opening with you." Raúl taps his shoulder.

"Hold on! I'll be there in two minutes." A surprised look on Raúl's face joins mine.

"Daniel, please, go in; the show is live. You can't..." I say, smiling.

"Bloody hell! Fine, but, Jade..." I just smile at him as he rushes off towards the stage that awaits him under the final chords of the show's opening music. I settle into my happy spot to watch the man I love sing my song.

"THAT WAS PRECISELY WHAT YOU HAD TO PREVENT; YOU SHOULD HAVE INTERRUPTED HER, SCARED HER, SHAMED HER, ANYTHING, BUT NOT ALLOWED HER TO SAY IT!"

"OF COURSE NOT! NOW HE KNOWS HE ALREADY HAS HER IN HIS HANDS, AND MAYBE HE'LL BEHAVE MORE COOPERATIVELY."

"LET ME ASK YOU A QUESTION. HOW MANY TIMES DO YOU THINK DANIEL HAS HEARD THOSE WORDS?"

"I HAVE NO IDEA. HUNDREDS, MAYBE."

Rocío Blisswealth

"WELL, YOU'RE RADICALLY MISTAKEN. WHAT HE'S HEARD, AND YES, MAYBE THOUSANDS OF TIMES, IS 'I LIKE YOU,' 'HOW HANDSOME YOU ARE,' 'I WANT YOU,' BUT NEVER, NEVER, AN 'I LOVE YOU.'"

"BUT THAT'S NOT POS..."

"YES, IT IS. DIDN'T YOU SEE HIS EYES? THIS HAS TURNED TERRIBLY WRONG BECAUSE NOW IT'S SHE WHO HAS HIM IN HER HANDS."

Daniel wraps up his part in the show and tries to come over to me, but the crowd surrounds him, asking for autographs, pictures, or just a simple handshake. Every now and then, he looks at me and smiles. Time rushes by, Raúl rescues him from the crowd, and we dash towards the van, heading to the airport. I hop in, and Raúl takes the seat next to me, leaving the front seat for Daniel. He tries to say something, but the engine's roar interrupts him, and he has no choice but to buckle up and stay put. He swivels in his seat and watches me chatting with Raúl, scanning my face for the usual red blush, but no, it doesn't show up this time. He can't take his eyes off me.

"Hey, is something wrong, Daniel?" Raúl looks at him. Daniel furrows his brow and replies with a half-smile.

"No, nothing, gorgeous."

One of two things: either the driver is a total pro at navigating this crazy traffic, or they moved the airport because we arrived pretty darn quickly. We park, and in one swift move, Daniel unbuckles his seatbelt and jumps down. The driver gets out to help with the bags. Daniel opens the door and commands, quite authoritatively:

"Raúl, get out of there, please." And addressing me. "As for you, don't even think about moving from that spot."

"But, Daniel..." Raúl starts to protest.

"Listen, Raúl, this isn't a live performance. I'm taking my two minutes, and if we happen to miss the plane, so be it! Understand?"

"No problem, brother." Even if there were, there's no choice but to obey.

Daniel gets in the vehicle and slams the door once he's sure it's almost welded shut. He then throws himself at me, hugging me tightly, burying his face between my shoulder and hair. I can feel his hands trembling against my back.

"I love you more, way more."

"Impossible." He lifts his head, searching for my eyes. I smile, and he kisses me slowly.

The Game...Jade

"I'll be back soon."

"I'll be right here." He turns and places his hand on the door handle, then pauses, looking at me with narrowed eyes.

"Would it be too much to ask you to say it again?" I lean in, taking his face in my hands to look him in the eyes.

"I love you, Daniel." Without breaking eye contact, he responds.

"I love you more, Jade."

"I already told you that's impossible." He brushes my cheek with his fingers.

"No blushing this time."

"There's no reason for it; I'd have to be embarrassed for that to happen, and it's not the case."

"Brillant." He smiles, gives me a quick kiss, and we get out of the van walking together, but not touching, as if nothing had happened.

Chapter XIX
As I said, be careful what you ask for; it might be granted

England.

"*Get out of the water! Everyone, get out of the water right now!*"

Several pairs of feet hastily exit the Elements Vault. However, one of them, moving a fraction of a second slower than the others, fails to pull back his left foot in time and ends up with a burn on the heel. The wound looks like a welt, leaving an exposed stretch of flesh without any skin to cover it.

"*¡Arghhh!*"

A muffled gasp escapes Boxwood, followed one by one by Mistletoe, Grapevine, Ebony, and Olive. Each one screams with the same intensity as the wound inflicted on their brother is mirrored in them. Their bodyguards rush to help them, although, in reality, there's nothing to be done. It's the kind of wound that only time can heal, a long time.

Boxwood: But what does he intend? To kill us?

Mistletoe: Oh, but do you still harbor doubts about it? Of course, that's what he would prefer, and if we hadn't left the water on time, perhaps...

Boxwood: No, it wasn't enough for that, but, as the saying goes, the intention alone is sufficient; this fundamentally alters the situation.

Ebony: The servant has arrived with information regarding Daniel's trip to Mexico; he was with Jade, and...

Mistletoe: Of course, he has been with her! If not, how the hell do you explain this? He says, revealing the sharp wound on his foot.

Ebony: She told him she loves him.

A deathly silence fills the place as they look at each other in bewilderment.

Boxwood: No, that's not possible; she must not love him.

Mistletoe: Can you find another explanation for what is happening?

Boxwood: There has to be. Daniel understands that, for this plan to succeed, for his fame to attain the starry heights he desires, and above all, for it to be eternal, solitude is an indispensable requirement. This fame thrives on loneliness, once it has settled, and...

The Game...Jade

Ebony: And are we entirely sure about that?

Boxwood: It has always been like this, or do you want me to go through the list of previous cases to cross-reference data?

Ebony: I don't mean that; I know it's always been like that. What I mean is if we're certain that it will work the same way with Jade. She wasn't supposed to love him; she had to desire him, nothing more, however...

Boxwood: Why didn't you prevent her from telling him? She brings things to life as soon as she puts them into words. He turns to the demon who just arrived with the news. It could have come earlier, but it was afraid, and with fear peeking through its eyes, it responds.

Demon: Lord, I thought with that, Daniel would have her in his hands, and perhaps, she'd be inclined to cooperate. I never imagined...

Grapevine, the one closest to the demon in that moment, lays his hand on it, and suddenly it starts convulsing. Its mouth widens beyond its limits, and its body flips inside out, revealing the gruesome interior amid screams that gradually fade until it disappears. Everyone watches in astonishment.

Ebony: What did you do to him? He asks with absolute calm.

Grapevine: I applied a touch of Jade's energy to him.

Boxwood: You shouldn't waste it like this, especially now when everything is so uncertain.

Grapevine: There are necessary expenses; I wanted to know what she is capable of.

Boxwood: And for that, isn't it sufficient to look at your own foot? Daniel did that to you when he jumped into the pool.

Grapevine: I want a clearer understanding of what we're dealing with.

Boxwood: We're not up against her; let me remind you that we're using her.

Grapevine: And let me remind you that nothing is as it's supposed to be. If we've managed to use her so far, it's been by chance. This case is entirely different from the rest. Let's admit it; we know nothing about her. It's fascinating.

Olive: We must study her to be able to steer her.

Grapevine: Certainly. There must be a way.

Olive: No doubt, it's all about knowing how to play our pieces.

Boxwood: Alright, let's calm down and get things in order.

Ebony: Before that... He says, pointing at the wound on his foot.

Mistletoe: *We need time to heal.*

Olive: *Bring him then! What are you waiting for?*

One of the bodyguards runs off, only to return seconds later with a man donned in Hindu-looking attire, very tall, almost a head taller than any of them, who are already quite tall. His face reflects disgust, and perhaps that's why his features appear bitter, as if a smile had never passed through there. His eyes are black and deep, completely lacking any luster, resembling those of a fish whose body rests on the ice of a market. His skin, of a perfect chocolate tone, is covered by a thin whitish layer caused by the lack of sunlight.

Strangely, his clothes remain whole, but the sets of thin fabrics, which were once of bright colors, are pale intertwined threads that partially allow seeing through them. He looks around and takes a glance at the water, which is not still as it would normally be; today, it reaches the edge of the tiles, swirling and forming small whirlpools. Curiously, this brings a smile to his face, or a semblance of one. However, for a fraction of a second, his eyes emit a small spark, and then nothing more.

He takes a couple of very slow steps; it's difficult for him to move due to the bracelet encircling one of his ankles—a metal circle in one piece as if it were once a ring belonging to a giant. It's golden, with inscriptions engraved in a very ancient language, nearly obsolete in this era. These inscriptions glow like flames when he walks, and it can be clearly seen that they hurt him, forming sores on his skin when the bracelet moves with each step, touching areas that have not yet formed scars under its contact. Still, he makes no sound of complaint as he approaches Boxwood, who looks at him with disdain.

Boxwood: *Come on! Do your job!*

The Hindu extends a finger towards Boxwood's heel, and the air around him ripples, much like when we peer through steam. Seconds later, his foot is completely healed, just like those of his brothers, who sigh in relief.

Boxwood: *Back off!*

With the same leisurely pace he came in with, he strolls out the door, but not before turning to look at the water once more.

Ebony: *It's been a long time since I've seen this one. How did we get him?*

Mistletoe: Speaking with all the cynicism he's capable of. *If I remember correctly, on one occasion, he asked us to keep the continent assigned to him unchanged; he considered that his people were happy, and that they lived in* *peace. Out of the kindness of my heart, I decided to help him. I made a pact with him and invited him to live with us for a while. He, being the Time of that continent, stayed here, and his land stood still in that instant, without Time to help it move towards the future. I don't know why he always wears that bitter expression; I did what he asked me to do.*

Ebony: *As I said, be careful what you ask for; it might be granted.* He responds with a laugh.

Mistletoe: *That's why it burns on his skin, so he doesn't forget his mistakes.*

Olive: *Gentlemen, let's focus on what matters, please. Let's review the information we have regarding Jade.*

Boxwood: *Very well. Jade's case has been unique from the beginning. We expected her at another time, and it took a lot of generations to prepare her. The demons were ready to interfere with her conception, but what we never considered was that the man, who in the visions played the role of her father, apart from never being able to provide her with the inheritance she needed, would decide to abandon her mother just days before her conception. Her mother conceived her with someone else, and by the time we realized it, the crucial first twenty-one days had passed, rendering the demons unable to act.*

Ebony: *Yes, they could, but her grandmother took it upon herself to protect the baby, twenty-four hours a day, years before she was born. Her mother would have been easy, but the grandmother had references about us, considering what happened with her brother, and...*

Mistletoe: *Another mistake of your demons.*

Ebony: *None of that, just the traditional procedure to test the resilience and inclinations of infants. It was necessary to know which side was predominant in Clemente, and he couldn't withstand even one of the most insignificant demons. That's how we realized he wouldn't be of much use, but his sister was present and waited until she recognized the symptoms in her own granddaughter.*

Olive: *Jade.*

Ebony: *That's right. It was she herself who tried to mark in Jade an inclination, the one that she thought could save her.*

Olive: *Save her from what? She wasn't really in any danger. What we take from her doesn't harm her; come on, it doesn't even wear her down* *spiritually or physically. Perhaps she wouldn't have noticed, and we would have taken care of her more than anyone; we would have been her family.*

Ebony: *Oh, but the damned ethic dictated to her soul that it was Jade who should choose, or rather, that Jade should choose what, from her point of view, was right.*

Olive: *And she protected her until she began to openly interfere with us, and we took matters into our own hands. By then, Jade had already passed all the tests; the demons only frightened her.*

Ebony: *And that just because they were asked to show themselves in their original form, without sweetening their appearance.*

Olive: *I know, that's what I mean. They never managed to provoke real terror in her; they just scared her, and she ended up getting used to them. When it was determined that it was necessary to remove her grandparents, and she was left alone, she even showed some affection for the demon that had been assigned to her; one could say she grew fond of him.*

Mistletoe: *This clearly shows us that, despite her grandmother's efforts, the scales tilt towards us.*

Boxwood: *It's not quite like that; she followed her instincts. Despite the enormous pain it caused her, she rid herself of it.*

Mistletoe: *So, where do we stand regarding her?*

Boxwood: *We chose Daniel because, according to Sara, he possessed all the physical characteristics to be the perfect lure for Jade. Since she considers demons the source of all her troubles, it is necessary to obtain her energy through other means. He worked wonderfully in the beginning, but greed has led him to believe he can have it all without sharing it with us.*

Olive: *But we don't know that for sure, do we?*

Boxwood: *Unfortunately, no. Jade protects him, causing interference when reading his thoughts. Although, it's easy to assume this is the case.*

Olive: *It was also easy to assume that he would awaken her lust, and, willingly or unwillingly, he surprised us by gaining her love, no less. A situation utterly unheard of; there are no records of anything similar, or are there?*

Boxwood: *No, they've all been easily swept away by their instincts; lust has been a powerful ally in keeping them at bay until their time runs out. They are then removed to become part of The Myths and Luminaries of the artistic scene, whose fame has endured even after their death.*

The Game…Jade

Olive: Why is it that everyone wants the same thing? Fame after death. If they're already dead, what does it matter if their fame endures or not?

Boxwood: Vanity, my dear friend! Vanity. Besides, you forget the last clause of their contracts. They want to witness their fame from the afterlife and end up, as humans say, haunting the world as long as someone remembers them.

Olive: They don't understand that no one will be able to see them anymore, and for them, that is hell in itself.

Ebony: We know that hell is different for everyone. And everyone designs their own.

Mistletoe: Gentlemen, we have deviated from the issue at hand, Jade. She protects Daniel; therefore, we won't try anything against him; it would be a waste of time. Nonetheless, it is imperative that her love stops flowing to him, or the consequences could be disastrous.

Olive: I still don't understand how he withstands it. According to the information we have, receiving it isn't straightforward without suffering the consequences, and so far, everything related to Daniel is working wonders; his career couldn't be better, and...

Mistletoe: Obviously, they complement each other, and that's precisely what we must prevent. We need to keep him away from her.

Ebony: Do you want to unleash Jade's wrath?

Mistletoe: That's not what I'm trying to do; I'm just trying to take advantage of the situation at hand. Fortunately, Jade is unaware of her capabilities, and it's necessary to keep it that way. In relation to Daniel, we can't endure either his anger or his love, but perhaps if we handle everything within a range of pain, we could achieve it. We can't risk losing her.

Boxwood: No, not yet. We've worked hard to secure her, and it wouldn't be in our best interest to lose her and start planning again. Let's exhaust all efforts to bring her back.

Grapevine: If only we could find a way to bring her closer to us; I could instruct her, shape her. If she grew fond of her demon, perhaps we could seduce her with something. She's intelligent and capable of great things.

Boxwood: Since her conception, you have shown a great preference for her over any other source of energy we have had access to.

Grapevine: She is different, unpredictable, courageous, inexhaustible.

Boxwood: Forget it! You said it yourself, too unpredictable to be safe. Pure nitroglycerin.

Rocío Blisswealth

412

Grapevine: But if we brought her here.

Boxwood: Stop the nonsense! Bring her here? That would be a death sentence.

Grapevine: Maybe not. Addressing the bodyguards. *Let's not waste this, gentlemen. Bring in the group, everyone; this energy will propel them forward significantly.*

Spain.

Daniel glides through the pool, back and forth, as if he were born in it. The water caresses him, sliding through his hair and tracing the curves of his body, almost as if it had missed him during the days he spent away from here.

Someone has been watching him for a few minutes, and he hasn't noticed. This person approaches slowly, never losing sight of him until reaching the poolside, right where Daniel places his hand after completing a stroke.

The visitor extends their hand and gently caresses his fingers. Startled, Daniel straightens up in the pool. Despite the difficulty of balancing himself, he manages to do so and meets Sara, who is crouched next to the edge of the pool.

"Hello, handsome!"

"What are you doing here?"

"I've missed you too, darling, thank you."

"Quit it with the name-calling."

"How would you prefer me to refrain from calling you? Handsome or darling?"

"Enough with the nonsense. Sara, what do you want?" He mutters a response.

"Oh dear, what a foul mood you're in today. Who got under your skin? Jade?"

"No, you've got that effect. I was perfectly fine until you showed up."

"Well, perhaps I can do something to counteract it." Daniel emerges from the water and dries his skin with a towel, attempting in vain to shield himself from Sara's uncomfortable gaze. She extends her hand and, with the tips of her fingers, traces Daniel's arm. He quickly pulls away and, trying to remain calm, says:

"Cut it out, Sara, please."

"Are you sure?" She asks, smiling.

"What brings you here?"

The Game...Jade

"I care about you, darl... that is, Daniel. How was your time in Aztec lands? Anything noteworthy?"

"All good, just as always."

"I don't know why, but I find that very hard to believe."

"Get to the point, Sara."

"Alright, Daniel, I don't think there's a better way to say this, so. We've decided to withdraw our support. Starting with your next album, if there is one, you'll have to find another record company. You won't have us backing you anymore."

Without looking at Sara, he smiles. Contrary to what she believes, the news doesn't bother him in the slightest. However, he doesn't want to show it openly and slightly hardens his features before making eye contact.

"Thanks, I've already got it noted, anything else?"

"Do you genuinely believe she loves you? I assume you've already revealed the true Daniel to her. Is that right?" Sara's voice carries a mocking tone.

He continues his attempts to control himself. Sara's words exasperate him, leading him down paths he refuses to tread. Finding some patience, he responds.

"I'm not going to hash out that point with you, Sara."

"Oh, no? Well, you should. How about if I, accidentally, of course, let her in on who you truly are?"

"Sara, leave her alone. Why do you insist on hurting me?" Daniel replies, attempting to steer the conversation away.

"I didn't realize that hurting her also hurt you; that's indeed a new revelation, considering you claim everything remains the same."

"Sara, this doesn't make sense. I won't be part of your ranks anymore, as you kindly informed me. Why should it matter if I believe she loves me? Or what part of me she loves? Shouldn't it be irrelevant to you? You won't see me again."

"You're mistaken. Support has been withdrawn, but I still have hope that you'll regain your sanity and return like the prodigal son to reclaim what is rightfully yours, the very thing we worked so hard for. Leave her, Daniel; someone else will handle the job, so you can enjoy the benefits without the obligations this girl brings. You could be with me. I could also tell you that I love you if that's what you fancy."

Rocío Blisswealth

"Sara, how can I make you understand that I don't...?"

"And you say I shouldn't care; no, Daniel, I'm not accustomed to working on something for someone else to enjoy it."

"I worked in this too, Sara. My career has cost me."

"I'm not referring to your career." She interrupts him. "I mean you."

"Sara, we'd better leave this behind, I'll walk you to the door." Now she's the one trying to contain herself. She knows Daniel well enough to understand that she won't achieve anything. She has to wait for the plans, already in motion, to take effect. Putting a damper on the fury and jealousy overwhelming her, she responds in a low voice.

"No need for that; we'll see each other soon." Speaking to himself, Daniel answers.

"I hope not."

Sara walks through the garden toward her car, and on the way, she encounters a demon very similar to the one that lived for decades in Jade's room. As he approaches her, he listens intently to her words.

"Give it a couple of days, then I'll give you instructions."

Daniel takes a seat at the edge of the pool, his feet dangling in the water. Carmen brings a stool and settles close to him, gently stroking his hair.

"How are you, my dear?"

"I've had brighter days." He responds with a sigh, without turning to look at her.

"But you returned from Mexico with such joy." Carmen's voice sounds concerned.

"Yes, I was still dreaming, Carmen, but Sara has this knack for grounding me in reality in less than a minute."

"Let's set aside Sara for now and share with me. What brought you such happiness? Can you tell me?"

"Carmen, I reckon there's nothing about me you don't know, and yes, I need to tell you; no one else knows."

"Well, end the suspense already and fill me in." She smiles.

"Jade told me she loves me."

Carmen extends her hand, gently stroking the head of the young man she loves like a son. Despite being his aunt, she has always been there for him, taking care of him, protecting him, and listening when he had no one else to talk to or trust. With his parents leaving him aside, each one preoccupied with

The Game...Jade

matters they deemed more important, Carmen stepped in, filling that void and earning the trust that no one else holds.

"We were already aware of that, Daniel."

"There's a world of difference between grasping it, feeling it in your gut, and having it spoken directly from her lips. Especially so when she told me, looking me in the eye, with no blush on her cheeks, completely honest. I yearned to bring her along, to sway her to join me, and allow me the chance to reciprocate, even if it's just a small portion of what she gives me."

"I don't believe it would have been too much trouble for you. Why didn't you do it?"

"And you ask me this? You're well aware I couldn't bring her here to be at the mercy of all of them, of Sara. Besides, I dare not plunge her into this decay that surrounds me." Daniel's voice has become deep, filled with sadness, as he acknowledges what he hasn't shown Jade.

"And do you prefer her to remain at the mercy of demons, my dear? You mentioned they use her however they please."

"She can stand up to demons, Carmen; she's been doing it all along, and she doesn't even notice them anymore."

"You can't be thinking like that, Daniel. What's happening?"

"What will she think of me if she finds out about my life, the deeds I've been capable of? I'm certain Carmen, she'll hate me, especially after what she's told me. I couldn't bear it if..." He stares straight ahead.

"Daniel, why not be honest with her? Jade loves you, and I believe it would be better to risk hearing what she might think of you than to lose everything. You could stand together and achieve something."

"At this moment, I'm not concerned about whatever they might do to me." He says with annoyance.

"I am, Daniel."

"I know, it's just that, as Sara puts it, what would Jade think if she learned I'm the one who handed her over to them? I should lay it out, admit that I'm somewhat of a predator, and she's my source of sustenance, and not only that, but I distribute what I get among the hungry pack of hyenas in exchange for fame. Fame, I might add, that I wouldn't have access to without her. How do I confront her with the fact that I'm like this house, where there's never been anything good, this resplendent dwelling where the most despicable acts have unfolded, and where the demons, despised by her, have held their most memorable revelries?

She would finally know that inside, I'm rotten, and the aroma I conceal with the lotion she so adores is the scent that the putridity exudes. She would know that with each of her hugs, I receive far more than she intends to give me. That she showers me with gifts meant solely for her. That I'm aware of it, and I do nothing to stop it, knowing I could keep my distance from her, and yet, out of sheer selfishness, I don't. I couldn't bear her gaze, Carmen."

"Let me ask you something. She's been in this house, as you told me. Didn't she notice anything then? Maybe she already knows something and you..."

"It doesn't work like that, you see. When you're astral traveling, your mind fixates on what piques your interest, that allows your soul to travel, and you only start picking up more things when you stay in one spot for a while. Otherwise, you just see what's essential, and trust me, she couldn't perceive these scents. If she had, she would've noticed the abundance of demons and wouldn't have gone any further; she would've bolted."

"I don't smell anything. Could it be that..."

"Carmen, I couldn't even see Salvador's demon myself. She sensed his scent in an instant, mere seconds before her eyes caught him."

"Oh."

"Now you see." Daniel says with a bitter smile.

"Daniel, when you talked to me about all of this, about what you could achieve through her, I thought about trying to persuade you otherwise, but then I convinced myself that if the girl didn't suffer any harm, what did it matter if you took a little, and I let you go ahead."

"You wouldn't have been able to convince me."

"What I mean is, at that time, you seemed very confident in your ability to handle it. What went wrong?"

"When Sara talked about her, she always called her 'the source.' She gave me details, names, dates as if it were a scientific experiment, and I ended up seeing her as a guinea pig. Soulless, conscienceless, someone you don't form a connection with because you always view them as an object. Someone to whom I could give..." Daniel avoids eye contact with Carmen, ashamed of the gaze of this woman, who watches him, waiting for him to finish what he's saying. "…my body, in exchange for what she'd give me. Back then, it seemed like a simple enough task."

Carmen remains silent and allows him to continue. There's no room for reproaches in this case. The chance to stop him disappeared long ago, and all that remains is to face the problem that has arisen.

"However, when I met her, she didn't even stretch out her hand to touch me. She thrust a notebook at me for an autograph. That's all she wanted. There I was, ready to tear her apart and toss her to the wolves for my trophy, and all she wanted was a few moments with me. I invited her to hang around, and she did, while I set up the snares to nab her. She sat beside me, waiting for the trap to be set, ready to calmly walk into it." He runs his fingers through his hair, pulling at it, desperate as he goes through again the worst of his actions, recounting to Carmen; the only thing that truly embarrasses him to say.

"I offered to jot down my address for her to write to me, but she dismissed it saying she had no plans to do so. She often claims she's not a fan of lost causes; I suppose she thought writing to me fell into that category. I then asked for her address so I could be the one to write to her; she looked at me indignantly, seemingly convinced I was mocking her. Why would someone like me want to stay in touch?

My surprise grew, along with my desperation to not let her go. It seemed that with every step I took forward, she took one back, distancing herself from me. I was moving too fast for her, and that was another chance to save her that I missed. As I escorted her to the car..."

"Did you go with her?"

"Yes, I made mistake after mistake. I could already sense her energy around me, but I craved more. Getting closer, I kissed her. The only kiss she's allowed me to give her in public, and it surprised her so much that she forgot about the people around us. It was then that I saw myself in her eyes, and I could see the image she had of me. To her, I was a normal man, maybe more attractive than the rest, but just normal. The very thing I'm not, yet I yearned to keep that perception. I held her hand, yet she was the one who freed herself, and, saying goodbye, she got into the car. Since then, that image has become addictive. No one had ever seen me like that, and I wanted more."

"Didn't she ask you, I don't know, to stay with you for a while, like the others do?"

Daniel smiles with the same bitterness that has filled him since this conversation began; the same bitterness left by Sara's verbal blows.

"She never has. I was the one who had to... I practically begged her to let me stay with her at night."

"Daniel, I thought you guys didn't..."

"And that's the truth, I swear. I wouldn't dare to drag her into the muck that I am when she's so pure. Can you fathom the level of trust she places in me to agree to stay without doubting that I wouldn't touch her without asking her first?" Carmen looks at Daniel again with eyes of surprise. "Those were her words. She said she knew I wouldn't, curled up next to me, and slept. That time with her allowed me to see myself in her eyes for a longer time, and I became fascinated by the image she had created of me. An image that, as if she were embroidering it, gains more and finer characteristics with each passing day we share. She adds and removes details; for her, I'm stubborn, whimsical, respectful, intelligent, talented, loving, trustworthy, but above all, worthy of being loved. And I crave to be just that, Carmen; I desire it with all my might."

"And I, who didn't believe this was true, could confirm that the closer you are to her, everything you dreamed about regarding your career comes true and then some. I think your fame has reached dimensions I didn't dare to dream of when you first told me about her." Daniel pulls at his hair again and rubs his hands, trying to distract himself from the thoughts that haunt him.

"It's true. I keep robbing her gift while she sleeps in my arms."

"I'm sorry, my dear, I didn't mean to..."

"Yet, that's what I do. Just by being by her side, and she doesn't know it, but I do. Do you get it now? How do I ask her to stay with me, to ignore the scent of demons and the filth that is all I can offer? How do I vow to her that I'll strive to be of value, to be what she wants me to be when I don't even know if I have the capacity to achieve such a thing? I can't, Carmen, and I can't distance myself from her either, not anymore."

"Daniel, there's much I don't understand, but one thing I do know is that if there's anyone capable of forgiving everything that torments you and keep loving you is her. But she needs to hear it from your lips, not Sara's, Daniel. To them, she's the treasure they sought for so long. I still don't know how they can use a person who has no idea of what she is. But if you're to achieve anything, it has to be with her, I'm sure of that. Don't let her feel betrayed."

The Game...Jade

"Yet, that's what I do, betray her minute after minute."

"Answer me one thing, dear. Do you love her?"

"More than she does me." Carmen's gaze, for the first time, shows serious concern.

"Then there's no other way. Talk to her, remove her from their reach, buy another house, a home cleansed of all bad memories, and find a way to rid yourself of all this."

"Why do you make it seem so easy?"

"It's not, dear. You're facing the most difficult situation you've encountered so far, but it's either that or letting her go."

Daniel despairs; these are words he doesn't want to hear, words that represent the only correct way out of this hole he has fallen into, dragging Jade with him. Once again, he will have to silence them to stay with her.

"Not that, Carmen! That would be like sacrificing her myself, handing her over for them to do with as they please. As long as they think they can still achieve something through me, maybe they'll lay off her. I don't want to entertain the possibility of someone else being thrown into her life, and that she..."

Carmen hesitates before asking him questions. However, while she let go of the possibility of stopping Daniel when it presented itself, she doesn't want to let go of the chance to help him in any way she can. He has already become involved in unthinkable things, things only spoken of in old horror stories, which she used to mock. However, they turned out to be more real than everything around her, and now it's her nephew who doesn't know how to escape them, adding sin upon his head by taking advantage of the girl who loves him. She must ask.

"Be honest, Daniel. Why don't you let her go?" Daniel loses his sight in the trees surrounding the garden. He doesn't want to think about what Carmen is asking him because he doesn't want to know the answer. "So they won't have her? So she won't be handed over to someone else? To not lose what you've achieved with her support? Or because you love her? What's the real reason, Daniel?"

"I don't know, I don't know." Tears stream down Daniel's face, and Carmen wipes them away with her fingers, just like when he was a child. But he's not anymore, and there's nothing she can do for him but sit next to him and keep him company, and that's what she does.

Rocío Blisswealth

Monterrey.

Strange as it might sound, things in this house have changed a lot. I returned to find that everything was still normal and quiet, which was truly weird for our family. Obviously, we're still dealing with the never-ending to-do list, something that increasingly makes me uneasy, but I diligently continue getting rid of any danger that worries Mara, all in an attempt to keep accumulating points.

Since the first time that possibility appeared before my eyes, my mind wandered with the expectation of where the next destination for those points might be. Whenever something good happened with Daniel, I always believed that's where they had ended up. However, for what I'm planning now, I need an incalculable amount of points; I don't see any other way to achieve it.

I want to leave with him and not come back. There must be some job I can do that allows me to be by his side more, all the time. And since I know I'd never dare to ask him, that's where I want my points to accumulate—I want him to be the one to do it.

Until recently, I wouldn't even have dared to even think about it. But after all that's happened, I want to give myself permission to dream; I don't lose anything by doing so. I lock myself in the bedroom, vainly hoping that Daniel will show up. I know he most likely won't; he usually takes a few days off before showing up here again. And it's only been thirty-six hours since I left him to catch the plane, so... I don't care, I'm still waiting.

I lie down on the bed with Tíber beside me, fully intending to wait for him awake. However, Mom's dinner was heavy, and that didn't help my eyelids stay open. Before I know it, I fall asleep.

I don't know how much time has passed; I feel someone sitting next to me. I open my eyes and see Daniel with Tíber in his arms, smiling at me.

"It's not fair."

"What's not fair, gorgeous?"

"I wanted to wait for you awake, but I couldn't."

"I'm relieved; it's nearly four in the morning. It would've been quite the wait. And tell me, how did you know I'd show up today?"

"Tíber told me." I speak in a hushed voice, as if trying not to let the puppy know.

The Game...Jade

"Are you suggesting he's some sort of fortune teller?" He asks, also in secret, and smiles.

"Of course not, he's psychic. Didn't you notice?"

"Blimey! Well, no, but let me ask him some things about you that I've always wanted to know."

"Like what? Hey! And why don't you ask me instead? I mean, you wouldn't want to tire out the psychic. Or do you?"

We both turn to look at Tíber, who just at that moment lets out a huge yawn, curls up in Daniel's arm, and closes his eyes. We laughed softly so as not to wake him up. Daniel gets up and places him in his doll's crib, in which, I still don't know if, fortunately or unfortunately, he still fits and has plenty of space.

"Can I?" He points to the space next to me on the bed.

"You don't have to ask; of course you can, always."

He settles in next to me, burying his hand behind my neck and guiding my head until I find myself lying on his shoulder. He hugs me tightly, and I feel his breath go through my hair until it reaches my cheek. As usual, I let the minutes go by, which seem to fly away when I'm with him. I lift my chin to reach his, and as I kiss him, I can feel the tension on his face. My heart races in less than a second, and I get down on my knees on the bed, sitting on my heels to look him straight in the eye. His eyes are fixed on a spot on the ceiling, and I watch him with terror.

"Daniel. What's the matter?" His gaze meets mine. He raises his hand, caresses my face as he always does, and smiles bitterly, with a smile I had never seen before and that I wish I never see again.

"Do you still feel the same way about me?" He asks in an effort to control his voice.

"Do you mean the fact that I love you?" I ask, intrigued and somewhat annoyed.

"That's right. Do you still love me?"

"No, to tell you the truth, I decided today that I don't love you, like alcoholics, you know? Just for today, tomorrow, I don't know."

"I'm being serious, gorgeous." I can't believe he's actually asking me that. What does he think? That I'm going to change my mind from one day to the next? I know he always questions my answers, but this one too?

Rocío Blisswealth

422

"Yes, Daniel, I still love you, unfortunately." He opens his eyes in surprise and anguish, straightens up until he is sitting facing me, and tries to take my hand, but withdraws it.

"Why, unfortunately?" He asks with fear.

"Because your question offends me, Daniel. Do you really think I'm so fickle? Or, worse, fake? What did I do to give you that idea?" Somehow, he gets some relief before he realizes the pain in the words. There are reasons why I could stop loving him like that overnight, but he forgets that I don't know them.

"No! Please don't think that. I didn't mean it like that, Jade." He tries to grab my arms, but I raise my hands, showing him my palms in a gesture he knows well; he must stop. He takes a breath and continues talking. "It's me who doesn't believe himself worthy even of your friendship, let alone your love, and I want to hear you say it, but I'm really clumsy; I'm sorry."

"You have such an incoherent way of asking for things. I'm going to ask you a favor, I don't want to go back to the paths we've already traveled and that hurt us. Daniel, that thing about worthiness... I don't want to talk about it anymore." I let my guard down a little and take his hand.

"I'm sorry, please forgive me."

"I love you, Daniel." I say, still serious, looking him in the eyes.

"Unfortunately." He says, smiling.

"No, irremediably." He gives me a quick kiss while saying, still with his lips on mine.

"I love you even more."

"Impossible." I reply, laughing.

"Oh, really?" He raises an eyebrow.

"Okay, let's call it unlikely."

"Still not quite right." He sits next to me on the edge of the bed and stares at a spot on the floor. He rubs his hands against his thighs in an obvious gesture of nervousness, but why is he like that? I watch him without speaking, not wanting to interrupt what he obviously wants to tell me, or maybe the problem is that he doesn't want to say it.

"Jade, there's something I need to talk to you about, but I'm not sure how to bring it up". I raise my hand and lightly touch his lips with my fingertips, signaling for him to hush. My whole body suddenly got goosebumps, and this time it wasn't because of his touch; there was something else. He looks at me

The Game...Jade

in surprise; I cover my lips with my index finger to make it clearer that he must stay quiet. He complies, and I listen closely. In the hallway, near the mirror, I hear flapping wings. In a fraction of a second, the sound becomes deafening. What I've been waiting for is arriving at the worst possible moment. Tíber straightens up and howls; I have no doubt now. I quickly get up, but he stops me by grabbing my wrist.

"What is it, Jade?! What's happening? Who is it?"

"He mustn't find you. Come on, Daniel! Get out of here." Terror fills his eyes; he knows what's happening. If I don't want him to be found here, it's because it's the same entity that attacked us before, and he doesn't want to leave me alone. He grabs my wrist again. My eyes are drawn to one of the corners of the bedroom as I let out a sigh of surprise.

"Get him out of here, Jade! He'll only make things worse. Make him go!" Ángel's voice is truly urgent; I know I must act and get him out of the demon's reach.

Daniel's eyes scan the space in front of us, but he doesn't move. I hit his chest with both hands in a desperate attempt to get his attention and shout over the sound of flapping wings.

"Go, Daniel! I beg you."

"No, Jade, I'm not going to leave you on your own."

"Now, Jade, he must go now!" Ángel shouts.

"Please, Daniel. I'm not alone." I grit through my teeth.

Finally, he gives in, kisses me, turns around, and leaves the room. I tense up, open the door, and there it is, those damn terrifying yellow eyes. With Ángel behind me, the demon smiles. For the first time, I feel my courage completely abandoning me. For the first time, I wish to live.

Chapter XX
Fame, akin to wealth, is insatiable; one can never have too much

England.

Sara arrives at the island with the group of singers she leads. Admiration quickly spreads as they begin to wander through the wide corridors of the mansion. They've been here before, but there are always changes; the house continuously adds new acquisitions to delight the eye. Several pairs of shoes are left behind on the boat as the bodyguards guide them to the Elements Vault to dip their feet into the still-rippling water.

They've never seen the lords; that's the kind of thing only a select few have access to. Sara escorts them to the door and watches as they, one by one, step into the water, smiling as they feel the abundant energy. They look like little kids in an amusement park or hyena pups to whom the mother has just delivered a fresh carcass, allowing them to savor every last bone; the rotting adds an exquisite flavor that only they can enjoy.

Boxwood: *Aren't you going into the water, Sara? It would be beneficial for you to take advantage of what our hunter so graciously brought us.*

Sara: Perhaps later, when the sensation of her essence isn't quite so intense.

Boxwood: *Suit yourself, but when it's as intense as it is now, that's when it's most enjoyable for those who can partake.*

Sara: Right now, I might not be able to enjoy it. It's as if her taste fills my mouth, and it's somewhat nauseating.

Boxwood: *You know everything serves a purpose. By sensing it on your... what shall we call it? Your spiritual palate, you'll always find it easy to trace. But, regardless, come with me, Sara.*

Boxwood leads her to one of the rooms near the vault, extravagant, just like the rest of the mansion, with large windows that offer a view of the amazing garden outside. If anyone saw the house from a distance, if that was even possible casually, they'd never imagine the kind of horrors hiding behind all that beauty.

Boxwood: *I want the composers to pay a visit to the muse.*

Sara: Are you sure? Daniel's latest songs are brimming with information, and Jade can't seem to stop listening to them constantly. Sooner or later, she'll realize everything they entail.

Boxwood: *That's why I want them to visit her. In case you've forgotten, this muse was acquired precisely because of Jade. We must provide her with the information she needs; it's part of the agreement. However, no one specified whether the information should be provided solely through Daniel or not, so we'll divide it among several singers. Haven't you heard the phrase "divide and conquer?" Well, that's precisely what we plan to do. What do you think of the idea?*

Sara: Excellent, like all of yours.

Boxwood: *Flatterer, we both know that's not entirely true. Sara, is something bothering you?*

Sara: I spent time with Daniel yesterday, and he's not himself. I can't help but wonder: when will the plans to separate him from Jade begin? He's our biggest star, and I wouldn't want to lose him. The financial gains through him have been substantial, and I would like him back with us by the time the next album recording begins.

Boxwood smiles mockingly. He can perfectly read Sara's intentions and has no trouble reducing her words to what she really meant, "I don't want to lose him."

Boxwood: *Plans were set in motion a few hours ago; they will soon take effect. And probably, if you're patient, you'll be able to claim it once Jade abandons him. Remember, Sara, she's what matters.*

Sara: They told me, when I introduced him, that I could have him.

Boxwood: *Allow me to remind you of a few points. You were told you could have him once he had fulfilled his purpose. And if we can bring him to his senses, his purpose still has so much life left that you might have to wait to satisfy your instincts. Furthermore, one of the key points of these agreements, as you well know, is to respect his free will, which for now, inevitably drives him towards Jade—a fact we, unfortunately, must respect. It might be simple;*

Rocío Blisswealth

when the time comes, a mere touch of my hand could bend his will, and you could have him. But that's not what you long for, am I mistaken?

Sara: No, I want him to desire to be with me; I want what she has achieved.

Boxwood: Humans, so akin to us, which is why I can understand you. "The grass is always greener on the other side," and you refuse to settle for anything less than what that girl has managed to achieve, without even trying. However, I tell you from experience, it won't happen. Once Daniel has felt what she can give him, he will never settle for less again, and you, my dear Sara, are less. If only there was someone who could see me as I want to be, as I was, I could never leave that person. And that's what Daniel sees in her eyes. Haven't you noticed that all the Muse's songs speak of that? That recurring and powerful idea. I can't blame Daniel; I identify with him.

Sara: Alright then, perhaps I might consider settling for less. When can we arrange that?

Boxwood: Patience. She will let him go, and then, when the pain overwhelms him, he'll be easier to handle. Remember the steps to bend someone: they must feel abandoned and hopeless, and then everything happens almost by itself. Now, come on, get into the water. Forget it's about Jade; just think that it was Daniel who presented you with this gift.

Spain.

Daniel's eyes snap open, drenched in sweat. Once again, he's overwhelmed by the terrible sensation that his body is too heavy, and he can't remember how his lungs start functioning. However, as awful as those sensations are, he's familiar with them, and he knows they'll fade away in a few seconds; not so with the other, the feeling of terror now coursing through every particle of his being.

He jumps out of bed quickly, grabbing the dresser to steady himself, his legs still not fully supporting him. He spins around, and he realizes where he is, thousands of kilometers away from Jade, safer in his home, while she faces the demon, who once almost killed them both, only this time, all his strength is directed against her. No! No! No! He cries out in desperation, understanding that they weren't going to stand idly by. He always thought he had time, that somehow, would be superior to them and would find a way for Jade to forgive him. But time ran out; he saw the last grains of sand from Jade's hourglass roll across the floor when the demon arrived, and she could hear him.

Questions pile up in his head. Why didn't Jade let him stay and face it with her? And the most pressing one now, what is happening right now? He's always known that something protects her, yet he doesn't know what they are capable of now that he has openly disobeyed them, now that they have withdrawn their support, and he means nothing to them anymore. But she is still important, still the most important thing to them, and he knows it. They won't dare to do away with an endless source of energy, as they had never found before. Although, perhaps, they want to teach her a lesson.

No, the lesson, in any case, would be for him and not for her. He's the one who disobeyed; she knows absolutely nothing and is not to blame. Why did the demon come to her, then? Damn it! If only he had seen her with an arrogant, almost rude attitude, like the last time they faced the demon; but no, this time, what he managed to see was pleading and a lot of fear.

He slumps into one of the corners of the room, wrapping his arms tightly around his legs, resting his head on his knees, trying to calm the tremors shaking his body. But no matter what, they refuse to ease even a bit. He knows that to return to Jade's side; he needs to fall into a deep sleep, but he's unable to achieve it. He can't even call her because it would wake up everyone in the house, and, even worse, it might distract Jade or make the demon go after someone else, forcing her to fight without thinking, and she needs to be completely concentrated to avoid being killed. That's why she asked him to leave, probably so she wouldn't have to think about anything other than confronting the demon with precision. He would've just been a distraction; he lacks the skills to attack demons, and she needed to do this alone; he would've only gotten in the way. Once again, he's a hindrance in her life; he should never have crossed her path.

He gets up and runs to the bathroom. His stomach, unable to bear so much anguish, refuses to keep the food down. He wets his face with plenty of water to ease the nausea, but there's nothing left inside him now, just the damn anguish. Looking at his reflection in the mirror, he sees the drops trickling down to his shirt. He can't shake the feeling that nothing turned out as it was supposed to. Sara painted him this picture where nobody got hurt, and the benefits were for everyone. In her version, Jade desired him; he paid her, and end of the story. Everyone would be happily ever after.

Rocío Blisswealth

But nothing is like that; in what fairy tale do demons play such an active role? A witch, maybe an ogre, roles that probably should've been his, but nothing more. It's like a sorceress, a stepsister; everything fits, but not demons. But he made mistake after mistake. If Jade survives after this demonic encounter—he prays that she does—and she no longer wants to see him, how could he dare to convince her otherwise? How, knowing that if he did convince her, it would only make these attacks more frequent and increasingly violent, until they managed to get her back?

However, he would do it; he would even beg her on his knees to forgive him and try to find a way to get rid of everyone to stay with her. He can't be without her; he doesn't want to. But she still has a way out: she got rid of a demon once, one she cared about because it had always been there for her, a demon she loved just like she loves him now, and maybe she would make the right decision again, and get rid of him for the right reasons.

No, no, there must be another way out. He's already done things that the lords and the demons haven't found out about; he's been smarter than them. If only Jade would remember, if she could open her mind and use all she was capable of, she'd wipe out any demon that came near her in a heartbeat, and he could be by her side in calm because they'd surely end up leaving them alone, "leaving them alone." Together and at peace, that sounds so good.

But a new terror takes hold of him, sending shivers down his spine, an option he hadn't considered. For all of his dreams to stand a chance of coming true, it would have to be him, and no one else, to fill Jade in on how things have been since she met him. He once tried to tell her something, and she didn't want to hear it, but now he'd make her listen, giving her all the information he knows. She'd know what to do with that info. But, looking her in the eyes so she could see the love in them, a strange mix of love with an absolute need to have her by his side.

Maybe like that, without losing sight of her, considering every change in her body language, always so explicit, he'd have a real chance to tell the truth and still keep her by his side. But, as Carmen said, the only possibility for that to happen is for her to hear everything from his lips. And if, instead, it's the demon who, right now, describes to her step by step what he's done, magnifying his mistakes and twisting his love for her into some shallow craving for fame, downplaying it until it vanishes, then everything would be lost.

The Game...Jade

He slumps onto the bed, staring at the ceiling, wishing he could be far away from there. However, he has to wait. There's no other option. From the shelf, Jade's photos stare at him; snapshots taken on the sly because, on one hand, she's against having her picture taken, and on the other, he wouldn't have dared to ask her to take photos together; with how suspicious she is, she would've never agreed.

And she would've been right. What he once told her was totally true: photos swipe a piece of your soul. Just staring into the camera is enough; that's all it takes, and they become a link to the person. Daniel turns to them whenever he wants to feel close to her, when he wants her to think of him. Not today; he has to wait, and then maybe it'll work.

Monterrey.

The light starts seeping in through the curtains' edge, but I couldn't care less; the darkness surrounding me is so dense that I'll never escape it. Even though Ángel is sitting at the foot of my bed, he seems so distant. It's like I'm stuck at the bottom of a well, and he's looking at me from the outside. I stopped hearing his voice a while ago, not sure if he stopped talking or if my brain just shut off to it. I don't want to hear anything more; I've already heard enough.

I can say to you for sure that the demon defeated me tonight; yes, victory is all his. I could hear his laughter as I writhed in pain, a victim of his attacks that, though not physical like before, were incredibly more painful than anything I've ever experienced. I could feel the fear of facing him leave me when the pain set in, leaving no room for any other sensation.

It only took a few minutes; he didn't need more. His worst weapon, which I now know, is his tongue; it was completely prepared to be used against me, and I had no armor against it, no possible defense. The energy in my hands? Yes, maybe it would have helped, but for what? To shut him up? No, I deserved every word he uttered; I ignored them every time my subconscious tried to speak up, but now it's time to listen, and they're wreaking havoc on me. I refused to accept that time was passing, giving me chances to turn around and run, yet here I am, fatally wounded. Maybe that's the only silver lining; I'll never have to recover.

As soon as I opened the door, he approached me, and I futilely took steps back, bumping into Ángel at every one of them. He didn't leave my side,

Rocío Blisswealth

covering my back at all times. Once inside the room, he let out his horrendous and guttural laughter.

"HE JUST LEFT, DIDN'T HE?"

I didn't respond to him; I knew perfectly well he was talking about Daniel, and I wasn't going to let him go after him.

"NO NEED TO RESPOND; I'M WELL AWARE. WONDERING HOW I KNOW?…" His smile grew wider. "BECAUSE HE COMES HERE BY OUR ORDERS."

This time, my stomach didn't fill with lead; it was hot steel that flooded it, burning, his words burned.

"Shut up!" Ángel yelled. The demon barely glanced away from me to respond to him.

"WHY?" He asked innocently. "OH, OF COURSE, I UNDERSTAND. THE INFORMATION ISN'T ENTIRELY ACCURATE. HOW CAN I EXPLAIN IT FOR YOUR COMPREHENSION, LITTLE GIRL? MY SUPERIORS DISPATCHED HIM TO ACCOMPANY YOU, WHICH IS WHY HE WAS ALWAYS SO COMPLIANT. HE WAS MERELY FOLLOWING ORDERS."

"I told you to be quiet." Ángel repeated; the demon replied with absolute calm.

"AND I HEARD YOU, BUT WE BOTH UNDERSTAND SHE MUST BE THE ONE TO SOLICIT ME, AND I SENSE SHE'S INCLINED TO LET ME SPEAK THIS TIME."

And so it was. I stood there, waiting for him to finish me off, and of course, he did.

"DO YOU RECALL OUR INITIAL ENCOUNTER, JADE? I MENTIONED I'VE KNOWN YOUR BLOOD FOR CENTURIES, AND INDEED I HAVE. YOUR BLOOD BEARS GIFTS CAPABLE OF EXTRAORDINARY FEATS, INCLUDING BESTOWING FAME UPON THOSE WHO DRAW NEAR. A GRAND, ENDURING, COVETED FAME. A FAME WHICH OUR DEAR DANIEL HAS ACCESSED. THAT TIME I ATTACKED YOU BOTH, IT WAS ORCHESTRATED TO EXPOSE HIS VULNERABILITY, ENSURING YOU WOULDN'T LEAVE HIM."

"You're lying!" Ángel shouted. The demon didn't even pay attention to him.

"AND WE ACHIEVED OUR PURPOSE; HE LAID THE SNARE, ENTWINING YOU FURTHER WITH EACH PASSING MOMENT. YOU CHOSE TO PLACE FAITH IN HIM, TO TRUST HIM, AND YOU BECAME ENSNARED. DO YOU UNDERSTAND? WITH EVERY BRUSH OF YOUR SKIN, YOU FILLED HIM WITH FAME, WITH GLORY, AND HE, WHO CAN BLAME HIM? HE FOREVER CRAVES MORE. FAME, AKIN TO

The Game…Jade

WEALTH, IS INSATIABLE; ONE CAN NEVER HAVE TOO MUCH. HOWEVER, FAME POSSESSES ANOTHER TRAIT; IT HAS A PROPENSITY TO UNVEIL THE DARKEST FACETS OF ONE'S NATURE. DANIEL IS NO EXCEPTION; HE'S TURNED PETTY AND IS EXPLOITING YOU TO THE FULLEST EXTENT. I KNOW YOU LOVE HIM, DAMN FORTUNATE BOY, BUT DO YOU GENUINELY BELIEVE HE CAN RECIPROCATE? UNFORTUNATELY, SUCH PURE EMOTIONS ARE BEYOND HIS REACH. NOW, CONSUMED BY HIS CAREER, HE'S FORSAKING IT TO EXPLOIT YOU, AND THAT'S WHY I'VE BEEN DISPATCHED. WOULDN'T YOU RATHER JOIN US, JADE? BE CLOSER TO HIM?"

"Leave her alone! Don't you dare...!" Ángel yelled, and for the first time, he got a strong response from the demon.

"YOU DARE NOT! FREE WILL, REMEMBER?" Whatever he meant, it was true, and Ángel fell silent.

"JADE, YOU COULD HAVE IT ALL. YOU'D HAVE DANIEL, REGARDLESS; THERE'S NOTHING HE DESIRES MORE THAN WHAT YOU OFFER, AND I'M CERTAIN HE'D WILLINGLY EXTEND HIS STAY WITH YOU IN EXCHANGE. WHAT SAY YOU? ACCEPT?" The demon asked, very close to me.

I didn't open my mouth; I didn't have an answer for that simply because nothing mattered anymore. The reason I had to live had suddenly abandoned me. I'd have Daniel, but for what? He doesn't want to be with me. What could I want him for, then? The blindfold had been lifted from my eyes, and now I could see the greed in his, his annoyance, his irritation; in short, I could see everything except the affection I wanted to believe existed, and that was the only thing that was never there. I didn't answer.

"VERY WELL. NEED TIME TO PONDER? IT'S PRUDENT; HASTY DECISIONS SELDOM YIELD FAVORABLE OUTCOMES. MEDITATE IT, AND WE'LL GATHER AGAIN LATER. A MESSAGE FOR DANIEL, PERHAPS? NONE? VERY WELL, AS YOU WISH." He disappeared into the mirror again.

A couple of seconds later, there was a knock on the door, as if they had been waiting for him to say goodbye. Mom came in to find me standing in the room despite the early hour, it was barely five in the morning.

"Jade, are you alright?"

Worse than ever, but no, even then, my mouth didn't open at all. Ángel moved restlessly around the room, rubbing his chest with desperation with his right hand. He had his gaze fixed on Mom; I guess he knew what she was coming to tell me.

Rocío Blisswealth

"Jade, I was awakened because there's something very important I need to tell you. It's a message from god and you must listen carefully."

She stopped, waiting for me to say something, but nothing came out of my mouth; I don't even have saliva in it. How could I say anything? With great seriousness, just as she said everything related to god, she continued.

"I was told it's important for me to tell you that you can't see Daniel anymore. He's involved with demons, and somehow, he's gaining his fame through you."

It was one thing for a demon to tell me; my brain could have protected itself by thinking that demons always lie, but how could I doubt it if it was god telling me? There was no doubt anymore; my head was spinning, and nausea was rising to my throat. I brought my hands to hold my head in a very vain attempt to stop this madness that was rushing over me.

"What's wrong?" Mom asked.

"I'm going crazy." It was all I could tell her.

"Jade, it will pass. I promise you; this will pass." She turned around and left, too.

My legs gave way to the whirlwind that had formed beneath me. I crumpled to the floor, witnessing all the pieces, big and small, of the life I'd crafted over the past few months vanish, each element reduced to mere dots in the swirling vortex at my feet. So much pain! How can a human being withstand it? I hoped it wasn't possible; I wished this pain would burst through my veins as it surged through them, putting an end to everything. A terrible tremor shook me, running through my legs and arms, and it didn't take long to figure out what caused it. It was the fear of emptiness, the unmistakable consequence of loss. It was coming.

I understood what loneliness was when I was in Daniel's arms and made the distinction. Now, it was creeping in through the soles of my feet, and emptiness was coming from its hand, ready to take possession of me, and here I was, not fighting it at all. Ángel ran towards me, trying to hold me, but my hand instinctively rose and stopped him. I didn't want him to touch me.

"Leave me alone."

"No, Jade."

"Nothing, not anymore." I begged him with the first sob that escaped my throat because, in a heroic act, I didn't allow the demon to see me cry.

However, he continued speaking; it didn't matter, madness prevented me from understanding what he was saying.

And that's how I ended up here, without moving from this piece of floor, which keeps moving beneath me, refusing to swallow me whole. Why doesn't it just finish me off at once? I no longer even hope to be with my grandparents, only to die, that's all. Today, I deeply envy those who have hit rock bottom because even that has been denied to me. In my fall, I still can't find it. If it's pain that's opened up at my feet, now I know I won't find it. My pain has no bottom; it has no end.

Spain.

Lying on the bed, in the same position he hasn't changed for a while, Daniel opens his eyes in surprise. He jumps out of bed and starts pacing around the room, which seems to be spinning.

"Arghhh!" He shouts, running his hands through his hair in desperation.

Carmen knocks on his door, asking if she can come in. When there's no answer, she slowly opens the door. Her eyes fill with anguish as she sees Daniel, tears streaming down his face, breathing heavily and rubbing his chest, sitting on the floor in the middle of the bedroom.

"What's wrong, my dear?!" She sits on the bed next to him and touches his shoulder. Daniel can't seem to find the breath to speak and answers in a whisper.

"They told her, Carmen. It's tearing her apart; this pain is unbearable."

"You've got to do something, Daniel. Go with her."

"She refuses to see me!" He lets out a scream. "Don't you get it? They've twisted it; she believes I don't love her."

"It doesn't matter, Daniel. Try to get her to listen to you. You can't stay like this."

"I won't be able to fall asleep; it's impossible."

"Is that all it takes? Just wait..." Carmen leaves the room and returns after a few minutes. She hands Daniel a bottle of pills that she takes when insomnia strikes her. "Take two, you'll sleep, I assure you."

Without thinking, Daniel goes to the bathroom and pours a glass of water to help swallow the pills. Still rubbing his chest, he sits down next to Carmen, tears still streaming down his face.

"Is it her pain you're feeling?"

Rocío Blisswealth

"I always sense what she feels, especially when it's this intense."

"How is that possible?"

"Jade and I have an unbreakable bond. It's only grown stronger as we've spent more time together."

"Can she feel what you feel? Maybe that will help, Daniel. She'll know you're not lying to her."

"Yes, Carmen, but it won't make a difference. Her feelings are so intense that they drown out everything else. If only she'd listen to me."

"Go to bed. It won't take long for the pills to take effect, and it will be quicker if you're lying down. I'm leaving you; I don't want to get in your way." She kisses him on the forehead and leaves the room. From the pocket of her sweater, she takes out a rosary and begins to recite her prayers. They won't be of much use this time. Daniel has navigated through very turbulent waters, and her prayers don't cross those kinds of oceans.

Monterrey.

I don't know how long I've been here, on this same spot of floor, but it must be a lot. My legs are so numb that I don't feel them anymore. If only that feeling could spread to my consciousness, so I wouldn't feel anything anymore, but I'm not that lucky. Ángel is still here, talking on and off, but I still can't hear him. His voice just sounds like noise to me.

He turns towards one of the walls, and I follow his gaze. Suddenly, my pain intensifies when I see Daniel standing in the corner of my room. Without remembering that my legs are numb, I try to get up. After several stumbles and resisting the strong stabs caused by the movement, I manage to reach the opposite corner from where he is. Now I realize that my legs were trying to take me as far away from him as possible. I raise both hands, even though they're shaking uncontrollably, showing him my palms to stop, although, in reality, he hasn't moved forward. My crying disrupts my breathing to the point where I struggle to get air into my lungs, yet I keep repeating a word non-stop.

"No, no, no... no."

"Jade, just hear me out, please."

Now, it's not just my hands that are shaking; my whole body is trembling without me being able to, or rather, without even trying to make it stop.

The Game...Jade

"You know, Daniel? This room was always the chamber of my torture, but I never would have imagined that you would be my executioner. How much longer are you going to torment me?" I say calmly, but my voice is choked with sobs.

Ángel doesn't move from where he is; he leans against the wall looking down at the floor as he waits.

"Jade..."

"What's it about now, Daniel? Can't you see that I'm falling apart? Oh, I guess you have to finish your job, you must be in charge of finishing me off, don't you? Fine, let's continue then; I'm not going to run away. I know my monsters will come after me until they catch up with me, so here I am."

"I've got to explain how things were." He says with tears in his eyes.

"There's no need, Daniel. I already got an extensive explanation a few hours ago, and even though I'm probably very stupid in your eyes, I managed to understand everything your friend explained to me."

"I need you to forgive me."

"Forgive you? Why should I? You gave me the only happy days of my life. You made me feel like I was worth something. And you lied to me so well, telling me you loved me. I don't know what you took from me, but it seemed like a fair trade. I just wish you had given me the final blow when I was in your arms. It wasn't necessary to do it face to face; that I would have forgiven you for."

"Jade. They fed you lies!" He says desperately.

"They lied to me? Don't you have dealings with demons?" I'm still speaking calmly; tears don't let me catch my breath for anything else. Besides, this can't end any other way than in death. After this, I'm sure there's no chance of life left for me, so staying calm seems like the only option right now.

"Yes." He responds with a sigh, closing his eyes.

"Did you take from me what you needed to be famous?"

"Yes."

"Did the demons send you to me?"

"Jade..."

Without giving me time for anything, he runs towards me, hugs me, and holds me tightly. Ángel watches me; I can only see pity in his eyes. Did he know this was waiting for me? If so, why didn't he stop it? I don't know if it's because he's witnessing my torment, but if so, why the pity?

Rocío Blisswealth

Daniel's closeness is unbearable, and to my surprise, it opens up new wounds in me. It's as if my physical skin is also injured, not just the inside. I can't think of anyone's touch I could bear right now, but his is the most unbearable—it hurts me.

I hold my breath as I feel his warm breath on my temple, his lips on my forehead, kissing me while repeating that I listen to him. His arms imprison me unnecessarily. I'm not running away; I just wish he would tell me where the guillotine blade is so I can lie down and rest until I can rid myself of this body that can no longer contain so much sadness.

"Jade, what they said is true. I struck a deal to gain fame, but that was before I knew you. It's not an excuse; I was aware I'd be taking something that wasn't rightfully mine, and who it affected didn't matter. I shouldn't have gone through with it; it was wrong, and the actions I've taken are infamous. But..."

"I don't care about that. I would have given you everything, absolutely everything, no strings attached, without asking for anything in return, just for the pleasure of reciprocating all your kindness. But why did you have to lie to me?"

"I never lied when I expressed my feelings for you. You brought out in me the person I never knew existed, and now..."

"Daniel, your touch burns me."

Slowly, he withdraws his arms and takes a short step back, pulling away from me. He turns to look at me with tears in his eyes, and it hurts to see him. It hurts to contain this stupid urge to hug him and stay where I am. It hurts terribly to need him so much, and it hurts that my body hasn't died yet, that this pain is not enough to end it. How much more must it hurt me?

"If I knew that staying in your arms would bring death sooner, I could bear it. But one thing I'm sure of is that death has decided to run away from me. If only it knew how much I long for it, maybe it would have compassion for me. Since it doesn't have it, could you have it? Please, Daniel. Leave me alone, I beg you... go away." He gets a little closer, but he doesn't touch me. He looks at me with narrowed eyes.

"I'm walking away, Jade, but I won't stop until you listen to me. You can't question my love for you. You sense it, you feel it, and I'll make sure you hear it."

Another heroic act: I didn't collapse until he left my room. I guess I owe it to the very little dignity left inside me. The pain I felt the first time I had to part from him was mild compared to this. It's the same invisible injuries that I felt then that have reopened, but with every word, that demon tore at my skin, leaving me morally raw. I fall on the bed and bury my face in the pillow, trying to silence my sobs, which don't seem to have an end in sight. Ángel sits down next to me and makes one last attempt to get me to listen to him.

"Jade, things aren't always what they appear to be. Remember my words: the enemy of your enemy is your ally."

"Ángel, kill me. You can do it. Nothing ties me here; I've already lost everything. I've even lost what I didn't consider mine. Kill me because the longing to see him doesn't allow me to take my own life. Don't let me die slowly."

"No, Jade, I won't rest until you listen to me, either." In the face of his refusal, I sink into the anguish that now surrounds me and weep without rest.

England.

Grapevine: *How are matters progressing?* He asks Olive as he stares at the water surrounding the mansion.

Olive: *Things couldn't be going any better. The demon knew exactly where to strike. His approach was so precise that she wouldn't even listen to the words that might save her; she was utterly shattered. I doubt she'll recover, and even if she does, she'll be easy to manipulate.*

Grapevine: *Nonetheless, her energy still courses through Daniel, doesn't it?*

Olive: *Of course, he's all she ever thinks about. Later, when the time's right, we can include someone else.*

Grapevine: *Do you believe she'll accept it?*

Olive: *Let's hope so, shall we? For now, Daniel's completely out of the picture.*

Grapevine: *I can't shake the feeling of uncertainty about that. Jade has proven to be unpredictable in myriad ways, and you're aware there's someone beside her.*

Olive: *Yes, someone who doesn't dare to bend the rules, follows them to the letter, and that puts everything in our favor. He hasn't allowed her to lose her life. He's kept death away from her since she was born, and this hasn't been an exception. She wants to die, but he won't allow it, and that's very useful to us. It's not in our interest for her to die and take all that energy with her.*

Rocío Blisswealth

Grapevine: What about Daniel?

Olive: All he desires is to be by her side; he wants to convince her to forgive him.

Grapevine: But why? He's already achieved what he set out to do; his body contains ample energy for decades of fame. Why doesn't he just enjoy it and leave her alone?

Olive: Actually, I don't know. I struggle to understand it. He got everything he needed to be happy, yet he, being the flawed human he is, grew fond of her. She reciprocates.

Grapevine: Is it indeed so? We need to be careful and keep him away from her; he might convince her, and she already knows far more than she should.

Olive: On the contrary, I want them to spend as much time together as possible. There's nothing that hurts them both more.

Grapevine: Careful, you might go too far.

Olive: It won't be like that as long as the other one doesn't allow death to come near her, and I know he won't; there's nothing to worry about. However, we might finally break her and perhaps fulfill a dream of yours at the same time.

Grapevine: Bring her here... He says hopefully.

Olive: That could only be achieved if she surrenders completely, which hasn't happened yet. But we'll make it happen, rest assured.

Grapevine: Fine then, proceed and crush her as soon as possible if that's what it takes to bring her here. And upon her arrival, I wish to be the first to lay eyes on her.

Olive: So it shall be, brother, so it shall be.

Monterrey.

The noise from the avenue keeps going. It's been hours since mom came in to bring me something to eat, not sure what it was, but as long as she left me alone, I ate it. She keeps saying it'll all pass, and I know it will once I find the courage to take control and leave this body behind. For now, everything remains the same.

Ángel is still here. It's the first time in my life he's stayed for more than a few minutes, but he hasn't managed to make me feel the peace he used to give me when I was little. He paces around the room and sits next to me every now and then, saying words that I don't hear; my brain just doesn't process them.

When it gets a little dark, my torment starts again. Daniel appears through the wall and kneels next to me, still sitting on the bed. I make a futile attempt not to see him, but it's useless. My gaze flies towards him without respecting my wishes or, perhaps, following them to the letter despite my weak orders. The trembling of my body, which had let me rest for a few hours, starts again, shaking the bed, and tears flow thicker than before.

"Jade, I beg you to just hear me out. A few minutes of your attention is all I ask."

"Daniel, you know what? I trained my brain to hold every moment I spent with you." I say with a choked voice. "I never thought those memories would be your best weapon against me. I replay them in my mind over and over without needing you to be here to relive them; you don't have to come."

"Amidst all those memories, search for the instances when I showed you how much I love you and analyze what you feel. I love you, Jade. You can't question that." My chest heaves as tears overwhelm me.

"I was wrong; you found something else to hurt me with. It hurts more... Don't say anything else... please."

He reaches out his hand and takes mine, but I pull away with a groan. I can't tell if the pain has become more intense or if my resistance to it has decreased. He leaves his hand on my thigh and closes his eyes.

"I always knew I was capable of the most despicable acts. Deep down, I've felt that sooner or later, I would pay for everything I had done, and believe me, Jade, with the pain I'm enduring now, I'm paying dearly. What I don't know is what I'll have to pay for the pain I've caused you, but I can't walk away. I need your forgiveness, even if you choose never to see me again afterward." He opens his eyes and locks them with mine, now swollen from crying. I say nothing; I just stare at him through the tears.

"I realize that I won't convince you. I don't blame you for that, but could you possibly find it within yourself to forgive me?"

"Will you stop coming to torment me? Let someone else come, anyone, but not you, not you." Tears choke me.

"Jade."

I turn over on the bed and cover my ears, falling asleep without realizing it, feeling his presence behind me. Mom wakes me up; Mara wants to know if

I'm up for a task she just came up with. I look around and notice that Daniel is missing, though Ángel is still there at the foot of my bed. I don't know how to read his gaze. Is he angry? It seems like it. While I think about what to tell Mom, anger takes hold of me, and this time, I don't try to control it—it's a welcome change after so much pain. At least it allows my lungs to fill completely and my skin to feel some warmth while my eyes remain dry.

I lose control of my emotions, knowing it will only last a few minutes, but it doesn't matter—it's like coming up for air after feeling like I was drowning, and I hear myself responding like I never have before. My voice is calm yet sharp with acidity.

"I guess this request comes from god, isn't that right?" Mom looks at me in surprise. Who else could it be from? Of course, it's from him.

"Absolutely." She replies.

"In that case, you can tell him I won't do anything else, ever. I've lost interest in accumulating points; there's nothing I care enough about to redeem them for."

"Jade, you shouldn't."

"Oh, but I can! The answer is no. And now, please leave me alone, and don't bother me again." I got out of bed, for the first time in over twenty-four hours or more, just to make my point clear and get her out of here. I turn to Ángel; he stares into my eyes, and even with anger coursing through my veins, I question him.

"Ángel, I've never known who you answer to, but I suppose it's god, isn't it?" He doesn't answer me. "Why don't you leave? You heard me; I'm not going to do anything else, and if I do, I won't leave this room either, so..." I open the door for him, too.

"I'm sorry, Jade, I won't leave. So you don't succeed."

"Darn it! How many tormentors am I stuck with? Let me die, Ángel, let me die already." Daniel returns just in time to hear my last sentence; I don't realize it because he's behind me. He wraps his arms around me from behind, and in just a second, pain and anguish overwhelm me again, but this time, the anger doesn't fade away; it's still here, pulsing through my veins. I can see his arms wrapped around my waist and feel his cheek against mine.

"No, Jade, please, don't do this. Don't talk about dying, I won't allow it."

The Game…Jade

I knew anger would come in handy, it always does, and this time wouldn't be any different. I try to free myself from his arms, but he doesn't allow it, so I twist within them to face him. Maybe this pain really is enough to end me; I'm not sure, but it's worth a shot. Being close to him has always been the most intense feeling I've ever experienced. Maybe today it's just as powerful, and it'll bleed me dry, finally.

"Daniel, are you back for my forgiveness?" I ask, holding his face in my hands. "I'm sorry, I don't have it. Can't you see? There's hardly anything left inside me. Actually, there never was, except what you recently made grow, and it all poured out through my wounds. You don't see them, do you? But they're here, and they let it all out. The weird thing about this is that even though I'm barely in one piece, I'm not leaving."

"Jade, please." He says, pressing me closer to him.

"They only left one thing inside me, and that's my love for you. Even now, I love you so much." I lean in to kiss him, he responds desperately, and moments later, I pull away and continue. "Do you feel it? It's still there, and I know why they left it. They knew it would be the thing that hurt me the most. It's making sure to tear me apart, and it's only a matter of time before it finishes the job. You got what you wanted, Daniel. So why don't you let me have what I want most now?"

"I don't want anything anymore. Nothing has meaning to me anymore after this. I just want to be with you. I won't let you die because of me. I'm not leaving, Jade. I'll always be by your side, because that's what I wish for, nothing else."

"I need to stop seeing you, Daniel, to make myself believe you don't exist anymore, and then, yes, let the pain do its work. Or maybe let madness convince me I imagined it all, that I was never in your arms, because that kind of thing doesn't happen to people like me, and so, the pain will have its way with me for being so naive. How? It's not important; I just want to go. One day, you asked me to hold on to you, do you remember? What am I supposed to do now that you don't exist? There's nothing left to hold on to."

"You don't want to see me? Fair enough, you won't see me, but I'll be here, looking after you, hoping for your forgiveness. Perhaps one day you'll understand the strength of my feelings for you and convince yourself that I do indeed exist."

Rocío Blisswealth

He lets go of his arms around me, and I stumble; my legs refuse to hold me up any longer. He tries to stop me, but I push his hand away, so he takes a step back, two, three, until he disappears into the wall. Ángel looks at me with pain in his eyes and starts talking to someone I don't listen to.

"Don't you dare do it; she has to go through this."

"Hasn't she been through enough already? And we both know there's more suffering to come."

"She can handle it. She'll know what to do, you know that."

"I'm the one who can't bear it anymore. We're treating her like a plaything. We're no better than them. She needs rest from the pain. In vain I keep death away from her if she doesn't strive to stay alive."

"Guide her, help her, don't prevent her from…"

"She doesn't listen to my words! She distrusts everyone. I'm sorry, but I can't." Ángel gets up and walks towards me; I step back and bump into the bed. I know what he's trying to do; he did it once before, and I lost hours I'll never get back. Not this time.

"No, Ángel." I plead. "Let death come, please. Don't help me if you don't want to but, leave me alone and don't try to stop it. I don't want it to hurt; just let me go."

"It won't hurt anymore." He reaches out and touches my face, and I fade into unconsciousness.

Chapter XXI
An endangered species

England.

Have you ever heard the phrase "when the waters find their way?" Well, that phrase perfectly describes what's happened. The intensity of Jade's love has faded away, and many singers have taken advantage of it. The water surrounding the mansion and reaching the Elements Vault is back to being calm and peaceful.

However, the atmosphere among the people here is nothing like that peaceful water. Their desperation to get what Jade can provide is growing. To them, Jade is just an energy source they need to nourish themselves. It's the energy that used to feed them constantly, but now they have to steal it if they want access to it. An even bigger problem: they need a human to filter it out. Their bodies, after all the transformation, lost the ability to resist or savor it, making the situation incredibly unpleasant for various reasons.

Firstly, humans are the beings they despise most for their perceived lack of wisdom. Even animals have it, but humans never value it enough to keep it, preferring to ignore it until they lose it completely. Secondly, human nature's fickleness means they can't rely on a steady supply of it, and getting it secondhand doesn't fully satisfy them. It's like eating a steak in mush, missing the pleasure of chewing before swallowing. The taste might be the same, but the presentation doesn't allow them to appreciate it as such.

Another issue is that humans with these kinds of gifts are becoming scarce. So, everything requires more planning, work, and time just to get what used to come easily. But there's no other option; if that's the way it has to be, so be it.

So, it's expected that a naive girl won't stand in the way of what they desire so intensely. Her pain, her anguish, means nothing to them; another aspect of human nature they detest is the agony of suffering. No, that won't stop them.

They understand the world's design hasn't changed since its creation. This is still the animal kingdom, where the biggest animal eats the smallest.

Rocío Blisswealth

Where most are prey, and few are the predators, the ones with the physical and mental capabilities to feed on them. Each predator seeks out the prey that satisfies its very particular appetite, and once it finds it, it doesn't rest until it eats it and feeds its offspring.

In the ecosystem of this blue marble suspended in space, Jade is an endangered species. Her kind only produces seven beings every seven years. They lack knowledge of the savage nature of their environment, at the mercy of predators who won't rest until they're caught and displayed as trophies. Maybe the only difference between this and the animal kingdom we know is that to feed on Jade, they need her alive, and she doesn't want to be. That could ruin their plans.

Boxwood: He stopped her! That fool stopped her; she was moments away from surrendering. She would have called upon the demon to surrender, only in exchange for a little relief from the pain, and now... Damn it!

Ebony: Don't worry, I'm not letting her go. He can do whatever he wants, but he'll only delay the inevitable. She's bound to give in; she has no other way out, and then we'll have everything we want.

Boxwood: Why has it been so difficult when it comes to her? We've never encountered so many obstacles before.

Ebony: The others were clueless about their potential. It was a breeze to snatch their gifts without them noticing, without disrupting their lives, that is, without them realizing they could have had different outcomes. They never deserved what they were given.

Boxwood: I never understood him. Why grant them such virtues only to allow them to decide whether to utilize them or not? A miserable waste! That's all it is. Most of them relinquished it for trivial reasons. A consort, an offspring, a voyage, wealth, and more recently, fame.

Ebony: "A bowl of lentils," that's what it's always been. Their narrow vision doesn't allow them to see beyond.

Boxwood: So, what happened to her?

Ebony: Well, you can't compare her; what she harbors is far more profound.

Boxwood: Nonetheless, everything was meticulously planned for ages. I know they protected her, and they protected the others, too, yet they never achieved anything for them. They were cannon fodder since birth, but her...

Ebony: Yes, everything was planned, but based on the assumption that she would be like the others. However, it was impossible to foresee, for example, that she would detect demons with unheard-of ease; the others never did. Also, she was always isolated; that's her inclination, which complicates things for us, and having used her gift at such an early age made her aware of it. That should never have happened. Not to mention, she embraces the supernatural and the macabre as if they were part of her life, without questioning the oddness of those situations. There was never a way to plant doubt; her instincts were more powerful than her reason, her logic, and even her sight. She'd rather be led by what she feels than what she sees. Remarkable, isn't it?

Boxwood: And then there's Daniel, another being unlike the rest. How could we misjudge him to such an extent? His sole desire was something as basic as fame, and we granted it to him, along with everything it provides, and then...

Ebony: He hungered for more. I think the genuine issue was that he glimpsed the possibility of being something greater. He could have it all—fame and distinction. She sees him as worthy, and he craves that validation. I don't know why. I would have to delve into his dull little brain to know what event from his childhood, as the stupid psychiatrists say, marked him to pursue something as futile as dignity. Nonetheless, he saw it reflected in Jade's eyes, and now, that image of himself, that Daniel he'll never embody, haunts him. He refuses to relinquish her. He's got everything he could ever desire, yet the stubborn fool clings to the one thing he'll never possess.

Boxwood: Perhaps the genuine issue is that he could potentially become one if he were to apply himself, hand in hand with Jade, of course, and his soul recognizes it. She's the one who clings to that notion. He should have never glimpsed that; everything would have been so simple. When you allow humans to catch a glimpse of what they can attain, it becomes harder to dissuade them.

Ebony: Harder but not impossible if time takes its course, coupled with despair, it could be attained. Just need to plant the concept of difficulty in their minds, and they'll believe it word for word. When we know that instigating an event requires energy, not difficulty or ease—just raw energy, a concept beyond their grasp.

Boxwood: Often, almost always, it's merely a matter of time, which is what terrifies humans the most—to witness time slipping away, beyond their

Rocío Blisswealth

control, as if they ever wielded control over it! And to contemplate the opportunity slipping through their fingers. They fail to grasp that opportunities and time are two parallel paths, never identical.

    Ebony: *Too many things to consider, and about which we can lament. I don't want to waste any more time on that; I have other plans.*

    Boxwood: *We also refuse to let her go, don't we? What do you plan to do now?*

    Ebony: *Pain, despair, loneliness.*

    Boxwood: *More?*

    Ebony: *I haven't even started yet.*

Spain.

Carmen sits on the bed next to Daniel as he opens his eyes. His gaze remains fixed on nothingness. Carmen takes his hand, trying to wake him up gently a couple of times. She was unsure whether she should do it or not, but he was complaining so much that she couldn't resist.

"Daniel." She waits for him to respond, but it seems like he doesn't hear her. "Daniel, what happened?"

He turns his head slightly to look at her as if he's just hearing her voice now. Anguish is evident in his eyes, and his skin looks extremely pale. His breathing is slow, perhaps too slow, as if his lungs are struggling to let air in. His hand remains in Carmen's, but he doesn't react to the force with which she's holding him; his fingers just lie there, still and motionless.

"You ask me what happened? Well, my worst nightmares don't even come close to what went down in that room. They used me to shatter her. They told her the truth, ripped off the blindfold, and showed her who I really was. That truth is tearing her apart, and it's all my fault."

"But there's another truth, Daniel. Did you tell her how you feel about her?" He smiles bitterly before responding.

"Do you have any idea of the impact everything else had on her? Yes, I told her, but it got lost in the rest of the filth she's now aware of. It didn't bring her any relief; if anything, my words just hurt her more. Everything that's tormenting her now is on me."

"It can't be, Daniel. She said she loved you. What she feels for you must count for something."

The Game…Jade

"Yes, it does serve a purpose; that's exactly what's finishing her off. That was the last thing she said before she asked me to leave her alone, that there's nothing left inside her but the love she still feels for me, despite everything. And that's what's going to keep on hurting her until it kills her. I don't know what's keeping her going or how much longer it'll last, but she's stopped fighting."

"Son…"

"Leave me alone, Carmen, please."

"What are you going to do?"

"Going back to her."

"But you just mentioned she asked you…"

"I can't. She won't see me, but I'll be there, always. I need to; it's all I have now."

"Keep going with the plans, buy another house, and get out of here. Perhaps, when the pain eases a little, you'll have somewhere to take her."

"Carmen, I can't think straight."

"Will you let me give it a try? I can start with the paperwork, and you…"

"Do as you please, but for now, leave me alone."

Carmen steps out into the hallway, clutching the rosary in her hand, knowing deep down it doesn't really help, but like Daniel, it's all she has now. There was a time when Daniel talked about buying a house in another country, a place where he could escape, even if just a little.

She'll dedicate herself to finding something that could serve him. Right now, it's something she needs to feel useful, too, to have a purpose to hold on to, especially now that she sees Daniel falling into a bottomless pit of despair. She's scared, though she doesn't want to admit it, not even to herself. She'd like someone to talk to about what's happening, but who would believe her? But even if someone does, how could she speak about it without exposing Daniel?

She's told herself countless times that she's losing it, that nothing makes sense, and then Daniel shows up with incredible news about his music career. Sure, it could all be a coincidence if it weren't for the fact that the prophecy he received almost ten years ago has been fulfilled to the very detail.

Daniel was careful to take notes of all the information he was given; he didn't trust his memory much, especially considering that, for the initial events to occur, he would have to wait seven years. When he met Jade and could prove to her that the first events had already happened, he let her read his notes.

Rocío Blisswealth

448

Dates, places, people, everything came true without fail. Before this, it was just Daniel's talks. Chats where he explained how he could achieve fame and his aspirations to be unlike any other Spanish artist. The craziness of a young man hungry for fame. And then, doors opened for him—doors to fame, recognition, fortune, and demons. The atmosphere in the house shifted dramatically, and the chills that ran down her spine became more frequent; it was hard to escape their presence.

She's never seen them, and for that, she's grateful to god, although she suspects it's not him preventing it; it must be just coincidence. Despite her closeness to the church, she knows it's not about them. She should have been an anchor to prevent Daniel from sinking so low. But honestly, she never fully believed in them.

She grew up in a home where talking about god was constant, but the devil was always like a character from a fairy tale—the villain of the movie, unreal and easy to defeat. But the reality is very different, and by the time she realized it, it was too late. Now, it turns out that what she never believed in is actually true. They're here everywhere, and once you've let them in, there's no way to run away from them.

She knows that god won't listen to her, at least not from where she is, in this house they've taken over. Her torment grows as Daniel's words echo in her head, "That's what's going to keep on hurting her until it kills her."

She can't let that happen; things have gone too far, but they don't owe a life yet. Yes, she's part of the debt; she didn't try to stop Daniel when she should've. So, if Jade dies because of the pain he caused her, it'll weigh on both of them, not just him.

She longed for the money Daniel would earn with his career, almost as much as he did, although not for the same reasons. She always watched him suffer because of the lack, the shortcomings his father imposed on him just for disobeying, and she wished he had the power to do and get everything money could buy. In recent months, things have been that way. Now, they have plenty of money, but it's only useful for planning an escape, with no guarantee that it will succeed. Can you really run away from the devil? There has to be a way, and she won't give up until she finds it.

She picks up the phone to contact the real estate agency. She mentions Daniel Montalvo's name. Done; in a few hours, they'll have the proposals. Now, all she has to do is wait.

The Game...Jade

Monterrey

Ángel's touch can bring out different feelings — calmness, peace, forgetfulness. His goal this time was to help Jade forget the pain of loss, betrayal, feelings she couldn't stand anymore. He's been taking care of her since before she was born, and it's been really hard, always facing so many obstacles.

Before giving him his assignment, they provided him with all the necessary information about it. They made it clear that she was one of The Seven, but they never mentioned the immense challenges that this girl's life would bring to him.

The demons showed up before he did; he'd never dealt with anything like that. And it got even worse when he had to share space with so many of them. His fights were always fierce, with no warnings or threats; they just wanted to take him out, and the scars all over his body were proof of his battles. Jade's life was always on the line until he finally figured out that they were testing how far he'd go to help her. And his response? He'd go as far as needed, as long as he's around. There were moments when they nearly got rid of him.

Maybe the toughest part for him was not being able to shield her without her realizing about the assaults. She was a kid so aware of the demonic presence that it made it harder to keep her spirit intact. She spotted them almost as quickly as he did, and that's not a usual thing, really harmful when you're trying to keep the sanity of a kid her age.

A few hours ago, his desperation led him to make a decision that didn't just mean bending a rule—he broke it completely. His partner has assigned him the job of going through their rules, weighing the risks of what he did, and he's on it, but till now, they have only served to reinforce the belief that his decision was the right one. He watches Jade sleep, or more like, lost in unconsciousness, and even then, she keeps on crying. The pain consumed her so much that he could only manage to disconnect her a bit.

His rules are:

1. ***Do not interfere in the person's life. You may advocate for them but do not prevent events from taking their course.***

So, what's the use of him being able to find out everything others are doing against her? Just to watch her suffer? Well, he's seen how her family made sure their home was anything but welcoming. And he knows that's the least they've dared to do; they've done terrible things to her, stuff she still doesn't realize, and it'll cause her pain almost as intense as Daniel's.

2. *Both demons and angels have the right to play their cards as they see fit, all in order to guide her towards the right decision.*

This reminds him of how he's seen demons harass her throughout her entire life, every single day, and sometimes almost every hour. They left her all alone and made her watch as she lost her grandparents, making her feel like her life was a path strewn with corpses, preparing the way for Daniel. When the time came, he found the road all set, and she was an easy target, with Ángel powerless to do anything to stop her.

3. *They can push her to extreme limits through their actions, but they are not allowed to touch her life.*

They've pushed her to her limits (and he's got to admit that his team, so to speak, also played a big role in it) to levels where most people would have given up. She's got two choices: give the demons what they want or fight to keep it; learn to use her gift and keep moving forward with the Game. But to choose the latter, she needs a purpose, a reason to keep going, at least to have a sharp survival instinct to stay alive. Yet, in her case, it's the opposite; she, unlike before, even more so now, wants to die, and he can't talk to her about a brighter future. Firstly, by mentioning it, they will know and might interfere, and secondly, because she simply wouldn't believe him, and he knows it too well.

Until now, Jade hasn't thought about giving in to the demons, but she also can't imagine life without Daniel anymore; she just can't picture it. He gave her the only love she's ever known, and whether it's love or not doesn't matter anymore; when there's no one else, the emotions he stirs up in her are what she calls love, and they make everything else fade away. Compared to the intensity of what he makes her feel, what she had with David was like watered-down sugar. A mere human can't match such depth of emotion, and Jade has experienced it for too long already. Obviously, that's something Daniel will have to deal with, too; no one else will make him feel the same feelings that Jade does, although that's not something Ángel is concerned about.

He watched as everything unfolded, grew. He was horrified when he realized how she felt about the demon in her room; she truly cared for him. At first, she was scared of him, then she got used to him, and before he knew it, she needed him around to feel secure. And that was just the beginning; later on, she found that security with Daniel, and Ángel was just there watching it all happen. He saw where everything was going and just had to let it play out. When possible, he used the circumstances in Jade's favor, but things took a turn, and now she's dealing with the fallout. Jade is lying there on the bed, barely conscious, just trying to hang on. She doesn't care if she shouldn't have done what she did, even though she's got a bunch of reasons. They shouldn't touch her life, and they definitely put her in danger; he knows her pretty well. So, he's not feeling guilty about it, not even a little. And...

4. Above all, respect her free will.

The decision, whatever it might be, whether it's right for Ángel or right for the demons, is hers to make. By the time she comes to a decision, all activity stops, and it must be respected. Free will.

"What is free will?" These are the first words Jade has said in many hours. Ángel is surprised; was he talking out loud? It's not like him. Seizing the opportunity, he responds.

"Free will is what humans use to follow the desires of their hearts."

"I'll keep that in mind." She closes her eyes again.

Ángel will still be there, next to her, just like Daniel, who he can clearly see sitting on the couch across from the bed. He won't let Jade see him; he wants to please her at least and not make the agony so much worse. Yet, Ángel knows that Jade can feel him and that simple fact continues to hurt her deeply. He wishes he could intervene and force him to stay away, to give her the time she needs to heal, but he won't dare to do it, nor will Daniel give up that space. Where will all this lead? The waiting and not getting Jade to completely disconnect overwhelms him.

Right now, he's completely committed to keeping the Angel of Death from getting too close to her. For hours now, he has been relentlessly asking for permission to take her away. He always heeds a strong call, especially when it involves Jade, well-known by all those beings, and, more than anyone else, by that angel, who has always shadowed her. But he respects Ángel's decision more than Jade's wish and stays out of it, though he's too close this time. It's the first time Jade has given up, and Ángel must find something to encourage her, or his orders won't be enough to prevent the Angel of Death from fulfilling his purpose. Ángel needs to give him a good reason to keep waiting and not take away this person who calls him so strongly.

Rocío Blisswealth

Spain.

Daniel's house feels empty, all appointments canceled, and activity reduced to nearly nothing. Carmen reported Daniel sick with a delayed case of chickenpox, hoping it would buy him some time. People will assume he needs to stay in bed, and with such a contagious disease, no one will dare to come near. The record company gave him twenty-one days, advising him to consult his doctor to speed up his recovery.

Daniel is already informed; Carmen goes into every little detail, not because she thinks he needs to know, but as an excuse to enter his room. Most of the time, she does. However, it doesn't serve her much; he sleeps too deeply. She regrets leaving him the pill bottle. She's searched for it when she feels free, without him noticing, but Daniel, sensing she would, hides it well.

Carmen has thought about different options concerning Jade, even calling her house on various occasions, at different times, sometimes pretending to be someone else and coming up with all sorts of excuses. The answer's always the same: someone claiming to be Mara says Jade's not home. She, better than anyone, knows that's a lie because the young man lying practically unconscious in the bed is with her in that room in Monterrey.

She hasn't quite figured out how this works, but she stopped caring about the "hows" days ago. Now, all she cares about is keeping Daniel healthy, at least that. She goes to the kitchen to oversee food preparations, even though no one eats with the same delight as Daniel when he's well. Something light yet nutritious is all he'll agree to. She got him to eat after a couple of days of not doing so, reminding him that if he got sick, he wouldn't be able to travel to be with Jade. She didn't know if that was true or not, but apparently, neither did Daniel because he agreed to eat as long as it was something light. Since he's not very aware of time, she feeds him as often as possible.

Besides that, she hasn't achieved much, like getting him to sleep fewer hours, for example. He keeps saying he wants to be with Jade, even if she can't see him. That's completely incomprehensible to Carmen, but she doesn't bother trying to figure it out. Deep down, she knows it'd be better if Daniel stopped trying to find Jade, but she doesn't try to convince him. It's not worth triggering his anger; she is all he has now.

England.

The Game...Jade

Grapevine wanders through the mansion, a magnificent construction that has been his home for a long time. Every detail of it is laden with beauty; it was built with care and dedication, though not with the intention of becoming his sanctuary, his hideaway, his prison.

When he realized that he might never be able to leave this space, that's when he began to want more, to crave more than what he could actually access. While the others may find it easy to accept their circumstances, for Grapevine, always haunted by his endless longing to have everything to which humans were entitled, it seems unbearable.

Having found a way to prolong his life, he observed how humans discard everything that makes them exceptional. Wisdom is a clear example of this; it led him to believe that other aspects of life were truly worth it. And so, he pursued them, even though he's never tasted a peach—his body isn't designed for it. But, like humans, he can appreciate art in all its forms, and among them, music is his favorite. Maybe that's why every seven years, he channels part of the energy of The Seven into the arts and music to have the pleasure of possessing more and better pieces over time.

The Seven, truly strange creatures, totally one-of-a-kind, created for some reason that, even after all this time, still doesn't make sense. So far, they've been sort of driven by their own limited human-like thoughts, but Jade is a whole different story, and he can't help but respect her. He doesn't pity her; he's incapable of it. Instead, he admires her more than the art pieces he's so proud to own.

His comrades have already noticed his preference for her despite his efforts to hide it. He always sensed she'd be different; her DNA carries a heavier weight than the others, and that's why he awaited her and watched over her even before she was born. He ensured that demons appeared to her more frequently than to others. His aim wasn't to attack her; he wanted to prepare her, to toughen her up, and he succeeded. It was he who drove away her grandparents prematurely. They interfered; they steered her away from the path he had planned for her, and he knew how to take advantage of it, using the slaves he's been meticulously collecting since time immemorial, almost as diligently as he selects a piece of art, all in anticipation of this day.

He occasionally strolls through the cells, housing muses of painters, sculptors, musicians, and writers for a change, even those of political strategists and religious leaders. He hoped Jade wouldn't be interested in dance; the Muses for dancers are so scarce that he has never managed to acquire one. Time, Space, even an Angel of Death and demons that could take care of the rest. He always worried that someone as insensitive as Ebony would be in charge of them, but there was no other choice; still, he managed to get what he needed.

And now she's in danger. How could he have missed that? She's still human, and Daniel focused precisely on that part of her nature. Why was that necessary? She possesses such a sublime energy, and he wants to steer it towards such wild paths. He's not going to allow it; he's taken care of her and trained her with such dedication that he won't let her waste away in ordinary ways; he has other plans. He wants her right here, beside him, to breathe life into this mansion and these pieces that have lost meaning for him, to be his creation. She bears his mark, the birthmark on her cheek, which he carefully placed there, being careful not to kill her in the process,
realizing that very day that she would withstand that and more, not even noticing. She's his living masterpiece.

He reaches a clearing in the forest, rarely allowing himself to come to these areas. Years ago, he wouldn't have cared, but now humans seem to be everywhere. Even though the demons guard the place to keep it from being located, he shouldn't risk it like this. Today, however, it's more necessary than ever. The demon from the mirror is already waiting for him, and as soon as he sees him, it bows almost to the ground.

Demon: MY LORD.

Grapevine: Rise.

Demon: I AM AT YOUR COMMAND.

Grapevine: What I'm about to request of you must be kept under the utmost secrecy.

Demon: WHATEVER YOU REQUEST, I AM AT YOUR DISPOSAL.

Grapevine: I must warn you that they shall not be informed of what I have asked of you.

The demon raises an eyebrow, knowing full well that they never act without the knowledge of others; too much is at stake. However, without saying a word, he keeps listening.

Grapevine: The situation with Jade has spiraled out of control, and they refuse to acknowledge it. That's why I am forced to take matters into my own hands without their consultation. If I delay any longer, we risk losing everything, and that's a gamble I'm no longer willing to take.

Demon: I'M LISTENING.

Grapevine: *You must accompany Sara to Daniel's residence and...*

Demon: MY LORD, YOU UNDERSTAND THAT JADE COULD DESTROY ME WITH JUST CAUSE. I WOULDN'T...

Grapevine: *Don't concern yourself with that. Once you've completed my task, she won't bother you anymore. She won't dare.*

The demon is afraid for his existence but doesn't want to miss the chance to escape Jade's attacks once and for all, so he obeys Grapevine's orders.

Demon: UNDERSTOOD, I AGREE.

Grapevine: *Excellent. Let me explain...*

The demon smiles at Grapevine's words and gets ready to execute his plan. Now, all he has to do is wait for Sara.

Spain.

Daniel wakes up, and Carmen hands him a glass of milk.

"I don't want to drink anymore, Carmen." He gets out of bed to take a few steps around the room. He hasn't even ventured into the garden in the past few days.

"Daniel, we had agreed on that..."

"Please, don't keep pushing."

"Alright, I'll leave it here for later. They called from the real estate agency; I think I found a house that you might like. It has some land where you could build the recording studio you've always wanted."

"Carmen."

"Please, dear, let me feel like I'm doing something. If I can't help you, what else do I have?"

"Where's the house?" He gives in to her.

"In Bruges, Belgium. They say it's a beautiful place."

"In Spanish, we call it "brujas" which means "witches" because the sound is similar, and with that name, it's quite fitting for me."

"Daniel, I don't..."

Rocío Blisswealth

"I'm sorry; I know you're trying to help me, but I don't think it makes sense. Nevertheless, if you reckon it could make a difference, have them send the papers your way and request the check from the bank to cover the full amount. Just go ahead and buy it."

"Don't you plan to see it, at least? What will happen if you don't like it?"

He turns his eyes towards her, those wonderful deep blue eyes that now lack their sparkle. He's been sleeping far longer than necessary, yet his dark circles are alarmingly pronounced. His gaze is deep and empty. He doesn't care about the house; he's only doing it to please her, to get her off his back. He doesn't want to spend another minute on it, and she can see it in his eyes filled with despair.

"If you could see her unconscious on that bed, yet the tears keep on flowing down her face."

"Unconscious? Have they given her something?"

"No, she's got someone looking after her, and I suppose he thought that was the only way to keep her alive; they're at least trying. I never thought that..."

"Daniel, how much longer do you plan to stay there? If she can feel you, and I'm afraid she can, don't you think it would be better for her if you didn't go anymore? You're prolonging her agony."

"My last words to her were to assure her that even if she couldn't spot me, I would always be there, waiting for her forgiveness, and I intend to fulfill that."

"That's suicide for both of you."

"A moment ago, you told me I'm dragging out her agony. As long as I'm prolonging anything that signifies there's life in her, I'll stay. For me to leave her, she'll have to ask me, but fully aware, with all her senses intact and with a determination to survive. As long as I see her as someone very close to becoming a corpse, I won't leave, Carmen. I owe her; she's done more for me than she can recall."

Tíber's barking can be heard in the garden. Carmen gets up and peers out the window. The barking becomes more intense as it approaches the house.

"I think it's Sara."

"Of course, she's here to throw her achievements in my face."

"Do you want me to get rid of her? I can tell her you're still in the contagious stage."

The Game...Jade

"No, she won't be bothered. She knows it's all lies. Don't interfere, Carmen. I deserve whatever she's coming to say; let's get it over with. Receive her and bring her here." Sara enters the room, her voice cheerful.

"No need, darling. I remembered the way perfectly, and because you are still recovering, I presumed I would find you here. Luckily, I was not mistaken. Good afternoon, Carmen." Her intention is not to respond at all, but Daniel's firm gaze compels her to. She doesn't want to cause any trouble.

"Good afternoon, Sara. Would you like something to drink?"

"Nothing, thank you. I'll just be here for a minute."

Carmen leaves the room, hoping it's true. However, she vividly remembers that Sara doesn't need much time to bring Daniel down, and with the distance between them now so short, it wouldn't take much effort.

Sara steps closer to Daniel, sizing up his condition, which is pretty sad no matter how you look at it. He hasn't showered in days, so his beard is creeping past the shadow stage, and his hair has lost its shine. His skin, once waxen and intense, now looks pale and ashen. And his eyes, usually the highlight of his handsome face, seem dimmed; the sparks that used to be in them have vanished.

Reaching out her hand, she gently touches his shoulder with a hint of pity. Daniel doesn't pull away; her touch is annoying, but he's not bothered enough to waste any energy defending a position that no longer matters. Perhaps a few days ago it did, but not now.

"Daniel, how are you feeling?"

He smiles bitterly, knowing that his appearance has never more clearly reflected the feelings overwhelming him. Sara's question seems unnecessary, yet he decides not to reply with what he truly wants to say: that it's none of her business. Instead, he settles into a spot on the floor, leaning against one of the large couches near the window in his bedroom. This puts some distance between them while she takes a seat on another couch opposite him.

"Badly."

"Why, Daniel?"

"Do I really have to spell it out?"

"Honestly, yes, I'd like to understand your perspective."

"Alright, I'll give it a shot, although it's unlikely to make a difference. I don't think you'll understand."

"I'll make an effort."

458

"Jade, she's deeply affected by what I did to her."

"It will pass, Daniel."

"I'm not sure how that's possible; I didn't think I'd hurt her that much."

"She clung to you, Daniel. You know more about her than I do, but I suppose her closeness to you made her trust you."

"And I betrayed her trust. I should've been more cautious and keep my distance from her." In their recent conversations with Sara, that was the key argument, the danger of being close to her and the risks it implied. He remains silent, expecting her to throw it in his face, but strangely, she doesn't.

"Daniel, they're unpredictable creatures, and Jade more so than any other, from what I've been told. I don't know what would have worked with her anymore; I mean, if preserving the image she had of you was what mattered to you, it's just that you..."

"I disobeyed; I know. I suppose I didn't leave them any other way out. As you said one day, being close to her, I felt like I could achieve many things, things that are far beyond my reach, and I've ruined everything."

"Not quite all, Daniel. Your career, which ultimately was the reason for all this, couldn't be better. Your fame has already spread throughout Latin America and Europe. TV shows keep calling us begging for exclusives with you, not to mention you now have more money than you could have ever imagined."

Daniel lifts his gaze from the floor, meeting Sara's eyes with the same bitter smile that seems to be the only one left to him as the others have faded from his lips, and he is no longer able to use them. She watches him and continues.

"Or don't you?"

Sara's face is flooded with curiosity. She spent long months with Daniel, analyzing everything he wanted to achieve, with the money and fame that obtaining Jade would bring him, and now he has everything he ever dreamed of. What more could he want? Daniel doesn't respond, and she keeps talking.

"I heard you bought a stunning house with plans to construct a recording studio. That's wonderful, Daniel. All your friends could produce their albums there, granting us more privacy for... well, for whatever might be necessary."

"Did you hear?"

The Game...Jade

"Darling, there's nothing you do that we don't find out about."

"Are you sure?" He smiles again.

"Daniel, stop with the games. You know who we're dealing with; they're monitoring every single one of your moves."

"Yet, you all don't know what's going on with me now, do you? Otherwise, you wouldn't be here."

"It's not that, they know it. I'm the one who's curious about your state, but you still haven't answered me. What's gotten into you? What exactly, I mean. You've achieved what you wanted, Daniel."

"No, Sara, I was never asked what I wanted. You asked me that night, at the burger stand where I worked, what I would be able to do for fame, huge, international fame. But you never asked me what I really desired. Maybe fame would have been the last thing on my list. Remember I mentioned to you that I didn't even sing? It was you who pushed me down that path."

"But I thought... what could be better?"

"You know, I think it all has to do with how we've grown. You know my parents have always had businesses and money. I just had to obey to have it, but my father always considered me rubbish. What were the words you used so accurately? 'Waste raw material,' that's it. And I wanted him to admire me, to consider me valuable.

When you presented me with the possibility of international fame, I thought it would finally make my father value me. Seeing how the rest of the world did, he would have no choice but to follow suit. And I became obsessed with the idea. One afternoon, while I was with Jade touring Mexico, my father showed up and forced me to invite him to lunch. Throughout the meal, with Jade by my side, he relentlessly belittled me, attacking me and reminding me that no matter what people thought of me, I meant nothing to him—I was still trash in his eyes. Nothing had changed, and what I desired so much had not happened. That's when Jade stood up to him, battered him just for defending me, and got up from the table, leaving him there, demonstrating what I meant to her. The upbringing she received from her grandparents is like gold to her, yet she threw it in the trash just to put him in his place so that I wouldn't feel so miserable. You can't imagine the turmoil I felt at that moment.

It dawned on me that what mattered most to me was being valuable to someone, to be worth in a way I never was to my family. I went to her room to see myself in her eyes and resolved to become the person she believed me to be—someone of worth. She, being one of the seven most significant figures on the planet, and I was the one who mattered to her, no one else. She loved me.

From then on, everything changed as I discovered my true dream. I began to fight for it, and, in the process, I forgot my recent past: what I had already been able to do, and what I already owed to Jade, above all, the fact that I could no longer ask more of her."

"Daniel, I didn't know that..."

"I didn't know either. I only realized it then, in her presence. People may wonder why I don't buy cars, clothes, jewelry, properties. It's because the image she holds of me isn't defined by material possessions. For her, what I represented was of far greater value than any worldly possessions I could offer. She never demanded anything from me, nor did she accept anything in return, except for my presence, up until now."

"Daniel, but there's something you need to consider: Jade loves music. That's precisely why I steered you down that path. She wouldn't have taken notice of you if you were just an ordinary person. You were tailored with everything she could possibly like, remember? You can't set aside your career now." Daniel laughs, a bit more eagerly this time, as he senses in Sara's words the path she wants him to take.

"You're saying I still have a chance for her to forgive me? I doubt it, Sara. The more I think about it, the less likely it seems. And honestly, I'm not in the mood for anything; I just want to..."

"To be with her, I already know. But they need her energy, Daniel, and you're the only one who possesses it. The only one who has acquired it."

"Sara, I'm drowning in guilt, can't you see? It's unlike anything I've ever felt before; it burns, it hurts, it suffocates. Don't ask me to make it any bigger; it's already massive, bursting at the seams. If I could get close to her and have her listen, I'd honestly just ask for her forgiveness, not to keep benefiting from her gifts. Please don't ask that of me, Sara. I can't do it anymore."

Sara stands up to sit next to him, placing her hands on his shoulders and squeezing them as if she pities him. Daniel doubts she actually feels that way, but maybe she's not like what he's seen before. Perhaps she understood his feelings and intended to leave him alone to deal with his guilt by himself.

"Daniel, I'm sorry. Truly, I'm so sorry."

The Game...Jade

"It doesn't matter anymore. Just leave me alone, will you?"

"It's not possible for me. I would lose what I have, but I can offer an alternative. I can make the pain, the guilt, vanish. The memories, everything, wouldn't trouble you again."

"No, Sara, trust me, I'm not in the mood. Take it as a plea and leave me be, please."

"There's something I need you to remember: our choices, our free will, it always matters. Regardless of whether we're deemed worthy or not, you've irreversibly committed yours. You've become their servant, Daniel. That commitment would only disappear with death, and that's not the case. I won't allow it to be; I like you too much. I'm truly sorry. I really am." Daniel is tired of Sara's presence. He needs to be alone, and if he has to force her to leave, he will. He already told her what she wanted to know, and he's not going to give in to her advances. She falls silent; he turns to look at her and asks her to leave. As he does, his eyes widen as he realizes what she means.

"No, Sara!"

"I'm sorry, Daniel."

Carmen watches through the kitchen window as Sara leaves and rushes to Daniel's bedroom. She's well aware of the chaos her visits usually cause and realizes he couldn't hold out much longer. She crosses the door but doesn't see him. Where could he have gone? She didn't see him leave with her.

Suddenly, she hears the sound of the shower. Really? What could this woman have said to him that convinced him to take a bath? All her previous efforts failed to achieve that. She takes a seat and waits to see him come out; she needs to see it with her own eyes. The sounds drifting from the bathroom suggest that Daniel's done with the shower and is now getting dressed. For the past few days, he's been wearing the same sweatpants, so seeing him in fresh clothes will be a welcome change, even if it's just another pair of similar pants. She knows he's not up for much more.

Daniel steps out of the bathroom, and Carmen's jaw practically hits the floor. Not only has he showered and changed his clothes, but he's also wearing jeans and a light blue shirt, a far cry from the somber black of the pants he has been using lately. He has also shaved, and although his face lacks a smile, the change is huge. He looks at her and, drawing closer, he gently strokes her cheek. Gathering her thoughts, she manages to say:

"Dear, what did Sara want? What did she say to you?"

Rocío Blisswealth

"She wanted to offer me choices; she wasn't pleased with the state she found me in."

"And how are you feeling now?"

"Better, I can't waste any more time focusing on what can't be."

Carmen stands up and takes his face in her hands; something about Daniel's attitude strikes her as very strange. Looking directly into his eyes, she asks:

"Daniel, what about Jade?" A flicker of pain briefly crosses his eyes, disappearing almost instantly, and then nothing, at least nothing she can identify.

"I don't know. I want to see her, but I don't know, Carmen. I don't know what's happening to me."

"What's going on with you about what, son?"

"What do you mean?"

"Are you going back to her side?"

"By whose side?"

"Jade, Daniel. We were talking about her, don't you remember?"

"I haven't got a trip scheduled to Mexico these days. Though given the success of the album, who knows, it might just happen. You like her, don't you?"

Carmen doesn't even try to get him to focus anymore. She doesn't understand what's happening, but it seems better than seeing him crumble under his mistakes, drowning in guilt. Even his absent state is a bit of a relief. Yes, it's all better than watching him sink into a deep depression. But now, what's going to happen to Jade? There's no way she'll find out, and maybe, if something really bad happens to her, they won't realize it until Daniel snaps out of it.

She needs to get her mind off all this and appreciate the peace that seems to have settled over him now. The awful thing is, she knows nothing good can come from Sara, and for sure, Daniel's change has something to do with her, maybe even with some demon's meddling. How can she just ignore what's going on? Maybe, just for tonight, sorting things out with a pillow might help them both.

"I'm going to have dinner. Would you like me to prepare something for you, Daniel?"

"No, Carmen, thanks, I'm going out. I'll grab a bite somewhere."

"Seriously?"

"Yes, why? Catch you later." He heads out the door. She stays in the bedroom, keeping her eyes on him as he crosses the garden to his car, starts it up, and disappears, leaving her in a kind of anguish she's never felt before.

Hours pass, and Carmen goes to bed. A few minutes later, she hears the sound of Daniel's car. She tracks the sound of his cowboy boots as he walks through the house and down the hallway to his bedroom. A shiver runs down her spine as Daniel's footsteps stop in front of her door, and without opening it, he says, "Rest well, Carmen."

How did he know she was awake with the lights off? How did he know she could hear him when she hadn't made a sound? She can almost see him smiling, and she hears his steps moving away again, towards his room, without her having said a word. Almost without thinking, she picks up the rosary resting on her bedside table and starts to pray. Today, more than ever, she feels like nobody's listening.

At dawn, as soon as she catches sight of the first rays of sunlight, she gets up and takes a bath, getting ready to go out. The long night helped her make decisions; things have reached such a point that she's not afraid to reveal what Daniel has been up to. What's happening with him is more dangerous than any trouble it could bring her, even if people think he's gone crazy. After all, with the depression he's been battling, that could be the path his mind took to disconnect. It seems Sara jumped the gun, and now he's being shadowed by demons; there's no other possible explanation.

She's heard about god's forgiveness, and that's her plan—start by seeking forgiveness, then speak to Father Julián. He's been her confessor for most of her life, and he may not understand or even want to forgive her when he finds out she turned a blind eye so Daniel could get his way with the demons. But he'll have to listen to her, at least. After that, everything will depend on what his heart tells her, and he'll have to guide her; he'll know what to do.

She snatches her purse to leave the house, but as she turns to approach the door of her room, her pulse races. For the first time, she's face to face with one of the demons she knew inhabited the house, visible to her human eye. She had never seen them before, something she had been thankful for until today, and now that blessing is nowhere to be found. There he stands, and she, in his presence, has forgotten how to pray, even how to speak.

Rocío Blisswealth

She is overwhelmed by the terrible smell of vomit, and she is petrified by the sight of that skeletal face with yellow eyes that never lose sight of her. Perhaps the most terrifying thing is its smile of sharp teeth, which can't mean anything good. It takes a step toward her, dragging his equally gruesome feet, and the grin widens. She reaches for her rosary in her purse; the demon slowly reaches out and snatches it, running the beads through his filthy fingers before uttering a simple "No," before throwing it to the ground.

It takes one more step to stand in front of her, extending his hand, and with the tip of his index finger—though he really only has four fingers—it touches her chest for a split second. What a terrible pain! She can't breathe anymore and falls to the ground. She tries to scream but only gets the same monosyllable: "No." Nothing more.

Another presence appears before her eyes; it looks human, although she knows it's not. Tall, pale, dressed in black, with worn-out wings as black as a crow's. It kneels beside her.

"It's not your time, yet your time has expired. The hour has arrived to settle the debts for every opportunity you've had to act but allowed to slip away. You will be judged based on your knowledge, and unfortunately for you, you hold too much information. Come with me, Carmen, Carmen, Carmen."

And that's the last thing she hears; her body lies lifeless on the ground where she fell. The next morning, the newspapers will carry her obituary:

* Carmen González passed away yesterday, within the embrace of our Holy Mother Church, succumbing to a massive heart attack. A series of three masses dedicated to the eternal rest of her soul will be held in the coming days, officiated by Priest Julián Domínguez, a childhood friend of the deceased. She is mourned by her beloved ones, among them the renowned singer Daniel Montalvo, who held a place in her heart akin to that of a son. May she rest in peace. *

Monterrey.

Jade's sobs echo through the room. Ángel rushes to her, placing his hand on her head and closing his eyes. He turns to Daniel, who remains seated on the couch, never taking his eyes off Jade, reacting to her cries with anguish, just like him.

"What have you done, Daniel?! What did they do?" Daniel hadn't left Jade's side for a second, so how did it happen what he saw in Jade's mind, the

The Game...Jade

haunting dreams that made her moan in anguish? How? Without Daniel ever leaving her side.

He leans back next to Jade and gently strokes her head, determined to bring her some peace. Despite his best efforts, the result is minimal; nevertheless, he'll keep trying. A death, they are already killing; they won't stop.

Ángel hadn't stopped to think, until now, that Daniel was spending so much time with Jade. It's not normal; it means he's sleeping too much, which isn't healthy, neither physically nor spiritually. Prolonged detachment like this isn't advisable. Why hadn't he noticed before?

Keeping Jade alive is consuming all of his attention, but he can't ignore the things around him, especially when they involve Daniel. Everything related to him directly concerns her, and he must be kept informed of what's happening.

She remains almost unconscious, occasionally eating a little before sinking back into that terrible, deep sleep. Days pass, leaving no sign of relief in her. Ángel can't understand why his efforts have no effect on her; every time he touches her, he only feels her pain, just as intensely as the first day. However, he won't give up; if he has to render her completely unconscious, he will. He's done it once before while her gestation approached its end.

Back then, her mother's human body couldn't handle the energy that composed the girl's body, and she had to be hospitalized for almost seven months. Meanwhile, Ángel had to isolate the baby just to keep her alive, practically holding the energy in his hands all that time. If he has to do something similar now, isolate her from the world around her, keep her away from Daniel's presence since he doesn't intend to leave, he will. He'll wait one more day, and then he'll act; there's not much time left.

Seventeen hours have gone by, and there's been no change. Seven more, and he'll have to get her out of there or at least bring her back to consciousness. The sound of the TV is blasting in Jade's room, which is weird since it's downstairs in the living room. How is the sound so loud? The kids probably left it on, but why with the volume so high? That's not normal. Music, laughter, and a voice. Jade opens her eyes with a blank look as if someone's calling her.

"Jade?"

She doesn't turn to look at him; all her attention is focused on the sounds she hears. She sits up in bed, leaning on her elbows, listening intently, and so does he.

"No, Jade. Stay where you are, don't move." She definitely doesn't hear him; she's probably chosen not to. She's already sitting on the bed, putting on her slippers. She stands up, her legs struggling to hold her up, but she persists until she convinces them of the importance of moving.

"Jade, listen to me. I beg you, don't go through with it."

It's totally useless; she's opened the door, and now the sounds, previously muffled, are crystal clear. Jade's footsteps are slow, but they've already reached halfway down the hallway, heading for the stairs. Why isn't anyone turning off the TV? Or at least lowering the volume so he can stop her.

"Tell us, Daniel, how's the new album coming along?"

"Brilliantly. The reception has been smashing, and I've already been awarded a platinum record for the soaring sales."

She reaches the first step and keeps going down. Ángel stands in front of her, trying once again to stop her. She looks at him for the first time and pushes him aside with her hand; she continues down.

"We hear you'll be kicking off a concert tour across Europe."

"Indeed; we'll start in Europe and then move on to Latin America."

On the last step, Jade makes a turn and enters the living room. The television is in front of her, with Daniel's image on the screen. She lets out a breath, shocked. But there are no more tears. She staggers, and Ángel holds her by the arm.

"Jade..."

"There it is, Ángel. Can you see it?"

"Yes, Jade, I see what you're seeing."

"Will this interview be seen in Mexico?"

"Absolutely, Daniel, it'll be broadcasted on various shows in that country."

"In that case, allow me to send a greeting. I want to blow a kiss to Monterrey; I'll be there soon."

"The demon from the mirror. Ángel, it's there."

The Game...Jade

"I know, Jade. It's under his skin."

"It's beneath the skin I love the most."

Her gaze, for the first time since the last visit of that demon, is filled with hope. Hope? It can't be; Ángel has to be wrong.

"Jade, there's no turning back; it's gone too far."

"That's right, there's no turning back."

"You need to let it go, Jade. There's nothing more to be done."

"You're wrong, Ángel. Free will, remember?"

"What?"

"You told me that free will is what humans use to follow our heart's desires."

"Of course, Jade, but..."

"Mine begs me to listen to my heart, and the only thing it says, what it has repeated for days, is that it prefers anything to be without Daniel, and, for once, I'm going to please it."

"Jade, that means death."

She doesn't answer anymore, just smiles, and heads to her room to get clothes for the shower. She'll just have to wait, but she knows what she's waiting for; it'll be worth it. Ángel tries to get in her way, but a hand stops him.

"Not anymore, Ángel. She's made her decision clear; she's exercising her free will. You can't intervene."

"They will put an end to her."

"If that's her wish, you must honor it."

"I can't bring myself to do it."

"Until the very end, Ángel."

Rocío Blisswealth

468

Chapter XXII
Cleft chin

I allow the shower water to loosen up my stiff muscles a little. Now I know how I've been able to deal with so many things: the loneliness, the terror, the loss. I was right to wonder how much pain someone can handle before they die, and it's probably way less than what I've been through. But whether I like it or not, I have Ángel by my side.

It's time to find out all the things I've been ignoring because even if I don't know about them, they still control me in some way. Ángel has spent these days—I can't even remember how many—keeping the Angel of Death away from me. I know it for sure because I've seen it. He's the one who kept showing up by my bedside, talking to him even though I couldn't hear. The response was always negative.

Sure, my body might not be in pain, but inside, I'm still falling, getting lower each time, without hitting anything, in a deep tunnel I can't escape. Daniel is no longer here, at least not fully, and he was undoubtedly my only reason to live. Now that he's gone, my whole purpose has flipped a hundred and eighty degrees. Now, all I want is to fulfill the desires my free will is shouting at me. I refuse to live without him, so there's only one way out for me, and I'll put all my efforts towards that goal.

That's a relief. My head, always so full of ideas that don't seem to clarify, has finally found one to hold onto. My life without Daniel makes no sense at all, at least not to me. I guess I'm important to the beings involved with Ángel and those who were on Daniel's side. So, one side will have to help me achieve what I set out to do.

Ángel mentioned something before, back when I was trying to offer something to that demon chasing Mara. He said there was actually something I could give, and he would be willing to accept it. I will dedicate myself to figure out what it is. Honestly, I don't know where to start looking. But before I dive into that, there's something more important I must do because, once I set off on this journey, I may not have time.

I step out of the shower and change into fresh clothes before heading into my room. Ángel's been sitting there the whole time, watching me. I walk over to him to talk.

The Game…Jade

"Ángel, I need to tell you something."

"Jade, you need to listen to me." He replies, taking my hand. I can see the pain, the anguish in his eyes, and it hurts, but this time, in a completely selfish way, I confess that I feel more sorry for myself.

"I will, I swear, but first, I need you to do it."

"Go ahead."

"I know you've kept my grandparents updated on my life so far."

"Until a few days ago."

"No, Ángel, I need them to know everything. Only then can they truly understand me. Maybe they won't forgive me, even with all the love they've always had for me; that would be too much to hope for. But I can't take it anymore, you know that, and I need them to know it too. My grandma knows me well. I'm sure that when you tell her what has happened, she will know without a doubt what I'm up to. Just let her know that I wish I could've been like Clemente, to have died before I let her down, but now, I just don't have the strength to continue on the path she taught me. Let my grandpa know that I've discovered everything he always talked about exists inside me; only I don't know if the path I plan to put this to work on is what he had in mind. Tell him that my biggest regret is not having him here to see what I'm capable of, to get what I want. And I don't think we'll meet again anytime soon. Just that. Can you pass that on?"

"I will."

"Okay, thank you. Now, what do you want to tell me?"

"Jade…" His gaze becomes very sweet, like when I was little, and he takes my hand again. "I understand what you're going through; trust me, I do. Yet, I also have a sense of what you might be contemplating, and I'm not willing to allow it. I've looked after you your whole life, and I believe that you deserve to keep living."

It's pretty obvious how human standards and those of someone like Ángel are totally opposite. "You deserve to," he says. I'm still trying to figure out what I could have done to deserve what's happening to me, and it turns out he sees it as some sort of reward. Maybe it would be if I had any plans to carry on with this lonely life without Daniel, but that's not the case. However, I'm not going to waste time trying to explain something he probably wouldn't get.

I know it hurts him to see me like this, and I wish I could thank him somehow, but all I can manage is this empty gaze. Without him, I'd probably

Rocío Blisswealth

have been done suffering minutes after that demon got me. But I plan to make use of his dedication to me, his loyalty, which I know will only end with death. So, I keep going, listening to him.

"There are countless things for you. You just have to ask for them." For the first time, something he said during these days caught my interest.

"I just have to ask?"

"That's correct." He says with hope in his voice.

"Do those things include Daniel?"

Ángel immediately looks over at the couch, and I follow his gaze, sending a shiver down my spine. Daniel is still here. I could feel him, but I wasn't completely sure because, as I asked him, he doesn't let me see him. It doesn't matter; I won't hold back anymore. Perhaps knowing he's here could even be helpful. Ángel gets all serious, but he doesn't want to miss this opportunity he finally has, and he answers me.

"No, Jade, I can only speak for the things within my domain."

Getting my brain to kick into gear is tough, but I know I won't get what I want if I don't first find out how many obstacles I'll have to face before I get it.

"Okay, then, if I ask for the truth, will you tell me?"

"I'll show you."

"I want it all. I want to understand why I am what I am."

"Alright. What else?"

"Where can I get information? Is it only through you?" His face twists with anguish as he looks around the room. I know he wants to see Daniel, but he doesn't want to make it obvious to me.

"You've always had access to the information." This time, my eyes change and pop wide open with surprise. My breath just speeds up like crazy, totally uncontrollable.

"What are you saying?"

"The issue is, we're obligated to provide you with the necessary information to make decisions, to influence your choices, and we do just that. However, even though we make it accessible to you, we're not obligated to instruct you on its application."

Just what I needed. Anger's knocking on the door. My heart pounds forcefully, sending a rush of heat to my whole body, intense heat mixing with this icy pain.

The Game…Jade

"Ángel, so if I had known, if they had told me where to look, none of this would've happened?"

"We may never truly uncover that. While information holds the power to modify the present and alter the future, it remains unable to change the past, so we'll never know."

The room swirls around me, but no, I'm done being a puppet, even to my own emotions. Not this time. I get up and start pacing the bedroom until I manage to shake off the dizziness caused by anger and surprise. As I return to my place next to Ángel, I make an effort to keep my tone steady as I address him. In the past, my impulse would have been to ask him to leave and lock myself away until I calmed down. But not this time. I've decided to skip those steps. Now, more determined than ever, I know my decision is the right one, and I'll do whatever it takes to achieve my purpose, even if it means going against myself.

"Where is the information, Ángel?" He hesitates before answering. I get it; he's stuck following his own rules, so he carries on.

"When it comes to you, in TV shows, movies, books, dreams, and especially there." He says as he points to my collection of Daniel's albums.

My breath catches in a sigh. How can this be possible? I've listened to those songs hundreds, no, thousands of times. What information? Daniel gets up from the couch. His astral body movement is perfectly clear to me. Ángel does the same, coming between him and me.

"Jade, you've listened to them, even sang them, but you never truly paid attention. You didn't know you had to." I focus on another one of his phrases and ask, sensing Daniel returning to the couch.

"When it comes to me? Are there more people like me?"

"Jade, please, take a moment to settle in. It's a long story, and I'd like you to take it calmly."

"Ángel, trust me, I'm trying hard not to offend you with what's on my mind. Quit messing with my plans and just tell me! I don't have time to waste."

"You have all the time in the world if you want it."

"Let's not play that game again, Ángel. If you've learned anything by now, it's that I can't imagine life without Daniel. You get that, right? I am pinned down by pins that you've put on me. I still don't get why, but I'm dead set on using my free will, and I don't want you to stop me anymore. If you notice I'm not crying anymore, it's because there's no longer a reason to do so, not because you're achieving something with me. I've lost hope, Ángel, so do your duty and tell me everything I need to know once and for all, please."

For the first time since I found out what the demon did to Daniel, I've found the strength to go after what I've set my mind to. I would've preferred if Ángel had just let the Angel of Death take me, putting an end to all this once and for all. But since that was a hard no, I've got no choice but to step into the Game and fight for the one thing I'm longing for now: to leave this life that feels pointless to me and hurts so much.

If I have to fight for that, I'll give it everything I've got. Just one thing I hope for: don't even think about telling me my destiny is to battle demons and save humanity because I'm not signing up for that. Nobody asked me if I wanted to be in this Game, and I don't see anyone else suffering alongside me or at least cheering me in this fight. So let humanity fend for itself and not expect a damn thing from me.

Yes, you heard me right. If this is a Game and I'm the player, think of it like a soccer match. No matter how hardcore a fan you are, only the players win, lose, or get paid, right? The spectators don't suffer or gain anything. Same deal here. Don't count on me for anything if it's about saving you. This is my Game, and I'll play it my way without caring about anyone else. The decision's all mine. I'll admit I've got one thing in my favor: I'm not scared. It's easy to go after an enemy when there's no fear holding you back. I've already lost everything, and I'm ready to do whatever it takes to get what I want. For the first time in my life, that's got to be enough. Ángel knows he's got to give me the info I need, whether he likes it or not, and he's struggling with it, but then he takes a seat again.

"First and foremost, let me caution you that there will be things outside my jurisdiction, things you'll have to discover for yourself. If you focus, it won't be difficult for you, but I won't be able to tell you, alright?"

I don't reply, just nod and get myself settled in front of him. I open my drawer, grab a small notebook and a pen, and get ready to listen and take notes. I won't leave anything to chance. My mind is a total mess right now, so I won't trust myself to remember things unless I jot them down. I take a deep breath, knowing for sure I won't like what's coming. I'll keep it together, follow my grandpa's advice: "Keep a level head. Anger messes with your brain when you need it most."

The Game…Jade

"Jade, you've always felt, deep within yourself, that you're different from the rest of humanity."

"Yes." I don't want to interrupt him; there'll be time for my questions later.

"You are, but not from all. Almost, but not entirely." He waits to see if I say something, but when I don't, he keeps going. "For thousands of years, some angels rebelled against the Creator due to the peculiar favoritism he's always had for humans. They were his creation, and they were totally loyal to him, obeying his every command and professing unconditional love. However, he created humans and endowed them with free will, they could choose to love him or not. This was exciting for the Creator, to gain something dependent on someone else's will, and he desired the love of his new children. The angels then, one of them in particular…"

"Luzbel."

"Well, that's how you refer to him, but in truth, his name was different. In summary, he became enraged when he felt like he wasn't enough for the Creator anymore. He refused to serve him, confronted him, and consequently, was expelled from paradise along with a few others who shared his views.

He spent a considerable amount of time seeking revenge. Eventually, he devised a plan to prove to the Creator that humans were not worthy of his love. His proposition was, 'Let me do as I please with humans, and we'll see if they still choose to love you.'

The Creator knew he would proceed regardless, so he decided to safeguard humanity from him. He proposed creating, every seven years, seven humans, specially designed by both sides with the necessary capabilities to resist and utilize their endowed gifts. Both factions would have unrestricted access to them, with exceptions agreed upon and respected by all. In this manner, the winner would be acquiring something truly valuable: the raw material with which the Creator endowed the first man on earth: his energy. Several rules were established, the primary one being the inviolable respect for…"

"Free will."

"Yes, free will. Initially, it functioned as intended. Each side provided their information, and we let conscience and free will determine the outcomes, so sometimes one side won, sometimes the other."

Rocío Blisswealth

"Ángel, this sounds to me like your Creator invented a breed of fighting dogs. They toss us into the ring until one of us finishes off the other; it's not fair. Can't he see that I'm raw? Couldn't he grant me euthanasia?" He doesn't look at me. I don't know what he's thinking, but I'm pretty sure if he had arguments to counter my comment, he'd be using them. "Go on, please."

"Not quite, Jade..." He looks at me and gets that there's no point trying to convince me things aren't the way I think. Honestly, I think that no matter my state, I'd still think the same. He decides to carry on.

"There were individuals who found ways to steal that energy, exploiting it for nefarious purposes, and that's when everything changed. The struggle became more intense as they began targeting these individuals from birth, all in pursuit of commodities that would become bargaining chips for the basest of instincts.

The demon had found a more potent weapon to inflict harm upon the one who had once been his beloved. He allowed the purest of his creations to be tarnished, feeding his horde with their energy."

"And then?"

"Then everything changed. They began pairing us with you for life."

"But the guardian angel..."

"No, Jade. While it's true that there's an angel assigned to humans, that's only during infancy. Once puberty arrives, they're left to their own devices, free to choose. We, however, remain with you throughout your life."

"As long as we're alive."

"Or until our end."

My shock at what I'm hearing is huge. My grandma always talked about angels like they're practically invincible. Angels can't be mortals; that's just not possible. My jaw drops in horror as I try to wrap my head around it. Even though I don't agree with what the Creator has done to me, now I realize that Ángel is also in danger, all because of a decision made by someone as insignificant as me. That just can't be right.

"No, you can't..."

"Jade, both sides are alike. You've defeated more demons than you can recall. What makes you think it's any different for us? We too perish, carrying the burden of not being able to save what was entrusted to us. We're with you until death, yours or ours. Your pain is ours; that's why I understand how much it hurts you, and I want to rescue you. You didn't deserve so much suffering."

The Game...Jade

That means he's my partner in this nightmare, which I've started calling the Game. At least I've got someone who's not just fighting alongside me but who's also feeling the same pain I do. The reasons don't matter as much; Ángel would give anything for me. So, from now on, he's the one I'll lean on as much as I can. I know the Creator sent him with me, but Ángel's the only one I've got, so it's between him and me now, and I'll do my best not to let him down. Terror starts to consume me. When will this ever stop getting worse? Every word, every piece of news, just adds more pain to my life, to what little is left of it.

"Ángel, you once said you could see my scars; I want to see yours." I'm afraid of what's in store for me, but I decide to face it.

"That's not necessary, Jade. Please, don't."

"It is. I have to know how much I owe you." I insist.

He stands up, pulling off his shirt over his head, and then I can see it all: his torso, his arms, his neck, his face. There's not an inch of smooth skin; it's all covered in scars. Scratches left long scars on his arms, and the healing process reveals that some are fresher than others. His right side and neck bear deep, massive bites. You can clearly see the marks of sharp teeth that caused them, tearing into his flesh. Pain, so much pain. His face is completely unrecognizable to me beneath that mass of scarred flesh. His mouth twists slightly to the left side, victim of a wound that crosses his face from the temple to the chin. His right eye has lost a piece of the eyelid that covered it, leaving the eyeball exposed in a monstrous way, yet his gaze remains sweet.

I get up from the bed and slowly walk towards his back; the same scars repeat on it. Perhaps his efforts to protect me left this area more exposed because the scars here are thicker. Rather, they're overlapped, one on top of the other, making the skin thicken to cover the exposed flesh. The left side appears the worst; it seems like a piece of his flesh was torn away, leaving thin scars that sink between his ribs. His skull is nearly bald, and as I finish turning him around, I notice his left hand is missing two fingers. I can't take it anymore.

"Ángel, forgive me." I whisper, covering my mouth with my hand; sobs choking me.

"Forgive you? You weren't the one who caused them; we were on the same side. Jade, I carry them with pride; they are, as you once said, scars of victory."

I slump to the floor and wrap my arms around my legs, hiding my embarrassed face between them. How could he do this for me? I don't want to think that I was the cause of all this. Me, such a stupid and insignificant being. I don't deserve it. Ángel kneels beside me, gently running his hand through my hair.

"You deserve it. The only thing I wish for is to be able to make you happy, but I can't. You've come to understand that happiness is something beyond my power to provide for you."

I raise my head slightly to thank him, relieved to see his skin back to normal. I couldn't handle much more of that image, though it doesn't matter now; it's etched into my mind. Now that I know how much I owe him, I'll repay him soon.

"Thank you."

"It's been a pleasure." He says as he puts his shirt back on.

"Ángel, is it always like this? I mean, for us." His expression turns serious as he responds.

"Your sixth sense is so intense. No, it's not always like that. You've been different since your conception; too much energy. I wouldn't know how to explain it. More perceptive than others, aware of many things you shouldn't know, more targeted than anyone."

"Why?"

"I don't know, we don't know, I mean... The Creator must know, but he won't tell us. That's one of the things you'll have to deduce if you still want to."

I pick my words carefully. I don't want to hurt him any more than he's already been hurt because of me, just because he was assigned to me. However, I need him to fully understand my view.

"Ángel, the Creator, as you call him, made me part of a Game where I'm the prize, and I didn't even know it; my opinion wasn't taken into account. But in all the madness of my life, I've learned to recognize loyalty. Forget about everything else; I know how much I owe you for that. But you know me well enough, so I hope you understand perfectly what drives me."

"Not living without Daniel." He says sadly.

"That's right, do you understand what that means? I really hope you do because it means freedom for both of us. Freedom from all the pain we've gone through, to forget about this prison, and above all, our release from our

The Game...Jade

tormentors. Can you see that? If not, I just ask two things: help me understand this Game as much as you can so I can gather the strength to end our participation in it, and two, stick with me till the very end, Ángel, until the last second. Can you promise me that?"

"Jade, you want me to..."

"Will you promise me?"

"Yes."

"Thanks. Can we continue? I have a lot of questions."

"Alright, Jade, but there's something I must tell you. Daniel is there; he hardly ever leaves." He points to the couch.

"I know, Ángel. If he wasn't, I couldn't breathe. I just couldn't keep going. It's stupid, I know, but I can't help it. Love it's still here."

"Shall we continue, then, Jade? I must warn you, there are still some very bitter pills ahead."

"Let's continue."

For the first time in my twenty-one years of life, I'm starting to learn things that I should have known all along; that would have been the honest thing to do. However, I wouldn't say they had me as part of a Game; rather, they kept me caught in the crossfire, and worse, not just me, but the people around me. That, of course, includes Ángel, although I can't exactly label him as a person.

In short, until now, I've been asking Ángel questions as they come to me. The sound under my bed was made by the demon assigned to me, trying to make its presence known, marking its territory, so to speak. The voice inside my head is one of Ángel's companions, only allowed to warn me in case of a truly serious danger, nothing more.

As for being able to know about things happening in other places, he tells me he didn't know I had that ability either. In fact, he was surprised when I told him. I thought he was with me twenty-four hours a day, but he clarified that no, they're usually absent sometimes, and they're not omnipresent, so there are things they don't know about.

There's something that makes me very curious: the attitude Dad always showed towards me. I know it doesn't matter anymore, but I would have liked to have had a good memory of him.

"Ángel, why didn't Dad love me?"

"There are things you don't want to know, Jade. Believe me, not right now, at least. You're not well."

"Ángel, the problem is that you keep trying to make me feel good, but that's a lost cause. Forget it; just tell me what I need to know."

"But you don't need to know that; it will only hurt."

"You yourself told me there are things I'll have to figure out. How do you expect me to do that if I don't have all the complete information?"

He stops and stares at me for a few seconds. I guess, thinking about how to explain things to me or resisting explaining them to me, but then he squints and continues.

"Your favorite subject in school was always Science. Do you remember?"

"Yes, but what's that got to do with...?"

"In one of your classes, they discussed the traits inherited from parents to children."

"I don't know where you're going with this."

"Please try to recall."

"Can't you just tell me?"

"No."

"Fine. Eye color, the ability to bend or roll the tongue, I don't know what else." I'm starting to get desperate.

"There's one characteristic, just one, that is one hundred percent hereditary from father to children."

My eyes widened with surprise, not at the memory but at the fact that I overlooked it when I studied.

"Cleft chin."

I didn't think it was possible; my stomach was still capable of churning with this kind of thing. I had already found some stability amidst all my pain and anguish, at least for a few hours. I had parked myself at a certain height in the well, but now I've lost the strength to hold on, and I'm starting to fall again.

I rush to the closet, knowing that somewhere in one of the boxes I've stored there over the years, there are photos of Dad, and I have to see them. The first ones I come across are of my grandparents, but I quickly pass them by, dropping photo after photo on the bed until I finally find it: Dad's picture, unmistakably showing his split chin. I didn't remember it anymore. In fact, I could hardly recall the general features of his face, but there it was. Mara has it, too, but not me.

The Game...Jade

The air leaves my lungs as I allow myself to grasp what I see before my eyes. That trait is one hundred percent hereditary, so I'm not his daughter. Tears, I didn't think I had any left, started rolling down my face.

"He knew." I turn to Ángel without really asking.

"Indeed."

"Why, then...?"

"Your mom had divorced him. After getting pregnant by another man, whom she never heard from again, he, still in love with her, proposed to recognize you, hoping she would come back to him."

"And I've always been the reminder of the other man in Mom's life."

"That's right."

"Why didn't Mom tell me?" I say, my voice choked with tears.

"I don't know."

"Who was my father?"

"No one knows. He was crucial for the DNA that runs through your veins; however, we have no idea of..."

"I have to know." I wipe my tears with my fingers and head for the door, but before I grab the doorknob, Ángel blocks my way.

"Jade, I warned you there were more bitter truths. Please, leave this for another day."

"I can't."

I control the tears and rush down the hallway. I don't understand why Ángel is so keen on stopping me. I know this was a bitter pill to swallow, but I've already faced it. Whatever else I might uncover will just be extra information, and I know I need it. I've practically lived in ignorance my whole life, and I can't afford to keep going like this, no matter how much it hurts.

Dad, well, he passed away several years ago, and there's nothing I can do about it. I mean, there never was. I had nothing to do with what happened in his life. My tears are because if I had known that he didn't have to love me, his lack of love wouldn't have hurt me so much. Anyway, now what matters to me is knowing who conceived me, giving me this DNA load, as Ángel calls it. Maybe it's him I owe all these misfortunes to. I don't know, but I have to find out as much as I can.

As I run, I almost bump into the mirror, but I don't care anymore. It holds no interest for me now; I know where the demon that came out of it is. I search the house, but I can't find Mom or Mara. I guess she's also in on the secret, so whoever I find first will have to help me clear up my doubts.

Unable to find them, I head down the hallway that connects the living room to Mara's room, which is at the back of the house, quite isolated from the other bedrooms. I start walking more slowly when I hear voices coming from inside; her door is closed. My feet hesitate, and suddenly, I stop dead in my tracks. The sensation of walking in icy water hits me, even before the smell of vomit does, freezing me in place.

The hairs on my neck stand on end, and fear starts to wash over me in waves down my spine. No matter how hard I listen, I can't make out clearly what they're saying. Those deep, guttural voices stir up the same terrors that have haunted me all my life; the demons are inside the bedroom.

Summoning the strength that still lingers within me, I wrench myself free from where my feet are rooted and cover the remaining distance to the door. Just before my hand reaches it, Ángel wraps me in a tight embrace, lifting me from the ground and pressing me against the wall, his hand covering my mouth, all in one swift motion. My breath hitches with the shock of it, and I stare at him with wide eyes. He doesn't budge an inch from his position, nor does he ease the pressure on me.

With a barely audible whisper, he says:

"Listen." I strain to catch what the demons are saying.

"YOU KNOW HER INSIDE OUT. WHAT'S HER NEXT MOVE? WHAT CAN WE EXPECT?"

"SHE ENDURED A SEVENTY-HOUR ATTACK." That voice! I know that voice. It's him, it's... it's... "AND SHE NEVER SURRENDERED; THE ONLY THING THAT HAS BROUGHT HER HAPPINESS HAS BEEN DANIEL. WITHOUT HIM, SHE'LL SEEK DEATH, I'M SURE OF IT."

It's my demon! But how? Where has he been all this time? I took him out of my room, and he disappeared, so?

"IT WOULD BE UTTERLY DEVASTATING IF SHE DIES. IMAGINE ALL THAT ENERGY GONE TO WASTE. IF ONLY WE COULD COMPEL HER TO SURRENDER, IT WOULD MARK A TRUE VICTORY FOR US. WE WOULD HAVE ACHIEVED WHAT NO ONE ELSE HAS BEEN ABLE TO ACCOMPLISH."

"FOR NOW, LET'S RECLINE IN THE ROCKING CHAIRS AND ENJOY THE SUNSET FOR A WHILE." I tremble at the thought of running into them the moment they open that door, but I don't have time to run. Even if I tried my best, I wouldn't make it down the hallway before they spotted me, assuming Ángel decided to let me go. It seems I have no choice but to face them, whether I like it or not.

"Don't move!"

Ángel quietly orders me, still covering my mouth, probably afraid that the insults I'm thinking might slip out, even against my will, and give us away. In just a split second, the door swings open, and I can see him. I have no doubt anymore: it's my demon and the one who followed Mara for several days without me being able to drive him away, the same one who killed Mrs. Rosy. They pass by us without seeing us, and I hear Ángel mutter so softly they couldn't hear.

"Allow her spirit to see what's invisible to her eyes."

My eyes, which until that moment were clearly focused on the figure of my demon, widened almost to the point of popping out, and my legs gave way under my weight, completely losing the strength that held them up. If it weren't for Ángel's arms still tight around me, I'd be on the floor watching my demon walk down the hallway under my mother's skin.

"Get me out of here." I plead to Ángel under the pressure of his hand, which he still holds over my mouth.

He pulls me close and runs down the hallway, leaving them behind and carrying me up the stairs to my room while my legs refuse to cooperate. This must be the bitter pill he was talking about because my mouth tastes like bile. It's a painfully bitter taste.

I collapse on the floor, curling up with my forehead against the ground, covering my head with my hands. Honestly, I don't know if I fell all at once or if Ángel interrupted my fall; it's impossible to feel anything amidst this whirlwind of terrible sensations flooding over me.

Everything spins once again, but this time, it's not the room. It's images, hundreds of images flashing behind my eyes all at once. Since when? I mentally trace back the images of the past few days, since when? I don't know. My breathing has turned into desperate gasps; every effort to breathe hurts.

I can feel Daniel's energy next to me and Ángel trying to lift me up. More images inside my head; the demon walking alongside mine was obviously inside Mara's skin. I trusted them; I defended them from the demons.

Rocío Blisswealth

Wait a second, wait a second, if only those images would stop flooding into my mind, and if Ángel would just stop insisting on lifting me up. I need to think, to focus my thoughts on something I can't quite decipher what it is.

The dream! The information is also given to me in dreams. In the dream, the demon said, "You're defending a demon from me." In my dream, I was defending him while he ran around the room, where Mom and Mara were also present, but when did he get inside her? How did he do it?

Why am I so stupid?! I stagger to my feet and rush to the bathroom, emptying my stomach. I couldn't contain all the bitterness inside any longer. Ángel helps me back and settles me on the bed. My body shakes with sobs and gasps. Finally, I open my eyes, fixing them on Ángel. Pain and fury consume me entirely, and I just want him to answer one thing: shouting at him.

"Why, Ángel?! Why didn't you protect them from them?! They killed them, Ángel. They killed them!" He calmly replies.

"No, they didn't kill them; they're still there."

My horror now is immense. I know what it's like to be in the same room with one of them. I can't imagine the terror of a soul confined within the same body alongside a nauseous demon. My screams persist, unable to express myself in any other way. I want answers. No! I demand answers!

"We have to help them, Ángel! Why didn't you help them?!" My sobs choke me.

"Jade, please, don't ask anymore."

"Answer me, I beg you, help them, please." My cries diminish as I struggle to find air to support them, reaching out and pressing my fingers against his forearm, leaving marks from my effort.

He looks at me with infinite pity, holding my head in his hand as if shaking it against the bed could cause me more harm, but no, that wouldn't be possible. My spirit is raw, on the brink of death without ever reaching it. Shaking me against the bed couldn't be worse than that. In a soft voice, he responds.

"I can't help them, Jade, and you're not holding up anymore. I don't want to tell you anything else."

"Can't you help them?" My voice has turned into a whisper.

"No."

Why?"

"They asked for it."

The Game...Jade

No, no, no. My ears start ringing, and the images slowly fade, plunging me into the deepest darkness I've ever experienced up to this point. It feels like every step I take in this search is destined to confirm that the conclusion I've come to is the most sensible one.

In the middle of all this madness, the tiny bit of sanity my mind is holding onto, must be enough to help me fulfill my purpose. But right now, as I'm tearing myself apart inside, it feels almost impossible to believe that I can even come close to achieving it. I'm discovering new kinds of pain. Ángel's words, "They asked for it," only mean one thing, even though I don't know the reasons; it tastes like betrayal.

I don't even consider the fact that they never loved me. That's a stupidity I won't allow myself anymore, despite all the mistakes I've made, because I trusted them. They knew how to manipulate me, and I fell for it. Now I can see that blood means nothing. Sharing the same blood doesn't guarantee unconditional love, doesn't guarantee trust, or protect you from getting stabbed in the back like this. This pain is different: it hurts, it burns, it's full of rage, not anguish. They took me for a fool, they used me, and I still don't understand why. But I kept believing in them and continued to defend them against demons. They must have laughed at me!

The only thing I can salvage from this consuming feeling is realizing that another tie, another obstacle to facing what's considered unimaginable, has disappeared, burned away, or rather burned onto me. That would be a clear way to explain the sensation of extreme burning in my skin.

I'm disgusted by the blood I share with them. I stop myself from cutting my veins open to let it all spill out on the floor, only because it's my grandparents' blood. That idea kind of washes away some of the filth I feel surrounded by. Daniel used to think I was... what were his words? "Pure"? What will he think now? He felt surrounded by filth, but I carried it within me. Ángel holds my hand, but I can't feel it anymore, can't even tell if he's still speaking or just keeping quiet. I'm leaving here, leaving this body that can't take it anymore, but where to? I have nowhere to go.

He looks at the couch where Daniel has spent the last few days, realizing he's not there. My hand stops its effort to press down on his arm and falls beside him on the bed. He desperately grabs it in an attempt to stop me, but that's impossible.

Rocío Blisswealth

Chapter XXIII
What might have been never was

The feeling of abandonment is quite nice, just letting yourself go. Your body lacks sensations, even emotions, giving me a break I've been craving. But it also scares me to think I could evade my anxieties. I think I might end up like when I felt myself floating in Daniel's arms, only to realize I'd always been alone when, for the first time, I wasn't. I've lost track of how long I've been sinking, experiencing all this pain, anguish, and betrayal. Now that I'm catching a break from it all, I'm afraid it'll hit me even harder in both, body and soul when I wake up. I'd rather stay here, caught in this fleeting moment of nothingness.

I guess this is what death feels like, though I'm not naive enough to think that Ángel decided to let me go. Now more than ever, he seems even more determined than ever to keep me alive, which is seriously torturous. So, this must be just a faint. My body shut down on its own without needing his help. But it seems like consciousness is coming back because I'm starting to notice that all the sensations that have been bombarding me since this morning, piling up one after another, are still ongoing without a pause. It looks like they never stopped; it was just me who didn't notice them.

As I become aware of what I'm feeling, I notice that Ángel's hand is still tightly wrapped around my wrist. Damn it! This means that this faint is useless. What's the point of wanting to be unconscious if everything is still here?

The sounds start to reach me, too. Since Ángel kept talking to me and encouraging me, I finally decided to open my eyes. Almost instantly, I shut them again and then try to open them, only this time, very slowly; the room is very bright. I suppose this was a prolonged faint; I don't remember there being so much light before. As my eyes slowly adapt to the bright light, I look around. It's not my bedroom, and yes, I'm definitely on the floor. Somewhere nearby, Ángel keeps talking. Can you please be quiet? I can't catch a word you're saying. The buzzing in my ears continues with the same intensity, making it impossible for me to hear you.

I give it one more shot, trying to focus my sight and choose Ángel's hand as a focal point to do so. I stare at it until my vision starts to clear, and...

The Game...Jade

No! Please. I quickly yank my hand away, struggling to push myself up to stand. The shivers caused by pain run through me again as I recognize first the hand and then the voice.

"Don't touch me, Daniel". Sobbing overtakes me once more.

"Alright, alright, I won't, but Jade, we can't afford to waste time." I furrow my brow and try to hold back my tears. I can't stand being so close to him, torn between two equally powerful feelings: the pain of loss and the desperate urge to throw myself into his arms and stay there. Yet, the concern in his eyes tells me that whatever he's trying to tell me is important. I pulled myself together just enough for my sobs to let me hear him and kept quiet. I don't have the strength for anything else.

"Jade, do you realize where we are?" I turn around, trying to recognize the place, but no. All I see, or rather all that surrounds me, is an intense blue color, much like his eyes, but I can't figure out where this space starts or finishes. My gaze doesn't settle anywhere, as if I suddenly found myself floating in the middle of the blue sky of a summer afternoon. Nothing here feels familiar. I shake my head, wishing my tears would stop; it would make things easier. He keeps going.

"We're in the Record of Time."

I shake my head once more, hoping the pieces will fall into place so I can make sense of it all, but nothing clicks. I just stare at him intently.

"Try to grasp it, Jade, because there's something you need to see."

"What thing?" I manage to ask.

"Here you can witness the past, present, and future, and right in this space lies your mother's life."

He reaches out a few inches, running his finger along one of the walls to demonstrate what happens when it's touched. The moment his finger makes contact, the wall ceases to feel solid. Instead, it vibrates, revealing that it's made up of thin sheets, like pages of a book, gently parting under his touch.

"I don't know what to look for."

"May I do this for you?"

I don't have the strength to say no, and I don't find a reason to either. After all, he's the one who brought me here, so I suppose he'll show me whatever he wants regardless of my decision. I look at his wonderful face, the one that sends new waves of pain through my spine, and I nod.

Rocío Blisswealth

"You have every right to know who conceived you. They owe you that, among other things."

He presses the wall a tad harder, and it swings open, unleashing a terrible noise as if all the day's noises break free at once for no reason. With a quick motion of his hand, he signals for me to come closer, and I do. Shoving me from behind, he places me right in front of the page, so to speak, that has unfolded before us and keeps pushing me until, with no idea of what I should do, I give in to his effort and take a step forward, stepping into that moment. I remain silent, holding my breath, afraid of being seen. Daniel approaches me and says in a normal tone:

"They can't see you or hear you."

That's a bit of a relief; at least I can lean against the wall and watch without worrying about being noticed. A few feet in front of me, I spot young Mom, meaning obviously this must have happened more than twenty-one years ago. She's at some kind of... personal growth conference? That's what it looks like.

The speaker grabs my attention; he's a tall man, impeccably groomed, dressed up in a suit that, by all appearances, is very expensive. The conference is coming to an end, and Mom applauds this guy's participation, along with the rest of the crowd filling the auditorium.

Some of her friends tag along, and even after all these years, it's easy for me to recognize them all. I never thought they would like this kind of thing. They grab the books they left on their chairs after applauding and head for another room nearby.

I take a few seconds to observe the space; this place seems to be in the United States. All the signs on the walls and the posters advertising upcoming events are in English, even though the conference is in Spanish. Mom and her friends are queuing up to get this guy's autograph; it's a long line, and they're right at the end, so it'll be a while before they get close to him. Despite the wait, their spirits remain high, probably because of the excitement of the conference. Finally, they reach him, and I'm faced with what I came here to see. As Mom approaches, he hugs her by the shoulders and gives her a gentle kiss on the lips, then goes on to greet her friends. Mom introduces them one by one, and I focus all my attention on him. I can't quite catch his name; I'm not even sure she said it since they all seem to know who he is.

"Can I get closer?" I ask Daniel, and he nods.

The Game...Jade

I head over to them, stopping just short of touching Mom's back; I want to get a close look at him. He's pretty tall, maybe even taller than Daniel, and his eyes are definitely like mine. Mom's eyes are medium-sized, Mara's too, but mine? They're big. Now I know why.

As if he knows I'm watching him, he stands still, and they discuss the details of the conference with him. Perfect! It gives me extra time to check him out. He definitely doesn't have a cleft chin, and all his features have something of mine, or rather, mine have something of his. It's strange to recognize a resemblance to someone. I don't really look much like Mom, and I grew up getting used to that. But now, seeing whose genes are running through me, it's of some relief. Even some of my gestures and mannerisms are his. It must have been tough for Mom to see so much of him in me! I don't know why they didn't stay together, but it must have been really hard, really painful. I can tell from the way she looks at him that she's very much in love with him.

"Jade, we ought to leave."

I turned to look at Daniel; just for a few seconds, I was able to forget the pain that having him so close caused me. I turn away and step out the page of time where I had the chance to meet, well, at least see, my biological father. As soon as we take a step out of it, it closes, seamlessly blending with the others, creating a wholly sky-blue continuum. Daniel walks over to me.

"It's time for you to go now." He says, caressing my face with his fingertips as he used to...

"Don't touch me, please." I say, tears streaming down my face.

"Jade..."

"It hurts."

"I know. It hurts me as well."

With a motion of his hand, he points the way, and soon after, I break down into sobs on my bed. Ángel gently strokes my head, saying nothing. After all, maybe that brief moment of unconsciousness did ease the pain slightly, because the ache I'm feeling now is definitely deeper, Daniel.

Thoughts swirl around in my head. What happened to this guy? Why didn't he stay with Mom? With me? Did he even know I existed? I'd like to believe my life could've been totally different. Maybe they could have raised me together, and my grandparents would have just been that: my grandparents, not the strange mix of parents, teachers, and even psychologists that they turned into. I would have grown up with a different last name, and I wouldn't have

Rocío Blisswealth

suffered the heartbreak of who I believed was my father until a few hours ago. Maybe I would've been happy. But I know: what might have been never was.

I wonder, if I could get answers to all my questions, what would be the first one? Or how many would there be? Probably thousands. Most people grow up clarifying their doubts over the years, but I only started figuring out who I am a few months ago, and I'm still nowhere near clear about it.

Maybe the first thing I'd ask is if there's something I could've done to change the way I have lived. Would there be something, anything, that could change things? If I knew, if it was really possible, I'd do it, whatever it was, I'm sure of that.

I roll on the bed to lie on my side; it's a position that makes it less painful for air to flow in and out of my lungs when I'm sobbing for a long time. Having Daniel so close made me realize I have a long period of crying ahead of me before I calm down or my eyes get tired of tears, whichever happens first.

What I still haven't figured out is how to stop my thoughts, how to stop replaying my hours with him over and over. They always seemed too short to me, but today, when each one brings a different torment, it feels like they go on forever. Maybe that's because every time it seems like I'm nearing the end, the memories start all over again, with all the sensations, smells, and sounds that keep tearing me apart inside.

For a ridiculous moment, I compare myself to Ángel, with one scar layered over another like there's no more room for new ones. It's a ridiculous comparison because his wounds could never match mine, especially when I think about how mine could've been avoided. If only I had given up my idea of looking for Daniel that first time, if at some point I had listened to the voice that told me it was "Too good to be true," if I had let my logic, not my heart, make the decisions. But there is no such thing as "what if"; I know that now. I would give anything to be able to kiss him again, to love him again, without it hurting.

Ángel touches my fingertips, and I raise my eyes to him. His brow is furrowed, and his eyes look quite concerned.

"How long was I gone?" I ask amid my tears.

"Almost two hours. Where did you go?"

"You don't know?" I replied, surprised.

"No."

"Daniel took me to the Record of Time."

The Game…Jade

"Daniel?" His surprise continues, and his gaze changes, becoming more intense, though his expression remains neutral, and he keeps questioning.

"What prompted you to go, Jade?"

"To see my father."

"He shouldn't have done that." He says, turning towards the couch. "If they realize he's giving you information..."

"Ángel, let's not talk about him anymore."

His words allow me to remember something I've set aside: gathering information. I've been caught between anguish and, if I decide to continue with my still vaguely defined plan, its resolution won't come for at least a couple of months. Since the pain is already tearing me apart, I figure I might as well try to find out everything I can about what will free me from all this torture.

I slowly get up from the bed and make my way to the bathroom. I wash my face with plenty of water, and, making an effort, I manage to hold back the tears. I know perfectly well that this won't ease the pain I'm feeling, but I refuse to allow the tears to flow endlessly. I won't let myself cry forever; I'll fight it for as long as I can.

Back in my room, I realize I hadn't taken notice of its state before. Daniel's posters are no longer on the walls. Where could they have gone? And when did this happen? I guess Ángel must have thought that having them around wasn't good for me, but honestly, I don't think it made me feel any worse than I already do. The walls now seem huge, dull, empty, lonely. I can't help but smile a little. Poor Ángel, by removing the posters, turned the walls into mirrors reflecting how I feel. I won't let him know that.

I open the closet door and pull out my CD player, placing it on the bed. From inside the drawer, my notebook emerges. Flipping to a blank page, as blank as my mind, which has no clue what to do, I gather Daniel's collection of albums and place them on the nightstand. I make sure to line them up in order of release, just to organize them somehow. Honestly, I don't know how I should listen to them; I'm hoping the information will somehow stand out, highlighted, or something, so I can identify it. Ángel watches me closely, probably wondering if I can handle the task I've set for myself.

"I guess it would be pointless to ask you to postpone this for another time, wouldn't it?" He asks in a low voice.

"And I guess this isn't exactly a life-threatening danger to me, right?"

"Jade..." I hear a hint of desperation in his voice.

Rocío Blisswealth

"So, you guess right. Any idea where to start or how to do it?" I think I know what he'll say, but it doesn't hurt to try.

"The instructions were crafted specifically for you and only you. So, if you're unable to comprehend them, nobody else will."

"Well, well! Thanks. So, it means, if I want to figure out the combination to get out of this vault, they've so kindly locked me in, no one can help me."

"Nobody."

"Got it."

With more determination than I thought I had, I grab the first CD and slot it into the player. Without a second thought, I press the Play button. This time, I refuse to let the pain confuse my thoughts. It'll always be there, anyway, if I don't uncover the hidden information right in front of me. So, I'll set it aside and study intensely.

Obviously, I never thought this task would be a piece of cake, but I figured the challenge would come from different areas. So, for the last hours, I've been listening—paying full attention, I must say—to every single one of Daniel's songs I've got. If things weren't so messed up, it'd be totally ridiculous. I locked myself in my room to block out any interruptions and let Daniel's voice flood the walls, the furniture, my entire mind, and even my subconsciousness. And then, I faced a series of challenges I hadn't seen coming.

First off, every song brings back memories that, even though they were the happiest moments of my life, now feel like the complete opposite given the current situation. So, I had to push them aside, and that was seriously tough. But after sort of dealing with that, even if only halfway, I hit another obstacle. I've listened to these songs so many times that I know them by heart. I can't seem to extract any information from them that would seem different from what they've always meant to me: just Daniel's thoughts with music playing in the background.

That's the really tough part. I never thought that after overcoming those obstacles, I'd have to listen to them as if I'd never heard them before. But I just can't seem to manage it, not even by accident, and what's worse, I don't see how I'm going to be able to.

One thing I have going for me: I haven't cried. I managed to keep it together, a small achievement, I know, but it's something. It's been tough. That was another thing I had to do while having to withstand the torture of listening to his voice for so long, and yet, it feels like it's all been for nothing. I'm lost.

I get up from the floor where I was sitting, maybe trying weakly to keep this whirlwind of emotions from pulling me under, and I walk impatiently across the room.

"Nothing?" Ángel asks far too calmly for my taste.

"Isn't it obvious?"

"It's interesting. I've been by your side for days, attempting to protect you from the most intense demon attack I've ever encountered. You've witnessed things few humans have. You possess knowledge that eludes others, and you even engage in constant conversation with me, fully aware of who I am and the fact that you're the only one who can see me. Yet, despite all this, you persist in approaching things in a purely human manner."

"Sorry! It's the only way I know."

"Oh, and have you ever mastered it?"

"Never, but..."

"And isn't it about time you learned something you can truly master?"

"How, Ángel? Be more specific, please."

"You know I can't do that." He shakes his head.

"I know, I know, just go as far as you can, okay?"

"All that surrounds you, it's not the entirety of existence. Your reality, at least, extends beyond this, but your eyes are limited in what they can perceive." His words bring me back to a time when I saw one of the most terrifying things ever: my demon inside my mom. What's coming might hurt just as bad, but it will only be for a while. My plan is moving forward; just a little more to go.

I sit back down, press the Play button again, and repeat Ángel's words.

"Let my spirit see what is invisible to my eyes." I close my eyes.

All of a sudden, I'm no longer lying on the floor; in fact, I'm not even in my room. It's tough to focus my sight; the place I've ended up in is very dark. What I'm scared of is that I've ended up at Daniel's house. I couldn't bear to see him again or come face to face with the demon hiding under his skin. The time will come to see him, but I'm not ready yet. I turn my head slowly and manage to see one of the walls closest to me; the texture is rough, like stone, as if this place were some kind of cave. I touch it with my fingertips, realizing it's not just stone; it's damp. Where am I?

Rocío Blisswealth

Shortly after, I can sense someone else's breathing here, too. Even though I can't see a thing and the lighting is barely there, I manage to keep my fear in check. After all, I'm already here, so I might as well make something happen. I look straight ahead and spot the dim light streaming in from a tiny window in the door, just a couple of feet in front of me. A shadow moves along the hallway, sometimes blocking the light, and I can't see much else. But I've got nothing else going on, so I might as well wait.

I don't have to wait long before I start hearing voices coming down the hallway. There are two people, both guys, one of them I've never heard of before, but the other, no doubt about it, is Daniel. It had to be him. The door swings open with a loud creak of rusty hinges; it is obvious it doesn't get used much. Light floods in, revealing the small cell before me. It's kind of like the ones you see on TV in the movie "The Count of Monte Cristo." And now, I can see the person breathing nearby.

Sitting on a wooden chair with no cushions is a girl about my age with long brown hair nearly reaching her waist. I don't know why, maybe it's the whole vibe of this place, but for a moment, my mind was picturing her in some vintage outfit. Turns out, she's just wearing blue jeans, a black long-sleeve shirt, and black shoes.

On her right ankle, there's this gold bracelet with lines that seem to burn, crossing each other like some weird letters. I can't make out what they say except for one word at the end: "Jade." The darn bracelet left thick scars where it touched her skin. What the heck do I have to do with her?

Without flinching at my presence, she calmly looks at me and whispers just before Daniel and his partner walk in.

"Pay attention and keep quiet."

Daniel doesn't look like how he does now; this scene took place years ago, back when I first met him. I can clearly spot the differences in his appearance. He walks in and settles on the floor, pretty close to the chair and me, even though he can't see me. I knew it; this was going to be tough. She watches him with no expression in her eyes, nothing. Daniel starts talking to her.

"I'm not quite sure how this works; they've informed me that you're the muse who'll be dictating the songs for the next album." His voice shakes, a clear sign that the situation's getting to him, but honestly, I think she's the one who should be scared, not him. She just nods and looks at him intently.

The Game...Jade

"Don't you know anything else?"

"Not really."

"I'll tell you what you need to know." For a split second, she looks at me, so it's clear I'm the one who needs to know it; got it. "My obligation isn't towards you; it's towards Jade. I must provide her with the necessary information so that, if she ever decides, she can break free from her chains. Therefore, you cannot interfere in the slightest with the texts I'm about to dictate to you, nor alter them in any way, because I must warn you, if you do, the truth will emerge even clearer to her, and no one can stop it.

If they don't want her to find out the information, it won't be because I'm hiding it; it doesn't work that way. You also can't suggest the approach or the theme of the songs; all I do is infuse the texts with Jade's feelings, love, joy, heartbreak, pain, betrayal. Whatever she's feeling will be reflected in them. If she's going through a happy phase, the album will be like that; if her mood is somber, it will reflect that, understand?"

"Yes." Daniel answers without looking her in the eye.

"All the songs I dictate to you will be hits because she's destined for that, but I want it to be very clear to you: your successes have nothing to do with you. Any questions?"

"Will all the songs contain information for Jade?" She continues to stare at him with no expression on her face. Seconds later, she smiles almost imperceptibly and replies.

"Almost all; I've already told you that she's the one feeding the texts. However, this information, in particular, is charged with emotion as if all the words were written in black and white and those specific lines in color. It doesn't matter. You will never be able to see the difference; only Jade can. Therefore, don't waste your time. Just take notes." Underlined! They're underlined, after all. Thank you!

While I've been here, I've listened to every album from when I first met Daniel up until the latest one. It was kind of weird seeing how his appearance, his clothes, and even his mood changed as year after year went by, especially because I was watching everything unfold in just a few hours. Listening to the lyrics sung by the muse made it way easier to get what they were about; it was like hearing them for the first time, and now, I think I understand a little. Every song holds some information, but there are seven in particular where the paragraphs, when pieced together, make up something bigger. I never imagined

Rocío Blisswealth

what those songs held; I thought they might be like some sort of code to undo what they've done to me, but no.

The songs tell my story, from the day I met him to the end. If I'm going to break free from these chains, that'll be another chapter. Here, the information just lays out the story, my story. How to change it? Well, it doesn't mention anything about that, not even if it's possible.

I wait for Daniel to leave the cell, and once back in the darkness, I speak up:

"Thanks."

"Figure it out, Jade. Free yourself from their chains."

"I will, one way or another."

When I got back to my room, it looked like Ángel had been playing the CDs in order while I was gone, probably not to mess with my journey. There's a couple of sandwiches on a plate and a Coke on the nightstand.

"What's this?"

"You haven't eaten in days. Don't worry, no one saw me."

"Thanks."

"Did you find anything?"

"Yes. Let me write them down, and I'll show you, okay?"

"I can wait. Eat."

"Alright." I just nod without saying anything. It's only then that I realize how hungry I am, so I start chowing down on the sandwiches.

Once the hunger I didn't even know I had is satisfied, I grab the notebook and start writing. The first part isn't too hard; I already know which songs they are, and lucky for me, I know them by heart. Now I remember that when my grandma wanted me to memorize something, like my phone number, for example, she'd turn it into a childish rhyme for me to sing until I knew it so well I couldn't forget it even if I tried. Funny thing is, I've changed my number a bunch of times since then, but I still can't forget the one I learned by singing. The same goes for this: I couldn't forget these songs even if I tried.

First, I write them down without worrying about the order, but getting that right will be crucial when piecing the fragments together if I want them to make sense. Before showing my notebook to Ángel, I number the fragments and arrange them in order while the feelings they stir up are still fresh. Now I get why some songs become hits, even if their lyrics don't make sense or, sometimes, if you really listen, they could be awful. They must be loaded with

The Game...Jade

the emotions of someone like me, and that's what people feel when they listen to them, unable to escape the grip of those feelings. For sure, I won't listen to music the same way again; it won't be just for chilling out and having fun, not anymore. Ángel reaches out for the notebook, and I hand it over. He reads it carefully.

The result, when piecing together the fragments from each song, was like this:

I.   Darkness and light, they melded into one gem
And time took its toll to make it shine so right
It became desirable, a dilemma to stem
But who would uncover it, in the end, who might?

But I've been the one
And for her, no one shows mercy
With my love as a guide, I've found her
And now she's my jade... my jade.

II.   You became my maze, always the same, always changing,
In the vice I can't shake, can't break away.
From now on, to share you or to end you,
Choices that'll drive me wild,
Craving to let myself fall off the edge.

III.   The struggle feels endless to me,
To be both your love and your foe,
Learning, fighting, uncovering,
How to become one with you.

IV.   And I believed in my own dream
To be able to shield your fragility
To become your owner... and I ended up
Being a nightmare turned into reality.

V.   How to conquer the terrors that surround me?
How to convince myself this horror is reality?
The demon of your farewell clings to me; it's not out there.

Rocío Blisswealth

It's here inside, next to me, eager for me to die...

VI.   I can't find anyone to take the sacrifice.
Someone who knows me inside and out,
Who shares my mind and takes me back to the start,
Who understands I'm dying without your love?

I included the entire last song, or rather, the muse poured a lot of information into it.

VII.   I'm sorry the day has come
When at last you realize
That everyone, saint and sinner, told lies
And your world's been turned upside down.

I'm sorry the day has come
When waves pound upon you,
When the lifebuoy I would become
Has vanished and you can't find it.

I'd give anything to be there,
To keep you from losing your mind,
But it was your choice, not mine.
It's my fault, I know, from the start.
It was impossible to dream that you would forgive me.

Now you find yourself alone
Facing truth on your own,
Riding high on the crest of the wave
Where the heavy sea shakes you without mercy.
I'm nothing but a shadow
Lost in the darkness
Unable to give you any peace.

Each strike takes a piece of you away
Each pain drains your strength
If only you'd remember that I'm still by your side

The Game…Jade

If you'd remember you can count on me.

Now you're feeling all alone
And can't find your way out
All that's left is to wait
For the nightmare to end...
And maybe, just maybe,
I'll find you in the afterlife.

I'm sorry the day has come,
I'm sorry I'm not there,
I'm sorry I'm not what I promised,
But if you think about it, I am here, always.

Ángel's expression screamed terror louder than anything. The songs tell a story with a beginning and an end. I guess, lucky for me—there had to be a stroke of luck at some point—the story's nearing its end. Now, if I'm not mistaken, I'm riding the wave the song talks about, waiting for the nightmare to end without Daniel, who's become a shadow that doesn't bring an ounce of peace, quite the opposite.

This just confirms my plan is the right one. Feels like there's nothing left, and this pain will finally kill me. But I'll keep pushing forward because there's no turning back. They've got me in their grip, like they do with the muse. It's like a fire burning every time I even think about moving, like taking a breath hurts. I'm determined to get out of there, even if it's the last thing I do. Every time I came face to face with a demon, I only hoped it wouldn't manage to kill me. I didn't want to die while their fierce eyes enjoyed watching me suffer. Now, maybe I'll be the one to give myself up if it means finally bringing this to an end. Ángel keeps on staring at me, waiting, but I've got nothing to say, just a smile. Daniel's energy stirs.

Rocío Blisswealth

Chapter XXIV
A death row last meal

For the first time in almost a month, according to Ángel's count, I can feel my lungs filling up completely. It's probably because the muscles in my chest have loosened up a bit, not entirely, but I'll take what I can get. It's kind of wild to think that it was precisely in this whirlwind of pain that I found some stability in my spirit. Looking back on the past has been helpful, too.

I think as I grew up, I wished for many things, though not all of them hit me with the same intensity; they all fell within the same range. Stuff like wanting a normal life, to stop seeing demons, for my dad to actually love me, for my grandparents not to die, and so on. And when those wishes didn't pan out, I just pushed them aside. That is until this massive, unstoppable desire to meet Daniel came true. That's when I realized that if you really want something, like, truly crave it, it's possible to make it happen. He totally raised the bar for my expectations, and thanks to that, I can recognize that I desire with that same intensity to make my plan a reality.

Like my grandpa always said, "Not worth the powder to blow it to Hell." I've decided to save it all up for one massive explosion. One that's capable of consuming me, to drive me to face off against the demon himself, the one that now stays beneath the skin I still love more than anything else. After what went down with Mom and Mara, it's no surprise I'm feeling this way. Well, I mean, you might think that what Daniel did against me is precisely what got me into this, but trust me, my mom and my sister take the cake when it comes to betrayal levels, don't you think? Daniel didn't even know me when everything was planned. But those two? One grew up with me almost all her life, and the other just brought me into this world.

One of these nights, three or four that I decided to take as a break before diving back into my search for information, I asked Ángel what made them want to share their body with a demon. It's been one of the toughest things for me to wrap my head around. As always, he resisted telling me, but eventually, he opened up. He told me what he knew.

Mom always knew there was something strange about me. During her church-hopping and all sorts of courses, she gathered information, connecting dots with the times I pulled off some miraculous healing, like with my grandma. The day she found herself seriously sick and convinced me to extend her life, she knew for sure. That's when the demons, who were always hanging around the house, figured out her interest in trading some of my energy for something she'd been longing for years: a chance to see my dad again.

That's how it went down for her. As for Mara, honestly, neither Ángel nor I can figure out what she wanted so badly that she'd trade her sister for it. Well, considering how much she always cared about me, I guess she would've swapped me for a pair of socks just for the pleasure of getting rid of me. The thing is, a demon told them the only way to control me was to let one of them into their body since my energy was so intense that they wouldn't make it otherwise, and they went for it.

When Mom found out that I was finally planning to get rid of the demon in my room, she saw it as a godsend: to harbor no less than the demon who knows me best in the whole world. Finally, I understood about the biscuits and lemonade; she didn't know, but my demon did.

As for Mara, they sent one in response to her request, a demon I couldn't banish from the house. I guess they asked for a life in return to make sure her decision was firm, and that's how Mrs. Rosy lost hers. So, they each got their own demon, which, I'm sorry to say to you, won't do them any good. One thing the demons didn't tell them is that once inside them, they couldn't track me without being seen, so their reach had been cut down a lot. They're probably already asking for a bigger demon to see if they can get what they want from me. Sorry to say, if their order isn't delivered promptly, they won't get it anymore.

As you know, my quest for information has filled me in on big chunks of events that shaped my life, like putting together a puzzle. But I want to make sure I have all the pieces and they are in place before I take that final step to what I've set out to do.

My plan, let me tell you now that Ángel isn't watching me for once, is to find Daniel. I mean, the demon who's got him now, and surrender. He'll know what to do, no doubt about it; there's a reason he's where he is. I don't want another demon; I need him precisely because he's known my blood for hundreds of years. Hope the bait, with me dangling from it, is too tempting for him to resist. Ángel will hold me up until the end, I know that, but all this will come to an end. It has to because it's what I want most: to not go on in this life

Rocío Blisswealth

without Daniel, which already in itself tastes like death to me, a long, painful death.

Why am I so determined to piece together this puzzle? I know it's dragging out the agony, but I owe it to my grandparents. I want Ángel to explain to them that there's nothing worth holding back for anymore, nothing at all, period. That way, they'll understand the decision I've made. Their opinion is the only one that still matters to me. I don't think I'm missing many pieces now. Three, if my calculations are right. First off, I want to know who's behind all this, who exactly. I'm done with vague explanations like good and evil or any of that nonsense. I want names, places, faces; I need to put a face to my tormentor.

Second, I need to talk to Daniel, face the awful pain of reaching out to him on my own, and have a real conversation like we used to. I owe him that much for all the happiness he brought into my life despite everything. Whether his actions were intentional or not, I don't care anymore. They happened, and that's more than I ever got from my mom, for instance. And finally, I'll have to search within myself, yes, sit down and have a chat with myself, and decide if the pieces I've gathered up to that point change my mind or not. Once that's done, everything will be laid out, and for the first time, the events of my life will be in my hands.

In these past few days, I've come face to face with Mom and Mara again, both of whom are "genuinely worried" about me. I've made sure they don't catch wind of what I know for two reasons. One, when the time comes to locate the demon inside Daniel, it won't do me any favors if they realize I already know who I'm really talking to; consider it training for that moment. And two, I don't want to start a war that could lead me down paths I haven't chosen. So, I've even put on a sweet act, believe it or not. Gross, right? I know, but it's an attempt to keep my true feelings under wraps, and that's all I've managed to achieve. They've clearly shown immense pity for me over the pain of not seeing Daniel anymore, and they keep saying everything will pass. Of course, it will! Because this time, I'll make sure it does.

One perk of this situation is that they've made sure I'm well-fed. I've been able to taste all the dishes my grandma used to make, my favorites. Apparently, even though I never paid much attention, my demon, on the other hand, always kept track of the ingredients in her cooking. And while they taste like a death row last meal, I admit I'd rather savor my grandma's seasoning than the sandwiches Ángel's been diligently preparing for me.

Another thing I found out is that Mara tracked down her ex-husband and decided to send my niece and nephews off to spend some time with him. At first, I thought it was a terrible idea; I'd rather have them here where I could protect them. But I ended up accepting that it's much better for them to be with their dad for a while. He loves them and will keep them safe from the demon Mara has become. Plus, it gives me time to figure things out without worrying about anyone else. The little one even asked for permission to take Tíber with her. Poor thing, he did nothing but howl every time one of them came near him. So, not only did I give my blessing, I practically begged her to take him. One less thing for me to worry about.

"Ángel, tell me something. You know who's behind all of this, don't you?" I ask from my spot on the bed.

"Yes."

"Are they the same ones chasing after all of us?"

"No, these are distinct factions. Knowledge of how to attain their blessings has been passed down through word of mouth, and those who discover them first…"

"Claim the prey."

"Something like that."

"Is there a way for me to see them without them knowing?"

He sits on the bed beside me and looks at me, then down at the floor. He shakes his head slightly in denial and falls silent. A few moments later, he whispers:

"Yes."

"That's another bitter pill to swallow, huh?"

"They all are, yet this one… I don't know how you might perceive it should you encounter them, and I know, no matter my words, I won't be able to stop you."

"So, how do I do it?"

"Now?"

"Why wait, Ángel? Yes, now."

He looks toward the couch, toward Daniel. He must know where I'm headed. I smile faintly.

"What's going on?"

Rocío Blisswealth

"You'll need to heed your essence, your energy, and Daniel's. He's been there too, so it'll be safer."

Of course! They're the ones who hired Daniel to get close to me. He knows them; he's been with them.

"Even easier, I know that one well." I lie back and close my eyes, breathing slowly until my essence and Daniel's materialize before me, like a weird blend of colors forming an orange line, easy to track. I push aside the pain of being enveloped in Daniel's essence and let myself go, eager this time, fueled by curiosity.

I should've figured it out: a mansion. I'm not exactly sure where I am, but it doesn't feel like México. The plants around here are very different, more like a forest, a weird, damp forest with huge oak trees. There's a lake, no, a narrow river circling the house grounds forming a ring around it, and the gardens are seriously incredible, stunning. When I finally reach the house, I slow my pace; I don't want to miss any detail that could come in handy.

Everything, absolutely everything I lay eyes on screams luxury. Art pieces are scattered all over the place; it seems like there's hardly any room left for them because, in some places, they're too close to each other. Maybe I'm just used to museums—the only reference I have of another place to admire such beauties—where they carefully display each piece. Here it's a mishmash of objects, paintings, sculptures, and other things that I can't even name, all jumbled up without any regard for where they're from or when they were made. And yes, some of them are antique, older than anything I've ever seen.

So far, I haven't come across anyone, so I keep walking. As I'm wandering around, I reach some stairs that lead down to what seems like a basement and follow them. I don't entirely like the idea, but then figure I better check it out; you never know if it could be useful. Once I'm down there, I'm struck by a strange feeling that I've been here before. This area is totally different from anywhere I've been before. It's dark, with this intense musty smell that hits you in the nose, and there's hardly any light. I start walking down this long hallway lit only by lamps on the walls on both sides.

Now I remember, yes, I've been here before. This is where I made the swap with Daniel, where they brought me to meet him inside one of these cells. Funny how I forgot about that; I'll add it to my list of pieces to find. I recognize the heavy doors with rusty hinges. There are loads of doors in front of me, including the one I pushed open to see Daniel. Two doors down, the muse's

The Game...Jade

door. I've been here, and not just once, but twice. I peek through the next door's window and can't see a thing, but I hear someone breathing. Every cell's got a prisoner.

Since I can't do anything to get them out of there, I turn around and retrace my steps until I come across the staircase again and climb it up. Once upstairs, I see a man in a dark suit and decide to follow him. He's moving fast, so I pick up the pace to catch up. He heads into the garden, where he meets a man who, from the way he addresses him with diligence and respect, seems to be the boss around here. This must be one of the guys hunting me down.

He's extremely good-looking, like seriously. If I'm guessing right, he's around forty, not older. I'm not sure why I thought they'd be older. His skin is really pale, and despite his hair being mostly gray, it's still shiny, silky, and styled perfectly. Overall, he's got this neat and tidy look, of course, which is probably easy to maintain with all the cash flowing around here. He's tall, maybe even taller than Daniel, and even though he's lean, his body looks sculpted. The clothes he's wearing, in shades of brown and sand, look amazing on him. His face is all sharp angles, with a straight and kind of prominent nose, like my grandpa's. He's got bushy eyebrows, and his big, almond-shaped, honey-colored eyes are strangely sweet.

I wasn't expecting that at all. I'm supposed to be his victim, his prey, and it's hard for me to reconcile his appearance with the feeling I thought it would draw out of me. He's so attractive that I find it difficult to feel contempt for him. He looks like a model or a TV heartthrob, although, to be honest, I've never seen one as attractive. I guess contempt is what I should feel, or at least fear, but I'm not feeling anything close to that.

The words from the guy, who I now get is one of his servants, grab my attention. Sara is looking for him because she wants to talk to him. Is it the same Sara? Come on, Jade, stop being silly! Of course, it must be the same Sara. I have to see this.

He walks gracefully to another area of the house, a cozy living room with two plush, pastel-colored couches where blue is the dominant hue and a tiny table in the middle for tea. Sunlight streams in through the huge window behind him, slightly dimmed by the thick foliage of the plants surrounding it. Without bothering with the formalities of politeness, at least mine, he takes a seat before Sara even shows up, and when he sees her, he just nods, doesn't greet her, or stands up. Alright, got it, she's another servant, and yes, she's the Sara I was expecting.

"*Good morning, Sara.*" Gods! What a voice he has, deep, soft as if he's caressing with it.

"Good morning, sir. You look remarkably refreshed; you appear very well."

"*Thanks to what you did with Daniel, the energy supply is coming regularly and in precise amounts. These are the results.*" What you did with Daniel. What did you do with Daniel?! How did that...? I have to focus on what's right in front of me. Concentrate.

"Is there any news about Jade?" She asks with a hint of doubt in her voice, as if she's not sure if she has the right to ask or not.

He raises an eyebrow. I guess he sees it as somewhat audacious, but he still responds.

"*She suffers too much for my taste. I don't want to think that could lead to a death we would all regret too much. Things definitely haven't gone the way we would have liked. However, we are in the process of fixing it.*"

"Would it be too bold of me to ask how?" He gives a slight smile, answering once again. I think she caught him in a good mood.

"*She refuses to live without Daniel. I hope she looks for him sooner or later. No, actually, I would prefer it to be sooner.*"

"But now it's the demon who occupies that body." Sara's voice trembles with anguish. Why? I doubt she cares what might happen to me.

"*They both occupy him, Sara. Daniel is still there; the demon has taken great care not to take away the vital space his spirit needs to remain tied to the body. It's not in our interest for him to die for now. We need him to be the one Jade perceives the day she decides to approach.*"

"According to Daniel, she's highly perceptive. What makes you think she won't realize it's not just Daniel living beneath that skin?"

"*I always remind myself not to underestimate that girl. However, Sara, let me remind you that we shouldn't overestimate her either. She's a human being, remember?*" His words come out harshly, clearly not pleased with Sara bringing up something that could be a terrible mistake for them, being too confident, which indeed it is. I already know the demon is there, and my whole plan is based on that fact. For the first time in a long time, I can feel a deep sense that I will achieve what I set out to do, finally breaking free from the

The Game...Jade

chains holding this body, much like the ones in the cells, as long as they don't catch on to what I know.

"It's just that I thought I could have him for myself." Now I get it; she wants to keep Daniel, and as long as he's with me, she can't.

He watches her carefully, as if analyzing her, and responds with a subtly authoritative yet extremely clear tone.

"*Sara, my words were, if I remember correctly, that you could stay with Daniel when Jade left him. She asked him, in every tone, to leave; however, he doesn't respect her decision and stays there.*" He smiles cynically and watches Sara's reaction shift from surprise to anger, then back to the emotionless facade she's worn, flawed as it may be since she arrived. He keeps talking.

"*There's not much we can do about it. We must respect free will. However, I doubt she'll take long to make a decision, although...*" He smiles more widely. "*If she decides to stay with him, demon and all, you'll have to find someone else to ease your loneliness. She is the most important thing, and if that makes her happy, so be it. Agreed?*"

"Of course." She manages to say, with a tone that's overly forced.

"*Now, tell me, who did you bring today?*"

"Víctor Arredondo and two other singers will be joining me. I was contemplating taking them to the Elements Vault. Is that alright?"

"*Of course! The energy today is of optimal quality; it will do them a lot of good.*"

"And what about the muse? Could Víctor stop by to see her? He needs to begin recording the new album within three months at the latest."

"*No problem, I'll arrange everything, come with me.*"

Both are making their way towards the entrance hall of the house, and of course, I'm following closely behind. Víctor Arredondo and two other young folks, whom I've seen on TV as rising stars, are there. They approached with the utmost respect to greet the man, and I could see they were already talking with another one of the bosses. They're incredibly alike, not like they're twins or anything. It's, I don't know, like they've been cast to play the same role in a movie. Their height, skin tone, hair color, complexion, and even their clothing style; it's all so similar. Only their faces differ, though not too much. Maybe they're brothers. I could tell them apart perfectly, but if I saw them from afar, it probably wouldn't be so easy.

There's a kind of mimicry between them, too; their gestures and their movements are very similar. And the way they briefly lock eyes for a fraction of a second. I know they're saying something to each other as if they could read each other's thoughts. Another person joins the gathering. It's incredible. Where did they find them? But I doubt it's the result of plastic surgery. This one's face, however, isn't as angular as the other two, and his eyes, if anything, stand out more, completely lacking in sweetness. His gaze is more cynical, making him stand out even more.

I watch the young visitors closely. Despite their smiles, they're terrified. That's what I should be feeling, I know, and yet, they're so easy on the eyes that I struggle to focus on the fact that they're my biggest enemies, the ones responsible for all my troubles.

The group heads towards some magnificent wooden doors with gold accents. It must be real gold; they wouldn't settle for anything less. As we make our way, I can see that the splendor of this hall surpasses that of the rest of the house, and that's saying quite a lot. It's then that I realize all the visitors are barefoot. Why is that? The hosts are about to do the same. Before stepping into the hall, they stop and remove their shoes, which the servants immediately collect and place on racks on the wall, arranged for that purpose. It must be something they do often.

We enter the hall, and another one of them is waiting, seated in an armchair that looks more like a throne. There are four more of these, so I figure there's one more of them left for me to meet or rather to see. The armchairs are just stunning, spacious, heavy, and made of smooth wood with high backs. Carved perfectly into the wood on the backrest is a plant. Each one has a different plant, and honestly, I don't recognize any of them, especially since the name of the plant is carved next to it, but it's in Latin or something; you can imagine I don't understand a thing.

Each of the hosts takes a seat, heading straight for their throne, so I guess the plant must be directly related to them, while the rest of the people stay standing in the center of the hall. I focus on the floor; it's extraordinary, and the tiles form perfect patterns. If I'm not mistaken, they represent air, earth, metal, and fire. I can't see all of them, but I guess water must be represented, too.

No. Now I realize they've dipped their feet into it; the tiles are covered with water, so clear and calm, I hadn't even noticed it. However, it's not very deep, just covering their feet up to their ankles, which explains why they all

The Game...Jade

enter here barefoot, although my doubt persists. What are they doing? I don't get it. It must be some kind of ritual; one I've never heard of.

The truth is, I don't understand anything I see, but I have no doubt that these people are the ones who are taking advantage of my gifts. To what end? Visitors, to gain fame or other things, I know that. I mean, these guys, the usual residents of this mansion, don't seem to need me to gain fame or money. In fact, I hardly think that kind of thing interests them.

Obviously, there's a part of this image that I'm missing, the most important part, since I'm captivated by the beauty of this place and its people that I can't see beyond what meets the eye. Fortunately, I know what I have to do, but it does scare me. Every time I've used that phrase, the results are terrible. Sometimes it's better to keep the blindfold on; ignorance is bliss, but that option is no longer available to me. I'm here to find out everything, so without overthinking it, I close my eyes and say:

"Let my spirit see what's invisible to my eyes." I open my eyes slowly, and in front of me, the young singers, including Víctor, remain unchanged. I stare at their figures from head to toe, but that's where things start to shift. The water has turned murky, and it's changing color; it's turning red, getting darker by the second. On top of that, small swirls are starting to form, and it's even bubbling slowly like it's about to boil. The whole scene's starting to become increasingly nauseating, and no one around seems to be noticing.

Struggling to tear my gaze away from the captivating image, I finally look up at the hosts. My stomach releases a burst of air as I can't help but be surprised by the change they've undergone. Each of them has spread a pair of wings on their back, massive, glossy, and stunning. Some have black wings, while others have white. Their faces remain mostly the same, except for their eyes, now white and iris-less, completely sightless, and terrifying.

Their arms still rest on the armchairs, but their legs are shaking gently. I trace their contours down to their feet, preferring that to look into their eyes. No, it's not true; this image is even worse. Their pants are lifted slightly, exposing part of their calves, showing their skin and allowing me to see how their veins have widened to an extreme degree, pulsating and expanding like leeches near their ankles. I notice small holes in their skin where they absorb the water, channeling it towards the rest of their bodies. I believe I'm witnessing the feeding process of a repulsive, terrifying Fallen Angel.

Rocío Blisswealth

I don't want to see it anymore. I want to get out of here, and yet, I can't move at all. It's as if I have shackles holding me by the ankles. Fear starts to overwhelm me as I fail to break free from here. I turn to my feet, searching for shackles or whatever holds me, and I see my body, my hands first, then my arms. They're covered in gaping wounds, as if invisible claws are holding the skin, preventing them from closing, and blood streams down my body, creating whirlpools in the water.

I try to hold back a scream stuck in my throat, making it hard to breathe. I desperately try to close the wounds, covering them with my hands, but as soon as I close one, an even larger one opens. Terror tightens my lungs, and my throat closes tighter with every passing second. Stop that! Stop doing that! It's the only thing my brain screams, but I can't manage to say a word. The doors open again, revealing the fifth host, the one I hadn't yet met. He takes a few steps, spreading his wings as if filled with great joy at what lies before him; he's just like the others, though not quite, more jovial.

"*Why did you start without me?*" He says amidst creepy laughter, and my heart jumps in my chest. Someone make him stop, please! Make it all stop right now! I can't handle it anymore.

I can't even breathe; I don't want to witness any more of this horror. Nausea churns in my stomach, and each breath feels like a sharp whistle in my lungs. They're feeding off me. I collapse into what used to be crystal-clear water, now tainted with my blood. I want to cry and scream at the same time. I want to die after what I've seen. I close my eyes, but their images continue to haunt me behind my eyelids. But I won't give in. I refuse to open them again. I won't subject myself to any more horror in this nightmare.

Again, I sense the heaviness in my body, the ringing in my ears. I half-open my eyes through tears and see the walls of my room. The urge to run hasn't faded, and I awkwardly hurl myself to the edge of the bed, landing painfully on my knees. On all fours, I crawl desperately, searching for any way out. Sobs choke my throat, blending with my screams, all desperate to break free.

Arms wrap around my waist, holding me tight. The urge to break free still rages within me, and my screams become more desperate, turning into desperate growls. I can't move forward; their grip is unreal. Finally, I give in, letting myself collapse sideways onto the ground. Ángel turns me to help me breathe easier, holding me in his arms. My vision, blurry until now, finally focuses on his gentle face. I release all the fight I had left and slump into his arms, seeing only him. I'd never seen tears in his eyes until today. He strokes my cheek, but I can't react. I try, but the strength has left me somewhere.

"Breathe, Jade, just keep breathing. Please, just do it." A terrifying image fills my mind, and then I blurt it out.

"They're... feeding... off me." The memory triggers the scream that my throat suppressed earlier, and I throw my head back to let it out. My back arches as if the weight of my head is too much to bear, the scream trying to burst out through my chest instead of my mouth. When it finally escapes, I cry uncontrollably.

Daniel, visible again, kneels next to us and takes my hand. His touch sends searing pain down my spine, but I hold on to him tightly, nonetheless. Ángel notices, and I can tell he's about to ask Daniel to let go, to disappear and leave me alone. But when he sees my white-knuckled grip on Daniel's hand, he says nothing, simply continues to stroke me gently, and begs me to keep breathing, not to give up.

The pain Daniel's causing is brutal, but I'd rather deal with that pain than the one I thought would finish me off just a few days ago. At least now, it helps me forget, kind of, about what I just witnessed... They're feeding off me.

Chapter XXV
Crying over spilled milk won't help

After a couple of hours, I was finally able to let go of Daniel's hand, and he retreated to his couch, fading from view as if he'd never been there. It seems like I've spent my whole life only seeing a fraction of what's around me as if, all this time, I'd been peeking through a keyhole. Until recently, that door was always locked, or maybe I just never tried opening it before.

Because of everything that's happened to me, I'm starting to believe more in my theory that people who can see the stuff I've seen are locked away somewhere, which honestly sounds like a relief. I can imagine having someone by my side, a doctor, a nurse, anyone, constantly telling me that everything I've seen is just my wild imagination, that none of those monsters are real. Trust me, I'd fight with all my might to let myself be convinced and just slip into the blissful ignorance most people live in. That'd be so sweet.

How many others out there are going through the same thing as me? I mean, I've been told the production is seven people every seven years, but how many of them have survived? How many have a guardian angel keeping them alive against all odds? How many have never realized that demons exist, even living normal lives without knowing? Man, I'm jealous! I think I would have liked to have a life like that.

But here I am, still stuck in bed, not even trying to get up; well, I have no reason to. I'm trying to figure out what I'm feeling, to put words to all these sensations flooding through me from head to toe. All I know until now is they're all seriously unpleasant. On top of that, I'm too aware of my body, as if I can feel every tiny part of it. I don't know if it's because of the pain, the anxiety, or if what I'm imagining is actually true.

If my blood really turned into acid, burning through my cells as it flowed, maybe that'd explain this agony. And if it's true, that'd be awesome. I'd love to see those damned creatures feeding on acid instead of blood, see if they're enjoying it as much as they were earlier.

Ángel has gone quiet for the first time since this whole thing started. After every bitter sip, the last thing he does is shut up. Instead, he spends hours trying to convince me that this life's worth living. But he's getting nowhere; my search is completely focused in the opposite direction. I'm gathering the pieces needed to confirm that it's not worth it, and I'm succeeding beyond measure.

Honestly, I didn't need this much. I never imagined that all the evidence I found would be too much for me. Yet here I am, obviously, thanks to Ángel who, for some reason I don't know, won't let me go. How many more horrors does he want me to uncover? Maybe he thinks if I've been through this and he keeps me alive, I'll finally think that I can just keep on living forever. That's not happening, but I don't bother telling him anymore; it wouldn't make sense to do so. He's not going to change his mind, and neither am I.

Inside my head, I keep replaying the scenes I saw, getting clearer each time. Sometimes, I focus on those terrifying, empty-eyed faces; other times, on the beauty of their figures with their gorgeous wings, but mostly, on the disgusting way those who used to be angels feed. I don't even try to stop the flood of images in my brain anymore; I know it wouldn't work. If I couldn't do it when they were softer, I sure won't, now that they're the most horrifying things I've ever seen. I don't fight it; I just keep going over them again and again, but now the screams only echo inside my head. I don't let them out into the real world anymore. They don't help me, and it could scare anyone; well, maybe the neighbors.

I have to admit that, despite everything I'm telling you, deep down I still hear it, faint but clear, the voice urging me to keep going, the one that repeats that this life isn't worth it and that it would take more courage to live it than to leave it.

My eyes wander over the walls, and now I notice Ángel isn't just quiet; he's holding my hand, but he's not looking at me. It's been a while since he looked at me. That's another weird thing about him; he always seeks out my eyes.

"Ángel."

"Yes?" He responds, his eyes fixed on the floor.

"Why won't you look at me?"

"I don't want to frighten you." This is weird. He's got my attention if that's what he was going for, and I'm taking the bait. I want to know what he's thinking. I sit up on the bed, leaning back against the headboard, but he stays the same, still looking at the floor.

"Scare me? Why?"

Rocío Blisswealth

"Jade, the beings you saw feeding, they were, and still are, in a manner of speaking, my brothers." I hadn't thought about it. Must be tough for him, too, dealing with people he knows so well, maybe even too well.

"I hadn't realized, but I still don't get it. Ángel, please, look at me." He turns his head partially, clearly worried about scaring me.

"I thought the similarity between us might bring back your memories more vividly, and you wouldn't want me by your side. Right now, I don't want to leave."

"It's true." I study him. "You kind of look like their son, a lot, but younger. You seem, like, twenty-five? While they look like they're in their forties, give or take." A shiver runs down my spine as I remember them.

"I remain as I was created; they, however, age. Not like you, but they do."

"Ángel, I couldn't compare you to them. To me, you are very different. Besides what you just pointed out, there's no resemblance between you and them, and I don't want you to leave. Remember, till the end?"

"How could I forget? You made me promise. I suppose now, with the hatred beginning to grow within you, it will be easier for you to achieve your goal."

Hate? Definitely! Amidst all these feelings overwhelming me, there's hate. They really got under my skin. I hadn't realized, amidst all the emotions, that one of them—one that could be very useful—is hate. A thousand times better than anger. Now I can feel it, sharp, boiling, strong, wonderful.

"I hadn't noticed."

"The hatred? How is that possible? I simply sensed it when I took your hand. It's very potent."

"Well, I still haven't figured out all that I'm feeling, but thanks. It helps."

"Jade, could you take a break from your search?"

"What for, Ángel?"

"I almost lost you. I'd like for you to regain some strength to... Actually, I'm not sure what your plans are now."

"The kind of strength you get from an energy drink or from a trip to Cancún? Which one are you talking about?" I smile; it's kind of funny to realize I can still do that.

The Game...Jade

"Well, you have the energy to mock me now. It's not a joke, Jade, I nearly... I mean emotional strength, and I still haven't figured it out."

"What thing?" I ask, even though I know exactly what he means.

"What do you plan to do now? Will you tell me?"

"To talk to Daniel." I say, almost whispering. It's hard for me to even think about it. He turns to face the couch this time, not bothering to hide his movement from me.

"For what purpose?" He asks very seriously.

"I need to know."

"This is suicidal. You know that, don't you?" I don't answer; I just look him straight in the eyes. "I don't know why I'm asking you."

"Ángel, I need to know. No one's ever bothered to give me any kind of information. Now, I've had to figure it all out at once. I don't have time for little doses or vacations anymore."

"I know; they should have given you the information when you were fourteen in another way. But back then, they took you from here and brought you to Ensenada. They didn't find you where you were supposed to be; they were constantly watching you, and we know how the rest happened."

"Crying over spilled milk won't help."

"Your grandmother used to say that phrase; you have a lot of her in you."

"I hope to have much more than learned phrases. I'll need it."

"There's a lot of them in you, I know for certain. If you believe you need it, trust me, it's there."

"Thank you."

"When will you talk to Daniel?"

"Tomorrow."

"I thought you'd tell me why wait." He smiles softly.

"I'm out of tears for today, and I think I'm going to need some, at least, besides a good night's sleep. Could you help me with that?"

"I can."

"No nightmares, no images of any kind."

"I don't normally enter your mind, except in very rare exceptions, but I can try."

"Enough."

I lie on my side, and Ángel moves behind me, lying down next to me like when I was a kid. As soon as he hugs me, I can feel tranquility enveloping me. This time, it's not quite peaceful, but I'm okay with that.

"One more favor." I don't want to push my luck by asking for too much, and saying it quietly makes it feel... I don't know, less demanding.

"Which one?"

"Could I, at least for today, see you?"

"Jade, I don't think that..."

"Please, just for today." My request turns into a plea. Today, more than ever, I need to convince myself that an angel is with me.

"Are you sure?"

"No, but yes."

"Mhm, alright. I hope so."

I hear a sound, like a sharp thud, and I turn slowly towards him. First out of the corner of my eye, then with my eyes wide open to their fullest, but I'm not looking for his eyes anymore; my gaze goes upwards. He's spread his wings, one of them above us, about half a meter above our bodies. Huge, white as freshly fallen snow, made up of thousands or millions of feathers, beautiful.

"Wow." I say with a sigh.

"It's not a scream of terror; we're fine, I suppose." He says, smiling.

"Can I?" I ask, bringing my fingertips closer to it. He brings it closer to me, covering me like a blanket, silky! There's no better word to describe it. I forget, if only for a few minutes, the images from this afternoon; now I can sleep.

The light filters through the curtains as I open my eyes. Thank you, thank you. It must have been more than eight hours, and yes, the sleep was deep, like I'd been knocked out by some sleeping pill. I disconnected, and now my body feels more refreshed. Morally, well, that would be asking too much, but I guess I'm managing to keep my head above water. Each blow drags me down deeper, but since I'm not trying to come up for air, I'm just getting used to this new state and trying to carry on from there.

I get up to open the curtains and see people walking along the sidewalk in front of my house. It's like the world operates backward for me. What I see through my windows is fiction, that normalcy that's impossible to exist, while my real life is what would be a horror movie for everyone else. I'm watching

The Game...Jade

the lives of regular people and thinking, "That's not real! People with simple lives are just a fantasy!"

Sometimes, I think maybe I would've liked to be like them, even if I wouldn't have noticed it. But as I brace myself for what today holds, I wonder, if I could turn back time, would I risk living a life where Daniel never existed? I don't know. Even after all this pain, I still don't know.

Ángel is sitting on the bed, keeping an eye on me. If he could interfere, what would he be capable of doing? I'd love to know. Sometimes, it frustrates me how strictly he follows the rules. Then again, maybe not entirely, because he's not willing to respect my decision and let me go. He hasn't respected my free will in that.

I have questions for him before I ask him to leave me alone with Daniel. I look him in the eyes, and I notice his shoulders tense up. In moments like these, he seems so human. I've never had the chance to watch him this closely before, but these days, I've learned a thing or two.

"Ángel."

"Yes?"

"Before I talk to Daniel, there's something I need to know."

"What is it, Jade?"

"Why did the Creator ask me to stop seeing him?"

"Jade, things..." Before he could finish, I cut him off.

"I'm not talking about what I already know. I want to know if there's any other reason behind it."

He looks me in the eye, and his gaze is soft, but he shifts it to the window as he responds.

"I believe at times you've let yourself be swayed by what you see, or what you hear, without considering what you feel, or what you already know. Consider it carefully: do you truly need to ask me that?"

I take a seat, bracing myself for what's coming. As I said before, I've learned to spot when Ángel's tensed up, and right now, he is, big time. I try to think, but I can't wrap my head around it. Honestly, I don't want to bother trying to figure it out; I'd rather he just tell me straight up.

"Why do you say that?" Without taking his eyes off the window, he continues.

"You're familiar with the concept of free will. You exercised it to ensure I respected your decision regarding this matter, and yet you still ask me?"

"Yes, even so, I'm asking you. My brain's been busy with something else. Please, Ángel."

"If the Creator had given you such a command, or even suggested you stop seeing him, it would have infringed upon your free will, overlooked one of the laws that weigh most heavily upon us: the non-intervention in your life." I don't need to ask him, but still, I want to hear it from his lips, no doubt about it.

"So?" Finally, he looks at me, and annoyed, he answers.

"No. He never said anything about it; it was a deception."

An ice block lodges in my stomach, or maybe I just froze solid because my brain can't process Ángel's crystal clear words. I don't want to understand them. I had another choice, and I didn't know it. Maybe I wouldn't have taken it, but now, I'll never know.

They played dirty; that was the final blow, just when I thought I was beginning to sink. I don't move; I don't yell; I don't even complain. I just let the anger grow inside me; I kind of enjoy the buzz it gives me; it's energizing. Without breaking eye contact with Ángel, a thousand thoughts race through my head about what I could've done differently, but they just pass; I've decided not to pay them any attention. I won't let the thirst for revenge, now bubbling up inside me, sidetrack me from my purpose, from the entirety of it. Now more than ever, I want a win that's all or nothing. They want my energy, right? If my only win, if my ultimate triumph, means completely put it out of their reach, then that's exactly what I'll do. Once again, the "what ifs" don't exist.

Ángel watches me closely. I guess he expected a more explosive reaction, and truthfully, I would've, too, given the circumstances. But it isn't happening. However, this information changes things. It gives me a fresh angle on the extent of free will. Now I know they won't interfere; they're forbidden to do so. And I can also see that Ángel, contrary to what I thought, has been stretching the rules like elastic bands, letting himself get away with everything he's done for me in the last month. Would knowing this earlier have made me change my mind about Daniel? I don't know anymore. After taking hit after hit these past few days, I'm not too sure about anything.

Chapter XXVI
Too much truth

"Are you alright?" Ángel finally asks.

"No, but I'm here. That's something, right?"

"Jade…"

"We keep going."

"I suspected as much." He says, with a hint of annoyance.

"Now, I want to see Daniel. Could you…?"

"No, I won't leave you alone under any circumstances. Not now, I'm sorry." Before he finishes the sentence, Daniel is already standing in front of me.

"If you're looking to have a private chat with me, don't worry." Without parting his lips, he says. "He won't be able to overhear us."

Wow! One surprise after another. My knees are shaking. Daniel still represents to me the most painful loss I've ever faced, and that pain, in particular, is sharp and intense, more than any other. I take a step back, searching for the bed. Once my calf hits it, without taking my eyes off him, I bend over, place my right hand on the mattress, and collapse. Ángel looks at us surprised, sensing something's up. He tries to get closer, but I gesture for him to stay back.

"What is happening, Jade?" He asks, his voice filled with anguish.

"I have no way of forcing you to leave me alone with him. I don't even know if there's a way to do it, but don't worry, I'm not going to try. Do you want to stay? Fine! Just don't interrupt."

"Jade, you don't have to face this alone. Allow me to..."

"I'm sorry, Ángel. You can't interfere in this, and I want you to be very clear about that."

He walks to the window and looks outside. I guess that's all the privacy he's willing to give me. If there's no other choice, I'll take it, especially if he won't be able to hear a thing we say.

With my hands, I pull myself back until I hit the headboard, then lean against it, crossing my legs. Daniel hesitates for a moment, then climbs onto the bed, sitting up like me, his knees almost touching mine. Not so close, please! I think, though I don't say it out loud. However, I hear his response immediately, echoing in my mind.

"I'm sorry, Jade. Let me stay like this, alright? I promise not to touch you." I just close my eyes in acceptance, wishing my response could be a no, but I need him close, as close as possible before his touch burns me. He looks exhausted, dark circles framing his eyes deeper than I've ever seen. Yet, those eyes are still the beautiful blue oceans I've desperately missed. I can't quite read his expression: it's not pain, not anger; it's defeat, I think.

"Daniel." I say, or rather, think finally.

"Can you forgive me, Jade?"

"Will you let me steer the conversation where I need it first? Then, I promise... Yes, I promise to listen to you and answer whatever you want to know. Okay? Would you do that?"

He nods, and Ángel picks up on it, watching us closely. Suddenly, he realizes what's going on. He doesn't say anything, just exhales sharply through his nose and turns his gaze back outside the room. He's figured out that, whether he likes it or not, this conversation is going to be between us since he can't read my mind. I take a deep breath and start firing off my questions.

"How come I can hear you like this?"

"Do you remember the exchange we had? What we carry inside allows us to have a different connection." I furrow my brow, not quite getting his answer, and he does the same, surprised by my reaction.

"You mentioned some kind of exchange, but it wasn't. You gave me something, but I never..."

"You're right... Jade, there are so many things I owe you an explanation for. I should've come clean about every single one of them, but out of cowardice, I didn't. It's my own weakness that led to losing you, and I fear it may be irreversible. But now, I need you to listen to me. I must tell you everything and give you all the information." His eyes, still filled with pain, also show a determination that convinces me to listen.

"So, I can have the whole puzzle, right?"

"Not only that, you also need to know who I am and, more importantly, what I am. All of that information will be crucial to you, Jade. I beg you to listen to me."

"Was this what you were going to tell me the night the demon showed up here?" Suddenly, I remember him sitting beside me, nervous, and that conversation got interrupted by the demon to expose him.

"Yes."

"Then talk. I want to know everything." I wish I could brace myself for the wave of pain I can already see coming, but there's no way. I've never been good at swimming in those deep waters, so I'll just drown, but not before swallowing everything he's going to tell me.

"Thank you, and if at any point you feel the need to ask me anything, please do; it could be important. I only have one more plea to make."

"Which one?"

"It's going to hurt, Jade, a lot, but please, don't ask me to stop."

"Okay." I take a deep breath and prepare to endure, no matter the cost.

"Jade, I was your predator, trained to snatch your energy and sustain myself with it. Please pay close attention to what I'm about to tell you because it's all vital. The demon told you he had known your blood for centuries, and he didn't lie. Both you and us, we are prepared for generations to be part of this."

"No one gave me a choice."

"I know."

"But did they give you one?"

"Yes."

"How unfair!" The pain has started.

"I want to explain something to you. In my case, my parents played a significant role in shaping me. They were always aware of what I was, and they instilled their teachings in me day after day. My wickedness ran deep; I was conceived and nurtured in evil. To be clear, I imbibed wickedness from minutes after birth, and that sustained me until I met you.

My birth was expected, and I can assure you there was a fierce battle between demons and angels who tried every means to prevent my arrival. I suppose it was an attempt to keep me from meeting you years later. But my defenses were formidable, and I managed to enter this world. I guess that makes it clear how significant my role is in this Game."

"Wait, it's just a Game, right?" I can't help but let a tear roll down my cheek. How can they play around like this with someone? He keeps on talking fast. I'm not sure if it's because he's afraid I'll cut him off or because he's scared he won't be able to keep going if he stops.

"Yes, a macabre Game indeed. My parents knew it, and they weren't surprised that death hovered over me on various occasions and under different circumstances. They fought for me to survive, and now, as expected, they expect much from me. I haven't lived up to it.

However, we could say I came into the world with a drawback. I've come to the conclusion that all of us are born with an Achilles' heel, something that doesn't quite fit with our DNA or our upbringing. A thorn that will pierce your skin if you don't learn to resist it, and that will be the advantage your opponent may seize upon. At least, that's my take. I didn't even bother asking because I knew I wouldn't get answers.

Now, in my case, that embarrassing thorn is the pursuit of what is just. As you can imagine, that impulse was vehemently discouraged every time it arose to dissuade me from demanding justice when something seemed unjust.

They succeeded in burying that impulse, almost making it disappear until I met you and realized you knew nothing, that you had no idea of who you are, of what you are. I couldn't bear it; it drove me to approach you in an attempt to protect you, to inform you of what you needed to know. Everything was so different from how they had explained it to me. I expected to find in you a formidable opponent, not a defenseless teenager.

I liked to think that my Game against you would be on level ground, where both of us would be in equal circumstances, and the most cunning would prevail. However, I soon realized they had dulled my bull's horns to ensure my victory, and I didn't consider it fair, nor did I want it or accept it that way. That caused significant trouble, and I didn't care.

It wasn't just a thorn I felt on my skin anymore; it was a damned porcupine lodged in the back of my neck, irritating me greatly. So, it began a different Game for me. No, that's not accurate. A different Game began for others, and I began mine.

In it, I hoped to find in you a worthy adversary, and as that wasn't the case, I started causing trouble. Just to start, and once I found out you didn't even know you were playing, I wanted you to know who you are, and once we reached that point, we would appreciate your abilities, and only then would the confrontation take place, not before. I may be wicked, but never unjust. I was

The Game…Jade

determined for you to be able to face me and defend your gift. I didn't want to take it like stealing candy from a baby; I wanted my bull with intact horns."

"How did you figure out that I didn't know anything about this Game or even about myself?"

"Do you recall that time you came to see me at the show we did in Mexico City, and Paty brought you over to ask for my autograph?"

"Yes."

"On that occasion, I tried to explain to you, in as much detail as I could gather, how they contacted me and what they told me about you. I got nothing in return; you just stared at me, not saying a word. What's worse, it all seemed to intrigue you; your furrowed brow wouldn't budge.

I paused and asked how you were, and you replied in a barely audible voice, claiming to be fine. I didn't believe you; you were uneasy. My demon was furious, wanting me to stop, threatening to cover your ears so you couldn't hear me. I moved in closer, glaring at him, and he backed off.

I had no idea if your confusion stemmed from not knowing the details I'd just shared with you or if, on the contrary, you felt exposed. I was curious about the strange expression on Ángel's face. He showed no concern, no threats; he was calm. I didn't understand anything. That was the moment to lay it all out on the table, and yet you continued to hide your game, or so I thought.

I watched you, locking eyes with yours, and you lifted your gaze to meet mine. Your eyes had glazed over, and that unsettled me greatly. Then you said, 'Daniel, I think you're mistaken. I'm not...' I glanced at your angel; I could swear he let out a sigh of relief. And I replied, 'You need to know; I'm not wrong.'

Right then, I felt the entire foundation of what I planned to build crumble until there was nothing left but sand beneath our feet. You weren't a bull; you were a small calf, unaware that I planned to slaughter you and distribute your remains among the pack of hyenas to which I belonged. What's worse, apparently, you trusted me. They had lied to me more than I realized. It wasn't fair.

I came to realize that everything about you, that marbled innocence enveloping you, draws its depth from a source within you, it's entirely and absolutely real. I had never met anyone quite like you. I drew closer and kissed you for the first time, not with the intention of going any further but driven by the tenderness you inspired in me.

Rocío Blisswealth

I didn't like this Game at all, not if I had to kill my opponent to win the match. No one told me about that. They spoke of us being equals, yet you showed up before me, completely defenseless. And I can confess, my wickedness had yet to be fully unleashed; I've refrained from murder, from rape, from theft, all in anticipation of facing you. How could I when I didn't dare?"

"Wait a second. Yes, it's true. You did mention that to me; you told me. I freaked out because I was scared I wouldn't be the person you expected and I'd have to leave. After that day, I totally forgot about it. How could I not remember all that?" My head's spinning. Now I remember another question I want to ask him.

"You... Did you have a demon?"

"Yes, just like you've got Ángel."

"And Ángel didn't stop you from talking to me about it because he figured it was in his best interest for me to have the info."

"I reckon so someone ought to have filled you in on that, but it seems they didn't bother. I came to realize that in this Game, the only time we're on a level playing field is when we're both lacking the full picture. In my case, they fed me only what they wanted me to know; in yours, it seems they didn't even bother with that, just left you in the dark. They spent seven years prepping me to face you, and you didn't even know I existed, let alone that you should fear me. I'm certain if you had known, fear would've kept you from seeking me out. You'd have stayed home that afternoon, safe and sound. All of this left a sour taste of injustice in my mouth, not just against you but against both of us.

That day, I made the decision that I'd be playing a third Game—not yours, not the one those recruiters had in mind, but ours—and in the process, I'd have to keep up appearances. I decided to bring you onto my team and spun a tale about Raúl being sick to ask for your help, and you agreed. In those days, I had got to learn a lot more about you and your angel."

"Like what?"

"Your abilities, in many ways and instances, surpass your understanding. The first time you were part of my team, when we went our separate ways at the airport..."

"I know; I was desperate to either go with you or have you stay. Couldn't stand the idea of not seeing you anymore." He smiles, well, kind of; his lips twitch a bit, but it's not a real smile.

The Game...Jade

"Without even realizing it, you split your soul, leaving a part of it within me. For others, that would require a huge effort and the intervention of immensely powerful forces, but for you, it was as simple as wishing for it."

"What? So, that means what you gave me to hold onto that day was part of your soul?"

"Yes, the same amount you gave me of yours to meld the two together. With that gesture, you made me far more resilient; perhaps that's how I've managed to endure all this, and it's also how I found out things about you that, though I knew them, I didn't realize their extent."

"Like what?"

"Your ability to sense what's happening over great distances, as if you were there. The power to use your energy to heal, or to inflict harm, even to kill, at your discretion." My brow furrows. That's definitely something I didn't know.

"I know you've never quite used it that way, but energy is just that; it doesn't take shape until you put some intent behind it. You've used it for healing because that's what you've been taught, but it'd be just as effective if you directed it elsewhere, maybe even more so. Hate is sometimes stronger than love. And then there's your ability to see demons, always, without fail."

"So that means, by sharing your soul, I must also know things about you that no one else does."

"You're starting to get it. That night at the hotel, when I said I wanted to deepen our connection, I meant to wake up your consciousness, teach you to squeeze every last drop from your gift, and show you everything you can now see and know."

"So, when I told you that you gave me what I was missing, I wasn't totally off."

"Not at all, but as it sometimes happens with you, you know the truth; you just don't acknowledge it. Everything matters."

"I still don't understand how I passed part of my soul to you. When did that happen?"

"Let me explain. When we said goodbye in that final hug, something happened that still astonishes me to this day. As I held you close, I felt as though a knife made of ice slid from my chest down to my gut, only to be stunned by a warm, smooth sphere that leaped inside me, resting right in front of my heart. The sensation was overwhelming, powerful, vital like I'd never been alive and was breathing for the first time in my life, as if I'd been reborn in that very moment in your arms. I didn't understand what was happening.

I lifted your chin and looked deep into your eyes. I could see clearly that you didn't know what had happened either. I wondered if you felt what I did."

"No, I didn't feel a thing."

"I lost sight of you and sank into the waiting room sofa at the airport, only to snap back up immediately, a victim of immense surprise."

"A surprise? What kind?" I can't believe that while all this was happening, I didn't even notice, and apparently, I'll keep finding out more things.

"Ángel appeared beside me." My eyes immediately shift to my angel, still gazing out the window. I don't interrupt and let him continue.

"I need to talk to you." Ángel said, looking directly into my eyes.

"Raúl will be back in a minute; he just went to see Jade off for her flight."

"Don't worry about time; we've got plenty." I glanced at my demon, motionless, eyes fixed on the door through which Raúl and you exited. I understood we had all the time in the world, and I intended to make the most of it. I'll try to recount the conversation as accurately as possible.

"What are you doing here?" I asked.

"You know they exterminated those of her generation. I'm doing everything I can to keep her safe."

"Handing her over to her predator on a silver platter?" I asked, dripping with sarcasm.

"Placing her within reach of the only person who, in pursuit of justice, can open her eyes, tell her who she is, so she can learn to defend herself. Indeed, you're her predator, but still, you're the only one I can rely on."

"Why don't you give her the information yourself?" I asked, intrigued.

"We are forbidden to intervene."

"What do you mean? I've been given the information I needed." His response caught me off guard.

"Daniel, you were told what was expected of you, but I'm sure you had no idea what you would face. Have they informed you how she's feeding them?" He had my full attention now; it was one of my biggest questions.

"No. Can you tell me?"

"One of the methods is similar to what has been used with you. When Jade focuses her attention on someone intensely and specifically, her energy flows toward that person uncontrollably. If, in addition to that, she touches or embraces the person, she inundates them with that same abundant energy."

"Just by touching me?" I was unaware of this detail.

"That's right." He answered.

I asked what the other way was. He observed me for long seconds, and finally, he dared to tell me.

"The demons terrorize her so that her fear unleashes a discharge of energy, which they then channel to your superiors. It's the same, but much more terrifying."

"And does she not know what we're doing?"

"Daniel, she knows nothing." He replied, irritated.

"Then why did she seek me out?" I had to know because until then nothing made sense to me.

"Your music has always been an escape for her, and she wanted exactly what she told you: to ask you for an autograph."

"I can't believe it." I replied, finding it utterly illogical.

"I didn't believe it either, but I couldn't avoid it; it's one of the rules of the Game. I knew she would go like a lamb among wolves."

"Why was I told to make a trade with her?"

"That was the initial plan; it would have been the easiest for them. However, Jade was raised by her grandparents, who instilled in her very solid values, shaping her into who she is."

"That protected her from me." I was finally starting to understand.

I cut in to ask.

"What was the exchange, Daniel?" I don't know that either. He looks down at his hands, then takes a deep breath before meeting my eyes.

"I was meant to take you to bed, share an intimate connection with you. That's what I'd put on the table in return."

"Oh, wow." Makes sense, but I kind of wish I hadn't asked.

Ángel kept on talking and said:

"A significant aspect of the challenge stems from her lack of knowledge about her own energy, coupled with the reality that there exist entities who covet it. She does things that, if she had possessed complete understanding, she wouldn't do."

Rocío Blisswealth

"What do you mean?" I asked.

"I'm referring precisely to what brought me here, talking to you. To what you felt when she hugged you." I placed a hand over my chest, in the same area he was observing.

"What did I feel? Did she feel it, too?" It intrigued me greatly.

"No, she didn't feel it. She has no idea what she just did. I didn't think she was capable of something like this either. She surprises me every day. I still don't know how she achieved it."

"Cut the crap and tell me straight! What did I feel?" I wasn't accepting any more beating around the bush.

"Daniel, you are the only person, beyond her grandparents, who has treated her with consideration, with an attitude she interprets as affection. You know, as the saying goes, 'When drowning, anyone extending a lifeline becomes your hero.' She, unplanned, entrusted half of her soul to you in a desperate attempt to escape with you and evade the tribulations awaiting her in Monterrey."

"How could she pass a piece of her soul to me?! Doesn't she understand I'm nearly a demon?" I couldn't believe anything he was telling me. I mean, I did, but I couldn't wrap my head around it. He kept talking.

"No, she doesn't understand it, and she wouldn't believe it either. She has lived with them her entire life, and for her, a demon couldn't behave like you do. She sees you as an honorable man; she even believes you are respectful. Frankly, it surprises me that her soul allowed itself to be fragmented."

"I know you're not lying, but I struggle to believe what you're saying. What I'm about to say sounds ridiculous, coming from someone like me, but this isn't normal, is it?"

"With her, nothing has been normal. I have resigned myself to accept what happens. Things are just like that, and that's all I can tell you. However, I must retrieve the fragment of her soul that resides within you; that should not have happened. So, if you'll allow me." He directed his hand toward my chest.

"No." I covered my chest with my hand, and he jumped.

"Daniel, you have no idea what you're getting yourself into by keeping it there."

"She wanted to give it to me."

"I can't leave you with it. If you don't hand it over, I'll have to take it by force." He observed me with a furrowed brow.

The Game...Jade

"She thinks I'm worthy enough to share this with me. I can't give it back." I kept resisting.

"Jade is going to need that other part." I came up with something and dared to suggest it.

"Wait, wait, what if I give her half of mine? Would it work? A part of me could be with her, not leave her alone. Please." He looked very surprised. I got up and started walking; I couldn't control myself.

"Daniel, have you lost your senses? Do you realize what you're saying? What leads you to make that decision?... What do you feel for her?"

"I couldn't say for certain; I've never felt anything like this before. Ángel, can we team up, her and I?" I couldn't describe the look on your angel's face; that definitely hadn't happened to him before.

"I ask you to be careful with what you say. You have a habit of speaking lightly, and I won't tolerate that." He warned me, but I persisted and tried to explain.

"These days I've spent with her, my mind has been toying with the idea of being able to free her from the things she goes through, to be able to help her in some way. I've stopped because I know that if I let them see what I'm thinking, well, I don't know what they'd be capable of doing."

"They would kill her." He replied without filters.

"No! We can't allow that." I shouted, getting more agitated by the minute.

"That's what I'm trying to prevent."

"I want to help her."

"Daniel, you have no idea what you're talking about. This hasn't even begun yet. The attacks will be brutal, and you are not prepared to fight."

"Alright, probably not; however, they told me they murdered her partner. I could be that for her. The person who helps her heal after the battles. Would that serve any purpose?" He couldn't take his surprised eyes off me. Honestly, I was more surprised than him by my own reaction.

"Whoa, hold up! I need to ask you something. Did they kill my partner? What are you talking about, Daniel?"

"Each of you has someone tailor-made, someone designed to be your emotional haven, to help you weather the storm. But they killed the one who was meant for you."

Rocío Blisswealth

"It's like this weird empty feeling, you know? Like, this ache for someone I never even got to meet, but somehow, I would've loved." I just stay quiet and keep listening.

Ángel persisted with his warnings, saying:

"Daniel, to achieve a place beside her, you would have to engage in a very dangerous Game. Pretend with those who recruited you, pretending that you are still in their Game. And, at the same time, be Jade's support. It would be terribly complicated. Furthermore, I cannot guarantee that she will reciprocate your feelings. I can't guarantee anything other than the fight will be fierce, and both of you could die. Very few have survived the final battle. So, if we do this, you would almost be accepting certain death."

"You still haven't given me an answer. Would it be of any use to Jade?" He still hadn't clarified what was important to me.

"Perhaps, if you are her anchor, the only one with enough weight to withstand what is to come. I must warn you; they could decide to use you against her."

"And they did it, Daniel. They're using you against me." I say with a sigh, feeling a lot of pain. He nods and keeps talking.

"I knew it from that moment. And there I was, striking a deal with your angel."

"If they find out what is happening, nothing can save you." He cautioned me.

"They won't find out, I assure you. What do I need to do?"

"I cannot accept this just like that. As Jade would say, one of us must be sane. And since it seems it won't be you, it must be me. I'll give you three days to think it over. If, at the end of that time, you still feel the same, I will help you share half of your soul with her. I hope I'm not mistaken in letting desperation guide me."

"Ángel..."

"Yes?"

"As you can imagine, I've been mulling over everything we discussed for months now. But what Jade did today only fueled my determination to help her. It's not merely a matter of wanting to be her support; it's a resolute decision. Do you understand now?"

"Yes, but still, I'll give you three days to think it over."

"I'll catch up with you in three days."

The Game...Jade

I settled in, a little calmer, knowing I had only three days to wait. I was certain a terrible war was coming, but I'd be by your side, on your team, doing the right thing, perhaps for the first time in my life.

Eventually, Ángel showed up and proposed leading me to one of the mansion's cells on the island. I'd been there a few times before, and your essence lingered strongly there too, so they wouldn't be able to detect us if we acted swiftly. And that's how it happened, just as you recall. You do remember, don't you?"

"Yes, I remember that well, even though I had no clue what it was about."

"You didn't hesitate for a moment; your response was resolute. No one had ever done anything like that for me before. My affection for you grew exponentially, and I felt absolutely reciprocated."

"You were. Tell me something, did your dad know who I was when he came to see you?"

"He always knew, more so than any of us. In fact, after you left the room, we had a massive fight and came to blows."

"Did he hit you? Why?"

"Because, well aware of what the supposed requirement was for you to give me your energy, he asked if I'd already taken you to bed, and I didn't respond. So, he requested some time alone with you, claiming he'd handle it... he's a pig." Another tear streams down my face, but this time out of anger. How stupid I must have looked to him, that damn jerk.

"Is there anything else I should know?"

"I'm not certain if you should know this, but I don't want to keep it from you."

"Go ahead."

"Do you recall that time on tour when your mother left a message for you to call her?"

"Yes."

"Your sister left a similar message for me." I cover my mouth with my hand in surprise; I didn't see that coming.

"And what did she tell you?"

"She wanted to make a deal with me, offering to sell you to me in exchange for something."

"In exchange for what?"

"I didn't know. I told her you were with me because you wanted to be, and I wouldn't engage in such a deal with her. After she threatened to never let me see you again, she hung up the phone."

"She knew."

"They both knew."

"I always thought she'd trade me for a pair of socks, just to get rid of me, but I was speaking metaphorically." A couple more tears follow the previous ones. "That's why they were interested in knowing if you'd taken me to bed."

"Did they ask you?"

"Yes, they probably wanted to know if the deal had already gone down." I shake my head from side to side; it's too much information to process in such a short time.

"Jade, are you alright? That was a lot to take in."

"Too much truth."

"You're right; too much truth."

"Alright, I'm trying to process everything you've told me, and I still haven't figured out where I stand on this. That'll be the next step for me. However, I need to know, what's your position on this whole thing?"

He responds quickly, having had time to think through answers to all my potential questions over these days. He reaches out to touch my leg, and my body flinches, realizing his intentions. He pulls his hand back.

"Everything changed for me when I could be with you. When I truly got to know you. When I saw myself in your eyes. And I was terrified by what I was capable of doing." He drops his gaze for a moment, then lifts it again, looking me straight in the eyes. "I can't tell you that at that moment I considered giving up everything and confessing the truth to you; I'd be lying. But my priorities shifted, putting you in the most important place. I can't bear the thought of being without you. I'm still here, waiting for you. Sooner or later, you'll understand how much I love you, and I hope that means something to you. That it weighs enough."

I can't stop the tears that suddenly overflow from my eyes. I quickly wipe them away with the back of my hand and try to keep it together. Nothing would please me more than to throw myself into his arms, but that's not an option for me anymore, not now.

"I guess you know what I intend to do."

The Game...Jade

"Which of the two options are you referring to?" He responds with a slight smile that lets me know he does indeed know everything.

"True, I haven't decided exactly which path to take, but there's one that, if I choose it, will put you at great risk because of what binds us. Now I know it's likely that death will catch up to both of us." He continues to smile, and his gaze softens.

"I've been by your side every step of the plan, and I've always known I want to be part of it. Death, you say, and isn't this what we're living through already? I have no way to turn back time, and even if I could, I've never been known for making the best decisions. I've always envied you for that. So now that I can, I'll go along with yours."

I know that with my decision, whatever it may be, I'm condemning him. Whether he deserves it or not, I'm not debating. It's just that a while ago if someone had asked me if I could ever put him in mortal danger—him, who has been and still is the person I love the most—I would undoubtedly have said no. And yet, here I am.

"Daniel, I don't have the strength to find another way out anymore. I don't know if I could live without you, but I refuse to do so, and we both know I couldn't live with you either. I'm sorry."

"I get it. My commitment to them let things go way too far. He's taken over my body, even if it's just partially. You could never live with something like that, and neither could I. Besides, there's no way for you to undo what you've done. What you're planning sounds infinitely better."

"Can I count on you then?"

"As your mate here would say." He says, pointing at Ángel with his index finger. "Till the very end, gorgeous."

"Thank you."

"Can you give me an answer now?" He gets serious.

"Yes."

"Will you forgive me?"

"I still don't know."

"Do you still love me?" I only have one answer to that question.

"Always."

"I love you even more." He says, smiling with a slightly raised corner of his lips.

Rocío Blisswealth

"Impossible." I can't manage a smile, only letting out more tears that I no longer bother to stop.

He moves in quickly, not giving me time to think, and plants a painful kiss on my lips, which I return amidst sobs, wondering if it could hurt anymore.

"Daniel, with what Ángel did, he put your life in danger. I'm so sorry."

"He warned me things might not work out. He was clear with me, and I accepted it. It's the only decision I'm proud to have made all on my own." He smiles softly.

And just like that, he fades back into his usual invisibility, leaving me still stunned. Ángel comes closer and runs his fingers through my hair. How far has he gone for me? How much do I really owe him? Now I can understand how he got all those scars; he's brave and reckless. Who would've thought? There's more to him than just the image of a sweet, attractive guy. Truly reckless, gods! What am I supposed to do now?

Chapter XXVII
Never, not once, none

It's been almost twenty-four hours since I had the nerve to talk to Daniel. I faced our conversation head-on, knowing that seeing him again, having him close visibly, wouldn't be easy. But surprisingly, I didn't even have time to think about it because now it's Ángel who's taking up almost all of my brain power. I haven't dared to talk to him; I'm scared of what answers he might give to my questions. Every time I ask something, no matter how simple, it just opens up more torment that I never saw coming.

I'm trying to cling to Daniel's idea that Ángel has done everything for my own good. I don't want to start doubting his loyalty to me right now because, honestly, I need him. He's pretty much all I've got left, and if I couldn't rely on him anymore, I don't know what I'd do.

I've managed to sort through the jumble of feelings inside me. Hate, anger, fear, anguish, pain, and now, guilt. I'm suffocating under the weight of guilt, thinking that Ángel has done way more for me than I realize, and yet all my efforts are aimed towards a goal with which I have completely failed him. He's gone above and beyond to keep me alive, and I want to risk it all without even considering, acknowledging, or even thanking him for everything he's done. Why did I have to ask? Why couldn't I have just stayed in blissful ignorance? I'd owe him the same, but I wouldn't have known, guilt wouldn't exist, and my reasoning would be clearer.

Instead, I've spent hours struggling to make a decision. A decision that I thought was already made, but now, thanks to this new information, it's back on the table, unresolved. The only thing I've figured out so far, and it seems to be the one thing that hasn't changed, no matter what I decide, is my conversation with myself. I need to really analyze my decision.

I thought the toughest part would be risking Daniel's life, but now I have to consider Ángel too, and what he once said, "We too perish, carrying the burden of not being able to save what was entrusted to us." How much pain could that really be? And, like in war, can they somehow reduce his rank or something? I'm too scared to ask him.

Rocío Blisswealth

I sit on my bed, leaning against the headboard, trying to get as comfortable as possible. I know that more pain likely awaits me as soon as I close my eyes, so being comfortable is the least I can aim for right now.

"What are you doing?" He asks, sounding a bit worried.

"I'm just getting comfortable." I reply calmly.

"I already saw that, but why are you getting comfortable?"

"I'm about to take the next step."

"The next step..." He mentions, sounding a little uneasy. "You said it was talking to yourself."

"That's right."

"I don't understand. Are you thinking of meditating?"

"Ángel, you know better than anyone that I've never done that." I smile.

"I know, Jade, but I don't understand what you're aiming for. Oh, no! Please tell me it's not what I'm thinking." I don't know if he has a heart like mine, I mean, but if he does, I could swear it's about to leap out of his chest.

"Just like you once told me, I can't get inside your head, so I don't know for sure, but I think you're on the right track."

"I can't believe it."

"Well, what did you think I was going to do?"

"I definitely prefer the idea of meditation."

"No, Ángel, I told you I would talk to myself."

"You never said it like that."

"I never said otherwise."

He takes a seat at the foot of the bed and watches me. Thankfully, I'm used to him doing that; if I weren't, I'd never be able to concentrate enough. I have no idea how to do this, but I remember what Daniel mentioned about achieving things I didn't know how to do just by wishing for them. Here goes nothing.

Gradually, I leave behind the sound of cars passing by my street and the scent of lavender from the air freshener I placed on my dresser a couple of months ago. I had thought it had lost its smell, but now that I'm not consciously aware of it, I realize it's still there. I try to tune into my surroundings; even before opening my eyes, I can tell that this place is quieter than my bedroom and smells like lavender. Well, some things haven't changed.

I open my eyes slowly and look around. I find myself sitting on a cozy brown couch, and in front of me is a table with a lamp and some sort of electronic device. A computer, perhaps? I guess so, although it's very strange, maybe too small. Across from me, I can see the wide closet doors. I'm itching to open them and see what's inside, but I don't dare, even though these must be my closet doors after all, right?

Suddenly, a doubt strikes me: what if I ended up in the wrong place? I've never done this before, and there's no guarantee that I've gone where I intended. Actually, I wanted to go to the Record of Time, the same place Daniel took me to, to see my future life and myself, of course. However, now that I think about it, the room I'm in bears no resemblance to the vast blue space I was in before. Besides, there's no evidence of my presence here: a photo, something with my name on it. Come to think of it, I've never been one for taking pictures. Maybe that hasn't changed. But if I have a family now, wouldn't I be in their photos?

I hear footsteps approaching the door, and fear overwhelms me. If the person coming isn't me, we're in for quite a scare! The door opens slowly, and I step inside. Or should I say, she does? Well, she didn't scream in surprise, and neither did I. She looks at me and smiles faintly.

"I wasn't sure what day it would be. I've been waiting for this since I got that lamp. And, to answer your question, twenty-eight years."

"Which question?" I say, barely audible.

"The one you thought of asking me when you saw me come in. I've been here before, remember? Only it was me sitting on the couch." I'm making an effort to control my confusion. However, I don't know how much time I have, so I better make sure my effort pays off.

Her hair is dyed a much darker shade than mine. She's wearing blue jeans, a white cotton blouse with buttons down the front, and brown loafers; apparently, my tastes haven't changed much. Her hair is shorter than mine, hers reaching only shoulder height, although it retains the same general style, more or less. Little makeup. Anyway, I don't see any significant changes in her, other than the normal ones caused by the twenty-eight years she mentioned, except for the eyes; there's sadness in her gaze. A shiver runs down my spine. How long have I been silent?

"Have you composed yourself yet? It's not like we're running out of time, but why wait?"

"I thought I was going to the Record of Time. How did...?"

Rocío Blisswealth

"You didn't think about the Record; you thought about talking to yourself when enough time had passed for me to give you concrete answers, and here you are. We always went above and beyond what we thought possible."

I keep making the effort; I really try. I remember a question; maybe that will help.

"I have two options. Which one did I... did you choose?" Without a second hesitation, she replies.

"For several days, I pondered what I knew about Ángel, letting guilt advise me; I felt indebted to him. Also, the idea of putting Daniel in mortal danger terrified me, as it does to you now, and I didn't dare to do it. I decided to please Ángel and keep my life."

"And?" I ask with a hint of anxiety in my voice. She talks about my future in the past tense, which is distressing.

"There's something you need to know; guilt serves no purpose and satisfies no one. Get rid of it as soon as possible."

"So, do you regret the decision you made?"

"Absolutely."

"Why?" She looks at me silently for a moment, then sighs.

"I'm not sure you want to know."

"Why do you say that?"

"Because I know myself. Also, because of that, I know you'll insist until I tell you, even if it puts you in a predicament even greater than the one you're in now, so..."

"I want to know everything."

"Okay. I lived with Mom and Mara for a while, maybe because I didn't really know what to do. I felt like attacking them or the demons they carry inside so many times, but I decided to let them suffer. After all, they brought it on themselves, and I saw it as my little revenge. Eventually, I got a job and threw myself into it, trying not to dwell on what I'd been through, but life without Daniel, you know, it just wasn't life anymore. So, I left home just like that."

"Just like that? But what about Ángel?"

"Oh, I'm still under his care, not as much around as he used to be for you these days, though. But every time I'm in mortal danger..."

My eyes are wide open. I can feel them, but I have no control over them.

"Mortal danger." I don't say it as a question; I think I always knew deep down.

"Continuing with my life meant not giving up my gift, which they've never been too thrilled about. I managed to keep it out of their reach, at least most of the time. But whenever they're hungry, I have to fight. My gift has evolved, and so have they."

"Daniel…" I can't seem to put a questioning tone in my voice; I don't think she cares; she answers anyway.

"He moved on with his career, well, the demon did. But his soul spends a lot of time here." She looks towards an empty chair in the corner.

"Still?"

"Until the end, remember? He's kept his promise. He's almost always here, and even though I can't always see him, I know it."

"But his life…"

"I know what you mean. He stayed alone, just like me, at least until today. I guess he was right."

"About what?"

"That he loves me more than I love him. I keep waiting for the day he won't show up anymore, but he always comes back."

"And for you, has there been anyone else?"

"Sometimes."

"And what happened?"

"You don't need to ask me that; you know it well, none of them is Daniel." I need to switch topics because I can't deal with what I'm feeling listening to her.

"I have a feeling Ángel is much more than what I've seen so far."

She frowns, focusing on something she doesn't seem to remember clearly.

"There was this time, about fifteen years ago, when demon attacks were brutal, really terrible. And I began to give vent to the sweet idea that I'd gone crazy, so I isolated myself. I fought to avoid anything that reminded me of demons in my life or Daniel in my room, and for a long time, I almost convinced myself of it. Even when the demons attacked me, I didn't fight back, just let them do whatever they wanted with me.

One day, this guy I sometimes talked to at work asked me to visit his friend. She was a psychic; it didn't seem like a big deal, so I went along. Once at her place, we talked for a while until, reaching out, she touched my hand. By the way, I still can't stand being touched by other people. Anyway, as soon as her hand touched mine, she jumped back, almost falling to the ground. Once she regained her balance, her eyes fixed on the wall behind me while she cried uncontrollably, repeating 'Who protects you?! Who protects you?!' Almost shouting. I didn't know what to do, so I just said, 'My guardian angel, I guess,' trying to smile so she wouldn't notice how startled I was. 'He's not an angel, he's an archangel. That's what he is! Didn't you know?' So that was it for my madness; I had a witness who could see my bodyguard. Unwillingly, I snapped back to reality that day."

"An archangel..." I say with a sigh.

"He's capable of way more than you think; don't underestimate him. For every wound he's received, I assure you he's dealt many, many more. If you think about it makes sense. I guess archangels have extra abilities to look after people like us. By the way, I've never directly asked him; I don't think he'd tell me."

I watch her in silence; well, I'm pretty dazed. This is the life I'm about to decide on, or at least the one I was leaning towards, and now, I'm not feeling it at all! I don't even know what I want, but I'm sure this isn't it, definitely not.

"Can you give me some advice? Anything you know that I don't, that could help us both."

She stares at me for a long moment, her lips holding a soft smile, barely there, really. I'm starting to think she learned to keep it there because her real expression would be too harsh for everyday life. Maybe it helps her avoid questions from the people around her, though I can't imagine who they might be.

"I can tell you, for instance, that over time, I found out that Grandma, who prayed for me all her life, was the one who arranged for Ángel to watch over me. He told me himself. She knew exactly what one of her descendants might suffer, having seen it in her childhood. So, she asked for a powerful enough angel to keep me alive no matter what. Archangel or not, Ángel is capable of great things. Don't forget that; always keep it in mind.

There's this phrase he said to me during my worst moments in that room, and I forgot it. It only came back to me recently: 'The enemy of your enemy is your friend.' I'm not sure what he meant by that, but it's something to

The Game...Jade

take seriously. He doesn't talk for the sake of it. Try to figure it out; you still have time.

Ángel is very cunning. I've come to know him well. Like a good warrior, he's an excellent strategist, and he likes to use the element of surprise. He did it with Daniel; that's another thing he told me. When you two met, he peeked into the future to see what could benefit him. He saw how things would play out, and he contacted Daniel back when he wasn't being watched so closely. Daniel agreed when he proposed exchanging a piece of his soul. He knew that by doing that, you wouldn't die without taking him down, too. And he also knew that you wouldn't dare to do it, even though he warned him of the possibility that there was a chance you might dare to cause his death. Daniel accepted; you know…"

"Free will." We both say.

"Exactly, and then he used him as an anchor, an unbreakable and heavy one, the only available. He taught him how to astrally transport himself and…" Her words trigger a memory in me; she must know, I need her to tell me.

"What was the demon searching for inside him that night in his chest?" She smiles a little more eagerly. I guess I'm on the right track.

"The demon was searching for the missing piece of Daniel's soul. He knew it messed up by leaving him alone for so long, considering it was supposed to be looking after him, and something seriously bad went down due to his negligence. He was eager to find that missing piece, but in his desperation and fear of the punishment it would face, he never stopped to question whose soul fragment it had swapped out the previous one with. He didn't even detect it because Daniel was already filled with your energy. He still doesn't know and hasn't said anything about it either. You get what I'm saying, right?"

"They don't know either." She doesn't respond, just flashes a big grin, though it lasts only for a few seconds.

"Now that demon dwells in his body, and you have an unbreakable connection with Daniel, so…"

"With him too."

"It should be easy to manipulate him if you connect with his essence. You'll know what to do and what not to. He's not very bright. No matter how much it tries to scare you, just ignore him."

I pause for a few seconds, thinking, trying to figure out the next move. She watches me and carries on.

"Remember the whole points accumulation thing?"

"Yes." Though now I'm not sure if that ever did me any good, it was Mom who handled it in the end.

"It works. That's another thing Ángel told me. Not because of Mom, he asked the Creator to back up your belief that it was Him changing your points, and for some reason, He found it amusing or something because He agreed. If I were to try to achieve what I want, for instance, I'd try to get something that gives me enough points to ensure success. Something significant enough."

Disappointment washes over me. I was starting to map out a plan, but now I have to rely on Him acting in my favor, and I haven't even managed to convince Ángel yet. Besides, what could I possibly get that would be worth so many points?

"I doubt He'll be on my side if it's something that doesn't exactly align with His plans for me."

"There's something you need to know. For Him, a deal's a deal; He won't back out, even if it's hard for Him. I know that now."

We lock eyes for what feels like forever; I don't know exactly how long. I have one last question, and I don't dare to ask it, but it's the only one that will clear things up enough for me to make an irreversible decision.

"Are you ready to go?"

"No, I have one more question." Her expression shows pure surprise. For some reason, she didn't expect it.

"Really? I didn't ask anything else. So, this must be the one that changes your future, away from mine. Go ahead, what is it?"

"When was the last time you were truly happy?"

She's staring right at me, and a tear slips from her eye, just one. I think by now there aren't many left. She's probably cried them all out by now. She wipes it away slowly with her fingertips, clearing her throat before answering me.

"Without a doubt, it was when I confessed my love to Daniel and got lost in his embrace, hearing him say he loved me more."

"Wasn't there any other moment?"

"Never, not once, none."

I get up from the couch, and before closing my eyes to leave, I ask:

"Anything else you want to tell me?"

"What you're about to do may be much harder than what I've faced so far. But trust me, you don't want to end up here." She places her right hand on

The Game...Jade

her chest, and I totally get what she means. "Gather your courage and do it. I have no clue how it'll turn out, but one thing I know for sure: I made the other choice, and it wasn't right; it wasn't. Good luck for both of us."

"Thank you."

Almost immediately, I open my eyes in my bed, facing Ángel, a single tear rolling down my cheek. I get it now. I don't need them anymore; they are just a waste of time. I can still dodge that future, and I will, no matter what. I know what I want now: escape!

Ángel watches me and says nothing, which I deeply appreciate. I lean over to the nightstand and grab the phone, the one that, as the little one said, seems like a decoration in my room because, with it hardly ever being used, it's even covered in a light layer of dust. I don't bother to dust it off; I couldn't care less. One by one, I dial the numbers; it starts ringing. The weight in my stomach is real, but I ignore it. Five rings, six, seven…

"Hello?" His voice! It's not, but at the same time, I could almost fool myself into thinking it's him.

"Hello, Daniel."

Daniel appears before me, probably wanting his image in my room to remind me who I'm dealing with, but it's unnecessary. I know well. My plan's already in motion.

"Jade? What a miracle, beautiful! Where on earth have you been hiding?"

"It's a long story. Daniel, I'm not okay; I miss you so much." I say this staring at Daniel, the real one, straight in the eyes. It's easier that way.

"There's no need for it to be like this, beautiful. You've got me here, and you know it. I've missed you terribly, too. And I was dreadfully worried after Carmen's tragic passing; I couldn't locate you anywhere. We tried calling you numerous times, but your family denied you. They always said you weren't there, and I didn't know what to do."

"My family has been a huge part of the problem, but I can't tell you now; they're listening."

"Don't worry, Jade, tell me what you want me to do, and I'll do it without a doubt."

He needs me to ask, to say it out loud, free will and all. No problem, but I have to act just like I would in any other situation; I don't want him to suspect anything.

Rocío Blisswealth

542

"I can't do it, Daniel. You know I've never wanted to bother you." The real Daniel winks at me. Thanks, I needed that.

"Ask me anything you want, my love, and I shall do it. Your desires are my commands; tell me."

"Come for me, please."

Ángel drops his head, staring at the ground; I can clearly see he's given up already. I'm sorry, there won't be any more explanations. I don't want him messing with my plans. I look at Daniel, and silently, deep inside me, I desperately plead with him to have my back, even though I know what it means for him, and to keep the secret from Ángel. He nods and lets out a sigh. "Until the end," I hear him say.

"Of course! Pack your bags. Do you have a way to get to Mexico City airport? I'll pick you up there tomorrow, before nightfall, and bring you home. How does that sound?"

"Yes, Daniel, I'll be there without fail, and… thank you."

"Jade, I love you."

His words, in Daniel's voice, send a shiver of horror down my spine. He's not capable of loving anyone, least of all me. Yet, with my eyes fixed on the love of my life, almost without blinking, I reply.

"I love you more. I'll be waiting for you, Daniel."

"It won't be long now, beautiful. See you there."

He hangs up. My future self was right: I had to connect with his essence. That's how I knew that all I had to do was tell him what he wanted to hear; that was easy. I get up and start packing, not even caring what goes in the suitcase anymore; it's no longer important.

Once on the plane, I buckled up my seatbelt. It's the first time Ángel's accompanying me, even though he's invisible to everyone but me. I've asked him to stay silent, and he's agreed, just holding my hand almost constantly. That's probably why I'm not feeling scared; I'm oddly calm. I'm pretty sure the decision I've made this time is better than the last one. Anything's got to be better than the previous path; that one really freaks me out.

The flight attendant announces over the loudspeaker that we're landing in Mexico City. It's the first time I've spoken to Ángel in hours.

"They'll be waiting for me, all of them. I need you to keep a low profile. It's crucial that they don't realize you're here."

"Don't worry." He responds seriously.

"Thanks."

The Game…Jade

We disembark, and there's an escort—a person I've never seen before—holding a sign with my name plastered on it, Jade Arias, missing the addition "condemned to death." A retinue of six demons, seeing me as something precious, wait patiently for me. I suppose handing me over will ensure them a great reward, maybe even a commendation. I can feel Ángel tensing up, but he keeps moving forward. They're huge, easily a head taller than me, and that's all I can see before they're too close. I don't want them to think I know they're there; any doubt I can cause them is worth it. They march surrounding Daniel, Ángel, and me. We head to a VIP waiting room, predictably empty, and take our seats.

I turn to the man and ask in a casual tone.

"Didn't Raúl come?"

"He wasn't available. I'm sorry."

"It's okay. Just curious." Of course, he wasn't available; if they hadn't called him to check, chances are he was busy doing laundry or something. I would've liked to see him, though it's probably better he didn't come.

A couple of hours later, the door to the room started to open; it hadn't moved the whole time, so I already knew who it was. Here goes. Daniel walks through the door, and without a second thought, I jump up and run into his arms. This time, it's not anxiety pushing me; it's just that if I don't do it now, I never will. He holds me tight, wrapping me in his arms, giving me a hug so strong it knocks the breath out of me, lifting my feet off the ground. Daniel's soul is still there, a faint whisper, but it's in there with him, moving forward with my plan. Thank you.

"I've missed you so much." I say almost in a whisper.

As he sets me down on the ground, he looks me straight in the eyes. Just as I thought, Daniel's soul isn't strong enough to peek through them; his eyes are kind of empty. I guess I notice it only because I know them so well. He comes up to me and kisses me slowly on the lips. All my effort, while I reciprocate it, is based on holding back the nausea. It would be terrible if I threw up right now. He runs his fingers through my hair.

"No more longing; we're finally together. Shall we be off?"

"Of course." I reply, flashing the fakest smile ever. I doubt he can tell the difference. "I've got a lot to fill you in on, Daniel, and there's something I need your help with."

His eyes light up, and a smile appears on his face. I can tell that, while the smile isn't fake, it's not Daniel's, not even close.

Rocío Blisswealth

544

"You'll tell me on the plane to Spain, and you can count on me to lend a hand with whatever you need, Jade."

"Thanks."

He hugs me around the waist, pulling me close, and I walk along, trying to keep up. The demons of our escort wear a smug smile mirroring his. The plane is waiting for us, with our first-class seats. No surprise there. What does surprise me is that he paid for them all. He didn't want anyone around us; I guess that's better. Everything's going smoothly; I'll be able to talk to him without worrying about anyone else listening. And when I say no one, I mean no one because even his secretary got sent to economy class. Only the demons are keeping us company, and well, I guess they'll find out sooner or later.

He orders some food and turns in his seat to face me more directly.

"What did you want to talk to me about, beautiful? How can I be of assistance to you?" He asks with a smile. No time to waste. Perfect, the sooner the better!

"Daniel, I'm not sure where to start, but you know I've never kept secrets from you." He nods, and I go on. "Remember the demon that attacked us that one time, both of us at the same time?"

He gets serious, way too serious, but he stays in character, doing his best.

"How could I forget? What's the deal with him?"

"My life's turned into a total mess. There are people and demons dead set on tearing us apart, and I can't live without you. I know you're trying to help me, and you came for me today, but I know this won't last long. They'll take you away from me, Daniel, and I..."

"And what's your plan?"

"The last time I saw him, before this long separation, he suggested that if I joined them, his bosses, I guess, and helped them with what I can do, they'd let me spend more time with you. So, I want to see him and tell him I agree. Anything to not live with this pain." I reach out and stroke his cheek, holding my fingertips against it for a few seconds before continuing. "But I just can't find him. He hasn't come back, and I can't take it anymore. I have to find him. Do you know anyone who could help me track him down?"

Damn it! His eyes light up in this amazing way. I hold back my anger, finally getting what I wanted. He manages a smile, or at least tries, and replies with a hint of joy in his voice.

The Game…Jade

"Jade, when demons meddle so boldly in one's life, there's often no easy way to banish them. If you've found a way to shake them off and bring us together, I'll do what I can to support you; you know that. I couldn't bear to be apart from you, and if this keeps us together, then it's undoubtedly the right path. I believe I know someone who can help us, but we'll need to travel to England. Do you agree?"

"Really, Daniel? Can we be together?" I say, smiling. I feel gross.

"Absolutely, beautiful, always together. Will you come to England?" He insists. He needs my consent for every step he plans to take with me.

"No doubt about it, I'm in. I need to see him, let him take what he wants, and leave me with you. That's all I want." I take his hand in mine.

"Me too, Jade. There's nothing I desire more than that."

They bring us food; it'll be hard to eat while holding back the nausea, but maybe the satisfaction of having convinced him so easily will help. So far, I'm doing great. This demon, on his own, is useless to me. I need to see the others, the ones back at the mansion, and I'm getting closer. I start eating to distract my stomach from feeling fear; I can't afford that luxury right now.

Daniel looks over, thinking I don't see, at one of his guards, and they share a look, probably communicating like Daniel and I do. And just like that, the demon vanishes from the plane. I hear Daniel's voice echoing inside me.

"He's sent it to the mansion and wants to know if they'll allow him to take you or if they'll see you elsewhere. He's feeling rather victorious, you see."

"Thanks. Let me know what they decide, please."

"As soon as I know anything."

It didn't take even five minutes before the demon came back. I try not to let it show, but I'm still waiting for Daniel's voice inside me.

"They've accepted. You'll be welcomed at the mansion. They're over the moon about it." I sigh and settle into my seat. Now, all I can do is wait. I guess once we land in Spain, we'll switch over to another flight headed for England. I better rest as much as I can, though I doubt it'll be much, with terror breathing down my neck. Luckily, it's only now that I can feel it, now that there's no turning back. At least I have something else to focus on—not trembling. Ángel comes over and whispers to me so only I can hear him.

"They will try to persuade you not to die; they have too much to lose. I want you to be prepared for anything." I just nod my head slightly. I'm aware it won't be easy.

Chapter XXVIII
What if her intention was not to surrender but to meet her end?

England.

Everyone has gathered in one of the huge rooms of the house. The vibe is buzzing; everything they've been waiting for, everything they've dreamt of, and what they never thought possible has happened. Just a couple more hours and Jade Arias will walk through those doors.

Olive sweeps his hand over the plant vases adorning the room, making them burst into bloom. Boxwood watches him with a furrowed brow.

> *Boxwood: What the hell are you doing?*
> *Olive: She likes plants; I want her to feel welcome.*
> *Boxwood: Don't be absurd! I doubt she'll even notice them or be in the mood for a party, and you're squandering valuable energy on that.*
> *Olive: Who cares! Starting tomorrow, we'll have all the energy at our disposal. Isn't that right?*
> *Boxwood: What do your demons say?* He asks, addressing Ebony.
> *Ebony: Well, it seems she finally succumbed to the pain we inflicted on her. I knew it would happen, and according to her words, what she wants is to ask us to take from her whatever we want in exchange for staying with Daniel. Everyone has a price.*
> *Grapevine: How did she request to come here?*
> *Ebony: No, it wasn't like that at all. She told Daniel that she couldn't find the demon who had made her the proposal anymore. If she only knew that he resides within the skin she caresses so lovingly! And she asked him if he knew anyone who could help her find it. Remember that the demon told her that Daniel was aware of everything, so it's not surprising that she knew he could help her.*
> *Grapevine: What's the plan moving forward? We must proceed with caution.*
> *Boxwood: Obviously, first and foremost, we need to remove the water from the vault and prevent her from getting her feet wet; the consequences*

would be absolutely terrible, and that will take time. That's why I don't want energy to be wasted. He directs his accusing gaze towards Olive, who, in response, only nods with annoyance.

Ebony: *I've already summoned a group of the strongest demons, just in case.*

Grapevine: *She is coming to surrender in a gesture of peace. I don't think that's necessary. Any eventuality, we are more than enough to control her.* He speaks annoyed.

Mistletoe: *Always with that predilection towards her. It's not about harming her; none of us wants that. It's just about being prepared. She probably expects us to take her energy and let her go with Daniel. We know that's absolutely impossible.*

Boxwood: *That reminds me, we need to prepare a cell to accommodate her.*

Grapevine: *Not in one of those cells! She wouldn't survive long!*

Ebony: *Everyone occupies cells, so why shouldn't she be?*

Mistletoe: *Simply because she's human. They have different needs, they're fragile, and they eat. Do you remember?*

Boxwood: *Alright, prepare a room for her, but with all the necessary security. I wouldn't want her to find a way out.*

Olive: *And I must assume that, in that cell, I mean, in that room, Daniel will have to stay with her.*

Boxwood: *Of course, we must give her what she wants in exchange. It can't be otherwise.*

Ebony: *I doubt the demon is thrilled about it.* He says with concern in his voice.

Mistletoe: *Well, for a moment there, your tone sounded like you actually care about what a foolish demon might think.* Laughter erupts in the room.

Ebony: *Sarcasm, brother, pure and vile sarcasm. It'll be a delight to witness his shock now that he's so gleefully in the skin of the famous and charming Daniel Montalvo. No doubt he's already thinking about the reward we'll bestow upon him for bringing our precious jewel home.*

Boxwood: *Reward? Our little girl comes to surrender. Reward? Bah!*

Olive: *There's something that concerns me.*

Grapevine: *What thing?* He asks, not paying attention.

Olive: Jade has always proven to be unpredictable in many ways.

Boxwood: What's going through your mind? Boxwood approaches him.

Olive: Jade has never been able to tolerate coexisting with demons.

Ebony: It's not quite as simple as that, at least not lately. Remember that she grew quite fond of the demon assigned to her.

Boxwood: Carry on... He becomes serious and raises his hand, signaling the others to be silent.

Olive: What if her intention was not to surrender but to meet her end?

Grapevine: That's out of the question! Impossible!

Everyone's gaze is fixed on Olive. The tension is so thick you can practically feel it in the air they breathe. Their long-awaited dream could turn into a nightmare.

Boxwood: Let him finish!

Olive: It occurs to me, thinking somewhat like I believe she does, that she couldn't bear living with a demon, even if it were under the skin of the man she loves. We know for sure that she is extremely perceptive. And what if she has already realized that the demon inhabits Daniel's body?

Mistletoe: But she hasn't said anything! She hasn't shown any hint of such a thing!

Olive: It's a hypothesis, so let's suppose she did. She cannot conceive her life without him, and he's no longer there. Her angel won't let her die. How could she leave this life unless aided by a force greater than her angel's? She knows she has something we want, something she can offer us in exchange for helping her to die.

Boxwood: Damn it! He rises from the chair and starts pacing around the room.

Grapevine: It's just a hypothesis. He speaks with a hint of terror in his voice, not wanting to believe that any of it could be real, let alone possible. He yearns to meet that girl in person, the one he admires with the same intensity he reserves for works of art.

Boxwood: You can't deny that it makes much more sense than a surrender, especially when it comes to Jade; suicide is more logical. She's seeking a firing squad with the strength to kill her.

Mistletoe: What's our course of action, then?

The Game...Jade

Grapevine: *If she dies, her energy will go with her. There's no entity here capable of containing it; she would end any of us. We would have to offer her an alternative.*

They stay silent for a few moments, pondering the options Jade might accept. Not a single sound can be heard in the room. It's Ebony who breaks the silence to put forward his idea.

Ebony: *Perhaps we could present her a clean Daniel. I can command the demon to leave him. She might just consider such an offer. We'd be granting her the life she craves with Daniel. After all, that's what she desires, isn't it?*

Boxwood: *That would be an option.*

Olive: *What if... It's another hypothesis, I warn you. If we were to try to convince her to stay, peacefully. After all, she has nowhere else to go.*

Mistletoe: *You forget the minuscule detail that we're fallen angels, and consequently, she despises us. If she dares to show up here, it's because she's left with no other recourse. I'm certain of that.*

Olive: *I know, however, she has no one—not her grandparents, not her mother; come on, she doesn't have Daniel anymore either. We could offer her a family. No one could love her more than us.*

Boxwood: *Assuming we were capable of such atrocity.*

Olive: *The mixture of envy and admiration we feel for her could pass for love. I don't think she would put up much objection. Perhaps someday, we could even get her to feed us by hand.*

Mistletoe: *Feed with her present? You must be truly delusional to entertain such a thought. That must never come to pass.*

Olive: *It's just speculation.*

Mistletoe: *No, it's an unattainable fantasy, at least the latter part.*

Boxwood: *Very well, this changes things. We'll allow her to arrive and assess her intentions. If it turns out she truly desires surrender, we'll offer her whatever she seeks in exchange. We'll propose she stays permanently, as you suggest.* Says, turning to Olive. *I wouldn't want to provoke her wrath; that's something we mustn't overlook. We're uncertain of her capabilities if provoked. Thus, we'll strive for a peaceful resolution. If, on the other hand, her intention is to die, we'll offer her our family. We'll be prepared to contain her fury should she refuse and confine her, understood?* He looks around, and everyone nods. But gone are the smiles; they are a thing of the past.

Rocío Blisswealth

Mistletoe: Very well, let's make preparations for both situations. We won't allow ourselves to be caught off guard.

They leave the room, each of them taking care of part of the reception for Jade. Grapevine heads towards the second floor; in the mansion, there are always plenty of empty rooms. He's chosen the largest one, next to his own—that'll be Jade's. He's sure of it. There's no room for gloominess now that everything is falling into place.

Never before had they considered the possibility of any of The Seven getting this close to them. The job was always done by demons or the humans in charge of their lives. But Jade is different. Anyone else in her shoes would freeze with fear just thinking about being here, especially knowing the demons like she does. Not her, though. She's capable of anything to achieve what she's set out to do.

Though they don't see themselves as demons—those are the outsiders born away from paradise. They were born within it, so they've never stopped considering themselves angels and referring to demons with disdain as inferior beings. Demons have never seen the Creator, but they're His offspring. It's like your DNA; it doesn't alter even if you change nationality. Jade needs to get that. Out of all humans, she's the only one who could understand. She won't see them as demons.

Supported by a group of them, he begins with the decorations. Light-colored walls and a big brass-backed bed. Thick pillows and lavender-scented candles. The bedspread is white, thick, quilted, like a cloud. Heavy wooden furniture and no mirrors; Jade doesn't like mirrors. The large window occupies the wall to the bed's right side and allows a view of the lush plants that he has grown on the terrace planters, dreaming of this day. The curtains should be lace, not to hide such a marvel. He'll convince her; it'll be his masterpiece, the crown jewel of his collection. A living piece of art, a wonderful source of energy.

Just a few hours, that's all there is to wait, and he'll have her in front of him. For hundreds of years, nothing has excited him like this.

The rest of them don't share his enthusiasm, especially Boxwood, tasked with ensuring there isn't a single drop of water inside the house. They need to restrict her energy as much as possible. Not that she necessarily needs water to harm them, but with it in the mix, she could kill them. He can't help but think of the endless scenarios that bringing Jade to the mansion entails. Something bothers him; he doesn't want to end her, but if there's no other way,

The Game...Jade

he'll have to. Confining her without her consent would be a major violation of free will; they can't afford one that big. He knows for sure that his own father would make them pay for it.

If she agrees to stay, which would be most convenient, they could conserve her energy forever. If not, he'll have to be prepared to kill her, and honestly, with the protection she carries, he doesn't know how to do it. Maybe if they all act together. Yes, that should work. He hopes he doesn't have to put that idea into practice because if it fails, things could take a disastrous turn.

How did they get this far? They've never had one of The Seven within reach, yet he can't find the strength to refuse to let Jade come here to their sanctuary. That would be having the energy of their Creator once again, close enough to smell, to see, to feel directly. None of them could say no, even knowing it was a mistake. It's been so many years since they've felt it that they've lost count. The risk is worth it; he just hopes he won't regret it.
Spain.

Finally, we hopped on the plane that will take us to England, although, it's not really a plane, it's a private jet. "To be more comfortable," were Daniel's words. As we wait for the last-minute checks to wrap up, he slips away to the restroom. Finally, after all those hours, I can breathe without inhaling his gross vomit smell. I should get a medal just for that and another for faking a loving smile every time he looks my way.

I take the opportunity to chat with Daniel briefly, with the real one, I mean. That way, nobody catches on to our conversation since, as you can imagine, my escort never loses sight of me, literally.

"Daniel."

"Tell me."

"We're almost there, right?"

"Altogether, it's about a three-hour journey to the mansion."

"There's something I want to ask you. Do you have a way to communicate with Ángel without anyone finding out?"

"Not really. Why do you ask? What's on your mind?"

"It's just that, once we get there, I'm not sure how things will play out. I need to ask him not to walk away, to stay close to me, that is, physically speaking, and so do you. I know it's a lot to ask, given my intentions, but I won't make it any other way."

552

"You don't have to worry. Ángel's choice and mine were settled ages ago. Here we are, and here we'll stay."

"Thanks. One more thing."

"Anything you fancy, gorgeous."

"I'll make you comply with what you just said. I need you to stay out of my head from this moment on. If I feel you, if I listen to you, I won't be able to make it to the end."

"Jade, please don't ask me that. Please, not like that. Just let me be with you. You don't know what you're getting into."

"I think I have a pretty clear idea. Daniel, you said, 'anything.'"

"Alright. I love you, Jade."

"I love you more, even though, with what I'm about to do, it might not seem like it."

My mind went quiet, a silence I now need to, as my future self advised me, gather the courage for what I have to do. Daniel comes back to me and, with a huge smile, informs me that we'll be taking off in five minutes. They are waiting for us with open arms in England and with all the willingness to help me with what I need. I try to smile; that's supposed to be good news.

"Daniel…"

"Tell me, sweetheart." He looks at me carefully. It wouldn't be good for him if I backed out at this point in the game.

"I want to ask you something. Stay close to me all the time, please. I'm scared, and if I don't have you there to hold my hand, I'm afraid I won't be able to do it. Will you?"

"Naturally, my love, never doubt it. I already told you that your wishes are my commands. Although, let me warn you: there's nothing to be afraid of. They simply wish to help you. They hold people like you, with such extraordinary gifts, in high regard. I can assure you that you have nothing to worry about. They value you; you're like a gem to them."

"Thanks."

I have nothing more to say; the second part of my plan is already underway, and there's nothing to stop it now. The plane takes off, and I have three hours to find within me what is necessary for everything to conclude according to my wishes. I lean my head, much to my regret, on Daniel's shoulder, who kisses my head in response, and pretend to sleep so he won't bother me.

The Game…Jade

"Jade, wake up, my love. We've landed."

"Thank you."

I unbuckle my seatbelt and get up from the seat. I take Daniel's hand tightly, and he responds. I won't let him go; I need him close. Our escort closes in on us, approaching. I'm ready now.

Rocío Blisswealth

Chapter XXIX
Life is full of twists and turns

The massive truck we're riding in is zooming along, racing to get to my destination, and I'm feeling that urgency, too. I don't know how much longer I can keep my emotions in check. I study my hand intertwined with Daniel's; his skin still has that waxy tone I'm so used to, but mine doesn't have that rosy hue anymore; it looks kind of greenish. It reminds me of what my grandpa used to say: when a person was under a lot of stress, their gallbladder released so much bile that their skin turned green. That must be what's happening because, despite everything I've been through, I've never seen it like this before.

I have no clue where we are; the road isn't even paved, so it's probably not used very often. All I can see on either side of it are trees, their branches brushing against the truck as we pass. The sound is like fingernails scraping against the surface. It's like huge monsters are trying to cling to the truck, and it's fighting to escape and take me to my creepy destination. Under the thick shadow of their foliage, the road gets darker, like it's rushing toward the night, which I might not get to see.

I try to keep my eyes on the truck's interior, but whenever I let it wander to the sides of the road, I notice a huge number of yellow eyes watching us from among the trees. Now I'm apparently a spectacle, something definitely worth seeing. I try to ignore them and focus on keeping it together. I've never felt so scared and panicked.

I can't stop thinking about Ángel; my brain can't even imagine what he must be feeling. To begin with, he's completely and utterly surrounded by demons, waiting for us to reap everything they've sown by attacking me so fiercely all my life, and now he has to watch me surrender. He's probably still figuring out how to get me out of here; that's just in his warrior nature.

A few hours ago, I was thinking about how hard it would be for him to deal with the disgust they cause him. But that's probably the least of his worries; he's probably mad at me, and he has every right to be. After everything he's done for me, I'm letting him down. I'm so sorry, Ángel. I hope you can forgive me.

The Game…Jade

My grandparents... During the flight hours, I had time to think about them, remembering everything they taught me, everything they put so much effort into ingraining in me, trying not to forget a single thing. They, better than anyone, will understand me. Now I see my time with them as so distant, like it happened in another life, many lives ago.

I can feel the truck starting to slow down until it comes to a complete stop. My survival instinct it's kind of funny; it keeps yelling at me to run. And I keep insisting that there's nowhere to go, there's no place on Earth where I could hide from them. It's better this way; at least I can still control something. I'm the one who sought them out; they didn't force me to come here; I'm the one surrendering. Like when a canary, not putting up any fight, just glides into the cat's mouth and the cat's already drooling, ready to gobble up the tasty treat.

The truck doors open, and Daniel helps me get out; three or four steps ahead, I jump into a boat, leaning on his arm; we'll cross the water in it. A minute, ninety seconds at most, separate me from the mansion grounds. He takes off his shoes; I watch him intrigued. He smiles and strokes my cheek to, just as he promised, take my hand again. I guess I don't have to worry about doing the same.

The boat stops. It surprises me that it does; there's still about three feet left to reach the shore. Daniel jumps, and he wades into the water up to his knees; he stretches out his arms and approaches to take me in them. He'll carry me up there; I don't question it. I approach, and I let him do it. Seconds later, and completely dry, he sets me down on solid ground a few feet away from the water. The third stage, the final stage, begins right now.

My steps are slow as I walk along the slabs that form the path through the garden. The scent of the flowers is so intense that it almost hides the smell of numerous demons of all sizes hiding in it. I don't lift my gaze from the ground, nor do I let go of Daniel's hand. They're watching me through the window, and I can feel them just a few steps away.

We stepped through the doorway, and I should've seen it coming—lesser demons aren't exactly welcome here, so they all stayed outside. I squeeze Daniel's hand tighter, and he squeezes back. We keep moving down the hallway, and this massive mahogany door, wide open, is right in front of us. I steal a quick glance up at Daniel, and his smile couldn't be wider, radiating satisfaction from every pore. He even seems taller, like the demon's trying to stretch his skin to show his real height.

Rocío Blisswealth

Suddenly, there's this rumble from inside the room, a noise so loud it makes me jump, and my heart races even faster than before. They're right there in front of me, all of them, with their wings spread out, looking threatening. But they're not looking at me; their icy stares are fixed on Ángel. Should've figured, they could actually see him. One of them, in a low but piercing voice, speaks to Daniel.

"How dare you bring him here?"

He looks at them with terror, clueless about what they're talking about. I turn my gaze to Ángel, who at that moment reveals his presence with his wings spread out, just like theirs, in front of Daniel and the rest of the bodyguards who are with us in the hall and who, until now, couldn't see him. It's my turn to speak up now; in a hushed voice, whether my distress is evident or not, I address them.

"If you'll allow me, gentlemen. I deeply regret that my visit might be bothering you, especially with the added inconvenience of my companion being unable to leave my side for a second — orders from above. In fact, he can't stray more than three feet from me." Ángel shoots me a quick glance and takes a step closer to me, keeping that exact distance. "However, once my business here is done, he'll leave, no doubt about it. Until then, you'll just have to ignore him."

They look at each other. Ángel must know them well, though I doubt he's seen them lately. It's still hard for me to wrap my head around the fact that they, at some point, looked similar to him. Right now, he just seems like a regular young guy, while they, on the other hand, not only look like adults despite their attractive appearance but have these bitter expressions. I didn't notice that the first time I saw them, probably because I didn't have Ángel around to make the comparison.

What do they feel seeing him so full of the same energy they so desperately seek in me? I suppose nostalgia. Do they regret what they did? Or is it more about what they lost? Their faces were blank; I couldn't tell. It takes a long minute before their wings fold back and become invisible, all except for Ángel's. But with their eyes locked on me, they choose to ignore him.

One of them takes a short step forward. His eyes immediately go to my hand intertwined with Daniel's, and he smiles almost imperceptibly. It must amuse him that I feel supported by one of their demons. Not at all, you damn

The Game...Jade

fool. Trust me, I know better than anyone whose hand I'm holding and why. In a soft voice, he says:

"Hello, Jade, welcome. I want to clarify that your visit is not bothersome to us at all. It's just that his presence caught us off guard." He says, pointing at Ángel without taking his eyes off me. *"We've been eagerly awaiting you; it's a pleasure to have you here. Would you like to take a seat?"*

Such kindness, I expected nothing less from them. They don't want to lose me, their main source of food, so they have no choice but to talk to me nicely. I glance around, furrowing my brow, and ask.

"Are we staying here?"

They look at each other, not understanding what I mean. The one speaking to me keeps going with intrigue and caution in his eyes. He carefully measures each word, aiming to keep everything under control. Let's see how well you can handle me.

"What do you mean, Jade? Where did you expect us to take you?" I smile slightly, or at least try to, and answer.

"Well, I thought... to the Elements Vault."

A sigh fills the room as everyone's gaze shifts between Daniel and me. I can't tell if it's just me or if it's taking too long for them to reply. I guess there are mental conversations going on that I'm not part of, which would explain the time slipping away from us. They're agreeing, exchanging ideas. Keeping his voice calm, he turns to Daniel.

"Did you talk to her about that room?" Before he could reply, I cut in.

"He didn't tell me anything, and I didn't ask. I saw it myself. I was here a few days ago."

They can't hide their surprise, looking to the bodyguards for confirmation, but they only get head shakes, indicating a negative response. Ángel, however, knows better than anyone that it's true. It's getting harder for them to control themselves; obviously, they're not used to facing situations slipping out of their hands, yet he manages once again and keeps talking.

"Jade, you'd better tell us the truth. How do you know about that room? It's completely impossible that you've been here without us knowing."

I try to keep my voice steady, even though I want to burst out laughing. I don't think I have many options left, and it bothers me to let this one slip, which seems perfect. Without looking at him, I say.

"It would probably be impossible for an in-person visit. It wasn't. It was an astral projection. Perhaps that would be possible? In my case, apparently, it was."

There are subtle movements among them, and this time, the bodyguards have no response. That's right, they didn't think of that, maybe because they never believed it was possible, firstly, for someone to know how to get here, and secondly, to control their fear enough to try, it slipped their minds; he keeps talking to me.

"*Let's suppose you tried projecting yourself if you know what you're talking about. You also know it's impossible to project yourself into an unknown place.*"

"Unless someone shows you the way." He immediately looks at Daniel, who emphatically shakes his head from side to side, and I continue.

"No, it wasn't him. It was someone else."

"*Who?*" This time, he doesn't hide his anxiety, and I quickly end the suspense.

"Sara. I came with her a few days ago."

His gaze remains fixed on me; however, I can feel he's not really seeing me. His thoughts have taken him far back to when Sara was indeed here. I know for sure because even though I didn't come with her; I saw and heard her talking to him. My grandpa used to say that for a lie to be believable, it had to have at least ten percent of truth. Well, that's my ten percent. I hope you're right, Grandpa.

"*With Sara...*" He says it in one breath, still not fully recovering from the surprise.

"Yes, she was sitting with you on the sofas by the entrance." I lean in to peek at them. "You know, the ones with the blue patterns. Then you headed to the Elements Vault with Víctor Arredondo and two other guys, whose names, honestly, are irrelevant."

"*And may I inquire why she brought you here?*"

His voice has gotten deeper, clearly uncomfortable with the surprise since he's used to pulling strings with humans like we're puppets. He's probably holding back his reaction not to scare me off, preferring that I finish telling him. He looks at me, raising an eyebrow. I see him from the corner of my eye like I've seen everyone else so far and keep going.

The Game...Jade

"She wanted to convince me that Daniel has a demon inside him, so I'd leave him. She wants him, you know it. You talked about it that day, and she brought me, trying to get me away from him." It's hard to take a breath, fear squeezing my lungs in this ridiculous way, but my voice stays steady.

"*And what happened next? Did you leave?*"

I glance at him for a split second, then back at the floor. I figured the last thing he expected was for me to witness what happened in that room. Well, he better be ready for a big letdown.

"Then all went into the Elements Vault, you know, at the end of that hallway, where the water reaches your ankles and..." I pause for a second to control my nausea, crossing my arm over my waist to try to keep my body from shaking with the memory of what happened behind that door. He takes a short step toward me and asks:

"*And?*"

I don't look up this time because I simply can't. The memory is too fresh, and it kills me that he's right there, yet I can't tear his eyes out with my nails. Almost breathless, I say:

"You fed."

He steps back, then another, exchanging surprised looks with the others. Looks that reveal fury coursing through them. Their fists are clenched tight, but the rest of their bodies stay stiff, avoiding showing what they must be feeling right now. Slowly, without my eyes lingering on them for more than a couple of seconds, I scan them one by one, always avoiding Ángel, who by now must be wondering what I'm up to.

"I shouldn't have found out about that, it seems. Although Sara was particularly keen on making sure I didn't miss a thing. She wanted to scare the living daylights out of me so I'd never want to see Daniel again. She almost pulled it off." I let my eyes fill with tears, but they don't overflow.

Another one of them steps forward, not fully facing me, and asks:

"*Jade, what was it that Sara almost achieved? That you would be horrified or that you would leave Daniel?*"

I don't lift my gaze; it's easier to address him if I hide it.

"Both things, but mostly, almost."

The atmosphere in the room is indescribable, total and absolute confusion. They look at each other more insistently, communicating among themselves.

Rocío Blisswealth

"*I don't comprehend.*"

"She wanted me to leave Daniel, but I still needed him. And was I horrified? Only at first, but life is full of twists and turns, and perceptions change."

"*I'm sorry, but I still don't understand.*"

"*Don't press her; we have time. Let her settle in.*" Boxwood, the first one who spoke to me, takes the floor again.

I slowly head towards one of the couches, still holding Daniel's hand. He remains by my side, but I opt to stand. I'm pretty sure if I sit down, I won't be able to control the trembling in my legs, so at least this way, I can hide it to some extent.

Daniel tries to sit, but seeing that I don't, he stays where he is. Ángel moves slowly as well, positioning himself on the other side of me. I avoid looking at him; I can't afford to be distracted even for a second. The threads I've woven in my mind are as delicate as they are intricate. I can't allow any of them to break; it took me effort to weave them, and my concentration keeps them in place as I go over them.

This time, the comments aren't conveyed through glances. They gather closer, exchanging phrases of surprise and annoyance, though incredibly well-controlled. I'm not sure if I achieved what I intended, not knowing them. I don't know if my words had the desired impact or if they're just annoyed. I need more, much more than that. They speak in such low tones that I can barely hear anything. At that moment, one of them, the one closest to me, turns to the bodyguards and gives them an order.

"*Locate Sara and eliminate her immediately.*"

They believe me, great! The first point on my list, the first thread I wove, has been firmly set in place. We're both sinking, Sara, but you're ahead. I won't leave you here to enjoy something I paid for. That's never happening. So far, so good.

The voices fade until silence returns. They decide to set the matter aside; there will be time to address it or not, depending on how things unfold. Returning to his position and, in a serious tone, though I could swear it's somewhat more relaxed, he addresses me again.

"*Jade, I would like to discuss with you more pressing matters, such as the reason for your presence here.*"

The Game…Jade

"I know." I say, still holding tightly to Daniel's hand, and he continues to smile.

"*Daniel informed us of your predicament, which suggests a surrender of your gift. Yet, I suspect amidst the torment inflicted by the demons, your intentions may be more serious.*"

My eyes well up with tears, but I manage to hold them back; I just need them to emphasize my words. Torment inflicted by demons? Damn wretch! And you, what are you then? I clear my throat to continue.

"Something more serious? Like... dying?"

His shoulders stiffen in a way I hadn't seen before. I suppose my words confirm his suspicions, but no, I am heading elsewhere. Ángel tilts his head, staring at the floor, awaiting the words he's feared hearing from my lips for months. Finally, the moment has come, and I know that even now, outnumbered as he is by countless demons and bodyguards, he hopes to save me.

"Well, I've thought about it many times. However, I've decided I don't want to die at twenty-one, maybe later, much later." My voice sounds firm, not tearful, despite the moisture in my eyes.

For the first time since I arrived here, I see smiles around me and Ángel's eyes wide open. I avoid his gaze.

There's no response from their end, no conversations, neither audible nor silent among them. All eyes are fixed on me. I can feel them. I hold Daniel's hand tightly; I need a point of balance. My legs have given out. I try to move my toes; the sensation slowly returns. Luckily, I don't consider the idea of running away at all; it would be totally and absolutely impossible for me.

Now I know why it's almost always the same character addressing me, not someone else. He seems to have the most self-control. He takes a step closer, and with more power in his voice than before, he asks:

"*So, what is your demand?*"

Right then, my grandpa's words echo in my mind like he's right there saying them again. "I don't know who convinced you that you were a Chihuahua when, in reality, it's a tiger inside you. If only you'd let it out." You better be right about this too, Grandpa, because it's the tiger I need right now. Despite the panic I feel, I lift my gaze, staring into his eyes, and hold my chin up high. With a firm and steady voice, I respond:

"Actually, it's a couple of things."

Rocío Blisswealth

For the first time in forever, I let go of Daniel's hand and stretch my fingers, trying to regain some mobility. I take a few steps away from him, approaching my interlocutor. Clearly surprised, he takes a step back and stops; fear is the last thing he wants to show me now. Without taking his eyes off me, he says:

"*And I suppose Daniel has ceased to be one of those two things.*"

"Yes, let's just say he was my ticket to get to you. But now that I'm here, I don't need him anymore."

The demon inside Daniel freaks out; he doesn't like this at all. It used to be crucial for him to stay where he is, but now he's on shaky ground. I turn to him, eyeing him with contempt. Finally! I've wanted to do this so many times in the last few hours, and now I don't hold back. I don't need to.

"*Well?*"

"It's just two things, but they're really important to me." The room falls silent; no one would dare interrupt me. "The first one is Power. Traveling with Daniel, the real one, not this weakling wearing his skin, I learned to enjoy it, seeing even the most important doors open before him. It's simply irresistible, addictive, delicious. That's what I want. Power."

They're all watching me, sizing me up. I hope they're way off with their guesses about me. Once again, there are long moments of silence as I wait, not patiently, but I wait. Finally, another one of them speaks up or rather snatches the opportunity from the last speaker.

"*That's easy, girl!*" Another one exclaims. "*One of the simplest tasks for us.*"

The others look at him, annoyed. I'm not sure if it's because he shouldn't be offering me anything yet or just because I haven't finished talking. I sneak a glance at him and wink. He winks back reflexively and smiles. Good, Jade, well done.

"*That's the first. What about the second?*"

He stares into my eyes, and I don't look away for a fraction of a second. He just has to believe me; it's a necessity that he does.

"As time has gone by, I've been left alone. First, my grandparents, then my mother and sister, although we were never close, they were something, and finally, Daniel."

Tears start welling up in my eyes again, this time involuntarily. I don't bother trying to hold back; after all, it's the only truth I've ever told so far, and they, better than anyone, know how much it hurts me.

"What I want most now is a family. A family whose members don't die, don't leave, who won't leave me alone. A family I can rely on and whose members can count on me. A family, that's what I want most. Now that's hard to come by. Isn't it? It's too much to ask, I know."

Expressions of approval come quickly. My interlocutor raises his hand, and everyone falls silent. I tense up, but I control the reaction and keep looking him in the eye.

"*Jade...*" His voice is softer, just a little, but I can detect it. I said what he wanted to hear. "*If it's love you seek, it's not within our capabilities, as I assume you mean us when you mention a family.*"

I take a quick step toward him. He can't help but take one back, showing that his reaction irritates him. I stay still and speak softly:

"I'm sorry, I didn't mean to... It's obvious that you don't want me around, but I'd like you to get a little closer so you can feel what's inside me, please. I'm not going to hurt you. You know well that someone like me couldn't hurt you. But if I repulse you, forget I dared to ask."

I don't release his gaze. I need to know how convincing I sounded. I know perfectly well that they're afraid of me, that if I could get closer than I should, I could at least harm him. But he doesn't need to know that I know.

"*No, Jade, it's not revulsion. It's just that human emotions can be quite unpleasant to us, overly intense, and touch conveys them in such an overwhelming way that I prefer to avoid it. But revulsion, never, I could never feel something like that for you. However, I believe some closeness would help to establish what you want to show me. Allow me to be the one to move. May I?*"

I stand with my arms at my sides, keeping myself still, even managing to control my knees so they don't shake, knowing he'll be closer than I think I can handle, but I'll have to bear it. Gathering courage, he moves towards me; there's only about ten inches between us. He closes his eyes and breathes in the air around me. What do I smell like, you fool? I want to scream at him, but I hold back, staying silent throughout. Seconds later, his eyes widen, and with a faint smile, he exclaims:

Rocío Blisswealth

564

"*Hatred, it's all that can be felt. Hatred.*" If they could, they would applaud.

"That's all that's left inside me. I'm not here for affection; I want a family. The only one who can accept me as I am now."

"*Well, Jade...*" This time, he speaks, looking me in the eye, not caring about the mere few inches that separate us now. "*As you've expressed before, life is full of twists and turns, and it appears yours has taken a particularly unforeseen one, at least from our perspective. The depth of your hatred, the fervor with which you embrace it, is a point of no return, an unmistakable sign of a deep, inner transformation. I must admit I had countless doubts about your motives for being here with us, but after sensing your emotions, those doubts have vanished.*"

I don't look away, leaning on, as he says, the hatred coursing through me, not letting a single particle of it escape, the hatred he inspires and fuels with every breath he takes near me. I say nothing, waiting for him to continue.

"*Well, speaking on behalf of everyone, I can assure you that you've stumbled upon your family. There may be some details to iron out, considering your human nature, but I don't foresee any major issues.*"

It's like the whole room is smiling. Everyone except Ángel. He keeps searching for my eyes, seeking something to understand what's going on, and I keep avoiding him. Sticking to my plan, I turn to them. With tears filling my eyes, I point to him as I ask:

"I'd like a few minutes to say goodbye to him, can I? There's no way around it, sorry. I think I have a knack for weird relationships; I've grown attached to him."

Boxwood raises a hand, indicating I can proceed, and as I approach, I hug Ángel. A few seconds is all I need. In the lowest voice possible, I say:

"I think I found something worth a lot of points. I want to know if He's willing to redeem them for me." I feel his breath pause momentarily. I look up, meeting his immensely surprised eyes, and ask, "Does He accept?" Without saying a word, he nods, and I kiss his cheek before stepping away.

My eyes continue to shed countless tears. My new family watches me, and Boxwood, with a concerned look, questions me:

"*Is something troubling you, Jade?*"

"Nothing, he will leave in a few minutes. It's just that I didn't expect to reach this point in the conversation without..."

The Game...Jade

I stop, and all eyes turn to me. Boxwood furrows his brow; he can't doubt what he feels inside me, but he doesn't understand what I mean, so he asks.

"At this point in the conversation without... what?"

For the first time, I swept my eyes over each of them, allowing myself a few seconds to rest my gaze on one before moving on to the next before continuing to speak.

"I mean, maybe there aren't that many details to sort out. I think I'll be able to adjust to this lifestyle easily."

My gaze continues to move over them while their anxiety increases. I know, because I can feel it, that Boxwood wants to scream at me to just finish what I want to say, but he holds back, not wanting to scare me. Finally, I stopped in front of the one who was the last to arrive to feed during my visit. His eyes are fixed on mine, listening carefully as I conclude my thoughts.

"Don't you think so, Dad?" I end with a sob.

His lungs fill up to their fullest, releasing a loud sigh. It's as if he has been waiting for that word for centuries. Where there was once tranquility, now there's only confusion; questions come and go, some quietly, others almost shouted. It can't be true, not without them noticing.

They no longer worry about keeping their composure; their movements, as well as their voices, have lost control. Four pairs of eyes are fixed on him, waiting for him to deny me, to clarify the madness they've just heard. He steps forward to speak to me, and everyone falls silent.

"Jade..."

"You knew, didn't you?" Tears continue to roll down my cheeks. Ángel looks at me with eyes full of pain; I can see he didn't know. Grapevine, my father, moves closer.

"Of course, I have. I've always known."

Boxwood and the others are closing the distance with us; my father has a lot to say, and he must do it now.

"You have a lot to explain. Start!"

He doesn't take his eyes off me; he looks at me with an expression in his eyes that I can't quite explain, as if he admires me. He smiles very softly and, without turning to look at them, he begins to speak. The explanation will be for me, before anyone else.

Rocío Blisswealth

"Jade, for many years, centuries to be precise, I yearned to give my life a purpose it lacked. Upon arriving here, I realized that we would never escape an intermediate point between the dimension in which we were created and the world we now inhabit. Being banished, we lose the most valuable of our world, and we will never have access to the best of the one we now occupy. We possess nothing of value, from either realm, only the ability to observe things from afar, to admire them."

He raises his hand and, without waiting, runs his fingers through my hair from root to tip. I don't know how I manage to hold myself back, but I do, unlike the others. Boxwood grabs his hand, pulls it away from my head, and yells at him.

"Don't be foolish! Have you lost your mind?"

He keeps smiling at me, even though it is impossible for me to reciprocate. He responds in a soft voice, speaking slowly; he is really calm.

"There's nothing to fear on her part. You've made the assessment yourself, and you know what lies within her. As for me, I touched her once, seconds after her birth, and she didn't even flinch. My touch doesn't affect her at all; it's incredibly unique."

"But..." He pays no attention; his only target is me.

"Gems like you, my dear, can be detected many years before birth. While I was researching your bloodline to determine if it was safe for us to approach, I discovered the special circumstances surrounding you and the genes that would form your body. I dreamed of being part of that DNA, of being, for the first time, a creator, not just an admirer of such an extraordinary, unique work of art. I dreamed of being your father."

Tears keep rolling down my face. That's what I am to him: a museum piece, something he managed to do on his first try, but still an object. I suspected it, but to confirm it is something else. He moves on, talking to his siblings for a moment before turning his attention back to me.

"I knew that if I informed you, you would never accept it. I know this goes entirely against the laws that govern us. We are not meant to procreate; it has been denied to us. But the temptation was too great.

I began to study your mother to see if she could withstand my proximity. She carries genetic material close to yours, albeit crude, completely unattractive, without the gifts, but with enough resilience for it. I had previously attempted approaches with humans; once I overcame the initial nausea, I tried

The Game...Jade

to get closer, but most of them didn't even pass the embrace. Their excessively fragile bodies are despicable and, in some cases, even malodorous. Their way of nourishing themselves makes them truly nauseating. However, I am capable of great achievements when it comes to obtaining something I desire, and in your case, I had desired you for so long that I would not allow the genes of a despicable human father to ruin what I could achieve if only your mother proved strong enough to conceive you with me, and not with one of them. Once I was sure she could do it, it was only a matter of time. I knew they..." He says, pointing at Ángel, *"wouldn't make contact until your gestation had begun; they wouldn't appear before that. I had a clear field, so I took advantage of it. With full knowledge of human nature and the path their desires take, I seduced your mother; it was extremely easy, and once I felt you beating inside her, I vanished from her life."*

It reminded me of a phrase my mother used when talking about someone who lacked charm, spiritually or physically—she'd call them "soulless," meaning they were "without an angel." I never paid much attention to that word, nor did I know where the expression came from, but now it holds a new meaning for me. That's how my father saw her—completely soulless, without any hint of an angel inside her. According to him, I'd be the opposite, I guess because of the way he looks at me. My legs tremble so much that I doubt they'll hold me up much longer. Ángel takes a step to support me, but my father raises his hand, signaling for him to stay back. Instead, he takes me by the elbow and helps me to the nearest chair.

"Are you alright?" He asks almost gently.

"Yes. Speaking of endurance, I think mine just bailed on me." I respond almost in a whisper.

"Don't worry, it's just the shock; it will pass soon. Remain seated." He smiles and carries on with the story. *"When your body reached five weeks of gestation, the demons reported to me that the energy within you was unprecedented. That's when I began to watch you closely. A few days later, at seven weeks, your mother couldn't contain you anymore. I was tempted to intervene again, to seek an option; I even considered the possibility of a demon harboring you."*

I try to control the anger his words stir up in me, but Ángel makes his disapproval more obvious, though it seems like no one cares what he thinks.

Rocío Blisswealth

"However, it wasn't necessary. While making rounds to check your mother's health, I saw him." His eyes turn towards Ángel. *"He was holding your unborn body in his hands, containing the energy that only someone like him could withstand without burning. The idea of seeing you in his hands, being mine, was unbearable. Nevertheless, I decided to accept it as a sacrifice; after all, it had been a long time since I made one, and having you, made it all worthwhile. From that moment on, the months passed without danger for you, and finally, I could touch you, caress you, and place that birthmark you have on your cheek."*

"My birthmark? And for what?" He smiles even wider, a smile that feels like it's mocking.

"It was a minor concession. Another one, you might say, akin to signing my name on my masterpiece."

I touch it with my fingertips. It's been there since that day, since the beginning, marking his claim over me. Boxwood talks to me; he's not sure how to handle all of this, but what choice does he have but to accept me as a legitimate part of the family now? Amidst all this chaos, he's trying to bring some order. He's trying to understand how he knows nothing about the one thing that truly matters in his life—it affects them all.

"Jade, how did you come to know?"

My father keeps watching me; I doubt he can stop now that nothing's holding him back, especially since he's not letting anything stand in his way anymore. I turn to him, just as he did to me.

"Once I knew that the other one wasn't my dad... genetics stuff, I started seeing your face in my dreams instead of his. I couldn't explain that, but when Sara brought me here, and I saw you and noticed the resemblance between us, I knew I needed you. I never had a father, and I wanted to be by your side. I wished with all my might that you wanted me by your side, too." He smiles broadly; there's no doubt my words are like music to his ears.

"Daughter..." He sighs as he calls me that. *"Believe me, there is nothing, nothing else, that I desire more than that."* This time, Ángel can't hold back, spitting out the words in a growl.

"Nothing you desire more. And what about nourishing yourself from her?"

The Game…Jade

When he hears this, his smile freezes, and a shadow passes over his face, making him look even more ominous. He turns slightly to face him and replies.

"Scruples, brother? Is that what you seek within me? I thought you knew I had left them forgotten in my old room. The one in our Father's house. I forgot them, among other things." He looks back at me to ask. *"Does that bother you, darling?"*

I rise to my feet, somehow managing it, and take a step towards him, smiling through the tears that keep flowing.

"Not at all, Dad. I told you just a few minutes ago that perceptions change. I'll gladly continue to do so, providing food for this family, and you; the support. Because I can already consider you my family. Right?" I turn around, looking at them all. Their faces reflect complete satisfaction.

Joy, if they're even capable of such a feeling, fills the room. So far, everything's gone very much their way, in both the literal and figurative sense. Amid laughter, one of them, who hadn't spoken until now, addresses me.

"Well, whenever a new member joins the family, adjustments must be made. I think we'll have to consider a change of residence, perhaps to a desert. You're dangerous with water nearby, precious! As much as having a dragon as a pet would be." I don't respond; just smile at him. My father looks at Ángel and asks.

"Jade, do you have any idea why he doesn't leave?"

"I suppose he hasn't lost hope of saving me. Maybe he needs proof that he has nothing to do here anymore. Perhaps if you let me hug you, Dad, maybe then he'll decide to leave." He doesn't hesitate for a second, coming closer to me, absolutely delighted to hear me call him that.

As I approach, I quickly glance at Ángel, who folds his wings and tenses his shoulders. He doesn't know what I have in mind or if I'm still proposing anything after everything that's been said, but he's ready to help me or die trying; I count on it. Another glance goes to Daniel; he feels lost, at least the demon inside him does. However, until he receives new orders, he doesn't move from here. Perfect, I need him around still.

I shorten the distance to my father, and with my fingers, I wipe away the tears from my cheeks. He holds me by the waist. I bring my hands to his face, and softly, affectionately, I say:

"You know something, Dad?... Tears are also water."

Rocío Blisswealth

In one swift move, I grab his face with my dripping hands. Everything happens in seconds; his eyes reflect sheer terror, the panic of having me so close, with water in between. The energy inside me is off the charts, making my whole body tremble, but I refuse to let go. If there's one thing I'll do right in this life, it's holding on to him till the bitter end.

His hands clenched into fists, clutching my clothes. He can't push me away, as much as I guess he's trying, because my energy works like a magnet for him, and my tears, like a conductor, give it more strength. The funny thing is, if they hadn't hammered on the water problem so much, I wouldn't have had a clue. Almost instantly, his skin starts forming red blisters under my touch, and his screams tear through the air, deep, raw, and demonic. I'm half expecting one of the others to come at me, but nothing. I hold his gaze with the same strength my hands hold his face; I want my eyes to be the last thing he sees.

The same screams start coming from the other four throats. They're united. I can't see them, but I can imagine what they're going through. The scene's crystal clear in front of me, five birds with one stone; talk about luck. I hope it's enough.

I catch a glimpse, partially, of Ángel's wings moving on either side of me. He's on guard, waiting for the demons to swoop in and stop what's happening. He won't give them a chance, though I don't see him fighting anyone; they must be frozen in their places.

The screams just keep pleading "*No!*" on repeat. Those screams only fill me with strength, reminding me of mine, the ones I cried out even when I had run out of tears, and I kept on begging endlessly not to have my loved ones taken away from me, my grandparents, Daniel. And yet, they didn't stop. They ripped them away from me, at least my grandparents. Now I've got a shot, a slim one but a shot nonetheless, to get Daniel back, and I won't let it slip away. And even if I don't succeed, I'll have the satisfaction of having killed my tormentors, even if their blood runs through my veins. I told them once, for me, that doesn't mean there must be love involved. He didn't earn my love or my respect; just this absolute and immense hatred, driving me and giving me strength to keep holding onto his face, squeezing tight, until I witnessed the life drain from him, from all of them. I don't want to miss that. I'll watch it from here, from the front row. I won't stop anymore. The bull outsmarted the matadors in this ring. His skin starts to swell under my hands, so much so that I feel as if I don't give him a little space, I'm going to make it burst. I don't care; I won't give in an inch. Hate, father, that hatred that they so enjoyed finding inside me. That's the driving force behind what you're suffering now. Enjoy it!

I've never felt so much energy inside me. I don't think I can resist it. My throat lets out a broken scream.

"Ángeeeel!"

He's the only one who can move in that room; maybe the bodyguards could, too, if they could shake off the shock from what they just saw. Ángel stretches his arm and, with one swift move, his hand goes right through my back; then he does the same to Daniel's chest, who's caught off guard and can't even fight back. The demon inside him starts squirming, but it's useless. If I don't free my father, Ángel won't let him go, even though he's already feeling the shocks. The energy's too much for him, and the demon inside Daniel is fighting for his life. Just hoping Daniel can hang on.

My body rests briefly. I knew that to handle this amount of energy I had to be complete. And the other part of my soul was in Daniel. That's why I needed him close. Bonus, the demon's kicking the bucket, too. Ángel's holding my soul together like when I was in my mother's womb, but now it's tougher. Dad's begging.

"Jade, no..."

His voice fades, barely audible. If I wasn't staring right at him so my eyes could lip-read, I wouldn't know what he was saying. I summon the strength to smirk and mutter back.

"Scruples, Dad? Is that what you're looking for in me? I'm sorry. After all, I'm a chip off the old block. No scruples".

His skin peels off in big chunks around my hands, like it's shedding, exposing something like a skeleton. Time's running out. Please, let this end soon; I can't take it anymore. I hear Ángel's voice behind me, must be yelling because, amidst the screams, I couldn't hear him otherwise.

"Jade, Daniel's in danger!"

"I know. Don't stop Ángel, he'll pull through!"

My jaw clenches even harder, teeth grinding with anguish, but I can't let it overwhelm me. Swore I wouldn't. Daniel knew what he was getting into. He was the only one who knew every step of the plan, and he chose to risk it for me, for us, whether it was our death or our survival if we made it out. I promised to fight for both of us to the end, no doubts, no fears. I won't back down.

My father's clothes are catching fire, but weirdly, it's not burning me. I can't even feel it. My hands stay put on the sides of his face. They seem to be the only part of my body that's not freaking out, shaking violently, making my teeth clench hard to keep it in check. Another thing that's not staying steady anymore is his face. It's losing bits and pieces with each passing moment. I can see the fire spreading behind me from the corner of my eye, they're going through the same thing. My whole body is hurting so bad, but I'm holding onto what's left of my father's face tightly. It's like he's only got enough left to keep his eyes locked on me. He's not making any noise now, just the crackling of the fire consuming their bodies while I'm inhaling this unbearable stench. How would you describe it, Dad? Nauseating? That's exactly how you smell right now. My heartbeat in my ears is drowning out everything else; if there's anything else to hear, I can't catch it.

His head gives in to the force of my hands, crumbling, and his eyes roll to my feet. My body keeps shaking. Ángel pulls his hand away, as does from Daniel. The demon finally left him, disappearing with cries of pain. Ángel holds me around the waist, and as the energy fades, my legs give out.

"Jade, Daniel..."

I drop to my knees beside him. He's still breathing. I put my hand on his chest, leaning in close to his ear, and say as loudly as I can manage:

"Daniel!... Daniel!... Daniel!"

That's what the Angel of Death did to Carmen when he wanted her soul, to take it from her body. Daniel has shared his body with the demon for too long now. I'm not sure if he knows where he should stay, so I called him three times to access his soul and make it stay. Please, let it stay inside him! I have no idea if that'll work. I just hope it does; it's the only thing I can think of. I wait for long, endless seconds. I'm aware, or at least I try to be, that we're surrounded by bodyguards and hundreds or thousands of demons. Getting out of here will be practically impossible. However, if I can get him to open his eyes, if I can keep him alive, I'll have the strength to try. If not, it's better they kill me, I won't defend myself.

My hand stays firm on his chest, sending him gentle waves of energy. I asked for a trade, and I gave up a lot of points; at least, that's what I believe. Five fallen angels, including my father, must be worth a lot, and He accepted them. This is what I want, my only wish: my life with Daniel or nothing at all. To escape that destiny I saw, the one my future self already lived through and the one I'm trying to dodge from, a life without Daniel, a life tasting like death. Ángel said You'd agree, so please! Show me that everything I've gone through was worth it. Honor Ángel's word with a nod, a sign that You're in. Give me what I asked for in exchange for all this!

My hand moves slightly, his lungs fill with air, and he slowly opens his eyes, those amazing pair of blue oceans. I lean over him, taking his face in my hands, locking my gaze into his eyes, and observing carefully. There's my reflection, and there he is, just him, thank you. A faint smile plays on his lips, and in a soft voice, he asks:

"Hey, gorgeous, was that level ten?"

A chuckle escapes my lips, more from the relief of hearing him than from the humor of his question.

"Yes, something like that."

"In that case, scratch what I mentioned earlier. I'd rather not experience it."

I chuckle again as Ángel and I help him up. Once he's on his feet, he wraps one arm around my waist, cradling the back of my neck with the other, and gives me a gentle kiss on the lips, a kiss that thankfully doesn't hurt at all. It brings me back to life, which is great because the worst is yet to come, and I must admit my plan didn't stretch this far. Every time I imagined it, I ended up dying in all sorts of terrible ways. I never made it this far, not even in my wildest dreams, so I hope Ángel's got some plan because if not, our chances are slim.

I turn to look at him; he's spread his wings again, shielding us as much as possible. Scanning the room, nobody moves. Bodyguards, servants, and demons all remain in their places, watching us intently. The windows are now covered by them; hundreds of yellow eyes are fixed on us. I search for Ángel's gaze, but he keeps his eyes locked on them, on some at least, on the bigger ones, without turning to me. He takes my hand, placing me between Daniel and him, preparing his right arm for a fight. I try to gather energy in my hands, but there's not much left; I don't have the strength for another brawl. Daniel holds my hand. Seconds turn into minutes, and nobody moves, not them, not us.

"Why aren't they attacking?" He whispers.

If only I knew. Though, knowing them as I do, they're probably waiting for us to make a move, a louder breath, an involuntary shake of the hand, to pounce on us all at once. Whatever it is, it's not good. Maybe they're even waiting for a higher-ranking demon to come and deal with this killer who took down their bosses. I don't know, but something like that must be it. I slowly lift my gaze to answer that I have no clue, but I'm cut off by a voice that freezes me inside.

A massive demon, easily ten inches taller than Daniel, steps forward. He looks, let's say, less aggressive than the others, almost human, and his eyes, though I haven't seen them clearly, aren't yellow; I can tell that much. His face and body have a human-like resemblance, but exaggeratedly tall, of course. Though being dressed in linen clothes helps maintain the effect, and his skin is smooth, almost silky, chocolate-colored. His hair falls over his shoulders to cover his entire back, like a bronze-colored waterfall. Yet, it's his unmistakably demonic voice that ruins any attempt at physical attractiveness.

Standing about three feet away from us, he addresses me without lifting his gaze from the ground. He must know the effect his voice has; it's really low, and yet, it feels strident to me.

"MISS JADE, DO YOU PLAN TO STAY?" A shiver runs down my spine. What's going on here? It's hard for me to take my eyes away from him, but I manage to glance at Ángel. The surprise in his eyes tells me everything; he doesn't know either. I can't tell if it's been a long time or a short one, but I can't pull myself together enough to answer him. Pushing myself to do so, I say:

"Look me in the eye and tell me, what do you mean by asking if I plan on staying?" I try to hide the terror in my voice, but I'm not sure I succeed.

"WE ARE NOT PERMITTED TO LOOK INTO YOUR EYES." He keeps his gaze on the ground.

"Who's not letting you?"

"WE SERVE THE BLOOD. WITH YOU BEING THE SOLE HEIRESS OF THE MASTERS NOW, IT IS OUR PLEASURE TO BE AT YOUR SERVICE. AND IN RESPONSE TO YOUR QUESTION, THE MASTERS HAVE NEVER ALLOWED US. THEY NEVER ALLOWED US TO LOOK INTO THEIR EYES, THEREFORE..."

What I'm hearing sounds completely unbelievable. It can't be true, but then again, it would explain why they haven't attacked us yet. I need answers. Finding more authority in my tone, I speak again.

"Well, nevertheless, I order you to look me in the eye when you talk to me."

The Game...Jade

Immediately, he complied, and I fought back a jump backward; that was my first reaction. Now I've got his expressionless, brown eyes locked on me. So, what next? All I can think to do is pick up on his question.

"Now, tell me. What do you mean when you ask if I plan to stay?"

"I WOULD NEVER DARE TO CHALLENGE ANY OF YOUR DECISIONS. HOWEVER, IF YOU PLAN TO STAY, YOUR FATHER PREPARED YOUR QUARTERS BEFORE DEPARTING, SO IT'S READY FOR YOU IF YOU INTEND TO STAY. BUT, IF..." he quickly glances at Daniel and Ángel before continuing, "YOUR GUESTS INTEND TO JOIN YOU, WE WILL NEED TO ARRANGE FOR TWO ADDITIONAL ROOMS. COULD YOU PLEASE INSTRUCT US ON WHAT TO DO?"

The excess of energy has definitely driven us all crazy because both Ángel and Daniel look just as shocked as me. My grandma always said that too much of anything is bad, but this is ridiculous. I turn to Ángel; he just raises his eyebrows, not saying a word, so I guess I'm still leading this. Looking for some support, some advice maybe, I turn to Daniel. He raises his shoulders and eyebrows at the same time, then lets them drop. Great, thanks for nothing.

My brain can't wrap around what this demon is saying. I've been a victim of the terror they've caused me all my life, and now it turns out they're under my commands? I don't get it, but my heart is screaming at me to get out of here, and if this is the only way, I'll do whatever it takes. Taking a look around for the first time, I see the unrecognizable but still smoldering remains of the house's inhabitants scattered on the floor. The stench they emit is still gross, but my attention is solely on the being in front of us, and I hardly register it. What do I do now?

"What do you mean I'm the sole heir?" I ask, looking into his eyes. Now, he's the one who doesn't understand my question, but he tries his best to clear up my doubt.

"INDEED, YOU ARE THE ONLY BEING IN THE WORLD WHOSE VEINS COURSE WITH THE MASTER'S LINEAGE. THERE IS NO ONE ELSE, AND YOUR FATHER ONCE ENTRUSTED ME, WITHOUT GIVING ANY DETAILS, NATURALLY, THAT YOU EXISTED. HE MENTIONED THAT IF HE COULD EVER HAVE YOU IN FRONT OF HIM, HE WOULD LET YOU KNOW THAT EVERYTHING HE POSSESSES... ONCE POSSESSED, IS YOURS. ABSOLUTELY EVERYTHING, ALTHOUGH THE MOST IMPORTANT, I BELIEVE, IS INHERITING OUR SERVITUDE. AMONG ALL THE THINGS HE HAD ACQUIRED, THIS SEEMED TO BE THE MOST VALUABLE TO HIM. WE HAVE FAITHFULLY SERVED HIM, ALWAYS FULFILLING HIS DESIRES. SOME

OF US, EVEN THOSE FAVORED BY THE MASTER, WERE CAREFULLY CHOSEN TO PARTICIPATE IN YOUR TRAINING."

"Which training?" I don't get what he means, or rather, I don't want to get it.

"YOURS, MISS." He gives a slight smile and keeps going. "THEY WERE CAREFUL NOT TO KILL YOU. DEFINITELY, THEY EXECUTED AN EXEMPLARY TASK." I'm furious; these are the demons who messed with me all through my childhood, my whole life, turning my days into nightmares and my nights into hell. Why don't you come closer, damn fool? Or, even better, tell them to line up so I can take them out. I just need a couple of seconds, that's all, to finish them off. My jaws clench audibly. Ángel reaches out and grabs my arm, stopping me. I hadn't even noticed I was already moving toward him.

"Not at this moment, Jade. I fear fortune may not favor us. We must leave this place."

I let out a forceful breath through my nostrils; I can't control myself. But then I look over at Daniel, who's looking at me with those sweet eyes, and it's enough to remind me that getting out of here, no matter what, is the most important thing right now. The demon, who heard Ángel, comes closer.

"IF YOU WISH TO GO SOMEWHERE, I CAN ORDER THE PLANE TO BE PREPARED FOR YOU. WOULD YOU LIKE ME TO DO SO?"

"Plane? What plane?" I ask, my voice tense.

"THE ONE... YOURS, MISS. SHALL I SUMMON THE CAPTAIN? IT WILL BE PREPARED IN A FEW MINUTES." He smiles at me; I almost regret asking him to look me in the eyes. His are strangely empty, expressing nothing, and it creeps me out.

"Yes." It's worth a shot.

"IT IS A PLEASURE." He seems genuinely happy to please me. I just hope this isn't some trick because, with no other way out, I have no choice but to accept.

Then I realize that the house is infested with demons, and I can't stand having them around for one more second. I turn back to him and order, my voice now thick with anger:

"I'm sick of them; tell them to leave. I can't stand seeing them." It didn't take even two seconds before they vanished from my sight. What a relief; I can breathe easier, though panic still courses just beneath my skin. I wish I could sit down and cry somewhere, but that's not an option right now. Two of the bodyguards are gathering up the remains of... them and putting them in a huge silver container, making sure there's no trace left on the ground. One of them turns and heads toward me.

"Miss, do you have any preference regarding the disposal of these remains?"

Honestly, what do you do with the remains of a fallen angel? I guess anything but give them a Christian burial. I have no idea; my eyes search for Ángel's.

"Let them be cast into the water surrounding the mansion; that should be adequate."

"You heard him. Get them out of here."

Once again, the response to my order was immediate; they both walked out the door, the container in hand, and I never saw them again. Now I remember something I want to do, something that will eventually show me just how faithfully they're really willing to serve me.

"There's something I want you to do." His eyes light up, and he pays full attention to me. "Open the cells, let them all out."

Contrary to what I thought, he didn't even dare to object to my order with his expression. He hastily left the massive room and headed for the cells. Moments later, a bunch of figures, because I can't call them people, start to fill the room; there are about twenty of them. I only recognized two: the Angel of Death, who took Carmen, and the muse. She comes up to me and takes my hand.

"Thanks."

"No problem."

I couldn't help but glance at her ankles, recalling the ring that once encircled one of them, burning her skin. It's gone now, but the scars remain. The rest of them have similar scars; I guess I spent a lot of time observing the ring's damage because she interrupted my thoughts.

"They're gone now, disappeared when they ceased to exist."

"But the scars..."

"They'll never vanish; they're the proof of what's been done, an unforgivable and grave mistake. We'd best remember it, or we might repeat it."

"They need to leave, and we'll do the same as soon as the plane arrives."

"If you authorize it, we'll go."

"If I... why?" I shake my head.

"It's because... We still owe you obedience, the..."

Rocío Blisswealth

"Blood."

"That's right."

This made me sick. Tears welled up in my eyes as I saw their faces filled with a mix of pain and fear. They're terrified that I won't let them go; that they'll have to obey me. How horrifying!

"Please, just go."

They all start to leave slowly. I wondered if there would be a way for them to move forward with what they were meant to do. I don't know, but it's not in my hands now, and I don't want it to be.

The muse stays beside me. Seeing my furrowed brow, she rushes to answer the unspoken question.

"I wonder if... Would you allow me to stay by your side? I was made for you; the path should have been different, but in the end, I'm yours. I wouldn't know what to do or where to go if it's not with you."

She's answered my question already; each of them had a purpose, a reason to exist, a place to be, and that's where they'll go, except for her. Her place is with me, like Ángel's. However, I want to believe that it's not me holding her back, that she follows the desires of her heart if she has one. And that her free will keeps her where she wants to be.

"I want you to do what you want. If that means staying with me, I'm fine with it, but I want you to know you can leave whenever you want, with whomever you want at any time." For the first time, I see a smile light up her face, and she takes my hand again.

"I'm staying."

The servant approaches me again, indicating that the plane is ready. Ángel smiles slightly and points me towards the exit, though his wings haven't folded.

"THE VAN AWAITS YOU UPON CROSSING THE WATER. THE DRIVER WILL TAKE YOU TO THE RUNWAY. ANY FURTHER INSTRUCTIONS, MISS?"

I don't look back; I wish I could forget his eyes, but I know that won't be possible.

"None. That's all."

Daniel hugs me, and we make our way to the garden. Despite the terror I still can't shake off, a laugh escapes my lips.

"What's so funny, gorgeous?"

"You know, I just realized I have nowhere to go."

The Game…Jade

"Don't you worry about that. If memory serves me right, I've got a place in Bruges, Belgium, that I've been itching to explore with you. Seems like I might just get to do that after all. Fancy joining me?" He smiles, such a sweet smile.

"I'd love that."

Epilogue

Once the plane lifts off the ground, I can feel part of my fear staying behind, at least some of it. I'm sitting next to Daniel, who hasn't let go of my hand, while Ángel occupies the seat in front of me, facing us since it's a private plane. The muse settled herself as far away as possible. I know the feeling; she doesn't want to intrude. Ángel never takes his eyes off me. I've never seen such sweetness in his eyes; it's like he's healing me with his gaze. Finally, he breaks the silence and asks:

"Jade, how long have you known?"

"About... my father?" He just nods in response.

"When Daniel took me to see my mother so I could meet the being who had conceived me, I saw him for the first time. Back then, his image meant nothing to me. However, when I went to the mansion to face my tormentors, he was the last one to enter the hall to feed on me. That's when I knew."

Nausea overwhelms me again. I cross my arms over my stomach to control it, and tears roll down my cheeks. Now, Ángel turns to Daniel.

"And you, did you know? Or was it merely chance?"

"When the demon took hold of me, I became privy to many things that initially made no sense, just a whirlwind of images in my mind. As the days passed, I realized I had access to everything the demon knew, and I delved into studying its mind, searching for anything that could aid Jade. That's when I found out. I also knew how incredibly painful it would be for her to find out, but it was necessary. She would never forgive me for withholding such a thing. Already, I had kept far too many secrets from her."

"I still don't understand. How did you come up with the idea of the exchange?" Ángel asks me.

"When I found out about my father, I was convinced your Creator would never listen to me, but when I spoke to my future self, she reminded me of the phrase you had told me, 'the enemy of your enemy is your friend.' I thought that, with the blood of a fallen angel in my veins, I had no hope that it would work, but remembering your phrase, I figured that if I became an enemy of His enemies, I would automatically be His friend and maybe He would listen to me." Ángel laughs, but what's so funny?

The Game…Jade

"Jade, with that phrase I wasn't referring to you. I was unaware of your lineage, remember?"

It's true, I had forgotten about that. He told me that before, so what did he mean? Without letting me ask, he responds to my puzzled expression.

"I was referring to Daniel. Despite his many grave mistakes, upon meeting you, he began to change, eventually becoming an adversary to your foe. What I meant to convey was that he was trustworthy. I thought you would come to see this in due time, but it seems I was mistaken."

"Wow."

"So, how did..."

"Daniel?"

"Yes."

"When I talked to myself in the future, the only feeling I felt with real intensity was her grief at having lost him. She learned to survive, to breathe from one day to the next, to fight without purpose, and not to cry. However, her happiest moment had been with him, one that I had just experienced, no other. If, after all those years, he was still my happiest moment, I no longer had doubts: no other life was worth living, none, if it didn't include him."

Daniel takes my hand again and kisses it as tears run down his cheeks.

"Once my plan was more or less finished, I brought it up to him, warning him that most likely neither of us would survive. I knew his demon would fight tooth and nail and maybe kill him before you or I could do anything to save him. In case that happened, I knew that I would let myself be killed by them. I prefer anything rather than living a life without him by my side. I had already decided that; I just never shared that part with him. Anyway, despite all that, and knowing that it would be a fierce fight and a truly terrifying death, he agreed. For me, that was more than enough."

"And how did you know what was necessary to end them?"

"It was also because of myself in the future. She mentioned that I had an infallible connection with Daniel and that the demon was inside his body. That if I could connect with his essence..."

"You would become aware of everything he knew."

"That's right. He knew a lot of facts, some he didn't. I had to wing it, guess, and cross my fingers hoping what I was about to do would work."

"But how was it that he only felt hatred within you?"

"On one occasion when I was furious, Daniel taught me to encapsulate my anger and get it out of me, as if it were a ball I threw somewhere far away. I did the same thing only I kept it inside so he could feel it. Believe me, it wasn't difficult."

"And you kept me out of everything."

"I'm sorry, but you weren't willing to let me die."

"Jade, everything is amendable except that."

"Án... gel" My voice cracks with sobs. He looks at me worriedly and straightens up in his seat to take my hand.

"What troubles you, Jade?"

"Do you have to... go?"

"Leave?! Where would I go? Why would I leave?" I can hardly control my voice to answer him.

"Because I'm the daughter of a demon." He squeezes my hand and answers.

"Throughout your life, even as I cradled your unborn form, the only sensation I could perceive was the blood of your grandparents. Even for Him, it's the singular matter He seems to cherish, or else He wouldn't have entrusted me in your care. In what you call the 'Game,' you inadvertently bestowed upon Him a significant triumph. Whatever the motivations, you took sides, waged war against your own lineage, and handed them to Him. You exercised your free will and renounced the blood coursing through you."

"But it wasn't for Him, it was for me."

"He knows, although you acted by His righteousness and that... No, I'm not going anywhere. Instead, you'll have to bear me along."

"Speaking of my grandparents, do they know?" My voice is still unsteady. Ángel smiles at me. Yes, they know, I don't know how or when, but he told them.

"Thank you."

"You're welcome." Turning a little to my left, I see Daniel and ask him.

"And you?" He furrows his brow to respond.

"And me, what about me?"

"Are you leaving?" He shakes his head from side to side, then takes my face in his hands.

"Because you're the daughter of a demon? Never, it never mattered to me whose daughter you were. It's always been about you and how you feel about me. If you still love me, despite everything, that's all that matters to me. And I'm not leaving either; you'll have to put up with me. Till the end, gorgeous."

"Jade, one more thing."

"Which one, Ángel?"

"About Sara."

"My grandpa always said that if you leave a problem unresolved, it means that if you let an enemy go alive, they will surely come back for you. I wanted to make sure that if we made it out of there alive, she wouldn't be able to bother us anymore. However, I knew I couldn't do it by my own hand; I wouldn't dare. It had to be them, so that was the first thing that had to happen."

"I understand." He smiles and gets up to sit with the muse. Daniel takes my chin in his hand, pulling me close for a kiss, a long kiss that I return without hesitation, letting him feel all the love I have and will have for him till the end.

He leans back on the backrest and indicates for me to lay on his chest. I do so eagerly, longing to lose myself there. He wraps his arms around me, and I hold them tightly. He buries his face in my hair and sighs. I dedicate myself to enjoying his long-awaited closeness. I know I could come up with a thousand reasons why I shouldn't be here with him. But do you really think that after everything my mother, my sister, and my father put me through, what Daniel dared to do without even knowing me would hold any weight against him? At least to my eyes, none. On the other hand, I indirectly got rid of Sara, and even if we don't consider the fact that my father was a demon, which, believe me, is heavy enough, I still killed him in cold blood. Not to mention, I traded him for something I desperately wanted.

I have decided not to think. Finally, I enjoy the tranquility, the peace that only his arms can give me, and I am happy; I don't care about anything else. I don't know what kind of life awaits me now, knowing what I know, being who I am, and with the understanding that my demons, my inheritance, await me there in the mansion.

"Daniel, can I ask you a favor?"

"Whatever you want."

"Don't you dare call me 'my love.'" The thought of hearing that from him gives me chills, especially after hearing the demon call me that.

"I had already thought about it. I swear, gorgeous, never."

For now, I lose myself in the arms of the man I love, my reward, what I managed to rescue from my battle. I look at my family—Daniel, Ángel, and the muse. I always knew I was weird, but I never realized it was this much.

End of book one...

www.ingramcontent.com/pod-product-compliance
Lightning Source LLC
Chambersburg PA
CBHW031334070726
47496CB00017B/872